CONFLUENCE

CONFLUENCE

Child of the River

Ancients of Days

Shrine of Stars

PAUL J. McAULEY

SCIENCE
FICTION

CHILD OF THE RIVER Copyright © 1997 by Paul J. McAuley
Publishing History: Eos hardcover, June 1998
Eos paperback, June 1999

ANCIENTS OF DAYS Copyright © 1998 by Paul J. McAuley
Publishing History: Eos hardcover, July 1999
Eos paperback, May 2000

SHRINE OF STARS Copyright © 1999 by Paul J. McAuley
Publishing History: Eos hardcover, September 2000

First SFBC Science Fiction Printing: September 2000

Published by arrangement with:
EOS
An Imprint of HarperCollins*Publishers*
10 East 53rd Street
New York, NY 10022

Visit The SFBC online at *http://www.sfbc.com*

Visit EOS online at *http://www.eosbooks.com*

ISBN 0-7394-1271-X

Contents

Child
of the
River

For Caroline,
shelter from the storm

Praise the Lord! for He hath spoken
Worlds his mighty voice obeyed
Laws, which never shall be broken
For their guidance He hath made.

Kempthorn

1

The White Boat

THE CONSTABLE OF Aeolis was a shrewd, pragmatic man who did not believe in miracles. In his opinion, everything must have an explanation, and simple explanations were best of all. "The sharpest knife cuts cleanest," he often told his sons. "The more a man talks, the more likely it is he's lying."

But to the end of his days, he could not explain the affair of the white boat.

It happened one midsummer night, when the huge black sky above the Great River was punctuated only by a scattering of dim halo stars and the dull red swirl, no bigger than a man's hand, of the Eye of the Preservers. The heaped lights of the little city of Aeolis and the lights of the carracks riding at anchor outside the harbor entrance were brighter by far than anything in the sky.

The summer heat was oppressive to the people of Aeolis. For most of the day they slept in the relative cool of their seeps and wallows, rising to begin work when the Rim Mountains clawed the setting sun, and retiring again when the sun rose, renewed, above the devouring peaks. In summer, stores and taverns and workshops stayed open from dusk until dawn, fishing boats set out at midnight to trawl the black river for noctilucent polyps and pale shrimp, and the streets of Aeolis were crowded and bustling beneath the flare of cressets and the orange glow of sodium vapor lamps. At night, in summer, the lights of Aeolis shone like a beacon in the midst of the dark shore.

That particular night, the Constable and his two eldest sons were rowing back to Aeolis in their skiff with two vagrant river traders who had been arrested while trying to run bales of cigarettes to the unchanged hill tribes of the wild shore downstream of Aeolis. Part of the traders' contraband cargo, soft bales sealed in plastic wrap and oiled cloth, was stacked in the forward well of the skiff; the traders lay in the stern, tied up like shoats for the slaughter. The skiff's powerful motor had been shot out in the brief skirmish, and the Constable's sons, already as big as their father, sat side by side on the center thwart, rowing steadily against the current. The Constable was perched on a button cushion in the skiff's high stern, steering for the lights of Aeolis.

The Constable was drinking steadily from a cruse of wine. He was a large man with loose gray skin and gross features, like a figure hastily molded from clay and abandoned before it was completed. A pair of tusks protruded like daggers from his meaty upper lip. One tusk had been broken when he had fought and killed his father, and the Constable had had it capped with silver; silver chinked against the neck of the cruse each time he took a swig of wine.

The Constable was not in a good temper. He would make a fair profit from his half of the captured cargo (the other half would go to the Aedile, if he could spare an hour or so from his excavations to pronounce sentence on the traders), but the arrest had not gone smoothly. The river traders had hired a pentad of ruffians as an escort, and they had put up a desperate fight before the Constable and his sons had managed to dispatch them. The Constable's shoulders had taken a bad cut, cleaving through blubber to the muscle beneath, and his back had been scorched by reflection of the pistol bolt which had damaged the skiff's motor. Fortunately, the weapon, which had probably predated the foundation of Aeolis, had misfired on the second shot and killed the man using it, but the Constable knew that he could not rely on good luck forever. He was getting old, ponderous and muddled when once he had been quick and strong. He knew that sooner or later one of his sons would challenge him, and he was worried that this night's botched episode was a harbinger of his decline. Like all strong men, he feared his own weakness more than death, for strength was how he measured the worth of his life.

Now and then he turned and looked back at the pyre of the smugglers' boat. It had burnt to the waterline, a flickering dash of light riding its own reflection far out across the river's broad black plain. The Constable's sons had run it aground on a mudbank, so that it would not drift amongst the banyan islands which at this time of year spun in slow circles in the shallow sargasso of the Great River's nearside shoals, tethered only by fine nets of feeder roots.

Of the two river traders, one lay as still as a sated cayman, resigned to his fate, but his mate, a tall, skinny old man naked but for a breech-clout and an unraveling turban, was trying to convince the Constable to let him go. Yoked hand to foot, so that his back was bent like a bow, he stared up at the Constable from the well, his insincere frightened smile like a rictus, his eyes so wide that white showed clear around their slitted irises. At first he had tried to gain the Constable's attention with flattery; now he was turning to threats.

"I have many friends, captain, who would be unhappy to see me in your jail," he said. "There are no walls strong enough to withstand the force of their friendship, for I am a generous man. I am known for my generosity across the breadth of the river."

The Constable rapped the top of the trader's turban with the butt of his whip, and for the fourth or fifth time advised him to be quiet. It was clear from the arrowhead tattoos on the man's fingers that he belonged to one of the street gangs which roved the ancient wharves of Ys. Any friends he might have were a hundred leagues upriver, and by dusk tomorrow he and his companion would be dead.

The skinny trader babbled, "Last year, captain, I took it upon myself to sponsor the wedding of the son of one of my dear friends, who had been struck down in the prime of life. Bad fortune had left his widow with little more than a rented room and nine children to feed. The son was besotted; his bride's family impatient. This poor lady had no one to turn to but myself, and I, captain, remembering the good company of my friend, his wisdom and his friendly laughter, took it upon myself to organize everything. Four hundred people ate and drank at the cele-bration, and I count them all as my friends. Quails' tongues in aspic we had, captain, and mounds of oysters and fish roe, and baby goats tender as the butter they were seethed in."

Perhaps there was a grain of truth in the story. Perhaps the man had been one of the guests at such a wedding, but he could not have spon-sored it. No one desperate enough to try to smuggle cigarettes to the hill tribes would have been able to lavish that kind of money on an act of charity.

The Constable flicked his whip across the legs of the prisoners. He said, "You are a dead man, and dead men have no friends. Compose yourself. Our city might be a small place, but it has a shrine, and it was one of the last places along all the river's shore where avatars talked with men, before the heretics silenced them. Pilgrims still come here, for even if the avatars are no longer able to speak, surely they are still listening. We'll let you speak to them after you've been sentenced. I suggest you take the time to think of what account you can give of your life."

One of the Constable's son's laughed, and the Constable gave their broad backs a touch of his whip. "Row," he told them, "and keep quiet." "Quails' tongues," the talkative trader said. "Anything you want, captain. You have only to name it and it will be yours. I can make you rich. I can offer you my own home, captain. Like a palace it is, right in the heart of Ys. Far from this stinking hole—"

The boat rocked when the Constable jumped into the well. His sons cursed wearily, and shipped their oars. The Constable knocked off the wretched trader's turban, pulled up the man's head by the greasy knot of hair that sprouted from his crown and, before he could scream, thrust two fingers into his mouth and grasped his writhing tongue. The trader gagged and tried to bite the Constable's fingers, but his teeth scarcely bruised their leathery skin. The Constable drew his knife, sliced the trader's tongue in half and tossed the scrap of flesh over the side of the skiff. The trader gargled blood and thrashed like a landed fish.

At the same moment, one of the Constable's sons cried out. "Boat ahead! Leastways, there's running lights."

This was Urthank, a dull-witted brute grown as heavy and muscular as his father. The Constable knew that it would not be long before Urthank roared his challenge, and knew too that the boy would lose. Urthank was too stupid to wait for the right moment; it was not in his nature to suppress an impulse. No, Urthank would not defeat him. It would be one of the others. But Urthank's challenge would be the beginning of the end.

The Constable searched the darkness. For a moment he thought he glimpsed a fugitive glimmer, but only for a moment. It could have been a mote floating in his eye, or a dim star glinting at the edge of the world's level horizon.

"You were dreaming," he said. "Set to rowing, or the sun will be up before we get back."

"I saw it," Urthank insisted.

The other son, Unthank, laughed.

"There!" Urthank said. "There it is again! Dead ahead, just like I said."

This time the Constable saw the flicker of light. His first thought was that perhaps the trader had not been boasting after all. He said quietly, "Go forward. Feathered oars."

As the skiff glided against the current, the Constable fumbled a clamshell case from the pouch hung on the belt of his white linen kilt.

The trader whose tongue had been cut out was making wet, choking sounds. The Constable kicked him into silence before opening the case and lifting out the spectacles that rested on the waterstained silk lining. The spectacles were the most valuable heirloom of the Constable's family; they had passed from defeated father to victorious son for more than a hundred generations. They were shaped like bladeless scissors, and the Constable unfolded them and carefully pinched them over his bulbous nose.

At once, the hull of the flat skiff and the bales of contraband cigarettes stacked in the forward well seemed to gain a luminous sheen; the bent backs of the Constable's sons and the supine bodies of the two prisoners glowed with furnace light. The Constable scanned the river, ignoring flaws in the old glass of the lenses which warped or smudged the amplified light, and saw, half a league from the skiff, a knot of tiny, intensely brilliant specks dancing above the river's surface.

"Machines," the Constable breathed. He stepped between the prisoners and pointed out the place to his sons.

The skiff glided forward under the Constable's guidance. As it drew closer, the Constable saw that there were hundreds of machines, a busy cloud swirling around an invisible pivot. He was used to seeing one or two flitting through the sky above Aeolis on their inscrutable business, but he had never before seen so many in one place.

Something knocked against the side of the skiff, and Urthank cursed and feathered his oar. It was a waterlogged coffin. Every day, thousands were launched from Ys. For a moment, a woman's face gazed up at the Constable through a glaze of water, glowing greenly amidst a halo of rotting flowers. Then the coffin turned end for end and was borne away.

The skiff had turned in the current, too. Now it was broadside to the cloud of machines, and for the first time the Constable saw what they attended.

A boat. A white boat riding high on the river's slow current.

The Constable took off his spectacles, and discovered that the boat was glimmering with a spectral luminescence. The water around it glowed too, as if it floated in the center of one of the shoals of luminous plankton that sometimes rose to the surface of the river on a calm summer night. The glow spread around the skiff; each stroke of the oars broke its pearly light into whirling interlocking spokes, as if the ghost of a machine lived just beneath the river's skin.

The tongue-cut trader groaned and coughed; his partner raised himself up on his elbows to watch as the white boat turned on the river's current, light as a leaf, a dancer barely touching the water.

The boat had a sharp, raised prow, and incurved sides that sealed it shut and swept back in a fan, like the tail of a dove. It was barely larger than an ordinary coffin. It made another turn, seemed to stretch like a cat, and then it was alongside the skiff, pressed right against it without even a bump.

Suddenly, the Constable and his sons were inside the cloud of machines. It was as if they had fallen headfirst into a nebula, for there were hundreds of them, each burning with ferocious white light, none bigger than a rhinoceros beetle. Urthank tried to swat one that hung in front of his snout, and cursed when it stung him with a flare of red light and a crisp sizzle.

"Steady," the Constable said, and someone else said hoarsely, "Flee."

Astonished, the Constable turned from his inspection of the glimmering boat.

"Flee," the second trader said again. "Flee, you fools!"

Both of the Constable's sons had shipped their oars and were looking at their father. They were waiting for his lead. The Constable put away his spectacles and shoved the butt end of his whip in his belt. He could not show that he was afraid. He reached through the whirling lights of the machines and touched the white boat.

Its hull was as light and close woven as feathers, and at the Constable's touch, the incurved sides peeled back with a sticky, crackling sound. As a boy, the Constable had been given to wandering the wild shore downriver of Aeolis, and he had once come across a blood orchid growing in the cloven root of a kapok tree. The orchid had made precisely the same noise when, sensing his body heat, it had spread its fleshy lobes wide to reveal the lubricious curves of its creamy pistil. He had fled in terror before the blood orchid's perfume could overwhelm him, and the ghost of that fear stayed his hand now.

The hull vibrated under his fingertips with a quick, eager pulse. Light poured out from the boat's interior, rich and golden and filled with floating motes. A body made a shadow inside this light, and the Constable thought at once that the boat was no more than a coffin set adrift on the river's current. The coffin of some lord or lady no doubt, but in function no different from the shoddy cardboard coffins of the poor or the enameled wooden coffins of the artisans and traders.

And then the baby started to cry.

The Constable squinted through the light, saw something move within it, and reached out. For a moment he was at the incandescent heart of the machines' intricate dance, and then they were gone, dispersing in flat trajectories into the darkness. The baby, a boy, pale and fat and hairless, squirmed in the Constable's hands.

The golden light was dying back inside the white boat. In moments, only traces remained, iridescent veins and dabs that fitfully illuminated the corpse on which the baby had been lying.

It was the corpse of a woman, naked, flat-breasted and starveling thin, and as hairless as the baby. She had been shot, once through the chest and once in the head, but there was no blood. One hand was three fingered, like the grabs of the cranes of Aeolis's docks; the other was monstrously swollen and bifurcate, like a lobster's claw. Her skin had a silvery-gray cast; her huge eyes, divided into a honeycomb of cells, were like the compound lenses of certain insects, and the color of blood rubies. Within each facet lived a flickering glint of golden light, and although the Constable knew that these were merely reflections of the white boat's fading light, he had the strange feeling that things, malevolently watchful things, lived behind the dead woman's strange eyes.

"Heresy," the second trader said. Somehow, he had got up on his knees and was staring wide-eyed at the white boat.

The Constable kicked the trader in the stomach; the man coughed and flopped back into the bilge water alongside his partner. The trader glared up at the Constable and said again, "Heresy. When they allowed the ship of the Ancients of Days to pass beyond Ys and sail downriver, our benevolent bureaucracies let heresy loose into the world."

"Let me kill him now," Urthank said.

"He's already a dead man," the Constable said.

"Not while he talks treason," Urthank said stubbornly. He was staring straight at his father.

"Fools," the trader said. "You have all seen the argosies and carracks sailing downriver to war with their cannons and siege engines. But there are more terrible weapons let loose in the world."

"Let me kill him," Urthank said.

The baby had caught at the Constable's thumb, although he could not close his fingers around it. He grimaced, as if trying to smile, but blew a saliva bubble instead.

The Constable gently disengaged the baby's grip and set him on the button cushion at the stern. He moved carefully, as if through air packed with invisible boxes, aware of Urthank's burning gaze at his back. He turned and said, "Let the man speak. He might know something."

The trader said, "The bureaucrats are trying to wake the Hierarchs from their reveries. Some say by science, some by witchery. The bureaucrats are so frightened of heresy consuming our world that they try anything to prevent it."

Unthank spat. "The Hierarchs are all ten thousand years dead. Everyone knows that. They were killed when the Insurrectionists threw down the temples and destroyed most of the avatars."

"The Hierarchs tried to follow the Preservers," the trader said. "They rose higher than any other bloodline, but not so high that they cannot be called back."

The Constable kicked the man and said roughly, "Enough theology. Is this one of their servants?"

"Ys is large, and contains a multitude of wonders, but I've never seen anything like this. Most likely it is a foul creature manufactured by the forbidden arts. Those trying to forge such weapons have become more corrupt than the heretics. Destroy it! Return the baby and sink the boat!"

"Why should I believe you?"

"I'm a bad man. I admit it. I'd sell any one of my daughters if I could be sure of a good profit. But I studied for a clerkship when I was a boy, and I was taught well. I remember my lessons, and I know that the existence of this thing is against the word of the Preservers."

Urthank said slowly, "We should put the baby back. It isn't our business."

"All on the river within a day's voyage is my business," the Constable said.

"You don't know everything," Urthank said. "You just think you do."

The Constable knew then that this was the moment poor Urthank had chosen. So did Unthank, who subtly shifted on the thwart so that he was no longer shoulder to shoulder with his brother. The Constable met Urthank's stare and said, "Keep your place, boy."

There was a moment when it seemed that Urthank would not attack. Then he inflated his chest and let out the air with a roar and, roaring, threw himself at his father.

The whip caught around Urthank's neck with a sharp crack that echoed out across the black water. Urthank fell to his knees and grabbed hold of the whip as its loop tightened under the slack flesh of his chin. The Constable gripped the whip's stock with both hands and jerked it sideways as if he held a line which a huge fish had suddenly struck. The skiff tipped wildly and Urthank tumbled headfirst into the glowing water. But the boy did not let go of the whip. He was stupid, but he was also stubborn. The Constable staggered, dropped the whip—it hissed over the side like a snake—and fell overboard too.

The Constable kicked off his loose, knee-high boots as he plunged down through the cold water, kicked out again for the surface. Something grabbed the hem of his kilt, and then Urthank was trying to swarm up his body. Light exploded in the Constable's eye as his son's hard elbow hit his face. They thrashed through glowing water and burst into the air, separated by no more than an arm's length.

The Constable spat a mouthful of water and gasped, "You're too quick to anger, my son. That was always your weakness."

He saw the shadow of Urthank's arm sweep through the milky glow, and countered the thrust with his own knife. The blades clashed and slid along each other, locking at their hilts. Urthank growled and pressed down. He was very strong. The Constable felt a terrific pain as his knife was twisted from his grasp and Urthank's blade buried its point in his forearm. He kicked backward in the water as Urthank slashed at his face; spray flew in a wide fan.

"Old," Urthank said. "Old and slow."

The Constable steadied himself with little circling kicks. He could feel his hot blood pulsing into the water; Urthank had caught a vein. There was a heaviness in his bones; the wound on his shoulder throbbed. He knew that Urthank was right, but he also knew that he was not prepared to die.

He said, "Come to me, son, and find out who is strongest."

Urthank grinned, freeing his tusks from his lips. He kicked forward, driving through the water with his knife held out straight, trying for a killing blow. But the water slowed him as the Constable had known it would, and the Constable kicked sideways, always just out of reach, while Urthank stabbed wildly, sobbing curses and uselessly spending his strength. Father and son circled each other. In the periphery of his vision, the Constable was aware that the white boat had separated from the skiff, but he could spare no thought for it as he avoided Urthank's next onslaught.

At last Urthank stopped, paddling to keep in one place and gasping heavily.

"Strength isn't everything," the Constable observed. "Come to me, son. I'll grant you a quick release and no shame."

"Surrender, old man, and I'll give you an honorable burial on land. Or I'll kill you here and let the little fishes strip your bones."

"O Urthank, how disappointed I am! You're no son of mine after all!"

Urthank lunged with a sudden, desperate fury, and the Constable punched precisely, hitting the boy's elbow where the nerve traveled over the bone. Urthank's fingers opened in reflex and his knife fluttered away through the water. He dove for it without thinking, and the Constable bore down on him with all his weight, enduring increasingly feeble blows to his chest and belly and legs. It took a long time, but at last he let go and Urthank's body floated free, facedown in the glowing water.

"You were the strongest of my sons," the Constable said when he had his breath back. "You were faithful after your fashion, but you never had a good thought in your head. If you had killed me and taken my wives, someone else would have killed you in a year."

Unthank paddled the skiff over and helped his father clamber into the well. The white boat was a dozen oar-lengths off, glimmering against the dark. The skinny trader whose tongue the Constable had cut out lay facedown in the bilgewater, drowned in his own blood. His partner was gone. Unthank shrugged, and said that the man had slipped over the side.

"You should have brought him back. He was bound hand and foot. A big boy like you should have had no trouble."

Unthank returned the Constable's gaze and said simply, "I was watching your victory, father."

"No, you're not ready yet, are you? You're waiting for the right moment. You're a subtle one, Unthank. Not like your brother."

"He won't have got far. The prisoner, I mean."

"Did you kill him?"

"Probably drowned by now. Like you said, he was bound hand and foot."

"Help me with your brother."

Together, father and son hauled Urthank's body into the skiff. The milky glow was fading out of the water. After the Constable had settled Urthank's body, he turned and saw that the white boat had vanished. The skiff was alone on the wide dark river, beneath the black sky and the smudged red whorl of the Eye of the Preservers. Under the arm of the tiller, on the leather pad of the button cushion, the baby grabbed at black air with pale starfish hands, chuckling at unguessable thoughts.

2

The Anchorite

ONE EVENING EARLY in spring, with the wheel of the Galaxy tilted waist-deep at the level horizon of the Great River, Yama eased open the shutters of the window of his room and stepped out onto the broad ledge. Any soldier looking up from the courtyard would have seen, by the Galaxy's blue-white light, a sturdy boy of some seventeen years on the ledge beneath the overhang of the red tile roof, and recognized the long-boned build, pale sharp face and cap of black hair of the Aedile's foundling son. But Yama knew that Sergeant Rhodean had taken most of the garrison of the peel-house on patrol through the winding paths of the City of the Dead, searching for the heretics who last night had tried to firebomb a ship at anchor in the floating harbor. Further, three men were standing guard over the laborers at the Aedile's excavations, leaving only the pack of watchdogs and a pentad of callow youths under the command of old one-legged Rotwang, who by now would have finished his nightly bottle of brandy and be snoring in his chair by the kitchen fire. With the garrison so reduced there was little chance that any of the soldiers would leave the warm fug of the guardroom to patrol the gardens, and Yama knew that he could persuade the watchdogs to allow him to pass unreported.

It was an opportunity for adventure too good to be missed. Yama was going to hunt frogs with the chandler's daughter, Derev, and Ananda, the sizar of the priest of Aeolis's temple. They had agreed on it that afternoon, using mirror talk.

The original walls of the Aedile's peel-house were built of smooth blocks of keelrock fitted together so cunningly that they presented a surface like polished ice, but at some point in the house's history an extra floor had been added, with a wide gutter ledge and gargoyles projecting into the air at intervals to spout water clear of the walls. Yama walked along the ledge as easily as if on a pavement, turned a corner, hooked his rope around the eroded ruff of a basilisk frozen in an agonized howl, and abseiled five stories to the ground. He would have to leave the rope in place, but it was a small risk.

No one was about. He darted across the wide, mossy lawn, jumped the ha-ha and quickly and silently threaded familiar paths through the dense stands of rhododendrons which had colonized the tumbled ruins of the ramparts of the peel-house's outer defensive wall. Yama had played endless games of soldiers and heretics with the kitchen boys here, and knew every path, every outcrop of ruined wall, all the holes in the ground which had once been guard rooms or stores and the buried passages between them. He stopped beneath a mature cork-oak, looked around, then lifted up a mossy stone to reveal a deep hole lined with stones and sealed with polymer spray. He pulled out a net bag and a long slender trident from this hiding place, then replaced the stone and hung the bag on his belt and laid the trident across his shoulders.

At the edge of the stands of rhododendrons, the ground dropped away steeply in an overgrown demilune breastwork to a barrens of tussock grass and scrub. Beyond was the patchwork of newly flooded paeonin fields on either side of the winding course of the Breas, and then low ranges of hills crowded with monuments and tombs, cairns and cists: league upon league of the City of the Dead stretching to the foothills of the Rim Mountains, its inhabitants outnumbered the living citizens of Aeolis by a thousand to one. The tombs glimmered in the cold light of the Galaxy, as if the hills had been dusted with salt, and little lights flickered here and there, where memorial tablets had been triggered by passing animals.

Yama took out a slim silver whistle twice the length of his forefinger and blew on it. It seemed to make no more than a breathy squeak. Yama blew three more times, then stuck his trident in the deep, soft leaf mold and squatted on his heels and listened to the peeping chorus of frogs that stitched the night. The frogs had emerged from their mucus cocoons a few weeks ago. They had been frantically feeding ever since, and now they were searching for mates, every male endeavoring to outdo his rivals with passionate froggy arias. Dopey with unrequited lust, they would be easy prey.

Behind Yama, the peel-house reared above the rhododendrons, lifting its freight of turrets against the Galaxy's blue-white wheel. A warm yellow light glowed near the top of the tall watchtower, where the Aedile, who had rarely slept since the news of Telmon's death last summer, would be working on his endless measurements and calculations.

Presently, Yama heard what he had been waiting for, the steady padding tread and faint sibilant breath of a watchdog. He called softly, and the strong, ugly creature trotted out of the bushes and laid its heavy head in his lap. Yama crooned to it, stroking its cropped ears and scratching the ridged line where flesh met the metal of its skullplate, lulling the machine part of the watchdog and, through its link, the rest of the pack. When he was satisfied that it understood it was not to raise the alarm either now or when he returned, Yama stood and wiped the dog's drool from his hands, plucked up his trident, and bounded away down the steep slope of the breastwork toward the barren ruins and the flooded fields beyond.

Ananda and Derev were waiting at the edge of the ruins. Tall, graceful Derev jumped down from her perch halfway up a broken wall cloaked in morning glory, and half-floated, half-ran across overgrown flagstones to embrace Yama. Ananda kept his seat on a fallen stele, eating ghostberries he had picked along the way and pretending to ignore the embracing lovers. He was a plump boy with dark skin and a bare, tubercled scalp, wearing the orange robe of his office.

"I brought the lantern," Ananda said at last, and held it up. It was a little brass signal lantern, with a slide and a lens to focus the light of its wick. The plan was to use it to mesmerize their prey.

Derev and Yama broke from their embrace and Ananda added, "I saw your soldiers march out along the old road this noon, brother Yama. Everyone in the town says they're after the heretics who tried to set fire to the floating harbor."

"If there are heretics within a day's march, Sergeant Rhodean will find them," Yama said.

"Perhaps they're still hiding here," Derev said. Her neck seemed to elongate as she turned her head this way and that to peer into the darkness around the ruins. Her feathery hair was brushed back from her shaven forehead and hung to the small of her back. She wore a belted shift that left her long, slim legs bare. A trident was slung over her left shoulder. She hugged Yama and said, "Suppose we found them! Wouldn't that be exciting?"

Yama said, "If they are stupid enough to remain near the place they have just attacked, then they would be easy to capture. We would need only to threaten them with our frog-stickers to force their surrender."

"My father says they make their women lie with animals to create monstrous warriors."

Ananda spat seeds and said, "Her father promised to pay a good copper penny for every ten frogs we catch."

"Derev's father has a price for everything," Yama said, smiling.

Derev smiled too—Yama felt it against his cheek. She said, "My father also said I should be back before the Galaxy sets. He only allowed me to come here because I told him that one of the Aedile's soldiers would be guarding us."

Derev's father was very tall and very thin and habitually dressed in black, and walked with his head hunched into his shoulders and his white hands clasped behind him. From the back he looked like one of the night storks that picked over the city's rubbish pits. He was invariably accompanied by his burly bodyservant; he was scared of footpads and the casual violence of sailors, and of kidnapping. The latter was a real threat, as his family was the only one of its bloodline in Aeolis. He was disliked within the tight-knit trading community because he bought favors rather than earned them, and Yama knew that Derev was allowed to see him only because Derev's father believed it brought him closer to the Aedile.

Ananda said, "The soldier would be guarding something more important than your life, although, like life, once taken it cannot be given back. But perhaps you no longer have it, which is why the soldier is not here."

Yama whispered to Derev, "You should not believe everything your father says," and told Ananda, "You dwell too much on things of the flesh. It does no good to brood on that which you cannot have. Give me some berries."

Ananda held out a handful. "You only had to ask," he said mildly.

Yama burst a ghostberry between his tongue and palate: the rough skin shockingly tart, the pulpy seed-rich flesh meltingly sweet. He grinned and said, "It is spring. We could stay out all night, then go fishing at dawn."

Derev said, "My father—"

"Your father would pay more for fresh fish than for frogs."

"He buys all the fish he can sell from the fisherfolk, and the amount he can buy is limited by the price of salt."

Ananda said, "It's traditional to hunt frogs in spring, which is why we're here. Derev's father wouldn't thank you for making her into a fisherman."

"If I don't get back before midnight he'll lock me up," Derev said. "I will never see you again."

Yama smiled. "You know that is not true. Otherwise your father would never have let you out in the first place."

"There should be a soldier here," Derev said. "We're none of us armed."

"The heretics are leagues away. And I will protect you, Derev."

Derev brandished her trident, as fierce and lovely as a naiad. "We're equally matched, I think."

"I cannot stay out all night either," Ananda said. "Father Quine rises an hour before sunrise, and before then I must sweep the naos and light the candles in the votary."

"No one will come," Yama said. "No one ever does any more, except on high days."

"That's not the point. The avatars may have been silenced, but the Preservers are still there."

"They will be there whether you light the candles or not. Stay with me, Ananda. Forget your duties for once."

Ananda shrugged. "I happen to believe in my duties."

Yama said, "You are scared of the beating you will get from Father Quine."

"Well, that's true, too. For a holy man, he has a fearsome temper and a strong arm. You're lucky, Yama. The Aedile is a kindly, scholarly man."

"If he is angry with me, he has Sergeant Rhodean beat me. And if he learns that I have left the peel-house at night, that is just what will happen. That is why I did not bring a soldier with me."

"My father says that physical punishment is barbaric," Derev said.

"It is not so bad," Yama said. "And at least you know when it is over."

"The Aedile sent for Father Quine yesterday," Ananda said. He crammed the last of the ghostberries into his mouth and got to his feet. Berry juice stained his lips; they looked black in the Galaxy's blue-white light.

Yama said unhappily, "My father is wondering what to do with me. He has been talking about finding a clerkship for me in a safe corner of the department. I think that is why Dr. Dismas went to Ys. But I do not want to be a clerk—I would rather be a priest. At least I would get to see something of the world."

"You're too old," Ananda said equitably. "My parents consecrated me a hundred days after my birth. And besides being too old, you are also too full of sin. You spy on your poor father, and steal."

"And sneak out after dark," Derev said.

"So has Ananda."

"But not to fornicate," Ananda said. "Derev's father knows that I'm here, so I'm as much a chaperon as any soldier, although more easily bribed."

Derev said, "Oh, Ananda, we really are here to hunt for frogs."

Ananda added, "And I will confess my sin tomorrow, before the shrine."

"As if the Preservers care about your small sins," Yama said.

"You're too proud to be a priest," Ananda said. "Above all, you're too proud. Come and pray with me. Unburden yourself."

Yama said, "Well, I would rather be a priest than a clerk, but most of all I would rather be a soldier. I will run away and enlist. I will train as an officer, and lead a company of myrmidons or command a corvette into battle against the heretics."

Ananda said, "That's why your father wants you to be a clerk."

Derev said, "Listen."

The two boys turned to look at where she pointed. Far out across the flooded fields, a point of intense turquoise light was moving through the dark air toward the Great River.

"A machine," Yama said.

"So it is," Derev said, "but that isn't what I meant. I heard someone crying out."

"Frogs fornicating," Ananda said.

Yama guessed that the machine was half a league off. It seemed to slide at an angle to everything else, twinkling as if stitching a path between the world and its own reality.

He said, "We should make a wish."

Ananda smiled, "I'll pretend you didn't say that, brother Yama. Such superstitions are unworthy of someone as educated as you."

Derev said, "Besides, you should never make a wish in case it is answered, like the story of the old man and the fox maiden. I know I heard something. It may be heretics. Or bandits. Quiet! Listen!"

Ananda said, "I hear nothing, Derev. Perhaps your heart is beating so quickly it cries out for relief. I know I'm a poor priest, Yama, but one thing I know is true. The Preservers see all; there is no need to invoke them by calling upon their servants."

Yama shrugged. There was no point debating such niceties with Ananda, who had been trained in theology since birth, but why shouldn't machines at least hear the wishes of those they passed by? Wishing was only an informal kind of praying, after all, and surely prayers were heard, and sometimes even answered. For if praying did not bring reward, then people would long ago have abandoned the habit of prayer, as farmers abandon land which no longer yields a crop. The priests taught that the Preservers heard and saw all, yet chose not to act because they did not wish to invalidate the free will of their creations; but machines were as much a part of the world which the Preservers had created as the Shaped bloodlines, although of a higher order. Even if the Preservers had withdrawn their blessing from the world after the affront of the Age of Insurrection, as the divaricationists believed, it was still possible that machines, their epigones, might recognize the justice of answering a particular wish, and intercede. After all, those avatars of the Preservers which had survived the Age of Insurrection had spoken with men as recently as forty years ago, before the heretics had finally silenced them.

In any event, better the chance taken than that lost and later regretted. Yama closed his eyes and offered up the quick wish, hostage to the future, that he be made a soldier and not a clerk.

Ananda said, "You might as well wish upon a star."

Derev said, "Quiet! I heard it again!"

And Yama heard it too, faint but unmistakable above the frogs' incessant chorus. A man's angry wordless yell, and then the sound of jeering voices and coarse laughter.

————

Yama led the others through the overgrown ruins. Ananda padded right behind him with his robe tucked into his girdle—the better to run away if there was trouble, he said, although Yama knew that he would not run. Derev would not run away either; she held her trident like a javelin.

One of the old roads ran alongside the fields. Its ceramic surface had been stripped and smelted for the metals it had contained thousands of years ago, but the long straight track preserved its geodesic ideal. At the crux between the old road and a footpath that led across the embankment between two of the flooded fields, by a simple shrine set on a wooden post, the Constable's twin sons, Lud and Lob, had ambushed an anchorite.

The man stood with his back to the shrine, brandishing his staff. Its metal-shod point flicked back and forth like a watchful eye. Lud and Lob yelled and threw stones and clods of dirt at the anchorite but stayed out of the staff's striking range. The twins were swaggering bullies who believed that they ruled the children of the town. Most especially, they picked on those few children of bloodlines not their own. Yama had been chased by them a decad ago, when he had been returning to the peel-house after visiting Derev, but he had easily lost them in the ruins outside the town.

"We'll find you later, little fish," they had shouted cheerfully. They had been drinking, and one of them had slapped his head with the empty bladder and cut a clumsy little dance. "We always finish our business," he had shouted. "Little fish, little fish, come out now. Be like a man."

Yama had chosen to stay hidden. Lud and Lob had scrawled their sign on a crumbling wall and pissed at its base, but after beating about the bushes in a desultory fashion they had grown bored and wandered off.

Now, crouching with Derev and Ananda in a thicket of chayote vine, Yama wondered what he should do. The anchorite was a tall man with a wild black mane and wilder beard. He was barefoot, and dressed in a crudely stitched robe of metallic-looking cloth. He dodged most of the stones thrown at him, but one had struck him on the head; blood ran down his forehead and he mechanically wiped it from his eyes with his wrist. Sooner or later, he would falter, and Lud and Lob would pounce.

Derev whispered, "We should fetch the militia."

"I don't think it's necessary," Ananda said.

At that moment, a stone struck the anchorite's elbow and the point of his staff dipped. Roaring with glee, Lob and Lud ran in from either side and knocked him to the ground. The anchorite surged up, throwing one of the twins aside, but the other clung to his back and the second knocked the anchorite down again.

Yama said, "Ananda, come out when I call your name. Derev, you set up a diversion." And before he could think better of it he stepped out onto the road and shouted the twins' names.

Lob turned. He held the staff in both hands, as if about to break it. Lud sat on the anchorite's back, grinning as he absorbed the man's blows to his flanks.

Yama said, "What is this, Lob? Are you and your brother footpads now?"

"Just a bit of fun, little fish," Lob said. He whirled the staff above his head. It whistled in the dark air.

"We saw him first," Lud added.

"I think you should leave him alone."

"Maybe we'll have you instead, little fish."

"We'll have him all right," Lud said. "That's why we're here." He cuffed the anchorite. "This culler got in the way of what we set out to do, remember? Grab him, brother, and then we can finish this bit of fun."

"You will have to deal with me, and with Ananda, too," Yama said. He did not look around, but by the shift in Lob's gaze he knew that Ananda had stepped out onto the road behind him.

"The priest's runt, eh?" Lob laughed, and farted tremendously.

"Gaw," his brother said, giggling so hard his triple chins quivered. He waved a hand in front of his face. "What a stink."

"Bless me your holiness," Lob said, leering at Ananda, and farted again.

"Even odds," Yama said, disgusted.

"Stay there, little fish," Lob said. "We'll deal with you when we've finished here."

"You wetbrain," Lud said, "we deal with him first. Remember?"

Yama flung his flimsy trident then, but it bounced uselessly off Lob's hide. Lob yawned, showing his stout, sharp tusks, and swept the staff at Yama's head. Yama ducked, then jumped back from the reverse stroke. The staff's metal tip cut the air a finger's width from his belly. Lob came on, stepping heavily and deliberately and sweeping the staff back and forth, but Yama easily dodged his clumsily aimed blows.

"Fight fair," Lob said, stopping at last. He was panting heavily. "Stand and fight fair."

Ananda was behind Lob now, and jabbed at his legs with his trident. Enraged, Lob turned and swung the staff at Ananda, and Yama stepped forward and kicked him in the kneecap, and then in the wrist. Lob howled and lost his balance, and Yama grabbed the staff when it clattered to the ground. He reversed it and jabbed Lob hard in the gut.

Lob fell to his knees in stages. "Fight fair," he gasped, winded. His little eyes blinked and blinked in his corpulent face.

"Fight fair," Lud echoed, and got off the anchorite and pulled a knife from his belt. It was as black as obsidian, with a narrow, crooked blade. He had stolen it from a drunken sailor, and claimed that it was from the first days of the Age of Enlightenment, nearly as old as the world. "Fight fair," Lud said again, and held the knife beside his face and grinned.

Lob threw himself forward then, and wrapped his arms around Yama's thighs. Yama hammered at Lob's back with the staff, but he was too close to get a good swing at his opponent and he tumbled over backward, his legs pinned beneath Lob's weight.

For a moment, all seemed lost. Then Ananda stepped forward and swung his doubled fist; the stone he held struck the side of Lob's skull with the sound of an axe sinking into wet wood. Lob roared with pain and sprang to his feet, and Lud roared too, and brandished his knife. Behind him, a tree burst into flame.

———

"It was all I could think of," Derev said. She flapped her arms about her slim body. She was shaking with excitement. Ananda ran a little way down the road and shouted after the fleeing twins, a high ululant wordless cry.

Yama said, "It was well done, but we should not mock them."

"We make a fine crew," Ananda said, and shouted again.

The burning tree shed sparks upward into the night, brighter than the Galaxy. Its trunk was a shadow inside a roaring pillar of hot blue flame. Heat and light beat out across the road. It was a young sweetgum tree. Derev had soaked its trunk with kerosene from the lantern's reservoir, and had ignited it with the lantern's flint when Lob had fallen on Yama.

"Even Lob and Lud won't forget this," Derev said gleefully.

"That is what I mean," Yama said.

"They'll be too ashamed to try anything. Frightened by a tree. It's too funny, Yama. They'll leave us alone from now on."

Ananda helped the anchorite sit up. The man dabbed at the blood crusted under his nose, cautiously bent and unbent his knees, then scrambled to his feet. Yama held out the staff, and the man took it and briefly bowed his head in thanks.

Yama bowed back, and the man grinned. Something had seared the left side of his face; a web of silvery scar tissue pulled down his eye and lifted the corner of his mouth. He was so dirty that the grain of his skin looked like embossed leather. The metallic cloth of his robe was filthy, too, but here and there patches and creases reflected the light of the burning tree. His hair was tangled in ropes around his face, and bits of twig were caught in his forked beard. He smelt powerfully of sweat and urine. He fixed Yama with an intense gaze, then made shapes with the fingers of his right hand against the palm of his left.

Ananda said, "He wants you to know that he has been searching for you."

"You can understand him?"

"We used hand speech like this in the seminary, to talk to each other during breakfast and supper when we were supposed to be listening to one of the brothers read from the Puranas. Some anchorites were once priests, and perhaps this is such a one."

The man shook his head violently, and made more shapes with his fingers.

Ananda said uncertainly, "He says that he is glad that he remembered all this. I think he must mean that he will always remember this."

"Well," Derev said, "so he should. We saved his life."

The anchorite dug inside his robe and pulled out a ceramic disc. It was attached to a thong looped around his neck, and he lifted the thong over his head and thrust the disc toward Yama, then made more shapes.

"You are the one who is to come," Ananda translated.

The anchorite shook his head and signed furiously, slamming his fingers against his palm.

"You will come here again. Yama, do you know what he means?"

And Derev said, "Listen!"

Far off, whistles sounded, calling and answering in the darkness.

The anchorite thrust the ceramic disc into Yama's hand. He stared into Yama's eyes and then he was gone, running out along the footpath between the flooded fields, a shadow dwindling against cold blue light reflected from the water, gone.

The whistles sounded again. "The militia," Ananda said, and turned and ran off down the old road.

Derev and Yama chased after him, but he soon outpaced them, and Yama had to stop to catch his breath before they reached the city wall.

Derev said, "Ananda won't stop running until he's thrown himself into his bed. And even then he'll run in his dreams until morning."

Yama was bent over, clasping his knees. He had a cramp in his side. He said, "We will have to watch out for each other. Lob and Lud will not forgive this easily. How can you run so fast and so far without getting out of breath?"

Derev's pale face glimmered in the Galaxy's light. She gave him a sly look. "Flying is harder work than running."

"If you can fly, I would love to see it. But you are teasing me again."

"This is the wrong place for flying. One day, perhaps, I'll show you the right place, but it's a long way from here."

"Do you mean the edge of the world? I used to dream that my people lived on the floating islands. I saw one—"

Derev suddenly grabbed Yama and pulled him into the long grass beside the track. He fell on top of her, laughing, but she put her hand over his mouth. "Listen!" she said.

Yama raised his head, but heard only the ordinary noises of the night. He was aware of the heat of Derev's slim body pressing against his. He said, "I think the militia have given up their search."

"No. They're coming this way."

Yama rolled over and parted the long dry grass so that he could watch the track. Presently a pentad of men went past in single file. None of them were of the bloodline of the citizens of Aeolis. They were armed with rifles and arbalests.

"Sailors," Yama said, when he was sure that they were gone.

Derev pressed the length of her body against his. "How do you know?"

"They were strangers, and all strangers come to Aeolis by the river, either as sailors or passengers. But there have been no passenger ships since the war began."

"They are gone now, whoever they are."

"Perhaps they were looking for the anchorite."

"He was crazy, that holy man, but we did the right thing. Or you did. I could not have stepped out and challenged those two."

"I did it knowing you were at my back."

"I'd be nowhere else." Derev added thoughtfully, "He looked like you."

Yama laughed.

"In the proportion of his limbs, and the shape of his head. And his eyes were halved by folds of skin, just like yours."

Derev kissed Yama's eyes. He kissed her back. They kissed for a long time, and then Derev broke away.

"You aren't alone in the world, Yama, no matter what you believe. It shouldn't surprise you to find one of your own bloodline."

But Yama had been looking for too long to believe it would be that easy. "I think he was crazy. I wonder why he gave me this."

Yama pulled the ceramic disc from the pocket of his tunic. It seemed no different from the discs the Aedile's workmen turned up by the hundred during their excavations: slick, white, slightly too large to fit comfortably in his palm. He held it up so that it faintly reflected the light of the Galaxy, and saw a distant light in the crooked tower that stood without the old, half-ruined city wall.

Dr. Dismas had returned from Ys.

3

Dr. Dismas

DR. DISMAS'S BENT-backed, black-clad figure came up the dry, stony hillside with a bustling, crabbed gait. The sun was at the height of its daily leap into the sky, and, like an aspect, he cast no shadow.

The Aedile, standing at the top of the slope by the spoil-heap of his latest excavation site, watched with swelling expectation as the apothecary drew near. The Aedile was tall and stooped and graying, with a diplomat's air of courteous reticence which many mistook for absent-mindedness. He was dressed after the fashion of the citizens of Aeolis, in a loose-fitting white tunic and a linen kilt. His knees were swollen and stiff from the hours he had spent kneeling on a leather pad brushing away dirt, hairfine layer after hairfine layer, from a ceramic disc, freeing it from the cerements of a hundred thousand years of burial. The excavation was not going well and the Aedile had grown bored with it before it was halfway done. Despite the insistence of his geomancer, he was convinced that nothing of interest would be found. The crew of trained diggers, convicts reprieved from army service, had caught their master's mood and worked at a desultory pace amongst the neatly dug trenches and pits, dragging their chains through dry white dust as they carried baskets of soil and limestone chippings to the conical spoil-heap. A drill rig taking a core through the reef of land coral which had overgrown the hilltop raised a plume of white dust that feathered off into the blue sky.

So far, the excavation had uncovered only a few potsherds, the corroded traces of what might have been the footings of a watchtower, and the inevitable hoard of ceramic discs. Although the Aedile had no idea what the discs had actually been used for (most scholars of Confluence's early history believed that they were some form of currency, but the Aedile thought that this was too obvious an explanation), he assiduously catalogued every one, and spent hours measuring the faint grooves and pits with which they were decorated. The Aedile believed in measurement. In small things were the gauge of the larger world which contained them, and of worlds without end. He believed that all measurements and constants might be arithmetically derived from a single number, the cypher of the Preservers which could unlock the secrets of the world they had made, and much else.

But here was Dr. Dismas, with news that would determine the fate of the Aedile's foundling son. The pinnace on which the apothecary had returned from Ys had anchored beyond the mouth of the bay two days before (and was anchored there still), and Dr. Dismas had been rowed ashore last night, but the Aedile had chosen to spend the day at his excavation site rather than wait at the peel-house for Dr. Dismas's call. Better that he heard the news, whatever it was, before Yama.

It was the Aedile's hope that Dr. Dismas had discovered the truth about the bloodline of his adopted son, but he did not trust the man, and was troubled by speculations about the ways in which Dr. Dismas might misuse his findings. It was Dr. Dismas, after all, who had proposed that he take the opportunity offered by his summons to Ys to undertake research into the matter of Yama's lineage. That this trip had been forced upon Dr. Dismas by his department, and had been entirely funded from the Aedile's purse, would not reduce by one iota the obligation which Dr. Dismas would surely expect the Aedile to express.

Dr. Dismas disappeared behind the tipped white cube of one of the empty tombs which were scattered beneath the brow of the hill like beads flung from a broken necklace—tombs of the dissolute time after the Age of Insurrection and the last to be built in the City of the Dead, simple boxes set at the edge of the low, rolling hills, crowded with monuments, tombs and statues of the ancient necropolis. Presently, Dr. Dismas reappeared almost at the Aedile's feet and labored up the last hundred paces of the steep, rough path. He was breathing hard. His sharp-featured face, propped amongst the high wings of his black coat's collar and shaded by a black, broad-brimmed hat, was sprinkled with sweat in which, like islands in the slowly shrinking river, the plaques of his addiction stood isolated.

"A warm day," the Aedile said by way of greeting.

Dr. Dismas took out a lace handkerchief from his sleeve and fastidiously dabbed sweat from his face. "It *is* hot. Perhaps Confluence tires of circling the sun and is falling into it, like a girl tumbling into the arms of her lover. Perhaps we'll be consumed by the fire of their passion."

Usually, Dr. Dismas's rhetorical asides amused the Aedile, but this wordplay only intensified his sense of foreboding. He said mildly, "I trust that your business was successful, doctor."

Dr. Dismas dismissed it with a flick of his handkerchief, like a conjuror.

"It was nothing. Routine puffed up with pomp. My department is fond of pomp, for it is, after all, a very old department. I am returned, my Aedile, to serve, if I may, with renewed vigor."

"I had never thought to withdraw that duty from you, my dear doctor."

"You are too kind. And more generous than the miserable termagants who nest amongst the dusty ledgers of my department, and do nothing but magnify rumor into fact."

Dr. Dismas had turned to gaze, like a conqueror, across the dry slope of the hill and its scattering of abandoned tombs, the patchwork of flooded fields along the Breas and the tumbled ruins and cluster of roofs of Aeolis at its mouth, the long finger of the new quay pointing across banks of green mud toward the Great River, which stretched away, shining like polished silver, to a misty union of water and air. Now he stuck a cigarette in his holder (carved, he liked to say, from the finger-bone of a multiple murderer; he cultivated a sense of the macabre), lit it and drew deeply, holding his breath for a count of ten before blowing a riffle of smoke through his nostrils with a satisfied sigh.

Dr. Dismas was the apothecary of Aeolis, hired a year ago by the same council which regulated the militia. He had been summoned to Ys to account for several lapses since he had taken up his position. He was said to have substituted glass powder for the expensive suspensions of tiny machines which cured river blindness—and certainly there had been more cases of river blindness the previous summer, although the Aedile attributed this to the greater numbers of biting flies which bred in the algae which choked the mud banks of the former harbor. More seriously, Dr. Dismas was said to have peddled his treatments amongst the fisherfolk and the hill tribes, making extravagant claims that he could cure cankers, blood cough and mental illness, and halt or even reverse aging. There were rumors, too, that he had made or grown chimeras of children and beasts, and that he had kidnapped a child from one of the hill tribes and used its blood and perfusions of its organs to treat one of the members of the Council for Night and Shrines.

The Aedile had dismissed all of these allegations as fantasies, but then a boy had died after blood-letting, and the parents, mid-caste chandlers, had lodged a formal protest. The Aedile had had to sign it. A field investigator of the Department of Apothecaries and Chirurgeons had arrived a hundred days ago, but quickly left in some confusion. It seemed that Dr. Dismas had threatened to kill him when he had tried to force an interview. And then the formal summons had arrived, which the Aedile had had to read out to Dr. Dismas in front of the Council of Night and Shrines. The doctor had been commanded to return to Ys for formal admonishment, both for his drug habit and (as the document delicately put it) for certain professional lapses. The Aedile had been informed that Dr. Dismas had been placed on probation, although from the doctor's manner he might have won a considerable victory rather than a reprieve.

The apothecary drew deeply on his cigarette and said, "The river voyage was a trial in itself. It made me so febrile that I had to lay in bed on the pinnace for a day after it anchored before I was strong enough to be taken ashore. I am still not quite recovered."

"Quite, quite," the Aedile said. "I am sure you came here as soon as you could."

But he did not believe it for a moment. The apothecary was up to something, no doubt about it.

"You have been working with those convicts of yours again. Don't deny it. I see the dirt under your nails. You are too old to be kneeling under the burning sun."

"I wore my hat, and coated my skin with the unguent you prescribed." The sticky stuff smelled strongly of menthol, and raised the fine hairs of the Aedile's pelt into stiff peaks, but it seemed uncharitable to complain.

"You should also wear glasses with tinted lenses. Cumulative ultraviolet will damage your corneas, and at your age that can be serious. I believe I see some inflammation there. Your excavations will proceed apace without your help. Day by day, you climb down into the past. I fear you will leave us all behind. Is the boy well? I trust you have taken better care of him than of yourself."

"I do not think I will learn anything here. There are the footings of a tower, but the structure itself must have been dismantled long ago. A tall tower, too; the foundations are very deep, although quite rusted away. I believe that it might have been made of metal, although that would have been fabulously costly even in the Age of Enlightenment. The geomancer may have been misled by the remains into thinking that a larger structure was once built here. It has happened before. Or perhaps there is something buried deeper. We will see."

The geomancer had been from one of the hill tribes, a man half the Aedile's age, but made wizened and toothless by his harsh nomadic life, one eye milky with a cataract which Dr. Dismas had later removed. This had been in winter, with hoarfrost mantling the ground each morning, but the geomancer had gone about barefoot, and naked under his red wool cloak. He had fasted three days on the hilltop before scrying out the site with a thread weighted with a sliver of lodestone.

Dr. Dismas said, "In Ys, there are buildings which are said to have once been entirely clad in metal."

"Quite, quite. If it can be found anywhere on Confluence, then it can be found in Ys."

"So they say, but who would know where to begin to look?"

"If there is any one person, then that would be you, my dear Dr. Dismas."

"I would like to think I have done my best for you."

"And for the boy. More importantly, the boy."

Dr. Dismas gave the Aedile a quick, piercing look. "Of course. That goes without saying."

"It is for the boy," the Aedile said again. "His future is constantly in my thoughts."

With the thumb and forefinger of his left hand, which were as stiffly crooked as the claw of a crayfish, Dr. Dismas plucked the stub of his cigarette from the bone holder and crushed its coal. His left hand was almost entirely affected by the drug; although the discrete plaques allowed limited flexure, they had robbed the fingers of all feeling.

The Aedile waited while Dr. Dismas went through the ritual of lighting another cigarette. There was something of Dr. Dismas's manner that reminded the Aedile of a sly, sleek nocturnal animal, secretive in its habits but always ready to pounce on some scrap or tidbit. He was a gossip, and like all gossips knew how to pace his revelations, how to string out a story and tease his audience—but the Aedile knew that like all gossips, Dr. Dismas could not hold a secret long. So he waited patiently while Dr. Dismas fitted another cigarette in the holder, and lit and drew on it. The Aedile was by nature a patient man, and his training in diplomacy had inured him to waiting on the whims of others.

Dr. Dismas blew streams of smoke through his nostrils and said at last, "It wasn't easy, you know."

"Oh, quite so. I did not think it would be. The libraries are much debased these days. Since the librarians fell silent, there is a general feeling that there is no longer the need to maintain anything but the most recent records, and so everything older than a thousand years is considerably compromised."

The Aedile realized that he had said too much. He was nervous, there on the threshold of revelation.

Dr. Dismas nodded vigorously. "And there is the present state of confusion brought about by the current political situation. It is most regrettable."

"Quite, quite. Well, but we are at war."

"I meant the confusion in the Palace of the Memory of the People itself, something for which your department, my dear Aedile, must take a considerable part of the blame. All of these difficulties suggest that we are trying to forget the past, as the Committee for Public Safety teaches we should."

The Aedile was stung by this remark, as Dr. Dismas had no doubt intended. The Aedile had been exiled to this tiny backwater city after the triumph of the Committee for Public Safety because he had spoken against the destruction of the records of past ages. It was to his everlasting shame that he had only spoken out, and not fought, as had many of his faction. And now his wife was dead. And his son. Only the Aedile was left, still in exile because of a political squabble mostly long forgotten.

The Aedile said with considerable asperity, "The past is not so easily lost, my dear Doctor. Each night, we have only to look up at the sky to be reminded of that. In winter, we see the Galaxy, sculpted by unimaginable forces in ages past; in summer, we see the Eye of the Preservers. And here in Aeolis, the past is more important than the present. After all, how much greater are the tombs than the mudbrick houses down by the bay? Even stripped of their ornaments, the tombs are greater, and will endure in ages to come. All that lived in Ys during the Golden Age once came to rest here, and much remains to be discovered."

Dr. Dismas ignored this. He said, "Despite these difficulties, the library of my department is still well-ordered. Several of the archive units are still completely functional under manual control, and they are amongst the oldest on Confluence. If records of the boy's bloodline could be found anywhere, it is there. But although I searched long and hard, of the boy's bloodline, well, I could find no trace."

The Aedile thought that he had misheard. "What is that? None at all?"

"I wish it were otherwise. Truly I do."

"This is—I mean to say, it is unexpected. Quite unexpected."

"I was surprised myself. As I say, the records of my department are perhaps the most complete on Confluence. Certainly, I believe that they are the only fully usable set, ever since your own department purged the archivists of the Palace of the Memory of the People."

The Aedile failed to understand what Dr. Dismas had told him. He said weakly, "There was no correspondence . . ."

"None at all. All Shaped bloodlines possess the universal sequence of genes inserted by the Preservers at the time of the remaking of our ancestors. No matter who we are, no matter the code in which our cellular inheritance is written, the meaning of those satellite sequences are the same. But although tests of the boy's self-awareness and rationality show that he is not an indigen, like them he lacks that which marks the Shaped as the chosen children of the Preservers. And more than that, the boy's genome is quite different from anything on Confluence."

"But apart from the mark of the Preservers we are all different from each other, doctor. We are all remade in the image of the Preservers in our various ways."

"Indeed. But every bloodline shares a genetic inheritance with certain of the beasts and plants and microbes of Confluence. Even the various races of simple indigens, which were not marked by the Preservers and which cannot evolve toward transcendence, have genetic relatives amongst the flora and fauna. The ancestors of the ten thousand bloodlines of Confluence were not brought here all alone; the Preservers also brought something of the home worlds of each of them. It seems that young Yamamanama is more truly a foundling than we first believed, for there is nothing on record, no bloodline, no plant, no beast, nor even any microbe, which has anything in common with him."

Only Dr. Dismas called the boy by his full name. It had been given to him by the wives of the old Constable, Thaw. In their language, the language of the harems, it meant *Child of the River*. The Council for Night and Shrines had met in secret after the baby had been found on the river by Constable Thaw, and it had been decided that he should be killed by exposure, for he might be a creature of the heretics, or some other kind of demon. But the baby had survived for ten days amongst the tombs on the hillside above Aeolis, and the women who had finally rescued him, defying their husbands, had said that bees had brought him pollen and water, proving that he was under the protection of the Preservers. Even so, no family in Aeolis would take in the baby, and so he had come to live in the peel-house, son to the Aedile and brother to poor Telmon.

The Aedile thought of this as he tried to fathom the implications of Dr. Dismas's discovery. Insects chirred all around in the dry grasses, insects and grass perhaps from the same long-lost world as the beasts which the Preservers had shaped into the ancestors of his own bloodline. There was a comfort, a continuity, in knowing that you were a part of the intricate tapestry of the wide world. Imagine then what it would be like to grow up alone in a world with no knowledge of your bloodline, and no hope of finding one! For the first time that day, the Aedile remembered his wife, dead more than twenty years now. A hot day then, too, and yet how cold her hands had been. His eyes pricked with the beginnings of tears, but he controlled himself. It would not do to show emotion in front of Dr. Dismas, who preyed on weakness like a wolf which follows a herd of antelope.

"All alone," the Aedile said. "Is that possible?"

"If he were a plant or an animal, then perhaps." Dr. Dismas pinched out the coal of his second cigarette, dropped the stub and ground it under the heel of his boot. Dr. Dismas's black calf-length boots were new, the Aedile noted, hand-tooled leather soft as butter.

"We could imagine him to be a stowaway," Dr. Dismas said. "A few ships still ply their old courses between Confluence and the mine worlds, and one could imagine something stowing away on one of them. Perhaps the boy is an animal, able to mimic the attributes of intelligence, in the way that certain insects mimic a leaf or a twig. But then we must ask, what is the difference between the reality and the mimic?"

The Aedile was repulsed by this notion. He could not bear to think that his own dear adopted son was an animal imitating a human being. He said, "Anyone trying to pluck such a leaf would know."

"Exactly. Even a perfect mimic differs from what it is imitating in that it *is* an imitation, with the ability to dissemble, to appear to be something it is not, to become something else. I know of no creature which is so perfect a mimic that it becomes the thing it is imitating. While there are insects which resemble leaves, they cannot make their food from sunlight. They cling to the plant, but they are not part of it."

"Quite, quite. But if the boy is not part of our world, then where is he from? The old mine worlds are uninhabited."

"Wherever he is from, I believe him to be dangerous. Remember how he was found. 'In the arms of a dead woman, in a frail craft on the flood of the river.' Those, I believe, were your exact words."

The Aedile remembered old Constable Thaw's story. The man had shamefully confessed the whole story after his wives had delivered the foundling to the peel-house. Constable Thaw had been a coarse and cunning man, but he had taken his duties seriously.

The Aedile said, "But my dear doctor, you cannot believe that Yama killed the woman—he was just a baby."

"Someone got rid of him," Dr. Dismas said. "Someone who could not bear to kill him. Or was not able to kill him."

"I have always thought that the woman was his mother. She was fleeing from something, no doubt from scandal or from her family's condemnation, and she gave birth to him there on the river, and died. It is the simplest explanation, and surely the most likely."

"We do not know all the facts of the case," Dr. Dismas said. "However, I did examine the records left by my predecessor. She performed several neurological tests on Yamamanama soon after he was brought to your house, and continued to perform them for several years afterward. Counting backward, and allowing for a good margin of error, I formed the opinion that Yamamanama had been born at least fifty days before he was found on the river. We are all marked by our intelligence. Unlike the beasts of the field, we must all of us continue our development outside the womb, because the womb does not supply sufficient sensory input to stimulate growth of neural pathways. I have no reason to doubt that this is not a universal law for all intelligent races. All the tests indicated that it was no newborn baby that Constable Thaw rescued."

"Well, no matter where he came from, or why, it seems that we are all he has, doctor."

Dr. Dismas looked around. Although the nearest workers were fifty paces away, chipping in a desultory way at the edge of the neat square of the excavated pit, he stepped closer to the Aedile and said confidingly, "You overlook one possibility. Since the Preservers abandoned Confluence, one new race has appeared, albeit briefly."

The Aedile smiled. "You scoff at my theory, doctor, but at least it fits with what is known, whereas you make a wild leap into thin air. The ship of the Ancients of Days passed downriver twenty years before Yama was found floating in his cradle, and no members of its crew remained on Confluence."

"Their heresies live on. We are at war with their ideas. The Ancients of Days were the ancestors of the Preservers, and we cannot guess at their powers." Dr. Dismas looked sideways at the Aedile. "I believe," he said, "that there have been certain portents, certain signs . . . The rumors are vague. Perhaps you know more. Perhaps it would help if you told me about them."

"I trust you have spoken to no one else," the Aedile said. "Talk like this, wild though it is, could put Yama in great danger."

"I understand why you have not discussed Yamamanama's troublesome origin before, even to your own department. But the signs are there, for those who know how to look. The number of machines that flit at the borders of Aeolis, for instance. You cannot hide these things forever."

The machines around the white boat. The woman in the shrine. Yama's silly trick with the watchdogs. The bees which had fed the abandoned baby had probably been machines, too.

The Aedile said carefully, "We should not talk of such things here. It requires discretion."

He would never tell Dr. Dismas everything. The man presumed too much, and he was not to be trusted.

"I am, and shall continue to be, the soul of discretion."

Never before had Dr. Dismas's dark, sharp-featured face seemed so much like a mask. It was why the man took the drug, the Aedile realized. The drug was a shield from the gaze and the hurts of the world.

The Aedile said sternly, "I mean it, Dismas. You will say nothing of what you found, and keep your speculations to yourself. I want to see what you found. Perhaps there is something you missed."

"I will bring the papers tonight, but you will see that I am right in every particular. Now, if I may have permission to leave," Dr. Dismas said, "I would like to recover from my journey. Think carefully about what I told you. We stand at the threshold of a great mystery."

When Dr. Dismas had gone, the Aedile called for his secretary. While the man was preparing his pens and ink and setting a disc of red wax to soften on a sunwarmed stone, the Aedile composed in his head the letter he needed to write. The letter would undermine Dr. Dismas's already blemished reputation and devalue any claims the apothecary might make on Yama, but it would not condemn him outright. It would suggest a suspicion that Dr. Dismas, because of his drug habit, might be involved with the heretics who had recently tried to set fire to the floating docks, but it must be the merest of hints hedged round with equivocation, for the Aedile was certain that if Dr. Dismas was ever arrested, he would promptly confess all he knew. The Aedile realized then that they were linked by a cat's cradle of secrets that was weighted with the soul of the foundling boy, the stranger, the sacrifice, the gift, the child of the river.

4

Yamamanama

YAMA REMEMBERED NOTHING of the circumstances of his birth, or of how he had arrived at Aeolis in a skiff steered by a man with a corpse at his feet and the blood of his own son fresh on his hands. Yama knew only that Aeolis was home, and knew it as intimately as only a child can, especially a child who has been adopted by the city's Aedile and so wears innocently and unknowingly an intangible badge of privilege.

In its glory, before the Age of Insurrection, Aeolis, named for the winter wind that sang through the passes of the hills above the broad valley of the river Breas, had been the disembarkation point for the City of the Dead. Ys had extended far downriver in those days, and then as now it was the law that no one could be buried within its boundaries. Instead, mourners accompanied their dead to Aeolis, where funeral pyres for the lesser castes burned day and night, temples rang with prayers and songs for the preserved bodies of the rich and altars shone with constellations of butter lamps that shimmered amongst heaps of flowers and strings of prayer flags. The ashes of the poor were cast on the waters of the Great River; the preserved bodies of the ruling and mercantile classes, and of scholars and dynasts, were interred in tombs whose ruined, empty shells still riddled the dry hills beyond the town. The Breas, which then had been navigable almost to its source in the foothills of the Rim Mountains, had been crowded with barges bringing slabs of land coral, porphyry, granite, marble and all kinds of precious stones for the construction of the tombs.

An age later, after half the world had been turned to desert during the rebellion of the feral machines, and the Preservers had withdrawn their blessing from Confluence, and Ys had retreated, contracting about its irreducible heart, funeral barges no longer ferried the dead to Aeolis; instead, bodies were launched from the docks and piers of Ys onto the full flood of the Great River, given up to caymans and fish, lammergeyers and carrion crows. As these creatures consumed the dead, so Aeolis consumed its own past. Tombs were looted of treasures; decorative panels and frescoes were removed from the walls; preserved bodies were stripped of their clothes and jewelery; the hammered bronze facings of doors and tomb furniture were melted down—the old pits of the wind-powered smelters were still visible along the escarpment above the little city.

After most of the tombs had been stripped, Aeolis became no more than a way station, a place where ships put in to replenish their supplies of fresh food on their voyages downriver from Ys. This was the city that Yama knew. There was the new quay which ran across the mudflats and stands of zebra grass of the old, silted harbor to the retreating edge of the Great River, where the fisherfolk of the floating islands gathered in their little coracles to sell strings of oysters and mussels, spongy parcels of red river moss, bundles of riverweed stipes, and shrimp and crabs and fresh fish. There were always people swimming off the new quay or splashing about in coracles and small boats, and men working at the fish traps and the shoals at the mouth of the shallow Breas where razorshell mussels were cultivated, and divers hunting for urchins and abalone amongst the holdfasts of stands of giant kelp whose long blades formed vast brown slicks on the surface of the river. There was the long road at the top of the ruined steps of the old waterfront, where tribesmen from the dry hills of the wild shore downriver of Aeolis squatted at blanket stalls to sell fruit and fresh meat, and dried mushrooms and manna lichen, and bits of lapis lazuli and marble pried from the wrecked facings of ancient tombs. There were ten taverns and two whorehouses; the chandlers' godowns and the farmers' cooperative; straggling streets of mudbrick houses which leaned toward each other over narrow canals; the one surviving temple, its walls white as salt, the gilt of its dome recently renewed by public subscription. And then the ruins of the ancient mortuaries, more extensive than the town, and fields of yams and raffia and yellow peas, and flooded paddies where rice and paeonin were grown. One of the last of Aeolis's mayors had established the paeonin industry in an attempt to revitalize the little city, but when the heretics had silenced the shrines at the beginning of the war there had been a sudden shrinkage in the priesthood and a decline in trade of the pigment which dyed their robes. These days, the mill, built at the downriver

point of the bay so that its effluent would not contaminate the silty
harbor, worked only one day in ten.

Most of the population of Aeolis were of the same bloodline. They
called themselves the Amnan, which meant simply *the human beings*;
their enemies called them the Mud People. They had bulky but well-
muscled bodies and baggy gray or brown skin. Clumsy on land, they
were strong swimmers and adept aquatic predators, and had hunted giant
otters and manatees almost to extinction along that part of the Great
River. They had preyed upon the indigenous fisherfolk, too, before the
Aedile had arrived and put a stop to it. More women were born than
men, and sons fought their fathers for control of the harem; if they won,
they killed their younger brothers or drove them out. The people of
Aeolis still talked about the fight between old Constable Thaw and his
son. It had lasted five days, and had ranged up and down the waterfront
and through the net of canals between the houses until Thaw, his legs
paralyzed, had been drowned in the shallow stream of the Breas.

It was a barbaric custom, the Aedile said, a sign that the Amnan
were reverting to their bestial nature. The Aedile went into the city as
little as possible—rarely more than once every hundred days, and then
only to the temple to attend the high day service with Yama and Telmon
sitting to the right and left side of their father in scratchy robes, on hard,
ornately carved chairs, facing the audience throughout the three or four
hours of obeisances and offerings, prayer and praise-songs. Yama loved
the sturdy square temple, with its clean high spaces, the black disc of
its shrine in its ornate gilded frame, and walls glowing with mosaics
picturing scenes of the end times, in which the Preservers (shown as
clouds of light) ushered the re-created dead into perfect worlds of parklands and immaculate gardens. He loved the pomp and circumstance of
the ceremonies, too, although he thought that it was unnecessary. The
Preservers, who watched all, did not need ritual praise; to walk and
work and play in the world they had made was praise enough. He was
happier worshipping at the shrines which stood near the edge of the
world on the far side of the Great River, visited every year during the
winter festival when the triple spiral of the Home Galaxy first rose in
its full glory above the Great River and most of the people of Aeolis
migrated to the farside shore in a swarm of boats to set up camps and
bonfires and greet the onset of winter with fireworks, and dance and
pray and drink and feast for a whole decad.

The Aedile had taken Yama into his household, but he was a remote,
scholarly man, busy with his official duties or preoccupied with his
excavations and the endless measurements and calculations by which he

tried to divide everything into everything else in an attempt to discover
the prime which harmonized the world, and perhaps the Universe. It
left him with little in the way of small talk. Like many unworldly,
learned men, the Aedile treated children as miniature adults, failing to
recognize that they were elemental, unfired vessels whose stuff was
malleable and fey.

As a consequence of the Aedile's benign neglect, Yama and Telmon
spent much of their childhood being passed from one to another of the
household servants, or running free amongst the tombs of the City of
the Dead. In summer, the Aedile often left the peel-house for a month
at a time, taking most of his household to one or another of his excavation sites in the dry hills and valleys beyond Aeolis. When they were
not helping with the slow, painstaking work, Yama and Telmon went
hunting and exploring amongst desert suburbs of the City of the Dead,
Telmon searching for unusual insects for his collection, Yama interrogating aspects—he had a knack for awakening them, and for tormenting
and teasing them into revealing details of the lives of the people on
whom they were based, and for whom they were both guardians and
advocates.

Telmon was the natural leader of the two, five years older, tall and
solemn and patient and endlessly inquisitive, with a fine black pelt shot
through with chestnut highlights. He was a natural horseman and an
excellent shot with bow, arbalest and rifle, and often went off by himself
for days at a time, hunting in the high ranges of hills where the Breas
ran white and fast through the locks and ponds of the old canal system.
He loved Yama like a true brother, and Yama loved him in turn, and
was as devastated as the Aedile by news of his death.

Formal education resumed in winter. For four days each decad
Yama and Telmon were taught fencing, wrestling and horsemanship by
Sergeant Rhodean; for the rest, their education was entrusted to the
librarian, Zakiel. Zakiel was a slave, the only one in the peel-house; he
had once been an archivist, but had committed an unspeakable heresy.
Zakiel did not seem to mind being a slave. Before he had been branded,
he had worked in the vast stacks of the library of the Palace of the
Memory of the People, and now he was librarian of the peel-house. He
ate his simple meals amongst dusty tiers of books and scrolls, and slept
in a cot in a dark corner under a cliff of quarto-sized ledgers whose
thin metal covers, spotted with corrosion, had not been disturbed for
centuries. All knowledge could be found in books, Zakiel declared, and
if he had a passion (apart from his mysterious heresy, which he had

never renounced) it was this. He was perhaps the happiest man in the Aedile's household, for he needed nothing but his work.

"Since the Preservers fully understand the Universe, and hold it whole in their minds, then it follows that all texts, which flow from minds forged by the Preservers, are reflections of their immanence," Zakiel told Yama and Telmon more than once. "It is not the world itself we should measure, but the reflections of the world, filtered through the creations of the Preservers and set down in these books. Of course, boys, you must never tell the Aedile I said this. He is happy in his pursuit of the ineffable, and I would not trouble him with these trivial matters."

Yama and Telmon were supposed to be taught the Summalae Logicales, the Puranas and the Protocols of the Department, but mostly they listened to Zakiel read passages from selected works of natural philosophy before engaging in long, formal discussions. Yama first learned to read upside-down by watching Zakiel's long, ink-stained forefinger tracking glyphs from right to left while listening to the librarian recite in a sing-song voice, and later had to learn to read all over again, this time the right way up, to be able to recite in his turn. Yama and Telmon had most of the major verses of the Puranas by heart, and were guided by Zakiel to read extensively in chrestomathies and incunabulae, but while Telmon dutifully followed the program Zakiel set out, Yama preferred to idle time away dreaming over bestiaries, prosopographies and maps—most especially maps.

Yama stole many books from the library. Taking them was a way of possessing the ideas and wonders they contained, as if he might, piece by piece, seize the whole world. Zakiel retrieved most of the books from various hiding places in the house or the ruins in its grounds, using a craft more subtle than the tracking skills of either Telmon or Sergeant Rhodean, but one thing Yama managed to retain was a map of the inhabited half of the world. The map's scroll was the width of his hand and almost twice the length of his body, wound on a resin spindle decorated with tiny figures of a thousand bloodlines frozen in representative poses. The map was printed on a material finer than silk and stronger than steel. At one edge were the purple and brown and white ridges of the Rim Mountains; at the other was the blue ribbon of the Great River, with a narrow unmarked margin at its far shore. Yama knew that there were many shrines and monuments to pillar saints on the farside shore—he visited some of them each year, when the whole city crossed the Great River to celebrate with fireworks and feasting the rise of the Galaxy at the beginning of winter—and he wondered why the map did not show them. For there was so much detail crammed into the map elsewhere. Between the Great River and the Rim Mountains was the long strip of inhabited land, marked with green plains and lesser mountain ranges and chains of lakes and ochre deserts. Most cities were scattered along the Great River's nearside shore, a thousand or more which lit up with their names when Yama touched them. The greatest of them all stood below the head of the Great River: Ys, a vast blot spread beyond the braided delta where the river gathered its strength from the glaciers and icefields which buried all but the peaks of the Terminal Mountains. When the map had been made, Ys had been at the height of its glory, and its intricate grids of streets and parks and temples stretched from the shore of the Great River to the foothills and canyons at the edge of the Rim Mountains. A disc of plain glass, attached to the spindle of the map by a reel of wire, revealed details of these streets. By squeezing the edges of the disc, the magnification could be adjusted to show individual buildings, and Yama spent long hours gazing at the crowded rooftops, imagining himself smaller than a speck of dust and able to wander the ancient streets of a more innocent age.

More and more, as he came into manhood, Yama was growing restless. He dreamed of searching for his bloodline. Perhaps they were a high-born and fabulously wealthy clan, or a crew of fierce adventurers who had sailed their ships downstream to the midpoint of the world and the end of the Great River, and fallen from the edge and gone adventuring amongst the floating islands; or perhaps they belonged to a coven of wizards with magic powers, and those same powers lay slumbering within him, waiting to be awakened. Yama elaborated enormously complicated stories around his imagined bloodline, some of which Telmon listened to patiently in the watches of the night, when they were camped amongst the tombs of the City of the Dead.

"Never lose your imagination, Yama," Telmon told him. "Whatever you are, wherever you come from, that is your most important gift. But you must observe the world, too, learn how to read and remember its every detail, celebrate its hills and forests and deserts and mountains, the Great River and the thousands of rivers that run into it, the thousand cities and the ten thousand bloodlines. I know how much you love that old map, but you must live in the world as it is to really know it. Do that, and think how rich and wild and strange your stories will become. They will make you famous, I know it."

This was at the end of the last winter Telmon had spent at home, a few days before he took his muster to war. He and Yama were on the high moors three days' ride inland, chasing the rumor of a dragon. Low clouds raced toward the Great River ahead of a cold wind, and a freezing rain, gritty with flecks of ice, blew in their faces as they walked at point with a straggling line of beaters on either side. The moors stretched away under the racing clouds, hummocky and drenched, grown over with dense stands of waist-high bracken and purple islands of springy heather, slashed with fast-running peaty streams and dotted with stands of windblasted juniper and cypress and bright green domes of bog moss. Yama and Telmon were walking because horses were driven mad by the mere scent of a dragon. They wore canvas trousers and long oilcloth slickers over down-lined jackets, and carried heavy carbon-fiber bows which stuck up behind their heads, and quivers of long arrows with sharply tapered ceramic heads. They were soaked and windblasted and utterly exhilarated.

"I will go with you," Yama said. "I will go to war, and fight by your side and write an epic about our adventures that will ring down the ages!"

Telmon laughed. "I doubt that I will see any fighting at all!"

"Your muster will do the town honor, Tel, I know it."

"At least they can drill well enough, but I hope that is all they will need to do."

After the Aedile had received the order to supply a muster of a hundred troops to contribute to the war effort, Telmon had chosen the men himself, mostly younger sons who had little chance of establishing a harem. With the help of Sergeant Rhodean, Telmon had drilled them for sixty days; in three more, the ship would arrive to take them down-river to the war.

Telmon said, "I want to bring them back safely, Yama. I will lead them into the fighting if I am ordered, but they are set down for working on the supply lines, and I will be content with that. For every man or woman fighting the heretics face to face, there are ten who bring up supplies, and build defenses, or tend the wounded or bury the dead. That is why the muster has been raised in every village and town and city. The war needs support troops as desperately as it needs fighting men."

"I will go as an irregular. We can fight together, Tel."

"You will look after our father, first of all. And then there is Derev."

"She would not mind. And it is not as if—"

Telmon understood. He said, "There are plenty of metic marriages, if it does become that serious."

"I think it might be, Tel. But I will not get married before you return, and I will not get married before I have had my chance to fight in the war."

"I'm sure you will get your chance, if that is what you want. But be sure that you really want it."

"Do you think the heretics really fight with magic?"

"They probably have technology given to them by the Ancients of Days. It might seem like magic, but that is only because we do not understand it. But we have right on our side, Yama. We are fighting with the will of the Preservers in our hearts. It is better than any magic."

Telmon sprang onto a hummock of sedge and looked left and right to check the progress of the beaters, but it was Yama, staring straight ahead with the rain driving into his face, who saw a little spark of light suddenly blossom far out across the sweep of the moors. He cried out and pointed, and Telmon blew and blew on his silver whistle, and raised both arms above his head to signal that the beaters at the far end of each line should begin to walk toward each other and close the circle. Other whistles sounded as the signal was passed down the lines, and Yama and Telmon broke into a run against the wind and rain, leaping a stream and running on toward the scrap of light, which flickered and grew brighter in the midst of the darkening plain.

It was a juniper set on fire. It was burning so fiercely that it had scorched the grass all around it, snapping and crackling as fire consumed its needle-laden branches and tossed yellow flame and fragrant smoke into the wind and rain. Telmon and Yama gazed at it with wonder, then hugged and pounded each other on the back.

"It is here!" Telmon shouted. "I know it is here!"

They cast around, and almost at once Telmon found the long scar in a stand of heather. It was thirty paces wide and more than five hundred long, burnt down to the earth and layered with wet black ashes.

It was a lek, Telmon said. "The male makes it to attract females. The size and regularity of it shows that he is strong and fit."

"This one must have been very big," Yama said. The excitement he had felt while running toward the burning tree was gone; he felt a queer kind of relief now. He would not have to face the dragon. Not yet. He paced out the length of the lek while Telmon squatted with the blazing tree at his back and poked through the char.

"Four hundred and twenty-eight," Yama said, when he came back. "How big would the dragon be, Tel?"

"Pretty big. I think he was successful, too. Look at the claw marks here. There are two kinds."

They quartered the area around the lek, moving quickly because the light was going. The tree had mostly burned out when the beaters arrived and helped widen the search. But the dragon was gone.

Three days later, Telmon and the muster from Aeolis boarded a carrack that had anchored at the floating harbor on its way from Ys to the war at the midpoint of the world. Yama did not go to see Telmon off, but stood on the bluff above the Great River and raised his fighting kite into the wind as the little flotilla of skiffs, each with a decad of men, rowed out to the great ship. Yama had painted the kite with a red dragon, its tail curled around its long body and fire pouring from its crocodile jaws, and he flew it high into the snapping wind and then lit the fuses and cut the string. The kite sailed out high above the Great River, and the chain of firecrackers exploded in flame and smoke until the last and biggest of all set fire to the kite's wide diamond, and it fell from the sky.

After the news of the death of Telmon, Yama began to feel an unfocused restlessness. He spent long hours studying the map or sweeping the horizons with the telescope in the tower which housed the heliograph, most often pointing it upriver, where there was always the sense of the teeming vast city, like a thunderstorm, looming beyond the vanishing point.

Ys! When the air was exceptionally clear, Yama could glimpse the slender gleaming towers rooted at the heart of the city. The towers were so tall that they rose beyond the limit of visibility, higher than the bare peaks of the Rimwall Mountains, punching through the atmosphere whose haze hid Ys itself. Ys was three days' journey by river and four times that by road, but even so the ancient city dominated the landscape, and Yama's dreams.

After Telmon's death, Yama began to plan his escape with meticulous care, although at first he did not think of it as escape at all, but merely an extension of the expeditions he had made, first with Telmon, and latterly with Ananda and Derev, in the City of the Dead. Sergeant Rhodean was fond of saying that most unsuccessful campaigns failed not because of the action of the enemy but because of lack of crucial supplies or unforeseeable circumstances, and so Yama made caches of stolen supplies in several hiding-places amongst the ruins in the garden of the peel-house. But he didn't seriously think of carrying out his plans until the night after the encounter with Lud and Lob, when Dr. Dismas had an audience with the Aedile.

Dr. Dismas arrived at the end of the evening meal. The Aedile and Yama customarily ate together in the Great Hall, sitting at one end of the long, polished table under the high, barrel-vaulted ceiling and its freight of hanging banners, most so ancient that all traces of the devices they had once borne had faded, leaving only a kind of insubstantial,

tattered gauze. They were the sigils of the Aedile's ancestors. He had
saved them from the great bonfires of the vanities when, after coming
to power, the present administration of the Department of Indigenous
Affairs had sought to eradicate the past.

Ghosts. Ghosts above, and a ghost unremarked in the empty chair
at the Aedile's right hand.

Servants came and went with silent precision, bringing lentil soup,
then slivers of mango dusted with ginger, and then a roast marmot
dismembered on a bed of watercress. The Aedile said little except to
ask after Yama's day.

Yama had spent the morning watching the pinnace which had anchored downriver of the bay three days ago, and now he remarked that
he would like to take a boat out to have a closer look at it.

The Aedile said, "I wonder why it does not anchor at the new quay.
It is small enough to enter the mouth of the bay, yet does not. No, I do
not think it would be good for you to go out to it, Yama. As well as
good, brave men, all sorts of ruffians are recruited to fight the heretics."

For a moment, they both thought of Telmon.

Ghosts, invisibly packing the air.

The Aedile changed the subject. "When I first arrived here, ships
of all sizes could anchor in the bay, and when the river level began to
fall I had the new quay built. But now the bigger ships must use the
floating harbor, and soon that will have to be moved farther out to
accommodate the largest of the argosies. From its present rate of shrinkage I have calculated that in less than five hundred years the river will
be completely dry. Aeolis will be a port stranded in a desert plain."

"There is the Breas."

"Quite, quite, but where does the water of the Breas come from,
except from the snows of the Rim Mountains, which in turn fall from
air pregnant with water evaporated from the Great River? I have sometimes thought that it would be good for the town to have the old locks
rebuilt. There is still good marble to be quarried in the hills."

Yama mentioned that Dr. Dismas was returned from Ys, but the
Aedile only said, "Quite, quite. I have even talked with him."

"I suppose he has arranged some filthy little clerkship for me."

"This is not the time to discuss your future," the Aedile said, and
retreated, as was increasingly his habit, into a book. He made occasional
notes in the margins of its pages with one hand while he ate with the
other at a slow, deliberate pace that was maddening to Yama. He wanted
to go down to the armory and question Sergeant Rhodean, who had
returned from his patrol just before darkness.

The servants had cleared away the great silver salver bearing the marmot's carcass and were bringing in a dish of iced sherbet when the majordomo paced down the long hall and announced the arrival of Dr. Dismas.

"Bring him directly." The Aedile shut his book, took off his spectacles, and told Yama, "Run along, my boy. I know you want to quiz Sergeant Rhodean."

Yama had used the telescope to spy on the Aedile and Dr. Dismas that afternoon, when they had met and talked on the dusty hillside at the edge of the City of the Dead. He was convinced that Dr. Dismas had been to Ys to arrange an apprenticeship in some dusty corner of the Aedile's department.

And so, although he set off toward the armory, Yama quickly doubled back and crept into the gallery just beneath the Great Hall's high ceiling, where, on feast days, musicians hidden from view serenaded the Aedile's guests. Yama thrust his head between the stays of two dusty banners and found that he was looking straight down at the Aedile and Dr. Dismas.

The two men were drinking port wine so dark that it was almost black, and Dr. Dismas had lit one of his cigarettes. Yama could smell its clove-scented smoke. Dr. Dismas sat stiffly in a carved chair, his white hands moving over the polished surface of the table like independently questing animals. Papers were scattered in front of him, and patterns of blue dots and dashes glowed in the air. Yama would have dearly loved to have had a spyglass just then, to find out what was written on the papers, and what the patterns meant.

Yama had expected to hear Dr. Dismas and the Aedile discuss his apprenticeship, but instead the Aedile was making a speech about trust. "When I took Yama into my household, I also took upon myself the responsibility of a parent. I have brought him up as best I could, and I have tried to make a decision about his future with his best interests in my heart. You ask me to overthrow that in an instant, to gamble my duty to the boy against some vague promise."

"It is more than that," Dr. Dismas said. "The boy's bloodline—"

Yama's heart beat more quickly, but the Aedile angrily interrupted Dr. Dismas. "That is of no consequence. I know what you told me. It only convinces me that I must see to the boy's future."

"I understand. But, with respect, you may not be able to protect him from those who might be interested to learn of him, who might believe that they have a use for him. I speak of higher affairs than those of the Department of Indigenous Affairs. I speak of great forces, forces

which your few decads of soldiers could not withstand for an instant.
You should not put yourself between those powers and that which they
may desire."

The Aedile stood so suddenly that he knocked over his glass of
port. High above, Yama thought that for a moment his guardian might
strike Dr. Dismas, but then the Aedile turned his back on the table and
closed his fist under his chin. He said, "Who did you tell, doctor?"

"As yet, only you."

Yama knew that Dr. Dismas was lying, because the answer sprang
so readily to his lips. He wondered if the Aedile knew, too.

"I notice that the pinnace which brought you back from Ys is still
anchored off the point of the bay. I wonder why that might be."

"I suppose I could ask its commander. He is an acquaintance of
mine."

The Aedile turned around. "I see," he said coldly. "Then you
threaten—"

"My dear Aedile, I do not come to your house to threaten you. I
have better manners than that, I would hope. I make no threats, only
predictions. You have heard my thoughts about the boy's bloodline.
There is only one explanation. I believe any other man, with the same
evidence, would come to the same conclusion as I, but it does not matter
if I am right. One need only raise the possibility to understand what
danger the boy might be in. We are at war, and you have been concealing him from your own department. You would not wish to have
your loyalty put to the question. Not again."

"Be careful, doctor. I could have you arrested. You are said to be
a necromancer, and it is well known that you indulge in drugs."

Dr. Dismas said calmly, "The first is only a rumor, and while the
second may be true, you have recently demonstrated your faith in me,
and your letter is lodged with my department. As, I might add, is a copy
of my findings. You could arrest me, but you could not keep me imprisoned for long without appearing foolish or corrupt. But why do we
argue? We both have the same interest. We both wish no harm to come
to the boy. We merely disagree on how to protect him."

The Aedile sat down and ran his fingers through the gray pelt which
covered his face. He said, "How much money do you want?"

Dr. Dismas laughed. It was like the creaking of old wood giving
beneath a weight. "In one pan of the scales is the golden ingot of the
boy; in the other the feather of your worth. I will not even pretend to
be insulted." He stood and plucked his cigarette from the holder and
extinguished it in the pool of port spilled from the Aedile's glass, then

reached into the glowing patterns. There was a click: the patterns vanished. Dr. Dismas tossed the projector cube into the air and made it vanish into one of the pockets of his long black coat. He said, "If you do not make arrangements, then I must. And believe me, you'll get the poorer part of the bargain if you do."

When Dr. Dismas had gone, the Aedile raked up the papers and clutched them to his chest. His shoulders shook. High above, Yama thought that his guardian might be crying, but surely he was mistaken, for never before, even at the news of Telmon's death, had the Aedile shown any sign of grief.

5

The Siege

YAMA LAY AWAKE long into the night, his mind racing with speculations about what Dr. Dismas might have discovered. Something about his bloodline, he was sure of that at least, and he slowly convinced himself it was something with which Dr. Dismas could blackmail the Aedile. Perhaps his real parents were heretics or murderers or pirates . . . but who then would have a use for him, and what powers would take an interest? He was well aware that like all orphans he had filled the void of his parents' absence with extreme caricatures. They could be war heroes or colorful villains or dynasts wealthy beyond measure; what they could not be was ordinary, for that would mean that he too was ordinary, abandoned not because of some desperate adventure or deep scandal, but because of the usual small tragedies of the human condition. In his heart he knew these dreams for what they were, but although he had put them away, as he had put aside his childish toys, Dr. Dismas's return had awakened them, and all the stories he had elaborated as a child tumbled through his mind in a vivid pageant that raveled away into confused dreams filled with unspecific longing.

As the sun crept above the ragged blue line of the Rim Mountains, Yama was woken by a commotion below his window. He threw open the shutters and saw that three pentads of the garrison, in black resin armor ridged like the carapaces of sexton beetles and kilts of red leather strips, and with burnished metal caps on their heads, were climbing onto their horses. Squat, shaven-headed Sergeant Rhodean leaned on the pommel of his gelding's saddle as he watched his men settle themselves and their restless mounts. Puffs of vapor rose from the horses' nostrils; harness jingled and hooves clattered on concrete as they stepped about.

Other soldiers were stacking ladders, grappling irons, siege rockets and coils of rope on the loadbed of the grimy black steam wagon. Two house servants maneuvered the Aedile's palanquin, which floated a handspan above the ground, into the center of the courtyard and then the Aedile himself appeared, clad in his robe of office, black sable trimmed with a collar of white feathers that ruffled in the cold dawn breeze.

The servants helped the Aedile over the flare of the palanquin's skirt and settled him in the backless chair beneath its red and gold canopy. Sergeant Rhodean raised a hand above his head and the procession, two files of mounted soldiers on either side of the palanquin, moved out of the courtyard. Black smoke and sparks shot up from the steam wagon's tall chimney; white vapor jetted from leaking piston sleeves. As the wagon ground forward, its iron-rimmed wheels striking sparks from concrete, Yama threw on his clothes; before it had passed through the arch of the gate in the old wall he was in the armory, quizzing the stable hands.

"Off to make an arrest," one of them said. It was the foreman, Torin. A tall man, his shaven bullet-head couched in the hump of muscle at his back, his skin a rich dark brown mapped with paler blotches. He had followed the Aedile into exile from Ys and, after Sergeant Rhodean, was the most senior of his servants. "Don't be thinking we'll saddle up your horse, young master," he told Yama. "We've strict instructions that you're to stay here."

"I suppose you are not allowed to tell me who they are going to arrest. Well, it does not matter. I know it is Dr. Dismas."

"The master was up all night," Torin said, "talking with the soldiers. Roused the cook hours ago to make him early breakfast. There might be a bit of a battle."

"Who told you that?"

Torin gave Yama an insolent smile. His teeth were needles of white bone. "Why it's plain to see. There's that ship still waiting offshore. It might try a rescue."

The party of sailors. What had they been looking for? Yama said, "Surely it is on our side."

"There's some that reckon it's for Dr. Dismas," Torin said. "That's how he came back to town, after all. There'll be blood shed before the end of it. Cook has his boys making bandages, and if you're looking for something to do you should join them."

Yama ran again, this time to the kitchens. He snatched a sugar roll from a batch fresh from the baking oven, then climbed the back stairs two steps at a time, taking big bites from the warm roll. He waited behind a pillar while the old man who had charge of the Aedile's bed-chamber locked the door and pottered off, crumpled towels over one arm, then used his knife to pick the lock, a modern mechanical thing as big as his head. It was easy to snap back the lock's wards one by one and to silence the machines which set up a chorus of protest at his entrance, although it took a whole minute to convince an alembic that his presence would not upset its delicate settings.

Quickly, Yama searched for the papers Dr. Dismas had brought, but they were not amongst the litter on the Aedile's desk, nor were they in the sandalwood traveling chest, with its deck of sliding drawers. Per-haps the papers were in the room in the watchtower—but that had an old lock, and Yama had never managed to persuade it to let him pass.

He closed the chest and sat back on his heels. This part of the house was quiet. Narrow beams of early sunlight slanted through the tall, nar-row windows, illuminating a patch of the richly patterned carpet, a book splayed upside-down on the little table beside the Aedile's reading chair. Zakiel would be waiting for him in the library, but there were more important things afoot. Yama went back out through the kitchen, cut across the herb garden and, after calming one of the watchdogs, ran down the steep slope of the breastwork and struck off through the ruins toward the city.

———

Dr. Dismas's tower stood just outside the city wall. It was tall and slender, and had once been used to manufacture shot. Molten blackstone had been poured through a screen at the top of the tower, and the drop-lets, rounding into perfect spheres as they fell, had plummeted into an annealing bath of water at the base. The builders of the tower had sought to advertise its function by adding slit windows and a parapet with a crenellated balustrade in imitation of the watchtower of a castellan, and after the foundry had been razed, the tower had indeed been briefly used as a lookout post. But then the new city wall had been built with the tower outside it, and the tower had fallen into disuse, its stones slowly pried apart by the tendrils of its ivy cloak, the platform where molten stone had been poured to make shot for the guns of soldiers and hunters becoming the haunt of owls and bats.

Dr. Dismas had moved into the tower shortly after taking up his apothecary's post. Once it had been cleaned out and joiners had fitted new stairs and three circular floors within it and raised a tall slender spire above the crenellated balustrade, Dr. Dismas had closed its door to the public, preferring to rent a room overlooking the waterfront as his office. There were rumors that he performed all kinds of black arts in the tower, from necromancy to the surgical creation of chimeras and other monsters. It was said that he owned a homunculus he himself had fathered by despoiling a young girl taken from the fisherfolk. The homunculus was kept in a tank of saline water, and could prophesy the future. Everyone in Aeolis would swear to the truth of this, although no one, of course, had actually seen it.

The soldiers had already begun the siege by the time Yama reached the tower, and a crowd had gathered at a respectful distance to watch the fun. Sergeant Rhodean stood at the door at the foot of the tower, his helmet tucked under one arm as he bawled out the warrant. The Aedile sat straight-backed under the canopy of the palanquin, which was grounded amongst the soldiers and a unit of the town's militia, out of range of shot or quarrel. The militiamen were a motley crew in mismatched bits of armor, armed mostly with homemade blunderbusses and rifles but drawn up in two neat ranks as if determined to put on a good show. The soldiers' horses tossed their heads, made nervous by the crowd and the steady hiss of the steam wagon's boiler.

Yama clambered to the top of a stretch of ruined wall near the back of the crowd. It was almost entirely composed of men; wives were not allowed to leave the harems. They stood shoulder to shoulder, gray- and brown-skinned, corpulent and four square on short, muscular legs, bare-chested in breechclouts or kilts. They stank of sweat and fish and stale riverwater, and nudged each other and jostled for a better view. There was a jocular sense of occasion, as if this were some piece of theater staged by a traveling mountebank. It was about time the magician got what he deserved, they told each other, and agreed that the Aedile would have a hard time of it winkling him from his nest.

Hawkers were selling sherbet and sweetmeats, fried cakes of riverweed and watermelon slices. A knot of whores of a dozen different bloodlines, clad in abbreviated, brightly colored nylon chitons, their faces painted dead white under fantastical conical wigs, watched from a little rise at the back of the crowd, passing a slim telescope to and fro. Their panderer, no doubt hoping for brisk business when the show was over, moved amongst the crowd, cracking jokes and handing out clove-flavored cigarettes. Yama looked for the whore he had lain with the night before Telmon had left for the war, but could not see her, and blushingly looked away when the panderer caught his eye and winked at him.

Sergeant Rhodean bawled out the warrant again, and when there was no reply set his helmet on his scarred, shaven head and limped back to where the Aedile and the other soldiers waited. He leaned on the skirt of the Aedile's palanquin and there was a brief conference.

"Burn him out!" someone in the crowd shouted, and there was a general murmur of agreement.

The steam wagon jetted black smoke and lumbered forward; soldiers dismounted and walked along the edge of the crowd, selecting volunteers from its ranks. Sergeant Rhodean spoke to the bravos and handed out coins; under his supervision, they lifted the ram from the loadbed of the steam wagon and, flanked by soldiers, carried it toward the tower. The soldiers held their round shields above their heads, but nothing stirred in the tower until the bravos applied the ram to its door.

The ram was the trunk of a young pine bound with a spiral of steel, slung in a cradle of leather straps with handholds for eight men and crowned with a steel cap shaped like a caprice, with sturdy, coiled horns. The crowd shouted encouragement as the bravos swung it in steadily increasing arcs. "One!" they shouted. "Two!"

At the first stroke of the ram, the door rang like a drum and a cloud of bats burst from the upper window of the tower. The bats swooped low, swirling above the heads of the crowd with a dry rustle of wings, and the men laughed and jumped up, trying to catch them. One of the whores ran down the road screaming, her hands beating at two bats which had tangled in her conical wig. Some in the crowd cheered coarsely. The whore stumbled and fell flat on her face and a militiaman ran forward and slashed at the bats with his knife. One struggled free and took to the air; the man stamped on the other until it was a bloody smear on the dirt. As if blown by a wind, the rest of the bats rose high and scattered into the blue sky.

The ram struck again and again. The bravos had found their rhythm now. The crowd cheered the steady beat. Someone at Yama's shoulder remarked, "They should burn him out."

It was Ananda. As usual, he wore his orange robe, with his left breast bare. He carried a small leather satchel containing incense and chrism oil. He told Yama that his master was here to exorcise the tower and, in case things got out of hand, to shrive the dead. He was indecently pleased about Dr. Dismas's impending arrest. Dr. Dismas was infamous for his belief that chance, not the Preservers, controlled the lives of men. He did not attend any high day services, although he was a frequent visitor to the temple, playing chess with Father Quine and spending hours debating the nature of the Preservers and the world. The priest viewed Dr. Dismas as a brilliant mind that might yet be saved; Ananda knew the doctor was too clever and too proud for that.

"He plays games with people," Ananda told Yama. "He enjoys making people believe that he's a warlock, although of course he has no such powers. No one has, unless they flow from the Preservers. It's time he was punished. He's been revelling in his notoriety too long."

"He knows something about me," Yama said. "He found it out in Ys. I think that he is trying to blackmail my father with it."

Yama described what had happened the night before, and Ananda said kindly, "I shouldn't think that Dismas has found out anything at all, but of course he couldn't return and tell the Aedile that. He was bluffing, and now his bluff has been called. You'll see. The Aedile will put him to question."

"He should have killed Dr. Dismas on the spot," Yama said. "Instead, he stayed his hand, and now he has this farce."

"Your father is a cautious and judicious man."

"Too cautious. A good general makes a plan and strikes before the enemy has a chance to find a place to make a stand."

Ananda said, "He could not strike Dr. Dismas dead on the spot, or even arrest him. It would not be seemly. He had to consult the Council for Night and Shrines—Dr. Dismas is their man, after all. This way, justice is seen to be done, and all are satisfied. That's why he chose volunteers from the crowd to break down the door. Everyone is involved in this."

"Perhaps," Yama said, but he was not convinced. That this whole affair was somehow hinged about his origin was both exciting and shameful. He wanted it over with, and yet a part of him, the wild part that dreamed of pirates and adventurers, exulted in the display of force, and he was more certain than ever that he could never settle into a quiet tenure in some obscure office within the Department of Indigenous Affairs.

The ram struck, and struck again, but the door showed no sign of giving way.

"It is reinforced with iron," Ananda said, "and it is not hinged, but slides into a recess. In any case we've a long wait even after they break down the door."

Yama remarked that Ananda seemed to be an expert on the prosecution of sieges.

"I saw one before," Ananda said. "It was in the little town outside the walls of the monastery where I was taught, in the high mountains upriver of Ys. A gang of brigands had sealed themselves in a house.

The town had only its militia, and Ys was two days' march away—long before soldiers could arrive, the brigands would have escaped under cover of darkness. The militia decided to capture the brigands themselves, but several were killed trying to break into the place, and at last they burned the house to the ground, and the brigands with it. That's what they should do here; otherwise the soldiers will have to break into every floor of the tower to catch Dismas. He could kill many of them before that—and suppose he has something like the palanquin? He could fly away."

"Then my father could chase him." Yama laughed at the vision this conjured up: Dr. Dismas fleeing the tower like a black beetle on the wing and the Aedile swooping behind in his richly decorated palanquin like a hungry bird.

The crowd cheered. Yama and Ananda pushed to the front, using their elbows and knees, and saw that the door had split from top to bottom.

Sergeant Rhodean raised a hand and there was an expectant hush. "One more time, lads," the sergeant shouted, "and put some back into it!"

The ram swung and the door shattered and fell away. The crowd surged forward, carrying Ananda and Yama with it, and soldiers pushed them back. One recognized Yama. "You should not be here, young master," he said. "Go back now. Be sensible."

Yama dodged away before the soldier could grab him and, followed by Ananda, retreated to his original vantage point on the broken bit of wall, where he could see over the heads of the crowd and the line of embattled soldiers. The team of bravos swung the ram with short brisk strokes, knocking away the wreckage of the door; then they stood aside as a pentad of soldiers (the leader of the militia trailing behind) came forward with rifles and arbalests at the ready.

Led by Sergeant Rhodean, this party disappeared into the dark doorway. There was an expectant hush. Yama looked to the Aedile, who sat upright under the canopy of his palanquin, his face set in a grim expression. The white feathers which trimmed the high collar of his sable robe fluttered in the morning breeze.

There was a muffled thump. Thick orange smoke suddenly poured from one of the narrow windows of the tower, round billows swiftly unpacking into the air. The crowd murmured, uncertain if this was part of the attack or a desperate defensive move. More thumps: now smoke poured from every window, and from the smashed doorway. The soldiers stumbled out under a wing of orange smoke. Sergeant Rhodean brought up the rear, hauling the leader of the militia with him.

Flames mingled with the smoke that poured from the windows, which was slowly changing from orange to deep red. Some of the crowd were kneeling, their fists curled against their foreheads to make the sign of the Eye.

Ananda said to Yama, "This is demon work."

"I thought you did not believe in magic."

"No, but I believe in demons. After all, demons tried to overthrow the order of the Preservers an age ago. Perhaps Dismas is one, disguised as a man."

"Demons are machines, not supernatural creatures," Yama said, but Ananda had turned to look at the burning tower, and did not seem to have heard him.

The flames licked higher; there was a ring of flames around the false spire that crowned the top of the tower. Red smoke hazed the air. Fat flakes of white ash fell through it. There was a stink of sulphur and something sickly sweet. Then there was another muffled thump and a tongue of flame shot out of the doorway. The tower's spire blew to flinders. Burning strips of plastic foil rained down on the heads of the crowd and men yelled and ran in every direction.

Yama and Ananda were separated by the sudden panic as the front ranks of the crowd tried to flee through the press of those behind and dozens of men clambered over the broken wall. A horse reared up, striking with its hooves at a man who had grabbed hold of its bridle. The steam wagon was alight from one end to the other. The driver jumped from its burning cab, rolled over and over to smother his smoldering clothes, and staggered to his feet just as the charges on its load-bed exploded and blew him to red ruin.

Siege rockets flew in crisscross trajectories, trailing burning lengths of rope. A cask of napalm burst in a ball of oily flame, sending a mushroom of smoke boiling into the air. Flecks of fire spattered in a wide circle. Men dived toward whatever cover they could find. Yama dropped to the ground, his arms crossed over his head, as burning debris pattered around.

There was a moment of intense quiet. As Yama climbed to his feet, his ears ringing, a heavy hand fell on his shoulder and spun him around.

"We've unfinished business, small fry," Lob said. Behind his brother, Lud grinned around his tusks.

6

The House of Ghost Lanterns

LUD TOOK YAMA'S knife and stuck it in his belt beside his own crooked blade. "Don't go shouting for help," he said, "or we'll tear out your tongue."

People were making a hasty retreat toward the gate in the city wall. Lob and Lud gripped Yama's arms and carried him along with them. The tower was burning furiously, a roaring chimney belching thick red fumes that, with the smoke of the burning wagon and countless lesser fires, veiled the sun. Several horses had thrown their riders and were galloping about wildly. Sergeant Rhodean strode amidst the flames and smoke, organizing countermeasures; already, soldiers and militiamen were beating at small grass fires with wet blankets.

The fleeing crowd split around Ananda and the priest. They were kneeling over a man and anointing his bloody head with oil while reciting the last rites. Yama turned to try and catch Ananda's eye, but Lud snarled and cuffed his head and forced him on.

The fumes of the burning tower hung over the crowded flat roofs of the little city. Along the old waterfront, peddlers were bundling wares into their blankets. Chandlers, tavern owners and their employees were locking shutters over windows and standing guard at doors, armed with rifles and axes. Men were already looting the building where Dr. Dismas had his office. They dragged furniture onto the second floor veranda and threw it into the street; books rained down like broken-backed birds; jars of simples smashed on the concrete, strewing arcs of colored powder. A man was methodically smashing all the windows with a heavy iron hammer.

Lob and Lud marched Yama through the riot and turned down a sidestreet that was little more than a paved walkway above the green water of a wide, stagnant canal. The single-story houses which stood shoulder to shoulder along the canal had been built with stone looted from older, grander buildings, and their tall, narrow windows were framed by collages of worn carvings and broken tablets incised with texts in long-forgotten scripts. Chutes led down into the scummy water; this part of the city was where the bachelor field laborers lived, and they could not afford private bathing places.

For a moment, Yama thought that the two brothers had dragged him to this shabby, unremarked sidestreet so that they could punish him for interfering with their fun with the anchorite. He braced himself, but was merely pushed forward. With Lud leading and Lob crowding behind, he was hustled through the street doorway of a tavern, under a cluster of ancient ghost lanterns that squealed and rustled in the fetid breeze.

A square plunge pool lit by green underwater lanterns took up half the echoing space. Worn stone steps led down into the slop of glowing water. An immensely fat man floated on his back in the middle of the pool; his shadow loomed across the galleries that ran around three sides of the room. As Lob and Lud hustled Yama past the pool, the man snorted and stirred, expelling a mist of oily vapor from his nostrils and opening one eye. Lob threw a coin. The fat man caught it in the mobile, blubbery lips of his horseshoe-shaped mouth. His lower lip inverted and the coin vanished into his maw. He snorted again and his eye closed.

Lud jabbed Yama with the point of his knife and marched him around a rack of barrels and along a narrow passage which opened into a tiny courtyard. The space, roofed with glass speckled and stained by green algae and black mold, contained a kind of cage of woven wire that fitted inside the whitewashed walls with only a handsbreadth to spare on either side. Inside the cage, beneath its wire ceiling, Dr. Dismas was hunched at a rickety table, reading a book and smoking a clove-scented cigarette stuck in his bone cigarette holder.

"Here he is," Lud said. "We have him, doctor!"

"Bring him inside," the apothecary said, and closed his book with an impatient snap.

Yama's fear had turned to paralyzing astonishment. Lob roughly pinioned his arms behind his back while Lud unlocked a door in the cage; then Yama was thrust through and the door was closed and locked behind him.

"No," Dr. Dismas said, "I am far from dead, although I have paid a heavy price for this venture. Close your mouth, boy. You look like one of the frogs you are so fond of hunting late at night."

Outside the cage, Lud and Lob nudged each other. "Go on," one muttered, and the other, "You do it!" At last, Lud said to Dr. Dismas, "You'll pay us. We done what you asked."

"You failed the first time," Dr. Dismas said, "and I haven't forgotten. There's work still to be done, and if I pay you now you'll turn any money I give you into drink. Go now. We'll start on the second part of this an hour after sunset."

After more nudging, Lob said, "We thought maybe we get paid for the one thing, and then we do the other."

"I told you that I would pay you to bring the boy here. And I will. And there will be more money when you help me take him to the man who has commissioned me. But there will be no money at all unless everything is done as I asked."

"Maybe we only do the one thing," Lob said, "and not the other."

"I would suggest it is dangerous to leave something unfinished," Dr. Dismas said.

"I don't know if this is right," Lud said. "We did what you asked—"

Dr. Dismas said sharply, "When did I ask you to begin the second part of your work?"

"Sunset," Lob said in a sullen mumble.

"An hour after. Remember that. You will suffer as much as I if the work is done badly. You failed the first time. Don't fail again."

Lud said sulkily, "We got him for you, didn't we?"

Lob added, "We would have got him the other night, if this old culler with a stick hadn't got in the way."

Yama stared at the brothers through the mesh of the cage. They would not meet his eyes. He said, "You should allow me to go. I will say you rescued me from the mob. I do not know what Dr. Dismas promised, but my father will pay double to have me safe."

Lud and Lob grinned, nudging each other in the ribs.

"Ain't he a corker," Lud said. "Like a proper little gentleman."

Lob belched, and his brother sniggered.

Yama turned to Dr. Dismas. "The same applies to you, doctor."

"My dear boy, I don't think the Aedile can afford my price," Dr. Dismas said. "I was happy in my home, with my research and my books." He put a hand on his narrow chest and sighed. He had six fingers, with long nails filed to points. "All gone now, thanks to you.

You owe me a great deal, Yamamanama, and I intend to have my price in full. I don't need the Aedile's charity."

Yama felt a queer mixture of excitement and fear. He was convinced that Dr. Dismas had found his bloodline, if not his family. "Then you really have found where I came from! You have found my family—that is, my real family—"

"O, far better than that," Dr. Dismas said, "but this is not the time to talk about it."

Yama said, "I would know it now, whatever it is. I deserve to know it."

Dr. Dismas said with sudden anger, "I'm no house servant, boy," and his hand flashed out and pinched a nerve in Yama's elbow. Yama's head was filled with pain as pure as light. He fell to his knees on the mesh floor of the cage, and Dr. Dismas came around the table and caught Yama's chin between long, stiff, cold fingers.

"You are mine now," he said, "and don't forget it." He turned to the twins. "Why are you two still here? You have your orders."

"We'll be back tonight," Lud said. "See you pay us then."

"Of course, of course." Once the twins had gone, Dr. Dismas said to Yama in a confiding tone, "Frankly, I would rather work alone, but I could hardly move amongst the crowd while everyone thought I was in the tower." He got his hands under Yama's arms and hauled him up. "Please, do sit. We are civilized men. There, that's better."

Yama, perched on the edge of the flimsy metal chair, simply breathed for a while until the pain had retreated to a warm throb in the muscles of his shoulder. At last he said, "You knew the Aedile was going to arrest you."

Dr. Dismas resumed his seat on the other side of the little table. As he screwed a cigarette into his bone holder, he said, "Your father is a man who takes his responsibilities seriously. Very properly, he confided his intentions to the Council for Night and Shrines. One of them owed me a favor."

"If there is any problem between you and my father, I am sure it can be worked out, but not while you hold me captive. Once the fire in the tower burns out, they will look for a body. When they do not find one, they will look for you. And this is a small city."

Dr. Dismas blew a riffle of smoke toward the mesh ceiling of the cage. "How well Zakiel has taught you logic. It would be a persuasive argument, except that they will find a body."

"Then you planned to burn your tower all along, and you should not blame me. I expect you removed your books before you left."

Dr. Dismas did not deny this. He said, "How did you like the display, by the way?"

"Some are convinced that you are a magician."

"There are no such creatures. Those who claim to be magicians delude themselves as much as their clients. My little pyrotechnic display was simply a few judiciously mixed salts ignited by electric detonators when the circuit was closed by some oaf stepping on a plate I'd hidden under a rug. No more than a jape which any apprentice apothecary worthy of the trade could produce, although perhaps not on such a grand scale." Dr. Dismas pointed a long forefinger at Yama, who stifled the impulse to flinch. "All this for you. You do owe me, Yamamanama. The Child of the River, yes, but which river, I wonder. Not our own Great River, I'm certain."

"You know about my family." Yama could not keep the eagerness from his voice. It was rising and bubbling inside him—he wanted to laugh, to sing, to dance. "You know about my bloodline."

Dr. Dismas reached into a pocket of his long coat and drew out a handful of plastic straws. He rattled them together in his long pale hands and cast them on the table. He was making a decision by appealing to their random pattern; Yama had heard of this habit from Ananda, who had reported it in scandalized tones.

Yama said, "Are you deciding whether to tell me or not, doctor?"

"You're a brave boy to ask after forbidden knowledge, so you deserve some sort of answer." Dr. Dismas tapped ash from his cigarette. "Oxen and camels, nilgai, ratites and horses—all of them work under the lash, watched by boys no older than you, or even younger, who are armed with no more than fresh-cut withes to restrain their charges. How is this? Because the part in those animals which yearns for freedom has been broken and replaced by habit. No more than a twitch of a stick is required to reinforce that habit; even if those beasts were freed of their harness and their burden, they would be too broken to realize that they could escape their masters. Most men are no different from beasts of burden, their spirits broken by fear of the phantoms of religion invoked by priests and bureaucrats. I work hard to avoid habits. To be unpredictable—that is how you cheat those who would be the masters of men."

"I thought you did not believe in the Preservers, doctor."

"I don't question their existence. Certainly they once existed. This world is evidence; the Eye of the Preservers and all the ordered Galaxy are evidence. But I do question the great lie with which the priests hypnotize the population, that the Preservers watch over us all, and that we must satisfy them so that we can win redemption and live forever after death. As if creatures who juggled stars in their courses would care about whether or not a man beats his wife, or the little torments one child visits upon another! It is a sop to keep men in their places, to ensure that so-called civilization can run on its own momentum. I spit on it."

And here Dr. Dismas did spit, as delicately as a cat, but nevertheless startling Yama.

The apothecary fitted his cigarette holder back between his large, flat-topped teeth. When he smiled around the holder, the plaques over his cheekbones stood out in relief, their sharp edges pressing through brown skin with the coarse, soft grain of wood-pulp.

Dr. Dismas said, "The Preservers created us, but they are gone. They are dead, and by their own hand. They created the Eye, and fell through its event horizon with all their worlds. And why? Because they despaired. They remade the Galaxy, and could have remade the Universe, but their nerve failed. They were cowardly fools, and anyone who believes that they watch us still, yet do not interfere in the terrible suffering of the world, is a worse fool."

Yama had no answer to this. There was no answer. Ananda was right. The apothecary was a monster who refused to serve anyone or anything except his own swollen pride.

Dr. Dismas said, "The Preservers are gone, but machines still watch us, and regulate the world according to out-of-date precepts. Of course, the machines can't watch everything at once, so they build up patterns and predict the behavior of men, and watch only for deviation from the norm. It works most of the time for most of the people, but there are a few men like me who defy their predictions by basing important decisions on chance. The machines cannot track our random paths from moment to moment, and so we become invisible. Of course, a cage such as the one in which we sit also helps hide us from them. It screens out the probing of the machines. I wear a hat for the same reason—it is lined with silver foil."

Yama laughed, because Dr. Dismas confessed this ridiculous habit with complete solemnity. "So you are afraid of machines."

"Not at all. But I am deeply interested in them. I have a small collection of parts of dead machines excavated from ruins in the deserts beyond the midpoint of the world—one is almost intact, a treasure beyond price." Dr. Dismas suddenly clutched his head and shook it violently for a moment, then winked at Yama. "But that's not to be spoken of. Not here! They might hear, even in this cage. One reason I came here is because machine activity is higher than anywhere else on Confluence—yes, even Ys. And so, my dear Yamamanama, I found you."

Yama pointed at the straws scattered on the table. They were hexagonal in cross-section, with red and green glyphs of some unknown language incised along their faces. He said, "You refuse to acknowledge the authority of the Preservers over men, yet you follow the guidance of these bits of plastic."

Dr. Dismas looked crafty. "Ah, but I choose which question to ask them."

Yama had only one question in his mind. "You found something about my bloodline in Ys, and told my father what you had learned. If you will not tell me everything, will you at least tell me what you told him? Did you perhaps find my family there?"

"You will have to look farther than Ys to find your family, my boy, and you may be given the opportunity to do so. The Aedile is a good enough man in his way, I suppose, but that is to say he is no more than a petty official barely capable of ruling a moribund little region of no interest to anyone. Into his hands has fallen a prize which could determine the fate of all the peoples of Confluence—even the world itself—and he does nothing about it. A man like that deserves to be punished, Yamamanama. And as for you, you are very dangerous. For you do not know what you are."

"I would like very much to know." Yama had not understood half of what Dr. Dismas had said. With a sinking heart, he was beginning to believe that the man was mad.

"Innocence is no excuse," Dr. Dismas said, but he appeared to be speaking to himself. He moved the plastic straws about the tabletop with a long, bony forefinger, as if seeking to rearrange his fate. He lit another cigarette and stared at Yama until Yama grew uncomfortable and looked away.

Dr. Dismas laughed, and with sudden energy took out a little leather case and opened it out on the table. Inside, held by elastic loops, were a glass syringe, an alcohol lamp, a bent silver spoon, its bowl blackened and tarnished, a small pestle and mortar, and several glass bottles with rubber stoppers. From one bottle Dr. Dismas shook out a single dried beetle into the mortar; from another he added a few drops of a clear liquid that filled the room with the smell of apricots. Dr. Dismas ground the beetle into a paste with finicky care and scraped the paste into the bowl of the spoon.

"Cantharides," he said, as if that explained everything. "You are young, and will not understand, but sometimes the world becomes too much to bear for someone of my sensibilities."

"My father said this got you into trouble with your department. He said—"

"That I had sworn to stop using it? Oh yes, of course I said that. If I had not said that, they would not have let me return to Aeolis."

Dr. Dismas lit the wick of the alcohol lamp with a flint and steel and held the spoon over the blue flame until the brown paste liquified and began to bubble. The smell of apricots intensified, sharpened by a metallic tang. Dr. Dismas drew the liquid into the hypodermic and tapped the barrel with a long thumbnail to loosen the bubbles which clung to the glass. "Don't think to escape," he said. "I have no key."

He spread his left hand on the tabletop and probed the web of skin between thumb and forefinger until he hit a vein. He teased back the syringe's plunger until a wisp of red swirled in the thin brown solution, then pressed the plunger home.

He drew in a sharp breath and stretched in his chair like a bow. The hypodermic dropped to the table. For a moment, his heels drummed an irregular tattoo on the mesh floor, and then he relaxed, and looked at Yama with half-closed eyes. His pupils, smeary crosses on yellow balls, contracted and expanded independently. He giggled. "If I had you long enough . . . ah, what I'd teach you . . ."

"Doctor?"

But Dr. Dismas would say no more. His gaze wandered around the cage and at last fixed on the spattered glass which roofed the courtyard. Yama tested the cage's wire mesh, but although he could deform its close-woven hexagons, they were all of a piece, and the door was so close-fitting Yama could not get his fingers into the gap between it and its wire frame. The sun crept into view above the little courtyard's glass ceiling, filling it with golden light, and began its slow reversal.

At last, Yama dared to touch the apothecary's outstretched hand. It was clammy, and irregular plates shifted under the loose skin. Dr. Dismas did not stir. His head was tipped back, his face bathed by the sunlight.

Yama found only one pocket inside the apothecary's long black coat, and it was empty. Dr. Dismas stirred as Yama withdrew his hand, and gripped his wrist and drew him down with unexpected strength. "Don't doubt," he murmured. His breath smelt of apricots and iron. "Sit and wait, boy."

Yama sat and waited. Presently the immensely fat man he had seen floating in the tavern's communal pool shuffled down the passage. He was naked except for blue rubber sandals on his broad feet, and he carried a tray covered with a white cloth.

"Stand back," he told Yama. "No, further back. Behind the doctor."

"Let me go. I promise you will be rewarded."

"I've already been paid, young master," the fat man said. He unlocked the door, set the tray down, and relocked the door. "Eat, young master. The doctor, he won't want anything. I never seen him eat. He has his drug."

"Let me go!" Yama banged at the cage's locked door and yelled threats at the fat man's retreating back before giving up and looking under the cloth that covered the tray.

A dish of watery soup with a cluster of whitened fish eyes sunk in the middle and rings of raw onion floating on top; a slab of black bread, as dense as a brick and almost as hard; a glass of small beer the color of stale urine.

The soup was flavored with chili oil, making it almost palatable, but the bread was so salty that Yama gagged on the first bite and could eat no more. He drank the sour beer and somehow fell asleep on the rickety chair.

He was woken by Dr. Dismas. He had a splitting headache and a foul taste in his mouth. The courtyard and the cage was lit by a hissing alcohol lantern which dangled from the cage's wire ceiling; the air beyond the glass that roofed the courtyard was black.

"Rise up, young man," Dr. Dismas said. He was filled with barely contained energy and hopped from foot to foot and banged his stiff fingers together. His shadow, thrown across the whitewashed walls of the courtyard, aped his movements.

"You drugged me," Yama said stupidly.

"A little something in the beer, to take away your cares." Dr. Dismas banged on the mesh of the cage and shouted, "Ho! Ho! Landlord!" and turned back to Yama and said, "You have been sleeping longer than you know. The little sleep just past is my gift to make you wake into your true self. You don't understand me, but it doesn't matter. Stand up! Stand up! Look lively! Awake, awake, awake! You venture forth to meet your destiny! Ho! Landlord!"

7

The Warlord

IN THE DARKNESS outside the door of the tavern, Dr. Dismas clapped a wide-brimmed hat on his head and exchanged a few words with the landlord, who handed something to the apothecary, knuckled his forehead, and shut the heavy street door. The cluster of ghost lanterns above the door creaked in the breeze, glimmering with a wan pallor that illuminated nothing but themselves. The rest of the street was dark, except for blades of light shining between a few of the closed shutters of the houses on the other side of the wide canal. Dr. Dismas switched on a penlight and waved its narrow beam at Yama, who blinked stupidly at the light; his wits were still dulled by sleep and the residue of the drugged beer.

"If you are going to be sick," Dr. Dismas said, "lean over and don't spatter your clothes or your boots. You must be presentable."

"What will you do with me, doctor?"

"Breathe, my dear boy. Slowly and deeply. Is it not a fine night? There is a curfew, I'm told. No one will be about to wonder at us. Look at this. Do you know what it is?"

Dr. Dismas showed Yama what the landlord had given him. It was an energy pistol, silver and streamlined, with a blunt muzzle and a swollen chamber, and a grip of memory plastic that could mold itself to fit the hands of most of the bloodlines of the world. A dot of red light glowed at the side of the chamber, indicating that it was fully charged.

"You could burn for that alone," Yama said.

"Then you know what it can do." Dr. Dismas pushed the muzzle into Yama's left armpit. "I have it at its weakest setting, but a single shot will roast your heart. We will walk to the new quay like two old friends."

Yama did as he was told. He was still too dazed to try to run. Besides, Sergeant Rhodean had taught him that in the event of being kidnapped he should not attempt to escape unless his life was in danger. He thought that the soldiers of the garrison must be searching for him; after all, he had been missing all day. They might turn a corner and find him at any moment.

The dose of cantharides had made Dr. Dismas talkative. He did not seem to think that he was in any danger. As they walked, he told Yama that originally the tavern had been a workshop where ghost lanterns had been manufactured in the glory days of Aeolis.

"The lanterns that advertise the tavern are a crude representation of the ideal of the past, being made of nothing more than lacquered paper. Real ghost lanterns were little round boats made of plastic, with a deep weighted keel to keep them upright and a globe of blown nylon infused with luminescent chemicals instead of a sail. Ghost lanterns were floated on the Great River after each funeral to confuse any restless spirits of the dead and make sure that they would not haunt their living relatives. There is, as you will soon see, an analogy to be made with your fate, my dear boy."

Yama said, "You traffic with fools, doctor. The owner of the tavern will be burnt for his part in my kidnap—it is the punishment my father reserves for the common people. Lud and Lob too, though their stupidity almost absolves them."

Dr. Dismas laughed. His sickly sweet breath touched Yama's cheek. He said, "And will I be burnt, too?"

"It is in my father's power. More likely you will be turned over to the mercies of your department. No one will profit from this."

"That's where you are wrong. First, I do not take you for ransom, but to save you from the pedestrian fate to which your father would consign you. Second, do you see anyone coming to your rescue?"

The long waterfront, lit by the orange glow of sodium vapor lamps, was deserted. The taverns, the chandlers' godowns and the two whorehouses were shuttered and dark. Curfew notices fluttered from doors; slogans in the crude ideograms used by the Amnan had been smeared on walls. Rubbish and driftwood had been piled against the steel doors of the big godown owned by Derev's father and set alight, but the fire had done no more than discolor the metal. Several lesser merchants' offices had been looted, and the building where Dr. Dismas had kept his office had been burnt to the ground. Smoldering timbers sent up a sharp stench that made Yama's eyes water.

Dr. Dismas marched Yama quite openly along the new quay, which ran out toward the mouth of the bay between meadows of zebra grass and shoals of mud dissected by shallow stagnant channels. The wide bay faced downriver. Framed on one side by the bluff on which the Aedile's house stood, and by the chimneys of the paeonin mill on the other, the triple-armed pinwheel of the Galaxy stood beyond the edge of the world. It was so big that when Yama looked at one edge he could not see the other. The Arm of the Warrior rose high above the arch of the Arm of the Hunter; the Arm of the Archer curved in the opposite direction, below the edge of the world, and would not be seen again until next winter. The structure known as the Blue Diadem, that Yama knew from his readings of the Puranas was a cloud of fifty thousand blue-white stars each forty times the mass of the sun of Confluence, was a brilliant pinprick of light beyond the frayed point of the outflung Arm of the Hunter, like a drop of water flicked from a finger. Smaller star clusters made long chains of concentrated light through the milky haze of the galactic arms. There were lines and threads and globes and clouds of stars, all fading into a general misty radiance notched by dark lanes which barred the arms at regular intervals. The core, bisected by the horizon, was knitted from thin shells of stars in tidy orbits concentrically packed around the great globular clusters of the heart stars, like layers of glittering tissue wrapped around a heap of jewels. Confronted with this ancient grandeur, Yama felt that his fate was as insignificant as that of any of the mosquitoes which danced before his face.

Dr. Dismas cupped his free hand to his mouth and called out, his voice shockingly loud in the quiet darkness. "Time to go!"

There was a distant splash in the shallows beyond the end of the quay's long stone finger. Then a familiar voice said, "Row with me, you bugger. You're making us go in circles."

A skiff glided out of the darkness. Lud and Lob shipped their oars as it thumped against the bottom of a broad stone stair. Lob jumped out and held the boat steady as Yama and Dr. Dismas climbed in.

"Quick as you like, your honor," Lud said.

"Haste makes waste," Dr. Dismas said. Slowly and fussily he settled himself on the center thwart, facing Yama with the energy pistol resting casually in his lap. He told the twins, "I hope that this time you did exactly as I asked."

"Sweet as you like," Lob said. "They didn't know we were there until the stuff went up." The skiff barely rocked when he vaulted back into it; he was surprisingly nimble for someone of his bulk. He and his brother settled themselves in the high seat at the stern and they pushed off from the rough stones of the quay.

Yama watched the string of orange lights along the waterfront swiftly recede into the general darkness of the shore. The cold breeze off the river was clearing his head, and for the first time since he had woken from his drugged sleep he was beginning to feel fear.

He said, "Where are you taking me, doctor?"

Dr. Dismas's eyes gleamed with red fire beneath the brim of his hat; his eyes were backed with a reflective membrane, like those of certain nocturnal animals. He said, "You return to the place of your birth, Yamamanama. Does that frighten you?"

"Little fish," Lud said mockingly. "Little fish, little fish."

"Fish out of water," Lob added.

They were both breathing heavily as they rowed swiftly toward the open water of the Great River.

"Keep quiet if you want to earn your money," Dr. Dismas said, and told Yama, "You must forgive them. Good help is so hard to find in backwater places. At times I was tempted to use my master's men instead."

Lud said, "We could tip you overboard, doctor. Ever think of that?"

Dr. Dismas said, "This pistol can kill you and your brother just as easily as Yamamanama."

"If you shoot at us, you'll set fire to the boat, and drown as neat as if we'd thrown you in."

"I might do it anyway. Like the scorpion who convinced the frog to carry him across the river, but stung his mount before they were halfway across, death is in my nature."

Lob said, "He don't mean anything by it, your honor."

"I just don't like bad-mouthing of our city," Lud said sullenly.

Dr. Dismas laughed. "I speak only the truth. Both of you agree with me, for why else would you want to leave? It is an understandable impulse, and it raises you above the rest of your kind."

Lud said, "Our father is young, that's all it is. We're strong, but he's stronger. He'd kill either of us or both of us, however we tried it, and we can't wait for him to get weak. It would take years and years."

Dr. Dismas said, "And Yamamanama wants to leave, too. Do not deny it, my boy. Soon you will have your wish. There! Look upriver! You see how much we do for you!"

The skiff heeled as it rounded the point of the shallow, silted bay and entered the choppier waters of the river proper. As it turned into the current, Yama saw with a shock that one of the ships anchored at the floating harbor half a league upstream was ablaze from bow to stern.

The burning ship squatted over its livid reflection, tossing harvests of sparks into the night, as if to rival the serene light of the Galaxy. It was a broad-beamed carrack, one of the fleet of transports which carried troops or bulk supplies to the armies fighting the heretics at the midpoint of the world. Four small boats were rowing away from it, sharply etched shadows crawling over water that shone like molten copper. Even as Yama watched, gape-mouthed, a series of muffled explosions in the ship's hold blew expanding globes of white flame high above the burning mastheads. The ship, broken-backed, settled in the water.

Lud and Lob cheered, and the skiff rocked alarmingly as they stood to get a better view.

"Sit down, you fools," Dr. Dismas said.

Lud whooped, and shouted, "We did it, your honor! Sweet as you like!"

Dr. Dismas said to Yama, "I devised a method so simple that even these two could carry it out successfully."

Yama said, "You tried to burn a ship a few days ago, did you not?"

"Two barrels of palm oil and liquid soap. One at the bow, one at the stern," Dr. Dismas said, ignoring the question, "armed with clockwork fuses. It makes a fine diversion, don't you think? Your father's soldiers are busy rescuing sailors and saving the rest of the floating harbor while we go about our business."

"There is a pinnace anchored farther out," Yama said. "It will investigate."

"I think not," Dr. Dismas said. "Its commander is most anxious to make your acquaintance, Yamamanama. He is a cunning warlord, and knows all about the fire. He understands that it is a necessary sacrifice. The heretics will be blamed for the burning of the ship, and also for your disappearance. Your father will receive a ransom note tomorrow, but even if he answers it there will, alas, be no reply. You will disappear without trace. Such things happen, in this terrible war."

"My father will search for me. He will not stop searching."

"Perhaps you won't want to be found, Yamamanama. You want to run away, and here you are, set on a great adventure."

Yama knew now who the sailors had been searching for. He said, "You tried to kidnap me two days ago. Those burning rafts were your work, so my father's soldiers would chase after imaginary heretics. But these two failed to get hold of me, and you had to try again."

"And here we are," Dr. Dismas said. "Now please be quiet. We have a rendezvous to keep."

The skiff drifted on a slow current parallel to the dark shore. The burning ship receded into the night. It had grounded on the river bottom, and only the forecastle and the masts were still burning. The fisherfolk were abroad, and the lanterns they used to attract fish to their lines made scattered constellations across the breast of the Great River, red sparks punctuating the reflected sheen of the Galaxy's light.

Dr. Dismas stared intently into the glimmering dark, swearing at Lud and Lob whenever they dipped their oars in the water. "We got to keep to the current, your honor," Lud said apologetically, "or we'll lose track of where we're supposed to be."

"Quiet! What was that?"

Yama heard a rustle of wings and a faint splash.

"Just a bat," Lud said. "They fish out here at night."

"We catch 'em with glue lines strung across the water," Lob explained. "Make good eating, bats do, but not in spring. After winter they're mainly skin and bone. They need to fatten up—"

"Do shut up!" Dr. Dismas said in exasperation. "One more word and I'll fry you both where you sit. You have so much fat on your bodies that you'll go up like candles."

The current bent away from the shore and the skiff drifted with it, scraping past young banyans that raised small crowns of leaves a handspan above the water. Yama glimpsed the pale violet spark of a machine spinning through the night. It seemed to be moving in short stuttering jerks, as if searching for something. At any other time he would have wondered at it, but now its remote light and unguessable motives only intensified his feeling of despair. The world had suddenly turned strange and treacherous, its wonders traps for the unwary.

At last Dr. Dismas said, "There! Row, you fools!"

Yama saw a red lamp flickering to starboard. Lud and Lob bent to their oars and the skiff flew across the water toward it. Dr. Dismas lit an alcohol lantern with flint and steel and held it up by his face. The light, cast through a mask of blue plastic, made his pinched face, misshapen by the plaques beneath its skin, look like that of a corpse.

The red lantern was hung from the stern of a lateen-rigged pinnace which swung at anchor beside a solitary banyan. It was the ship which had returned Dr. Dismas to Aeolis. Two sailors had climbed into the branches of the tree, and they watched over the long barrels of their rifles as the skiff came alongside. Lob stood and threw a line up to the stern of the pinnace. A sailor caught the end and made the skiff fast, and someone vaulted the pinnace's rail, landing so suddenly and lightly in the well of the skiff that Yama half rose in alarm.

The man clamped a hand on Yama's shoulder. "Easy there, lad," he said, "or you'll have us in the river." He was only a few years older than Yama, bare-chested, squat and muscular, with an officer's sash tied at the waist of his tight, white trousers. His broad, pugnacious face, framed by a cloud of loose, red-gold hair, was seamed with scars, like a clay mask someone had broken and badly mended, but his look was frank and appraising, and enlivened by good-humored intelligence.

The officer steadied the skiff as Dr. Dismas unhandily clambered up the short rope ladder dropped down the side of the pinnace, but when it was his turn Yama shook off the officer's hand and sprang up and grabbed the stern rail. His breath was driven from him when his belly and legs slammed against the clinkered planks of the pinnace's hull, and pain shot through his arms and shoulders as they took his weight, but he pulled himself up, got a leg over the rail and rolled over, coming up in a crouch on the deck of the stern platform at the bare feet of an astonished sailor.

The officer laughed and sprang from a standing jump to the rail and then, lightly and easily, to the deck. He said, "He has spirit, doctor."

Yama stood up. He had banged his right knee, and it throbbed warmly. Two sailors leaned on the steering bar and a tall man in black stood beside them. The pinnace's single mast was rooted at the edge of the stern platform; below it, three decads of rowers, naked except for breechclouts, sat in two staggered rows. The sharp prow was upswept, with a white stylized hawk's eye painted on the side. A small, swivel-mounted cannon was set in the prow's beak; its gunner had turned to watch Yama come aboard, one arm resting on the cannon's fretted barrel.

Yama looked at the black-clad man and said, "Where is the warlord who would buy me?"

Dr. Dismas said querulously, "I dislike doing business with guns pointed at me."

The officer gestured, and the two sailors perched in the banyan branches above the pinnace put up their rifles. "Just a precaution, Dismas, in case you had brought along uninvited guests. If I had wanted you shot, Dercetas and Diomedes would have picked you off while you were still rowing around the point of the bay. But have no fear of that, my friend, for I need you as much as you need me."

Yama said again, loudly, "Where is he, this warlord?"

The bare-chested officer laughed. "Why here I am," he said, and stuck out his hand.

Yama took it. The officer's grip was firm, that of a strong man who is confident of his strength. His fingers were tipped with claws that slid a little from their sheaths and pricked the palm of Yama's hand.

"Well met, Yamamanama," the officer said. His large eyes were golden, with tawny irises; the only beautiful feature of his broken face. The lid of the left eye was pulled down by a deep, crooked scar that ran from brow to chin.

"This war breeds heroes as ordure breeds flies," Dr. Dismas remarked, "but Enobarbus is a singular champion. He set sail last summer as a mere lieutenant. He led a picket boat smaller than his present command into the harbor of the enemy and sank four ships and damaged a dozen others before his own boat was sunk under him."

"It was a lucky venture," Enobarbus said. "We had a long swim of it, I can tell you, and a longer walk afterward."

Dr. Dismas said, "If Enobarbus has one flaw, it is his humility. After his boat was sunk, he led fifteen men—his entire crew—through twenty leagues of enemy lines, and did not lose one. He was rewarded with command of a division, and he is going downriver to take it up. With your help, Yamamanama, he will soon command much more."

Enobarbus grinned. "As for humility, I always have you, Dismas. If I have any failing, you are swift to point it out. How fortunate, Yamamanama, that we both know him."

"More fortunate for you, I think," Yama said.

"Every hero must be reminded of his humanity, from time to time," Dr. Dismas said.

"Fortunate for both of us," Enobarbus told Yama. "We'll make history, you and I. That is, of course, if you are what Dismas claims. He has been very careful not to bring the proof with him, so that I must keep him alive. He is a most cunning fellow."

"I've lied many times in my life," Dr. Dismas said, "but this time I tell the truth. For the truth is so astonishing that any lie would pale before it, like a candle in the sun. I think we should leave. My diversion was splendid while it lasted, but already it is almost burned out, and while the Aedile of that silly little city may be a weak man, he is no fool. His soldiers searched the hills after my men set fire to the first ship, and they will search the water this time."

"You should have trusted my men, Dismas," Enobarbus said. "We could have taken the boy two nights ago."

"And the game would have been up at once if anyone had seen

you. We should move on at once, or the Aedile will wonder why you do not come to the aid of the burning ship."

"No," Enobarbus said, "we'll tarry here a while. I have brought my own physician, and he'll take a look at your lad."

Enobarbus called the man in black forward. He was of the same bloodline as Enobarbus, but considerably older. Although he moved with the same lithe tread, he had a comfortable swag of a belly and his mane, loose about his face, was streaked with gray. His name was Agnitus.

"Take off your shirt, boy," the physician said. "Let's see what you're made of."

"It's better you do it yourself," Dr. Dismas advised. "They can tie you down and do it anyway, and it will be more humiliating, I promise you. Be strong, Yamamanama. Be true to your inheritance. All will be well. Soon you will thank me."

"I do not think so," Yama said, but pulled his shirt over his head. Now he knew that he was not going to be killed, he felt a shivery excitement. This was the adventure he had dreamed of, but unlike his dreams it was not under his control.

The physician, Agnitus, sat Yama on a stool and took his right arm and turned the joints of his fingers and wrist and elbow, ran cold hard fingers down his ribs and prodded at his backbone. He shone a light in Yama's right eye and gazed closely at it, then fitted a kind of skeletal helmet over Yama's scalp and turned various screws until their blunt ends gripped his skull, and recorded the measurements in a little oilskin-covered notebook.

Dr. Dismas said impatiently, "You'll see that he has a very distinctive bone structure, but the real proof is in his genotype. I hardly think you can conduct that kind of test here."

Agnitus said to Enobarbus, "He's right, my lord. I must take a sample of the boy's blood and a scraping of the skin from the inside of his cheek. But I can tell you now that his bloodline is not one I recognize, and I've seen plenty in my time. And he's not a surgical construct, unless our apothecary is more cunning than I am."

"I would not presume," Dr. Dismas said.

"A proof by elimination is less satisfactory than one by demonstration," Enobarbus said. "But unless we storm the library of the Department of Apothecaries and Chirurgeons, we must be content with what we have."

"It is true," Dr. Dismas said. "Haven't I sworn it so? And does he not fulfil the prophecy made to you?"

Enobarbus nodded. "Yamamanama, you've always believed your-self special. Do you have a clear view of your destiny?"

Yama pulled his shirt over his head. He liked Enobarbus's bold candor, but mistrusted him because he was clearly an ally of Dr. Dismas. He realized that everyone was looking at him, and he said defiantly, "I would say that you are a proud and ambitious man, Enobarbus, a leader of men who would seek a prize greater than mere promotion. You be-lieve that I can help you, although I do not know how—unless it is to do with the circumstances of my birth. Dr. Dismas knows about that, I think, but he likes to tease."

Enobarbus laughed. "Well said! He reads us both as easily as read-ing a book, Dismas. We must be careful."

"The Aedile would have made him a clerk," Dr. Dismas said with disgust.

"The Aedile belongs to a part of our department that is not noted for its imagination," Enobarbus said. "It is why men like him are en-trusted with the administration of unimportant towns. They can be relied upon precisely because they have no imagination. We should not con-demn him for what, in his office, is a virtue.

"Yamamanama, listen to me. With my help, the world itself lies within your grasp. Do you understand? You have always considered yourself to be of special birth, I know. Well, Dismas has discovered that you are unique, and he has convinced me that you are a part of my destiny."

And then this powerful young man did an extraordinary thing. He knelt before Yama and bowed his head until his forehead touched the deck. He looked up through the tangle of his mane and said, "I will serve you well, Yamamanama. I swear with my life. Together we will save Confluence."

"Please get up," Yama said. He was frightened by this gesture, for it marked a solemn moment whose significance he did not fully under-stand. "I do not know why I have been brought here, or why you are saying these things, but I did not ask for any of it, and I do not want it."

"Stand fast," Dr. Dismas hissed, and grasped Yama's upper arm in a cruel pinch.

Enobarbus stood. "Let him alone, Dismas. My lord . . . Yamaman-ama . . . we are about to embark upon a hard and perilous journey. I have worked toward it all my life. When I was a cub, I was blessed by a vision. It was in the temple of my bloodline, in Ys. I was praying for my brother, who had died in battle a hundred days before. The news had just reached me. I was praying that I could avenge him, and that I could play my part in saving Confluence from the heretics. I was very young, as you might imagine, and very foolish, but my prayers were answered. The shrine lit and a woman arrayed in white appeared, and told me of my destiny. I accepted, and I have been trying my best to carry it out ever since.

"Yamamanama, to know one's fate is a privilege granted only to a few men, and it is a heavy responsibility. Most men live their lives as they can. I must live my life in pursuit of an ideal. It has stripped me of my humanity as faith strips an eremite of worldly possessions, and honed my life to a single point. Nothing else matters to me. How often have I wished that the obligation be lifted, but it has not, and I have come to accept it. And here we are, as was predicted long ago."

Enobarbus suddenly smiled. It transformed his wrecked face as a firework, bursting across the dark sky, transforms the night. He clapped his hands. "I have spoken enough for now. I will speak more, Yama-manama, I promise, but it must wait until we are safe. Pay your men, Dismas. We are at last embarked on our journey."

Dr. Dismas pulled out his pistol. "It would be well if your boat put some distance between their miserable skiff. I'm not sure of the range of this thing."

Enobarbus nodded. "It's probably for the best," he said. "They might guess, and they'll certainly talk."

"You overestimate them," Dr. Dismas said. "They deserve to die because they endangered my plans by their stupidity. Besides, I cannot stand boorishness, and I have been exiled amongst these uncivilized creatures for an entire year. This will be a catharsis."

"I'll hear no more. Kill them cleanly, and do not seek to justify yourself."

Enobarbus turned to give his orders, and at that moment one of the sailors perched in the branches of the banyan to which the pinnace was moored cried out.

"Sail! Sail ahead!"

"Thirty degrees off the starboard bow," his mate added. "Half a league and bearing down hard."

Enobarbus gave his orders without missing a beat. "Cut the mooring ropes fore and aft. Dercetas and Diomedes, to your posts at once! Ready the rowers, push off on my word! I want thirty beats a minute from you lads, and no slacking or we're dead men."

In the midst of the sudden rush of activity, as oars were raised and sailors hacked at mooring lines, Yama saw his opportunity. Dr. Dismas made a grab for him, but was too slow. Yama vaulted the rail and landed hard in the well of the skiff.

"Row!" Yama yelled to Lob and Lud. "Row for your lives!"

"Catch hold of him!" Dr. Dismas shouted from above. "Catch him and make sure you don't let go!"

Lud started forward. "It's for your own good, little fish," he said. Yama dodged Lud's clumsy swipe and retreated to the stern of the little skiff. "He wants to kill you!"

"Get him, you fools," Dr. Dismas said.

Yama grabbed hold of the sides of the skiff and rocked it from side to side, but Lud stood foursquare. He grinned. "That won't help, little fish. Keep still, and maybe I won't have to hurt you."

"Hurt him anyway," Lob said.

Yama picked up the alcohol lantern and dashed it into the well of the skiff. Instantly, translucent blue flames licked up. Lud reared backward, and the skiff pitched violently. Unbearable heat beat at Yama's face; he took a deep breath and dived into the river.

He swam as far as he could before he came up and drew a gulp of air that burned all the way down the inverted trees of his lungs. He pulled at the fastenings of his heavy boots and kicked them off.

The skiff was drifting away from the side of the pinnace. Flames flickered brightly in its well. Lud and Lob were trying to beat out the fire with their shirts. Sailors threw ropes down the side of the pinnace and shouted to them to give it up and come aboard. A tremendous glow was growing brighter and brighter beyond the pinnace, turning everything into a shadow of its own self. The cannon in the prow of the pinnace spoke: a crisp rattling burst, and then another.

Yama swam as hard as he could, and when he finally turned to float on his back, breathing hard, the whole scene was spread before him. The pinnace was sliding away from the banyan tree, leaving the burning skiff behind. A great glowing ship was bearing down toward the pinnace. She was a narrow-hulled frigate, her three masts crowded with square sails, and every part of her shone with cold fire. The pinnace's cannon spoke again, and there was a crackling of rifle fire. And then Dr. Dismas fired his pistol, and for an instant a narrow lance of red fire split the night.

8

The Fisherman

DR. DISMAS'S SHOT must have missed the glowing frigate, for it bore down on the pinnace relentlessly. The bristling oars of the pinnace set a steady, rapid beat as it left the burning skiff behind and began to turn toward its pursuer. Yama saw that Enobarbus was planning to come around to the near side of the frigate, to pass beneath its cannons and rake its sides with her own guns, but before he could complete his maneuver the frigate swung about like a leaf blown by the wind. In a moment, its bow loomed above the stricken pinnace. The pinnace's cannon hammered defiantly, and Yama heard someone cry out.

But at the instant the frigate struck the pinnace, it dissolved into a spreading mist of white light. Yama backstroked in the cold water, watching as the pinnace was engulfed by a globe of white fog that boiled up higher than the outflung arm of the Galaxy. A point of violet light shot up from this spreading bank of luminous fog, rising into the night sky until it had vanished from sight.

Yama did not stop to wonder at this miracle, for he knew that Enobarbus would start searching for him as soon as the pinnace had escaped the fog. He turned in the water and began to swim. Although he aimed for the dark, distant shore, he quickly found himself in a swift current that took him amongst a scattered shoal of banyans. They were rooted in a gravel bank that at times Yama could graze with his toes; if he had been as tall as the Aedile he could have stood with his head clear of the swiftly running water.

At first, the banyans were no more than handfuls of broad, glossy leaves that stood stiffly above the water, but the current carried Yama deeper into a maze of wide channels between stands of bigger trees.

Here, they rose in dense thickets above prop roots flexed in low arches. The prop roots were fringed by tangled mats of feeder roots alive with schools of tiny fish that flashed red or green dots of luminescence as they darted away from Yama.

With the last of his strength, Yama swam toward one of the largest of the banyans as he was swept past it. The cold water had stolen all feeling from his limbs and the muscles of his shoulders and arms were tender with exhaustion. He threw himself into floating nets of feeder roots and, scraping past strings of clams and bearded mussels, dragged himself onto a smooth horizontal trunk, and lay gasping like a fish that had just learned the trick of breathing air.

———

Yama was too cold and wet and scared to sleep, and something in the tangled thickets of the tree had set up a thin, irregular piping, like the fretting of a sick baby. He sat with his back against an arched root and watched the uppermost arm of the Galaxy set beyond the bank of faintly luminescent fog that had spread for leagues across the black river. Somewhere in the fog was Enobarbus's pinnace, lost, blinded. By what strange allies, or stranger coincidence? The top of the wide fog bank seethed like boiling milk; Yama watched the black sky above it for the return of the machine's violet spark. Answered prayers, he thought, and shivered.

He dozed and woke, and dozed again, and jerked awake from a vivid dream of standing on the flying bridge of the ghostly frigate as it bore down on the pinnace. The frigate was crewed neither by men nor even by ghosts or revenants, but by a crowd of restless lights that responded to his unspoken commands with quick unquestioning intelligence. Zakiel had taught him that although dreams were usually stitched from fragments of daily experience, sometimes they were more, portents of the future or riddles whose answers were keys to the conduct of the dreamer's life. Yama did not know if this dream was of the first or second kind, let alone what it might mean, but when he woke it left him with a clinging horror, as if his every action might somehow be magnified, with terrible consequences.

The Galaxy had set, and dawn touched the flood of the river with flat gray light. The bank of fog was gone; there was no sign of the pinnace. Yama dozed again, and woke with sunlight dancing on his face, filtered through the restless leaves of the banyan. He found himself on a wide limb that gently sloped up from the water and ran straight as an old road into the dense leafy tangles of the banyan's heart, crossed by arching roots and lesser branches that dropped prop roots straight down into the water. The banyan's glossy leaves hung everywhere like the endlessly deep folds of a ragged green cloak, and the bark of its limbs, smoothly wrinkled as skin, was colonized by lichens that hung like curtains of gray lace, the green barrels of bromeliads, and the scarlet and gold and pure white blossoms of epiphytic orchids.

Yama ached in every muscle. He drew off his wet shirt and trousers and hung them on a branch, then set to the exercises Sergeant Rhodean had taught him until at last his joints and muscles loosened. He drank handfuls of cold water, startling shoals of fairy shrimp that scattered from his shadow, and splashed water on his face until his skin tingled with racing blood.

Yama had come ashore on the side of the banyan that faced toward the far side of the river. He slung his damp clothes over his shoulder and, naked, set off through the thickets of the tree, at first following the broad limb and then, when it joined another and bent upward into the high, sunspeckled canopy, scrambling through a tangle of lesser branches. There was always still, black water somewhere beneath the random lattice of branches and prop roots. Tiny hummingbirds, clad in electric blues and emerald greens, as if enameled by the most skillful of artists, darted from flower to flower. When Yama blundered through curtains of leaves, clouds of blackflies rose up and got in his eyes and mouth. At last, he glimpsed blue sky through a fall of green vines. He parted the soft, jointed stems and stepped through them onto a sloping spit of mossy ground, where a round coracle of the kind used by the fisherfolk was drawn up on the miniature shore.

The blackened, upturned shell of a snapping turtle held the ashes of a small fire, still warm when Yama sifted them through his fingers. Yama drew on his damp shirt and trousers and called out, but no one answered his call. He cast around and quickly found a winding path leading away from the spit. And a moment later found the fisherman, tangled in a crude net of black threads just beyond the second bend.

The threads were the kind that Amnan used to catch bats and birds, resin fibers as strong as steel covered with thousands of tiny blisters that exuded a strong glue at a touch. The threads had partly collapsed when the fisherman had blundered into them, and he hung like a corpse in an unraveling shroud, one arm caught above his head, the other bound tightly to his side.

He did not seem surprised to see Yama. He said, in a quiet, hoarse voice, "Kill me quick. Have mercy."

"I was hoping for rescue," Yama said.

The fisherman stared at him. He wore only a breechclout, and his pale skin was blotched with islands of pale green. Black hair hung in greasy tangles around his broad, chinless froggy face. His wide mouth hung open, showing rows of tiny triangular teeth. He had watery, protuberant eyes, and a transparent membrane flicked over their balls three times before he said, "You are not one of the Mud People."

"I come from Aeolis. My father is the Aedile."

"The Mud People think they know the river. It's true they can swim a bit, but they're greedy, and pollute her waters."

"One of them seems to have caught you."

"You're a merchant's son, perhaps. We have dealings with them, for flints and steel. No, don't come close, or you'll be caught too. There is only one way to free me, and I don't think you carry it."

"I know how the threads work," Yama said, "and I am sorry that I do not have what is needed to set you free. I do not even have a knife."

"Even steel will not cut them. Leave me. I'm a dead man, fit only to fill the bellies of the Mud People. What are you doing?"

Yama had discovered that the surface of the path was a spongy thatch of wiry roots, fallen leaves and the tangled filaments of epiphytic lichens. He lay on his belly and pushed his arm all the way through the thick thatch until his fingers touched water. He looked at the fisherman and said, "I have seen your people use baited traps to catch fish. Do you have one on your coracle? And I will need some twine or rope, too."

While Yama worked, the fisherman, whose name was Caphis, told him that he had blundered into the sticky web just after dawn, while searching for the eggs of a species of coot which nested in the hearts of banyan thickets. "The eggs are good to eat," Caphis said, "but not worth dying for."

Caphis had put into the banyan shoal last night. He had seen a great battle, he explained, and had thought it prudent to take shelter. "So I am doubly a fool."

While the fisherman talked, Yama cut away a section of lichenous thatch and lashed the trap upright to a prop root. He had to use the blade of the fisherman's short spear to cut the twine, and several times sliced his palm. He sucked at the shallow cuts before starting to replace the thatch. It was in the sharp bend of the path; anyone hurrying down it would have to step there to make the turn.

He said, "Did you see much of the battle?"

"A big ship caught fire. And then the small boat which has been lying offshore of the Mud People's city for three days must have found an enemy, because it started firing into the dark."

"But there was another ship—it was huge and glowing, and melted into fog . . ."

The fisherman considered this, and said at last, "I turned for shelter once the firing started, as anyone with any sense would. You saw a third ship? Well, perhaps you were closer than I, and I expect that you saw more than you wanted to."

"Well, that is true enough." Yama stood, leaning on the stout shaft of the spear.

"The river carries all away, if you let it. That's our view. What's done one day is gone the next, and there's a new start. He might not come today, or even tomorrow. You will not wait that long. You will take the coracle and leave me to the fate I deserve."

"My father outlawed this."

"They are a devious people, the Mud People." Sunlight splashed through the broad leaves of the banyan, shining on the fisherman's face. Caphis squinted and added, "If you could fetch water, it would be a blessing."

Yama found a resin mug in the coracle. He was dipping it into the water at the edge of the mossy spit when he saw a little boat making its way toward the island. It was a skiff, rowed by a single man. By the time Yama had climbed into a crotch of the banyan, hidden amongst rustling leaves high above the spit, the skiff was edging through the slick of feeder roots that ringed the banyan.

Yama recognized the man. Grog, or Greg. One of the bachelor laborers who tended the mussel beds at the mouth of the Breas. He was heavy and slow, and wore only a filthy kilt. The gray skin of his shoulders and back was dappled with a purple rash, the precursor of the skin canker which affected those Amnan who worked too long in sunlight.

Yama watched, his mouth dry and his heart beating quickly, as the man tied up his boat and examined the coracle and the cold ashes in the turtle shell. He urinated at the edge of the water for what seemed a very long time, then set off along the path.

A moment later, while Yama was climbing down from his hiding place, made clumsy because he dared not let go of the fisherman's short spear, someone, the man or the fisherman, cried out. It startled two white herons which had been perching amongst the topmost branches of the banyan; the birds rose up into the air and flapped away as Yama crept down the path, clutching the spear with both hands.

There was a tremendous shaking in the leaves at the bend of the path. The man was floundering hip-deep amongst the broken thatch which Yama had used to conceal the trap. The big trap was wide-mouthed and two spans long, tapering to a blunt point. It was woven from pliable young prop roots, and bamboo spikes had been fastened on the inside, pointing downward, so that when a fish entered to get at the bait it could not back out. These spikes had dug into the flesh of the man's leg when he had tried to pull free, and he was bleeding hard and grunting with pain as he pushed down with his hands like a man trying to work off a particularly tight boot. He did not see Yama until the point of the spear pricked the fat folds of speckled skin at the back of his neck.

———

After Yama had used the spray which dissolved the threads' glue, Caphis wanted to kill the man who would have killed and eaten him, but Yama kept hold of the spear, and at last Caphis satisfied himself by tying the man's thumbs together behind his back and leaving him there, with his leg still in the trap.

The man started to shout as soon as they were out of sight. "I gave you the stuff, didn't I? I didn't mean no harm. Let me go, master! Let me go and I'll say nothing! I swear it!"

He was still shouting when Caphis and Yama put out from the banyan.

The fisherman's scrawny shanks were so long that his knees jutted above the crown of his head as he squatted in the coracle. He paddled with slow, deliberate strokes. The threads of the trap had left a hundred red weals across the mottled yellow skin of his chest. He said that once he had warmed up his blood he would take Yama across to the shore.

"That is, if you don't mind helping me with my night lines."

"You could take me to Aeolis. It is not far."

Caphis nodded. "That's true enough, but it would take me all day to haul against the current. Some of us go there to trade, and that's where I got that fine spear-point last year. But we never leave our boats when we go there, because it is a wicked town."

Yama said, "It is where I live. You have nothing to fear. Even if the man gets free, he would be burnt for trying to murder you."

"Perhaps. But then his family would make a vendetta against my family. That is how it is." Caphis studied Yama, and said at last, "You'll help me with my lines, and I'll take you to the shore. You can walk more quickly to your home than I can row. But you'll need some breakfast before you can work, I reckon."

They landed at the edge of a solitary grandfather banyan half a league downstream. Caphis built a fire of dried moss in the upturned turtle shell and boiled up tea in the resin mug, using friable strips of the bark of a twiggy bush that grew, he said, high up in the tangled tops of the banyans. When the tea started to boil he threw in some flat seeds that made it froth, and handed Yama the mug.

The tea was bitter, but after the first sip Yama felt it warm his blood, and he quickly drained the mug. He sat by the fire, chewing on a strip of dried fish, while Caphis moved about the hummocky moss of the little clearing where they had landed. With his long legs and short barrel of a body, and his slow, deliberate, flatfooted steps, the fisherman looked something like a heron. The toes of his feet were webbed, and the hooked claws on his big toes and spurs on his heels helped him climb the banyan's smooth, interlaced branches. He collected seeds and lichens and a particular kind of moss, and dug fat beetle grubs from rotten wood and ate them at once, spitting out the heads.

All anyone could want could be found in the banyans, Caphis told Yama. The fisherfolk pounded the leaves to make a fibrous pulp from which they wove their clothes. Their traps and the ribs of their coracles were made from young prop roots, and the hulls were woven from strips of bark varnished with a distillation of the tree's sap. The kernels of banyan fruit, which set all through the year, could be ground into flour. Poison used to stun fish was extracted from the skin of a particular kind of frog that lived in the tiny ponds cupped within the living vases of bromeliads. A hundred kinds of fish swarmed around the feeder roots, and a thousand kinds of plants grew on the branches; all had their uses, and their own tutelary spirits which had to be individually appeased.

"There's hardly anything we lack, except metals and tobacco, which is why we trade with you land folk. Otherwise we're as free as the fish, and always have been. We've never risen above our animal selves since the Preservers gave us the banyans as our province, and that is the excuse the Mud People use when they hunt us. But we're an old folk, and we've seen much, and we have long memories. Everything comes to the river, we say, and generally that's true."

Caphis had a tattoo on the ball of his left shoulder, a snake done in black and red that curled around so that it could swallow its own tail. He touched the skin beneath this tattoo with the claw of his thumb and said, "Even the river comes to its own self."

"What do you mean?"

"Why, where do you think the river goes, when it falls over the edge of the world? It swallows its own self and returns to its beginning, and so renews itself. That's how the Preservers made the world, and we, who were here from the first, remember how it was. Lately, things are changing. Year by year the river grows less. Perhaps the river no longer bites its own tail, but if that is so I cannot say where it goes instead."

"Do you—your people, do they remember the Preservers?"

Caphis's eyes filmed over. His voice took on a sing-song lilt. "Before the Preservers, the Universe was a plain of ice. The Preservers brought light that melted the ice and woke the seeds of the banyans which were trapped there. The first men were made of wood, carved from a banyan tree so huge that it was a world in itself, standing in the universe of water and light. But the men of wood showed their backs to the Preservers, and did not respect animals or even themselves, and destroyed so much of the world-tree that the Preservers raised a great flood. It rained for forty days and forty nights, and the waters rose through the roots of the banyan and rose through the branches until only the youngest leaves showed above the flood, and at last even these were submerged. All of the creatures of the world-tree perished in the flood except for a frog and a heron. The frog clung to the last leaf which showed above the flood and called to its own kind, but the lonely heron heard its call and stooped down and ate it.

"Well, the Preservers saw this, and the frog grew within the heron's stomach until it split open its captor, and stepped out, neither frog nor heron but a new creature which had taken something from both its parents. It was the first of our kind, and just as it was neither frog nor heron, neither was it man or woman. At once the flood receded. The new creature lay down on a smooth mudbank and fell asleep. And while it slept, the Preservers dismembered it, and from its ribs fifty others were made, and these were men and women of the first tribe of my people. The Preservers breathed on them and clouded their minds, so that unlike the men of wood they would not challenge or be disrespectful to their creators. But that was long ago, and in another place. You, if you don't mind me saying so, look as if your bloodline climbed down from the trees."

"I was born on the river, like you."

Caphis clacked his wide flat lower jaw—it was the way the fisherfolk laughed. "Sometime I'd like to hear that story. But now we should set to. The day does not grow younger, and there is work to do. It is likely that the Mud Man will escape. We should have killed him. He would bite off his own leg, if he thought that would help him escape. The Mud People are treacherous and full of tricks—that is how they are able to catch us, we who are more clever than they, as long as our blood is warmed. That is why they generally hunt us at night. I was caught because my blood had the night chill, you see. It made me slow and stupid, but now I am warm, and I know what I must do."

Caphis pissed on the fire to extinguish it, packed away the cup and the turtle shell beneath the narrow bench which circled the rim of the coracle, and declared himself ready.

"You will bring me luck, for it was by luck that you saved yourself from the phantom and then found me."

With Yama seated on one side and Caphis wielding a leaf-shaped paddle on the other, the coracle was surprisingly stable, although it was so small that Yama's knees pressed against Caphis's bony shins. As the craft swung out into the current, Caphis paddled with one hand and filled a long-stemmed clay pipe with ordinary tobacco with the other, striking a flint against a bit of rough steel for a spark.

It was a bright clear afternoon, with a gentle wind that barely ruffled the surface of the river. There was no sign of the pinnace; no ships at all, only the little coracles of the fisherfolk scattered across the broad river between shore and misty horizon. As Caphis said, the river bore all away. For a while, Yama could believe that none of his adventures had happened, that his life could return to its normal routines.

Caphis squinted at the sun, wet a finger and held it up to the wind, then drove his craft swiftly between the scattered tops of young banyans (Yama thought of the lone frog in Caphis's story, clinging to the single leaf above the universal flood, bravely calling but finding only death, and in death, transfiguration).

As the sun fell toward the distant peaks of the Rim Mountains, Yama and Caphis worked trotlines strung between bending poles anchored in the bottom of the gravel bank. Caphis gave Yama a sticky, odorless ointment to rub on his shoulders and arms to protect his skin from sunburn. Yama soon fell into an unthinking rhythm, hauling up lines, rebaiting hooks with bloodworms and dropping them back. Most of the hooks were empty, but gradually a pile of small silver fish accumulated in the well of the coracle, frantically jinking in the shallow puddle there or lying still, their gill flaps pulsing like blood red flowers as they drowned in air.

Caphis asked forgiveness for each fish he caught. The fisherfolk believed that the world was packed with spirits which controlled everything from the weather to the flowering of the least of the epiphytic plants of the banyan shoals. Their days were spent in endless negotiations with these spirits to ensure that the world continued its seamless untroubled spinning out.

At last Caphis declared himself satisfied with the day's catch. He gutted a pentad of fingerlings, stripped the fillets of pale muscle from their backbones, and gave half to Yama, together with a handful of fleshy leaves.

The fillets of fish were juicy; chewed, the leaves tasted of sweet limes and quenched Yama's thirst. Following Caphis's example, he spat the leaf pulp overboard, and tiny fish promptly swarmed around this prize as it sank through the clear dark water.

Caphis picked up his paddle and the coracle skimmed across the water toward a bend of the stony shore, where cliffs carved and socketed with empty tombs rose from a broad pale beach.

"There's an old road that leads along the shore to Aeolis," Caphis told Yama. "It will take you the rest of this day, and a little of the next, I reckon."

"If you would take me directly to Aeolis, I can promise you a fine reward. It is little enough in return for your life."

"We do not go there unless we must, and never after nightfall. You saved my life, and so it is always in your care. Would you risk it so quickly, by taking me into the jaws of the Mud People? I do not think you would be so cruel. I have my family to consider. They'll be watching for me this night, and I don't want to worry them further."

Caphis grounded his frail craft in the shallows a little way from the shore. He had never set foot on land, he said, and he wasn't about to start now. He looked at Yama and said, "Don't walk after dark, young master. Find shelter before the sun goes down and stick to it until first light. Then you'll be all right. There are ghouls out there, and they like a bit of live meat on occasion."

Yama knew about the ghouls. He and Telmon had once hidden from a ghoul on one of their expeditions into the foothills of the City of the Dead. He remembered the way the man-shaped creature's pale skin had glimmered in the twilight like wet muscle, and how frightened he had been as it stooped this way and that, and the stench it had left. He said, "I will be careful."

Caphis said, "Take this. No use against ghouls, but I hear tell there are plenty of coneys on the shore. Some of us hunt them, but not me."

It was a small knife carved from a flake of obsidian. Its hilt was wrapped with twine, and its exfoliated edge was as sharp as a razor.

"I reckon you can look after your own self, young master, but maybe a time will come when you need help. Then my family will remember that you helped me. Do you recall what I said about the river?"

"Everything comes around again."

Caphis nodded, and touched the tattoo of the self-engulfing snake on his shoulder. "You had a good teacher. You know how to pay attention."

Yama slid from the tipping coracle and stood knee-deep in ooze and brown water. "I will not forget," he said.

"Choose carefully where you camp this night," Caphis said. "Ghouls are bad, but ghosts are worse. We see their lights sometimes, shining softly in the ruins."

Then he pushed away from the shallows and the coracle waltzed into the current as he dug the water with his leaf-shaped paddle. By the time Yama had waded to shore, the coracle was already far off, a black speck on the shining plane of the river, making a long, curved path toward a raft of banyan islands far from shore.

9

The Knife

THE BEACH WAS made of deep, soft drifts of white shell fragments; it was not until Yama began to climb the worn stone stair that zigzagged up the face of the carved cliff that he remembered how difficult it was to walk on firm ground, where each step sent a little shock up the ladder of the spine. At the first turn of the stair, a spring welled inside a trough cut from the native stone. Yama knelt on the mossy ground by the trough and drank clear sweet water until his belly sloshed, knowing that there would be little chance of finding any potable water in the City of the Dead. Only when he stood did he notice that someone else had drunk there recently—no, to judge by the overlapping footprints in the soft red moss, it had been two people.

Lud and Lob. They had also escaped Dr. Dismas. Yama had tucked the obsidian knife into his belt under the flap of his shirt, snug against the small of his back. He touched the handle for reassurance before he continued his ascent.

An ancient road ran close to the edge of the cliff, its flat pavement, splashed with the yellow and gray blotches of lichens, so wide that twenty men could have ridden abreast along it. Beyond, the alkaline, shaley land shimmered in the level light of the late afternoon sun. Tombs stood everywhere, casting long shadows toward the river. This was the Silent Quarter, which Yama had rarely visited—he and Telmon preferred the ancient tombs of the foothills beyond the Breas, where aspects could be wakened and the flora and fauna was richer. Compared to the sumptuously decorated mausoleums of the older parts of the City of the Dead, the tombs here were poor things, mostly no more than low boxes with domed roofs, although here and there memorial steles and columns rose amongst them, and a few larger tombs stood on artificial stepped mounds, guarded by statues that watched the river with stony eyes. One of these was as big as the peel-house, half hidden by a small wood of yews grown wild and twisted. In all the desiccated landscape nothing stirred except for a lammergeyer high in the deep blue sky, riding a thermal on outspread wings.

When Yama was satisfied that he was not about to be ambushed, he set off down the road toward the distant smudge that must surely be Aeolis, halfway toward the vanishing point where the Rim Mountains and the misty horizon of the farside seemed to converge.

Little grew in the stone gardens of this part of the City of the Dead. The white, sliding rocks weathered to a bitter dust in which only a few plants could root, mostly yuccas and creosote bushes and clumps of prickly pear. Wild roses crept around the smashed doorways of some of the tombs, their blood-red blooms scenting the warm air. The tombs had all been looted long ago, and of their inhabitants scarcely a bone remained. If the cunningly preserved bodies had not been carted away to fuel the smelters of old Aeolis, then wild animals had long ago dismembered and consumed them once they had been disinterred from their caskets. Ancient debris was strewn everywhere, from fragments of smashed funeral urns and shards of broken furniture fossilized on the dry shale, to slates which displayed pictures of the dead, impressed into their surfaces by some forgotten art. Some of these were still active, and as Yama went past, scenes from ancient Ys briefly came to life or the faces of men and women turned to watch him, their lips moving soundlessly or shaping into a smile or a coquettish kiss. Unlike the aspects of older tombs, these were mere recordings without intelligence; the slates played the same meaningless loop over and over, whether for the human eye or the uncomprehending gaze of any lizard that flicked over the glazed surfaces in which the pictures were embedded.

Yama was familiar with these animations; the Aedile had an extensive collection of them. They had to be exposed to sunlight before they would work, and Yama had always wondered why, for they were normally found inside the tombs. But although he knew what these mirages were, their unpredictable flicker was still disturbing. He kept looking behind him, fearful that Lud and Lob were stalking him through the quiet solitude of the ruins.

The oppressive feeling of being watched grew as the sun fell toward the ragged blue line of the Rim Mountains and the shadows of the tombs lengthened and mingled across the bone-white ground. To be walking through the City of the Dead in the bright sunshine was one thing, but as the light faded Yama increasingly glanced over his shoulder as he walked, and sometimes turned and walked backward a few paces, or stopped and slowly scanned the low hills with their freight of empty tombs. He had often camped in the City of the Dead with the Aedile and his retinue of servants and archaeological workers, or with Telmon and two or three soldiers, but never before alone.

The distant peaks of the Rim Mountains bit into the reddened disc of the sun. The lights of Aeolis shimmered in the distance like a heap of tiny diamonds. It was still at least half a day's walk to the city, and would be longer in darkness. Yama left the road and began to search the tombs for one that would give shelter for the night.

It was like a game. Yama knew that the tombs he rejected now would be better than the one he would choose of necessity when the last of the sun's light fled the sky. But he did not want to choose straightaway because he still felt that he was being watched and fancied, as he wandered the network of narrow paths between the tombs, that he heard a padding footfall behind him that stopped when he stopped and resumed a moment after he began to move forward again. At last, halfway up a long, gentle slope, he turned and called out Lud and Lob's names, feeling both fearful and defiant as the echoes of his voice died away amongst the tombs spread below him. There was no answer, but when he moved on he heard a faint squealing and splashing beyond the crest of the slope.

Yama drew the obsidian knife and crept forward like a thief. Beyond the crest, the ground fell away in an abrupt drop, as if something had bitten away half the hill. At the foot of the drop, a seep of brackish water gleamed like copper in the sun's last light, and a family of hyraces were sporting in the muddy shallows.

Yama stood and yelled and plunged down the steep slope. The hyraces bolted in every direction and a youngster ran squealing in blind panic into the middle of the shallow pond. It saw Yama charging toward it and stopped so suddenly that it tumbled head over heels. Before it could change direction, he threw himself on its slim, hairy body and wrestled it onto its back and slit its throat with his knife.

Yama built a fire of twisted strands of dried wood picked from the centers of prickly pear clumps and lit it using a friction bow made from two twigs and a sinew from the hyrax's carcass. He cleaned and skinned and jointed the hyrax, roasted its meat in the hot ashes, and ate until his stomach hurt, cracking bones for hot marrow and licking the fatty juices from his fingers. The sky had darkened to reveal a scattering of dim halo stars, and the Galaxy was rising, salting the City of the Dead with a blue-white glow and casting a confusion of shadows.

The tomb Yama chose as a place to sleep was not far from the seep, and as he rested against its granite façade, which still held the day's heat, he heard something splash in the pool—an animal come to drink. Yama laid the remains of the hyrax on a flat stone a hundred paces from the tomb and took the precaution of dragging a screen of rose stems across the tomb's entrance before curling up to sleep on the empty catafalque inside, his head pillowed on his folded shirt, the obsidian knife in his hand.

———

Yama awoke from bad dreams at first light, stiff and cold. The golden sun stood a handspan above the Rim Mountains. The tomb in which he had slept was one of a row that stretched along the ridge above the pool, each with a gabled false front of rosy granite; they glowed like so many hearths in the sun's early light. Yama warmed himself with a set of exercises before pulling on his shirt and walking down to the pool.

His offering was gone; only a dark stain was left on the flat white stone. There was a confusion of tracks around the water's edge, but he could find no human ones, only the slots of hyraces and antelopes, and what looked like the impress of the pads of some large cat, most likely a spotted panther.

The seep water of the pool was chalky with suspended solids, and so bitter that Yama spat out the first mouthful. He chewed a strip of cold meat and skinned and ate new buds taken from a prickly pear stand, but the cool juices did not entirely quench his thirst. He put a pebble in his mouth to stimulate the flow of saliva and walked back toward the river, thinking that he would climb down the cliff to drink and bathe at the water's edge.

He had wandered farther than he had thought when he had been looking for shelter the previous evening. The narrow paths that meandered between the tombs and memorials and up and down the gentle slopes of the low hills were all alike, and not one ran for more than a hundred paces before meeting with another, or splitting into two, but Yama kept the sun at his back, and by midmorning had reached the wide straight road again.

The cliffs there were sheer and high; if the peel-house had stood in the seething water at their bases, its tallest turret would not have reached to their tops. Yama got down on his belly and hung over the edge and looked right and left, but could not see any sign of a path or of stairs, although there were many tombs cut into the cliff faces—there was one directly below him. Birds nested in the openings, and thousands floated on the wind that blew up the face of the cliff, like flakes of restlessly sifting snow. Yama spat out the pebble and watched it bounce from the ledge in front of the tomb directly below and dwindle away; it vanished from sight before it hit the tumbled slabs of rock that were covered and uncovered by the heave of the river's brown water.

Behind him, someone said, "A hot morning."

And someone else: "Watch you don't fall, little fish."

Yama jumped to his feet. Lud and Lob stood on top of a bank of white shale on the far side of the road. Both wore only kilts. Lob had a coil of rope over his bare shoulder; the skin of Lud's chest was reddened and blistered by a bad burn.

"Don't think of running," Lud advised. "It's too hot for you to get far without water, and you know you can't get away."

Yama said, "Dr. Dismas tried to have you killed. There is no enmity between us."

"I wouldn't know about that," Lud said. "I reckon we've a score to settle."

"You owe us," Lob said.

"I do not see it."

Lud explained patiently, "Dr. Dismas would have paid us for our trouble, and instead we had to swim for our lives when you pulled that trick. I got burnt, too."

"And he lost his knife," Lob added. "He loved that knife, you miserable culler, and you made him lose it."

Lud said, "And then there was the boat you put on fire. You owe for that, I reckon."

"That was not yours."

Lud scratched at the patch of reddened skin on his chest and said, "It's the principle of the thing."

"In any case, I can only pay you when I get home," Yama said.

" 'In any case,' " Lud echoed in a mocking voice. "That's not how we see it. How do we know we can trust you?"

"Of course you can."

Lud said, "You haven't even asked how much we want, and then you might just think to tell your father. I don't think he'd pay us then, would he, brother?"

"It's doubtful."

"Very doubtful, I'd say."

Yama knew that there was only one chance to escape. He said, "Then you do not trust me?"

Lud saw Yama's change in posture. He started down the slope, raising a cloud of white dust, and yelled, "Don't—"

Yama did. He turned and took two steps backward, and then, before he could have second thoughts, ran forward and jumped over the edge of the cliff.

He fell in a rush of air, and as he fell threw back his head and brought up his knees. (Sergeant Rhodean was saying, "Just let it happen to you. If you learn to trust your body it's all a matter of timing.") Sky and river revolved around each other, and then he landed on his feet, knees bent to take the shock, on the ledge before the entrance to the tomb.

The ledge was no wider than a bed, and slippery with bird excrement. Yama fell flat on his back at once, filled with a wild fear that he would tumble over the edge—there had been a balustrade once, but it had long ago fallen away. He caught a tuft of wiry grass and held on, although the sharp blades of grass reopened the wounds made by Caphis's spearhead.

As he carefully climbed back to his feet, a stone clipped the ledge and tumbled away toward the heaving water far below. Yama looked up. Lob and Lud capered at the top of the cliff, silhouetted against the blue sky. They shouted down at him, but their words were snatched away by the wind. One of them threw another stone, which smashed to flinders scarcely a span from Yama's feet.

Yama ran forward, darting between the winged figures, their faces blurred by time, which supported the lintel of the gaping entrance to the tomb. Inside, stone blocks fallen from the high ceiling littered the mosaic floor. An empty casket stood on a dais beneath a canopy of stone carved to look like cloth rippling in the wind. Disturbed by Yama's footfalls, bats fell from one of the holes in the ceiling and dashed around and around above his head, chittering in alarm.

The tomb was shaped like a wedge of pie, and behind the dais it narrowed to a passageway. It had once been sealed by a slab of stone, but that had been smashed long ago by robbers who had discovered the path used by the builders of the tomb. Yama grinned. He had guessed that the tombs in the cliffs would have been breached and stripped just like those above. It was his way of escape. He stepped over the sill and, keeping one hand on the cold dry stone of the wall, felt his way through near darkness.

He had not gone far when the passage struck another running at right angles. He tossed an imaginary coin and chose the left-hand way. A hundred heartbeats later, in pitch darkness, he went sprawling over a slump of rubble. He got up cautiously and climbed the spill of stones until his head bumped the ceiling of the passage. It was blocked.

Then Yama heard voices behind him, and knew that Lud and Lob had followed him. He should have expected it. They would lose their lives if he was able to escape and tell the Aedile about the part they had played in Dr. Dismas's scheme.

As Yama slid down the rubble, his hand fell on something cold and hard. It was a metal knife, its curved blade as long as his forearm. It was cold to the touch and gave off a faint glow; motes of light seemed to float in the wake of its blade when Yama slashed at the darkness. Emboldened, he felt his way back to the tomb.

The dim light hurt his eyes; it spilled around one of the twins, who stood in the tomb's narrow entrance.

"Little fish, little fish. What are you scared of?"

Yama held up the long knife. "Not you, Lud."

"Let me get him," Lob said, peering over his brother's shoulder.

"Don't block the light, stupid." Lud pushed Lob out of the way and grinned at Yama. "There isn't a way out, is there? Or you wouldn't have come back. We can wait. We caught fish this morning, and we have water. I don't think you do, or you would have set out for the city straight away."

Yama said, "I killed a hyrax last night. I ate well enough then."

Lud started forward. "But I bet you couldn't drink the water in the pool, eh? We couldn't, and we can drink just about anything."

Yama was aware of a faint breath of air at his back. He said, "How did you get down here?"

"Rope," Lob said. "From the boat. I saved it. People say we're stupid, but we're not."

"Then I can climb back up," Yama said, and advanced on Lud, making passes with the knife as he came around the raised casket. The knife made a soft hum, and its rusty hilt pricked his palm. He felt a coldness flowing into his wrist and along his arm as the blade brightened with blue light.

Lud retreated. "You wouldn't," he said.

Lob pushed at his brother, trying to get past him. He was excited. "Break his legs," he shrieked. "Break his legs! See how he swims then!" "A knife! He's got a knife!"

Yama swung the knife again. Lud crowded backward into Lob and they both fell over.

Yama yelled, words that hurt his throat and tongue. He did not know what he yelled and he stumbled, because suddenly his legs seemed too long and bony and his arms hung wrong. Where was his mount and where was the rest of the squad? Why was he standing in the middle of what looked like a ruined tomb? Had he fallen into the keelways? All he could remember was a tremendous crushing pain, and then he had suddenly woken here, with two fat ruffians threatening him. He struck at the nearest and the man scrambled out of the way with jittery haste; the knife hit the wall and spat a shower of sparks. It was screaming now. He jumped onto the casket—yes, a tomb—but his body betrayed him and he lost his balance; before he could recover, the second ruffian caught his ankles and he fell heavily, striking the stone floor with hip and elbow and shoulder. The impact numbed his fingers, and the knife fell from his grasp, clattering on the floor and gouging a smoking rut in the stone.

Lud ran forward and kicked the knife out of the way. Yama scrambled to his feet. He did not remember falling. His right arm was cold and numb, and hung from his shoulder like a piece of meat; he had to pull the obsidian knife from his belt with his left hand as Lud ran at him. They slammed against the wall and Lud gasped and clutched at his chest. Blood welled over his hand and he looked at it dully. "What?" he said. He stepped away from Yama with a bewildered look and said again, "What?"

"You killed him!" Lob said.

Yama shook his head. He could not get his breath. The ancient knife lay on the filthy floor exactly between him and Lob, sputtering and sending up a thick smoke that stank of burning metal.

Lud tried to pull the obsidian knife from his chest, but it snapped, leaving a finger's width of the blade protruding. He blundered around the tomb, blood all over his hands now, blood running down his chest and soaking into the waistband of his kilt. He didn't seem to understand what had happened to him. He kept saying over and over again, "What? What?" and pushed past his brother and fell to his knees at the entrance to the tomb. Light spilled over his shoulders. He seemed to be searching the blue sky for something he could not find.

Lob stared at Yama, his gray tongue working between his tusks. At last he said, "You killed him, you culler. You didn't have to kill him." Yama took a deep breath. His hands were shaking. "You were going to kill me." "All we wanted was a bit of money. Just enough to get away. Not much to ask, and now you've gone and killed my brother." Lob stepped toward Yama and his foot struck the knife. He picked it up—and screamed. White smoke rose from his hand and then he was not holding the knife but a creature fastened to his arm by clawed hands and feet. Lob staggered backward and slammed his arm against the wall, but the creature only snarled and tightened its grip. It was the size of a small child, and seemed to be made of sticks. A kind of mane of dry, white hair stood around its starveling face. A horrid stink of burning flesh filled the tomb. Lob beat at the creature with his free hand and it vanished in a sudden flash of blue light.

The ancient knife fell to the floor, ringing on the stone. Yama snatched it up and fled down the passage, barely remembering to turn right into the faint breeze. He banged from wall to wall as he ran, and then the walls fell away and he was tumbling through a rush of black air.

10

The Curators of the City of the Dead

THE ROOM WAS in some high, windy place. It was small and square, with whitewashed stone walls and a ceiling of tongue-and-groove planking painted with a hunting scene. The day after he first woke, Yama managed to raise himself from the thin mattress on the stone slab and stagger to the deep-set slit window. He glimpsed a series of stony ridges stepping away beneath a blank blue sky, and then pain overcame his will and he fainted.

"He is ill and he does not know it," the old man said. He had half-turned his head to speak to someone else as he leaned over Yama. The tip of his wispy white beard hung a finger's width from Yama's chin. The deeply wrinkled skin of his face was mottled with brown spots, and there was only a fringe of white hair around his bald pate. Glasses with lenses like small mirrors hid his eyes. Deep, old scars cut the left side of his face, drawing up the side of his mouth in a sardonic rictus. He said, "He does not know how much the knife took from him."

"He's young," an old woman's voice said. She added, "He'll learn by himself, won't he? We can't—"

The old man curled and uncurled the end of his wispy beard around his fingers. At last, he said, "I cannot remember."

Yama asked them who they were, and where this cool white room was, but they did not hear him. Perhaps he had not spoken at all. He could not move even a single fingertip, although this did not scare him. He was too tired to be scared. The two old people went away and Yama was left to stare at the painted hunting scene on the ceiling. His thoughts would not fit together. Men in plastic armor over brightly colored jerkins and hose were chasing a white stag through a forest of leafless tree trunks. The turf between the trees was starred with flowers. It seemed to be night in the painting, for in every direction the slim trunks of the trees faded into darkness. The white stag glimmered amongst them like a fugitive star. The paint had flaked away from the wood in places, and a patch above the window was faded. In the foreground, a young man in a leather jacket was pulling a brace of hunting dogs away from a pool. Yama thought that he knew the names of the dogs, and who their owner was. But he was dead.

Some time later, the old man came back and lifted Yama up so that he could sip thin vegetable soup from an earthenware bowl. Later, he was cold, so cold that he shivered under the thin gray blanket, and then so hot that he would have cast aside the blanket if he had possessed the strength.

Fever, the old man told him. He had a bad fever. Something was wrong with his blood. "You have been in the tombs," the old man said, "and there are many kinds of old sicknesses there."

Yama sweated into the mattress, thinking that if only he could get up he would quench his thirst with the clear water of the forest pool. Telmon would help him.

But Telmon was dead.

In the middle of the day, sunlight crept a few paces into the little room before shyly retreating. At night, wind hunted at the corners of the deep-set window, making the candle gutter inside its glass sleeve. When Yama's fever broke it was night. He lay still, listening to the wuthering of the wind. He felt very tired but entirely clearheaded, and spent hours piecing together what had happened.

Dr. Dismas's tower, burning like a firework. The strange cage, and the burning ship. The leonine young war hero, Enobarbus, his face as ruined as the old man's. The ghost ship, and his escape—more fire. The whole adventure seemed to be punctuated by fire. He remembered the kindness of the fisherman, Caphis, and the adventure amongst the dry tombs of the Silent Quarter, which had ended in Lud's death. He had run from something terrible, and as for what had happened after that, he remembered nothing at all.

"You were carried here," the old woman told him, when she brought him breakfast. "It was from a place on the shore somewhere downstream of Aeolis, I'd judge. A fair distance, as the fox said to the hen, when he gave her a head start."

Her skin was fine-grained, almost translucent, and her white, feathery hair reached to the small of her back. She was of the same bloodline as Derev, but far older than either of Derev's parents.

Yama said, "How did you know?"

The old man smiled at the woman's shoulder. As always, he wore his mirrored lenses. "Your trousers and your shirt were freshly stained with river silt. It is quite distinctive. But I believe that you had been wandering in the City of the Dead, too."

Yama asked why he thought that.

"The knife, dear," the woman said.

The old man pulled on his scanty white beard and said, "Many people carry old weapons, for they are often far more potent than those made today."

Yama nodded, remembering Dr. Dismas's energy pistol.

"However, the knife you carried has a patina of corrosion that suggests it had lain undisturbed in some dark, dry place for many years. Perhaps you have carried it around without scrupling to clean it, but I think that you are more responsible than that. I think that you found it only recently, and did not have time to clean it. You landed at the shore and began to walk through the City of the Dead, and at some point found the knife in an old tomb."

"It's from the Age of Insurrection, if I'm a judge," the woman said. "It's a cruel thing."

"And she has forgotten a good deal more than I ever knew," the old man said fondly. "You will have to learn its ways, or it could kill you."

"Hush!" the old woman said sharply. "Nothing should be changed!"

"Perhaps nothing can be changed," the old man said.

"Then I would be a machine," the old woman said, "and I don't like that thought."

"At least you would not need to worry. But I will be careful. Pay no attention to me, youngster. My mind wanders these days, as my wife will surely remind you at every opportunity."

They had been married a long time. They both wore the same kind of long, layered shifts over woollen trousers, and shared the same set of gestures, as if love were a kind of imitation game in which the best of both participants was mingled. They called themselves Osric and Beatrice, but Yama suspected that these were not their real names. They both had an air of sly caution which suggested that they were withholding much, although Yama felt that Osric wanted to tell him more than he was allowed to know. Beatrice was strict with her husband, but she favored Yama with fond glances, and while he had been stricken with fever she had spent hours bathing his forehead with wet cloths infused with oil of spikenard, and had fed him infusions of honey and herbs, crooning to him as if he were her child. While Osric was bent by age, his tall, slender wife carried herself like a young dancer.

Later, husband and wife sat side by side on the ledge beneath the narrow window of the little room, watching Yama eat a bowl of boiled maize. It was his first solid food since he had woken. They said that they were members of the Department of the Curators of the City of the Dead, an office of the civil service which had been disbanded centuries ago.

"But my ancestors stayed on, dear," Beatrice explained. "They believed that the dead deserved better than abandonment, and fought against dissolution. There was quite a little war. Of course, we're much diminished now. Most would say that we had vanished long ago, if they had heard of us at all, but we still hold some of the more important parts of the city."

"You might say that I am an honorary member of the department, by marriage," Osric said. "Here, I cleaned the knife for you."

Osric laid the long, curved knife at the foot of the bed. Yama looked at it and discovered that although it had saved his life he feared it; it was as if Osric had set a live snake at his feet. He said, "I found it in a tomb in the cliffs by the river."

"Then it came from somewhere else," Osric said, and laid a bony finger beside his nose. The tip of the finger was missing. He said, "I used a little white vinegar to take the bloom of age from the metal, and every decad or so you should rub it down with a cloth touched to mineral oil. But it will not need sharpening, and it will repair itself, within limits. It had been imprinted with a copy of the personality of its previous owner, but I have purged that ghost. You should practice with it as often as you can, and handle it at least once a day, and so it will come to know you."

"Osric—"

"He needs to know," Osric told his wife. "It will not hurt. Handle it often, Yama. The more you handle it, the better it will know you. And leave it in the sunlight, or between places of different temperature—placing the point in a fire is good. Otherwise it will take energy from you again. It had lain in the dark a long time—that was why you were hurt by it when you used it. I would guess it belonged to an officer of the cavalry, dead long ages past. They were issued to those fighting in the rain forests two thousand leagues downriver."

Yama said stupidly, "But the war started only forty years ago."

"This was another war, dear," Beatrice said.

"I found it by the river. In a tomb there. I put out my hand in the dark."

Yama remembered how the knife had kindled its eldritch glow when he had held it up, wonderingly, before his face. But when Lob had picked it up, the horrible thing had happened. The knife was different things to different people.

Yama had been brought a long way from the river. This was the last retreat of the last of the curators of the City of the Dead, deep in the foothills of the Rim Mountains. He had not realized until then the true extent of the necropolis.

"The dead outnumber the living," Osric said, "and this has been the burial place for Ys since the construction of Confluence. Until this last, decadent age, at least."

Yama gathered that there were not many curators left now, and that most of those were old. This was a place where the past was stronger than the present. The Department of the Curators of the City of the Dead had once been responsible for preparation and arrangement of the deceased, whom they called clients, and for the care and maintenance of the graves, tombs and memorials, the picture slates and aspects of the dead. It had been a solemn and complex task. For instance, Yama learned that there had been four methods of dealing with clients: by interment, including burial or entombment; by cremation, either by fire or by acids; by exposure, either in a byre raised above the ground or by dismemberment; and by water.

"Which I understand is the only method used these days," Osric said. "It has its place, but many die a long way from the Great River, and besides, many communities are too close together, so that the corpses of those upriver foul the water of those below them. Consider, Yama. Much of Confluence is desert or mountain. Interment in the soil is rare, for there is little enough land for cultivation. For myriad upon myriad days, our ancestors built tombs for their dead, or burned them on pyres or dissolved them in tanks of acid, or exposed them to the brothers of the air. Building tombs takes much labor and is suitable only for the rich, for the badly constructed tombs of the poor are soon ransacked by wild animals. Firewood is in as short supply as arable land, for the same reasons, and dissolution in acid is usually considered aesthetically displeasing. How much more natural, in the circumstances, to expose the client to the brothers of the air. It is how I wish my body to be disposed, when my time comes. Beatrice has promised it to me. The world will end before I die, of course, but I think there will still be birds . . ."

"You forgot preservation," Beatrice said sharply. "He always does," she told Yama. "He disapproves."

"Ah, but I did not forget. It is merely a variation on interment. Without a tomb, the preserved body is merely fodder for the animals, or a curiosity in a sideshow."

"Some are turned into stone," Beatrice said. "It is mostly done by exposing the client to limy water."

"And then there is mummification, and desiccation, either by vacuum or by chemical treatment, and treatment by tar, or by ice." Osric ticked off the variations on his fingers. "But you know full well that I mean the most common method, and the most decadent. Which is to say, those clients who were preserved while still alive, in the hope of physical resurrection in ages to come. Instead, robbers opened the tombs and took what there was of value, and threw away the bodies for wild animals to devour, or burned them as fuel, or ground them up for fertilizer. The brave cavalry officer who once wielded your knife in battle, young Yama, was in all probability burned in some furnace to melt the alloy stripped from his tomb. Perhaps one of the tomb robbers picked up the knife, and it attacked him. He dropped it where you would find it an age later. We live in impoverished times. I remember that I played amongst the tombs as a child, teasing the aspects who still spoke for those beyond hope of resurrection. There is a lesson in folly. Only the Preservers outrun time. I did not know then that the aspects were bound to oblige my foolishness; the young are needlessly cruel because they know no better."

Beatrice straightened her back, held up her hand, and recited a verse:

Let fame, that all hunt after in their lives,
Live registered upon our brazen tombs,
And then grace us in the disgrace of death;
When, spite of the cormorant devouring time,
The endeavor of this present breath may buy
That honor which shall bate his scythe's keen edge,
And makes us heirs to all eternity.

Yama guessed that this was from the Puranas, but Beatrice said that it was far older. "There are too few of us to remember everything left by the dead," she said, "but we do what we can, and we are a long-lived race."

There was much more to the tasks of the curators than preparation of their clients, and in the next two days Yama learned something about care of tombs and the preservation of the artifacts with which clients had been interred, each according to the customs of their bloodline. Osric and Beatrice fed him vegetable broths, baked roots and succulent young okra, corn and green beans fried in airy batter. He was getting better, and was beginning to feel a restless curiosity. He had not broken any bones, but his ribs were badly bruised and muscles in his back and arms had been torn. There were numerous half-healed cuts on his limbs and torso, too, and the fever had left him very weak, as if most of his blood had been drained.

Beatrice cleaned out the worst of his wounds; she explained that the stone dust embedded in them would otherwise leave scars. As soon as he could, Yama started to exercise, using the drills taught him by Sergeant Rhodean. He practiced with the knife, too, mastering his instinctive revulsion. He handled it each day, as Osric had suggested, and otherwise left it on the ledge beneath the narrow window, where it would catch the midday sun. To begin with, he had to rest for an hour or more between each set of exercises, but he ate large amounts of the curators' plain food and felt his strength return. At last, he was able to climb the winding stairs to the top of the hollow crag.

He had to stop and rest frequently, but finally stepped out of the door of a little hut into the open air under an achingly blue sky. The air was clean and cold, as heady as wine after the stuffy room in which he had lain for so long.

The hut was set at one end of the top of the crag, which was so flat that it might have been sheared off by someone wielding a gigantic blade. Possibly this was more or less what had been done, for during the construction of Confluence, long before the Preservers had abandoned the ten thousand bloodlines, energies had been deployed to move whole mountains and shape entire landscapes as easily as a gardener might set out a bed of flowers.

The flat top of the crag was no bigger than the Great Hall of the peel-house, and divided into tiny fields by low drystone walls. There were plots of squash and yams, corn and kale and cane fruits. Little paths wandered between these plots, and there was a complicated system of cisterns and gutters to provide a constant supply of water to the crops. At the far end, Beatrice and Osric were feeding doves which fluttered around a round-topped dovecote built of unmortared stone.

The crag stood at the edge of a winding ridge above a gorge so deep that its bottom was lost in shadow. Other flat-topped crags stood along the ridge, their smooth sides fretted with windows and balconies. There was a scattering of tombs on broad ledges cut into the white rock of the gorge's steep sides, huge buildings with blind, whitewashed walls under pitched roofs of red tile that stood amidst manicured lawns and groves of tall trees. Beyond the far side of the gorge, other ridges stepped up toward the sky, and beyond the farthest ridge the peaks of the Rim Mountains seemed to float free above indistinct blue and purple masses, shining in the light of the sun.

Yama threaded the winding paths to the little patch of grass where Beatrice and Osric were scattering grain. Doves rose up in a whir of white wings as he approached. Osric raised a hand in greeting and said, "This is the valley of the kings of the first days. Some maintain that Preservers are buried here, but if that is true, the location is hidden from us."

"It must be a lot of work, looking after these tombs."

The mirror lenses of Osric's spectacles flashed light at Yama. "They maintain themselves," the old man said, "and there are mechanisms which prevent people from approaching too closely. It was once our job to keep people away for their own good, but only those who know this place come here now."

"Few know of it," Beatrice added, "and fewer come."

She held out a long, skinny arm. A dove immediately perched on her hand, and she drew it to her breast and stroked its head with a bony forefinger until it began to coo.

Yama said, "I was brought a long way."

Osric nodded. His wispy beard blew sideways in the wind. "The Department of the Curators of the City of the Dead once maintained a city that stretched from these mountains to the river, a day's hard ride distant. Whoever brought you here had a good reason."

Beatrice suddenly flung out her hands. The dove rose into the wind and circled high above the patchwork of tiny fields. She watched it for a minute and then said, "I think it's time we showed Yama why he was brought here."

"I would like to know who brought me here, to begin with."

"As long as you do not know who saved you," Osric said, "there is no obligation."

Yama nodded, remembering that after he had saved Caphis from the trap, the fisherman had said that his life was forever in Yama's care. He said, "Perhaps I could at least know the circumstances."

"Something had taken one of our goats," Beatrice said. "It was in a field far below. We went to look for her, and found you. It is better if you see for yourself why you have been brought here. Then you'll understand. Having climbed so high, you must descend. I think that you are strong enough."

Descending the long spiral of stairs was easier than climbing up, but Yama felt that if not for him, Osric and Beatrice would have bounded away eagerly, although he was so much younger than they. The stairs ended at a balcony that girdled the crag halfway between its flat top and its base. A series of arched doorways opened off the balcony, and Osric immediately disappeared through one. Yama would have followed, but Beatrice took his arm and guided him to a stone bench by the low wall of the balcony. Sunlight drenched the ancient stone; Yama was grateful for its warmth.

"There were a hundred thousand of us, once," Beatrice said, "but we are greatly reduced. This is the oldest part of all that still lies within our care, and it will be the last to fall. It will fall eventually, of course. All of Confluence will fall."

Yama said, "You sound like those who say that the war at the midpoint of the world may be the war at the end of all things."

Sergeant Rhodean had taught Yama and Telmon the major battles, scratching the lines of the armies and the routes of their long marches in the red clay floor of the gymnasium.

Beatrice said, "When there is a war, everyone believes that it will end in a victory that will bring an end to all conflict, but in a series of events there is no way of determining which is to be the last."

Yama said stoutly, "The heretics will be defeated because they challenge the word of the Preservers. The Ancients of Days revived much old technology which their followers use against us, but they were lesser creatures than the Preservers because they were the distant ancestors of the Preservers. How can a lesser idea prevail against a greater one?"

"I forget that you are young," Beatrice said, smiling. "You still have hope. But Osric has hope, too, and he is a wise man. Not that the world will not end, for that is certain, but that it will end well. The Great River fails day by day, and at last all that my people care for will fall away."

"With respect, perhaps you and your husband live for the past, yet I live for the future."

Beatrice smiled. "Ah, but which future, I wonder? Osric suspects that there might be more than one. As for us, it is our duty to preserve the past to inform the future, and this place is where the past is strongest. There are wonders interred here which could end the war in an instant if wielded by one side, or destroy Confluence, if used by both against each other.

"The living bury the dead and move on, and forget. We remember. Above all, that is our duty. There are record keepers in Ys who claim to be able to trace the bloodlines of Confluence back to their first members. My family preserves the tombs of those ancestors, their bodies and their artifacts. The record keepers would claim that words are stronger than the phenomena they describe, and that only words endure while all else fails, but we know that even words change. Stories are mutable, and in any story each generation finds a different lesson, and with each telling a story changes slightly until it is no longer the thing it was. The king who prevails against the hero who would have brought redeeming light to the world becomes after many tellings of the story a hero saving the world from fire, and the light-bringer becomes a fiend. Only things remain what they are. They are themselves. Words are merely representations of things; but we have the things themselves. How much more powerful they are than their representations!"

Yama thought of the Aedile, who put so much trust in the objects that the soil preserved. He said, "My father seeks to understand the past by the wreckage it leaves behind. Perhaps it is not the stories that change but the past itself, for all that lives of the past is the meaning we invest in what remains."

Behind him, Osric said, "You have been taught by a record keeper. That is just what one of those beetle-browed near-sighted bookworms would say, bless them all, each and every one. Well, there is more of the past than can be found in books. That is a lesson I had to learn over and over, young man. All that is ordinary and human passes away without record, and all that remains are stories of priests and philosophers, heroes and kings. Much is made of the altar stones and sacraria of temples, but nothing of the cloisters where lovers rendezvoused and friends gossiped, and the courtyards where children played. That is the false lesson of history. Still, we can peer into random scenes of the past and wonder at their import. That is what I have brought you."

Osric carried something square and flat under his arm, covered with a white cloth. He removed the cloth with a flourish, revealing a thin rectangle of milky stone which he laid in a pool of sunlight on the tiled floor of the balcony.

Yama said, "My father collects these picture slates, but this one appears blank."

"He collected them for important research, perhaps," Osric said, "but I am sorry to hear of it. Their proper resting place is not in a collection, but in the tomb in which they were installed."

"I have always wondered why they need to drink sunlight to work, when they were buried away in darkness."

"The tombs drink sunlight, too," Osric said, "and distribute it amongst their components according to need. The pictures respond to the heat given off by a living body, and in the darkness of the tomb would waken in the presence of any watcher. Outside the tomb, without their usual power source, the pictures also require sunlight."

"Be quiet, husband," Beatrice said. "It wakens. Watch it, Yama, and learn. This is all we can show you."

Colors mingled and ran in the slate, seeming to swirl just beneath its surface. At first they were faint and amorphous, little more than pastel flows within the slate's milky depths, but gradually they brightened, running together in a sudden silvery flash.

For a moment, Yama thought that the slate had turned into a mirror, reflecting his own eager face. But when he leaned closer, the face within the slate turned as if to speak to someone beyond the frame of the picture, and he saw that it was the face of someone older than he was, a man with lines at the corners of his eyes and grooves at either side of his mouth. But the shape of the eyes and their round blue irises, and the shape of the face, the pale skin and the mop of wiry black hair: all these were so very like his own that he cried out in astonishment.

The man in the picture was talking now, and suddenly smiled at someone beyond the picture's frame, a frank, eager smile that turned Yama's heart. The man turned away and the view slid from his face to show the night sky. It was not the sky of Confluence, for it was full of stars, scattered like diamond chips carelessly thrown across black velvet. There was a frozen swirl of dull red light in the center of the picture, and Yama saw that the stars around it seemed to be drawn into lines that curved in toward the red swirl. Stars streaked as the viewpoint of the picture moved, and for a moment it steadied on a flock of splinters of light hung against pure black, and then it faded.

Osric wrapped the white cloth around the slate. Immediately, Yama wanted to strip the cloth away and see the picture blossom within the slate again, wanted to feast on the stranger's face, the stranger who was of his bloodline, wanted to understand the strange skies under which his long-dead ancestor had stood. His blood sang in his ears.

Beatrice handed him a square of lace-trimmed cloth. A handkerchief. Yama realized then that he was weeping.

Osric said, "This is the place where the oldest tombs on Confluence can be found, but the picture is older than anything on Confluence, for it is older than Confluence itself. It shows the first stage in the construction of the Eye of the Preservers, and it shows the lands which the Preservers walked before they fell into the Eye and vanished into the deep past or the deep future, or perhaps into another universe entirely."

"I would like to see the tomb. I want to see where you found this picture."

Osric said, "The Department of the Curators of the City of the Dead has kept the picture a long time, and if it once rested in a tomb, then it was so long ago that all records of that tomb are lost. Your bloodline walked Confluence at its beginning, and now it walks it again."

Yama said, "This is the second time that someone has hinted that I have a mysterious destiny, but no one will explain why or what it is."

Beatrice told her husband, "He'll discover it soon enough. We should not tell him more."

Osric tugged at his beard. "I do not know everything. What the hollow man said, for instance, or what lies beyond the end of the river. I have tried to remember it all over again, and I cannot!"

Beatrice took her husband's hands in her own and told Yama, "He was hurt, and sometimes gets confused about what might happen and what has happened. Remember the slate. It's important."

Yama said, "I know less than you. Let me see the slate again. Perhaps there is something—"

Beatrice said, "Perhaps it is your destiny to discover your past, dear. Only by knowing the past can you know yourself."

Yama smiled, because that was precisely the motto which Zakiel used to justify his long lessons. It seemed to him that the curators of the dead and the librarians and archivists were so similar that they amplified slight differences into a deadly rivalry, just as brothers feuded over nothing at all simply to assert their individuality.

"You have seen all we can show you, Yama," Osric said. "We preserve the past as best we can, but we do not pretend to understand everything we preserve."

Yama said formally, "I thank you for showing me this wonder." But he thought that it proved only that others like him had lived long ago—he was more concerned with discovering if they still lived now. Surely they must—he was proof of that—but where? What had Dr. Dismas discovered in the archives of his department?

Beatrice stood with a graceful flowing motion. "You cannot stay, Yama. You are a catalyst, and change is most dangerous here."

Yama said, "If you would show me the way, I would go home at once."

He said it with little hope, for he was convinced that the two curators were holding him prisoner. But Beatrice smiled and said, "I will do better than that. I will take you."

Osric said, "You are stronger than you were when you arrived here, but not, I think, as strong as you can be. Let my wife help you, Yama. And remember us. We have served as best we can, and I feel that we have served well. When you discover your purpose, remember us."

Beatrice said, "Don't burden the poor boy, husband. He is too young. It is too early."

"He is old enough to know his mind, I think. Remember that we are your friends, Yama."

Yama bowed from the waist, as the Aedile had taught him, and turned to follow Beatrice, leaving her husband sitting in a pool of sunlight, his ravaged face made inscrutable by the mirror lenses of his spectacles, the blue uncharted mountain ridges framed by the pillars behind him, and the picture slate, wrapped in white cloth, on his lap.

Beatrice led Yama down a long helical stair and through chambers where machines as big as houses stood half-buried in the stone floor. Beyond these were the wide, circular mouths of pits in which long narrow tubes, made of a metal as clear as glass, fell into white mists a league or more below. Vast slow lightnings sparked and rippled in the transparent tubes. Yama felt a slow vibration through the soles of his feet, a pulse deeper than sound.

He would have stayed to examine the machines, but Beatrice urged him past and led him down a long hall with black keelrock walls, lit by balls of white fire that spun beneath a high curved ceiling. Parts of the floor were transparent and Yama saw, dimly, huge machines crouched in chambers far below his feet.

"Don't gawp," Beatrice said. "You don't want to wake them before their time."

Many narrow corridors led off the hall. Beatrice ushered Yama down one of them into a small room which, once its door slid shut, began at once to hum and shake. Yama felt for a moment as if he had stepped over a cliff, and clutched at the rail which ran around the curved walls of the room.

"We fall through the keelways," Beatrice said. "Most people live on the surface now, but in ancient times the surface was a place where they came to play and meet, while they had their dwelling and working places underground. This is one of the old roads. It will return you to Aeolis in less than an hour."

"Are these roads everywhere?"

"Once. No more. We have maintained a few beneath the City of the Dead, but many more no longer function, and beyond the limits of our jurisdiction things are worse. Everything fails at last. Even the Universe will fall into itself eventually."

"The Puranas say that is why the Preservers fled into the Eye. But if the Universe will not end soon, then surely that is not why they fled. Zakiel could never explain that. He said it was not for me to question the Puranas."

Beatrice laughed. It was like the tinkling of old, fragile bells. "How like a librarian! But the Puranas contain many riddles, and there is no harm in admitting that not all the answers are obvious. Perhaps they are not even comprehensible to our small minds, but a librarian will never admit that any text in his charge is unfathomable. He must be the master of them all, and is shamed to admit any possible failure."

"The slate showed the creation of the Eye. There is a sura in the Puranas, the forty-third sura, I think, which says that the Preservers made stars fall together, until their light grew too heavy to escape."

"Perhaps. There is much we do not know about the past, Yama. Some have said that the Preservers set us here for their own amusement, as certain bloodlines keep caged birds for amusement, but I would not repeat that heresy. All who believed it are safely dead long ago, but it is still a dangerous thought."

"Perhaps because it is true, or contains some measure of the truth."

Beatrice regarded him with her bright eyes. She was a head taller than he was. "Do not be bitter, Yama. You will find what you are looking for, although it might not be where you expect it. Ah, we are almost there."

The room shuddered violently. Yama fell to his knees. The floor was padded with a kind of quilting, covered in an artificial material as slick and thin as satin.

Beatrice opened the door and Yama followed her into a very long room that had been carved from rock. Its high roof was held up by a forest of slender pillars and wan light fell from narrow slits in the roof. It had once been a stonemasons' workshop, and Beatrice led Yama around half-finished carvings and benches scattered with tools, all abandoned an age ago and muffled by thick dust. At the door, she took out a hood of soft, black cloth and said that she must blindfold him.

"We are a secret people, because we should not exist. Our department was disbanded long ago, and we survive only because we are good at hiding."

"I understand. My father—"

"We are not frightened of discovery, Yama, but we have stayed hidden for so long that knowledge of where we are is valuable to certain people. I would not ask you to carry that burden. It would expose you to unnecessary danger. If you need to find us again, you will. I can safely promise that, I think. In return, will you promise that you won't mention us to the Aedile?"

"He will want to know where I have been."

"You were ill. You recovered, and you returned. Perhaps you were nursed by one of the hill tribes. The Aedile will be so pleased to see you that he won't question you too closely. Will you promise?"

"As long as I do not have to lie to him. I think that I am done with lies."

Beatrice was pleased by this. "You were honest from the first, dear heart. Tell the Aedile as much of the truth as is good for him, and no more. Now, come with me."

Blinded by the soft, heavy cloth of the hood, Yama took Beatrice's hot, fine-boned hand, and allowed himself to be led once more. They walked a long way. He trusted this strange old woman, and he was thinking about the man of his bloodline, dead ages past.

At last she told him to stand still. Something cold and heavy was placed in his right hand. After a moment of silence, Yama lifted the hood away and saw that he was in a dark passageway walled with broken stone blocks, with stout tree roots thrust between their courses. A patch of sunlight fell through a narrow doorway at the top of a stair whose stone treads had been worn away in the center. He was holding the ancient metal knife he had found in the tomb by the river's shore— or which had found him. A skirl of blue sparks flared along the outer edge of its blade and sputtered out one by one.

Yama looked around for Beatrice and thought he saw a patch of white float around the corner of a passageway. But when he ran after it, he found a stone wall blocking his way. He turned back to the sunlight. This place was familiar, but he did not recognize it until he climbed the stair and stepped out into the ruins in the Aedile's garden, with the peel-house looming beyond masses of dark green rhododendrons.

11

Prefect Corin

LOB AND THE landlord of *The House of Ghost Lanterns* were arrested
before Yama had finished telling his story to the Aedile, and the next
day were tried and sentenced to death for kidnap and sabotage. The
Aedile also issued a warrant for the arrest of Dr. Dismas, although he
confided to Yama that he did not expect to see the apothecary again.

Although it took a long time to explain his adventures, Yama did
not tell the whole story. He suppressed the part about Enobarbus, for
he had come to believe that the young warlord had somehow been
caught by Dr. Dismas's spell. He kept his promise to Beatrice, too, and
said that after he had escaped from the skiff and had been helped ashore
by one of the fisherfolk, he had fallen ill after being attacked by Lob
and Lud amongst the ransacked tombs of the Silent Quarter, and had
not been able to return to the peel-house until he had recovered. It was
not the whole truth, but the Aedile did not question him closely.

Yama was not allowed to attend the trial; nor was he allowed to
leave the grounds of the peel-house, although he very much wanted to
see Derev. The Aedile said that it was too dangerous. The families of
Lob and the tavern landlord would be looking for revenge, and the city
was still on edge after the riots which had followed the failed siege of
Dr. Dismas's tower. Yama tried to contact Derev using mirror talk, but
although he signaled for most of the afternoon there was no answering
spark of light from the apartments Derev's father had built on top of
his godown by the old waterfront of the city. Sick at heart, Yama went
to plead with Sergeant Rhodean, but the Sergeant refused to provide an
escort.

"And you're not to confuse the watchdogs and go sneaking out on your own, neither," Sergeant Rhodean said. "Oh yes, I know all about that trick, lad. But see here, you can't rely on tricks to keep yourself out of trouble. They're more likely to get you into it instead. I won't risk having any of my men hurt rescuing you from your own foolishness, and think how it would look if we took you down there in the middle of a decad of armed soldiers. You'd start another riot. My men have already spent too much time looking for you when you were lost in the City of the Dead, and they'll have their hands full in a couple of days. The department is sending a clerk to deal with the prisoners, but no extra troops. Pure foolishness on their part, and I'll get blamed if something goes wrong."

Sergeant Rhodean was much exercised by this. As he talked, he paced in a tight circle on the red clay floor of the gymnasium. He was a small, burly man, almost as wide as he was tall, as he liked to say. As always, his gray tunic and blue trousers were neatly pressed, his black knee-boots were spit-polished, and the scalp of his heavy, ridged skull was close-shaven and burnished with oil. He favored his right leg, and the thumb and forefinger of his right hand were missing. He had been the Aedile's bodyguard long before the entire household had been exiled from the Palace of the Memory of the People, and had celebrated his hundredth birthday two years ago. He lived quietly with his wife, who was always trying to overfeed Yama because, she said, he needed to put some muscle on his long bones. They had two married daughters, six sons away fighting the heretics, and two more who had been killed in the war; Sergeant Rhodean had mourned Telmon's death almost as bitterly as Yama and the Aedile.

Sergeant Rhodean suddenly stopped pacing and looked at Yama as if for the first time. He said, "I see you're wearing that knife you found, lad. Let's take a look at it."

Yama had taken to hanging the knife from his belt by a loop of leather, with its blade tied flat against his thigh by a red ribbon. He undid the ribbon, unhooked the loop and held out the knife, and Sergeant Rhodean put on thick-lensed spectacles, which vastly magnified his yellow eyes, and peered closely at it for a long time. At last, he blew reflectively through his drooping mustache and said, "It's old, and sentient, or at least partly so. Maybe as smart as one of the watchdogs. A good idea to carry it around. It will bond to you. You said you were ill after using it?"

"It gave out a blue light. And when Lob picked it up, it turned into something horrible."

"Well now, lad, it had to get its energy from somewhere for tricks like that, especially after all the time in the dark. So it took it from you."

"I leave it in sunlight," Yama said.

"Do you?" Sergeant Rhodean gave Yama a shrewd look. "Then I can't tell you much more. What did you clean it with? White vinegar? As good as anything, I suppose. Well, let's see you make a few passes with it. It will stop you brooding over your true love."

For the next hour, Sergeant Rhodean instructed Yama on how to make best use of the knife against a variety of imaginary opponents. Yama found himself beginning to enjoy the exercises, and was sorry when Sergeant Rhodean called a halt. He had spent many happy hours in the gymnasium, with its mingled smell of clay and old sweat and rubbing alcohol, its dim underwater light filtered through green-tinted windows high up in the whitewashed walls, the green rubber wrestling mats rolled up like the shed cocoons of giant caterpillars and the rack of parallel bars, the open cases of swords and knives, javelins and padded staves, the straw archery targets stacked behind the vaulting horse, the battered wooden torsos of the tilting dummies, the frames hung with pieces of plastic and resin and metal armor.

"We'll do some more work tomorrow, lad," Sergeant Rhodean said at last. "You need to work on your backhand. You aim too low, at the belly instead of the chest, and any opponent worth their salt would spot that in an instant. Of course, a knife like this is really intended for close work by a cavalryman surrounded by the enemy, and you might do better carrying a long sword or a revolver when walking about the city. It's possible that an old weapon like this might be proscribed. But now I have to drill the men. The clerk is coming tomorrow, and I suppose your father will want an honor guard for him."

But the clerk sent from Ys to oversee the executions slipped unnoticed into the peel-house early the next morning, and the first time Yama saw him was when the Aedile summoned him to an audience that afternoon.

"The townspeople already believe that you have blood on your hands," the Aedile said. "I do not wish to see any more trouble. So I have come to a decision."

Yama felt his heart turn over, although he already knew that this was no ordinary interview. He had been escorted to the Aedile's receiving chamber by one of the soldiers of the house guard. The soldier now stood in front of the tall double doors, resplendent in burnished helmet and corselet and scarlet hose, his pike at parade rest.

Yama perched on an uncomfortable curved backless seat before the central dais on which the Aedile's canopied chair stood. The Aedile did not sit down but paced about restlessly. He was dressed in a tunic embroidered with silver and gold, and his sable robe of office hung on a rack by his chair.

There was a fourth person in the room, standing in the shadows by the small private door which led, via a stairway, to the Aedile's private chambers. It was the clerk who had been sent from Ys to supervise the executions. Yama watched him out of the corner of his eye. He was a tall, slender man of the Aedile's bloodline, bareheaded in a plain homespun tunic and gray leggings. A close-clipped black pelt covered his head and face, with a broad white stripe, like a badger's marking, on the left side of his face.

Yama's breakfast had been brought to his room that morning, and this was the first chance he had to study the man. He had heard from the stable hands that the clerk had disembarked from an ordinary lugger, armed with only a stout ironshod staff and with no more than a rolled blanket on his back, but the Aedile had prostrated himself at the man's feet as if he were a Hierarch risen from the files.

"I don't think he expected someone so high up in the Committee for Public Safety," the foreman, Torin, had said.

But the clerk did not look like an executioner, or anyone important. He could have been any one of the thousands of ordinary scribes who plied pens in cells deep in the Palace of the Memory of the People, as indistinguishable from each other as ants.

The Aedile stood before one of the four great tapestries that decorated the high, square room. It depicted the seeding of Confluence. Plants and animals rained out of a blaze of light toward a bare plain crossed by silvery loops of water. Birds soared through the air, and little groups of naked men and women of various bloodlines stood on wisps of cloud, hands modestly covering their genitals and breasts.

Yama had always loved this tapestry, but now that he had talked with the curators of the City of the Dead he knew that it was a lie. Since he had returned, everything in the peel-house seemed to have changed. The house was smaller; the gardens cramped and neglected; the people preoccupied with small matters, their backs bent to routine labor so that, like peasants planting a paddy field, they failed to see the great events of the world rushing above their heads.

At last, the Aedile turned and said, "It was always my plan to apprentice you to my department, Yama, and I have not changed my mind. You are perhaps a little young to begin proper apprenticeship, but I have great hopes of you. Zakiel says that you are the best pupil he has known, and Sergeant Rhodean believes that in a few years you will be able to best him in archery and fencing, although he adds that your horse riding still requires attention.

"I know your determination and ambition, Yama. I think that you will be a great power in the department. You are not of my bloodline, but you are my son, now and always. I would wish that you could have stayed here until you were old enough to be inducted as a full apprentice, but it is clear to me that if you stay here you are in great danger."

"I am not afraid of anyone in Aeolis."

But Yama's protest was a formality. Already he was dizzy with the prospect of kicking the dust of this sleepily corrupt little city from his heels. In Ys, there were records which went back to the foundation of Confluence. Beatrice had said as much. She and Osric had shown him a slate which had displayed the likeness of an ancestor of his bloodline; in Ys, he might learn who that man had been. There might even be people of his bloodline! Anything was possible. After all, surely he had come from Ys in the first place, borne downstream on the river's current. For that reason alone he would gladly go to Ys, although more than ever he knew that he could not serve as a clerk. But he could not tell his father that, of course, and it burned in his chest like a coal.

The Aedile said, "I am proud that you can say that you are unafraid with such conviction, and I think that you truly believe it. But you cannot spend your life looking over your shoulder, Yama, and that is what you would have to do if you stayed here. One day, sooner or later, Lob and Lud's brothers will seek to press their need for revenge. That they are the sons of the Constable of Aeolis makes this more likely, not less, for if any one of them killed you, it would not only satisfy their family's need for revenge, it would also be a triumph over their father.

"It is not the townspeople I fear, however. Dr. Dismas has fled, but he may try to revive his scheme, or he may sell his information to others. In Aeolis you are a wonder; in Ys, which is the fount of all the wonders of the world, less so. Here, I command only three decads of soldiers; there, you will be in the heart of the department."

"When will I go?"

The Aedile clasped his hands and bowed his head. It was a peculiarly submissive gesture. "You will leave with Prefect Corin, after he has concluded his business here."

The man in the shadows caught Yama's gaze. "In cases like this," he said in a soft, lilting voice, "it is not advisable to linger once duty has been done. I will leave tomorrow."

No, the clerk, Prefect Corin, did not look like an executioner, but he had already visited Lob and the landlord of the tavern, who had been held in the peel-house's oubliette since their trial. They were to be burned that evening outside the town's walls, and their ashes would be scattered on the wind so that their families would have no part of them as a memorial and their souls would never have rest until the Preservers woke all the dead at the end of the Universe. Sergeant Rhodean had been drilling his men ever since the trial. If there was any trouble, he could not rely on the Constable and the city militia for aid. Every bit of armor had been polished, and every weapon cleaned or sharpened. Because the steam wagon had been destroyed in the siege of Dr. Dismas's tower, an ordinary wagon had been sequestered to transport the condemned men from the peel-house to the place of execution. It had been painted white, and its axles greased and its wheels balanced, and the two white oxen which would draw it had been brushed until their coats shone. The entire peel-house had been filled with bustle over the affair, but as soon as he had arrived, Prefect Corin had become its still center.

The Aedile said, "It is abrupt, I know, but I will see you in Ys, as soon as I can be sure that there will be no more trouble here. In the meantime, I hope you will remember me with affection."

"Father, you have done more for me than I ever can deserve." It was a formal sentiment, and sounded trite, but Yama felt a sudden flood of affection for the Aedile then, and would have embraced him if Prefect Corin had not been watching.

The Aedile turned to study the tapestry again. Perhaps Prefect Corin made him uncomfortable, too. He said, "Quite, quite. You are my son, Yama. No less than Telmon."

Prefect Corin cleared his throat, a small sound in the large room, but father and son turned to stare at him as if he had shot a pistol at the painted ceiling.

"Your pardon," he said, "but it is time to shrive the prisoners."

Two hours before sunset, Father Quine, the priest of the temple of Aeolis, came in his orange robes, walking barefoot and bareheaded up the winding road from the city to the peel-house. Ananda accompanied him, carrying a chrism of oil. The Aedile greeted them formally and escorted them to the oubliette, where they would hear the final confessions of the prisoners.

Again, Yama had no part in the ceremony. He sat in one corner of the big fireplace in the kitchen, but that had changed, too. He was no longer a part of the kitchen's bustle and banter. The scullions and the kitchen boys and the three cooks politely replied to his remarks, but their manner was subdued. He wanted to tell them that he was still Yama, the boy who had wrestled with most of the kitchen boys, who had received clouts from the cooks when he had tried to steal bits of food, who had cheeked the scullions to make them chase him. But he was no longer that boy.

After a while, oppressed by polite deference, Yama went out to watch the soldiers drilling in the slanting sunlight, and that was where Ananda found him.

Ananda's head was clean-shaven; there was a fresh cut above his right ear, painted with yellow iodine. His eyes were enlarged by clever use of blue paint and gold leaf. He gave off a smell of cloves and cinnamon. It was the scent of the oil with which the prisoners had been anointed.

Ananda knew how to judge Yama's mood. For a while, the two friends stood side by side in companionable silence and watched the soldiers make squares and lines in the dusty sunlight. Sergeant Rhodean barked orders which echoed off the high wall of the peel-house.

At last, Yama said, "I have to go away tomorrow."

"I know."

"With that little badger of a clerk. He is to be my master. He will teach me how to copy records and write up administrative reports. I will be buried, Ananda. Buried in old paper and futile tasks. There is only one consolation."

"You can look for your bloodline."

Yama was astonished. "How did you know?"

"Why, you've always talked about it." Ananda looked at Yama shrewdly. "But you've learnt something about it, haven't you? That's why it's on your mind."

"A clerk, Ananda. I will not serve. I cannot. I have more important things to do."

"Not only soldiers help fight the war. And don't change the subject."

"That is what my father would say. I want to be a hero, Ananda. It is my destiny!"

"If it's your destiny, then it will happen." Ananda pulled a pouch from inside his robe and spilled hulled pistachios into his meaty palm. "Want some?"

Yama shook his head. He said, "It has all changed so quickly."

Ananda put his palm to his lips and said, around a mouthful of pistachios, "Is there time to tell me all that happened? I'm never going to leave here, you know. My master will die, and I will take his place, and begin to teach the new sizar, who will be a boy just like me. And so on."

"I am not allowed to go to the execution."

"Of course not. It would be unseemly."

"I want to prove that I am brave enough to see it."

"What did happen, Yama? You couldn't have been lost for so long, and they couldn't have taken you far if you said you escaped on the night you were taken."

"A lot of things happened after that. I do not understand all of them, but one thing I do understand. I found something . . . something important."

Ananda laughed. "You mustn't tease your friends, Yama. Share it with me. Perhaps I can help you understand everything."

"Meet me tonight. After the executions. Bring Derev, too. I tried to send a message to her by mirror talk, but no one replied. I want her to hear my story. I want to . . ."

"I know. There will be a service. We have to exculpate Prefect Corin after he sets the torch to . . . well, to the prisoners. Then there's a formal meal, but I'm not invited to that, of course. It begins two hours after sunset, and I'll come then. And I'll find a way of bringing Derev."

"Have you ever seen an execution, Ananda?"

Ananda poured more pistachios into his palm. He looked at them and said, "No. No, I haven't. Oh, I know everything that will happen, of course, and I know what I have to do, but I'm not sure how I'll act."

"You will not disgrace your master. I will see you two hours after sunset. And make sure to bring Derev."

"As if I would forget." Ananda tipped the pistachios into the dirt and brushed his hands together. "The landlord of the tavern was an addict of the drug that Dismas used, did you know that? Dismas supplied him with it, and he'd do anything asked of him. It didn't lessen the sentence, of course, but it was how he pleaded."

Yama remembered Dr. Dismas grinding dried beetles and clear, apricot-scented liquid into paste, the sudden relaxation of his face after he had injected himself.

"Cantharides," he said. "And Lob and Lud did it for money."

"Well, Lob had his payment, at least," Ananda said. "He was drunk when he was arrested, and I hear he'd been buying the whole town drinks for several days before that. I think he knew that you'd be back."

Yama remembered that Lob and Lud had not been paid by Dr.

Dismas. Where then had Lob got the money for his drinking spree? And who had rescued him from the old tomb, and taken him to the tower of Beatrice and Osric? With a cold pang, he realized who it must have been, and how she had known where to find him.

Ananda had turned to watch the soldiers wheel out on the parade square, one line becoming two that marched off side by side toward the main gate, with Sergeant Rhodean loudly counting the pace as he marched at their head. After a while, Ananda said, "Did you ever think that Lob and Lud were a little bit like you? They wanted to escape this place, too."

———

Yama wanted to watch Lob and the landlord of the tavern leave the peel-house for the place of execution, but even that was denied him. Zakiel found him at a window, staring down at the courtyard where soldiers were harnessing the stamping horses to the white wagon, and took him off to the library.

"We have only a little time, master, and there is so much to tell you."

"Then why begin to try? Are you going to the executions, Zakiel?"

"It is not my place, master."

"I suppose that my father told you to keep me occupied. I want to see it, Zakiel. They are trying to exclude me from it all. I suppose it is to spare my feelings. But imagining it is worse than knowing."

"I have taught you something, then. I was beginning to wonder."

Zakiel rarely smiled, but he smiled now. He was a tall, gaunt man, with a long, heavy-browed face and a shaven skull with a bony crest. His black skin shone in the yellow light of the flickering electric sconce, and the muscles of his heavy jaws moved under the skin on either side of the crest when he smiled. As a party piece, on high day feasts, he would crack walnuts between his strong square teeth. As always, he wore a gray tunic and gray leggings, and sandals soled with rubber that squeaked on the polished marquetry of the paths between the library stacks. He wore a slave collar around his neck, but it was made of a light alloy, not iron, and covered with a circlet of handmade lace.

Zakiel said, "I could tell you what will happen, if you like. I was instructed in it, because it is believed that to tell the prisoner exactly what will happen to him will make it endurable. But it was the cruellest thing they did, far crueller than being put to question."

Zakiel had been sentenced to death before he had come to work for the Aedile. Yama, who had forgotten that, was mortified. He said, "I was not thinking. I am sorry. No, do not tell me."

"You would rather see it. You believe your senses, but not words. Yet the long-dead men and women who wrote all these volumes which stand about us had the same appetites as us, the same fears, the same ambitions. All we know of the world passes through our sensory organs and is reduced to electric impulses in certain sensory nerve fibers. When you open one of these books and read of events that happened before you were born, some of those nerve fibers are stimulated in exactly the same way."

"I want to see for myself. Reading about it is different."

Zakiel cracked his knuckles. They were swollen, like all of his joints. His fingers looked like strings of nuts.

"Why, perhaps I have not taught you anything after all. Of course it is different. What books do is allow you to share the perceptions of those who write them. There are certain wizards who claim to be able to read minds, and mountebanks who claim to have discovered ancient machines that print out a person's thoughts, or project them in a sphere of glass or crystal metal, but the wizards and mountebanks lie. Only books allow us to share another's thoughts. By reading them, we see the world not through our senses, but through those of their authors. And if those authors are wiser than us, or more knowing, or more sensitive, then so are we while we read. I will say no more about this. I know you would read the world directly, and tomorrow you will no longer have to listen to old Zakiel. But I would give you something, if I may. A slave owns nothing, not even his own life, so this is in the nature of a loan, but I have the Aedile's permission."

Zakiel led Yama deeper into the stacks, where books stood two-deep on shelves that bent under their weight. He pulled a ladder from a recess, set its hooked top on the lip of the highest shelf, and climbed up. He fussed there for a minute, blowing dust from one book after another, and finally climbed down with a volume no bigger than his hand.

"I knew I had it," he said, "although I have not touched it since I first cataloged the library. Even the Aedile does not know of this. It was left by one of his predecessors; that is the way this library has grown, and why there is so much of little value. Yet some hold that gems are engendered in mud, and this book is such a gem. It is yours."

It was bound in a black, artificial stuff that, although scuffed at the corners, shone as if newly made when Zakiel wiped away the dust with the hem of his tunic. Yama riffled the pages of the book. They were stiff and slick, and seemed to contain a hidden depth. When he tilted the pages to the light, images came and went in the margins of the crisp double-columned print. He had expected some rare history of Ys, or a bestiary, like those he had loved to read when he was younger, but this was no more than a copy of the Puranas.

Yama said, "If my father told you to give me this book, then how is it that he does not know he owns it?"

"I asked if I could give you a volume of the Puranas, and so I have. But this edition is very old, and differs in some details from that which I have taught you. It is an edition that has long been suppressed, and perhaps this is the only copy of that edition which now exists."

"It is different?"

"In some parts. You must read it all to find out, and remember what I have taught you. So perhaps my teachings will continue, in some fashion. Or you could simply look at the pictures. Modern editions do not, of course, have pictures."

Yama, who had been tilting the pages of the book to the light as he turned them, suddenly felt a shock of recognition. There in the margin of one of the last pages was the view he had glimpsed behind the face of his ancestor, of stars streaming inwards toward a dull glow.

He said, "I will read it, Zakiel. I promise."

For a moment Zakiel stared at Yama in silence, his black eyes inscrutable beneath the bony shelf of his brow. Then the librarian smiled and clapped dust from his big, bony hands. "Very good, master. Very good. Now we will drink some tea, and talk on the history of the department of which, when you reach Ys, you will be the newest and youngest member."

"With respect, Zakiel, I am sure that the history of the department will be the first thing I will be taught when I arrive in Ys, and no doubt the clerk will have some words on it during our journey."

"I do not think that Prefect Corin is a man who wastes words," Zakiel said. "And he does not see himself as a teacher."

"My father would have you occupy my mind. I understand. Well then, I would like to hear something of the history of another department. One that was broken up a long time ago. Is that possible?"

12

The Execution

AFTER SUNSET, YAMA climbed to the heliograph platform that circled the top of the tallest of the peel-house's towers. He uncapped the observation telescope and, turning it on the heavy steel gimbals which floated in sealed oil baths, lined up its declinational and equatorial axes in a combination he knew as well as his own name.

Beyond the darkening vanishing point, the tops of the towers that rose up from the heart of Ys shone in the last light of the sun like a cluster of fiery needles floating high above the world, higher than the naked peaks of the Rim Mountains. Ys! In his room, Yama had spent a little time gazing at his old map before reluctantly rolling it up and putting it away. He had traced the roads that crossed the barrens of the coastal plains, the passes through the mountains that embraced the city. He vowed now that in a handful of days he would stand at the base of the towers as a free man.

When he put up the telescope and leaned at the rail, with warm air gusting around him, he saw prickles of light flickering in the middle distance. Messages. The air was full of messages, talking of war, of faraway battles and sieges at the midpoint of the world.

Yama walked to the other side of the tower and stared out across the wide shallow valley of the Breas toward Aeolis, and saw with a little shock that the execution pyre had already been kindled. The point of light flickered like a baleful star fallen to the ground outside the wall of the little city.

"They would have killed me," he said, trying out the words, "if there was money in it."

Yama watched for a long time, until the distant fire began to dim and was outshone by the ordinary lights of the city. Lob and the landlord of *The House of Ghost Lanterns* were dead. The Aedile and the colorless man, the clerk, Prefect Corin, would be in grave procession toward the temple, led by Father Quine and flanked by Sergeant Rhodean's men in polished black armor.

His supper had been set out in his room, but he left it and went down to the kitchen and, armored by his new authority, hacked a wedge from a wheel of cheese and took a melon, a bottle of yellow wine, and one of the heavy date loaves that had been baked that morning. He cut through the kitchen gardens, fooled the watchdogs for the last time, and walked along the high road before plunging down the steep slope of the bluff and following the paths along the tops of the dikes which divided the flooded paeonin fields.

The clear, shallow Breas made a rushing noise in the darkness as it ran swiftly over the flat rocks of its bed. At the waterlift, two oxen plodded side by side around their circle, harnessed to the trimmed trunk of a young pine. This spar turned the shaft that, groaning as if in protest at its eternal torment, lifted a chain of buckets from the river and tipped them in a never-ending cascade into the channels which fed the irrigation system of the paeonin fields. The oxen walked in their circle under a roof of palm fronds, their tails rhythmically slapping their dung-spattered flanks. Now and then they snatched a mouthful of the fodder scattered around the perimeter of their circular path, but mostly they walked with their heads down, from nowhere to nowhere.

No, Yama thought, I will not serve.

He sat on an upturned stone a little distance off the path and ate meltingly sweet slices of melon while he waited. The oxen plodded around and around, turning the groaning shaft. Frogs peeped in the paeonin fields. Beyond the city, at the mouth of the Breas, the misty light of the Arm of the Warrior was lifting above the farside horizon. It would rise a little later each night, a little farther downriver. Soon it would not rise at all, and the Eye of the Preservers would appear above the upriver vanishing point, and it would be summer. But before then Yama would be in Ys.

Two people were coming along the path, shadows moving through the Galaxy's blue twilight. Yama waited until they had gone past before he whistled sharply.

"We thought you might not be here," Ananda said as he walked up to where Yama sat.

"Well met," Derev said, at Ananda's shoulder. The Galaxy put blue shadows in the unbound mass of her white hair and a spark in each of her large, dark eyes. "O, well met, Yama!"

She rushed forward and hugged him. Her light-boned body, her long slim arms and legs, her heat, her scent. Yama was always surprised to discover that Derev was taller than himself. Despite the cold certainty he had nursed ever since Ananda's remark about Lob's drunken spree, his love rekindled in her embrace. It was an effort not to respond, and he hated himself because it seemed a worse betrayal than anything she might have done.

Derev drew back a little and said, "What's wrong?"

Yama said, "I am glad you came. There is something I want to ask you."

Derev smiled and moved her arms in a graceful circle, making the wide sleeves of her white dress floatingly glimmer in the half-dark. "Anything! As long, of course, as I can hear your story. All of it, not just the highlights."

Ananda found the wedge of cheese and began to pare slices from it. "I've been fasting," he explained. "Water for breakfast, water for lunch."

"And pistachios," Yama said.

"I never said I would make a good priest. I am supposed to be cleaning out the narthex while Father Quine dines with the Aedile and Prefect Corin. This is a strange place to meet, Yama."

"There was something Dr. Dismas once said to me, about the habits we fall into. I wanted to be reminded of it."

Derev said, "But you are all right. You have recovered from your adventures."

"I learned much from them."

"And you will tell all," Ananda said. He handed around slices of bread and cheese, and pried the cork out of the wine bottle with his little knife. "I think," he said, "that you should start at the beginning."

The story seemed far stranger and more exciting than the actual experience. To tell it concisely, Yama had to miss out the fear and tension he had felt during every moment of his adventures, the long hours of discomfort when he had tried to sleep in wet clothes on the trunk of the banyan, his growing hunger and thirst while wandering the hot shaly land of the Silent Quarter of the City of the Dead.

As he talked, he remembered a dream he had had while sleeping on the catafalque inside the old tomb in the Silent Quarter. He had dreamed that he had been swimming in the Great River, and that a current had suddenly caught him and swept him toward the edge of the world, where the river fell away in thunder and spray. He had tried to swim against the current, but his arms had been trapped at his sides and he had been helplessly swept through swift white water toward the tremendous noise of the river's fall. The oppressive helplessness of the dream had stayed with him all that morning, right up to the moment when Lud and Lob had caught up with him, but he had forgotten about it until now. And now it seemed important, as if dream and reality were, during the telling of his tale, coterminous. He told his two friends about the dream as if it were one more part of his adventures, and then described how Lob and Lud had surprised him, and how he had killed Lud by accident.

"I had found an old knife, and Lob got hold of it, ready to kill me because I had killed his brother. But the knife hurt him. It seemed to turn into something like a ghoul, or a giant spider. I ran, I am ashamed to say. I left him with his dead brother."

"He would have killed you," Derev said. "Of course you should have run."

Yama said, "I should have killed him. The knife would have done it for me if I had not taken it, I think. It helped me, like the ghost ship."

"Lob escaped," Ananda said. "He wanted his father to condemn you for the murder of his brother, the fool, but then you came back. Lob had already convicted himself, and Unprac confessed to his part as soon as he was arrested."

Unprac was the name of the landlord of *The House of Ghost Lanterns*. Yama had not known it until the trial.

"So I killed Lob anyway. I should have killed him then, in the tomb. It would have been a cleaner death. It was a poor bargain he got in the end."

"That's what they said about the farmer," Derev said, "after the girl fox had lain with him and took his baby in payment."

Suddenly, with a feeling like falling, Yama saw Derev's face as a stranger might. All planes, with large dark eyes and a small mouth and a bump of a nose, framed by a fall of white hair that moved in the slightest breeze as if possessed with an independent life. They had pursued each other all last summer, awakened to the possibilities of each other's bodies. They had lain in the long dry grasses between the tombs and tasted each other's mouths, each other's skin. He had felt the swell of her small breasts, traced the bowl of her pelvis, the elegant length of her arms, her legs. They had not made love; they had sworn that they would not make love together until they were married. Now, he was glad that they had not.

He said, "Do you keep doves, Derev?"

"You know that my father does. For sacrifice. Some palmers still come here to pray at the temple's shrine. Mostly they don't want doves, though, but flowers or fruit."

"There were no palmers this year," Ananda said.

"When the war is over, they'll come again," Derev said. "My father clips the wings of the doves. It would be a bad omen if they escaped in the middle of the sacrifice."

Ananda said, "You mean that it would be bad for his trade."

Derev laughed. "Then the desires of the Preservers are equal to those of my father, and I am glad."

"There is one more mystery," Yama said, and explained that he had been knocked unconscious by a fall and had woken elsewhere, in a little room of a hollowed crag far from the Great River's shore, watched by an old man and an old woman who claimed to be curators of the City of the Dead.

"They showed me a marvel. It was a picture slate from a tomb, and it showed someone of my bloodline. It was as if they had been waiting for me, and I have been thinking about what they showed me ever since I was returned here."

Derev had the bottle of wine. She took a long swallow from it and said, "But that's good! That's wonderful! In less than a decad you have found two people of your bloodline."

Yama said, "The man in the picture was alive before the building of Confluence. I imagine he is long dead. What is interesting is that the curators already knew about me, for they had the picture slate ready, and they also had prepared a route from their hiding place to the very grounds of the peel-house. That was how I returned. One of them, the woman, was of your bloodline, Derev."

"Well, so are many. We are traders and merchants. We are to be found throughout the length and breadth of Confluence."

Derev looked coolly at Yama when she said this, and his heart meltingly turned. It was hard to continue, but he had to. He said, "I did not think much of it for that very reason, and I did not even make very much of the fact that, like you, they had a fund of cautionary sayings and stories concerning magical foxes. But they kept doves. I wonder, if I looked amongst your father's doves, if I would find some that were not clipped. I think you use them to keep in touch with your people."

Ananda said, "What is this, Yama? You make a trial here."

Derev said, "It's all right, Ananda. Yama, my father said that you might have guessed. That was why he did not allow me to go to the peel-house, or to talk with you using the mirror. But I came here anyway. I wanted to see you. Tell me what you know, and I'll tell you what we know. How did you guess that I helped you?"

"I think that the old woman, Beatrice, had a son, and that he is your father. When Lob returned to Aeolis, you gave him money and got him drunk to learn his story. I know that he had not been paid by Dr. Dismas, so he had to get the money from somewhere. You found me, and took me to your grandparents. They made up a story about looking for a lost goat and finding me instead, but they ate only vegetables. As do you and your parents, Derev."

"They make cheese from goats' milk," Derev said. "And they *did* lose one last year, to a leopard. But you more or less have the truth. I'm not sure what scared me more, getting Lob drunk, or climbing down the cliff using the rope he had left behind and picking my way through the dark tomb to find you."

"Did your family come here because of me? Am I so important, or am I merely foolish to believe it? Why are you interested in me?"

"Because you are of a bloodline which vanished from the world long ago. My family have stayed true to the old department as no others of my bloodline have. We revere the dead, and keep the memory of their lives as best we can, but we do not remember your bloodline, except in legends from the beginning of the world. Beatrice isn't my grandmother, although she and her husband came to live at the tower after my great-grandparents died. My grandparents wanted a normal life, you see. They established a business downriver and my father inherited it, but Beatrice and her husband persuaded him to move here because of you." She paused. She said, "I know you are destined for great things, but it doesn't change what I feel for you."

Yama remembered Beatrice's verse and recited, "*Let fame, that all hunt after in their lives, Live registered upon our brazen tombs.*"

Derev said, "Yes, it's a favorite verse of Beatrice's. She has always said that it was far older than Confluence. But we keep the memory of all the dead alive, even if no one else will."

Yama said, "Am I then of the dead?"

Derev walked about, pumping her elbows in and out as was her habit when agitated. Her white dress glimmered in the light of the outflung arm of the Galaxy. "You were very ill when I found you. You had been lying there all night. I took you to Beatrice and Osric by the keel road and they saved your life, using old machines. I didn't know what else to do. I thought you might die if I took you to Aeolis, or if I went to fetch the soldiers who were looking for you. Well, it is time you knew that my family have been watching over you. After all, Dr. Dismas found out about you and put you in peril. So might others, and you should be ready."

Ananda said, "What are you saying, Derev? That you're some kind of spy? On which side?"

Yama laughed. "Derev is no spy. She is anxious that I should receive my inheritance, such as it is."

"My father and mother know, too. It isn't just me. At first, I didn't even know why we came here."

Ananda had drunk most of the wine. He tipped the bottle to get the last swallow, wiped his mouth on his sleeve, and said gravely, "So you don't want to sell rubbish to sailors and Mud Men, Derev? There's no harm in that. It's good that you want to keep to the old ways of your people."

"The Department of the Curators of the City of the Dead was disbanded long ago," Yama said, looking at Derev.

"It was defeated," Derev said, "but it endures. There are not many of us now. We mostly live in the mountains, or in Ys."

"Why are you interested in me?"

"You've seen the picture," Derev said. She had turned her back to Yama and Ananda, and was looking out across the swampy fields toward the ridge at the far side of the Breas's valley. "I don't know why you're important. My father thinks that it is to do with the ship of the Ancients of Days. Beatrice and Osric know more, I think, but won't tell even me all they know. They have many secrets."

Ananda said, "The ship of the Ancients of Days passed downriver years before Yama was born."

Derev ignored his interruption. "The Ancients of Days left to explore the neighboring galaxy long before the Preservers achieved godhead. They left more than five million years ago, while the stars of the Galaxy were still being moved into their present patterns. It was long before the Puranas were written, or the Eye of the Preservers was made, or Confluence was built."

"So they claimed," Ananda said. "But there is no word of them in the Puranas."

"They returned to find all that they knew had passed into the Eye of the Preservers, and that they were the last of their kind. They landed at Ys, traveled downriver and sailed away from Confluence for the galaxy they had forsaken so long ago, but they left their ideas behind."

"They turned innocent unfallen bloodlines against the word of the

Preservers," Ananda said. "They woke old technologies and created armies of monsters to spread their heresies."

"And twenty years later you were born, Yama."

"So were many others," Ananda said. "All three of us here were born after the war began. Derev makes a fantasy."

"Beatrice and Osric think that Yama's bloodline is the one which built Confluence," Derev told Ananda. "Perhaps the Preservers raised his bloodline up for just that task and then dispersed it, or perhaps as a reward it passed over with the Preservers when they fell into the Eye and vanished from the Universe. In any event, it disappeared from Confluence long ago. And yet Yama is here now, at a time of great danger."

Ananda said, "The Preservers needed no help in creating Confluence. They spoke a word, and it was so."

"It was a very long word," Derev said. She lifted her arms above her head, and raised herself up on the points of her toes, as graceful as a dancer. She was remembering something she had learned long ago. She said, "It was longer than the words in the nuclei of our cells which define what we are. If all the different instructions for all the different bloodlines of Confluence were put together it would not be one hundredth of the length of the word which defined the initial conditions necessary for the creation of Confluence. That word was a set of instructions or rules. Yama's bloodline was part of those instructions."

Ananda said, "This is heresy, Derev. I'm a bad priest, but I know the sound of heresy. The Preservers needed no help in making Confluence."

"Let her explain," Yama said.

Ananda stood. "It's lies," he said flatly. "Her people deceive themselves that they know more of Confluence and the Preservers than is written in the Puranas. They spin elaborate sophistries, and delude themselves with dreams of hidden power, and they have snared you, Yama. Come with me. Don't listen any more. You leave for Ys tomorrow. Don't be fooled into thinking that you are more than you are."

Derev said, "We don't pretend to understand what we remember. It is simply our duty. It was the duty of our bloodline since the foundation of Confluence, and my family are among the last to keep that duty. After the defeat of the department, my bloodline were scattered the length and breadth of the Great River. They became traders and merchants. My grandparents and my father wanted to be like them, but my father was called back."

Yama said, "Sit down, Ananda. Please. Help me understand."

Ananda said, "I don't think you're fully recovered, Yama. You've been ill. That part I believe. You have always wanted to see yourself as the center of the world, for you have no center to your own life. Derev is treating you cruelly, and I'll hear no more. You've even forgotten about the execution. Let me tell you that Unprac died badly, screaming to the Preservers for aid with one breath, and cursing them and all who watched with the next. Lob was stoic. For all his faults, he died a man."

"That is cruel, Ananda," Yama said.

"It's the truth. Farewell, friend Yama. If you must dream of glory, dream of being an ordinary soldier and of giving your life for the Preservers. All else is vanity."

Yama did not try to stop Ananda. He knew how stubborn his friend could be. He watched as Ananda walked away beside the noisy river, a shadow against the blue-white arch of the Galaxy. Yama hoped that the young priest would at least turn and wave farewell.

But he did not.

Derev said, "You must believe me, Yama. At first I became your friend because it was my duty. But that quickly changed. I would not be here if it had not."

Yama smiled. He could not stay angry at her; if she had deceived him, it was because she had believed that she was helping him.

They fell into each other's arms and breathlessly kissed and re-kissed. He felt her heat pressing through their clothes, the quick patter of her heart like a bird beating at the cage of her ribs. Her hair fell around his face like a trembling veil: he might drown in its dry scent.

After a while, he said, "If you took me to Beatrice and Osric, and they nursed me back to health, then what of the ghost ship? Do they claim that, too?"

Derev's eyes shone a handspan from his. She said, "I'd never heard of it before you told me your story. But there are many strange things on the river, Yama. It is always changing."

"Yet always the same," Yama said, remembering Caphis's tattoo, the snake swallowing its own tail. He added, "You thought that the anchorite we saved from Lud and Lob was one of my bloodline."

"Perhaps he was the first generation, born just after the ship of the Ancients of Days arrived."

"There may be hundreds of my bloodline by now, Derev. Thousands!"

"That's what I think. I told Beatrice and Osric about the anchorite, but they didn't seem to be very interested. Perhaps I was mistaken about him being of your bloodline, but I do not think I was. He gave you a coin. You should take it with you."

"So he did. I had forgotten it."

13

The Palmers

YAMA DISCOVERED THE knife at the bottom of his satchel on the first evening of his journey to Ys in the company of Prefect Corin. Yama had given the knife to Sergeant Rhodean that morning, because Prefect Corin had said that it was not the kind of thing an apprentice should own. The Prefect had been quite specific about what Yama could and could not carry; before they had set off he had looked through Yama's satchel and had removed the knife and the carefully folded map of Ys and the horn-handled pocket-knife which had once belonged to Telmon. Yama had been able to take little with him but a change of clothes and the money given to him by the Aedile. He had the copy of the Puranas and the anchorite's coin, which he wore around his neck, inside his shirt, but because they had been given to him so recently they did not yet seem like proper possessions.

Sergeant Rhodean must have slipped the knife back into the satchel when Yama had been making his farewells. It was sheathed in brown and white goatskin and tucked beneath Yama's spare shirt and trousers. Yama was pleased to see it, even though it still made him uneasy. He knew that all heroes carried weapons with special attributes, and he was determined to be a hero. He was still very young.

Prefect Corin asked him what he had found. Reluctantly, Yama slipped the knife from its sheath and held it up in the firelight. A blue sheen slowly extended from its hilt to the point of its curved blade. It emitted a faint high-pitched buzz, and a sharp smell like discharged electricity.

"I am certain that Sergeant Rhodean meant well," Prefect Corin said, "but you will not need that. If we are attacked, it will do nothing but put you in danger. In any case, it is very unlikely that we will be attacked."

Prefect Corin sat crosslegged on the other side of the small campfire, neat and trim in his homespun tunic and gray leggings. He was smoking a long-stemmed clay pipe which he held clenched between his small even teeth. His ironshod staff was stuck in the ground behind him. They had walked all day at a steady pace, and this was the most he had said to Yama at any one time.

Yama said, "That is why I gave it away, dominie, but it has come back."

"It is not regulation."

"Well, but I am not yet an apprentice," Yama said. He added, "Perhaps I could make a gift of it to the department."

"That is possible," Prefect Corin allowed. "Tributes are not unknown. Weapons like that are generally loyal to their owner, but loyalty can be broken with suitable treatment. Well, we cannot leave it here. You may carry it, but do not think to try to use it."

But after Prefect Corin had fallen asleep, Yama took out the knife and practiced the passes and thrusts that Sergeant Rhodean had taught him, and later slept sweetly and deeply, with the point of the knife thrust into the warm ashes of the campfire.

The next day, as before, Yama dutifully walked three paces behind Prefect Corin along raised paths between the flooded fields that made an intricate green and brown quilt along the margin of the river. It was the planting season, and the fields were being ploughed by teams of water buffalo commanded by small, naked boys who controlled their charges with no more than shouts and vigorous application of long bamboo switches.

A cool wind blew from the Great River, ruffling the brown waters which flooded the fields, stirring the bright green flags of the bamboos and the clumps of elephant grass that grew at the places where the corners of four fields met. Yama and Prefect Corin rose just before dawn and prayed and walked until it was too hot, and sheltered in the shade of a tree until early evening, when, after a brief prayer, they walked again until the Galaxy began to rise above the river.

Ordinarily, Yama would have enjoyed this adventure, but Prefect Corin was an impassive, taciturn companion. He did not comment on anything they saw, but was like a machine moving implacably through the sunlit world, noticing only what was necessary. He responded with no more than a grunt when Yama pointed to a fleet of argosies far out across the glittering waters of the Great River; he ignored the ruins they passed, even a long sandstone cliff-face which had been carved with pillars and friezes and statues of men and beasts around gaping doors; he ignored the little villages which could be glimpsed amongst stands of palms, flowering magnolias and pines on the ridge of the old river bank in the blue distance, or which stood on islands of higher ground amongst the mosaic of flooded fields; he ignored the fishermen who worked the margin of the Great River beyond the weedy gravel banks and mud flats revealed by the river's retreat, fishermen who stood thigh-deep in the shallows and cast circular nets across the water, or who sat in tiny bark boats further out, using black cormorants tethered by one leg to catch fish. (Yama thought of the verse which the old curator, Beatrice, had recited to him. Had its author seen the ancestors of these fishermen? He understood then a little of what Zakiel had tried to teach him, that books were not obdurate thickets of glyphs but transparent windows, looking out through another's eyes on to a familiar world, or on to a world which lived only when the book was read, and vanished when it was set down.)

The mud walls of the straw-thatched huts of the villages often incorporated slates stolen from tombs, so that pictures from the past (as often as not sideways or upside down) flashed with vibrant colors amongst the poverty of the peasants' lives. Chickens and black pigs ran amongst the huts, chased by naked toddlers. Women pounded grain or gutted fish or mended fishing nets, watched by impassive men sitting in the doorways of their huts or beneath shade trees, smoking clay pipes or sipping green tea from chipped glasses.

In one village there was a stone pen with a small dragon coiled on the white sand inside it. The dragon was black, with a double row of diamond-shaped plates along its ridged back, and it slept with its long, scaley snout on its forelegs, like a dog. Flies clustered around its long-lashed eyes; it stank of sulphur and marsh gas. Yama remembered the abortive hunt at the end of last winter, before poor Telmon went away, and would have liked to see more of this wonder, but Prefect Corin strode past without sparing it a single glance.

Sometimes the villagers came out to watch Yama and Prefect Corin go by, and little boys ran up to try and sell them wedges of watermelon or polished quartz pebbles or charms woven of thorny twigs. Prefect Corin ignored the animated crowds of little boys; he did not even trouble to use his staff to clear a way but simply pushed through them as through a thicket. Yama was left behind to apologize and ask for indulgence, saying over and over that they had no money. It was almost true. Yama had the two gold rials which the Aedile had given him, but one of those would buy an entire village, and he had no smaller coins. And Prefect Corin had nothing but his staff and his hat, his leggings and his homespun tunic, his sandals and his blanket, and a few small tools packed inside the leather purse that hung from his belt.

"Be careful of him," the Aedile had whispered, when he had embraced Yama in farewell. "Do all he asks of you, but no more than that. Reveal no more than is necessary. He will seize on any weakness, any difference, and use it against you. It is their way."

The Prefect was a spare, ascetic man. He drank tea made from fragments of dusty bark and ate only dried fruit and the yeasty buds of manna lichen picked from rocks, although he let Yama cook the rabbits and lizards he caught in wire snares set each evening. As he walked, Yama ate ghostberries picked from thickets which grew amongst ruined tombs, but the ghostberries were almost over now and difficult to find under the new leaves of the bushes, and Prefect Corin would not allow Yama to move more than a few paces from the edge of the path. There were traps amongst the tombs, he said, and ghouls and worse things at night. Yama did not argue with him, but apart from the necessities of toilet he was never out of Prefect Corin's sight. There were a hundred moments when he wanted to make a run for it. But not yet. Not yet. He was learning patience, at least.

The stretches of uncultivated country between the villages grew wider. There were fewer flooded fields and more ruined tombs, overgrown with creepers and moss amidst rustling stands of bamboo or clumps of date or oil palms, or copses of dark green swamp cypress. Then they passed the last village and the road widened into a long, straight pavement. It was like the ancient road that ran between the river and the edge of the Silent Quarter downriver of Aeolis, Yama thought, and then he realized that it was the same road.

It was the third day of the journey. They camped that night in a hollow with tall pines leaning above. Wind moved through the doffing branches of the pines. The Great River stretched away toward the Galaxy, which even at this late hour showed only the upper part of the Arm of the Warrior above the horizon, with the Blue Diadem gleaming cold and sharp at the upflung terminus of the lanes of misty starlight. Halo stars were like dimming coals scattered sparsely across the cold hearth of the sky; the smudged specks of distant galaxies could be seen here and there.

Yama lay near the little fire on a soft, deep layer of brown pine needles and thought of the Ancients of Days and wondered what it might be like to plunge through the emptiness between galaxies for longer than Confluence had been in existence. And the Ancients of Days had not possessed one hundredth of the power of their distant children, the Preservers.

Yama asked Prefect Corin if he had ever seen the Ancients of Days after they had arrived at Ys. For a long time, the man did not answer, and Yama began to believe that he had not been heard, or that Prefect Corin had simply ignored the question. But at last the Prefect knocked out his pipe on the heel of his boot and said, "I saw two of them once. I was a boy, a little older than you, and newly apprenticed. They were both tall, and as alike as brothers, with black hair and faces as white as new paper. We say that some bloodlines have white skin—your own is very pale—but we mean that it has no pigmentation in it, except that it is suffused by the blood in the tissues beneath. But this was a true white, as if their faces had been powdered with chalk. They wore long white shirts that left their arms and legs bare, and little machines hung from their belts. I was in the Day Market with the oldest of the apprentices, carrying the spices he had bought. The two Ancients of Days walked through the aisles at the head of a great crowd and passed by as close to me as you are now.

"They should have been killed, all of them. Unfortunately, it was not a decision the Department could make, although even then, in Ys, it was possible to see that their ideas were dangerous. Confluence survives only because it does not change. The Preservers unite us because it is to them that each department swears its loyalty, and so no department shows particular favor to any of the bloodlines of Confluence. The Ancients of Days have infected their allies with the heresy that each bloodline, indeed every individual, might have an intrinsic worth. They promote the individual above society, change above duty. You should reflect on why this is wrong, Yama."

"Is it true that there are wars in Ys now? That different departments fight each other, even in the Palace of the Memory of the People?"

Prefect Corin gave him a sharp look across the little fire and said, "You have been listening to the wrong kind of gossip."

Yama was thinking of the curators of the City of the Dead, whose resistance had dwindled to a stubborn refusal to yield to the flow of history. Perhaps Derev would be the last of them. He said, trying to draw out the Prefect, "But surely there are disputes about whether one department or another should carry out a particular duty. I have heard

that outmoded departments sometimes resist amalgamation or disband-
ment, and I have also heard that these disputes are increasing, and that
the Department of Indigenous Affairs is training most of its apprentices
to be soldiers."

"You have a lot to learn," Prefect Corin said. He tamped tobacco
into the bowl of his pipe and lit it before adding, "Apprentices do not
choose the way in which they serve the Department, and you are too
young to be an apprentice in any case. You have had an odd childhood,
with what amounts to three fathers and no mother. You have far too
much pride and not enough education, and most of that in odd bits of
history and philosophy and cosmology, and far too much in the arts of
soldiering. Even before you can be accepted as an apprentice, you will
have to catch up in all the areas your education has neglected."

Yama said, "I think I might make a good soldier."

Prefect Corin drew on his pipe and looked at Yama with narrowed
eyes. They were small and close together, and gleamed palely in his
black-furred face. The white stripe ran past the outer corner of his left
eye. Eventually he said, "I came down here to execute two men because
their crimes involved the Aedile's private life. That is the way it is done
in the Department. It demonstrates that the Department supports the
action of its man, and it ensures that none of the local staff have to do
the job. That way, there is no one for the locals to take revenge on,
with the exception of the Aedile himself, and no one will do that as
long as he commands his garrison, because he has the authority of the
Preservers. I agreed to bring you to Ys because it is my duty. It does
not mean I owe you anything, especially answers to your questions.
Now get some sleep."

Later, long after the Prefect had rolled himself in his blanket and
gone to sleep, Yama cautiously stood and backed away from the fire,
which had burnt down to white ash around a dimming core of glowing
coals. The road stretched away between hummocks of dry friable stone
and clumps of pines. Its paved surface gleamed faintly in the light of
the Galaxy. Yama settled his pack on his shoulders and set off. He
wanted to go to Ys, but he was determined not to become an apprentice
clerk, and after the final dismissal of his worth he thought that he could
not bear Prefect Corin's company a day longer.

He had not gone very far down the road when he heard a dry rattle
in the darkness ahead. Yama put his hand on the hilt of his knife, but
did not draw it from its sheath in case its light betrayed him. He advanced cautiously, his eyes wide, his whole skin tingling, his blood
rustling in his ears. Then a stone smashed onto the paved road behind

him! He whirled around, and another stone exploded at his feet. A fragment cut his shin, and he felt blood trickle into his boot.

He gripped the knife tightly and said, "Who is it? Show yourself."

Silence, and then Prefect Corin stepped up behind Yama and gripped the wrist of his right hand and said in his ear, "You have a lot to learn, boy."

"A clever trick," Yama said. He felt oddly calm, as if he had expected this all along.

After a moment Prefect Corin released him and said, "It is lucky for you I played it, and no one else." Yama had never seen Prefect Corin smile, but in the blue light of the Galaxy he saw the man's lips compress in what might have been the beginning of a smile. "I promised to look after you, and so I will. Meanwhile, no more games. All right?"

"All right," Yama said.

"Good. You need to sleep. We still have a long way to go."

Early the next day, Yama and Prefect Corin passed a group of palmers. They soon left the group behind, but the palmers caught up with them that night and camped a little way off. They numbered more than two decads, men and women in dust-stained orange robes, their heads cleanly shaven and painted with interlocked curves which represented the Eye of the Preservers. They were a slightly built people, with pinched faces under swollen, bicephalic foreheads, and leathery skin mottled with brown and black patches. Like Prefect Corin, they carried only staffs, bedrolls, and little purses hung from their belts. They sang in clear high voices around their campfire, welding close harmonies that carried a long way across the dry stones and the empty tombs of the hillside.

Yama and Prefect Corin had made camp under a group of fig trees beside the road. A little spring rose amongst the trees, a gush of clear water that fell from the gaping mouth of a stone carved with the likeness of a fierce, bearded face into a shallow pool curbed with flat rocks. The road had turned away from the Great River, climbing a switchback of low, gentle hills dotted with creosote scrub and clumps of saw-toothed palmettos as it rose toward the pass.

The priest who was in charge of the palmers came over to talk with Prefect Corin. His group was from a city a thousand leagues downriver. They had been traveling for half a year, first by a merchant ship and then by foot after the ship had been laid up for repairs after having been attacked by water bandits. The palmers were archivists on their way to the Palace of the Memory of the People, to tell into the records the stories of all those who had died in their city in the last ten years, and to ask for guidance from the prognosticators.

The priest was a large smooth-skinned man by the name of Belarius. He had a ready smile and a habit of mopping sweat from his bare scalp and the fat folds of skin at the back of his neck with a square of cloth. His smooth, chrome-yellow skin shone like butter. He offered Prefect Corin a cigarette and was not offended when his offer was refused, and without prompting started to talk about the risks of traveling by foot. He had heard that there were roving bands of deserters abroad in the land, in addition to the usual bandits.

"Near the battlelines, perhaps," Prefect Corin said. "Not this far upriver." He drew on his pipe and stared judiciously at the fat priest. "Are you armed?"

Belarius smiled—his smile was as wide as a frog's, and Yama thought that he could probably hold a whole watermelon slice in his mouth. The priest said, "We are palmers, not soldiers."

"But you have knives to prepare your food, machetes to cut fire-wood, that kind of thing?"

"Oh yes."

"A large group like yours need not worry. It is people traveling alone, or by two or by three, who are vulnerable."

Belarius mopped at his scalp. His smile grew wider. He said eagerly, "And you have seen nothing?"

"But for the chattering of this boy, it has been a quiet journey."

Yama smarted at Prefect Corin's remark, but said nothing. Belarius smoked his cigarette—it smelt overpoweringly of cloves—and gave a rambling account of exactly how the ship on which he had hoped to take his charges all the way to Ys had been ambushed one night by water bandits in a decad of small skiffs. The bandits had been beaten off when the ship's captain had ordered pitch spread on the water and set on fire.

"Our ship put every man to the oars and rowed free of the flames," Belarius said, "but the bandits were consumed."

Prefect Corin listened, but made no comment.

Belarius said, "The bandits fired chainshot. It damaged the mast and rigging and struck the hull at the waterline. We were taking on water in several places, and so we limped to the nearest port. My charges did not want to wait out the repairs, so we walked on. The ship will meet us at Ys, when we have finished our business there. A ghoul has been following us the past week, but that is the only trouble we have had. Such are the times, when the road is safer than the Great River."

After Belarius had filled his waterskin from the spring and taken his leave, Yama said, "You do not like him."

Prefect Corin considered this, then said in a measured tone, "I do not like veiled insults about the competence of the Department. If the Great River is no longer safe, it is because of the war, and those who travel on it should take suitable precautions and travel in convoy. Not only that, but our well-upholstered priest did not hire any bodyguards as escort on the road, which would have been prudent, and it would have been more prudent to have waited until the ship was repaired than to have gone forward on foot. I rather think that he has told us only half of the story. Either he does not have the money to hire men or to pay for repairs to the ship, or he is willing to risk the lives of his charges to make extra profit. And he put aboard with a bravado captain, which says little for his judgement. If the ship was able to outdistance the fire it set on the water, then it could have outdistanced the bandits. Often flight is better than fight."

"If less honorable."

"There is no honor in needless fighting. The captain could have destroyed his ship as well as the bandits with his trick."

"Will we stay with these people?"

"Their singing will wake every bandit in a hundred leagues," Prefect Corin said. "And if there are any bandits, then they will be attracted to the larger group rather than to the lesser."

14

The Bandits

THE NEXT DAY, Yama and Prefect Corin drew ahead of the group of palmers, but never so far ahead that the dust cloud the palmers raised was lost from sight. That night, the palmers caught up with them and camped nearby, and Belarius came over and talked to Prefect Corin about the day's journey for the length of time it took him to smoke two of his clove-flavored cigarettes. The palmers' songs sounded clear and strong in the quiet evening.

When Prefect Corin woke Yama from a deep sleep it was past midnight, and the fire was no more than warm ashes. They had camped by a square tomb covered in the scrambling thorny canes of roses, on top of a bluff that overlooked the Great River. He was leaning on his staff. Behind him, the white roses glimmered like ghosts of their own selves. Their strong scent filled the air.

"Something bad nearby," Prefect Corin said in a quiet voice. Galaxy light put a spark in each of his close-set eyes. "Take up your knife and come with me."

Yama whispered, "What is it?"

"Perhaps nothing. We will see."

They crossed the road and circled the palmers' camp, which had been pitched in a grove of eucalyptus. Low cliffs loomed above. The openings of tombs carved into the rock were like staggered rows of hollow eyes: a hiding place for an army. Yama heard nothing but the rustle of eucalyptus leaves, and, far off, the screech of a hunting owl. In the camp, one of the palmers groaned in his sleep. Then the wind shifted, and Yama caught a faint, foul odor above the medicinal tang of the eucalyptus.

Prefect Corin pointed toward the camp with his staff and moved forward, dry leaves crackling beneath his feet. Yama saw something scuttle away through the trees, man-sized yet running on all fours with a lurching sideways movement. He drew his knife and gave chase, but Prefect Corin overtook him and sprang onto an outcrop of rock beyond the trees with his staff raised above his head. He held the pose for a moment, then jumped down.

"Gone," he said. "Well, the priest is right about one thing. They have a ghoul following them."

Yama sheathed his knife. His hand was trembling. He was out of breath and his blood sang in his head. He remembered the time he and Telmon had hunted antelope, armed only with stone axes like the men of the hill tribes. He said, "I saw it."

"I will tell them to bury their rubbish and to make sure that they hang their food in branches."

"Ghouls can climb," Yama said. He added, "I am sorry. I should not have chased after it."

"It was bravely done. Perhaps we scared it off."

Yama and Prefect Corin reached the pass the next day. It was only a little wider than the road, cutting through a high scarp of rough-edged blocks of gray granite which rose abruptly from the gentle slope they had been climbing all morning. A cairn of flat stones stood at the edge of the road near the beginning of the pass, built around a slab engraved with a list of names. Prefect Corin said that it was the memorial of a battle in the Age of Insurrection, when those few men whose names were engraved on the slab had held the pass against overwhelming odds. Every man defending the pass had died, but the army they had fought had been held up long enough for reinforcements from Ys to arrive and drive them back.

Across the road from the shrine was a house-sized platform of red rock split down the middle by a single, straight-edged crack. Prefect Corin sat in the shade of the rock's overhang and said that they would wait for the palmers to catch up before they tried the pass.

"Safety in numbers," Yama said, to provoke a reaction.

"Quite the reverse, but you do not seem to understand that." Prefect Corin watched as Yama restlessly poked about, and eventually said, "There are supposed to be footprints on top of this rock, one either side of the crack. It is said that an aesthetic stood there an age past, and ascended directly to the Eye of the Preservers. The force of his ascent cracked the rock, and left his footprints melted into it."

"Is it true?"

"Certainly a great deal of energy would be required to accelerate someone so that they could fall beyond the influence of Confluence's gravity fields, more than enough to melt rock. But if the energy was applied all at once a normal body would be flash-heated into a cloud of steam by friction with the air. I do not blame you for not knowing that, Yama. Your education is not what it should be."

Yama did not see any point replying to this provocation, and continued to wander about in the dry heat, searching for nothing in particular. The alternative was to sit by Prefect Corin. Small lizards flicked over the hot stones; a scarlet and gold hummingbird hung in the air on a blur of wings for a few moments before darting away. At last, Yama found a way up a jumble of boulders to the flat top of the outcrop. The fracture was straight and narrow, and its depths glittered with shards of what looked like melted glass. The fabled prints were just as Prefect Corin had described them, no more than a pair of foot-sized oval hollows, one on either side of the crack.

Yama lay down on warm, gritty rock and looked up at the empty blue sky. His thoughts moved lazily. He started to read his copy of the Puranas, but did not find anything that was different from his rote learning and put the book away. It was too bright and hot to read, and he had already looked long and hard at the pictures; apart from the one which showed the creation of the Eye of the Preservers, they were little different from the scenes of the lost past captured in the slates of tombs—and unlike the pictures in the slates, the pictures in the book did not move.

Yama idly wondered why the ghoul was following the palmers, and wondered why the Preservers had created ghouls in the first place. For if the Preservers had created the world and everything in it, as was written in the Puranas, and had raised up the ten thousand bloodlines from animals of ten thousand worlds, then what were the ghouls, which stood between animals and the humblest of the indigenous races?

According to the argument from design, which Zakiel had taught Yama and Telmon, ghouls existed because they aided the processes of decay, but there were many other scavenger species, and ghouls had a particular appetite for the flesh of men, and would take small children and babies if they could. Others said that ghouls were only imperfectly raised up, their natures partaking of the worst of men and of beasts, or that their bloodline had not advanced like those of other kinds of men, or remained unchanged, like the various indigenous races, but had run backward until they retained nothing of the gifts of the Preservers but the capacity for evil. Both arguments suggested that the world which the Preservers had created was imperfect, although neither denied the possibility of perfectibility. Some claimed that the Preservers had chosen not to create a perfect world because such a world would be unchanging, and only an imperfect world allowed the possibility of evil and, therefore, of redemption. By their nature, Preservers could do only good, but while they could not create evil, the presence of evil was an inevitable consequence in their creation, just as light casts shadows when material objects are interposed. Others argued that since the light of the Preservers had been everywhere at the construction of the world, where then could any shadows lie? By this argument, evil was the consequence of the rebellion of men and machines against the Preservers, and only by rediscovering the land of lost content which had existed before that rebellion could evil be banished and men win redemption.

Still others argued that evil had its use in a great plan that could not be understood by any but the Preservers themselves. That such a plan might exist, with past, present and future absolutely determined, was one reason why no one should rely on miracles. As Ananda would say, no use praying for intercession if all was determined from the outset. If the Preservers wanted something to be so, then they would have created it already, without waiting to hear prayers asking for intercession, without needing to watch over every soul. Everything was predestined in the single long word which the Preservers had spoken to bring the world into existence.

Yama's mind rebelled against this notion, as a man buried before his death might fight against a winding sheet. If everything was part of a predetermined plan, then why should anyone in it do anything at all, least of all worship the Preservers? Except that too was a part of the plan, and everyone in the world was a wind-up puppet ratcheting from birth to death in a series of preprogrammed gestures.

It was undeniable that the Preservers had set the world in motion, but Yama did not believe that they had abandoned it in disgust or despair, or because, seeing all, they knew every detail of its destiny. No, Yama preferred to think that the Preservers had left the world to grow as it would, as a fond parent must watch a child grow into independence. In this way, the bloodlines which the Preservers had raised up from animals might rise further to become their equals, and that could not occur if the Preservers interfered with destiny, for just as a man cannot make another man, so gods cannot make other gods. For this reason, it was necessary that individuals must be able to choose between good and evil—they must be able to choose, like Dr. Dismas, not to serve goodness, but their own appetites. Without the possibility of evil, no bloodline could define its own goodness. The existence of evil allowed bloodlines to fail and fall, or to transcend their animal natures by their own efforts.

Yama wondered if ghouls had chosen to fall, reveling in their bestial nature as Dr. Dismas reveled in his rebellion against the society of men. Animals did not choose their natures, of course. A jaguar did not delight in the pain it caused its prey; it merely needed to eat. Cats played with mice, but only because their mothers had taught them to hunt by such play. Only men had free will and could choose to wallow in their base desires or by force of will overcome them. Were men little different from ghouls, then, except they struggled against their dark side, while ghouls swam in it with the innocent unthinking ease of fish in water? By praying to the Preservers, perhaps men were in reality doing no more than praying to their own as yet unrealized higher natures, as an explorer might contemplate the untraveled peaks he must climb to reach his goal.

If the Preservers had left the world to its own devices and there were no miracles, except the existence of free will, what then, of the ghost ship? Yama had not prayed for it, or at least had not known that he had done so, and yet it had come precisely when he had needed a diversion to make good his escape. Was something watching over him? If so, to what purpose? Or perhaps it was no more than a coincidence: some old machinery had been accidentally awakened, and Yama had seized the moment to escape. It was possible that there was another world where the ghost ship had not appeared, or had appeared too early or too late, and Yama had gone with Dr. Dismas and the warlord, Enobarbus. He would be traveling downriver on the pinnace even now, a willing or unwilling participant in their plans, perhaps to death, perhaps to a destiny more glorious than the apprenticeship which now lay ahead of him.

Yama's speculations widened and at some point he was no longer in control of them but was carried on their flow, like a twig on the Great River's flood. He slept, and woke to find Prefect Corin standing over him, a black shadow against the dazzling blue of the sky.

"Trouble," the man said, and pointed down the long gentle slope of the road. A tiny smudge of smoke hung in the middle distance, trembling in the heat haze, and at that moment Yama realized that all along Prefect Corin had been protecting the palmers.

———

They found the dead first. The bodies had been dragged off the road and stacked and set on fire. Little was left but greasy ash and charred bones, although, bizarrely, a pair of unburnt feet still shod in sandals protruded from the bottom of the gruesome pyre. Prefect Corin poked amongst the hot ashes with his staff and counted fourteen skulls, leaving nine unaccounted for. He cast about in one direction, bending low as he searched the muddle of prints on the ground, and Yama, although not asked, went in the other. It was he, following a trail of blood speckles, who found Belarius hiding inside a tomb. The priest was cradling a dead woman, and his robe was drenched in her blood.

———

"They shot at us from hiding places amongst the tombs," Belarius said. "I think they shot Vril by accident because they did not shoot any of the other women. When all the men had been killed or badly wounded, they came for the women. Small fierce men with bright red skin and long arms and legs, some on foot, some on horse, three or four decads of them. Like spiders. They had sharp teeth, and claws like thorns. I remember they couldn't close their hands around their weapons."

"I know the bloodline," Prefect Corin said. "They are a long way from home."

"Two came and looked at me, and jeered and went away again," Belarius said.

"They would not kill a priest," Prefect Corin said. "It is bad luck."

"I tried to stop them despoiling the bodies," Belarius said. "They threatened me with their knives or spat on me or laughed, but they didn't stop their work. They stripped the bodies and dismembered them, cut what they wanted from the heads. Some of the men were still alive. When they were finished, they set the bodies on fire. I wanted to shrive the dead, but they pushed me away."

"And the women?"

Belarius started to cry. He said, "I meant no harm to anyone. No harm. No harm to anyone."

"They took the women with them," Prefect Corin said. "To despoil or to sell. Stop blubbering, man! Which way did they go?"

"Toward the mountains. You must believe that I meant no harm. If you had stayed with us instead of getting ahead—no, forgive me. That is unworthy."

"We would have been killed, too," Prefect Corin said. "These bandits strike quickly, and without fear. They will attack larger groups better armed than themselves if they think that the surprise and fury of their assault will overcome their opponents. As it is, we may yet save some of your people. Go and shrive your dead, man. After that you must decide whether you want to come with us or stay here."

When Belarius was out of earshot, Prefect Corin said to Yama, "Listen carefully, boy. You can come with me, but only if you swear that you will do exactly as I say."

"Of course," Yama said at once. He would have promised anything for the chance.

It was not difficult to track the bandits and the captured women across the dry, sandy land. The trail ran parallel to the granite scarp across a series of flat, barren salt pans. Each was higher than the next, like a series of giant steps. Prefect Corin set a relentless pace, but the priest, Belarius, kept up surprisingly well; he was one of those fat men who are also strong, and the shock of the ambush was wearing off. Yama supposed that this was a chance for Belarius to regain face. Already, the priest was beginning to speak of the attack as if it was an accident or natural disaster from which he would rescue the survivors.

"As if he did not invite the lightning," Prefect Corin said to Yama, when they stopped to rest in the shade of a tomb. "At the best of times, bringing a party of palmers on the land route to Ys without proper escort is like herding sheep through a country of wolves. And these were archivists, too. Not proper archivists—those are from the Department, and are trained in the art of memory. These use machines to record the lives of the dying. If you had looked closely at the skulls, you would have seen that they had been broken open. Some bandits eat the brains of their victims, but these wanted the machines in their heads."

Yama laughed in disbelief. "I have never heard of such a thing!"

Prefect Corin passed a hand over his black-furred face, like a grooming cat. "It is an abomination, promulgated by a department so corrupt and debased that it seeks to survive by coarse imitation of the tasks properly carried out by its superiors. Proper archivists learn how to manage their memories by training; these people would be archivists in a few days, by swallowing the seeds of machines which migrate to a certain area of the brain and grow a kind of library. It is not without risks. In one in fifty of those who swallow the seeds, the machines grow unchecked and destroy their host's brains."

"But surely only the unchanged need archivists? Once changed, everyone is remembered by the Preservers."

"Many no longer believe it, and because the Department will not supply archivists to the cities of the changed, these mountebanks make fortunes by pandering to the gullible. Like real archivists, they listen to the life stories of the dying and promise to transmit them to the shrines of the Palace of the Memory of the People."

Yama said, "No wonder the priest is upset. He believes that many more died than we saw."

"They are all remembered by the Preservers in any event," Prefect Corin said. "Saints or sinners, all men marked by the Preservers are remembered, while true archivists remember the stories of as many of the unchanged bloodlines as they can. The priest is upset because his reputation will be blemished, and he will lose trade. Hush. Here he comes."

Belarius had ripped away the blood-soaked part of his orange robe, leaving only a kind of kilt about his waist. The smooth yellow skin of his shoulders and his fat man's breasts had darkened in the sun to the color of blood oranges, and he scratched at his sunburnt skin as he told Yama and Prefect Corin that he had found fresh horse droppings.

"They are not more than an hour ahead of us. If we hurry, we can catch them before they reach the foothills."

Prefect Corin said, "They make the women walk. It slows them down."

"Then their cruelty will be their undoing." Belarius curled his right hand into a fist and ground it into the palm of his left. "We will catch them and we will crush them."

Prefect Corin said calmly, "They are cruel but not stupid. They could tie the women to their horses if they wanted to outpace us, yet they do not. They taunt us, I think. They want sport. We must proceed carefully. We will wait until night, and follow them to their camp."

"They will leave us behind in the darkness!"

"I know this bloodline. They do not travel by night, for their blood slows as the air cools. Meanwhile we will rest. You will pray for us, Belarius. It will set our minds to the struggle ahead."

———

They waited until the sun had fallen behind the Rim Mountains and the Galaxy had begun to rise above the farside horizon before they set off. The tracks left by the bandits ran straight across the flat white land into a tangle of shallow draws which sloped up toward a range of low hills. Yama tried his best to imitate Prefect Corin's ambling gait, and remembered to go flatfooted on loose stones, as Telmon had taught him. Belarius was less nimble, and every now and then would stumble and send stones clattering away downslope. There were tombs scattered at irregular intervals along the sides of the draws, unornamented and squarely built, with tall narrow doors which had been smashed open an age ago. A few had picture slates, and these wakened when the three men went by, so that they had to walk along the tops of the ridges between the draws to avoid being betrayed by the light of the past. Belarius fretted that they would lose the trail, but then Yama saw a flickering dab of light brighten ahead.

It was a dry tree set on fire in the bottom of a deep draw. It burned with a white intensity and a harsh crackling, sending up volumes of acrid white smoke. Its tracery of branches made a web of black shadows within the brightness of its burning. The three men looked down on it, and Prefect Corin said, "Well, they know that we are following them. Yama, look after Belarius. I will not be long."

He was gone before Yama could reply, a swift shadow flowing down the slope, circling the burning tree and disappearing into the darkness beyond. Belarius sat down heavily and whispered, "You two should not die on my account."

"Let us not talk of death," Yama said. He had his knife in his hand—he had drawn it upon seeing the burning tree. It showed not a spark, and he sheathed it and said, "A little while ago, I was taken aboard a pinnace by force, but a white ship appeared, glowing with cold fire. The pinnace attacked the white ship and I was able to escape. Yet the white ship was not real; even as it bore down on the pinnace it began to dissolve. Was this a miracle? And was it for my benefit? What do you think?"

"We shouldn't question the plan of the Preservers. Only they can say what is miraculous."

It was a rote reply. Belarius was more intent on the darkness beyond the burning tree than on Yama's tale. He was smoking one of his clove-scented cigarettes, cupping it hungrily to his wide mouth. The light of the burning tree beat on him unmercifully; shadows in his deep eye sockets made a skull of his face.

Prefect Corin came back an hour later. The tree had burnt down to a stump of glowing cinders. He appeared out of the darkness and knelt between Belarius and Yama. "The way is clear," he said.

Yama said, "Did you see them?"

Prefect Corin considered this. Yama thought he looked smug, the son-of-a-bitch. At last he said, "I saw our friend of last night."

"The ghoul?"

"It is following us. It will feed well tonight, one way or the other. Listen carefully. This ridge rises and leads around to a place above a canyon. There are large tombs at the bottom of the canyon, and that is where the bandits are camped. They have stripped the women and tied them to stakes, but I do not think they have used them." Prefect Corin looked directly at Belarius. "These people come into heat like dogs or deer, and it is not their season. They display the women to make us angry, and we will not be angry. They have built a big fire, but away from it the night air will make them sluggish. Yama, you and Belarius will create a diversion, and I will go in and cut the women free and bring them out."

Belarius said, "It is not much of a plan."

"Well, we could leave the women," Prefect Corin said, with such seriousness that it was plain he would do just that if Belarius refused to help.

"They'll sleep," the priest said. "We wait until they sleep, and then we take the women."

Prefect Corin said, "No. They never sleep, but simply become less active at night. They will be waiting for us. That is why we must make them come out, preferably away from their fire. I will kill them then. I have a pistol."

It was like a flat, water-smoothed pebble. It caught the Galaxy's cold blue light and shone in Prefect Corin's palm. Yama was amazed. The Department of Indigenous Affairs was surely greater than he had imagined, if one of them could carry a weapon not only forbidden to most but so valuable, because the secret of its manufacture was lost an age past, that it could ransom a city like Aeolis. Dr. Dismas's energy pistol, which merely increased the power of light by making its waves march in step, had been a clumsy imitation of the weapon Prefect Corin held.

Belarius said, "Those things are evil."

"It has saved my life before now. It has three shots, and then it must lie in sunlight all day before it will fire again. That is why you must get them into the open, so I have a clear field of fire."

Yama said, "How will we make the diversion?"

"I am sure you will think of something when you get there," Prefect Corin said.

His lips were pressed together as if he was suppressing a smile, and now Yama knew what this was all about.

Prefect Corin said, "Follow the ridge, and be careful not to show yourself against the sky."

"What about guards?"

"There are no guards," Prefect Corin said. "Not any more."

And then he was gone.

———

The canyon was sinuous and narrow, a deeply folded crevice winding back the hills. The ridge rose above it to a tabletop bluff dissected by dry ravines. Lying on his belly, looking over the edge of the drop into the canyon, Yama could see the fire the bandits had lit on the canyon floor far below. Its red glow beat on the white faces of the tombs that were set into the walls of the canyon, and the brushwood corral where a decad of horses milled, and the line of naked women tied to stakes.

Yama said, "It is like a test."

Belarius, squatting on his heels a little way from the edge, stared at him.

"I have to show initiative," Yama said. "If I do not, Prefect Corin will not try to rescue the women."

He did not add that it was also a punishment. Because he carried the knife; because he wanted to be a soldier; because he had tried to run away. He knew that he could not allow himself to fail, but he did not know how he could succeed.

"Pride," Belarius said sulkily. He seemed to have reached a point where nothing much mattered to him. "He makes himself into a petty god, deciding whether my poor clients live or die."

"That is up to us, I think. He is a cold man, but he wants to help you."

Belarius pointed into the darkness behind him. "There's a dead man over there. I can smell him."

It was one of the bandits. He was lying on his belly in the middle of a circle of creosote bushes. His neck had been broken and he seemed to be staring over his shoulder at his doom.

Belarius mumbled a brief prayer, then took the dead man's short, stout recurved bow and quiver of unfledged arrows. He seemed to cheer up a little, and Yama asked him if he knew how to use a bow.

"I'm not a man of violence."

"Do you want to help rescue your clients?"

"Most of them are dead," Belarius said gravely. "I will shrive this poor wight now."

Yama left the priest with the dead man and quartered the ground along the edge of the canyon. Although he was tired, he felt a peculiar clarity, a keen alertness sustained by a mixture of anger and adrenalin. This might be a test, but the women's lives depended on it. That was more important than pleasing Prefect Corin, or proving to himself that he could live up to his dreams.

A round boulder stood at the edge of the drop. It was half Yama's height and bedded in the dirt, but it gave a little when he put his back to it. He tried to get Belarius to help him, but the priest was kneeling as if in prayer and either did not understand or did not want to understand, and he would not stand up even when Yama pulled at his arm. Yama groaned in frustration and went back to the boulder and began to attack the sandy soil around its base with his eating knife. He had not been digging for long when he struck something metallic. The little knife quivered in his hands and when he drew it out he found that the point of the blade had been neatly cut away. He had found a machine.

Yama knelt and whispered to the thing, asking it to come to him. He did it more from reflex than hope, and was amazed when the soil shifted between his knees and the machine slid into the air with a sudden slipping motion, like a squeezed watermelon seed. It bobbed in the air before Yama's face, a shining, silvery oval that would have fitted into his palm, had he dared touch it. It was both metallic and fluid, like a big drop of hydrargyrum. Flecks of light flickered here and there on its surface. It emitted a strong smell of ozone, and a faint crepitating sound.

Yama said, slowly and carefully, shaping the words in his mind as well as his mouth as he did when instructing the peel-house's watchdogs, "I need to make this part of the edge of the canyon fall. Help me."

The machine dropped to the ground and a little geyser of dust and small stones spat up as it dug down out of sight. Yama sat on his heels, hardly daring to breathe, but although he waited a long time, nothing else seemed to happen. He had started to dig around the base of the boulder again when Belarius found him.

The priest had uprooted a couple of small creosote bushes. He said, "We will set these alight and throw them down onto those wicked men."

"Help me with this boulder."

Belarius shook his head and sat by the edge and began to tie the bushes together with a strip of cloth torn from remnants of his robe.

"If you set fire to those bushes, you will make yourself a target," Yama said.

"I expect that you have a flint in your satchel."

"Yes, but—"

In the canyon below, horses cried to each other. Yama looked over the edge and saw that the horses were running from one corner of the corral to the other. They moved in the firelight like water running before a strong, choppy wind, bunched together and flicking their tails and tossing their heads. At first, Yama thought that they had been disturbed by Prefect Corin, but then he saw something white clinging upside-down to the neck of a black mare in the middle of the panicky herd. The ghoul had found the bandits. Men were running toward the horses with a scampering crabwise gait, casting long crooked shadows because the fire was at their backs, and Yama threw his weight against the boulder, knowing he would not have a better chance.

The ground moved under Yama's feet and he lost his footing and fell backward, banging the back of his head against the boulder. The blow dazed him, and he was unable to stop Belarius pawing through his satchel and taking the flint. The ground moved again and the boulder stirred and sank a handspan into the soil. Yama realized what was happening and scrambled out of the way just as the edge of the canyon collapsed.

The boulder dropped straight down. A cloud of dust and dirt shot up and there was a crash when the boulder struck the side of the canyon, and then a moment of silence. The ground was still shaking. Yama tried to get to his feet, but it was like trying to stand up in a boat caught in cross-currents. Belarius was kneeling over the bundle of creosote bushes, striking the flint against its stone. Dust puffed up behind him, defining a long crooked line, and a kind of lip opened in the ground. Little lights swarmed in the churning soil. Yama saw them when he snatched up his satchel and jumped the widening gash. He landed on hands and knees and the ground moved again and he fell down. Belarius was standing on the other side of the gash, his feet planted wide apart as he swung two burning bushes around his head. Then the edge of the canyon gave way and fell with a sliding roar into the canyon. A moment later a vast cloud of dust boiled up amidst a noise like a thunderclap, and lightning lit the length of the canyon at spaced intervals. Once, twice, three times.

15

The Magistrate

AT FIRST THE houses were no more than empty tombs that people had moved into, making improvised villages strung out along low cliff terraces by the old edge of the Great River. The people who lived there went about naked. They were thin and very tall, with small heads and long, glossy black hair, and skin the color of rust. The chests of the men were welted with spiral patterns of scars; the women stiffened their hair with red clay. They hunted lizards and snakes and coneys, collected the juicy young pads of prickly pear and dug for tuberous roots in the dry tableland above the cliffs, picked samphire and watercress in the marshes by the margin of the river and waded out into the river's shallows and cast circular nets to catch fish, which they smoked on racks above fires built of creosote bush and pine chips. They were cheerful and hospitable, and gave food and shelter freely to Yama and Prefect Corin.

Then there were proper houses amongst the tombs, foursquare and painted yellow or blue or pink, with little gardens planted out on their flat roofs. The houses stepped up the cliffs like piles of boxes, with steep narrow streets between. Shanty villages had been built on stilts over the mudbanks and silty channels left by the river's retreat, and beyond these, sometimes less than half a league from the road, sometimes two or three leagues distant, was the river, and docks made of floating pontoons, and a constant traffic of little cockle-shell sailboats and barges and sleek fore-and-aft rigged cutters and three-masted xebecs hugging the shore. Along the old river road, street merchants sold fresh fish and oysters and mussels from tanks, and freshly steamed lobsters and spiny crabs, samphire and lotus roots and water chestnuts, bamboo and little red bananas and several kinds of kelp, milk from tethered goats, spices, pickled walnuts, fresh fruit and grass juice, ice, jewelery made of polished shells, black seed pearls, caged birds, bolts of brightly patterned cloth, sandals made from the worn rubber tread of steam wagon tires, cheap plastic toys, tape recordings of popular ballads or prayers, and a thousand other things. The stalls and booths of the merchants formed a kind of ribbon market strung along the dusty margin of land at the shoulder of the old road, noisy with the cries of hawkers and music from tape recorders and itinerant musicians, and the buzz of commerce as people bargained and gossiped. When a warship went past, a league beyond the crowded tarpaper roofs of the shanty villages and the cranes of the floating docks, everyone stopped to watch it. As if in salute, it raised the red and gold blades of its triple-banked oars and fired a charge of white smoke from a cannon, and everyone watching cheered.

That was when Yama realized that he could see, for the first time, the farside shore of the Great River, and that the dark line at the horizon, like a storm cloud, were houses and docks. The river here was deep and swift, stained brown along the shore and dark blue farther out. He had reached Ys and had not known it; the city had crept up on him like an army in the night, the inhabited tombs like scouts, these painted houses and tumbledown shanty villages like the first ranks of footsoldiers. It was as if, after the fiasco of the attempted rescue of the palmers, he had suddenly woken from a long sleep.

Prefect Corin had said little about the landslide which had killed the bandits, the kidnapped women and their priest, Belarius. "You did what you could," he had told Yama. "If we had not tried, the women would be dead anyway."

Yama had not told Prefect Corin about the machine. Let him think what he liked. But Yama had not been able to stop himself reliving what had happened as he had trudged behind the Prefect on the long road to Ys. Sometimes he felt a tremendous guilt, for it had been his foolish pride which had prompted him to use the machine, which had led to the deaths of the bandits and the kidnapped women. And sometimes he felt a tremendous anger toward Prefect Corin, for having laid such a responsibility upon him. He had little doubt that the Prefect could have walked into the bandits' camp, killed them all, and freed the women. Instead he had used the situation to test Yama, and Yama had failed, and felt guilt for having failed, and then anger for having been put to an impossible test.

Humiliation or anger. At last, Yama settled for the latter. As he walked behind Prefect Corin, he often imagined drawing his knife and hacking the man's head from his shoulders with a single blow, or picking a stone from the side of the road and using it as a hammer. He dreamed of running fast and far and, until the warship passed, had been lost in his dreams.

Yama and Prefect Corin ate at a roadside stall. Without being asked, the owner of the stall brought them steamed mussels, water lettuce crisply fried in sesame oil with strands of ginger, and tea made from kakava bark; there was a red plastic bowl in the center of the table into which fragments of bark could be spat. Prefect Corin did not pay for the food—the stall's owner, a tall man with loose, pale skin and rubbery webs between his fingers, simply smiled and bowed when they left.

"He is glad to help someone from the Department," Prefect Corin explained, when Yama asked.

"Why is that?"

Prefect Corin waved a hand in front of his face, as if at a fly. Yama asked again.

"Because we are at war," the Prefect said. "Because the Department fights that war. You saw how they cheered the warship. Must you ask so many questions?"

Yama said, "How am I to learn, if I do not ask?"

Prefect Corin stopped and leaned on his tall staff and stared at Yama. People stepped around them. It was crowded here, with two- and three-story houses packed closely together on either side of the road. A string of camels padded past, their loose lips curled in supercilious expressions, little silver bells jingling on their leather harness.

"The first thing to learn is when to ask questions and when to keep silent," Prefect Corin said, and then he turned and strode off through the crowd.

Without thinking, Yama hurried after him. It was as if this stern, taciturn man had made him into a kind of pet, anxiously trotting at his master's heels. He remembered what Dr. Dismas had said about the oxen, trudging endlessly around the water lift because they knew no better, and his resentment rose again, refreshed.

For long stretches, now, the river disappeared behind houses or godowns. Hills rose above the flat roofs of the houses on the landward side of the road, and after a while Yama realized that they were not hills but buildings. In the hazy distance, the towers he had so often glimpsed using the telescope on the peel-house's heliograph platform shone like silver threads linking earth and sky.

For all the long days of traveling, the towers seemed as far away as ever.

There were more and more people on the road, and strings of camels and oxen, and horse-drawn or steam wagons bedecked with pious slogans, and sleds gliding at waist height, their loadbeds decorated with intricately carved wooden rails painted red and gold. There were machines here, too. At first, Yama mistook them for insects or hummingbirds as they zipped this way and that above the crowds. No one in Aeolis owned machines, not even the Aedile (the watchdogs were surgically altered animals, and did not count) and if a machine strayed into the little city's streets everyone would get as far away from it as possible. Here, no one took any notice of the many machines that darted or spun through the air on mysterious errands. Indeed, one man was walking toward Yama and Prefect Corin with a decad of tiny machines circling above his head.

The man stopped in front of the Prefect. The Prefect was tall, but this man was taller still—he was the tallest man Yama had ever seen. He wore a scarlet cloak with the hood cast over his head, and a black tunic and black trousers tucked into thigh-high boots of soft black leather. A quirt like those used by ox drivers was tucked into the belt of his trousers; the ends of the quirt's hundred strands were braided with diamond-shaped metal tags. The man squared up to Prefect Corin and said, "You're a long way from where you should be."

Prefect Corin leaned on his staff and looked up at the man. Yama stood behind the Prefect. People were beginning to form a loose circle with the red-cloaked man and Prefect Corin in its center.

The man in the red cloak said, "If you have business here, I haven't heard of it."

A machine landed on Prefect Corin's neck, just beneath the angle of his jaw. Prefect Corin ignored it. He said, "There is no reason why you should."

"There's every reason." The man noticed the people watching and slashed the air with his quirt. The tiny, bright machines above his head widened their orbits and one dropped down to hover before the man's lips.

"Move on," the man said. His voice, amplified by the machine, echoed off the faces of the buildings on either side of the street, but most of the people only stepped back a few paces. The machine rose and the man told Prefect Corin in his ordinary voice, "You're causing a disturbance."

Prefect Corin said, "There was no disturbance until you stopped me. I would ask why."

"This is the road, not the river."

Prefect Corin spat in the dust at his feet. "I had noticed."

"You are carrying a pistol."

"By the authority of my Department."

"We'll see about that. What's your business? Are you spying on us?"

"If you are doing your duty, you have nothing to fear. But do not worry, brother, I am no spy. I am returning from a downriver city where I had a task to perform. It is done, and now I return."

"Yet you travel by road."

"I thought I would show this boy something of the countryside. He has led a very sheltered life."

A machine darted forward and spun in front of Yama's face. There was a flash of red light in the backs of Yama's eyes and he blinked, and the machine flew up to rejoin the spinning dance above the man's head. The man said, "This is your catamite? The war is going badly if you can't find better. This one has a corpse's skin. And he is carrying a proscribed weapon."

"Again, by the authority of my Department," Prefect Corin said.

"I don't know the bloodline, but I'd guess he's too young for an apprenticeship. You had better show your papers to the officer of the day."

The man snapped his fingers and the machines dropped and settled into a tight orbit around the Prefect's head, circling him like angry silver wasps. The man turned then, slashing the air with his quirt so that those nearest him fell back, pressing against those behind. "Make way!" the man shouted as he hacked a path through the crowd with his quirt. "Make way! Make way!"

Yama said to Prefect Corin, as they followed the man, "Is this the time to ask a question?"

"He is a magistrate. A member of the autonomous civil authority of Ys. There is some bad blood between his department and mine. He will make a point about who is in charge here, and then we will be on our way."

"How did he know about the pistol and my knife?"

"His machines told him."

Yama studied the shuttling weave of the little machines around Prefect Corin's head. One still clung to the Prefect's neck, a segmented silver bead with four pairs of wire-like legs and mica wings folded along its back. Yama could feel the simple thoughts of the machines, and wondered if he might be able to make them forget what they had been ordered to do, but he did not trust himself to say the right thing to them, and besides, he was not about to reveal his ability by helping the Prefect.

The road opened onto a square lined with flame trees just coming into leaf. On the far side, a high wall rose above the roofs of the buildings and the tops of the trees. It was built of closely fitted blocks of black, polished granite, with gun platforms and watch-towers along its top. Soldiers lounged by a tall gate in the wall, watching the traffic that jostled through the shadow of the gate's arch. The magistrate led Prefect Corin and Yama across the square and the soldiers snapped to attention as they went through the gate. They climbed a steep stair that wound widdershins inside the wall to a wide walkway at the top. A little way along, the wall turned at a right-angle and ran beside the old bank of the river, and a faceted blister of glass, glittering in the sunlight, clung there.

It was warm and full of light inside the glass blister. Magistrates in red cloaks stood at windows hung in the air, watching aerial views of the road, of ships moored at the docks or passing up and down the river, of red tile rooftops, of a man walking along a crowded street. Machines zipped to and fro in the bright air, or spun in little clouds. At the center of all this activity, a bareheaded officer sat with his boots up on a clear plastic table, and after the magistrate had talked with him the officer called Prefect Corin over.

"Just a formality," the officer said languidly, and held out his hand. The eight-legged machine dropped from the Prefect's neck and the officer's fingers briefly closed around it. When they opened again, the machine sprang into the air and began to circle the magistrate's head.

The officer yawned and said, "Your pass, Prefect Corin, if you please." He ran a fingernail over the imprinted seal of the resin tablet Prefect Corin gave him, and said, "You didn't take return passage by river, as you were ordered."

"Not ordered. I could have taken the river passage if I chose to, but it was left to my discretion. The boy is to be apprenticed as a clerk. I thought that I would show him something of the country. He has led a sheltered life."

The officer said, "It's a long, hard walk." He was looking at Yama now. Yama met his gaze and the officer winked. He said, "There's nothing here about this boy, or his weapon. Quite a hanger for a mere apprentice."

"An heirloom. He is the son of the Aedile of Aeolis." Prefect

Corin's tone implied that there was nothing more to be said about the matter.

The officer set the tablet on the desk and said to the magistrate, "Nym, fetch a chair for Prefect Corin."

Prefect Corin said, "There is no need for delay."

The officer yawned again. His tongue and teeth had been stained red by the narcotic leaf he had wadded between gum and cheek. His tongue was black, long and sharply pointed. "It'll take a little while to confirm things with your department. Would you like some refreshment?"

The tall, red-cloaked magistrate set a stool beside Prefect Corin. The officer indicated it, and after a moment Prefect Corin sat down. He said, "I do not need anything from you."

The officer took out a packet of cigarettes and put one in his mouth and lit it with a match he struck on the surface of the desk. He did all this at a leisurely pace; his gaze did not leave the Prefect's face. He exhaled smoke and said to the magistrate, "Some fruit. And iced sherbet." He told Prefect Corin, "While we're waiting, you can tell me about your long walk from—" he glanced at the tablet "—Aeolis. A party of palmers has gone missing somewhere around there, I believe. Perhaps you know something. Meanwhile, Nym will talk with the boy, and we'll see if the stories are the same. What could be simpler?"

Prefect Corin said, "The boy must stay with me. He is in my charge."

"Oh, I think he will be safe with Nym, don't you?"

"I have my instructions," Prefect Corin said.

The officer stubbed out his half-smoked cigarette. "You cleave to them with admirable fidelity. We'll take care of the boy. You'll tell your story to me. He'll tell his to Nym. Then we'll see if the stories are the same. What could be simpler?"

Prefect Corin said, "You do not know—"

The officer raised an eyebrow.

"He is in my charge," Prefect Corin said. "We will go now, I think."

He started to rise, and for an instant was crowned with a jagged circle of sparks. There was a sudden sharp smell of burnt hair and he fell heavily onto the stool. The little machines calmly circled his head, as if nothing had happened.

"Take the boy away, Nym," the officer said. "Find out where he's been and where he's going."

Prefect Corin turned and gave Yama a dark stare. His shoulders were hunched and his hands were pressed between his knees. A thin line of white char circled his sleek black head, above his eyes and the tops of his tightly folded ears. "Do what you are told," he said. "No more than that."

The magistrate, Nym, took Yama's arm and steered him around the windows in the air. The machines quit their orbits around Prefect Corin's head and followed the magistrate in a compact cloud. In the hot sunlight outside the dome, Nym looked through Yama's satchel and took out the sheathed knife.

"That was a gift from my father," Yama said. He half-hoped that the knife would do something to the magistrate, but it remained inert. Yama added, "My father is the Aedile of Aeolis, and he told me to take good care of it."

"I'm not going to steal it, boy." The magistrate pulled the blade halfway out of its sheath. "Nicely balanced. Loyal, too." He dropped it into Yama's satchel. "It tried to bite me, but I know something about machines. You use it to cut firewood, I suppose. Sit down. There. Wait for me. Don't move. Try to leave, and the machines will knock you down, like they did with your master. Try to use your weapon and they'll boil you down to a grease spot. I'll come back and we'll have a little talk, you and me."

Yama looked up at the magistrate. He tried not to blink when the machines settled in a close orbit around his head. "When you fetch refreshments for my master, remember that I would like sherbet, too."

"Oh yes, we'll have a nice talk, you and me. Your master doesn't have a pass for you, and I'll bet you don't have a permit for your knife, either. Think about that."

Yama waited until Nym had gone down the stairway, then told the machines to leave him alone. They wanted to know where they should go, so he asked them if they could cross the river, and when they said that they could he told them to go directly across the river and to wait there.

The machines gathered into a line and flew straight out over the edge of the wall, disappearing into the blue sky above the crowded roofs of the stilt shanties and the masts of the ships anchored at the floating docks. Yama went down the stairs and walked boldly past the soldiers. None of them spared him more than a glance, and he walked out of the shadow of the gate into the busy street beyond the wall.

16

The Cateran

AT FIRST THE landlord of the inn did not want to rent a room to Yama. The inn was full, he said, on account of the Water Market. But when Yama showed him the two gold rials, the man chuckled and said that he might be able to make a special arrangement. Perhaps twice the usual tariff, to take account of the inconvenience, and if Yama would like to eat while waiting for the room to be made up . . . ? The landlord was a fat young man with smooth brown skin and short, spiky white hair, and a brisk, direct manner. He took one of the coins and said that he'd bring change in the morning, seeing as the money changers were closed up for the day.

Yama sat in a corner of the taproom, and presently a pot boy brought him a plate of shrimp boiled in their shells and stir-fried okra and peppers, with chili and peanut sauce and flat discs of unleavened bread and a beaker of thin rice beer. Yama ate hungrily. He had walked until the sun had fallen below the roofs of the city, and although he had passed numerous stalls and street vendors he had not been able to buy any food or drink—he had not realized that there were men whose business was to change coins like his into smaller denominations. The landlord would change the coin tomorrow, and Yama would begin to search for his bloodline. But now he was content to sit with a full stomach, his head pleasantly lightened by the beer, and watch the inn's customers.

They seemed to fall into two distinct groups. There were ordinary working men of several bloodlines, dressed in homespun and clogs, who stood at the counter drinking quietly, and there was a party of men and a single red-haired woman eating at a long table under the stained glass window which displayed the inn's sign of two crossed axes. They made a lot of noise, playing elaborate toasting games and calling from one end of the table to the other. Yama thought that they must be soldiers, caterans or some other kind of irregulars, for they all wore bits of armor, mostly metal or resin chestplates painted with various devices, and wrist guards and greaves. Many were scarred, or had missing fingers. One big, bare-chested man had a silver patch over one eye; another had only one arm, although he atc as quickly and as dextrously as his companions. The red-haired woman seemed to be one of them, rather than a concubine they had picked up; she wore a sleeveless leather tunic and a short leather skirt that left her legs mostly bare.

The landlord seemed to know the caterans, and when he was not busy he sat with them, laughing at their jokes and pouring wine or beer for those nearest him. He whispered something in the one-eyed man's ear and they both laughed, and when the landlord went off to serve one of the other customers, the one-eyed man grinned across the room at Yama.

Presently, the pot boy told Yama that his room was ready and led him around the counter and through a small hot kitchen into a courtyard lit by electric floodlights hung from a central pole. There were white-washed stables on two sides and a wide square gate shaded by an avocado tree in which green parrots squawked and rustled. The room was in the eaves above one of the stable blocks. It was long and low and dark, with a single window at its end looking out over the street and a tumble of roofs falling toward the Great River. The pot boy lit a fish-oil lantern and uncovered a pitcher of hot water, turned down the blanket and fussed with the bolster on the bed, and then hesitated, clearly reluctant to leave.

"I do not have any small coins," Yama said, "but tomorrow I will give you something for your trouble."

The boy went to the door and looked outside, then closed it and turned to Yama. "I don't know you, master," he said, "but I think I should tell you this, or it'll be on my conscience. You shouldn't stay here tonight."

"I paid for the room with honest money left on account," Yama said.

The boy nodded. He wore a clean, much-darned shirt and a pair of breeches. He was half Yama's height and slightly built, with black hair slicked back from a sharp, narrow face. His eyes were large, with golden irises that gleamed in the candlelight. He said, "I saw the coin you left on trust. I won't ask where you got it, but I reckon it could buy this whole place. My master is not a bad man, but he's not a good man either, if you take my meaning, and there's plenty better that would be tempted by something like that."

"I will be careful," Yama said. The truth was that he was tired, and a little dizzy from the beer.

"If there's trouble, you can climb out the window onto the roof," the boy said. "On the far side there's a vine that's grown up to the top of the wall. It's an easy climb down. I've done it many times."

After the boy left, Yama bolted the door and leaned at the open window and gazed out at the vista of roofs and river under the darkening sky, listening to the evening sounds of the city. There was a continual distant roar, the blended noise of millions of people going about their business, and closer at hand the sounds of the neighborhood: a hawker's cry; a pop ballad playing on a tape recorder; someone hammering metal with quick sure strokes; a woman calling to her children. Yama felt an immense peacefulness and an intense awareness that he was there, alone in that particular place and time with his whole life spread before him, a sheaf of wonderful possibilities.

He took off his shirt and washed his face and arms, then pulled off his boots and washed his feet. The bed had a lumpy mattress stuffed with straw, but the sheets were freshly laundered and the wool blanket was clean. This was probably the pot boy's room, he thought, which was why the boy wanted him to leave.

He intended to rest for a few minutes before getting up to close the shutters, but when he woke it was much later. The cold light of the Galaxy lay on the floor; something made a scratching sound in the rafters above the bed. A mouse or a gecko, Yama thought sleepily, but then he felt a feathery touch in his mind and knew that a machine had flown into the room through the window he had carelessly left open.

Yama wondered sleepily if the machine had woken him, but then there was a metallic clatter outside the door. He sat up, groping for the lantern. Someone pushed at the door and Yama, still stupid with sleep, called out.

The door flew open with a tremendous crash, sending the broken bolt flying across the room. A man stood silhouetted in the doorway. Yama rolled onto the floor, reaching for his satchel, and something hit the bed. Wood splintered and straw flew into the air. Yama rolled again, dragging his satchel with him. He cut his hand getting his knife out but hardly noticed. The curved blade shone with a fierce blue light and spat fat blue sparks from its point.

The man turned from the bed, a shadow in the blue half-light. He had broken the frame and slashed the mattress to ribbons with the long, broad blade of his sword. Yama threw the pitcher of water at him and he ducked and said, "Give it up, boy, and maybe you'll live."

Yama hesitated, and the man struck at him with a sudden fury. Yama ducked and heard the air part above his head, and slashed at the man's legs with the knife, so that he had to step back. The knife howled and Yama felt a sudden coldness in the muscles of his arm.

"You fight like a woman," the man said. Knife-light flashed on something on his intent face.

Then he drove forward again, and Yama stopped thinking. Reflexes, inculcated in the long hours in the gymnasium under Sergeant Rhodean's stern instruction, took over. Yama's knife was better suited to close fighting than the man's long blade, but the man had the advantage of reach and weight. Yama managed to parry a series of savage, hacking strokes—fountains of sparks spurted at each blow—but the force of the blows numbed his wrist, and then the man's longer blade slid past the guard of Yama's knife and nicked his forearm. The wound was not painful, but it bled copiously and weakened Yama's grip on his knife.

Yama knocked the chair over and, in the moment it took the man to kick it out of the way, managed to get out of the corner into which he had been forced. But the man was still between Yama and the door. In a moment he pressed his attack again, and Yama was driven back against the wall. The knife's blue light blazed and something white and bone-thin stood between Yama and the man, but the man laughed and said, "I know that trick," and kicked out, catching Yama's elbow with the toe of his boot. The blow numbed Yama's arm and he dropped the knife. The phantom vanished with a sharp snap.

The man raised his sword for the killing blow. For a moment, it was as if he and Yama stood in a tableau pose. Then the man grunted and let out a long sighing breath that stank of onions and wine fumes, and fell to his knees. He dropped his sword and pawed at his ear, then fell on his face at Yama's feet.

Yama's right arm was numb from elbow to wrist; his left hand was shaking so much that it took him a whole minute to find the lantern and light it with his flint and steel. By its yellow glow he tore strips from the bedsheet and bound the shallow but bloody wound on his forearm and the smaller, self-inflicted gash on his palm. He sat still then, but heard only horses stepping about in the stables below. If anyone had heard the door crash open or the subsequent struggle, which was unlikely given that the other guests would be sleeping on the far side of the courtyard, they were not coming to investigate.

The dead man was the one-eyed cateran who had looked at Yama across the taproom of the inn. Apart from a trickle of dark, venous blood from his right ear he did not appear to be hurt. For a moment, Yama did not understand what had happened. Then the dead man's lips parted and a machine slid out of his mouth and dropped to the floor.

The machine's teardrop shape was covered in blood, and it vibrated with a brisk buzz until it shone silver and clean. Yama held out his left hand and the machine slid up the air and landed lightly on his palm.

"I do not remember asking you for help," Yama told it, "but I am grateful."

The machine had been looking for him; there were many of its kind combing this part of Ys. Yama told it that it should look elsewhere, and that it should broadcast that idea to its fellows, then stepped to the window and held up his hand. The machine rose, circled his head once, and flew straight out into the night.

Yama pulled on his shirt and fastened his boots and set to the distasteful task of searching the dead cateran. The man had no money on him and carried only a dirk with a thin blade and a bone hilt, and a loop of wire with wooden pegs for handles. He supposed that the man would have been paid after he had done his job. The pot boy had been right after all. The landlord wanted both coins.

Yama sheathed his knife and tied the sheath to his belt, then picked up his satchel. He found it suddenly hard to turn his back on the dead man, who seemed to be watching him across the room, so he climbed out of the window sideways.

A stout beam jutted above the window frame; it might once have been a support for a hoist used to lift supplies from the street. Yama grasped the beam with both hands and swung himself once, twice, and on the third swing got his leg over the beam and pulled himself up so that he sat astride it. The wound on his forearm had parted a little, and he retied the bandage. Then it was easy enough to stand on the beam's broad top and pull himself on to the ridge of the roof.

17

The Water Market

THE VINE WAS just where the pot boy had said it would be. It was very large and very old—perhaps it had been planted when the inn had been built—and Yama climbed down its stout leafy branches as easily as down a ladder. He knew that he should run, but he also knew that Telmon would not have run. It was a matter of honor to get the coin back, and there in the darkness of the narrow alley at the back of the inn Yama remembered the landlord's duplicitous smile and felt a slow flush of anger.

He was groping his way toward the orange lamplight at the end of the alley when he heard footsteps behind him. For a moment he feared that the cateran's body had been found, and that his friends were searching for his killer. But no cry had been raised, and surely the city was not so wicked that murder would go unremarked. He forced himself not to look back, but walked around the corner and drew his knife and waited in the shadows by the inn's gate, under the wide canopy of the avocado tree.

When the pot boy came out of the alley, Yama pushed him against the wall and held the knife at his throat. "I don't mean any harm!" the boy squealed. Above them, a parrot echoed his frightened cry, modulating it into a screeching cackle.

Yama took away the knife. The thought came to him that if the one-eyed cateran had crept into the room to cut his throat or use the strangling wire, instead of bursting in with his sword swinging wildly, he, and not the cateran, would now be dead.

"He came for you," the pot boy said. "I saw him."

"He is dead." Yama sheathed his knife. "I should have listened to you. As it is, I have killed a man, and your master still has my coin."

The pot boy fussily straightened his ragged jerkin. He had regained his dignity. He looked up at Yama boldly and said, "You could call the magistrates."

"I do not want to get you into trouble, but perhaps you could show me where your master sleeps. If I get back the coin, half of it is yours."

The boy said, "Pandaras, at your service, master. For a tenth of it, I'll skewer his heart for you. He beats me, and cheats his customers, and cheats his provisioners and wine merchants, too. You are a brave man, master, but a poor judge of inns. You're on the run, aren't you? That's why you won't call on the magistrates."

"It is not the magistrates I fear most," Yama said, thinking of Prefect Corin.

Pandaras nodded. "Families can be worse than any lock-up, as I know too well."

"As a matter of fact, I have come here to search for my family."

"I thought you were from the wrong side of the walls—no one born in the city would openly carry a knife as old and as valuable as yours. I'll bet that dead man in your room was more interested in the knife than your coins. I may not be much more than a street urchin, but I know my way around. If hunting down your family is what you want, why then I can help you in a hundred different ways. I'll be glad to be quit of this place. It never was much of a job anyway, and I'm getting too old for it."

Yama thought that this pitch was little more than a gentler form of robbery, but said that for the moment he would be glad of the boy's help.

"My master sleeps as soundly as a sated seal," Pandaras said. "He won't wake until you put your blade to his throat."

Pandaras let Yama into the inn through the kitchen door and led him upstairs. He put a finger to his black lips before delicately unlatching a door. Yama's knife emitted a faint blue glow and he held it up like a candle as he stepped into the stuffy room.

The landlord snored under a disarrayed sheet on a huge canopied bed that took up most of the space; there was no other furniture. Yama shook him awake, and the man pushed Yama's hand away and sat up. The sheet slipped down his smooth naked chest to the mound of his belly. When Yama aimed the point of the knife at his face, the man smiled and said, "Go ahead and kill me. If you don't, I'll probably set the magistrates on you."

"Then you will have to explain that one of your guests was attacked in his room. There is a dead man up there, by the way."

The landlord gave Yama a sly look. The knife's blue glow was liquidly reflected in his round, black eyes and glimmered in his spiky white hair. He said, "Of course there is, or you wouldn't be here. Cyg wasn't working for me, and you can't prove different."

"Then how did you know his name?"

The landlord's shrug was like a mountain moving. "Everyone knows Cyg."

"Then everyone will probably know about the bargain he made with you. Give me my coin and I will leave at once."

"And if I don't, what will you do? If you kill me you won't find it. Why don't we sit down over a glass of brandy and talk about this sensibly? I could make use of a sharp young cock like you. There are ways to make that coin multiply, and I know most of them."

"I have heard that you cheat your customers," Yama said. "Those who cheat are always afraid that they will be cheated in turn, so I would guess that the only place you could have hidden my coin is somewhere in this room. Probably under your pillow."

The landlord lunged forward then, and something struck at Yama's knife. The room filled with white light and the landlord screamed.

———

Afterwards, the landlord huddled against the headboard of his bed and wouldn't look at Yama or the knife. His hand was bleeding badly, for although he had wrapped his sheet around it before grabbing at the knife, the blade had cut him deeply. But he took no notice of his wound, or Yama's questions. He was staring at something which had vanished as quickly as it had appeared, and would only say, over and over, "It had no eyes. Hair like cobwebs, and no eyes."

Yama searched beneath the bolster and the mattress, and then, re-membering the place where he had hidden his map in his own room in the peel-house, rapped the floor with the hilt of his knife until he found the loose board under which the landlord had hidden the gold rial. He had to show the landlord his knife and threaten the return of the appa-rition to make the man roll onto his belly, so that he could gag him and tie his thumbs together with strips torn from the bedsheet.

"I am only taking back what is mine," Yama said. "I do not think you have earned any payment for hospitality. The fool you sent to rob me is dead. Be grateful you are not."

Pandaras was waiting outside the gate. "We'll get some breakfast by the fishing docks," he said. "The boats go out before first light and the stalls open early."

Yama showed Pandaras the gold rial. His hand shook. Although he had felt quite calm while looking for the coin, he was now filled with an excess of nervous energy. He laughed and said, "I have no coin small enough to pay for breakfast."

Pandaras reached inside his ragged shirt and lifted out two worn iron pennies hung on a string looped around his neck. He winked. "I'll pay, master, and then you can pay me."

"As long as you stop calling me master. You are hardly younger than I am."

"Oh, in many ways I'm much older," Pandaras said. "Forgive me, but you're obviously of noble birth. Such folk live longer than most; relatively speaking, you're hardly weaned from the wet nurse's teat." He squinted up at Yama as they passed through the orange glow of a sodium vapor lamp. "Your bloodline isn't one I know, but there are many strange folk downriver of Ys, and many more in her streets. Everything may be found here, it's said, but even if you lived a thousand years and spent all your time searching you'd never find it all. Even if you came to the end of your searching so much would have changed that it would be time to start all over again."

Yama smiled at the boy's babble. "It is the truth about my bloodline I have come to discover," he said, "and fortunately I think I know where to find it."

As they descended toward the waterfront, down narrow streets that were sometimes so steep that they were little more than flights of shallow steps, with every house leaning on the shoulder of its neighbor, Yama told Pandaras something of the circumstances of his birth, of what he thought Dr. Dismas had discovered, and of his journey to Ys. "I know the Department of Apothecaries and Chirurgeons," Pandaras said. "It's no grand place, but stuck as an afterthought on the lower levels of the Palace of the Memory of the People."

"Then I must go there after all," Yama said. "I thought I had escaped it."

"The place you want is on the roof," Pandaras said. "You won't have to go inside, if that's what's worrying you."

The sky was beginning to brighten when Yama and Pandaras reached the wide road by the old waterfront. A brace of camels padded past, loaded with bundles of cloth and led by a sleepy boy, and a few merchants were rolling up the shutters of their stalls or lighting cooking fires. On the long piers which ran out to the river's edge between shacks raised on a forest of stilts above the wide mud flats, fishermen were coiling ropes and taking down nets from drying poles and folding them in elaborate pleats.

For the first time, Yama noticed the extent of the riverside shanty town. The shacks crowded all the way to the edge of the floating docks, half a league distant, and ran along the river edge for as far as the eye could see. They were built mostly of plastic sheeting dulled by smoke and weather toward a universal gray, and roofed with tarpaper or sagging canvas. Channels brimming with thick brown water ran between mudbanks under the tangle of stilts and props. Tethered chickens pecked amongst threadbare grass on drier pieces of ground. Already, people were astir, washing clothes or washing themselves, tending tiny cooking fires, exchanging gossip. Naked children of a decad or more different bloodlines chased each other along swaybacked rope walkways.

Pandaras explained that the shanty towns were the home of refugees from the war. "Argosies go downriver loaded with soldiers, and return with these unfortunates. They are brought here before they can be turned by the heretics."

"Why do they live in such squalor?"

"They know no better, master. They are unchanged savages."

"They must have been hunters once, or fishermen or farmers. Is there no room for them in the city? I think that it is much smaller than it once was."

"Some of them may go to the empty quarters, I suppose, but most would be killed by bandits, and besides, the empty quarters are no good for agriculture. Wherever you dig there are stones, and stones beneath the stones. The Department of Indigenous Affairs likes to keep them in one place, where they can be watched. They get dole food, and a place to live."

"I suppose many become beggars."

Pandaras shook his head vigorously. "No, no. They would be killed by the professional beggars if they tried. They are nothing, master. They are not even human beings. See how they live!"

In the shadows beneath the nearest of the shacks, beside a green, stagnant pool, two naked men were pulling pale guts from the belly of a small cayman. A boy was pissing into the water on the other side of the pool, and a woman was dipping water into a plastic bowl. On a platform above, a woman with a naked baby on her arm was crumbling gray lumps of edible plastic into a blackened wok hung over a tiny fire.

Beside her, a child of indeterminate age and sex was listlessly sorting through wilted cabbage leaves.

Yama said, "It seems to me that they are an army drawn up at the edge of the city."

"They are nothing, master. We are the strength of the city, as you will see."

Pandaras chose a stall by one of the wide causeways that ran out to the pontoon docks, and hungrily devoured a shrimp omelette and finished Yama's leavings while Yama warmed his hands around his bowl of tea. In the growing light Yama could see, three or four leagues downriver, the wall where he and Prefect Corin had been taken yesterday, a black line rising above red tile roofs like the back of a sleeping dragon. He wondered if the magistrates' screens could be turned in this direction. No, they had set machines to look for him, but he had dealt with them. For now he was safe.

Pandaras called out for more tea, and told Yama that there was an hour at least before the money changers opened.

Yama said, "I will make good my debt to you, do not worry. Where will you go?"

"Perhaps with you, master," Pandaras said, grinning. "I'll help you find your family. You do not know where you were born, and wish to find it, while I know my birthplace all too well, and want to escape it."

The boy had small, sharp teeth all exactly the same size. Yama noticed that his black, pointed fingernails were more like claws, and that his hands, with leathery pads on their palms and hooked thumbs stuck stiffly halfway up the wrists, resembled an animal's paws. He had seen many of Pandaras's bloodline yesterday, portering and leading draft animals and carrying out a hundred other kinds of menial jobs. The strength of the city.

Yama asked about the caterans who had been eating in the taproom of the inn, but Pandaras shrugged. "I don't know them. They arrived only an hour before you, and they'll leave this morning for the Water Market by the Black Temple, looking for people who want to employ them. I thought that you might be one of them, until you showed my master the coin."

"Perhaps I am one, but do not yet know it," Yama said, thinking of his vow. He knew that he was still too young to join the army in the usual way, but his age would be no bar to becoming an irregular. Prefect Corin might think him young, but he had already killed a man in close combat, and had had more adventures in the past two decads than most people could expect in a lifetime. He said, "Before we go anywhere else, take me to the Water Market, Pandaras. I want to see how it is done."

"If you join up then I'll go with you, and be your squire. You've enough money to buy a good rifle, or better still, a pistol, and you'll need armor, too. I'll polish it bright between battles, and keep your devices clean—"

Yama laughed. "Hush! You build a whole fantasy on a single whim. I only want to find out about the caterans; I do not yet want to become one. After I know more about where I come from, then, yes, I intend to enlist and help win the war. My brother was killed fighting the heretics. I have made a vow to fight in his place."

Pandaras drained his cup of tea and spat fragments of bark onto the ground. "We'll do the first before the Castellan of the Twelve Devotions sounds its noon gun," he said, "and the second before the Galaxy rises. With my help, anything is possible. But you must forgive my prattle. My people love to talk and to tell stories, and invent tall tales most of all. No doubt you see us as laborers little better than beasts of burden. And that is indeed how we earn our bread and beer, but although we may be poor in the things of the world, we are rich in the things of imagination. Our stories and songs are told and sung by every bloodline, and a few of us even gain brief fame as jongleurs to the great houses and the rich merchants, or as singers and musicians and storytellers of cassette recordings."

Yama said, "It would seem that with all their talents, your people deserve a better station than they have."

"Ah, but we do not live long enough to profit from them. No more than twenty years is the usual; twenty-five is almost unheard of. You're surprised, but that's how it is. It is our curse and our gift. The swiftest stream polishes the pebbles smoothest, as my grandfather had it, and so with us. We live brief but intense lives, for from the pace of our living comes our songs and stories."

Yama said, "Then may I ask how old you are?"

Pandaras showed his sharp teeth. "You think me your age, I'd guess, but I've no more than four years, and in another I'll marry. That is, if I don't go off adventuring with you."

"If you could finish my search in a day, I would be the happiest man on Confluence, but I think it will take longer than that."

"A white boat and a shining woman, and a picture of one of your ancestors made before the building of Confluence. What could be more distinctive? I'll make a song of it soon enough. Besides, you said that you know to begin your search in the records of the Department of Apothecaries and Chirurgeons."

"If Dr. Dismas did not lie. He lied about much else."

The sky above the crowded rooftops was blue now, and traffic was thickening along the road. Fishing boats were moving out past the ends of the piers of the floating docks, their russet and tan sails bellying in the wind and white birds flying in their wake as they breasted the swell of the morning tide. As he walked beside Pandaras, Yama thought of the hundred leagues of docks, of the thousands of boats of the vast fishing fleets which put out every day to feed the myriad mouths of the city, and began to understand the true extent of Ys.

How could he ever expect to find out about his birth, or of the history of any one man, in such a mutable throng? And yet, he thought, Dr. Dismas had found out something in the records of his department, and he did not doubt that he could find it too, and perhaps more. Freshly escaped from his adventure with the cateran and from the fusty fate the Aedile and Prefect Corin had wished upon him, Yama felt his heart rise. It did not occur to him that he might fail in his self-appointed quest. He was, as Pandaras had pointed out, still very young, and had yet to fail in anything important.

The first money changer refused Yama's rials after a mere glance. The second, whose office was in a tiny basement with a packed dirt floor and flaking pink plaster walls, spent a long time looking at the coins under a magnifying screen, then scraped a fleck from one coin and tried to dissolve it in a minim of aqua regia. The money changer was a small, scrawny old man almost lost in the folds of his black silk robe. He clucked to himself when the fleck of gold refused to dissolve even when he heated the watchglass, then motioned to his impassive bodyguard, who fetched out tea bowls and a battered aluminium pot, and resumed his position at the foot of the steps up to the street.

Pandaras haggled for an hour with the money changer, over several pots of tea and a plate of tiny honeycakes so piercingly sweet that they made Yama's teeth ache. Yama felt cramped and anxious in the dank little basement, with the tramp of feet going to and fro overhead and the bodyguard blocking most of the sunlight that spilled down the stair, and was relieved when at last Pandaras announced that the deal was done.

"We'll starve in a month, but this old man has a stone for a heart," he said, staring boldly at the money changer.

"You are quite welcome to take your custom elsewhere," the money changer said, thrusting his sharp face from the fold of black silk over his head and giving Pandaras a fierce, hawkish look. "I'd say your coins were stolen, and any price I give you would be fair enough. As it is, I risk ruining my reputation on your behalf."

"You'll not need to work again for a year," Pandaras retorted. Despite the money changer's impatience, he insisted on counting the slew of silver and iron coins twice over. The iron pennies were pierced—for stringing around the neck, Pandaras said. He demonstrated the trick with his share before shaking hands with the money changer, who suddenly smiled and wished them every blessing of the Preservers.

The street was bright and hot after the money changer's basement. The road was busier than ever, and the traffic crowding its wide asphalt pavement moved at walking pace. The air was filled with the noise of hooves and wheels, the shouts and curses of drivers, the cries of hawkers and merchants, the silver notes of whistles and the brassy clangor of bells. Small boys darted amongst the legs of beasts and men, collecting the dung of horses, oxen and camels, which they would shape into patties and dry on walls for fuel for cooking fires. There were beggars and thieves, skyclad mendicants and palmers, jugglers and contortionists, mountebanks and magicians, and a thousand other wonders, so many that as he walked along amongst the throng Yama soon stopped noticing any but the most outrageous, for else he would have gone mad with amazement.

A black dome had been raised up amongst the masts of the ships and the flat roofs of the godowns at the edge of the river, and Yama pointed to it. "That was not there when we first came here this morning," he said.

"A voidship," Pandaras said casually, and expressed surprise when Yama insisted that they go and look at it. He said, "It's just a lighter for a voidship really. The ship to which it belongs is too big to make riverfall and hangs beyond the edge of Confluence. It has been there a full year now, unloading its ores. The lighter will have put in at the docks for fresh food. It's nothing special."

In any case, they could not get close to the lighter; the dock was closed off and guarded by a squad of soldiers armed with fusiliers more suited to demolishing a citadel than keeping away sightseers. Yama looked up at the lighter's smooth black flank, which curved up to a blunt silver cap that shone with white fire in the sunlight, and wondered at what other suns it had seen. He could have stood there all day, filled with an undefined longing, but Pandaras took his arm and steered him away.

"It's dangerous to linger," the boy said. "The star-sailors steal children, it's said, because they cannot engender their own. If you see one, you'll understand. Most do not even look like men."

As they walked on, Yama asked if Pandaras knew of the ship of the Ancients of Days.

Pandaras touched his fist to his throat. "My grandfather said that he saw two of them walking through the streets of our quarter late one night, but everyone in Ys alive at that time claims as much." He touched his fist to his throat and added, "My grandfather said that they glowed the way the river water sometimes glows on summer nights, and that they stepped into the air and walked away above the rooftops. He made a song about it, but when he submitted it to the legates he was arrested for heresy, and he died under the question."

The sun had climbed halfway to zenith by the time Yama and Pandaras reached the Black Temple and the Water Market. The Black Temple had once been extensive, built on its own island around a protrusion or plug of keelrock in a wide deep bay, but it had been devastated in the wars of the Age of Insurrection and had not been rebuilt, and now the falling level of the Great River had left it stranded in a shallow muddy lagoon fringed with palm trees. The outline of the temple's inner walls and a row of half-melted pillars stood amongst outcrops of keelrock and groves of flame trees; the three black circles of the temple's shrines glittered amongst grassy swales where the narthex had once stood. Nothing could destroy the shrines, not even the energies deployed in the battle which had won back Ys from the Insurrectionists, for they were only partly of the world of material existence. Services were still held at the Black Temple every New Year, Pandaras said, and Yama noticed the heaps of fresh flowers and offerings of fruits before the shrines. Although most of the avatars had disappeared in the Age of Insurrection, and the last had been silenced by the heretics, people still came to petition them.

At the mouth of the bay which surrounded the temple's small island, beyond wrinkled mudflats where flocks of white ibis stalked on delicate legs, on rafts and pontoons and barges, the Water Market was in full swing. The standards of a hundred condottieri flew from poles, and there were a dozen exhibition duels under way, each at the center of a ring of spectators. There were stalls selling every kind of weapon, armorers sweating naked by their forges as they repaired or reforged pieces, provisioners extolling the virtue of their preserved fare. A merchant blew up a water bottle and jumped up and down on it to demonstrate its durability. Newly indentured convicts sat in sullen groups on benches behind the auction block, most sporting fresh mutilations. Galleys, pinnaces and picket boats stood offshore, their masts hung with bright flags that flapped in the strong, hot breeze.

Yama eagerly drank in the bustle and the noise, the exotic costumes of the caterans and the mundane dove-gray uniforms of regular soldiers mingled together, the ringing sound of the weapons of the duelists, and the smell of hot metal and plastic from the forges of the armorers. He wanted to see everything the city had to offer, to search its great temples and the meanest of its alleys and courts for any sign of his bloodline.

As he followed Pandaras along a rickety gangway between two rafts, someone stepped out of the crowd and hailed him. His heart turned over. It was the red-haired woman who last night had sat eating with the man he had killed. When she saw that he had heard her, she shouted again and raised her naked sword above her head.

18

The Thing in the Bottle

"THEY ARE YOURS by right of arms," Tamora, the red-haired cateran, said. "The sword is too long for you, but I know an armorer who can shorten and rebalance it so sweetly you'd swear afterwards that's how it was first forged. The corselet and the greaves can be cut down to suit, and you can sell the trimmings. That way it pays for itself. Old armor is expensive because it's the best. Especially plastic armor, because no one knows how to make the stuff anymore. You might think my breast-plate is new, but that's only because I polished it this morning. It's a thousand years old if it's a day, but even if it's better than most of the clag they make these days, it's still only steel. But, see, these greaves are real old. I could have taken them, but that wouldn't be right. Every-one says we're vagabonds and thieves, but even if we don't belong to any department, we have our traditions. So these are your responsibility now. You won them by right of arms. You can do what you want with them. Throw them in the river if you want, but it would be a fucking shame if you did."

"She wants you to give them back to her as a reward for giving them to you," Pandaras said.

"I talk to the master," Tamora said, "not his fool."

Pandaras struck an attitude. "I am his squire."

"I was the fool," Yama said to Tamora, "and because I was a fool your friend died. That is why I cannot take his things."

Tamora shrugged. "Cyg was no friend of mine, and as far as I'm concerned he was the fool, getting himself killed by a scrap of a thing like you. Why, you're so newly hatched you probably still have eggshell stuck to your back."

Pandaras said, "If this is to be your career, then you must arm yourself properly, master. As your squire, I strongly suggest it."

"Squire, is it?" Tamora cracked open another oyster with her strong, ridged fingernails, slurped up the flesh and wiped her mouth with the back of her hand. The cateran's bright red hair, which Yama suspected was dyed, was cut short over her skull, with a long fringe in the back that fell to her shoulders. She wore her steel breastplate over a skirt made of leather strips and a mesh shirt which left her muscular arms bare. There was a tattoo of a bird sitting on a nest of flames on the tawny skin of her upper arm, the flames in red ink, the bird, its wings outstretched as if drying them in the fire which was consuming it, in blue.

They were sitting in the shade of an umbrella at a table by a food stall on the waterfront, near the causeway that led from the shore to the island of the Black Temple. It was sunstruck noon. The owner of the stall was sitting under the awning by the ice-chest, listening with half-closed eyes to a long antiphonal prayer burbling from the cassette recorder under his chair.

Tamora squinted against the silver light that burned off the wet mudflats. She had a small, triangular, feral face, with green eyes and a wide mouth that stretched to the hinges of her jaw. Her eyebrows were a single brick-red rope; now the rope dented in the middle and she said, "Caterans don't have squires. That's for regular officers, and their squires are appointed from the common ranks. This boy has leeched onto you, Yama. I'll get rid of him if you want."

Yama said, "It is just a joke between the two of us."

"I *am* his squire," Pandaras insisted. "My master is of noble birth. He deserves a train of servants, but I'm so good he needs no other."

Yama laughed.

Tamora squinted at Pandaras. "You people are all the same to me, like fucking rats running around underfoot, but I could swear you're the pot boy of the crutty inn where I stayed the night." She told Yama, "If I was more suspicious, I might suspect a plot."

"If there was a plot, it was between your friend and the landlord of the inn."

"Grah. I suspected as much. If I survive my present job, and there's no reason why I shouldn't, then I'll have words with that rogue. More than words, in fact."

Tamora's usual expression was a sullen, suspicious pout, but when she smiled her face came to life, as if a mask had suddenly dropped, or the sun had come out from behind a cloud. She smiled now, as if at the thought of her revenge. Her upper incisors were long and stout and sharply pointed.

Yama said, "He did not profit from his treachery."

Pandaras kicked him under the table and frowned.

Tamora said, "I'm not after your fucking money, or else I would have taken it already. I have just now taken on a new job, so be quick in making up your mind on how you'll dispose of what is due to you by right of arms. As I said before, you can throw it in the river or leave it for the scavengers if you want, but it's good gear."

Yama picked up the sword. Its broad blade was iron and had seen a lot of use. Its nicked edge was razor sharp. The hilt was wound with bronze wire; the pommel an unornamented plastic ball, chipped and dented. He held the blade up before his face, then essayed a few passes. The cut on his forearm stickily parted under the crude bandage he had tied and he put the sword down. No one sitting at the tables around the stall had looked at the display, although he had hoped that they would.

He said, "I have a knife that serves me well enough, and the sword is made for a strong unsubtle man more used to hewing wood than fighting properly. Find a woodsman and give it to him, although I suspect he would rather keep his axe. But I will take the armor. As you say, old armor is the best."

"Well, at least you know something about weapons," Tamora said grudgingly. "Are you here looking for hire? If so, I'll give some advice for free. Come back tomorrow, early. That's when the best jobs are available. Condottieri like a soldier who can rise early."

"I had thought to watch a duel or two," Yama said.

"Grah. Exhibition matches between oiled cornfed oafs who wouldn't last a minute in real battle. Do you think we fight with swords against the fucking heretics? The matches draw people who would otherwise not come, that's all. They get drunk with recruiting sergeants and the next day find themselves indentured in the army, with a hangover and the taste of the oath like a copper penny in their mouth."

"I am not here to join the army. Perhaps I will become a cateran eventually, but not yet."

"He's looking for his people," Pandaras said.

It was Yama's turn to kick under the table. It was green-painted tin, with a bamboo and paper umbrella. He said, "I am looking for certain records in one of the departmental libraries."

Tamora swallowed the last oyster and belched. "Then sign up with the department. Better still, join the fucking archivists. After ten years' apprenticeship you might just be sent to the Palace of the Memory of the People; more likely you'll be sent to listen to the stories of un-changed toads squatting in some mudhole. But that's a better chance than trying to bribe your way into their confidence. They're a frugal lot, and besides, if any one of them was caught betraying his duty he'd be executed on the spot. The same penalty applies to any who try to bribe them. Those records are all that remains of the dead, kept until they're resurrected at the end of time. It's serious shit to even look at them the wrong way."

"The Puranas say that the Preservers need no records, for at the end of time an infinite amount of energy becomes available. In the last instant as the Universe falls into itself all is possible, and everyone who ever lived or ever could have lived will live again forever, in that eternal now. Besides, the records I am looking for are not in the Palace of the Memory of the People, but in the archives of the Department of Apoth-ecaries and Chirurgeons."

"That's more or less the same place. On the roof rather than inside, that's all."

"Just as I told you, master," Pandaras said. "You don't need her to show you what I already know!"

Tamora ignored him. "Their records are maintained by archivists, too. Unless you're a sawbones or a sawbones' runner, you can forget about it. It's the same in all the departments. The truth is expensive and difficult to keep pure, and so getting at it without proper authority is dangerous." Tamora smiled. "But that doesn't mean that there aren't ways of getting at it."

Pandaras said, "She is baiting a hook. Be careful."

Yama said to Tamora, "Tell me this. You have fought against the heretics—that is what the tattoo on your arm implies, anyway. In all your travels, have you ever seen any other men and women like me?"

"I fought in two campaigns, and in the last I was so badly wounded that I took a year recovering. When I'm fit I'll go again. It's better pay than bodyguard or pickup work, and more honorable, although honor has little to do with it when you're there. No, I haven't seen anyone like you, but it doesn't signify. There are ten thousand bloodlines on Confluence, not counting all those hill tribes of indigens, who are little more than animals."

"Then you see how hard I must search," Yama said.

Tamora smiled. It seemed to split her face in half. "How much will you pay?"

"Master—"

"All I have. I changed two gold rials for smaller coins this morning. It is yours, if you help me."

Pandaras whistled and looked up at the blue sky.

"Grah. Against death, that is not so much."

Yama said, "Do they guard the records with men, or with machines?"

"Why, mostly machines of course. As I said, the records of any department are important. Even the poorest departments guard their archives carefully—often their archives are all they have left."

"Well, it might be easier than you suppose."

Tamora stared at Yama. He met her luminous green gaze and for a long moment the rest of the world melted away. Her pupils were vertical slits edged with closely crowded dots of golden pigment that faded to copper at the periphery. Yama imagined drowning in that green-gold gaze, as a luckless fisherman might drown in the Great River's flood. It was the heart-stopping gaze that a predator turns upon its prey.

Tamora's voice said from far away, "Before I help you, if I do help you, you must prove yourself."

Yama said faintly, "How?"

"Don't trust her," Pandaras said. "If she really wanted the job, she'd have asked for all your money. There are plenty like her. If we threw a stone in any direction, we'd hit at least two."

Tamora said, "In a way, you owe it to me."

Yama was still looking into Tamora's gaze. He said, "Cyg was going to partner you, I think. Now I know why you came here. You were not looking for me, but for a replacement. Well, what would you have me do?"

Tamora pointed over his shoulder. He turned, and saw the black, silver-capped dome of the voidship lighter rising beyond the flame trees of the island of the Black Temple. The cateran said, "We have to bring back a star-sailor who jumped ship."

━━━━━━━

They sold the sword to an armorer for rather more than Yama expected, and left the corselet and the greaves with the same man to be cut down. Tamora insisted that Yama get his wounds treated by one of the leeches who had set up their stalls near the duelling arena, and Yama sat and watched two men fence with chainsaws ("Showboat juggling," Tamora sneered) while the cut on his forearm was stitched, painted with blue gel and neatly bandaged. The shallow cut on Yama's palm should be left to heal on its own, the leech said, but Tamora made him bandage it anyway, saying that the bandage would help Yama grip his knife. She bought Pandaras a knife with a long thin round blade and a fingerguard chased with a chrysanthemum flower; it was called a kidney puncher.

"Suitable for sneaking up on someone in the dark," Tamora said. "If you stand on tiptoe, rat-boy, you should be able to reach someone's vitals with this."

Pandaras flexed the knife's blade between two clumsy, clawed fingers, licked it with his long, pink tongue, then tucked it in his belt. Yama told him, "You do not have to follow me. I killed the man who would have helped her, and it is only proper that I should take his place. But there is no need for you to come."

"Well put," Tamora said.

Pandaras showed his small sharp teeth. "Who else would watch your back, master? Besides, I have never been aboard a voidship."

<hr>

One of the guards escorted them across the wharf to the voidship lighter. Cables and flexible plastic hoses lay everywhere, like a tangle of basking snakes. Laborers, nearly naked in the hot sunlight, were winching a cavernous pipe toward an opening which had dilated in the lighter's black hull. An ordinary canvas and bamboo gangway angled up to a smaller entrance.

Yama felt a distinct pressure sweep over his skin as, following Tamora up the gangway, he ducked beneath the port's rim. Inside, a passageway sloped away to the left, curving as it rose so that its end could not be seen. Yama supposed that it spiralled around the inside of the hull of the lighter like the track a maggot leaves in a fruit. It was circular in cross-section, and lit by a soft directionless red light that seemed to hang in the air like smoke. Although the lighter's black hull radiated the day's heat, inside it was as chilly as the mountain garden of the curators of the City of the Dead.

Another guard waited inside. He was a short, thickset man with a bland face and a broad, humped back. His head was shaven, and ugly red scars criss-crossed his scalp. He wore a many-pocketed waistcoat and loose-fitting trousers, and did not appear to be armed. He told them to keep to the middle of the passageway, not to touch anything, and not to talk to any voices which might challenge them.

"I've been here before," Tamora said. She seemed subdued in the red light and the chill air of the passageway.

"I remember you," the guard said, "and I remember a man with only one eye, but I do not remember your companions."

"My original partner ran into something unexpected. But I'm here, as I said I would be, and I vouch for these two. Lead on. This place is like a tomb."

"It is older than any tomb," the guard said.

They climbed around two turns of the passageway. Groups of colored lights were set at random in the black stuff which sheathed the walls and ceiling and floor. The floor gave softly beneath Yama's boots, and there was a faint vibration in the red-lit air, so low-pitched that he felt it more in his bones than in his ears.

The guard stopped and pressed his palm against the wall, and the black stuff puckered and pulled back with a grating noise. Ordinary light flooded through the orifice, which opened onto a room no more than twenty paces across and ringed round with a narrow window that looked out across the roofs of the city in one direction and the glittering expanse of the Great River in the other. Irregular clusters of colored lights depended from the ceiling like stalactites in a cave, and a thick-walled glass bottle hung from the ceiling in the middle of the clusters of lights, containing some kind of red and white blossom in turgid liquid.

Yama whispered to Tamora, "Where is the captain?"

He had read several of the old romances in the library of the peel-house, and expected a tall man in a crisp, archaic uniform, with sharp, bright eyes focused on the vast distances between stars, and skin tanned black with the fierce light of alien suns.

Pandaras snickered, but fell silent when the guard looked at him.

The guard said, "There is no captain except when the crew meld, but the pilot of this vessel will talk with you."

Tamora said, "The same one I talked with two days ago?"

"Does it matter?" the guard said. He pulled a golden circlet from one of his pockets and set it on his scarred scalp. At once, his body stiffened. His eyes blinked, each to a different rhythm, and his mouth opened and closed.

Tamora stepped up to him and said, "Do you know who I am?"

The guard's mouth hung open. Spittle looped between his lips. His tongue writhed behind his teeth like a wounded snake and his breath came out as a hiss that slowly shaped itself into a word.

"Yesssss."

Pandaras nudged Yama and indicated the bottled blossom with a crooked thumb. "There's the star-sailor," he said. "It's talking through the guard."

Yama looked more closely at the thing inside the bottle. What he had thought were fleshy petals of some exotic flower were the lobes of a mantle that bunched around a core woven of pink and gray filaments. Feathery gills rich with red blood waved slowly to and fro in the thick liquid in which they were suspended. It was a little like a squid, but instead of tentacles it had white, many-branching fibers that disappeared into the base of its bottle.

Pandaras whispered, "Nothing but a nervous system. That's why it needs puppets."

The guard jerked his head around and stared at Yama and Pandaras. His eyes were no longer blinking at different rates, but the pupil of the left eye was much bigger than that of the right. Speaking with great effort, as if forcing the words around pebbles lodged in his throat, he said, "You told me you would bring only one other."

Tamora said, "The taller one, yes. But he has brought his . . . servant."

Pandaras stepped forward and bowed low from the waist. "I am Yama's squire. He is a perfect master of fighting. Only this night past he killed a man, an experienced fighter better armed than he, who thought to rob him while he slept."

The star-sailor said through its puppet, "I have not seen the bloodline for a long time, but you have chosen well. He has abilities you will find useful."

Yama stared at the thing in the bottle, shocked to the core.

Tamora said, "Is that so?"

"I scanned all of you when you stepped aboard. This one—" the guard slammed his chest with his open hand "—will see to the contract, following local custom. It will be best to return with the whole body, but if it is badly damaged then you must bring a sample of tissue. A piece the size of your smallest finger will be sufficient. You remember what I told you."

Yama said, "Wait. You know my bloodline?"

Tamora ignored him. She closed her eyes and recited, " 'It will be lying close to the spine. The host must be mutilated to obliterate all trace of occupation. Burn it if possible.' " She opened her eyes. "Suppose we're caught? What do we tell the magistrates?"

"If you are caught by your quarry, you will not live to tell the magistrates anything."

"He'll know you sent us."

"And we will send others, if you fail. I trust you will not."

"You know my bloodline," Yama said. "How do you know my bloodline?"

Pandaras said, "We aren't the first to try this, are we?"

"There was one attempt before," Tamora said. "It failed. That is why we're being so well paid."

The guard said, "If you succeed."

"Grah. You say I have a miracle worker with me. Of course we'll succeed."

The guard was groping for the circlet on his head. Yama said quickly, "No! I want you to tell me how you know my bloodline!"

The guard's head jerked around. "We thought you all dead," he said, and pulled the circlet from his scalp. He fell to his knees and retched up a mouthful of yellow bile which was absorbed by the black floor, then got to his feet and wiped his mouth on the sleeve of his tunic. He said in his own voice, "Was it agreed?"

Tamora said, "You'll make the contract, and we put our thumbs to it."

"Outside," the guard said.

Yama said, "He knew who I was! I must talk with him!"

The guard got between Yama and the bottled star-sailor. He said, "Perhaps when you return."

"We should get started straightaway," Tamora said. "It's a long haul to the estate."

The door ground open. Yama looked at the star-sailor in its bottle, and said, "I will return, and with many questions."

19

Iachimo

WHEN THE GIANT guard went past the other side of the gate for the third time, Tamora said, "Every four hundred heartbeats. You could boil an egg by him."

She lay beside Yama and Pandaras under a clump of thorny bushes in the shadows beyond the fierce white glare of a battery of electric arc lamps that crackled at the top of the wall. The gate was a square lattice of steel bars set in a high wall of fused rock, polished as smoothly as black glass. The wall stretched away into the darkness on either side, separated from the dry scrub by a wide swathe of barren sandy soil.

Yama said, "I still think we should go over the wall somewhere else. The rest of the perimeter cannot be as heavily guarded as the gate."

"The gate is heavily guarded because it's the weakest part of the wall," Tamora said. "That's why we're going in through it. The guard is a man. Doesn't look it, but he is. He decides who to let in and who to keep out. Elsewhere, the guards will be machines or dogs. They'll kill without thinking and do it so quick you won't know it until you find yourself in the hands of the Preservers. Listen. After the guard goes past again, I'll climb the wall, kill him, and open the gates to let you in."

"If he raises the alarm—"

"He won't have time for that," Tamora said, and showed her teeth.

"Those won't do any good against armor," Pandaras said.

"They'll snap off your head if you don't swallow your tongue. Be quiet. This is warrior work."

They were all tired and on edge. It had been a long journey from the waterfront. Although they had traveled most of the distance in a public calash, they had had to walk the final three leagues. The merchant's estate was at the top of one of a straggling range of hills that, linked by steep scrub-covered ridges, rose like worn teeth at the edge of the city's wide basin. An age ago, the hills had been part of the city. As Yama, Tamora and Pandaras had climbed through dry, fragrant pine woods, they had stumbled upon an ancient paved street and the remains of the buildings which had once lined it. They had rested there until just after sunset. Yama and Pandaras had eaten the raisin cakes they had bought hours before, while Tamora had prowled impatiently amongst the ruins, wolfing strips of dried meat and snicking off the fluffy seeding heads of fireweed with her rapier.

The merchant who owned the estate was a star-sailor who had jumped ship the last time it had lain off the edge of Confluence, over forty years ago. He had amassed his wealth by surreptitious deployment of technologies whose use was forbidden outside the voidships. For that alone, quite apart from the crime of desertion, he had been sentenced to death by his crewmates, but they had no jurisdiction outside their ship and, because of the same laws which the merchant had violated, could not use their powers to capture him.

Tamora was the second cateran hired to carry out the sentence. The first had not returned, and was presumed to have been killed by the merchant's guards. Yama thought that this put them at a disadvantage, since the merchant would be expecting another attack, but Tamora said it made no difference.

"He has been expecting this ever since his old ship returned. That's why he has retreated to this estate, which has better defenses than the compound he maintains in the city. We're lucky there aren't patrols outside the walls."

In fact, Yama had already asked several machines to ignore them as they had toiled up the hill through the pine woods, but he did not point this out. There was an advantage in being able to do something no one suspected was possible. He already owed his life to this ability, and it was to his benefit to have Tamora believe that he had killed the cateran by force of arms rather than by lucky sleight of hand.

Now, crouched between Tamora and Pandaras in the dry brush, Yama could faintly sense other machines beyond the high black wall, but they were too far away to count, let alone influence. He was dry-mouthed, and his hands had a persistent uncontrollable tremor. All his adventures with Telmon had been childhood games without risk, inadequate preparation for the real thing. His suggestion to try another part of the wall was made as much from the need to delay the inevitable as to present an alternative strategy.

Pandaras said, "I have an idea. Master, lend me your satchel, and that book you were reading."

Tamora said fiercely, "Do as I say. No more, no less."

"I can have the guard open the gates for me," Pandaras said. "Or would you rather break your teeth on steel bars?"

"If you insist that we have to go through the gate," Yama told Tamora, as he emptied out his satchel, "at least we should listen to his idea."

"Grah. Insist? I *tell* you what to do, and you do it. This is not a democracy. Wait!"

But Pandaras stood up and, with Yama's satchel slung around his neck, stepped out into the middle of the asphalt road which ran through the gateway. Tamora hissed in frustration as the boy walked into the glare of the arc lights, and Yama told her, "He is cleverer than you think."

"He'll be dead in a moment, clever or not."

Pandaras banged on the gate. A bell trilled in the distance and dogs barked closer at hand. Yama said, "Did you know there were dogs?"

"Grah. Dogs are nothing. It is easy to kill dogs."

Yama was not so sure. Any one of the watchdogs of the peel-house could bring down an ox by clamping its powerful jaws on the windpipe of its victim and strangling it—and to judge by the volume and ferocity of the barking there were at least a dozen dogs beyond the gate.

The guard appeared on the other side of the gate. In his augmented armor, painted scarlet as if dipped in fresh blood, he was more than twice Pandaras's height. His eyes were red embers that glowed in the shadow beneath the bill of his flared helmet. Energy pistols mounted on his shoulders trained their muzzles on Pandaras and the guard's amplified bass voice boomed and echoed in the gateway.

Pandaras stood his ground. He held up the satchel and opened it and showed it to the guard, then took out the book and flipped through its pages in an exaggerated pantomime. The guard reached through the gate's steel lattice, his arm extending more than a man's arm should reach, but Pandaras danced backward and put the book back in the satchel and folded his arms and shook his head from side to side.

The guard conferred with himself in a booming mutter of subsonics; then the red dots of his eyes brightened and a bar of intense red light swept up and down Pandaras. The red light winked out and with a clang the gate sprang open a fraction. Pandaras slipped through the gap. The gate slammed shut behind him and he followed the monstrously tall guard into the shadows beyond.

"He's brave, your fool," Tamora remarked, "but he's even more of a fool than I thought possible."

"Let us wait and see," Yama said, although he did not really believe that the pot boy could do anything against the armored giant. He was as astonished as Tamora when, a few minutes later, the dogs began to bark again, the gate clanged open, and Pandaras appeared in the gap and beckoned to them.

The giant guard sprawled on his belly in the roadway a little way beyond the gate. His helmet was turned to one side, and one of his arms was twisted behind him, as if he was trying to reach something on his back. Yama knew that the guard was dead, but he could feel a glimmer of machine intelligence in the man's skull, as if something still lived there, gazing with furious impotence through its host's dead eyes.

Pandaras returned Yama's satchel with a flourish, and Yama stuffed his belongings into it. Tamora kicked the guard's scarlet cuirass, then turned on Pandaras.

"Tell me how you did it later," she said. "Now we must silence the dogs. You're lucky they weren't set on you."

Pandaras calmly stared up at her. "A harmless messenger like me?"

"Don't be so fucking cute."

"Let me deal with the dogs," Yama said.

"Be quick," Pandaras said. "Before I killed him, the guard sent for someone to escort me to the house."

The dogs were baying loudly, and other dogs answered them from distant parts of the grounds. Yama found the kennel to the left of the gate, cut into the base of the wall. Several dogs thrust their snouts through the kennel's barred door with such ferocity that their skull caps and the machines embedded in their shoulders struck sparks from the iron bars. They howled and whined and snapped in a ferocious tumult, and it took Yama several minutes to calm them down to a point where he could ask them to speak with their fellows and assure them that nothing was wrong.

"Go to sleep," he told the dogs, once they had passed on the message, and then he ran back to the road.

Tamora and Pandaras had rolled the guard under the partial cover of a stand of moonflower bushes beside the road. Tamora had stripped the guard's heavy pistols from their shoulder mountings. She handed one to Yama and showed him how to press two contact plates together to make it fire.

"I should have one of those," Pandaras said. "Right of arms, and all that."

Tamora showed her teeth. "You killed a man in full powered armor twice your height and armed with both of these pistols. I'd say you are dangerous enough with that kidney puncher I chose for you. Follow me, if you can!"

She threw herself into the bushes, and Yama and Pandaras ran after her, thrashing through drooping branches laden with white, waxy blossoms. Tamora and Pandaras quickly outpaced Yama, but Pandaras could not sustain his initial burst of speed and Yama soon caught up with him. The boy was leaning against the trunk of a cork oak, watching the dark stretch of grass beyond while he tried to get his breath back.

"She has the blood rage," Pandaras said, when he could speak again. "No sense in chasing after her."

Yama saw a string of lights burning far off through a screen of trees on the far side of the wide lawn. He began to walk in that direction, with Pandaras trotting at his side.

Yama said, "Will you tell me how you killed the guard? I might need the trick myself."

"How did you calm the watchdogs?"

"Do you always answer a question with a question?"

"We say that what you know makes you what you are. So you should never be free with what you know, or strangers will take pieces of you until nothing is left."

"Nothing is free in this city, it seems."

"Only the Preservers know everything, master. Everyone else must pay or trade for information. How did you calm the dogs?"

"We have similar dogs at home. I know how to talk to them."

"Perhaps you'll teach me that trick when we have time."

"I am not sure if that is possible, Pandaras, but I suppose that I can try. How did you get through the gate and kill the guard?"

"I showed him your book. I saw you reading in it when we rested in the ruins. It's very old, and therefore very valuable. My former master—" Pandaras spat on the clipped grass "—and that stupid cateran you killed would have taken the gold rials and left the book, but my mother's family deals in books, and I know a little about them. Enough to know that it is worth more than the money. I talked with someone through the guard, and they let me in. The rich often collect books. There is power in them."

"Because of the knowledge they contain."

"You're catching on. As for killing the guard, it was no trick. I'll tell you how I did it now, master, and you must tell me something later. The guard seemed a giant, but he was an ordinary man inside that armor. Without power, he could not move a step; with it, he could sling a horse over his shoulders and still run as fast as a deer. I jumped onto his back, where he couldn't reach me, and pulled the cable that connected the power supply to the muscles in his armor. Then I stuck my knife in the gap where the cable went in, and pierced his spinal cord. A trick one of my stepbrothers taught me. The family of my mother's third husband work in a foundry that refurbishes armor. I helped out there when I was a kit. You get to know the weak points that way—they're where mending is most needed. Do we have to go so fast?"

"Where is the house, Pandaras?"

"This man is rich, but he is not one of the old trading families, who have estates upriver of the city. So he has a compound by the docks where he does his business, and this estate in the hills on the edge of the city. That is why the wall is so high and strong, and why there are many guards. They all fear bands of robbers out here, and arm their men as if to fight off a cohort."

Yama nodded. "The country beyond is very wild. It used to be part of the city, I think."

"No one lives there. No one important, anyhow. The robbers come from the city."

"The law is weaker here, then?"

"Stronger, master, if you fall foul of it. The rich make their own laws. For ordinary people, it's the magistrates who decide right and wrong. Isn't that how it was where you come from?"

Yama thought of the Aedile, and of the militia. He said, "More or less. Then the house will be fortified. Sheer force of arms might not be the best way to try and enter it."

"Fortified and hidden. That's the fashion these days. We could wander around for a day and not find it. Those lights are probably where the servants live, or a compound for other guards." Pandaras stopped to untangle the unraveling edge of his sleeve from the thorny canes of a bush. "If you ask me, this crutty greenery is all part of the defenses."

Yama said, "There is a path through there. Perhaps that will lead to the house."

"If it was that simple, we'd all be rich, and have big houses of our own, neh? It probably leads to a pit full of caymans or snakes."

"Well, someone is coming along it, anyway. Here."

Yama gave the pistol to Pandaras. It was so heavy that the boy needed both hands to hold it. "Wait," he said, "you can't—"

But Yama ran toward the lights and the sound of hooves, carried by a rush of exhilaration. It was better to act than to hide, he thought, and in that moment understood why Tamora had charged off so recklessly. As he ran, he took the book from his satchel; when lights swooped toward him through the dark air, he stopped and held it up. A triplet of machines spun to a halt above his head and bathed him in a flood of white light. Yama squinted through their radiance at the three riders who had pulled up at the edge of the road.

Two guards in plastic armor reined in their prancing mounts and levelled light lances at him. The third was a mild old man on a gray palfrey. He wore a plain black tunic and his long white hair was brushed back from the narrow blade of his face. His skin was yellow and very smooth, stretched tautly over high cheekbones and a tall, ridged brow.

Yama held the book higher. The white-haired man said, "Why aren't you waiting at the gate?"

"The guard was attacked, and I got scared and ran. Thieves have been after what I carry ever since I have come to this city. Only last night I had to kill a man who wanted to steal from me."

The white-haired man jogged his palfrey so that it stepped sideways toward Yama, and he leaned down to peer at the book. He said, "I can certainly see why someone would want to steal this."

"I have been told that it is very valuable."

"Indeed." The white-haired man stared at Yama for a full minute. The two guards watched him, although their lances were still pointed at Yama, who stood quite still in the light of the three machines. At last, the man said, "Where are you from, boy?"

"Downriver."

Did he know? And if he knew, how many others?

"You've been amongst the tombs, have you not?"

"You are very wise, dominie."

It was possible that the Aedile knew. Perhaps that was why he had wanted to bury Yama in a drab clerkship, away from the eyes of the world. And if the Aedile had known, then Prefect Corin had known too.

One of the guards said, "Take the book and let us deal with him. He won't be missed."

"I allowed him in," the white-haired man said. "Although he should have waited by the gate, I will continue to be responsible for him. Boy, where did you get that book? From one of the old tombs downriver? Did you find anything else there?"

Before Yama could answer, the second guard said, "He has the pallid look of a tomb-robber."

The white-haired man held up a hand. His fingers were very long, with nails filed to points and painted black. "It isn't just the book. I'm interested in the boy too."

The first guard said, "He carries a power knife in his satchel."

"More loot, I expect," the white-haired man said. "You won't use it here, will you, boy?"

"I have not come to kill you," Yama said.

The second guard said, "He's a little old for you, Iachimo."

"Be silent," the white-haired man, Iachimo, said pleasantly, "or I'll slice out your tongue and eat it in front of you." He told Yama, "They obey me because they know I never make an idle threat. I wish it were otherwise, but you cannot buy loyalty. You must win it by fear or by love. I find fear to be more effective."

The second guard said, "We should check the gate."

Iachimo said, "The dogs have not raised any real alarm, and neither has the guard."

The first guard said, "But here's this boy wandering the grounds. There might be others."

"Oh, very well," Iachimo said, "but be quick." He swung down from his palfrey and told Yama, "You'll come with me, boy."

As they crossed the road and plunged into a stand of pine trees beyond, Iachimo said, "Is the book from the City of the Dead? Answer truthfully. I can smell out a lie, and I have little patience for evasion."

Yama did not doubt it, but he thought to himself that Iachimo was the kind of man who believed too strongly in his cleverness, and so held all others in contempt and did not pay as much attention to them as he should. He said, "It was not from the City of the Dead, dominie, but a place close by."

"Hmm. As I remember, the house occupied by the Aedile of Aeolis has an extensive library." Iachimo turned and looked at Yama and smiled. "I see I have hit the truth. Well, I doubt that the Aedile will miss it. The library is a depository of all kinds of rubbish, but as the fisherfolk of that region have it, rubies are sometimes engendered in mud by the light of the Eye of the Preservers. Nonsense, of course, but despite that it has a grain of truth. In this case, the fisherfolk are familiar with pearls, which are produced by certain shellfish when they are irritated by a speck of grit, and secrete layers of slime to enclose the irritation. This slime hardens, and becomes the black or red pearls so eagerly sought by gentlemen and ladies of high breeding, who do not know of the base origin of their beloved jewels. Your book is a pearl, without doubt. I knew it as soon as I saw it, although I do not think it was you who held it up at the gate."

"It was my friend. But he got scared and ran off."

"The guards will catch him. Or the dogs, if he is unlucky."

"He's only a pot boy from one of the inns by the waterfront. I struck up a friendship with him."

"From which he hoped to profit, I expect," Iachimo said, and then stopped and turned to look back at the way they had come.

A moment later, a thread of white light lanced through the darkness, illuminating a distant line of trees. Yama felt the ground tremble beneath his feet; a noise like thunder rolled through the grounds.

Iachimo grasped Yama's shoulders and pushed him forward. "One of the weapons mounted by the gatekeeper, unless I am mistaken. And I am never mistaken. Your friend has been found, I believe. Do not think of running, boy, or you'll suffer the same fate."

Yama did not resist. Both Tamora and Pandaras were armed with the pistols taken from the gatekeeper, and Iachimo did not yet know that the gatekeeper was dead. Besides, he was being taken to the very place the others were looking for.

Yama and Iachimo descended into a narrow defile between steep rock walls studded with ferns and orchids. Another white flash lit the crack of sky above. Pebbles rattled down the walls in the aftershock. Iachimo tightened his grip on Yama's shoulder and pushed him on. "This matter is consuming more time than I like," he said.

"Are you in charge of the guards? They do not seem to be doing a very good job."

"I am in charge of the entire household. And do not think I turned out for you, boy. It was the book. But I admit you are a curiosity. There could be some advantage here."

Yama said boldly, "What do you know about my bloodline? You recognized it, and that was why I was not killed."

"You know less than I, I think. I wonder if you even know your parents."

"Only that my mother is dead."

A silver lady in a white boat. The old Constable, Thaw, had said that he had plucked Yama from her dead breast, but as a young boy Yama had dreamed that she had only been profoundly asleep, and was searching for him in the wilderness of tombs around Aeolis. Sometimes he had searched for her there—as he was searching still.

Iachimo said, "Oh, she's dead all right. Dead ages past. You're probably first generation, revived from a stored template."

The narrow defile opened out into a courtyard dimly lit by a scattering of floating lanterns, tiny as fireflies, that drifted in the black air. Its tiled floor was crowded with gray, life-sized statues of men and animals in a variety of contorted poses. Iachimo pushed Yama forward. Horribly, the statues stirred and trembled, sending up ripples of gray dust and a dry scent of electricity. Some opened their eyes, but the orbs they rolled toward Yama were like dry, white marbles.

Iachimo said in Yama's ear, "There's worse that can happen to you than being returned to storage. Do we understand each other?"

Yama thought of his knife. It occurred to him that there were situations in which it might be more merciful to use it against himself rather than his enemies. He said, "You are taking me to your master."

"He wants only to see the book. You will be a surprise gift. We'll see what shakes out, and afterwards we'll talk."

Iachimo smiled at Yama, but it was merely a movement of certain muscles in his narrow, high-browed face. He was lost in his own thoughts, Yama saw, a man so clever that he schemed as naturally as other men breathed.

Yama said, "How do you know about my bloodline?"

"My master's bloodline is long-lived, and he is one of the oldest. He has taught me much about the history of the world. I know that he will be interested in you. Of course, he may want you killed, but I will try to prevent it. And so you owe me your life twice over. Think of that, when you talk with him. We can do things for each other, you and I."

Yama remembered that the pilot of the voidship lighter had said that it knew his bloodline, and understood that he was a prize which Iachimo would offer to his master in the hope of advancement or reward. He said, "It seems to me that this is a very one-sided bargain. What will I gain?"

"Your life, to begin with. My master may want to kill you at once, or use you and then kill you, but I can help you, and you can help me. Damn these things!"

Iachimo was standing beside the statue of a naked boy—or perhaps it had once been a living boy, encased or transformed in some way— and the statue had managed to grasp the hem of his tunic. Iachimo tugged impatiently, then broke off the statue's fingers, one by one. They made a dry snapping sound, and fell to dust when they struck the floor.

Iachimo brushed his hands together briskly and said, "My master has revived certain technologies long thought forgotten. It is the basis of his fortune and his power. You understand why you will be of considerable interest to him."

Yama realized that this was a question, but he did not know how to begin to answer it. Instead, he said, "It is a very old edition of the Puranas."

"Oh, the book. Like you, it is not an original, but it is not far removed. You have read it?"

"Yes."

"Don't tell my master that. Tell him you stole it, nothing more. Lie if you must; otherwise he may well have you killed on the spot, and that is something that will be difficult for me to prevent. He controls the guards here. Let us go. He is waiting."

On the far side of the courtyard was an arched doorway and a broad flight of marble steps that led down toward a pool of warm white light. Iachimo's long, pointed nails dug into Yama's shoulder, pricking his skin through his shirt.

"Stand straight," Iachimo said. "Use your backbone as it was intended. Remember that you were made in the image of the Preservers, and forget that your ancestors were animals that went about on all fours. Good. Now walk forward, and do not stare at anything. Most especially, do not stare at my master. He is more sensitive than he might appear. He has not always been as he is now."

20

The Hollow Man

EVEN BEFORE YAMA reached the bottom of the stairs, he knew that there was a large number of machines ahead of him, but the size of the room was still surprising. Golden pillars twisted into fantastic shapes marched away across an emerald green lawn, lending perspective to a space perhaps a thousand paces long and three hundred wide. The lawn was studded with islands of couches upholstered in brilliant silks, and fountains and dwarf fruit trees and statues—these last merely of red sandstone or marble, not petrified flesh. Displays of exotic flowers perfumed the air. Constellations of brilliant white lights floated in the air beneath a high glass ceiling. Above the glass was not air but water—schools of golden and black carp lazily swam through illuminated currents, and pads of water lilies hung above them like the silhouettes of clouds.

Thousands of tiny machines crawled amongst the closely trimmed blades of grass or spun through the bright air like silver beetles or dragonflies with mica wings, their thoughts a single rising harmonic in Yama's head. Men in scarlet and white uniforms and silver helmets stood in alcoves carved into the marble walls. They were unnaturally still and, like the fallen guard at the gate, emitted faint glimmers of machine intelligence, as if machines inhabited their skulls.

As Yama walked across the lawn, with Iachimo following close behind, he heard music in the distance: the chiming runs of a tambura like silver laughter over the solemn pulse of a tabla. A light sculpture twisted in the air like a writhing column of brightly colored scarves seen through a heat haze.

The two musicians sat in a nest of embroidered silk cushions to one side of a huge couch on which lay the fattest man Yama had ever seen. He was naked except for a loincloth, and as hairless as a seal. A gold circlet crowned his shaven head. The thick folds of his belly spilled his flanks and draped his swollen thighs. His black skin shone with oils and unguents; the light of the sculpture slid over it in greasy rainbows. He was propped on his side amongst cushions and bolsters, and pawed in a distracted fashion at a naked woman who was feeding him pastries from a pile stacked high on a silver salver. Without doubt, this was the master of the house, the merchant, the rogue star-sailor.

Yama halted a few paces from him and bowed from the waist, but the merchant did not acknowledge him. Yama stood and sweated, with Iachimo beside him, while the musicians played through the variations of their raga and the merchant ate a dozen pastries one after the other and stroked the gleaming pillows of the woman's large breasts with swollen, ring-encrusted fingers. Like her master, the woman was quite without hair. The petals of her labia were pierced with rings; from one of these rings a fine gold chain ran to a bracelet on the merchant's wrist.

When the concluding chimes of the tambura had died away, the merchant closed his eyes and sighed deeply, then waved at the musicians in dismissal. "Drink," he said in a high, wheezing voice. The woman jumped up and poured red wine into a bowl which she held to the merchant's lips. He slobbered at the wine horribly and it spilled over his chin and chest onto the grassy floor. Yama saw now that the cushions of the couch were stained with old spillages and littered with crumbs and half-eaten crusts; underlying the rich scents of spikenard and jasmine and the sweet smoke of candles which floated in a bowl of water was a stale reek of old sweat and spoiled food.

The merchant belched and glanced at Yama. His cheeks were so puffed with fat that they pushed his mouth into a squashed rosebud, and his eyes peered above their ramparts like sentries, darting here and there as if expecting a sudden attack from any quarter. He said petulantly, "What's this, Iachimo? A little old for your tastes, isn't he?"

Iachimo inclined his head. "Very amusing, master, but you know that I would never trouble you with my bed companions. Perhaps you might look more closely. I believe that you will find he is a rare type, one not seen on Confluence for many an age."

The merchant waved a doughy paw in front of his face, as if trying to swat a fly. "You are always playing games, Iachimo. It will be your downfall. Tell me and have done with it."

"I believe that he is one of the Builders," Iachimo said.

The merchant laughed—a series of grunts that convulsed his vast, gleaming body as a storm tosses the surface of the river. At last he said, "Your inventive mind never ceases to amaze me, Iachimo. I'll grant he has the somatype, but this is some river-rat a mountebank has surgically altered, no doubt inspired by some old carving or slate. You've been had."

"He came here of his own accord. He brought a book of great antiquity. I have it here."

The merchant took the copy of the Puranas from Iachimo and pawed through it, grunting to himself, before casually tossing it aside. It landed facedown and splayed open amongst the cushions on which the merchant sprawled. Yama made a move to retrieve it, but Iachimo caught his arm.

"I've seen better," the merchant said. "If this fake says he brought you an original of the Puranas, then that too will be a fake. I'm no longer interested. Take this creature away, Iachimo, and its book. Dispose of it in the usual way, and dispose of its companion, too, once you've caught it. Or do I have to take charge of the guards and do that myself?"

"It won't be necessary, master. The other boy is certainly no more than a river-rat. He won't be missed. But this one is something rarer." Iachimo prodded Yama in the small of the back with a fingernail as sharply pointed as a stiletto and whispered, "Show him what you can do."

"I do not understand what you want of me."

"Oh, you understand," Iachimo hissed. "I know what you can do with machines. You got past the gatekeeper, so you know something of your inheritance."

The merchant said, "I'm in an indulgent mood, Iachimo. Here's your test. I'm going to order my soldiers to kill you, boy. Do you understand? Stop them, and we'll talk some more. Otherwise I'm rid of a fraud."

Four of the guards started forward from their niches. Yama stepped back involuntarily as the guards, their faces expressionless beneath the bills of their silver helmets, raised their gleaming falchions and marched stiffly across the lawn toward him, two on the right, two on the left.

Iachimo said in a wheedling tone, "Master, surely this isn't necessary."

"Let me have my fun," the merchant said. "What is he to you, eh?"

Yama put his hand inside his satchel and found the hilt of his knife, but the guards were almost upon him and he knew that he could not fight four at once. He felt a tingling expansion and shouted at the top of his voice. "Stop! Stop now!"

The guards froze in midstep, then, moving as one, knelt and laid down their falchions, and bent until their silver helmets touched the grass.

The merchant reared up and squealed, "What is this? Do you betray me, Iachimo?"

"Quite the reverse, master. I'll kill him in a moment, if you give the word. But you see that he is no mountebank's fake."

The merchant glared at Yama. There was a high whine, like a bee trapped in a bottle, and a machine dropped through the air and hovered in front of Yama's face. Red light flashed in the backs of his eyes. He asked the machine to go away, but the red light flashed again, filling his vision. He could see nothing but the red light and held himself still, although panic trembled in his breast like a trapped dove. He could feel every corner of the machine's small bright mind, but by a sudden inversion, as if a flower had suddenly dwindled down to the seed from which it had sprung, it was closed to him.

Somewhere beyond the red light, the merchant said, "Recently born. No revenant. Where is he from, Iachimo?"

"Downriver," Iachimo said, close by Yama's ear. "Not far downriver, though. There's a small town called Aeolis amongst the old tombs. The book at least comes from there."

The merchant said, "The City of the Dead. There are older tombs elsewhere on Confluence, but I suppose you aren't to know that. Boy, stop trying to control my machines. I have told them to ignore you, and fortunately for you, you don't know the extent of your abilities. Fortunate for you, too, Iachimo. You risked a great deal bringing him here. I'll not forget that."

Iachimo said, "I am yours to punish or reward, master. As always. But be assured that this boy does not understand what he is. Otherwise I would not have been able to capture him."

"He's done enough damage. I have reviewed the security systems, something you haven't troubled to do. He blinded the watchdogs and the machines patrolling the grounds, which is why he and his friend could wander the grounds with impunity. I have restored them. He has killed the gatekeeper too, and his friend is armed. Wait—there are two of them, both armed, and loose in the grounds. The security system was told to ignore them, but I'm tracking them now. You have let things get out of hand, Iachimo."

"I had no reason to believe the security system was not operating correctly, master, but it proves my point. Here is a rare treasure."

Yama turned his head back and forth, but could see nothing but red mist. There was a splinter of pain in each of his eyes. He said, "Am I blinded?" and his voice was smaller and weaker than he would have liked.

"I suppose it isn't necessary," the merchant said, and the red mist was gone.

Yama knuckled his stinging eyes, blinking hard in the sudden bright light. Two of the guards stood at attention behind the merchant's couch, their red and white uniforms gleaming, their falchions held before their faces as if at parade.

The merchant said, "Don't mind my toys. They won't harm you as long as you're sensible." His voice was silkily unctuous now. "Drink, eat. I have nothing but the best. The best vintages, the finest meats, the tenderest vegetables."

"Some wine, perhaps. Thank you."

The naked woman poured wine as rich and red as fresh blood into a gold beaker and handed it to Yama, then poured another bowl for the merchant, who slobbered it down before Yama could do more than sip his. He expected some rare vintage, and was disappointed to discover that it was no better than the ordinary wine of the peel-house's cellars.

The merchant smacked his lips and said, "Do you know what I am? And do stop trying to take control of my servants. You will give me a headache."

Yama had been trying to persuade one of the machines which illuminated the room to fly down and settle above his head, but despite his sense of expansion, as if his thoughts had become larger than his skull, he might as well have tried to order an ossifrage to quit its icy perch in the high foothills of the Rim Mountains. He stared at the gold circlet on the merchant's fleshy, hairless pate, and said, "You are really one of those things which crew the voidships. I suppose that you stole the body."

"As a matter of fact I had it grown. Do you like it?"

Yama took another sip of wine. He felt calmer now. He said, "I am amazed by it."

"You have been raised to be polite. That's good. It will make things easier, eh, Iachimo?"

"I'm sure he could stand a little more polishing, master."

"I've yet to find a body that can withstand my appetites," the merchant told Yama, "but that's of little consequence, because there are always more bodies. This is my—what is it, Iachimo? The tenth?"

"The ninth, master."

"Well, there will soon be need for a tenth, and there will be more, an endless chain. How old are you, boy? No more than twenty, I'd guess. This body is half that age."

The merchant pawed at the breasts of the woman. She was feeding him sugared almonds, popping them into his mouth each time it opened. He chewed the almonds mechanically, and a long string of pulp and saliva drooled unheeded down his chin.

He said, "I've been male and female in my time, too. Mostly male, given the current state of civilization, but now that I've made my fortune and have no need to leave my estate, perhaps I'll be female next time. Are there others like you?"

"That is what I want to discover," Yama said. "You know of my bloodline. You know more than me, it seems. You called me a builder. A builder of what?"

But he already knew. He had read in the Puranas, and he remembered the man in the picture slate which Osric and Beatrice had shown him.

Iachimo said, " 'And the Preservers raised up a man and set on his brow their mark, and raised up a woman of the same kind, and set on her brow the same mark. From the white clay of the middle region did they shape this race, and quickened them with their marks. And those of this race were the servants of the Preservers. And in their myriads this race shaped the world after the ideas of the Preservers.' There's more, but you get the general idea. Those are your people, boy. So long dead that almost no one remembers—"

Suddenly, the room brightened: white light flashed beyond the lake which hung above the long room. Rafts of waterlily pads swung wildly on clashing waves and there was a deep, heavy muffled sound, as if a massive door had slammed in the keel of the world.

The merchant said, "No hope there, boy. You put some of my guards to sleep, but they're all under my control again, and almost have your two friends. Iachimo, you did not say that one of them was a cateran."

"There was another boy, master. I knew of no other."

The merchant closed his eyes. For a moment, Yama felt that a thousand intelligences lived in his head. Then the feeling was gone and the merchant said, "She has killed several guards, but one caught a glimpse of her. She's of the Fierce People, and she's armed with one of the gatekeeper's pistols."

"There are still many guards, master, and many machines. Besides, the lake will absorb any blast from the pistol."

The merchant pulled the woman close to him. "He's an assassin's tool, you idiot! Why else would a cateran come here? You know I have been expecting this ever since my old ship returned through the manifold."

"There was the man who broke into the godown," Iachimo said, "but we dealt with him easily enough."

"It was just the beginning. They won't rest—"

There was another flash of white light. A portion of water above the glass ceiling seethed into a spreading cloud of white bubbles, and the glass rang like a cracked bell.

The merchant closed his eyes briefly, then relaxed and drew the naked woman closer. "Well, it doesn't matter now. There's a weapon in his satchel, Iachimo. Take it out and give it to me."

The white-haired man lifted out the sheathed knife and said, "It is only a knife, master."

"I know what it is. Bring it here."

Iachimo offered the sheathed knife, hilt first. Yama implored it to manifest the horrible shape which had frightened Lob and the landlord of *The Crossed Axes,* but he was at the center of a vast muffling silence. The merchant squinted at the knife's goatskin sheath, and then the woman drew it and plunged it into Iachimo's belly.

Iachimo grunted and fell to his knees. The knife flashed blue fire and the woman screamed and dropped it and clutched her smoking hand. The knife embedded itself point first in the grass, sizzling faintly and emitting a drizzle of fat blue motes. Iachimo was holding his belly with both hands. There was blood all over his fingers and the front of his black tunic.

The merchant looked at the woman and she fell silent in mid-scream. He said to Yama, "So die all those who think to betray me. Now, boy, you'll answer all my questions truthfully, or you'll join your two friends. Yes, they have been captured. Not dead, not yet. We'll talk, you and I, and decide their fate."

Iachimo, kneeling over the knife and a pool of his own blood, said something about a circle, and then the guards seized him and jerked him upright and cut his throat and lifted him away from the merchant, all in one quick motion. They dropped the body onto the neatly trimmed

grass beneath the light sculpture and returned to their position behind
the merchant's couch.

"You're trouble, boy," the merchant said. The woman tremblingly
placed the mouthpiece of a clay pipe between his rosebud lips and lit
the scrap of resin in its bowl. He drew a long breath and said, dribbling
smoke with the words, "Your people were the first. The rest came later,
but you were the first. I had never thought to see your kind again, but
this is an age of wonders. Listen to me, boy, or I'll have you killed too.
You see how easy it is."

Yama was holding the wine goblet so tightly that he had reopened
the wound in his palm. He threw it away and said as boldly as he could,
"Will you spare my friends?"

"They came to kill me, didn't they? Sent by my crewmates, who
are jealous of me."

Yama could not deny it. He stared in stubborn silence at the merchant, who calmly drew on his pipe and contemplated the wreaths of
smoke he breathed out. At last, the merchant said, "The woman is a
cateran, and their loyalty is easily bought. I might have a use for her.
The boy is no different from a million other river-rats in Ys. I could
kill him and it would be as if he had never been born. I see that you
want him to live. You are very sentimental. Well then. You must prove
your worth to me, and perhaps the boy will live. Do you know exactly
what you are?"

Yama said, "You say that I am of the bloodline of the Builders,
and I have seen an ancient picture showing one of my kind before the
world was made. But I also have been told that I might be a child of
the Ancients of Days."

"Hmm. It's possible they had something to do with it. In their brief
time here they meddled in much that didn't concern them. They didn't
achieve anything of consequence, of course. For all that they might have
appeared as gods to the degenerate population of Confluence, they predated the Preservers by several million years. Their kind were the ancestors of the Preservers, but with about as much relation to them as
the brainless plankton grazers which were the ancestors of my own
bloodline have to me. It is only because the Ancients of Days were
timeshifted while travelling to our neighboring galaxy and back at close
to the speed of light that they appeared so late, like an actor delayed
by circumstance who incontinently rushes on stage to deliver his lines
and finds that he has interrupted the closing soliloquy instead of beginning the second act. We are in the end times, young builder. This whole

grand glorious foolish experiment has all but run its course. The silly little war downriver begun by the Ancients of Days is only a footnote."

The merchant seemed exhausted by this speech, and drank more wine before he continued. "Do you know, I haven't thought about this for a long time. Iachimo was a very clever man, but not a brave one. He was doomed to a servant's role, and resented it. I thought at first you were some scheme of his, and I haven't fully dismissed the thought from my mind. I do not believe that it was through simple carelessness that he allowed the cateran to roam free, or that you were allowed to carry a knife into my presence."

"I have never seen him before tonight. I am not the servant of any man."

The merchant said, "Don't be a fool. Like most here, your bloodline was created as servants to the immediate will of the Preservers."

"We all serve the Preservers as we can," Yama said.

"You've been in the hands of a priest," the merchant said. His gaze was shrewd. "You parrot his pious phrases, but do you really believe them?"

Yama could not answer. His faith was never something he had questioned, but now he saw that by disobeying the wishes of his father he had rebelled against his place in the social hierarchy, and had not that hierarchy proceeded from the Preservers? So the priests taught, but now Yama was unsure. For the priests also taught that the Preservers wanted their creations to advance from a low to a high condition, and how could that happen if society was fixed, eternal and unchanging?

The merchant belched. "You are just a curiosity, boy. A revenant. An afterthought or an accident—it's all the same. But you might be useful, even so. You and I might do great things together. You asked why I am here. It is because I have remembered what all others of my kind have long forgotten. They are lost in ascetic contemplation of the mathematics of the manifolds and the secrets of the beginning and end of the cosmos, but I have remembered the pleasures of the real world, of appetite and sex and all the rest of the messy wonderful business of life. They would say that mathematics is the reality underlying everything; I say that it is an abstraction of the real world, a ghost." He belched again. "There is my riposte to algebra."

Yama made a wild intuitive leap. He said, "You met the Ancients of Days, didn't you?"

"My ship hailed theirs, as it fell through the void toward the Eye of the Preservers. They had seen the Eye's construction by ancient light while hundreds of thousands of years out, and were amazed to discover that organic intelligent life still existed. We merged our mindscapes and talked long there, and I followed them out into the world. And here I am. It is remarkably easy to make a fortune in these benighted times, but I'm finding that merely satisfying sensual appetites is not enough. If you're truly a Builder, and I am not quite convinced that you are, then perhaps you can help me. I have plans."

"I believe that I am no man's servant. I cannot serve you as Iachimo did."

The merchant laughed. "I would hope not. You will have to unlearn your arrogance to begin with; then I will see what I can make of you. I can teach you many things, boy. I can realize your potential. There are many like Iachimo in the world, intelligent and learned and quite without the daring to act on their convictions. There is no end to natural followers like him. You are something more. I must think hard about it, and so will you. But you will serve, or you will die, and so will your friends."

The twisting scarves of color in the light sculpture ran together into a steely gray and widened into a kind of window, showing Tamora and Pandaras kneeling inside tiny cages suspended in dark air.

For a moment, Yama's breath caught in his throat. He said, "Let them go, and I will serve you as I can."

The merchant shifted his immense oiled bulk. "I think not. I'll give you a taste of their fate while I decide how I can make use of you. When you can make that promise from your heart, then we can talk again."

The two guards turned toward Yama, who stared in sudden panic into their blank, blind faces. His panic inflated into something immense, a great wild bird he had loosed, its wings beating at the edges of his sight. In desperation, quite without hope, his mind threw out an immense imploring scream for help.

The merchant pawed at his head and far down the room something struck the glass ceiling with a tremendous bang. For a moment, all was still. Then a line of spray sheeted down, and the glass around it gave with a loud splintering crash. The spray became a widening waterfall that poured down and rebounded from the floor and sent a tawny wave flooding down the length of the room, knocking over pillars and statues and sweeping tables and couches before it.

The merchant's couch lurched into the air. The woman gave a guttural cry of alarm, and clung to her master's flesh as a shipwrecked sailor clings to a bit of flotsam. Yama dashed forward through surging water (for a moment, Iachimo's corpse clutched at his ankles; then it was swept away), made a desperate leap and caught hold of one end of the rising couch. His weight rocked it on its long axis, so violently that for one moment he hung straight down, the next tipped forward and fell across the merchant's legs.

The merchant roared and his woman clawed at Yama with sudden fury, her long nails opening his forehead so that blood poured into his eyes. The couch turned in a dizzy circle above the guards as they struggled to stay upright in the seething flood. The merchant caught at Yama's hands, but his grasp was feeble, and Yama, half-blinded, grabbed the golden circlet around the man's fleshy scalp and pulled with all his strength.

For a moment, he feared that the circlet would not give way. Then it snapped in half and unravelled like a ribbon. All the lights went out. The couch tipped and Yama and the merchant and the woman fell into the wash of the flood. Yama went under and got a mouthful of muddy water and came up spitting and gasping.

The guards had fallen; so had all the machines.

Yama asked a question, and after a moment points of intense white light flared down the length of the room, burning through the swirling brown flood. Yama wiped blood from his eyes. The current swirled around his waist. He was clutching a tangle of golden filaments tipped with stringy fragments of flesh.

At the far end of the huge room, something floated a handspan above the water, turning slowly end for end. It was as big as Yama's head, and black, and decorated all over with spikes of varying lengths and thickness, some like rose thorns, others long and finely tapered and questing this way and that with blind intelligence. The thing radiated a black icy menace, a negation not only of life, but of the reality of the world. For a moment, Yama was transfixed; then the machine rose straight up, smashing through the ceiling. Yama felt it rise higher and higher, and for a moment felt all the machines in Ys turn toward it— but it was gone.

The merchant sprawled across the fallen couch like a beached grampus. A ragged wound crowned his head, streaming blood; he snorted a jelly of blood and mucus through his nose. The woman lay beneath him, entirely submerged. Her head was twisted back, and her eyes looked up through the swirling water. Up and down the length of the room, the guards were dead, too.

Yama held the frayed remnants of the circlet before the merchant's eyes, and said, "Iachimo told me about this with his last breath, but I had already guessed its secret. I saw something like it on the lighter."

"The Preservers have gone away," the merchant whispered.

The floodwaters were receding, running away into deeper levels of the sunken house. Yama knelt by the couch and said, "Why am I here?"

The merchant drew a breath. Blood ran from his nostrils and his mouth. He said wetly, "Serve no one."

"If the Preservers are gone, why was I brought back?"

The merchant tried to say something, but only blew a bubble of blood. Yama left him there and went to find Tamora and Pandaras.

21

The Fierce People

TAMORA CAME BACK to the campfire at a loping run. She was grinning broadly and there was blood around her mouth. She threw a brace of coneys at Yama's feet and said proudly, "This is how we live, when we can. We are the Fierce People, the Memsh Tek!"

Pandaras said, "Not all of us can live on meat alone."

"Your kind have to exist on leaves and the filth swept into street gutters," Tamora said, "and that is why they are so weak. Meat and blood are what warriors need, so be glad that I give you fine fresh guts. They will make you strong."

She slit the bellies of the conies with her sharp thumbnail, crammed the steaming, rich red livers into her mouth and gulped them down. Then she pulled the furry skins from the gutted bodies, as someone might strip gloves from their hands, and set about dismembering them with teeth and nails.

She had attacked the merchant's carcass with the same butcher's skill, using a falchion taken from one of the dead guards to fillet it from neck to buttocks and expose the thing which had burrowed into the fatty flesh like a hagfish. It was not much like the bottled creature Yama had seen on the lighter. Its mantle was shrunken, and white fibers had knitted around its host's spinal column like cords of fungus in rotten wood.

Tamora kept most of the coney meat for herself and ate it raw, but she allowed Yama and Pandaras to cook the haunches over the embers of the fire. The unsalted meat was half-burned and half-raw, but Yama and Pandaras hungrily stripped it from the bones.

"Burnt meat is bad for the digestion," Tamora said, grinning at them across the embers of the fire. She wore only her leather skirt. Her two pairs of breasts were little more than enlarged nipples, like tarnished coins set on her narrow ribcage. In addition to the bird burning in a nest of fire on her upper arm, inverted triangles were tattooed in black ink on her shoulders. There was a bandage around her waist; she had been seared by backflash from a guard's pistol shot. She took a swallow of brandy and passed the bottle to Yama. He had bought the brandy in a bottleshop and used a little to preserve the filaments Tamora had flensed from the merchant's body and placed in a beautiful miniature flask, cut from a single crystal of rose quartz, which Yama had found in the wreckage left by the flood when he had been searching for his copy of the Puranas.

Yama drank and passed the bottle to Pandaras, who was cracking coney bones between his sharp teeth.

"Drink," Tamora said. "We fought a great battle today."

Pandaras spat a bit of gristle into the fire. He had already made it clear how unhappy he was to be in the Fierce People's tract of wild country, and he sat with his kidney puncher laid across his lap and his mobile ears pricked. He said, "I'd rather keep my wits about me."

Tamora laughed. "No one would mistake you for a coney. You're about the right size, but you can't run fast enough to make the hunt interesting."

Pandaras took the smallest possible sip from the brandy bottle and passed it back to Yama. He told Tamora, "You certainly ran when the soldiers came."

"Grah. I was trying to catch up with you to make sure you went the right way."

"Enough stuff to set a man up for life," Pandaras said, "and we had to leave it for the city militia to loot."

"I'm a cateran, not a robber. We have done what we contracted to do. Be happy." Tamora grinned. Her pink tongue lolled amongst her big, sharp teeth. "Eat burnt bones. Drink. Sleep. We are safe here, and tomorrow we are paid."

Yama realized that she was drunk. The bottle of brandy had been the smallest he could buy, but it was still big enough, as Pandaras put it, to drown a baby. They had needed only a few minims to fill the crystal flask, and Tamora had drunk about half of what was left.

"Safe?" Pandaras retorted. "In the middle of any number of packs of bloodthirsty howlers like you? I won't sleep at all tonight."

"I will sing a great song of our triumph, and you will listen. Pass that bottle, Yama. It is not your child."

Yama took a burning swallow of brandy, handed the bottle over, and walked out of the firelight to the crest of the ridge. The sandy hills where the Fierce People maintained their hunting grounds looked out across the wide basin of the city toward the Great River. The misty light of the Arm of the Warrior was rising above the farside horizon. It was past midnight. The city was mostly dark, but many campfires flickered amongst the scrub and clumps of crown ferns, pines and eucalyptus of the Fierce People's hunting grounds, and from every quarter came the sound of distant voices raised in song.

Yama sat on the dry grass and listened to the night music of the Fierce People. The feral machine still haunted him, like a ringing in the ears or the afterimage of a searingly bright light. And beyond this psychic echo he could feel the ebb and flow of the myriad machines in the city, like the flexing of a great net. They had also been disturbed by the feral machine, and the ripples of alarm caused by the disturbance were still spreading, leaping from cluster to cluster of machines along the docks, running out toward the vast bulk of the Palace of the Memory of the People, clashing at the bases of the high towers and racing up their lengths out of the atmosphere.

Yama still did not know how he had called down the feral machine, and although it had saved him he feared that he might call it again by accident, and feared too that he had exposed himself to discovery by the network of machines which served the magistrates, or by Prefect Corin, who must surely still be searching for him. The descent of the feral machine was the most terrifying and the most shameful of his adventures. He had been paralyzed with fear when confronted with it, and even now he felt that it had marked him in some obscure way, for some small part of him yearned for it, and what it could tell him. It could be watching him still; it could return at any time, and he did not know what he would do if it did.

The merchant—Yama still found it difficult to think of him as the parasitic bundle of nerve fibers burrowed deep within that tremendously fat body—had said that he was a Builder, a member of the first bloodline of Ys. The pilot of the voidship had said something similar, and the slate that Beatrice and Osric had shown him had suggested the same thing. His people had walked Confluence in its first days, sculpting the world under the direct instruction of the Preservers, and had died out or ascended ages past, so long ago that most had forgotten them. And yet he was here, and he still did not know why; nor did he know the full extent of his powers.

The merchant had hinted that he knew what Yama was capable of, but he might have been lying to serve his own ends, and besides, he was dead. Perhaps the other star-sailors knew—Iachimo had said that they were very long-lived—or perhaps, as Yama had hoped even before he had set out from Aeolis, there were records somewhere in Ys that would explain everything, or at least lead him to others of his kind. He still did not know how he had been brought into the world, or why he had been found floating on the river on the breast of a dead woman who might have been his mother or nurse or something else entirely, but surely he had been born to serve the Preservers in some fashion. After the Preservers had fallen into the event horizon of the Eye, they could still watch the world they had made, for nothing fell faster than light, but they could no longer act upon it. But perhaps their reach was long—perhaps they had ordained his birth, here in what the merchant had called the end times, long before they had withdrawn from the Universe. Perhaps, as Derev believed, many of Yama's kind now walked the world, as they had at its beginning. But for what purpose? All through his childhood he had prayed for a revelation, a sign, a hint, and had received nothing. Perhaps he should expect nothing else. Perhaps the shape of his life was the sign he sought, if only he could understand it.

But he could not believe he was the servant of the feral machines. That was the worst thought of all.

Yama sat on a hummock of dry grass, with the noise of crickets everywhere in the darkness around him, and leafed through his copy of the Puranas. The book had dried out well, although one corner of its front cover was faintly but indelibly stained with the merchant's blood. The pages held a faint light, and the glyphs stood out like shadows against this soft effulgence. Yama found the sura which Iachimo had quoted, and read it from beginning to end.

The world first showed itself as a golden embryo of sound. As soon as the thoughts of the Preservers turned to the creation of the world, the long vowel which described the form of the world vibrated in the pure realm of thought, and re-echoed on itself. From the knots in the play of vibrations, the crude matter of the world curdled. In the beginning, it was no more than a sphere of air and water with a little mud at the center.

And the Preservers raised up a man and set on his brow their mark, and raised up a woman of the same kind, and set on her brow the same mark. From the white clay of the middle region did they shape this race, and quickened them with their marks. And those of this race were the servants of the Preservers. And in their

*myriads this race shaped the world after the ideas of the Pre-
servers.*

Yama read on, although the next sura was merely an exhaustive
description of the dimensions and composition of the world, and he
knew that there was no other mention of the Builders, nor of their fate.
This was toward the end of the Puranas. The world and everything in
it was an afterthought at the end of the history of the Galaxy, created
in the last moment before the Preservers fell into the Eye and were
known no more in the Universe. Nothing had been written about the
ten thousand bloodlines of Confluence in the Puranas; if there had been,
then there would have never been a beginning to the endless disputations
amongst priests and philosophers about the reason for the world's creation.

Tamora said, "Reading, is it? There's nothing in books you can't
learn better in the world, nothing but fantastic rubbish about monsters
and the like. You'll rot your mind and your eyes, reading too much in
books."

"Well, I met a real monster today."

"And he's dead, the fucker, and we have a piece of him in brandy
as proof. So much for him."

Yama had not told Tamora and Pandaras about the feral machine.
Tamora had boasted that one of her pistol shots had weakened the ceiling and so caused the flood which had saved them, and Yama had not
corrected her error. He felt a rekindling of shame at this deception, and
said weakly, "I suppose the merchant was a kind of monster. He tried
to flee from his true self, and let a little hungry part of himself rule his
life. He was all appetite and nothing else. I think he would have eaten
the whole world, if he could."

"You want to be a soldier. Here's some advice. Don't think about
what you have to do and don't think about it when it's done."

"And can you forget it so easily?"

"Of course not. But I try. We were captured, your rat-boy and me,
and thrown into cages, but you had it worse, I think. The merchant was
trying to bend you toward his will. The words of his kind are like thorns,
and some of them are still in your flesh. But they'll wither, and you'll
forget them."

Yama smiled and said, "Perhaps it would be no bad thing, to be the
ruler of the world."

Tamora sat down close beside him. She was a shadow in the darkness. She said, "You would destroy the civil service and rule instead? How would that change the world for the better?"

Yama could feel her heat. She gave off a strong scent compounded of fresh blood and sweat and a sharp musk. He said, "Of course not. But the merchant told me something about my bloodline. I may be alone in the world. I may be a mistake thrown up at the end of things. Or I may be something else. Something *intended*."

"The fat fuck was lying. How better to get you to follow him than by saying that you are the only one of your kind, and he knows all about you?"

"I am not sure that he was lying, Tamora. At least, I think he was telling part of the truth."

"I haven't forgotten what you want, and I was a long time hunting coneys because I really went to ask around. Listen. I have a way of getting at what you want. There is a job for a couple of caterans. Some little pissant department needs someone to organize a defense of its territory inside the Palace of the Memory of the People. There are many disputes between departments, and the powerful grow strong at the expense of the weak. That's the way of the world, but I don't mind defending the weak if I get paid for it."

"Then perhaps they may be stronger than you after all."

"Grah. Listen. When a litter is born here, the babies are exposed on a hillside for a day. Any that are weak die, or are taken by birds or foxes. We're the Fierce People, see? We keep our bloodline strong. The wogs and wetbacks and snakes and the rest of the garbage down there in the city, they're what we prey on. They need us, not the other way around." Tamora spat sideways. Yes, she had drunk a lot of brandy. She said, "There's prey, and there's hunters. You have to decide which you are. You don't know, now is the time you find out. Are you for it?"

"It seems like a good plan."

"Somewhere or other you've picked up the habit of not speaking plain. You mean yes, then say it."

"Yes. Yes, I will do it. If it means getting into the Palace of the Memory of the People."

"Then you got to pay me, because I found it for you, and I'll do the work."

"I know something about fighting."

Tamora spat again. "Listen, this is a dangerous job. This little department is certain to be attacked and they don't have a security office or they wouldn't be hiring someone from outside. They're bound to lose, see, but if it's done right then only their thralls will get killed. We can probably escape, or at worse lose our bond when we're ransomed, but I won't deny there's a chance we'll get killed, too. You still want it?"

"It is a way in."

"Exactly. This department used to deal in prognostication, but it is much debased. There are only a couple of seers left, but it is highly placed in the Palace of the Memory of the People, and other more powerful departments want to displace it. It needs us to train its thralls so they can put up some kind of defense, but there will be time for you to search for whatever it is you're looking for. We will agree payment now. You'll pay any expenses out of your share of the fees for killing the merchant and for this new job, and I keep my half of both fees, and half again of anything that's left of yours."

"Is that a fair price?"

"Grah. You're supposed to bargain, you idiot! It is twice what the risk is worth."

"I will pay it anyway. If I find out what I want to know, I will have no need of money."

"If you want to join the army as an officer, you'll need plenty, more than you're carrying around now. You'll have to buy the rest of your own armor, and mounts, and weaponry. And if you're looking for information, there will be bribes to be paid. I'll take a quarter of your fees, bargaining against myself like a fool, and share expenses with you. You'll need the rest, believe me."

"You are a good person, Tamora, although I would like you better if you were more tolerant. No one bloodline should raise itself above any other."

"I'll do well enough out of this, believe me. One other thing. We won't tell the rat-boy about this. We do this without him."

"Are you scared of him because he killed the gatekeeper?"

"If I was scared of any of his kind, I would never dare spit in the gutter again, for fear of hitting one in the eye. Let him come if he must, but I won't pretend I like it, and any money he wants comes from you, not me."

"He is like me, Tamora. He wants to be other than his fate."

"Then he's certainly as big a fool as you." Tamora handed Yama the brandy bottle. It was almost empty. "Drink. Then you will listen to me sing our victory song. The rat-boy is scared to sit with my brothers and sisters, but I know you won't be."

———

Although Yama tried not to show it, he was intimidated by the proud, fierce people who sat around the campfire: an even decad of Tamora's kin, heavily muscled men and women marked on their shoulders by identical tattoos of inverted triangles. Most intimidating of all was a straight-backed matriarch with a white mane and a lacework of fine scars across her naked torso, who watched Yama with red-backed eyes from the other side of the fire while Tamora sang.

Tamora's victory song was a discordant open-throated ululation that rose and twisted like a sharp silver wire into the black air above the flames of the campfire. When it was done, she took a long swig from a wine skin while the men and women murmured and nodded and showed their fangs in quick snarling smiles, although one complained loudly that the song had been less about Tamora and more about this whey-skinned stranger.

"That is because it was his adventure," Tamora said.

"Then let him sing for himself," the man grumbled.

The matriarch asked Tamora about Yama, saying that she had not seen his kind before.

"He's from downriver, grandmother."

"That would explain it. I'm told that there are many strange peoples downriver, although I myself have never troubled to go and see, and now I am too old to have to bother. Talk with me, boy. Tell me how your people came into the world."

"That is a mystery, even to myself. I have read something in the Puranas about my people, and I have seen a picture of one in an old slate, but that is all I know."

"Then your people are very strange indeed," the matriarch said. "Every bloodline has its story and its mysteries and its three names. The Preservers chose to raise up each bloodline in their image for a particular reason, and the stories explain why. You won't find your real story in that book you carry. That's about older mysteries, and not about this world at all." She cuffed one of the women and snatched a wine skin from her. "They keep this from me," she told Yama, "because they're frightened I'll disgrace myself if I get drunk."

"Nothing could make you drunk, grandmother," one of the men said. "That's why we ration your drinking, or you'd poison yourself trying."

The matriarch spat into the fire. "A mouthful of this rotgut will poison me. Can no one afford proper booze? In the old days we would have used this to fuel our lamps."

Yama still had the brandy bottle, with a couple of fingers of clear, apricot-scented liquor at its bottom. "Here, grandmother," he said, and handed it to the matriarch.

The old woman drained the bottle and licked her lips in appreciation. "Do you know how we came into the world, boy? I'll tell you."

Several of the people around the fire groaned, and the matriarch said sharply, "It'll do you good to hear it again. You young people don't know the stories as well as you should. Listen, then.

"After the world was made, some of the Preservers set animals down on its surface, and kindled intelligence in them. There are a people descended from coyotes, for instance, whose ancestors were taught by the Preservers to bury their dead. This odd habit brought about a change in the coyotes, for they learned to sit up so they could sit beside the graves and mourn their dead properly. But sitting on cold stone wore away their bushy tails, and after many generations they began standing upright because the stone was uncomfortable to their naked arses. When that happened, their forepaws lengthened into human hands, and their sharp muzzles shortened bit by bit until they became human faces. That's one story, and there are as many stories as there are bloodlines descended from the different kinds of animals which were taught to become human. But our own people had a different origin.

"Two of the Preservers fell into an argument about the right way to make human people. The Preservers do not have sexes as we understand them, nor do they marry, but it is easier to follow the story if we think of them as wife and husband. One, Enki, was the Preserver who had charge of the world's water, and so his work was hard, for in those early times all there was of the world was the Great River, running from nowhere to nowhere. He complained of his hard work to his wife, Ninmah, who was the Preserver of earth, and she suggested that they create a race of marionettes or puppets who would do the work for them. And this they did, using the small amount of white silt that was suspended in the Great River. I see that you know this part of the story."

"Someone told me a little of it today. It is to be found in the Puranas."

"What I tell you is truer, for it has been told from mouth to ear for ten thousand generations, and so its words still live, and have not become dead things squashed flat on plastic or pulped wood. Well then, after this race was produced from the mud of the river, there was a great celebration because the Preservers no longer needed to work on their creation. Much beer was consumed, and Ninmah became especially light-headed. She called to Enki, saying, 'How good or bad is a human body? I could reshape it in any way I please, but could you find tasks for it?' Enki responded to this challenge, and so Ninmah made a barren woman, and a eunuch, and several other cripples.

"But Enki found tasks for them all. The barren woman he made into a concubine; the eunuch he made into a civil servant, and so on. Then in the same playful spirit he challenged Ninmah. He would do the shaping of different races, and she the placing. She agreed, and Enki first made a man whose making was already remote from him, and so the first old man appeared before Ninmah. She offered the old man bread, but he was too feeble to reach for it, and when she thrust the bread into his mouth, he could not chew it for he had no teeth, and so Ninmah could find no use for this unfortunate. Then Enki made many other cripples and monsters, and Ninmah could find no use for them, either.

"The pair fell into a drunken sleep, and when they wakened all was in uproar, for the cripples Enki had made were spreading through the world. Enki and Ninmah were summoned before the other Preservers to explain themselves, and to escape punishment Enki and Ninmah together made a final race, who would hunt the lame and the old, and so make the races of the world stronger by consuming their weak members.

"And so we came into the world, and it is said that we have a quick and cruel temper, because Enki and Ninmah suffered dreadfully from the effects of drinking too much beer when they made us, and that was passed to us as a potmaker leaves her thumbprint in the clay."

"I have heard only the beginning of this story," Yama said, "and I am glad that now I have heard the end of it."

"Now you must tell a story," one of the men said loudly. It was the one who had complained before. He was smaller than the others, but still a head taller than Yama. He wore black leather trousers and a black leather jacket studded with copper nails.

"Be quiet, Gorgo," the matriarch said. "This young man is our guest."

Gorgo looked across the fire at Yama, and Yama met his truculent, challenging gaze. Neither was willing to look away, but then a branch snapped in the fire and sent burning fragments flying into Gorgo's lap. He cursed and brushed at the sparks while the others laughed.

Gorgo glowered and said, "We have heard his boasts echoed in Tamora's song. I simply wonder if he has the heart to speak for himself. He owes that courtesy, I think."

"You're a great one for knowing what's owed," someone said.

Gorgo turned on the man. "I only press for payment when it's needed, as you well know. How much poorer you would be if I didn't find you work! You are all in my debt."

The matriarch said, "That is not to be spoken of. Are we not the Fierce People, whose honor is as renowned as our strength and our temper?"

Gorgo said, "Some people need reminding about honor."

One of the women said, "We fight. You get the rewards."

"Then don't ask me for work," Gorgo said petulantly. "Find your own. I force no one, as is well known, but so many ask for my help that I scarcely have time to sleep or catch my food. But here is our guest. Let's not forget him. We hear great things of him from Tamora. Hush, and let him speak for himself."

Yama thought that Gorgo could speak sweetly when he chose, but the honey of his words disguised his envy and suspicion. Clearly, Gorgo thought that Yama's was one of the trash or vermin bloodlines.

Yama said, "I will tell a story, although I am afraid that it might bore you. It is about how my life was saved by one of the indigens."

Gorgo grumbled that this didn't sound like a true story at all. "Tell something of your people instead," he said. "Please do not tell me that such a fine hero as yourself, if we are to believe the words of our sister here, is so ashamed of his own people that he has to make up stories of sub-human creatures which do not carry the blessing of the Preservers."

Yama smiled. This at least was easy to counter. "I wish I knew such stories, but I was raised as an orphan."

"Perhaps your people were ashamed of you," Gorgo said, but he was the only one to laugh at his sally.

"Tell your story," Tamora said, "and don't let Gorgo interrupt you. He is jealous, because he hasn't any stories of his own."

When Yama began, he realized that he had drunk more than he intended, but he could not back out now. He described how he had been kidnapped and taken to the pinnace, and how he had escaped (making no mention of the ghostly ship) and cast himself upon a banyan island far from shore.

"I found one of the indigenous fisherfolk stuck fast in a trap left by one of the people of the city which my father administers. The people of the city once hunted the fisherfolk, but my father put a stop to it. The unfortunate fisherman had become entangled in a trap made of strong, sticky threads of the kind used to snare bats which skim the surface of the water for fish. I could not free him without becoming caught fast myself, so I set a trap of my own and waited. When the hunter came to collect his prey, as a spider sidles down to claim a fly caught in its web, it was the hunter who became the prey. I took the spray which dissolves the trap's glue, and the fisherman and I made our escape and left the foolish hunter to the torments of those small, voracious hunters who outnumber their prey, mosquitoes and blackflies. In turn, the fisherman fed me and took me back to the shore of the Great River. And so we saved each other."

"A tall tale," Gorgo said, meeting Yama's gaze again.

"It is true I missed out much, but if I told everything then we would be up all night. I will say one more thing. If not for the fisherman's kindness, I would not be here, so I have learnt never to rush to judge any man, no matter how worthless he might appear."

Gorgo said, "He asks us to admire his reflection in his tales. Let me tell you that what I see is a fool. Any sensible man would have devoured the fisherman and taken his coracle and escaped with a full belly."

"I simply told you what happened," Yama said, meeting the man's yellow gaze. "Anything you see in my words is what you have placed there. If you had tried to steal the hunter's prey, you would have been stuck there too, and been butchered and devoured along with the fisherman."

Gorgo jumped up. "I think I know something about hunting, and I do know that you are not as clever as you imagine yourself to be. You side with prey, and so you're no hunter at all."

Yama stood too, for he would not look up from a lesser to a higher position when he replied to Gorgo's insult. Perhaps he would not have done it if he had been less drunk, but he felt the sting of wounded pride. Besides, he did not think that Gorgo was a threat. He was a man who used words as others use weapons. He was taller and heavier than Yama, and armed with a strong jaw and sharp teeth, but Sergeant Rhodean had taught Yama several ways by which such differences could be turned to an advantage.

"I described what happened, no more and no less," Yama said. "I hope I do not need to prove the truth of my words."

Tamora grabbed Yama's hand and said, "Don't mind Gorgo. He has always wanted to fuck me, and I've always refused. He's quick to anger, and jealous."

Gorgo laughed. "I think you have me wrong, sister. It is not your delusion I object to, but his. Remember what you owe me before you insult me again."

"You will both sit down," the matriarch said. "Yama is our guest, Gorgo. You dishonor all of us. Sit down. Drink. We all lose our temper, and the less we make of it the better."

"You all owe me," Gorgo said, "one way or another." He glared at the circle of people, then spat into the fire and turned and stalked away into the night.

There was an awkward pause. Yama sat down and apologized, saying that he had drunk too much and lost his judgment.

"We've all slapped Gorgo around one time or another," one of the women said. "He grows angry if his advances are ignored."

"He is more angry than fierce," someone said, and the rest laughed.

"He's a fucking disgrace," Tamora said. "A sneak and a coward. He never hunts, but feeds off the quarry of us all. He shot a man with an arbalest instead of fighting fair—"

"Enough," the matriarch said. "We do not speak of others to their backs."

"I'd speak to his face," Tamora said, "if he'd ever look me in the eye."

"If we say no more about this," Yama said, "I promise to say no more about myself."

There were more drinking games, and more songs, and at last Yama begged to be released, for although Tamora's people seemed to need little sleep, he was exhausted by his adventures. He found his way back to his own campfire by the faint light of the Arm of the Warrior, falling several times but feeling no hurt. Pandaras was curled up near the warm ashes, his kidney puncher gripped in both hands. Yama lay down a little way off, on the ridge which overlooked the dark city. He did not remember wrapping himself in his blanket, or falling asleep, but he woke when Tamora pulled the blanket away from him. Her naked body glimmered in the near dark. He did not resist when she started to undo the laces of his shirt, or when she covered his mouth with hers.

22

The Country of the Mind

THE NEXT MORNING, Pandaras watched with unconcealed amusement as Tamora swabbed the scratches on Yama's flanks and the sore places on his shoulders and neck where she had nipped him. Pandaras sleeked back his hair with wrists wet by his own saliva, slapped dust from his ragged jerkin, and announced that he was ready to go.

"We can buy breakfast on the way to the docks. With all the money we have earned, there's no reason to live like unchanged rustics."

"You slept soundly last night," Yama said.

"I was not sleeping at all. When I had not fainted away with fright I was listening to every sound in the night, imagining that some hungry meat-eater was creeping up on me. My people have lived in the city forever. We were not made for the countryside."

Yama held up his shirt. It was stained with silt from the flood which had fallen through the ceiling of the merchant's house, and flecked with chaff where he and Tamora had used it as a pillow. He said, "I should wash out my clothes. This will make no impression on our new employers."

Pandaras looked up. "Are we away then? We'll collect our reward, and go to our new employer in the Palace of the Memory of the People, and find your family, all before the mountains eat the sun. We could already be there, master, if you had not slept so late."

"Not so quickly," Yama said, smiling at Pandaras's eagerness.

"I'll be an old man before long, and no use to you at all. At least let me wash your clothes. It will take but a minute, and I am, after all, your squire."

Tamora scratched at reddened skin at the edge of the bandage around her waist. "Grah. Some squire you'd make," she said, "with straws in your hair and dirt on your snout. Come with me, Yama. There's a washing place farther up."

Pandaras flourished his kidney puncher and struck an attitude and smiled at Yama, seeking his approval. He had an appetite for drama, as if all the world were a stage, and he was the central player. He said, "I will guard your satchel, master, but do not leave me alone for long. I can fight off two or three of these ravenous savages, but not an entire tribe."

A series of pools in natural limestone basins stepped away down the slope of the hill, with water rising from hot springs near the crest and falling from one pool to the next. Each pool was slightly cooler than the one above. Yama sat with Tamora in the shallow end of the hottest pool he could bear and scrubbed his shirt and trousers with white sand. He spread them out to dry on a flat rock already warm from the sun, and then allowed Tamora to wash his back. Little fish striped with silver and black darted around his legs in the clear hot water, nipping at the dirt between his toes. Other people were using pools higher up, calling cheerfully to each other under the blue sky.

Tamora explained that the water came from the Rim Mountains. "Everyone in the city who can afford it uses mountain water; only beggars and refugees drink from the river."

"Then they must be the holiest people in Ys, for the water of the Great River is sacred."

"Grah, holiness does not cleanse the river of all the shit put into it. Most bathe in it only once a year, on the high day celebrated by their bloodline. Otherwise those who can avoid it, which is why water is brought into the city. One of the underground rivers which transports the mountain water passes close by. It's why we have our hunting grounds here. There are waterholes where animals come to drink and where the hunting is good, and at this place we have hidden machines to heat the water."

"It is a wonderful place," Yama said. "Look, a hawk!"

Tamora lifted the thong around Yama's neck and fingered the coin which hung from it. "What's this? A keepsake?"

"Someone gave it to me. Before I left Aeolis."

"You find them everywhere, if you bother to dig for a few minutes. We used to play with them when we were children. This is less worn than most, though. Who gave it to you? A sweetheart, perhaps?"

Derev. This was the second time Yama had betrayed her trust. Although he did not know if he would ever see Derev again, and although he had been drunk, he felt suddenly ashamed that he had allowed Tamora to take him.

Tamora's breath feathered his cheek. It had a minty tang from the leaf she had plucked from a bush and folded inside her mouth between her teeth and her cheek. She fingered the line of Yama's jaw and said, "There's hair coming in here."

"There is a glass blade in my satchel. I should have brought it to shave. Or perhaps I will grow a beard."

"It was your first time, wasn't it? Don't be ashamed. Everyone must have a first time."

"No. I mean, no, it was not the first time."

Telmon's high, excited voice as he threw open the door of the brothel's warm, scented, lamp-lit parlor. The women turning to them like exotic orchids unfolding. Yama had gone with Telmon because he had been asked, because he had been curious, because Telmon had been about to leave for the war. Afterwards, he had suspected that Derev had known all about it, and if she had not condoned it, then perhaps at least she had understood. That was why Yama had been so fervent with his promises on the night before he left Aeolis, and yet how easily he had broken them. He felt a sudden desolation. How could he even think of being a hero?

Tamora said, "It was your first time with one of the Fierce People. That should burn away the memory of all others." She nipped his shoulder. "You have a soft skin, and it tastes of salt."

"I sweat everywhere, except the palms of my hands and the soles of my feet."

"Really? How strange. But I like the taste. That's why I bit you last night."

"I heal quickly."

Tamora said, "Yama, listen to me. It won't happen again. Not while we're working together. No, stay still. I can't clean your back if you turn around. We celebrated together last night, and that was good. But I won't let it interfere with my work. If you don't like that, and think yourself used, then find another cateran. There are plenty here, and plenty more at the Water Market. You have enough money to hire the best."

"I was at least as drunk as you were."

"Drunker, I'd say. I hope you didn't fuck me just because you were drunk."

Yama blushed. "I meant that I lost any inhibitions I might otherwise have had. Tamora—"

"Don't start on any sweet talk. And don't tell me about any sweetheart you might have left at home, either, or about how sorry you are. That's there. This is here. We're battle companions. We fucked. End of that part of the story."

"Are all your people so direct?"

"We speak as we find. Not to do so is a weakness. I like you, and I enjoyed last night. We're lucky, because some bloodlines are only on heat once a year—imagine how miserable they must be—and besides, there's no danger of us making babies together. That's what happens when my people fuck, unless the woman is already pregnant. I'm not ready for that, not yet. In a few years I'll find some men to run with and we'll raise a family, but not yet. A lot of us choose the metic way for that reason."

Yama was interested. He said, "Can you not use prophylactics?"

Tamora laughed. "You haven't seen the cock of one of our men! There are spines to hold it in place. Put a rubber on that? Grah! There's a herb some women boil into a tea and drink to stop their courses, but it doesn't work most of the time."

"Women of your people are stronger than men."

"It's generally true of all bloodlines, even when it doesn't seem so. We're more honest about it, perhaps. Now you clean my back, and I'll go use the shittery, and then we'll find the rat-boy. If we're lucky, he's run back to where he belongs."

As they went back down the hill, along the path that wandered between stands of sage and tall sawgrasses, Yama saw someone dressed in black watching them from the shade at the edge of a grove of live oaks. He thought it might have been Gorgo, but whoever it was stepped back into the shadows and was gone before Yama could point him out to Tamora.

———

The city was still disturbed by Yama's drawing down of the feral machine. Magistrates and their attendant clouds of machines were patrolling the streets, and although Yama asked the machines to ignore him and his companions, he was fearful that he would miss one until it was too late, or that Prefect Corin would lunge out of the crowds toward him. He kept turning this way and that until Tamora told him to stop it, or they'd be arrested for sure. Little groups of soldiers lounged at every major intersection. They were the city militia, armed with fusils and carbines, and dressed in loose red trousers and plastic cuirasses as slick and cloudily transparent as ice. They watched the crowds with hard, insolent eyes, but they did not challenge anyone. They did not dare, Pandaras said, and Yama asked how that could be, if they had the authority of the Preservers.

"There are many more of us than there are of them," Pandaras said, and made the sign Yama had noticed before, touching his fist to his throat.

The boy did not seem scared of the soldiers, but instead openly displayed a smoldering contempt, and Yama noticed that many of the other people made the same sign when they went by a group of soldiers. Some even spat or shouted a curse, safe in the anonymity of the crowd.

Pandaras said, "With the war downriver, there are even fewer soldiers in the city, and they must keep the peace by terror. That's why they're hated. See that cock there?"

Yama looked up. An officer in gold-tinted body armor stood on a metal disc that floated in the air above the dusty crowns of the ginkgoes which lined one side of the broad, brawling avenue.

"He could level a city block with one shot, if he had a mind to," Pandaras said. "But he wouldn't unless he had no other choice, because there'd be riots and even more of the city would be burned. If someone stole a pistol and tried to use it against soldiers or magistrates, then he might do it."

"It seems an excessive punishment."

Tamora said, "Energy weapons are prohibited, worse luck. I'd like one right now. Clear a way through these herds of grazers in a blink."

"One of my uncles on my mother's side of the family was caught up in a tax protest a few years back," Pandaras said. "It was in a part of the city a few leagues upriver. A merchant bought up a block and levelled it to make a park, and the legates decided that every tradesman living round about should pay more tax. The park made the area more attractive, neh? The legates said that more people would come because of the open space, and spend more in the shops round about. So the tradesmen got together and declared a tax strike in protest. The legates called up the magistrates, and they came and blockaded the area. Set their machines spinning in the air to make a picket line, so no one could get in or out. It lasted a hundred days, and at the end they said people inside the picket line were eating each other. The food ran out, and there was no way to get more in. A few tried to dig tunnels, but the magistrates sent in machines and killed them."

Yama said, "Why did they not give up the strike?"

"They did, after twenty days. They would have held out longer, but there were children, and there were people who didn't live there at all but happened to be passing through when the blockade went up. So they presented a petition of surrender, but the magistrates kept the siege going as punishment. That kind of thing is supposed to make the rest of us too frightened to spit unless we get permission."

Tamora said, "There's no other way. There are too many people living in the city, and most are fools or grazers. An argument between neighbors can turn into a feud between bloodlines, with thousands killed. Instead, the magistrates or the militia kill two or three, or even a hundred if necessary, and the matter is settled before it spreads. There are a dozen bloodlines they could get rid of and no one would notice."

"We're the strength of Ys," Pandaras said defiantly, and for once Tamora didn't answer back.

———

They reached the docks late in the afternoon. The same stocky, shaven-headed guard met them in the shadow of the lighter. He looked at the brandy-filled flask and the strings of nerve tissue that floated inside and said that he had already heard that the merchant was dead.

Tamora said, "Then we'll just take our money and go."

Yama said to the guard, "You said you would need to test what we brought."

The guard said, "The whole city knows that he was killed last night. To be frank, we would have preferred less attention drawn to it, but we are happy that the task was done. Do not worry. We will pay you."

"Then let's do it now," Tamora said, "and we'll be on our way."

Yama said quickly, "But we have made an agreement. I would have it seen through to the letter. Your master wanted to test what we brought, and I would have it done no other way, to prove that we are honest."

The guard stared hard at Yama, then said, "I would not insult you by failing to carry out everything we agreed. Come with me."

As they followed the guard up the gangway, Tamora caught Yama's arm and whispered fiercely, "This is a foolish risk. We do the job, we take the money, we go. Who cares what they think of us? Complications are dangerous, especially with the star-sailors, and we have an appointment at the Water Market."

"I have my reasons," Yama said stubbornly. "You and Pandaras can wait on the dock, or go on to the Water Market, just as you please."

He had thought it over as they had walked through the streets of the city to the wharf where the voidship lighter was moored. The star-sailor who piloted the lighter had said that it knew something of Yama's bloodline, and even if it was only one tenth of what the merchant had claimed to know, it was still worth learning. Yama was prepared to pay for the knowledge, and he thought that he knew a sure way of getting at it if the star-sailor refused to tell him anything.

Inside the ship, in the round room at the top of the spiral corridor, the guard uncapped the crystal flask and poured its contents onto the black floor, which quickly absorbed the brandy and the strings of nervous tissue. He set the gold circlet on his scarred, shaven scalp and jerked to attention. His mouth worked, and he said in a voice not his own, "This one will pay you. What else do you want of me?"

Yama addressed the fleshy blossom which floated inside its bottle. "I talked with your crewmate before he died. He said that he knew something of my bloodline."

The star-sailor said through its human mouthpiece, "No doubt he said many things to save his life."

"This was when he had me prisoner, and my friends, too."

"Then perhaps he was boasting. You must understand that he was mad. He had corrupted himself with the desires of the flesh."

"I remember you said that I had abilities that might be useful."

"I was mistaken. They have proved . . . inconvenient. You have no control over what you can do."

Tamora said, "We should leave this. Yama, I'll help you find out what you want to know, but in the Palace of the Memory of the People, not here. We made a deal."

Yama said stubbornly, "I have not forgotten. The few questions I want to ask will not end my quest, but they may aid it." He turned back to the thing in the bottle. "I will waive my part of the fee for the murder of your crewmate if you will help me understand what he told me."

Tamora said, "Don't listen to him, dominie! He hasn't the right to make that bargain!"

The guard's mouth opened and closed. His chin was slick with saliva. He said, "He was driven mad by the desires of the flesh. I, however, am not mad. I have nothing to say to you unless you can prove that you know what you are. Return then, and we can talk."

"If I knew that, I would have nothing to ask you."

Tamora grabbed Yama's arm. "You're risking everything, you fool. Come on!"

Yama tried to free himself, but Tamora's grip was unyielding and her sharp nails dug into his flesh until blood ran. He stepped in close, thinking to throw her from his hip, but she knew that trick and butted

him on the bridge of his nose with her forehead. A blinding spike of
pain shot through his head and tears sprang to his eyes. Tamora twisted
his arm up behind his back and started to drag him across the room to
the dilated doorway, but Pandaras wrapped himself around her legs and
fastened his sharp teeth on her thigh. Tamora howled and Yama pulled
free and flung himself at the guard, ripping the gold circlet from the
man's head and jamming it on his own.

White light.

White noise.

Something was in his head. It fled even as he noticed it and he
turned in a direction he had not seen before and flew after it. It was a
woman, a naked, graceful woman with pale skin and long black hair
that fanned out behind her as she soared through clashing currents of
light. Even as she fled, she kept looking back over her bare shoulder.
Her eyes blazed with a desperate light.

Yama followed with mounting exhilaration. He seemed to be connected to her through a kind of cord that was growing shorter and
stronger, and he twisted and turned after his quarry without thought as
they plunged together through interlaced strands of light.

Others were pacing them on either side, and beyond these unseen
presences Yama could feel a vast congregation, mostly in clusters as
distant and faint as the halo stars. They were the crews of the voidships,
meeting together in this country of the mind, in which they swam as
easily as fish in the river. Whenever Yama turned his attention to one
or another of these clusters, he felt an airy expansion and a fleeting
glimpse of the combined light of other minds, as if through a window
whose shutters are flung back to greet the rising sun. In every case the
minds he touched with his mind recoiled; the shutters slammed; the light
faded.

In his desperate chase after the woman through the country of the
mind, Yama left behind a growing wake of confused and scandalized
inhabitants. They called on something, a guardian or watchdog, and it
rose toward Yama like a pressure wave, angling through unseen dimensions like a pike gliding effortlessly through water toward a duckling
paddling on the surface. Yama doubled and redoubled his effort to catch
the woman, and was almost on her when white light blinded him and
white noise roared in his ears and a black floor flew up and struck him
with all the weight of the world.

The Temple of the Black Well

WHEN YAMA WOKE, the first thing he saw was Pandaras sitting cross-legged by the foot of the bed, sewing up a rip in his second-best shirt. Yama was naked under the scratchy starched sheet, and clammy with old sweat. His head ached, and some time ago a small animal seemed to have crept into the dry cavern of his mouth and died there. Perhaps it was a cousin of the bright green gecko which clung upside down in a patch of sunlight on the far wall, its scarlet throat pulsing. This was a small room, with ochre plaster walls painted with twining patterns of blue vines, and dusty rafters under a slanted ceiling. Afternoon light fell through the two tall windows, and with it the noise and dust and smells of a busy street.

Pandaras helped him up, fussing with the bolster, and brought him a beaker of water. "It has salt and sugar in it, master. Drink. It will make you stronger."

Yama obeyed the boy. It seemed that he had been asleep for a night and most of the day that followed. Pandaras and Tamora had brought him here from the docks.

"She has gone out to talk with the man we should have met yesterday. And we didn't get paid by the star-sailor, so she's angry with you."

"I remember that you tried to help me." Yama discovered that at some time he had bitten his tongue and the insides of his cheeks. He said, "You killed the guard with that kidney puncher she gave you."

"That was before, master. At the gate of the merchant's estate. After that there was the voidship lighter, when you snatched the circlet from the guard and put it on your head."

"The merchant was wearing the circlet. It was how he controlled his household. But I broke it when I took it away from him."

"This was in the voidship lighter. Please try and remember, master! You put the circlet on your head and straightaway you collapsed with foam on your lips and your eyes rolled right back. One of my half-sisters has the falling sickness, and that's what it looked like."

"A woman. I saw a woman. But she fled from me."

Pandaras pressed on with his story. "I snatched the circlet from your head, but you didn't wake. More guards came, and they marched us off the lighter. The first guard, the one you took the circlet from, he and Tamora had an argument about the fee. I thought she might kill him, but he and his fellows drew their pistols, and there was no argument after that. We took some of your money to pay for the room, and for the palanquin that carried you here. I hope we did right."

"Tamora must be angry with you, too."

"She doesn't take any account of me, which is just as well. I bit her pretty badly when she tried to stop you taking the circlet, but she bandaged up her legs and said nothing of it. Wouldn't admit I could hurt her, neh? And now I'm not frightened of her because I know I can hurt her, and I'll do it again if I have to. I didn't want to fight with her, master, but she shouldn't have tried to stop you. She didn't have the right."

Yama closed his eyes. Clusters of lights hanging from the ceiling of the round room at the top of the voidship lighter. The thing in the bottle, with rose-red gills and a lily-white mantle folded around a thick braid of naked nerve tissue. "I remember," he said. "I tried to find out about my bloodline. The country of the mind—"

Pandaras nodded eagerly. "You took the circlet from the guard and put it on your own head."

"Perhaps it would have been better if Tamora had stopped me. She was worried that I would no longer have any need of her."

Pandaras took the empty beaker from Yama and said, "Well, and do you need her, master? You stood face to face with that thing and talked to it direct. Did it tell you what you wanted to know?"

It seemed like a dream, fading even as Yama tried to remember its details. The woman fleeing, the faint stars of other minds. Yama said, "I saw something wonderful, but I did not learn anything about myself, except that the people who crew the voidships are scared of me."

"You scared me too, master. I thought you had gone into the place where they live and left your body behind. I'll have some food sent up. You haven't eaten in two days."

"You have been good to me, Pandaras."

"Why, it's a fine novelty to order people about in a place like this. A while ago it was me running at any cock's shout, and I haven't forgotten what it was like."

"It was not that long ago. A few days."

"Longer for me than for you. Rest, master. I'll be back soon."

But Pandaras was gone a long time. The room was hot and close, and Yama wrapped the sheet around himself and sat at one of the windows, where there was a little breeze. He felt weak, but rested and alert. The bandage was gone from the wound on his forearm and the flesh had knitted about the puckers made by the black crosses of the stitches; the self-inflicted wound on his palm was no more than a faint silvery line. All the bruises and small cuts from his recent adventures were healed, too, and someone, presumably Pandaras, had shaved him while he had been sleeping.

The inn stood on a broad avenue divided down the center by a line of palm trees. The crowds which jostled along the dusty white thoroughfare contained more people than Yama had ever seen in his life, thousands of people of a hundred different bloodlines. There were hawkers and skyclad mendicants, parties of palmers, priests, officials hurrying along in groups of two or three, scribes, musicians, tumblers, whores and mountebanks. An acrobat walked above the heads of the crowd on a wire strung from one side of the avenue to the other. Vendors fried plantains and yams on heated iron plates, or roasted nuts in huge copper basins set over oil burners. Ragged boys ran amongst the people, selling flavored ice, twists of licorice, boiled sweets, roast nuts, cigarettes, plastic trinkets representing one or another of the long-lost aspects of the Preservers, and medals stamped with the likenesses of official heroes of the war against the heretics. Beggars exhibited a hundred different kinds of mutilation and deformity. Messengers on nimble genets or black plumaged ratites rode at full tilt through the crowds. A few important personages walked under silk canopies held up by dragomen, or were carried on litters or palanquins. A party of solemn giants walked waist high amidst the throng as if wading in a stream. Directly across the avenue, people gathered at a stone altar, burning incense cones bought from a priest, muttering prayers and wafting the smoke toward themselves. A procession of ordinands in red robes, their freshly shaven heads gleaming with oil, wound in a long straggling line behind men banging tambours.

In the distance, the sound of braying, discordant trumpets rang above the noise of the crowded avenue, and presently the procession heralded by the trumpeters hove into view. It was a huge cart pulled by a team of a hundred sweating, half-naked men, with priests swinging fuming censers on either side. It was painted scarlet and gold and bedecked with garlands of flowers, and amidst the heaps of flowers stood a screen, its black oval framed by ornate golden scrollwork. The cart stopped almost directly opposite Yama's window, and people gathered on the rooftops and threw down bucketfuls of water on the men who pulled it, and dropped more garlands of flowers onto the cart and around the men and the attendant priests in a soft, multicolored snowstorm. Yama leaned out farther to get a better view, and at that moment heard a noise in the room behind him and turned, thinking it was Pandaras.

A patch of ocher plaster on the wall opposite the window was cracked in a spiderweb pattern, and in the center of the web stood an arbalest bolt.

The bolt was as long as Yama's forearm, with a shaft of dense, hard wood and red flight feathers. From the downward pointing angle at which the bolt had embedded itself in the plaster, it must have been fired from one of the flat roofs on the other side of the avenue, for all of them were higher than the window. Yama crouched down and scanned the rooftops, but there were hundreds of people crowded along their edges, scattering flowers and pitching silvery twists of water at the cart. He tried to find a machine which might have been watching, but it seemed that there were no magistrates here.

Still crouching, Yama closed and bolted the heavy slatted shutters of both windows, then pulled the arbalest bolt from the wall.

A few minutes later, Pandaras returned ahead of a pot boy who set a tray covered in a white cloth on the low, round table which, apart from the bed and the chair in which Yama sat, were the only pieces of furniture in the room. Pandaras dismissed the pot boy and whipped away the tray's cover like a conjuror, revealing a platter of fruit and cold meat, and a sweating earthenware pitcher of white wine. He poured wine into two cups, and handed one to Yama. "I'm sorry it took so long, master. There's a festival. We had to pay double rates just to get the room."

The wine was cold, and as thickly sweet as syrup. Yama said, "I saw the procession go by."

"There's always some procession here. It's in the nature of the place. Eat, master. You must break your fast before you go anywhere."

Yama took the slice of green melon Pandaras held out. "Where are we?"

Pandaras bit into his own melon slice. "Why, it's the quarter that runs between the river and the Palace of the Memory of the People."

"I think we should go and find Tamora. Where are my clothes?"

"Your trousers are under the mattress, to keep them pressed. I am mending one of your shirts; the other is in your pack. Master, you should eat, and then rest."

"I do not think so," Yama said, and showed Pandaras the arbalest bolt.

The landlady called to Yama and Pandaras as they pushed through the hot, crowded taproom of the inn. She was a plump, broad-beamed, brown-skinned woman, her long black hair shiny with grease and braided into a thick rope. She was sweating heavily into her purple and gold sarong, and she waved a fretted palm leaf to and fro as she explained that a message had been left for them.

"I have it here," she said, rummaging through the drawer of her desk. "Please be patient, sirs. It is a very busy day today. Is this it? No. Wait, here it is."

Yama took the scrap of stiff paper. It had been folded four times and tucked into itself, and sealed with a splash of wax. Yama turned it over and over, and asked Pandaras, "Can Tamora read and write?"

"She put her thumb to the contract, master, so I'd guess she has as much reading as I have, which is to say none."

The landlady said helpfully, "There are scribes on every corner. The seal is one of theirs."

"Do you know which one?"

"There are very many. I suppose I could have one of my boys . . ." The landlady patted her brow with a square of yellow cloth that reeked of peppermint oil. Her eyes were made up with blue paint and gold leaf and her eyebrows had been twisted and stiffened with wax to form long tapering points, giving the effect of a butterfly perched on her face. She added, "That is, when we are less busy. It is a festival day, you see."

Yama said, "I saw the cart go by."

"The cart? Oh, the shrine. No, no, that is nothing to do with the festival. It passes up and down the street every day, except on its feast day, of course, when it is presented at the Great River. But that is a hundred days off, and just a local affair. People have come here from all over Ys for the festival, and from downriver, too. A very busy time, although of course there are not so many people as there once were. Fewer travel, you see, because of the war. That is why I was able to find you a room at short notice."

"She moved two palmers into the stables, and charges us twice what they paid," Pandaras remarked.

"And now they are paying less than they would have," the landlady said, "so it all evens out. I hope that the message is not bad news, sirs. The room is yours as long as you want it." Despite her claim to be busy, it seemed that she had plenty of time to stick her nose in other people's business.

Yama held up the folded paper and said, "Who brought this?"

"I didn't see. One of my boys gave it to me. I could find him, I suppose, although it's all a muddle today—"

"Because of the festival." Yama snapped the wax seal and unfolded the paper.

The message was brief, and written in neatly aligned glyphs with firm and decisive downstrokes and fine feathering on the upstrokes. Most likely it had been set down by a scribe, unless Tamora had spent as long as Yama learning the finer nuances of penmanship.

I have gone on. The man you want is at the Temple of the Black Well.

Pandaras said, "What does it say?"

Yama read the message to Pandaras, and the landlady said, "That's not too far from here. Go down the passage at the left side of the inn and strike toward the Palace. I could get you a link boy if you'd like to wait . . ."

But Yama and Pandaras were already pushing their way through the crowded room toward the open door and the sunlit avenue beyond.

———

The narrow streets that tangled behind the inn were cooler and less crowded than the avenue. They were paved with ancient, uneven brick courses, and naked children played in the streams of dirty water that ran down the central gutters. The houses were flat-roofed and none were more than two stories high, with small shuttered windows and walls covered in thick yellow or orange plaster, walls that were crumbling and much-patched. Many had workshops on the ground floor, open to the street, and Yama and Pandaras passed a hundred tableaus of industry, most to do with the manufacture of the religious mementoes which were displayed in shops which stood at every corner of every street, although none of the shops seemed to be open.

It was a secretive, suspicious place, Yama thought, noting that people stopped what they were doing and openly stared as he and Pandaras went past. But he liked the serendipitous geography, so that a narrow street might suddenly open onto a beautiful square with a white fountain splashing in its center, and liked the small neighborhood shrines set into the walls of the houses, with browning wreaths of flowers and pyramids of ash before a flyspotted circle of black glass that poorly mimicked the dark transparency of true shrines.

The domes and pinnacles and towers of temples and shrines reared up amongst the crowded flat roofs of the ordinary houses like ships foundering in the scruffy pack ice of the frozen wilderness at the head of the Great River hundreds of leagues upstream. And beyond all these houses and temples and shrines, the black mountain of the Palace of the Memory of the People climbed terrace by terrace toward its distant peak, with the setting sun making the sky red behind it.

Pandaras explained that this part of the city was given over to the business of worship of the Preservers and of the governance of Ys. Civil service departments displaced from the interior of the Palace of the Memory of the People occupied lesser buildings on its outskirts, and a thousand cults flourished openly or skulked in secret underground chambers.

"At night it can be a dangerous place for strangers," Pandaras said.

"I have my knife. And you have yours."

"You should have worn your armor. We collected it from the Water Market, cut down neatly and polished up as good as new."

Yama had found it when he had taken his shirt from the satchel. He said, "It would attract attention. Someone might take a fancy to it. Already I feel as if I am a procession, the way people turn to stare."

"They might want our blood. Or want to scoop out our brains and put them in tanks, all alive-o like the star-sailors."

Yama laughed at these fantasies.

Pandaras said darkly, "This is a place of good and evil, master. It is the New Quarter, built on a bloody battleground. You are a singular person. Don't forget it. You would be a great prize for a blood sacrifice."

"New? It seems to me very old."

"That's because nothing here has been rebuilt since the Age of Insurrection. The rest of the city is far older, but people are always knocking down old buildings and putting up new ones. The Hierarchs ordered clearance of the ruined buildings where the last battle between machines was fought, and the bones and casings of all the dead were tipped into great pits and the ground around about was flattened and these houses were built."

"I know there was a battle fought near Ys, but I thought it was much farther upriver." Yama remembered now that the Temple of the Black Well had something to do with that last battle, although he could not quite remember what it was.

Pandaras said, "They built the houses over the battleground, and nothing's changed since, except for the building of shrines and temples."

"I had thought the houses were built around them."

"Houses have to be knocked down each time a new temple is built. It's a dangerous business. There are old poisons in the ground, and old weapons too, and sometimes the weapons discharge when they are uncovered. There's a department which does nothing but search by divination for old weapons, and make them safe when they're found. And some parts of the quarter are haunted, too. It's why the people are so strange hereabouts, neh? The ghosts get inside their heads, and infect them with ideas from ages past."

Yama said, "I have never seen a ghost." The aspects which haunted the City of the Dead did not count, for they were merely semi-intelligent projections. And while the Amnan claimed that the blue lights sometimes seen floating amongst the ruins below the peel-house were wights, the eidolons of the restless dead, Zakiel said that they were no more than wisps of burning marsh gas.

Pandaras said, "These are machine ghosts mostly, but some were human, once, and they say that those are the worst. That's why they make so many icons hereabouts, master. If you were to look inside one of these houses, you'd find layer upon layer of them on the walls."

"To keep out the ghosts."

"They don't usually work. That's what I heard, anyway."

"Look there. Is that our temple?"

It reared up a few streets ahead, a giant cube built of huge, roughly hewn stone blocks stained black with soot, and topped by an onion dome lapped in scuffed gilt tiles.

Pandaras squinted at it, then said, "No, ours has a rounder roof, with a hole in the top of it."

"Of course! Where the machine fell!"

The Temple of the Black Well had been built long after the feral machine's fiery fall, but its dome had been left symbolically uncompleted, with the aperture at its apex directly above the deep hole made when the machine had struck the surface of the world and melted a passage in the rock all the way down to the keel. Yama had been told the story by the aspect of a leather merchant who had had his tannery near the site of the temple's construction. Mysyme, that had been the merchant's name. He had had two wives and six beautiful daughters, and had done much charitable work amongst the orphaned river-rats of the docks. Mysyme was dead an age past, and Yama had lost interest in the limited responses of his aspect years ago, but now he remembered them all over again. Mysyme's father had seen the fall of the machine, and had told his son that when it hit, a plume of melted rock had been thrown higher than the atmosphere, while the smoke of secondary fires had darkened the sky above Ys for a decad.

"It's a little to the left," Pandaras said, "and maybe ten minutes' walk. That place with the gold roof is a tomb of a warrior-saint. It's solid all the way through except for a secret chamber."

"You are a walking education, Pandaras."

"I have an uncle who used to live here, and one time I stayed with him. He was on my mother's side, and this was when my father ran off and my mother went looking for him. She was a year at it, and never found him. And a year is a long time for my people. So she came back and married another man, and when that didn't work out she married my stepfather. I don't get on with him, and that's why I took the job of pot boy, because it came with a room. And then you came along, and here we are." Pandaras grinned. "For a long time after I left this part of the city, I thought maybe I was haunted. I'd wake up and think I'd been hearing voices, voices that had been telling me things in my sleep. But I haven't heard them since I met up with you, master. Maybe your bloodline is a cure for ghosts."

"All my bloodline are ghosts, from the little I have learned," Yama said.

The Temple of the Black Well stood at the center of a wide, quiet plaza of mossy cobbles. It had been built in the shape of a cross, with a long atrium and short apses; its dome, covered in gold leaf that shone with the last light of the sun, capped the point where the apses intersected the atrium. The temple was clad in lustrous black stone, although here and there parts of the cladding had fallen away to reveal the grayish limestone beneath. Yama and Pandaras walked all the way around the temple and saw no one, and then climbed the long flight of shallow steps and went through the tall narthex.

It was dark inside, but a thick slanted column of reddish light fell through the open apex of the dome at the far end of a long atrium flanked by colonnades. Yama walked toward the light. There was no sign of Tamora or her mysterious contact; the whole temple seemed deserted. The pillars of the colonnades were intricately carved and the ruined mosaics of the floor sketched the outlines of heroic figures. The temple had been splendid once, Yama thought, but now it had the air of a place that was no longer cared for. He thought it an odd choice for a rendezvous—far better for an ambush.

Pandaras clearly felt the same thing, for his sleek head continually turned this way and that as they went down the atrium. The reddish light, alive with swirling motes of dust, fell on a waist-high wall of undressed stone which ringed a wide hole that plunged down into darkness. It was the well, the shaft the fallen machine had melted. The wide coping on top of the wall was covered in the ashy remnants of incense cones, and here and there were offerings of fruit and flowers. A few joss sticks jammed into cracks in the wall sent up curls of sweet-smelling smoke, but the flowers were shrivelled and brown, and the little piles of fruit were spotted with decay.

"Not many come here," Pandaras said. "The ghost of the machine is powerful, and quick to anger."

Yama gripped the edge of the coping and looked into the depths of the well. A faint draught of cold, stale air blew up around him from the lightless depths. The walls of the shaft were long glassy flows of once-melted rock, veined with impurities, dwindling away to a vanishing point small as the end of his thumb. It was impossible to tell how deep the well really was, and in a spirit of inquiry Yama dropped a softening pomegranate into the black air.

"That isn't a good idea," Pandaras said uneasily.

"I do not think a piece of fruit would wake this particular machine. It fell a long way as I recall—at least, it was two days in falling, and appeared in the sky as a star clothed in burning hair. When it struck the ground, the blow knocked down thousands of houses and caused a wave in the river that washed away much of the city on the farside shore. And then the sky turned black with smoke from all the fires."

"There might be other things down there," Pandaras said. "Bats, for instance. I have a particular loathing of bats."

Yama said, "I should have thrown a coin. I might have heard it hit."

But a small part of his mind insisted that the fruit was still falling through black air toward the bottom, two leagues or more to the keel. He and Pandaras walked around the well, but apart from the smoking joss sticks there was no sign that Tamora or anyone else had been there recently, and the hushed air was beginning to feel oppressive, as if it held a note endlessly drawn out just beyond the range of hearing.

Pandaras said, "We should go on, master. She isn't here." He added hopefully, "Perhaps she has run off and left us."

"She made a contract with me. I should think that is a serious thing for someone who lives from one job to the next. We will wait a little longer." He took out the paper and read it again. " 'The man you want . . .' I wonder what she meant."

"It'll be dark soon."

Yama smiled, and said, "I believe that you are scared of this place."

"You might not believe in ghosts, master, but there are many who do—most of the people in the city, I reckon."

"I might have more cause to believe in ghosts, because I was brought up in the middle of the City of the Dead, but I do not. Just because a lot of people believe in ghosts does not make them real. I might believe that the Preservers have incarnated themselves in river turtles, and I might persuade a million people to believe it, too, but that does not make it true."

"You shouldn't make jokes like that," Pandaras said. "Especially not here."

"Surely the Preservers will forgive a small joke."

"There's many who would take offense on their account," Pandaras said stubbornly. He had a deep streak of superstition, despite his worldly-wise air. Yama had seen the care with which he washed himself in a ritual pattern after eating and upon waking, the way he crossed his fingers when walking past a shrine—a superstition he shared with the citizens of Aeolis, who believed that it disguised the fact that you had come to a shrine without an offering—and his devotion at prayer. Like the Amnan, who could not or would not read the Puranas and so only knew them secondhand through the preaching of priests and iconoclasts, Pandaras and the countless millions of ordinary folk of Ys believed that the Preservers had undergone a transubstantiation, disappearing not into the Eye but dispersing themselves into every particle of the world which they had made, so that they were everywhere at once, immortal, invisible and, despite their limitless power, quick to judge and requiring constant placation. It was not surprising, then, that Pandaras believed in ghosts and other revenants.

Pandaras said, "Ghosts are more like ideas than you might think. The more people believe in them, the more powerful they become. Listen! What was that?"

"I heard nothing," Yama said, but even as he said it there was a faint brief rumble, as if the temple, with all its massy stones, had briefly stirred and then settled again. It seemed to come from the well, and Yama leaned over and peered into its depths. The wind which blew out of the darkness seemed to be blowing a little more strongly, and it held a faint tang, like heated metal.

"Come away," Pandaras pleaded uneasily. He was shifting his weight from foot to foot, as if ready to run.

"We will look in the apses. If anything was going to happen, Pandaras, it would have happened by now."

"If it does happen, it'll be all the worse for waiting."

"You go left and I will go right, and if we find nothing I promise we will go straight out of this place."

"I'll come with you, master, if you don't mind. I've no liking for being left alone in this hecatomb."

The archway which led into the apse to the right of the well was curtained by falls of fine black plastic mesh. Beyond was a high square space lit by shafts of dim light striking through knotholes that pierced the thick walls just beneath the vaulted roof. There was a shrine set in the center of the space, a glossy black circle like a giant's coin or eyeglass stood on its side.

Statues three times the height of a man stood in recesses all around the four walls, although they were not statues of men, and nor were they carved from stone, but were made of the same slick, translucent stuff as ancient armor. Yama could dimly see shapes and catenaries inside their chests and limbs.

Pandaras went up to a statue and knocked his knuckles against its shin: it rang with a dull note. "There's a story that these things fought against the Insurrectionists."

"More likely they were made in the likeness of great generals," Yama said, looking up at their grim visages.

"Don't worry," a woman's voice said. "They've been asleep so long they've forgotten how to wake."

24

The Woman in White

YAMA TURNED, AND streamers of blazing white light suddenly raced through the shrine's black disc. He raised an arm to shade his eyes, but the white light had already faded into a swirling play of soft colors.

Pandaras's clenched paw fluttered under his open mouth. He said, "Master, this is some horrid trick."

Cautiously, Yama stepped through polychromatic light and touched the shrine's slick, cold surface. He was possessed by the mad idea that he could slip into it as easily as slipping into the cool water of the river.

Like a reflection, a hand rose through swirling colors to meet his own. For a moment he thought that he felt its touch, like a glove slipping around his skin, and he recoiled in shock.

Laughter, like the chiming of small silver bells. Streaks and swirls and dabs of a hundred colors collapsed into themselves, and a woman was framed in the disc of the shrine. Pandaras shouted and ran, flinging himself in a furious panic through the black mesh curtains which divided the apse from the main part of the temple.

Yama knelt before the shrine, fearful and amazed. "Lady . . . what do you want from me?"

"Oh do get up. I can't talk to the top of your head."

Yama obeyed. He supposed that the woman was one of the avatars of the Preservers, who, as was written in the Puranas, stood between the quotidian world and the glory of their masters, facing both ways at once. She was tall and slender, with a commanding, imperious gaze, and wore a white one-piece garment which clung to her limbs and body. Her skin was the color of newly forged bronze, and her long black hair was caught in a kind of net at her right shoulder. A green garden receded behind her: smooth lawns and a maze of high, trimmed hedges. A stone fountain sent a muscular jet of water high into the sunlit air.

"Who are you, domina? Do you live in this shrine?"

"I don't know where I live, these days. I'm scattered, I suppose you could say. But this is one of the places where I can look out at the world. It's like a window. You live in a house made of rooms. Where I live is mostly windows, looking out to different places. You drew me to this window and I looked out and found you."

"Drew you? Domina, I did not mean to."

"You wear the key around your neck. You have discovered that, at least."

Yama lifted out the coin which hung on the thong around his neck, the coin which the anchorite had given him the spring night when Dr. Dismas had returned to Ys, and everything had changed. Yama had gone out to hunt frogs, and caught something far stranger. The coin was warm, but perhaps only because it had lain next to his skin.

The woman in the shrine said, "It works by light, and briefly talked with this transceiver. I heard it, and came here. Don't be afraid. Do you like where I live?"

Yama said, with reflexive politeness, "I have never seen a garden like yours."

"Of course you haven't. It is from some long-vanished world, perhaps even from Earth. Do you wish me to change it? I could live anywhere, you know. Or at least anywhere on file that hasn't been corrupted. The servers are very old, and there's much that has been corrupted. Atoms migrate; cosmic rays and neutrinos disrupt the lattices . . . Anyway, I like gardens. It stirs something in my memory. My original ruled many worlds once, and surely some of those possessed gardens. It's possible she owned a garden just like this, once upon a time. But I've forgotten such a lot, and I was never really whole in the first place. There are peacocks. Do you know peacocks? No, I suppose not. Perhaps there are autochthonous creatures like peacocks somewhere on Confluence, but I don't have the files to hand. If we talk long enough perhaps one will come past. They are birds. The cocks have huge fan-shaped tails, with eyes in them."

Yama was suddenly overwhelmed by the image of an electric blue long-necked bird with concentric arcs of fiery eyes peering over its tiny head. He turned away, the heels of his palms pressed into his eye sockets, but the vision still beat inside his head.

"Wait," the woman said. Was there a note of uncertainty in her voice? "I didn't mean . . . The gain is difficult to control . . ."

The sheaves of burning eyes vanished; there was only ordinary bloodwarm darkness behind his eyelids. Cautiously, Yama turned back to the shrine.

"It isn't real," the woman said. She stepped up to the inner surface of the shrine and pressed her hands against it and peered between them as if trying to see through the window of a lighted room into a dark landscape. Her palms were dyed red. Paeonin. She said, "That it isn't real is the important thing to remember. But isn't everything an illusion? We're all waves, and even the waves are really half-glimpsed strings folded deeply into themselves."

She seemed to be talking to herself, but then she smiled at Yama. Or no, her eyes were not quite focused on him, but at a point a little to one side of the top of his head.

Yama said, prompted by a flicker of suspicion, "Excuse me, domina, but are you really an avatar? I have never seen one before."

"I'm no fragment of a god, Yamamanama. The clade of my original ruled a million planetary systems, once upon a time, but she never claimed to be a god. None of the transcendents ever claimed that, only their enemies."

Fear and amazement collapsed into relief. Yama laughed and said, "An aspect. You are an aspect. Or a ghost."

"A ghost in the machine. Yes, that's one way of looking at it. Why not? Even when my original walked the surface of this strange habitat she was a copy of a memory, and I suppose that would make me a kind of a ghost of a ghost. But you're a ghost, too. You shouldn't be here, not at this time. You're either too young, or too old, a hundred thousand years either way . . . Do you know why you are here?"

"I wish with all my heart to find out," Yama said, "but I do not believe in ghosts."

"We have spoken before." The woman tilted her head with a curiously coquettish gesture, and smiled. "You don't remember, do you?" she said. "Well, you were very young, and that foolish man with you hid your face in a fold of his robes. I think he must have done something to the shrine, afterwards, because that window has been closed to me ever since, like so many others. There is much old damage in the system from the war between the machines. I could only glimpse you now and then as you grew up. How I wish I could have spoken to you! How I wish I could have helped you! I am so happy to meet you again, but you should not be here, in this strange and terrible city. You should be on your way downriver, to the war."

"What do you know about me? Please, domina, will you tell me what you know?"

"There are gates. Manifolds held open by the negative gravity of strange matter. They run in every direction, even into the past, all the way back to when they were created. I think that is where you come from. That, or the voidships. Perhaps your parents were passengers or stowaways on a voidship, time-shifted by the velocity of some long voyage. We did not learn where the voidships went. There was not enough time to learn a tenth of what we wanted to know. In any case, you come from the deep past of this strange world, Yamamanama, but although I have searched the records, I do not know who sent you, or why. Does it matter? You are here, and there is much to be done."

Yama could not believe her. For if he had been sent here from the deep past when his people, the Builders, had been constructing the world according to the desires of the Preservers, then he could never find his family or any others like him. He would be quite alone, and that was unthinkable.

He said, "I was found on the river. I was a baby, lying on the breast of a dead woman in a white boat." He suddenly felt that his heart might burst with longing. "Please tell me! Tell me why I am here!"

The woman in the shrine lifted her hands, wrists cocked in an elegant shrug. She said, "I'm a stranger here. My original walked out into your world and died there, but not before she started to change it. And before she died part of her came here, and here I am still. I sometimes wonder if you're part of what she did after she left me here. Would that make you my son, if it were true?"

Yama said, "I am looking for answers, not more riddles."

"Let me give an example. You see the statues? You think them monuments to dead heroes, but the truth is simpler than any story."

"Then they are not statues?"

"Not at all. They are soldiers. They were garrisoned here after the main part of the temple was built, to guard against what the foolish little priests of the temple call the Thing Below. I suppose that when the apses were remodelled many years later it was easier to incorporate the soldiers into the architecture than to move them. Most of their kind have been smelted down, and small pieces of armor have been cast from their remains, so in a sense they still defend the populace. But the soldiers around us are the reality, and the human soldiers who wear reforged scraps of the integuments of their brothers are but the shadows of that reality, as I am a shadow of the one for whom I speak. Unlike the soldiers, she is quite vanished from this world, and only I remain."

Yama looked up at the nearest of the figures. It stared above his head at one of its fellows on the opposite side of the square apse, but Yama fancied that he saw its eyes flicker toward him for an instant. They were red, and held a faint glow that he knew had not been there before.

He said, "Am I then a shadow too? I am searching for others like me. Can I find them?"

"I would be amazed and delighted if you did, but they are all long dead. I think that you will be sufficient, Yamamanama. Already you have discovered that you can control the machines which maintain this habitat. There is much more I can teach you."

"My bloodline was made by the Preservers to build the world, and then they went away. That much I have learnt, at least. I will discover more in the Palace of the Memory of the People."

"They were taken back," the woman said. "You might say that if I am a shadow of what I was, then your kind were a shadow of what you call the Preservers and what I suppose I could call my children, although they are as remote from me as I am from the plains apes which walked out of Afrique and set fire to the Galaxy."

Someone had recently said something similar to Yama. Who? Trying to remember, he said automatically, "All are shadows of the Preservers."

"Not quite all. There are many different kinds of men on this strange world—I suppose I must call it a world—and each has been reworked until it retains only a shadow of its animal ancestors. Most, but not all, have been salted with a fragment of inheritable material derived from the Preservers. The dominant races of this habitat are from many different places and many different times, but they all are marked by this attribute, and all believe that they can evolve to a higher state. Indeed, many seem to have evolved out of existence, but it is not clear if they have transcended or merely become extinct. But the primitive races, which resemble men but are little better than animals, are not marked, and have never advanced from their original state. There is much I still do not understand about this world, but that much I do know."

"If you can help me understand where I came from, perhaps I can help you."

The woman smiled. "You try to bargain with me. But I have already told you where you came from, Yamamanama, and I have already helped you. I have sung many songs of praise in your honor. I have told many of your coming. I have raised up a champion to fight for you. You should be with him now, sailing downriver to the war."

Yama remembered the young warlord's story. He said, "With Enobarbus?"

"The soldier too. But I meant Dr. Dismas. He found me long ago, long before I spoke with Enobarbus. You should be with them now. With their help, and especially with mine, you could save the world."

Yama laughed. "Lady, I will do what I can against the heretics, but I do not think I can do more than any other man."

"*Against* the heretics? Don't be silly. I have not been able to speak to you, but I have watched you. I heard your prayers, after your brother's death. I know how desperately you wish to become a hero and avenge him. Ah, but I can make you more than that."

After the news of Telmon's death, Yama had prayed all night before the shrine in the temple. The Aedile had sent two soldiers to watch over him, but they had fallen asleep, and in the quiet hour before dawn Yama had asked for a sign that he would lead a great victory in Telmon's name. He had thought then that he wanted to redeem his brother's death, but he understood now that his prayers had been prompted by mere selfishness. He had wanted a shape to his own life, to know its beginning and to be given a destiny. He realized that perhaps his prayer had been answered after all, but not in the way he had hoped.

"You must take up your inheritance," the woman said. "I can help you. Together we can complete the changes my original began. I think you have already begun to explore what you can do. There is much more, if you will let me teach you."

"If you had listened to me, domina, you would know that I pledged to save the world, not change it."

Did her gaze darken? For a moment, it seemed to Yama that her strange beauty was merely a mask or film covering something horrible.

She said, "If you want to save the world, it must be changed. Change is fundamental to life. The world will be changed whichever side wins the war, but only one side can ensure that stasis is not enforced again. Stasis preserves dead things, but it suffocates life. A faction of the servants of this world realized that long ago. But they failed, and those which survived were thrown into exile. Now they are our servants, and together we will succeed where they alone did not."

Yama remembered the cold black presence of the feral machine he had inadvertently called down at the merchant's house, and it took all his will not to run from the woman, as Pandaras had run at first sight. He knew now which side this avatar was on, and where Enobarbus and Dr. Dismas would have taken him if he had not escaped. Dr. Dismas had lied about everything. He was a spy for the heretics, and Enobarbus was not a champion against them, but a warlord secretly fighting on their side. He had not escaped when his ship had been sunk, but had been captured by the heretics and made into one of them. Or perhaps he had been granted safe passage because he already was one of them— for had he not spoken of a vision which had spoken to him from the shrine of the temple of his people? Yama knew now who had spoken to the young soldier, and knew what course he had been set upon. Not against the heretics, but for them. What a fool he had been to believe otherwise!

He said, "The world cannot be saved by contesting the will of those who made it. I will fight the heretics, not serve them."

Silver bells, ringing in the air all around. "You are still so young, Yamamanama! You still cling to the beliefs of your childhood! But you will change your mind. Dr. Dismas has promised that he has already sown the seeds of change. Look on this, Yamamanama. All this can be ours!"

The shrine flashed edge to edge with white light. Yama closed his eyes, but the white light was inside his head, too. Something long and narrow floated in it, like a needle in milk. It was his map. No, it was the world.

Half was green and blue and white, with the Great River running along one side and the ranges of the Rim Mountains on the other, and the icecap of the Endpoint shining in the sunlight; half was tawny desert, splotched and gouged with angry black and red scars and craters, the river dry, the icecap gone.

It floated before Yama, serene and lovely, for a long moment. And then it was gone, and the woman smiled at him from the window of the shrine, with the green lawn and the high hedges of the garden receding behind her.

"Together we will do great things," she said. "We will remake the world, and everyone in it, as a start."

Yama said steadfastly, "You are an aspect of one of the Ancients of Days. You raised up the heretics against the will of the Preservers. You are my enemy."

"I am no enemy of yours, Yamamanama. How could an enemy speak from a shrine?"

"The heretics silenced the last avatars of the Preservers. Why shouldn't something else take their place? Why do you tempt me with foolish visions? No one can rule the world."

The woman smiled. "No one does, and there is its problem. Any advanced organism must have a dominating principle, or else its different parts will war against each other, and it will be paralyzed by inaction. As with organisms, so with worlds. You have so many doubts. I understand. Hush! Not another word! Someone comes. We'll talk again. If not here, then at one of the other transceivers that are still functioning. There are many on the farside shore."

"If I talk with you again, it will be because I have found some way of destroying you."

She smiled. "I think you will change your mind about that."

"Never!"

"Oh, but I think that you will. Already it has begun. Until then."

And then she was gone, and with her the light. Once more, Yama could see through the darkly transparent disc of the shrine. On the far side of the apse, the curtain of black mesh stirred as someone pushed it aside.

25

The Assassin

IT WAS NOT Pandaras, nor even Tamora, but a barechested giant of a man in black leather trews. His skin was the color of rust and his face was masked with an oval of soft black moleskin. He carried a naked falchion, and there was a percussion pistol tucked into his waistband. His muscular arms were bound tightly with leather thongs; plastic vambraces, mottled with extreme age, were laced around his forearms.

As soon as he saw Yama, the man quickly advanced around the shrine. Yama stepped backward and drew his long knife. It ran with blue fire, as if dipped in flaming brandy.

The man smiled. His mouth was red and wet inside the slit in his black mask. The pointed teeth of a small fierce animal made a radiating pattern around the mask's mouth slit and little bones made a zig-zag pattern around the eyeholes, exaggerating their size. The man's rust-colored skin shone as if oiled, and a spiral pattern of welts was raised on the skin of his chest. Yama thought of the friendly people who had colonized the abandoned tombs at the edge of Ys. This was one of their sons, corrupted by the city. Or perhaps he had left his people because he was already corrupted.

"Who sent you?" Yama said. He was aware that one of the statues was only a few paces from his back. Remembering what Sergeant Rhodean had taught him, he carefully watched as the man moved toward him, looking for weaknesses he might exploit if it came to a fight.

"Put up that silly pricking blade, and I'll tell you," the man said. His voice was deep and slow, and set up echoes in the vaulted roof of the apse. "I was asked to kill you slowly, but I promise to make it quick if you don't struggle."

"It was Gorgo. He hired you at the Water Market."

The man's eyes widened slightly under the mask and Yama knew that he had guessed right, or had struck close to the truth.

He said, "Or you are a friend of Gorgo, or someone who owes him a favor. In any case, it is not an honorable act."

The man said, "Honor has nothing to it."

Yama's fingers sweated on the hilt of the knife and the skin and muscles of his forearm tingled as if held close to a fire, although the knife blade gave off no heat. Pandaras had not known to leave the knife in sunlight while I was ill, he thought. Now it takes the energy it needs from me, and I must strike soon.

He said, "Did Gorgo tell you who I killed? He cannot have forgotten, because it was only two nights ago. It was a rich and powerful merchant, with many guards. I was his prisoner, and my knife was taken from me, but he is dead and I stand here before you. Go now, and I will spare you."

He was calling out to any machine for help, but there were none close by. He could only feel their distant, directionless swarm, as a man hears the many voices of a city as an unmodulated roar.

The assassin said, "You think to keep me talking, that I may spare you or help will come. Those are foolish hopes. Put up your knife and it'll be a quick dispatch. You have my word."

"And perhaps you talk because you do not have the stomach for it."

The assassin laughed, a rumble like rocks moving over each other in his belly. "It's the other way around. I was paid to kill you as slowly as possible, and to withhold the name of my client until the last possible moment. You won't put away your silly little blade? You choose a slow death, then."

Yama saw that the assassin favored his right arm; if he ran to the left, the man must turn before striking. In that instant Yama might have a chance at a successful blow. Although the shrine was dark and fading sunlight had climbed halfway up the walls, laying a bronze sheen on the cloudily opaque torsoes of the gigantic soldiers, everything in the square apse shone with an intense particularity. Yama had never felt more alive than now, at the moment before his certain death.

He yelled and ran, striking at the man's masked face. His opponent whirled with amazing speed and parried automatically with such force that Yama was barely able to fend off the blow. The knife screamed and spat a stream of sparks, and notched the assassin's sword.

The assassin did not press his advantage, but stared distractedly at something above Yama's head. Yama struck again, lunging with the point of his knife; Sergeant Rhodean had taught him that the advantage of a shorter blade is the precision with which it can be directed. The assassin parried with the same casual, brutal force as before and stepped back, pulling the percussion pistol from his waistband.

Suddenly, dust boiled around them in a dry, choking cloud. Chips of stone rained down like hail, ringing on the stone flags of the floor. In the midst of this, Yama lunged again. It was a slight, glancing blow that barely grazed the assassin's chest, but the knife flashed and there was a terrific flash of blue light that knocked the man down. Yama's arm was instantly numbed from wrist to shoulder. As he shifted the knife to his left hand, the assassin got to his feet and raised the percussion pistol.

The man's mouth was working inside the mask's slit, and his eyes were wide. He fired and fired again at something behind Yama. The pistol failed on the third shot and the assassin threw it hard over Yama's head and ran, just as Pandaras had run when the woman had appeared in the shrine.

Yama chased after the assassin, his blood singing in his head, but the man plunged through the curtain of black mesh and Yama stopped short, fearing an ambush on the other side. He turned and looked up at the soldier which had stepped from its niche, and asked it to go back to sleep until it was needed again. The soldier, its eyes glowing bright red in its impassive face, struck its chestplate with a mailed fist, and the apse rang like a bell with the sound.

26

The Thing Below

A LONG WAY down the shadow-filled atrium, in the glow of a palm-oil lantern which had been lowered on a chain from the lofty ceiling, two men bent over something. Yama ran forward with his knife raised, but they were only priests tending to Pandaras. The boy lay sprawled on the mosaic floor, alive but unconscious. Yama knelt and touched his face. His eyes opened, but he seemed unable to speak. There was a bloody gash on his temple; it seemed to be his only wound.

Yama sheathed his knife and looked up at the two priests. They wore homespun robes and had broad, wide-browed faces and tangled manes of white hair: the same bloodline as Enobarbus. Although Yama had guessed that this was the place where the young warlord had received his vision, he still felt a small shock of recognition.

He asked the priests if they had seen who had wounded his friend, and they looked at each other before one volunteered that a man had just now run past, but they had already discovered this poor boy. Yama smiled to think of the spectacle the masked assassin must have made, running through the temple with a sword in his hand and blood running down his bare chest. Gorgo must be nearby—if he had sent the assassin, surely he would want to witness what he had paid for—and he would have seen the rout of his hireling.

The priests looked at each other again and the one who had spoken before said, "I am Antros, and this is my brother, Balcus. We are keepers of the temple. There is a place to wash your friend's wound, and to tend to your own wounds, too. Follow me."

Yama's right arm had recovered most of its strength, although it now tingled as if it had been stung by a horde of ants. He gathered up

Pandaras and followed the old priest. The boy's skin was hot and his heartbeat was light and rapid, but Yama had no way of knowing whether or not this was normal.

Beyond the colonnade on the left-hand side of the atrium was a little grotto carved into the thick stone of the temple's outer wall. Water trickled into a shallow stone trough from a plastic spout set in the center of a swirl of red mosaic. Yama helped Pandaras kneel, and bathed the shallow wound on his temple. Blood which had matted the boy's sleek hair fluttered into the clear cold water, but the bleeding had already stopped and the edges of the wound were clean.

"You will have a headache," Yama told Pandaras, "but nothing worse. I think he struck you with the edge of his vambrace, or with his pistol, rather than with his falchion. You should have stayed with me, Pandaras."

Pandaras was still unable to speak, but he clumsily caught Yama's hand and squeezed it.

The old priest, Antros, insisted on cleaning the shallow cuts on Yama's back. As he worked, he said, "We heard two pistol shots. You are lucky that he missed you, although I would guess that he did not miss you by much, and you were hurt by stone splinters knocked from the wall."

"Fortunately, he was not aiming at me," Yama said.

Antros said, "This was a fine place once. The pillars were painted azure and gold, and beeswax candles as tall as a man scented the air with their perfume. Our temple was filled with mendicants and palmers from every town and city along the length of the river. That was long before my time, of course, but I do remember when an avatar of the Preservers still appeared in the shrine."

"Was this avatar a woman, dressed in white?"

"It was neither man nor woman, and neither young nor old." The old priest smiled in recollection. "How I miss its wild laughter—it was filled with fierce joy, and yet it was a gentle creature. But it is gone. They have all gone. Men still come to pray at the shrine, of course, but although the Preservers hear every prayer, men have fallen so far from grace that there are no longer answers to their questions. Few come here now, and even fewer to bare themselves humbly before their creators. Most who come do so to ask the one below to curse their enemies, but there are not even very many of them."

"I suppose that most people fear this place."

"Just so, although we do have problems with cultists from time to time, for they are attracted by the same thing which the ordinary folk fear. My brother and I come here each evening to light the lamps, but otherwise the temple is not much used, even by our own bloodline. Of course, we have our high day when the atrium is decorated with palm fronds and wreaths of ivy and there is a solemn procession to aspurge every corner and to propitiate the Thing Below. But otherwise, as I have said, most people keep away. You are a stranger here. A palmer, perhaps. I am sorry that you and your friend were attacked. No doubt a footpad followed you, and saw his chance."

Yama asked Antros if the Thing Below was the machine which had fallen in the final battle at the end of the Age of Insurrection.

"Indeed. You must not suppose it was destroyed. Rather, it was entombed alive in rock made molten by its fall. It stirs, sometimes. In fact, it has been very restless recently. Listen! Do you hear it?"

Yama nodded. He had supposed that the high singing in his head was his own blood rushing through his veins with the excitement of his brief skirmish.

"It is the second time in as many days," Antros said. "Most of our bloodline are soldiers, and part of our duty is to guard the well and the thing entombed at its bottom. But many have gone downriver to fight in the war, and many of those have been killed there."

"I met one," Yama said. He did not need to ask when the machine had begun to be restless, and felt a chill in his blood. He had called for help in the merchant's house, and the feral machine which had answered his call was not the only one to have heard him. What else? What else might he have inadvertently awakened?

Out in the atrium, someone suddenly started to shout, raising overlapping echoes. The old priest looked alarmed, but Yama said, "Do not be afraid, dominie. I know that voice."

———

Tamora had returned to the inn, she said, and had had to threaten the painted witch who ran it to find out where Yama and Pandaras had gone. "Then I realized what the game was, and came straightaway."

"It was Gorgo," Yama said, as he tied the laces of his torn, bloodstained shirt. "I appear to have a knack of making enemies."

"I hope you gouged out his eyes before you killed him," Tamora said.

"I have not seen him. But someone shot an arbalest bolt at me earlier, and I remember that you said Gorgo had killed someone with an arbalest. He missed, and then he sent another man to kill me. Fortunately, I had some help, and was able to scare off the assassin."

"I will have his eyes," Tamora said with venomous passion, "if I ever see him again! His balls and his eyes! He is a disgrace to the Fierce People!"

"He must be very jealous, to want to kill me because of you."

Tamora laughed, and said, "O Yama, at last you show some human weakness, even if it is only conceit about your cockmanship. The truth is, I owe Gorgo money. He's not one for fighting, but for making deals. He finds work for others, and takes a cut of the fees for his trouble. And he loans money, too. I borrowed from him to buy new armor and this sword after I was wounded in the war last year. I lost my kit then, you see. I was working on commission to pay off the debt and the interest. I got enough to live on, and he took the rest."

"Then the job I did with you—"

"Yes, yes," Tamora said impatiently. "On Gorgo's commission. He didn't really expect me to succeed, but he was still angry when I told him that we'd killed the merchant and hadn't been able to collect the fee."

"And that is why you agreed to help me."

"Not exactly. Yama, we don't have time for this."

"I need to know, Tamora."

Yama understood now why Tamora had embarked on such a risky enterprise, but he still did not understand why Gorgo wanted him dead.

Tamora hung her head for a moment, then said with a mixture of vulnerability and defiance, "I suppose it's only fair. The star-sailor job would have paid well, but we lost the fee because you went crazy and grabbed that circlet. And I still owe Gorgo, and I was going off to work for you, as he saw it. I said he should wait and I'd pay back everything, but he's greedy. He wants the liver and the lights as well as the meat and bones."

Yama nodded. "He decided to kill me and steal the money I have."

"He said that he would rob you, not kill you. He said it was only fair, because you'd lost him the fee for killing the merchant. I didn't know he'd try and kill you. I swear it."

"I believe you," Yama said. "And I know that Gorgo found someone else to help you with the job in the Palace of the Memory of the People. He wanted me out of the way."

"A man with red skin and welts on his chest. I told Gorgo that I was going to work with you, Yama, and no other, but Gorgo said the man would be waiting for me at the Palace gate. I went there, but I couldn't find the man and I went back to the inn and found that you had come here."

"Well, the man you were waiting for was here. It was he who tried to kill me."

"I was going to tell you everything," Tamora said. "I decided something, while I was waiting. Hear me out. I made an agreement with you, and I will stick with it. Fuck Gorgo. When the job is finished I'll find him and kill him."

"Then you will work for me, and not Gorgo?"

"Isn't that what I said?" Tamora said impatiently. "But there isn't time to stand and talk a moment longer, not now! You've been lying around in bed, and then fooling about in this mausoleum, and meanwhile I have been busy. We have already missed one appointment, and we must not miss the second, or the contract will be voided. Can you ride?"

"A little."

"That had better mean you can ride like the wind." Tamora seemed to notice Pandaras for the first time. "What happened to the rat-boy?"

"A blow to the head. Luckily, the assassin Gorgo hired had some scruples."

"Maybe it'll have knocked some of his airs out and let some sense in. I suppose you still want to bring him? Well, I'll carry him for you. Why are you staring at me? Do you call off our contract after all this?"

"I have already woken things best left sleeping. If I go on, what else might I do?"

Tamora said briskly, "Would you emasculate yourself, then? If you don't know who you are and where you came from, then you can't know what you can become. Come with me, or not. I'm taking the job anyway, because I'll get paid for it with you or without you. And when I've finished there, I'll kill Gorgo."

She slung Pandaras over her shoulder and walked away with a quick, lithe step, as if the boy weighed nothing at all. After a moment, Yama followed.

It was dusk. Warm lights glowed in windows of the houses around the mossy plaza. Two horses were tethered to a pole topped by a smoky, guttering cresset. Tamora and Yama lifted Pandaras onto the withers of her mount, and then she vaulted easily into the saddle behind him. She leaned down and told Yama, "I had to pay the painted witch a fortune for the hire of these. Don't stand and gape. Already it may be too late."

The horses were harnessed cavalry fashion, with light saddles and high stirrups. Yama had just grasped the horn of his mount's saddle and fitted his left foot in the stirrup, ready to swing himself up, when the ground shook. The horse jinked and as Yama tried to check it, he saw a beam of light shoot up through the aperture of the domed roof of the Black Temple.

The light was as red as burning sulphur, with flecks of violet and vermilion whirling in it like sparks flying up a chimney. It burned high into the sky, so bright that it washed the temple and the square in bloody light.

Yama realized at once what was happening, and knew that he must confront what he had wakened. He was horribly afraid of it, but if he did not face it then he would always be afraid.

He threw the reins of his mount to Tamora and ran up the steps into the temple. As he entered the long atrium, the floor groaned and heaved, like an animal tormented by biting flies. Yama fell headlong, picked himself up, and ran on toward the column of red light that burned up from the well and filled the temple with its fierce glare.

The temple was restless. The stone of its walls squealed and howled; dust and small fragments rained down from the ceiling. Several of the pillars on either side had cracked from top to bottom; one had collapsed across the floor, its heavy stone discs spilled like a stack of giant's coins. The intricate mosaics of the floor were fractured, heaved apart in uneven ripples. A long ragged crack ran back from the well, and the two old priests stood on either side of it, silhouetted in the furnace light. Balcus had drawn his sword and held it above his head in pitiful defiance; Antros knelt with the heels of his hands pressed to his eyes, chanting over and over an incantation or prayer.

The language was a private dialect of the priests' bloodline, but its rhythm struck deep in Yama. He fell to his knees beside the old priest and began to chant too.

It was not a prayer, but a set of instructions to the guards of the temple.

He was repeating it for a third time when the black mesh curtain which divided the right-hand apse from the atrium was struck aside. Two, four, five of the giant soldiers marched out. The red light gleamed like fresh blood on their transparent carapaces.

The two old priests immediately threw themselves full-length on the floor, but Yama watched with rapt fascination. The five soldiers were the only survivors of the long sleep of the temple's guards. One dragged a stiff leg, and another was blind and moved haltingly under the instructions of the others, but none of them had forgotten their duty. They took up position, forming a five-pointed star around the well, threw open their chest-plates and drew out bulbous silver tubes as long as Yama was tall. Yama supposed that the soldiers would discharge their weapons into the well, but instead they aimed at the coping and floor around it and fired as one.

One of the weapons exploded, blowing the upper part of its owner to flinders; from the others, violet threads as intensely bright as the sun raked stone until it ran like water into the well. Heat and light beat at Yama's skin; the atrium filled with the acrid stench of burning stone. The floor heaved again, a rolling ripple that snapped mosaics and paving slabs like a whip and threw Yama and the priests backward.

And the Thing Below rose up from the white-hot annulus around its pit.

It was brother to the feral machine that Yama had inadvertently drawn down at the merchant's house, although it was very much larger. It barely cleared the sides of the well—black, spherical, and bristling with mobile spines. It had grown misshapen during its long confinement, like a spoiled orange that flattens under its own weight.

The giant soldiers played violet fire across the machine, but it took no notice of them. It hung in the midst of its column of red light and looked directly into Yama's head. *You have called me. I am here. Now come with me, and serve.*

Pain struck through Yama's skull like an iron wedge. His sight was filled with red and black lightnings. Blind, burning inside and out, he gave the soldiers a final order.

They moved as one, and then Yama could see again. The four soldiers were clinging to the machine as men cling to a bit of flotsam from a wreck. They were shearing away the machine's spines with the blades of their hands.

The spines were what enabled the machine to bend the gravity field of the world to its will. It spun and jerked, like a hyrax attacked by dire wolves, but it was too late. It fell like a stone into the well, and the temple shuddered again. There was a long roaring sound, and the column of red light flickered and then went out.

27

The Palace of the Memory of the People

YAMA AND THE two priests helped each other through the smoky wreckage of the temple. A great cheer went up when they emerged into the twilight, scorched, blinking, coughing on fumes and covered in soot. The people who lived in the houses around and about the temple had run out of their homes convinced that the last day of the world was at hand, and now they knew that they were saved. Men of the priests' bloodline ran up and helped them away; Tamora urged her horse up the shallow steps, leading Yama's mount by its reins.

Yama fought through the crowd. "It is gone!" he shouted to her. "I woke the soldiers and I defeated it!"

"We may be too late!" Tamora shouted back. "If you're done here, follow me!"

By the time Yama had climbed into the saddle of his horse, she was already galloping away across the square. He whooped and gave chase. His horse was a lean, sure-footed gelding, and needed little guidance as he raced Tamora through the narrow streets. The rush of warm evening air stung his scorched skin but cleared his head. His long hair, uncut since he had left Aeolis, streamed out behind him.

A bell began to toll, and Tamora looked back and yelled, "The gate! Ten minutes before it closes!"

She lashed the flanks of her mount with her reins, and it laid back its ears and raised its tail and doubled its speed. Yama shouted encouraging words in the ear of his own horse, and it took heart and gave chase. A minute later, they shot out of the end of the narrow street and began to plough through crowds that clogged a wide avenue beneath globes of blue fire floating high in the air.

They were petitioners, penitents and palmers trying to gain entrance to the Palace of the Memory of the People, their numbers swelled by those panicked by earth tremors and strange lights. Tamora laid about her with bunched reins, and people pressed back into each other as she forced a way through, with Yama close behind. The tolling of the bell shivered the air, drowning the screams and shouts of the crowd.

When Tamora and Yama reached the end of the avenue, they found a picket line of machines spinning in the air, burning with fierce radiance like a cord of tiny suns. Overhead, more machines flitted through the dusk like fireflies. They filled Yama's head with their drowsy hum, as if he had plunged head-first into a hive of bees. Robed and hooded magistrates stood behind the glare of the picket line. Beyond them the avenue opened out into a square so huge it could easily have contained the little city of Aeolis. At the far side of the square a high smooth cliff of keelrock curved away to the left and right, punctuated by a gateway that was guarded by a decad of soldiers in silvery armor who stood on floating discs high in the blue-lit air.

The black mountain of the Palace of the Memory of the People loomed above all of this, studded with lights and blotting out the sky. Its peaks vanished into a wreath of clouds. Yama stared up at it. He had come so far in a handful of days, from the little citadel of the peel-house of the Aedile of Aeolis to this, the greatest citadel of all, which the preterites claimed was older than the world itself. He had learned that his bloodline was older than the world, and that he could bend to his will the machines which maintained the world. He had learned that the heretics considered him a great prize, and had resolved to fight against them with all his might—and he had confronted and defeated one of their dark angels.

He had left behind his childhood. Ahead lay the long struggle by which he would define himself. Perhaps it would end in death; certainly, countless men had already died in the war, and many more would die before the heretics were defeated. But at this moment, although he was exhausted and bruised, his clothes scorched and tattered, he felt more alive than ever before. Somewhere in the great citadel that reared above him, in the stacks of its ten thousand libraries, in the labyrinths of the hundreds of temples and shrines and departments, must be the secret of his origin. He did not doubt it. The woman in the shrine had said that he had come from the deep past, but she was his enemy, and surely she had been lying. He would prove her wrong. He would find the secrets that Dr. Dismas had uncovered and discover where his bloodline still lived, and learn from them how to use his powers against the heretics.

Tamora caught the bridle of Yama's horse and shouted that they would do better to return tomorrow. "The gates are about to close!"

"No! We must go now! It is my destiny!"

Pandaras raised his head and said weakly, "My master wills it."

Tamora grinned, showing the rack of her sharp white teeth, and held up something that flashed with red light. The picket line of incandescent machines spun apart before her. People started toward the gap and magistrates moved forward, lashing out with their quirts, driving those at the front into those pressing forward from behind. In the midst of the mêlée, a fat woman reclining on a pallet born by four oiled, nearly naked men suddenly clutched at the swell of her bosom. Under her plump hands, a vivid red stain spread over her white dress. She slumped sideways and the pallet tipped and foundered, sending a wave of confusion spreading out through the close-packed people.

Yama did not understand what had happened until a man right by his horse's flank flew forward and folded over and fell under the feet of his neighbors. Yama glimpsed the red fletching of the bolt in the dead man's back, and then the crowd closed over him.

Tamora had drawn her sword and was brandishing it about her as she forced a way through the crowd. Yama kicked at hands which tried to grasp the bridle of his plunging mount, and fought through the tumult to her side.

"Gorgo!" he shouted at Tamora. "Gorgo! He is here!"

But Tamora did not hear him. She was leaning against Pandaras and shouting at the magistrates who barred her way. Yama reached for her shoulder and something went past his ear with a wicked crack, and when he jerked around to see where it had come from another bolt smashed the head of a man who had been trying to catch hold of the bridle of his horse.

Yama lashed out in panic and anger then. Red and black lightning filled his head. And suddenly he saw the square from a thousand points of view that all converged on a figure on a flat roof above the crowded avenue. Gorgo screamed and raised the arbalest in front of his face as hundreds of tiny machines smashed into him, riddling his torso and arms and legs. He must have died in an instant, but his body did not fall. Instead, it rose into the air, the sole of one boot brushing the parapet as it drifted out above the packed heads of the crowd.

Yama came to himself and saw that Tamora had forced her way through the line of magistrates. He galloped after her. On the far side of the vast square, the great iron gates of the Palace of the Memory of the People were closing. The bell fell silent, and there was a shocking moment of silence. Then people felt drops of blood falling on them and looked up and saw Gorgo's riddled body sustained high above, head bowed and arms flung wide, the arbalest dangling by its strap against his ruined chest.

A woman screamed and the crowd began to yell again, ten thousand voices shouting against each other. The discs which bore the soldiers swooped toward the crowd as Yama and Tamora raced their horses across the square and plunged through the gates into the darkness beyond.

Ancients
of
Days

For Kim Newman,
compañero

In books lies the soul of the whole Past Time; the articulate audible voice of the Past, when the body and material substance of it has altogether vanished like a dream.

Thomas Carlyle

1

The Whisperers

PANDARAS ENTERED THE shadowy arena of the Basilica just as one half of the defense force charged at the other. Tamora led the point of the attacking wedge, screaming fearsomely; Yama ran up and down behind the double rank of the defending line and shouted at his thralls to stand firm.

The two sides met with a rattle of padded staves against round arm shields. Shadows shifted wildly as fireflies swooped overhead like a storm of sparks. For a moment it seemed that the attack must fail, but then one of the thralls in the defending line gave ground to Tamora's remorseless blows. Instead of closing the gap as the man went down in the press, the first rank wavered and broke, stumbling backward into the second. Yama shouted the order to regroup, but his thralls fell over each other or simply dropped their shields and staves and ran, and the wedge formation of the attacking force dissolved as thralls began to chase each other around the Basilica.

In the middle of the confusion, Tamora threw down her stave in disgust, and Yama blew and blew on his whistle until everyone stopped running. Pandaras came toward them, trotting over the pattern of chalked lines Tamora had carefully drawn on the marble floor that morning. His two fireflies spun above his small sleek head. He said cheerfully, "Did they do something wrong? I thought it was very energetic."

"You should be in the kitchen with the rest of the pan scourers," Tamora said, and went off to round up the thralls so that she could tell them exactly what they had done wrong. Her own fireflies seemed to have caught some of her anger; they flared with bright white light and whirled around her head like hornets sprung in defense of their nest.

Her long queue of red hair gleamed like a rope of fresh blood. She wore a plastic corselet, much scratched and scored, and a short skirt of over-lapping strips of scuffed leather that left her powerfully muscled legs mostly bare.

Pandaras said, "They are armed with sticks, master. Is that part of your plan?"

"We do not dare give them proper weapons yet," Yama told the boy. Like the thralls, he wore only a breechclout. The floor was cold and gritty under his bare feet, but he was sweating in the chill air, and his blood sang. He could feel it thrilling under his skin. His vigorous black hair was bushed up by the bandage around his forehead. A ceramic disc, of the kind believed to have been used as coins in the Age of Enlightenment, hung from his neck on a leather thong. At his back, his knife hung in its goatskin sheath from a leather harness that went over his shoulders and fastened across his chest.

He said, "We had them at drill most of the day. You should see how they keep in step!"

Pandaras looked up at his master, affecting concern. "How is your head, master? Is the wound making you feverish? You seem to think an army of polishers and floor sweepers, armed only with sticks, can frighten away the crack troops of the Department of Indigenous Affairs by putting on a marching display."

Yama smiled. "Why are you here, Pandaras? Do you really have something to tell me, or have you come expressly to annoy Tamora? I hope not. She is doing the best she can."

Pandaras looked to either side, then drew himself up until his sleek head was level with Yama's chest. He said, "I have learned something. You may have exiled me to the bowels of this broken-backed, bankrupt and debauched department, but I have still been working hard for you."

"You chose your place, as I remember."

Pandaras said, "And now you may thank me for my foresight. I have news which affects our whole scheme here, and I beg to be allowed to lay my prize at your feet. I don't think you'll be displeased."

"You have been spying, Pandaras. What did you find?"

"It was in the mausoleum they call the Hall of the Tranquil Mind," Pandaras said. "While you two have been playing soldiers with the hewers of wood and drawers of water, I've been risking my life in intrigue. A deadly game with the worst of penalties for losing, but I have had the good fortune to learn something that affects our whole scheme."

The Hall of the Tranquil Mind was a black, windowless edifice carved out of the basalt wall of the big cavern which housed the Department of Vaticination. Yama had thought that it was locked up and derelict, like so much of the Department.

He said, "I suppose you went there to meet your sweetheart. Are you still chasing that scullion? You are dressed for the part."

Pandaras had washed and mended his ragged clothes and polished his boots. He had found or stolen a red silk scarf which was knotted around his long, flexible neck with such casual elegance that Yama suspected he had spent half the morning getting it just so. His two fireflies spun above his head like living jewels.

He winked and said, "Chased, caught, wooed, won. I didn't come to boast of my conquests, master. It's an old tale oft told, and there's not time. We're in mortal peril here, if I'm any judge of the situation."

Yama smiled. His self-appointed squire loved to conjure drama from the slightest of events.

Pandaras said, "There is a gallery that runs along one side of the Hall of the Tranquil Mind, under the rim of the dome. If you happen to be standing at the top of the stairs to the gallery, and if you place your ear close to the wall, then you can hear anything said by those below. A device much favored by tyrants, I understand, who know that plotters often choose public buildings to meet, for any gathering in a public place can be easily explained away. But fortune favors the brave, master. Today I was placed in the role of tyrant, and I overheard the whispered plotting of a pair of schemers."

Pandaras paused. Yama had turned away to look across the shadowy Basilica. Tamora was marshalling the reluctant thralls into three ranks. Her voice raised echoes under the shabby grandeur of the vaulted dome.

Pandaras said, "It is more important, master, than playing at soldiers."

"But this is important, too. It is why we are here, to begin with, and besides, it is useful to stay in practice."

Yama did not add that it helped satisfy something in him that hungered for action. His sleep had been troubled by bloodthirsty dreams ever since he had entered the Palace of the Memory of the People, and sometimes an unfocused rage stirred up headaches that filled his sight with jagged red and black lightnings, and left him weak and ill. He had been hard-used since he had reached Ys and escaped Prefect Corin, and he had been wounded in an ambush when they had first arrived outside the gates of the Department of Vaticination. He needed rest, but there was no time for it.

He said, "I must hear what Tamora has to say. Walk with me, Pandaras."

"The blow to the head has given you delusions, master. You believe yourself a soldier."

"And you believe that you are my squire, so we are equally deluded. Hush, now. We will speak of what you heard when Tamora has finished with our poor warriors."

Tamora had jumped on to a square stone plinth which had once supported a statue—only its feet remained, clad in daintily pointed slippers which still retained traces of yellow pigment. She looked at the six decads of thralls who had gathered around her, allowing scorn to darken her small, triangular face. It was a trick she had taught Yama. To be a teacher, she said, was to be an actor first. Unless delivered from the heart, no lesson could be convincing.

The thralls were all of the same bloodline, lean and long-armed and bowlegged, with loose gray skin that hung in heavy folds from bony joints. They had long, vulpine faces, untidy manes of coarse black or umber hair that tumbled down their bent backs and muddy yellow or green eyes that peered out from beneath heavy brows. They were a stupid and frustratingly obdurate bloodline. According to Syle, the Secretary of the Department of Vatication, their families had served here for more than twenty thousand years. But although they were naturally servile, the unaccustomed drill had made them sullen and mutinous, and they took every opportunity to make it clear that Tamora and Yama had no real authority over them. They glared at Tamora, sharp teeth pricking their thin black lips, as she told them how badly they had done.

She said, "You have all taken your turn at defense, and you have all taken your turn at attack. You should know that if you are to win through or stand firm, you must stay in formation. A defending rank is only as strong as its weakest member. If he falls, someone must immediately take his place. If an attacking formation breaks through a line, it must stay together."

One of the thralls said, "They ran and we chased 'em down, mistress. What's wrong with that?"

Tamora stared at the man until he lowered his gaze. She said, "There might be reserves waiting behind a turn in a corridor. If your disorganized rabble ran into them, then you'd be quickly slaughtered."

"But there wasn't anyone else," the thrall mumbled, and those around him muttered in agreement.

Tamora raised her voice. "This is an exercise. When you fight for real, you can't assume anything. That's why you must fight as you're told, not as you want. It's very easy to kill one man on his own, much harder to kill him when he's part of a formation. When you fight shoulder to shoulder, you defend those on either side of you, and they defend you. That way you don't have to worry about the enemy getting behind your back, because to do that they'd have to get around the line. And they won't, not in the corridors. Elsewhere, in the open, you fight in squares, as you tried yesterday."

When Tamora paused for breath, a thrall stepped out of the front rank and said, "We'd do better, mistress, if we had proper weapons."

"I'll break open the armory when you've mastered those sticks," Tamora said. "From what I've just seen, I've a mind to take the sticks away."

The thrall did not back down. He was taller than the rest, if only because he was straight-backed. There were streaks of gray in his long mane. Most of the thralls possessed only one or two dim fireflies, but six hung in a neat cluster above his head, burning nearly as brightly as Tamora's. He said, "We won't be fighting with these sticks, so why do we practice with them?"

The thralls muttered and nudged each other, and Pandaras told Yama, "That's what they've been complaining about, down in the kitchens."

Yama felt a sudden hot anger. He strode forward and confronted the gray-maned thrall. "It is discipline, not weapons, that makes a fighting force," he said loudly. "Between all of you, there is not the discipline to attack a nest of rats."

The thrall returned Yama's glare. He said, "Beg your pardon, dominie, but we do know a bit about rat-catching."

Some of the other thralls laughed and Yama lost the last of his temper; it was easily lost these days. "Come on," he said. "Come on then, rat-catcher! Show me how well you fight!"

The thrall looked around at his fellows, but none were willing to support him. He said uneasily, "It's not you I want to fight, dominie."

"You cannot choose who to fight!" Yama asked Tamora to lend him her sword, and presented it hilt-first to the thrall. "Take this! Take it right now!"

The thrall dropped his stave and spread his empty hands. "Dominie . . ."

From above, Tamora said sharply, "Do as he commands or slink away like the cur you are."

Yama thrust the hilt of the sword at the thrall until he had to take it or have it fall on his feet. "Take it! Good. Now hold it up. It is not a broom. It is a weapon. You can kill with the point or with the cutting edge, and if you do not have the taste for blood, you can render your enemy insensible with a blow to the head with the flat of the blade. However, I do not recommend you try the last against anyone less skilled than you. The man who wounded me that way lost most of his fingers when I countered his stroke. Hold it up. Keep the tip of the blade level with your eyes."

Tamora said, "If you're any kind of man, you must know that the higher the angle the better the thrust. Obey your master! Show him you're a man!"

The other thralls had broken ranks and backed away, forming a rough circle around Yama and the gray-maned thrall. They laughed now, and Yama scowled at them and told them what Sergeant Rhodean had told him so many times.

"Do not mock an armed man unless you wish to fight him." He pointed at the gray-maned thrall and thumped himself just below the breastbone. "Now thrust at me. Aim here. If you miss the heart, you might get a lung. Either way you will have killed me. Come on!"

The thrall made a tentative jab that did not carry more than halfway. Yama batted the square point of the sword aside and leaned forward and shouted in the thrall's face.

"Come on! Kill me, or I will tear out your eyes as a lesson! Do it!"

The thrall yelled and sprang forward, swiping wildly. Yama stepped inside the swing and caught the thrall's arm at the elbow, pivoted in a neat half-turn and threw him from his hip. The thrall let go of the sword when he fell; Yama had it before it could ring on the marble floor and with a smooth swing laid the edge at the thrall's throat. For a moment, he struggled against the urge to complete the motion.

The thrall looked up at him, his yellow slitted eyes glaring behind the agitated orbits of his six fireflies. In the moment of shocked silence, Yama looked around. None of the other thralls would meet his gaze. He smiled and reversed the sword and presented it to Tamora.

She sheathed it, jumped down from the pedestal, and helped the thrall to his feet. "Bravely tried. Better than anything anyone else has done." She looked around at the others. "I don't mind if you hate us, but I do mind if you can't get angry. Without anger you'll have only fear when it comes to a fight. We can't teach you how to get angry, but if you can manage it we can teach you how to direct your anger. To-morrow we begin again. Now get out of my sight. Go on! Run!"

Pandaras applauded languidly as the thralls dispersed around him, their claws clicking on marble. He said, "A bold display, master. I had not thought you could play-act so well."

Yama shrugged. Now it was over he felt self-conscious. His head wound throbbed. He said, "I was not play-acting. I lost my temper."

Tamora said, "Like I said, that's what's needed. You're getting an edge to you, Yama. That's good. We'll make you into something like one of the Fierce People, eh? The thralls have been servants for thousands of generations, and we've been treating them like volunteers. We have been too kind. They take up arms not because they want to, but because they have been told to. Grah, they will not do anything unless they are told, and then they do what they are told and no more. They can march in perfect formation all day long without losing step, but they haven't the heart to fight."

Tamora was angry with herself, and so all the more unforgiving. Nothing had gone right since they had been ambushed by hired ruffians when they had arrived at the Gate of Double Glory.

She added, "We're just a couple of caterans. We'll do our best with what we've been given, but in the end it won't matter. Indigenous Affairs will march right in and slaughter the thralls and take this place inside a day. This is a poor diversion in your search, Yama. I'm sorry for it."

"Without this subterfuge, I would not have been able to enter the Palace without being questioned. Besides," Yama said, "I enjoy these exercises."

It was true. The sound of padded staves thumping on shields and the smell of chalk and sweat had brought back happy memories of all the afternoons he had spent training with Telmon and Sergeant Rhodean in the gymnasium of the peel-house. The practice fights satisfied a fierceness he had not known he had possessed.

Tamora said, "I forget how young you are, and how hopeful. We might make these poor fools believe they have the heart for a fight, but it'll delay their deaths by no more than a minute. They know they're going to die, and they know that their wives and children will be killed too, or put into slavery. We'll be ransomed, but because our ransoms have already been paid into bond with the Department of Internal Harmony, we'll be freed and given our wages, and that'll be the end of that."

"I pray you are right. I think that Prefect Corin is still searching for me, and he is a high official in Indigenous Affairs."

They had talked about this before. Tamora said with exaggerated patience, "Of course I am right. It is how it has always been, since the world was made. If it were not for the ancient protocols, there would be constant civil war here. Your Prefect will not be able to interfere. I am sure the Indigenous Affairs sent those fools to ambush us, and perhaps Prefect Corin had a hand in it, but now we are inside the boundary of this Department he will dare do nothing else.

"Listen. Here is the problem. Not your Prefect, but the real problem. We fight because we're paid. Once captured no harm will come to us. But the thralls fight because they've been told to fight, and they've been told to fight because that fat fool who rules this place and claims to see into the future predicts victory. The thralls know in their guts that she is wrong. That is why they are so sullen."

Yama said, "We do not know that Luria does not have the powers she claims."

"Grah. *She* knows that she doesn't, and so does Syle, and so do the thralls. And the other pythoness is no more than a whey-faced wet-brained child stolen from her cradle. I have not heard her speak a single word since we came here."

Pandaras said, "From what I hear, Daphoene might be young, but she does have power, and that's why she is forbidden to speak. Luria fears her because she thinks that one day innocent Daphoene will expose her fraud. Master, I must speak with you about what I heard."

Yama said, "Daphoene is very young. She may appear to keep her own counsel, but perhaps she has none to offer."

Tamora laughed. "Yama, you're so innocent that you're a danger to all around you. For once your pet rat has said something sensible. If Daphoene does have true foresight, then Luria has every reason to keep her quiet. Syle too, and that bloodless wife of his. For Daphoene will know how badly the defense of this place will go."

Yama said, "Well, we will see her at work soon enough."

In two days, the oracle would be opened for public inquisition, and the pythonesses would answer the questions of their petitioners. It might be the last time the ceremony was held, for ten days after that the deadline for challenging the quit claim would run out. The Department of Indigenous Affairs would be allowed to march on the crumbling glory of the High Morning Court of the Department of Vaticination, and occupy the place where once Hierarchs had swum amongst maps of the Galaxy's stars, ordering the voyages of ships that fell from star to star through holes in space and time.

Pandaras told Tamora, "My master has paid you to help him find his bloodline, and it is a better and more honorable task than this game of soldiers. As you will at once see, if you let me tell my tale."

"You run if you want," Tamora said. "I'd like to see you run, rat-boy. It would prove what I've always thought about you."

Pandaras said, with an air of affronted dignity, "I'll ignore the slights on my character, except to say that those who attribute base motives to all around them do so because they expect no better of themselves. But while you have been playing at soldiers, I have been risking my life. Master, please hear me out, I must tell you what I heard."

"If this is more kitchen gossip," Tamora said, "then hold your yap. You'd inflate the breaking of a glass into an epic tragedy."

"Neh, and why not? It's a painful death for the glass concerned, leaves its fellows bereft of a good companion, and makes them aware of their own mortality."

Yama said, "Pandaras claims to have overheard a conspiracy."

"Master, she will not believe me. It is not worth telling her."

"Out with it, Pandaras," Yama said. "Forget your injured dignity."

"There were two of them. They were whispering together, but I heard one say, 'Tomorrow, at dawn. Go straightaway, and come straight back.' This was a woman. The other may have been a servant, for he simply made a noise of assent, and the first said, 'Do this, and I see a great elevation. Fail, and she lives. And if she lives we all may die.' Then they both moved off, master, and I heard no more. But it is enough, don't you think?"

Tamora said, "We should expect nothing less. These old departments are rats' nests of poisonous intrigues and feuds over trifles."

Pandaras said, "If we can trust no one here, why must we stay? We should cut our losses and run."

Yama said, "You have not told us who these plotters were."

"Ah, as to that . . ."

Tamora scowled. "Grah. You were scared, and didn't dare look."

"Had I leaned out over the gallery rail, I might have been seen, and the game would have been up." Pandaras batted at the pair of fireflies which circled his head; they dipped away and circled back. "These cursed things we must use instead of candles would have given me away."

"As I said, you were scared."

Yama said, "It does not matter. The gate is closed at night, and opens again at sunrise. Whoever leaves when it opens tomorrow will be our man."

Tamora said, "And when we catch him we can cut the truth from him."

"No," Yama said. "I will follow him, and learn what I can. If there is a conspiracy, of course. There may be an innocent explanation."

Drilling the thralls was all very well, but Yama had done little else in the three days since they had arrived here. He was beginning to feel as if he was suffocating in the stale air of the Department of Vaticination, with its meaningless ceremonies and its constant reverent evocation of the dead days of its long-lost glory. He wanted to see more of the Palace. He wanted to find the records of his bloodline and move on. He wanted to go downriver and plunge into the war at the midpoint of the world.

"It's obviously some plot against the fat bitch," Tamora said thoughtfully. "It's because of Luria's refusal to bargain with the Department of Indigenous Affairs that we're here. Without her, there would be no dispute."

" 'Fail, and she lives. And if she lives we all may die,' " Pandaras said.

"When your rat-boy agrees with me," Tamora told Yama, "then you know I must be right. Perhaps the best thing to do would be to do nothing. In any case, you should not leave this place, Yama. We are protected by law and custom only as long as we stay within the boundaries of the Department of Vaticination. I know that you want to begin your search for the records of your bloodline. But be patient. In a decad, the Department of Indigenous Affairs will take this place, no matter how well we train the thralls. Then we can search together, as we agreed. You're already wounded, and we have been misled about the kind of troops we were to command, and our employers plot against each other. It's clear someone here has allied themselves to Indigenous Affairs, and hopes to make a bargain after assassinating their rivals. It doesn't matter who is plotting against who, for there's no honor to be won here. The defense is simply a matter of form before the inevitable surrender. Like all of Gorgo's little jobs, this has nothing to commend it. Another reason to kill him, when we are done here."

Gorgo was the broker who had given Tamora this contract. He had tried to kill Yama because Yama had cost him the commission on a previous job and because he suspected that, with Yama's help, Tamora might free herself of her obligation to him. Yama had killed him instead, riddling him with a hundred tiny machines, but Tamora had not seen it and she did not or would not believe in what she called Yama's magic tricks.

"If we find out more," Yama said, "then we can end the plot before it begins."

"Grah! And if you leave here before the end of the contract, you'll be assassinated. You will stay here, for your own safety."

"I can take care of myself."

Tamora said sharply, "How is your wound? Does it trouble you?"

"A headache now and then," Yama admitted.

He had the beginning of a headache now. He felt as if his skull was too small to contain his thoughts, as if his brain was a bladder pumped up by a growing anger. Red and black sparks crawled at the edge of his vision. He had to stifle an impulse to draw his knife and do some harm.

He said, "I will not make the same mistake again. And I will do as I will."

Pandaras said, "Perhaps my master should leave now. Go and find the records of his bloodline, for that's why he is really here."

Tamora suddenly whirled, smashing her stave against the plinth with such force that it snapped in two. She glared at the splintered stub in her hand, then threw it hard and fast down the length of the Basilica. "Grah! Go then! Both of you! Go, and accept what falls out. Death, most likely. Even if you dodge the hirelings of the Department of Indigenous Affairs, you know nothing about the Palace, and it is a dangerous place."

"I will come back," Yama said. "I promised that I would help you and I was taught to keep my promises. Besides, I hope to learn something here. Is not one of the attributes of this Department the ability to find lost things?"

2

The Eye of the Preservers

IT WAS THE custom of the Department of Vaticination that everyone, from senior pythoness to lowliest collector of nightsoil, took their evening meal together in the refectory hall of the House of the Twelve Front Rooms. The pythonesses and their domestic staff—the secretary, the bursar, the chamberlain, the librarian, the sacristan, and a decad of holders of ancient offices which had dwindled to purely ceremonial functions or nothing more than empty titles—raised up on a platform at one end of the refectory; the thralls ranged around the other three sides. The refectory was not a convivial place. Yama supposed that there had once been tapestries muffling the bare stone walls—the hooks were still in place—and perhaps rugs on the flagstone floor, but now the gloomy high-ceilinged hall was undecorated, and lit only by the fireflies which danced attendance above the heads of every man and woman. The thralls ate in silence; only the chink and scrape of their knives underlay the high, clear voice of the praise-sayer, who, at a lectern raised in one corner of the refectory, recited suras from the Puranas. Alone amongst several hundred sullen servants, only Pandaras dared glance now and then at the people on the platform.

Although the refectory was bleak, Yama found the formal style of the meals, a decad of courses presented at intervals by liveried thralls, comfortingly familiar. It reminded him of suppers at the long banqueting table in the Great Hall of the peel-house. He sprawled in a nest of silk cushions (their delicate embroidery tattered, stained and musty) at a low square table he shared with Syle, the secretary of the Department of Vaticination, and Syle's pregnant wife, Rega. The rest of the domestic staff were grouped around other tables, and all were turned toward the couches on which the two pythonesses reclined.

The Department of Vaticination was one of the oldest in the Palace of the Memory of the People, and although it had fallen on hard times, it kept up its traditions. The food was poor, mostly rice and glutinous vegetable sauces eaten with wedges of unleavened bread (the thralls had it even worse, with only lentils and edible plastic), but it was served on fine, translucent porcelain, and accompanied by thin, bitter wine in fragile cups of blown glass veined with gold and silver.

Luria, the senior pythoness, overflowed her couch, looking, as Tamora liked to say, like a grampus stranded on a mudbank. Crowned by a tower of red and gold fireflies, she ate with surprising delicacy but ferocious appetite; usually, she had finished her portion and rung the bell to signal that the dishes should be taken away before the others on the platform were halfway done. Swags of flesh hung from her jowls and from her upper arms, and her eyes were half-hidden by the puffy ramparts of her cheeks. They were large, her eyes, and a lustrous brown, with long, delicate lashes. Her black hair was greased and tied in numerous plaits with colored silk ribbons, and she wore layers of colored gauze that floated and stirred on the faintest breeze. Whenever she chose to walk, she had to be supported by two thralls, but usually she was carried about on a chair. She had been pythoness for more than a century. She was the imperturbable center of such power that remained in the faded glory of the Department of Vaticination, like a bloated spider brooding in a tattered web in a locked, airless room. Yama knew that she did not miss a single nuance of the whispered conversations around her.

The junior pythoness, Daphoene, was Luria's starveling shadow. Only a single wan firefly flickered above her flat, pale face, as if she were no better than the least of the kitchen thralls. She wore a long white shift that, girdled with a belt of gold wires, covered her body from neck to ankles. Her head was shaven, and lumpy scars wormed across her scalp. She was blind. Her eyes, white as stones, were turned toward the ceiling while her fine-boned hands moved amongst the bowls and cups on the tray a servant held before her, questing independently like small restless animals. She never spoke, and did not appear to hear any of the conversations around her.

Yama suspected that Daphoene was inhabited by more than one person. Lately, he had begun to sense that everyone had folded within themselves a small irreducible kernel of self, the soul grown by the invisibly small machines which infected all of the changed bloodlines.

But Daphoene was a vessel for an uncountable number of kernels, a constant ferment of flickering fragments.

The formal evening meals were a trial to Tamora, and she guyed her unease by playing up the part of an uncouth cateran. That evening, after the argument in the Basilica, she had chosen to sit alone at a table at the far end of the platform, and was more restless than ever. But the more she played the barbarian, the more she endeared herself to Syle, who would incline his head toward Yama and comment in an admiring, mock-scandalized whisper on the way Tamora tossed and caught her knife over and over, or yawned widely, or noisily spat a bit of gristle onto the floor, or drank from the fingerbowl, or, as now, scratched herself with a cat's lazy self-indulgence.

"Quite wonderfully untamed," Syle murmured to Yama. "Isn't she so thrillingly physical?"

"She comes from a people not much given to formalities," Yama whispered back.

"Fortunately, we didn't hire her for her manners," Syle's wife, Rega, said. Rega was older than Syle, with a pointed wit and a sharp gaze that measured everyone it fell upon and usually found them wanting. She was tremendously pregnant; as round as an egg, as her husband fondly put it, in a shift of purple satin that stretched like a drumhead over her distended belly. She had twisted her feathery hair into a tall cone that sat like a shell on top of her small head.

"She is tired, too," Yama said. "We have both been working hard."

The praise-sayer had been reciting from the sura which described how the Preservers had altered the orbits of every star in the Galaxy, as a feoffer might replant a forest as a formal garden. A monument, a game, a work of art—who could say? Who could understand the minds of those who had become gods, so powerful that they had escaped this Universe of things?

Yama knew these suras by heart, and had been paying little attention to the praise-singer. But now the man paused, and began to recite a sura from the last pages of the Puranas.

The world first showed itself as a golden embryo of sound. As soon as the thoughts of the Preservers turned to the creation of the world, the long vowel which described the form of the world vibrated in the pure realm of thought, and re-echoed on itself. From the knots in the play of vibrations, the crude matter of the world curdled. In the beginning, it was no more than a sphere of air and water with a little mud at the center.

And the Preservers raised up a man and set on his brow their mark, and raised up a woman of the same kind, and set on her brow the same mark. From the white clay of the middle region did they shape this race, and quickened them with their marks. And those of this race were the servants of the Preservers. And in their myriads this race shaped the world after the ideas of the Preservers.

Yama's blood quickened. It was a description of how the Preservers had created the first bloodline of Confluence: the Builders, his own bloodline, long thought to have vanished with their masters into the black hole at the heart of the Eye of the Preservers. He saw that Syle was watching him, and knew that Syle knew. Knew what he was. Knew why he was here. The sura had been chosen deliberately.

Luria rang her little bell. The attendants cleared away the bowls of rice and the dishes of sauces, and sprinkled the diners with water perfumed with rose petals.

"You will watch the exercises tomorrow," Luria told Syle. "I want to know how the training of our defense force is proceeding."

Without looking away from Yama, Syle said, "I am sure that it is in capable hands, pythoness." Yes, he knew. But what did he want?

Tamora said loudly, "Well, we didn't kill anyone today, and I believe my friend's wound is healing."

She had spoken out of turn. Luria took no more notice than if she had belched.

Syle said, "I watched the exercises yesterday, pythoness, but I will do so again tomorrow. It is very diverting. You should see how well the thralls march."

"It's a pity they can't fight," Tamora said.

"I have had a presentiment," Luria told Syle. "You will see to it that all is well."

Tamora said, "If you've seen something with your cards or dice, perhaps you could share it with us. It could help our plans."

There was a silence. Syle turned very pale. At last, Luria said in a soft croak, "Not dice, dear. Dice and cards are for street performers who take your money and promise anything they think will make you happy. I deal in the truth."

Syle said, "The pythoness entered a trance today. If she has said little to you, it is because she is exhausted. You will see how hard divination is in two days' time, at the public inquisition."

"Syle likes to explain things," Luria said. "You will show him the progress you have made. He will then explain it to me."

"Oh, pythoness, you should see how the thralls march!" Syle said again, and began to describe the precision of the martial drills at length, falling silent only when the last course, iced fruits and sweet yellow wine, was served.

Luria ate a token mouthful, then rang her bell. The praise-sayer fell silent. The meal was over. Luria's chair arrived and she was helped into it by two tall strong attendants and carried away. Another attendant took Daphoene's arm, and she rose and followed him with the childlike trust of a sleepwalker. Her mouth hung open and there was a slick of drool on her chin.

As the thralls began to move out of the hall, followed by flocks of faint fireflies, Rega told her husband, "You are kinder to Luria than she deserves. Certainly kinder to her than she is to you, who works so hard for her."

Syle said mildly, "She worries all the time about the quit claim, and of course about the public inquisition. We are all a little short of patience, these days."

Rega said, "Luria has her fine troops, who can march in formation all day long without missing a step. Why should she worry about the quit claim?" She smiled sweetly at Tamora and said, "You're doing your best, I'm sure, but you must wish for proper soldiers."

"We only have what we have," Syle said, again gazing at Yama. "I'm sure the thralls will fight to the death."

"I'm sure they will," Rega said. She held out her hand, and her husband helped her to her feet. Her round belly swayed, stretching the panels of her satin dress. She added, "A very quick death it will be, too. Yama, Tamora, I don't blame either of you. Our good pythoness has said that there will be victory, and so she does not trifle to provide the means to ensure it. Of course, it isn't possible to sell even one tenth of her jewels and trinkets. Although she does not wear or use any of them, they are heirlooms and cannot be sacrificed for anything as trivial as the defense of the Department. And so we must make do, with the fate of the Department in the balance."

Tamora drew herself up. She was very angry. She showed her sharp white teeth and said, "If you find anything I have done that does not satisfy you, then I will resign at once."

Syle made fluttering motions with his hands. "Please. Nothing of the sort is intended. I myself have seen how well you have drilled our thralls. A thrilling sight, to see them march!"

"Then perhaps your reports have been misunderstood," Tamora said. "Excuse me. I have work to do."

Syle caught Yama's arm and said quietly, "Walk with me, if you will."

Yama looked after Tamora, but she had leapt from the platform and was already halfway across the refectory, the crowd of thralls parting before her as rice parts before the scythe. He said, "Of course."

Syle's touch, its implication of familiarity, excited him. He felt the same quickening nervousness which had possessed him whenever he had attempted a dive off the end of the new quay into the strong river currents in which the children of the Amnan sported so easily. Not precisely fear, but an anticipation that heightened his senses. He liked Syle too much to be afraid of him, and not only because the tall, slightly built man, with his delicate bones, fine features, and white, feathery hair, reminded him of his sweetheart, Derev.

Syle had taught him much about the history of the Department of Vaticination and of its trade of prognostication. There were very many ways of gaining foresight, Syle said, but almost all of them were false, and those that remained could be divided into no more than three types. The least of these was sortilege, the drawing of lots, or astragalomancy, the use of dice or huckle-bones or sticks, neither of which, as Luria had pointed out, were practiced in the Department, although they were much abused by charlatans. Of more merit were those methods classed as divination, in which signs were scried in the client's physiogonomy, as in metascopy or chiromancy, or in the landscape, or in dust cast on a mirror (Syle said that gold was best, but the finings of any metal were better than ordinary dust or the husks of rice grains used by village witches). The form most often performed by the Department was rhabdomancy, or dowsing, used to find lost property or to find the best place for the site of a house or to locate a hidden spring. Finally, there was true foresight obtained through visions, either in dreams or in waking trances. It was the most difficult and most powerful method of all, and it was by custom what the pythonesses would attempt in two days' time at the public inquisition, although these days most clients wanted answers to trivial questions, to find things that were lost or hidden (wills were a perennial favorite, for many slighted by the wishes of rich, dead relatives came to believe that, hidden somewhere, there was a true will which would favor them), to speak with the dead, or to gain assurance of the success of a new business or a marriage.

The problem was that, as Syle put it, the business of the future was a thing of the past. The ordinary citizens of Ys would believe a roadside

cartomancer as readily as the pythonesses of the Department of Vaticination, and other departments no longer called upon its services when
planning their business.

"Syle wants to ask you something," Rega told Yama. "Be good
enough to humor him."

"This is not the place," her husband told her.

"We will be able to say anything we like soon enough. Don't do
anything to ruin it." Rega gave her husband a cold look, but allowed
him to kiss her on her forehead before she took her leave.

As Syle steered him toward the broad stair at the far end of the hall,
Yama said, "Where are we going?" Thralls made way for them. Pandaras had disappeared, no doubt in pursuit of another amatory conquest.

"I have something to show you," Syle said. He had the tentative
touch of an old man, although he was not much more than twice Yama's
age, and much younger than his wife. "I promise not to keep you long.
Is your wound healing? You should let brother Apothecary attend to it."

"Tamora said that the dressing should not be disturbed," Yama said.
"Besides, it is mostly bruising."

He had been embarrassed in the brief fight. The ruffians had rushed
up from behind as Tamora, Pandaras, and Yama had climbed toward
the Gate of Double Glory. One had struck Yama with the flat of a blade;
dazed and half-blinded by blood, Yama had saved himself with a lucky
swipe that had hit his opponent's sword-hand, severing two fingers and
causing the man to drop his weapon. By the time Yama had wiped
blood from his eyes, Tamora had killed three of the ruffians and the
two survivors had fled, with Pandaras chasing after them and screaming
insults.

"We have lodged a protest with the Department of Internal Harmony over the incident," Syle said. "If it is successful, then we may
move on to a formal hearing. Unfortunately, the petition of protest must
be read and approved by a clerk of court in the first instance, and then
a committee will be deputized to discuss it. That may take no more than
fifty or sixty days if the business is rushed, but I do not suppose it will
be rushed. Nothing ever is rushed in the Palace, but of course that is
only proper. These are serious matters, and must be taken seriously.
After that, well, the process of establishing a hearing usually takes at
least two years."

"And in twelve days the ultimatum delivered by the Department of
Indigenous Affairs will expire."

Syle said, "Yes, but I have faith in you, Yama."

Yama had learned a little of the art of diplomacy from his stepfather, the Aedile of Aeolis. Nothing must be said directly; to ask a question is to lose advantage. He said, "I have never been in this part of the Department before."

"This was the main entrance, once upon a time. Now no one uses it but me. It leads to the roof."

They reached the top of the stairway and went down a long corridor. Its walls were paneled in dark, heavily carved wood and hung with big square paintings whose pigments were so blackened by time that it was impossible to discern what scenes or persons they might once have depicted. A rat fled from their footsteps, pursued by a single wan firefly. It disappeared into a hole in the paneling, and rolled the end of a broken bottle across the hole to stop it. The feeble light of the firefly flickered behind the thick roundel of glass as the rat lay still and watched the two men pass.

The corridor ended at a pair of round metal doors, with a metal-walled antechamber sandwiched between them. The inner door was open, the outer dogged shut. Syle shut the inner door behind them and talked to the lock of the outer door—Yama felt its dim intelligence briefly waken—then instructed Yama to spin a wheel and pull the door open. It moved sweetly on its counterbalanced track, and Yama followed Syle over the high sill.

They were on the wide, flat roof of the House of the Twelve Front Rooms. It was lapped with metal plates that fitted together like the scales of a fish. Behind it was the cavern, dark except for a few tiny stars where people walked, attended by fireflies. The other buildings of the Department of Vatication—the Basilica, the Hall of the Tranquil Mind, the Hall of Great Achievements, and the Gate of Double Glory— were set symmetrically around the edge of this great hollow, dark shapes sunk deep in darkness. On the other side of the House of the Twelve Front Rooms, beyond the looming arch of the cavern's mouth, was the night sky. A cold wind blew past skeletal towers which jutted from the outer edge of the roof. Syle explained that in ancient times drugged pythonesses lashed to platforms on top of these towers had searched for intimations of the future in the patterns of clouds and the flight of birds. Beyond the towers, a narrow walkway projected from a corner of the roof into the windy darkness. It was along this walkway that Syle now led Yama, who clung to the single railing with sweating hands.

The House of the Twelve Front Rooms faced toward the Great River; even at noon, only a shallow curtain of light fell into the mouth of the cavern. Directly below the walkway, a long steep slope of scrub and bare rock fell to the spurs and spires and towers which had accreted around the ragged hem of the Palace, covering it as corals will cover a wreck in the warm lower reaches of the river. Beyond, the lights of Ys were spread along the edge of the broad river; Yama could see, across a hundred leagues of water, the flat edge of the world itself against the empty darkness of the night sky. Downriver, where the world narrowed to its vanishing point, was a dim red glow, as if a fire had been kindled beneath the horizon.

In the windy dark, his mild face illuminated by his crown of fireflies, Syle said, "In a few hours the Preservers will look upon us for the first time this year."

"I had forgotten. Will there be celebrations?"

"Amongst the rabble of the city, yes. If we stay out long enough we'll see their fireworks and bonfires. And later, perhaps, the fires of riots, and then the flashes of the weapons of the magistrates as they restore order."

"Ys is a strange and terrible city."

"It is a very large city, and there can only be order by suppressing any disorder at once, by whatever force is necessary. The Department of Indigenous Affairs has raised an army to fight the heretics; that is why they want new territory. But the magistrates are a greater army, one which constantly strives against a greater enemy. It is because we have fallen from grace that the people war against themselves with more hatred than against the heretics."

Yama remembered Pandaras's story of how his uncle had been trapped when magistrates had laid siege to a block of the city which had refused to pay an increase in taxes. He said, "In the city where I grew up, the people celebrate the setting of the Eye of the Preservers, not its rising. They sail across the river to the farside shore and hold a winter festival. They polish and repair the settings of the shrines, and renew the flags of the prayer strings. They light bonfires, and feast and dance, and lay flowers and other offerings at the shrines."

"The ordinary people of Ys celebrate the rising of the Eye because they think that once more they are beneath the beneficent gaze of the Preservers, and all evil must flee away. They bang gongs, rattle their pots and pans, and light firecrackers to drive evil into the open. I am not familiar with your city, Yama, but I wonder why its people are glad to believe that they are free of this gaze. Surely they must worship the Preservers, for else they would be unique amongst the ten thousand bloodlines of the Shaped."

"They celebrate the beginning of winter. They dislike the summer's heat."

"Ah. In any case, although the Eye is named because it has the appearance of the organ of sight, it does not share the function of its namesake. Anyone with a little learning knows that when the Preservers vanished beyond the horizon of the Universe, they left behind servants to watch over us, their poor creatures. Were not the shrines once the homes of countless avatars who guided and inspired us? Are not all of the changed bloodlines infected with the particles of the breath of the Preservers, who will cherish our memories after we die?"

"I am glad to see the Eye. I have always preferred summer to winter. Is it what you brought me to see?"

"I would like to talk with you in private. Do not be afraid. This walkway has stood for longer than the Department. It was built long before Confluence entered its present orbit."

But Yama felt a chill vertigo, for they were now so far out that the buildings heaped along the hem of the Palace were directly below. A cold wind buffeted him; the walkway hummed like a plucked wire. All he could see of it was that part of its mesh floor beneath his feet, illuminated by the intense light of the single firefly above his head. He could lose his grip on the slender rail and fall like a stone through someone's roof. Slip, or perhaps be pushed.

"You are the first to come here with me," Syle said, "but then, you are a singular young man. Take your firefly, for instance. You should have allowed them to choose you, and not taken the brightest anyone has ever seen."

"But it did choose me." Yama had kept others from joining it because he feared that he would be blinded inside their ardent orbits.

"Some say that fireflies multiply in dark places hidden from our sight, but I think not. Every year there are fewer and fewer people in the Palace proper—by which I mean the corridors and chambers and cells, and not the newer buildings built over the lower floors. Once, even the least of bloodlines were crowned with twenty or thirty fireflies, and the Palace blazed with their light. Now, many fireflies are so feeble that they have become tropically fixed on members of the indigenous tribes which infest the roof, or on rats and other vermin. I doubt that there is another firefly as bright as the one you wear, except perhaps within the chambers of the Hierarchs. It will attract much attention, but it is fixed now, and will not leave you until you leave this place."

Yama said, "I hope that it does not put me in danger." He could order the firefly to leave, and then choose others more ordinary—but that might be worse than having selected it in the first place.

Syle did not answer at once. At last, he said, "You know that I find the cateran is very amusing, but I do not think that she will be able to marshal a successful defense of the Department."

Yama remembered what Rega had said. "If you gave us more men—"

"How would you train them? Indigenous Affairs will send an army of its best troops to enforce the quit claim."

"That is what Tamora thinks, too."

"Then at least she has some sense. But she is an ordinary cateran. I believe that you are capable of greater things."

Yama said warily, "You do?"

Yama's wise but unworldly stepfather had not known what Yama was. He had sent the apothecary, Dr. Dismas, to the Palace of the Memory of the People to discover what he could about Yama's bloodline, but Dr. Dismas had lied to the old man and claimed to have found nothing, and then tried to kidnap Yama for his own purposes. For the first time Yama wondered whether Syle, kin to his sweetheart and to one of the curators of the City of the Dead, who had shown him that he was of the bloodline which had built the world according to the will of the Preservers, was part of their conspiracy.

Syle said, "We have forgotten how to speak plainly here. In a department as old as this, words raise such echoes that their meaning might never be clear. Forgive me."

"But we are in the open air now."

"Luria has been pythoness for more than a century, but the Department is more than two hundred times older. I must be loyal to the Department first."

Yama saw the man's distress. He said, "No one can overhear us here."

"Except the Preservers."

"Yes. We must always speak truthfully to them." Syle gripped the fragile rail and stared into the night, toward the first light of the Eye of the Preservers. He said, "The truth then. I know what you are, Yama. You are one of the Builders. Your bloodline was the first of all the bloodlines the Preservers raised up to populate Confluence, and the machines which maintain this world have not forgotten your kind. All machines obey you, even those that follow the orders of other men. Even those which will not obey anyone else." He laughed. "There, I have said it. Rega thought I could not, but I have. And the world has not ended."

Yama said, "How did you find out what I am?"

Wind blew Syle's white, feathery hair back from the narrow blade of his face. He said, "Our library is very extensive."

Yama's heart turned over. Perhaps his quest was already over, before he had hardly begun. He said, "I came to Ys to search for my bloodline, and would very much like to see that book. Will you show me now?"

Syle said, "No, not yet. The library is closed to all but the pythonesses and the highest officers of the domestic staff. I would show you all I can, Yama, but I fear that I am more in need of help than you. I'm told that the Preservers act through you. If that's true, then whatever you do cannot be evil. You cannot help but do good. Don't deny the powers you have. I know, for instance, that the Temple of the Black Well was burned down on the day you entered the Palace. It seemed that someone woke the thing in the well and then destroyed it. As for us, a lesser miracle would suffice."

Yama had encountered two feral machines since he had arrived in Ys. In a desperate moment, he had called down the first without knowing what he was doing. The second had fallen in the wars of the Age of Insurrection, and men had later built a temple over the hole it had burnt through the keelrock. The machine had lain brooding within a tomb of congealed lava for an age, until woken by the same call which had brought down the first. With the help of the ancient guardians of the temple, Yama had reburied it. Machines like those had destroyed half the world in the Age of Insurrection, and although their time was long past, and their powers had faded as the lights of the fireflies had faded, they were still powerful. They shadowed the world from which they had been expelled, waiting, some said, for the Preservers to return to begin the final battle when the just, living and dead, would be raised up, and the damned thrown aside.

Beyond dismissing the fireflies which had eagerly flocked to him when he had entered the Palace, Yama had not tried to influence a machine since. He was scared that he might inadvertently wake more monsters from the past.

He told Syle, "I signed as a cateran, for a cateran's wages. That is the duty I will discharge to you, dominie, nothing more and nothing less. What you have learned from your library is your own affair. You have not shared it with the pythonesses, or you would not have brought me here to talk in secret. Perhaps I should ask them about it."

Syle turned to Yama and said with sudden passion, "Listen to me! If you can help me, then I can help you find out about your bloodline. True pythonesses can see the past as well as the future. Just as our actions and wishes contain the seeds of the future, so the present also holds the echoes of actions and wishes of the past. Indeed, since there was only one past but there are many possible futures it is easier to read the past from the present than it is to predict the future. It is said that the Preservers could travel from the future into the past as easily as starships slip from star to star, but that they could not travel into the future because from the point of view of the past the future does not yet exist. And so with prediction."

"Yet it is said that the Preservers will return from the future, so there can only be one future, as there is only one past."

"Our world has only one past, but there are many possible worlds arrayed in the future. Some say that every step we take creates new worlds, which contain all the directions in which we could have turned. When looking into the future, a pythoness must encompass all these possible states and choose the most likely, which is to say the one which is most common. But the past is a straight road, because the world has traveled along it to reach the present."

"You do not speak of Luria, do you? You speak of Daphoene."

Syle nodded. "Daphoene has true sight. The business of this Department is to tell people what they want to hear, or what they most need to hear, which is not always the same thing. And so most of our business is concerned with collecting intelligence about our clients, so that we can satisfy their inquiries."

"You are very candid."

"If you will not help us, then what I tell you will do no harm, for the Department will cease to exist. If you do help us, then you will need to know these things. Some say that we practice magic, but in truth ours is a rational science."

Yama thought of the buzzing confusion in Daphoene's head. Perhaps she was able to scry a path through the sheaves of possible futures because she was many people inhabiting a single mind, or perhaps what he glimpsed within her were futures continually appearing and dying.

Syle said, "Daphoene tells only the truth, and that is what scares Luria. She sees our clients driven away by the truth. Oh, do not think that Luria does not believe in her own powers. Of course she does. If her predictions come true, then she is satisfied; if not, then she will find some condition of the ceremony to be at fault, or she will say that something more powerful intervened to change events from the course she had divined. There can never be any blame on her part if what she predicts does not happen. But Daphoene is always right, and needs no ceremony. She speaks directly. I brought her here, Yama. I am responsible for her. I had hoped that she would be a true pythoness, and it seems that she is much more than I had hoped. Daphoene frightens Luria, and I fear that because of that Luria will destroy her. I would rather die than bear that."

No doubt this confession was supposed to win Yama's trust, but instead it made him wary. Syle was so accustomed to deceiving the clients of the Department of Vaticination that he habitually deceived himself, too, by pretending that everything he did was for the good of the Department and never for his own gain. But Yama suspected that Syle wanted to use him for his own ends. If Syle had been a little less clever, his motives might simply be venal, but nothing Syle did was simple. This seemed to be a straightforward bargain—a miracle in exchange for revelation—but Yama remembered the plot Pandaras had uncovered, and Tamora's harsh words. *These old departments are rats' nests of poisonous intrigues and feuds over trifles.*

He said, "If Daphoene can see into the future, then what does she say about the Department? Will it be saved?"

"She knows, but will not say. Do not think I have not asked, but she has set her heart against revealing what she knows. She says that if she speaks, then the future may be changed, and the fate of the world with it. All she will say is that it will not be saved by force of arms. I understand that to mean that you will intervene."

"But if I asked her, would she speak plainly of my fate? Would she look into the future and see where I might meet my people?"

"She has already said something. That is why you must help us, Yama. If you do not, then yours will be a tragic fate."

There, in the windy dark high above the oldest city in the world, Yama knew that Syle had baited a hook to set in his heart. But he had to ask.

"Tell me what she said, and perhaps I will know whether I should help you."

Syle turned to regard the panorama spread far below. The darkling plain of Ys, the wide ribbon of the Great River stretching away toward the vanishing point, where the Eye of the Preservers had risen a finger-breadth above the edge of the world. He inclined his head, and said, "There are two parts. The first is that you will either save the world or destroy it. She said that both things were connected. Do not ask me what she meant—she would not explain it to me."

Yama said, "Perhaps the first is more likely than the second. The world will continue as before, but some might say that I am responsible. I think that people have more faith in me than I have in myself."

"Then it's time you learned to trust yourself," Syle said briskly. "The second part is this: if you do not help me, then you will be betrayed to those you have already escaped. As I said, if you do not help the Department, then yours is a dark fate."

Yama felt a chill of presentiment. His stepfather had sent him to Ys to become an apprentice to the Department of Indigenous Affairs, the same department he was now contracted to fight against. Although he had escaped Prefect Corin, the man to whom the Aedile had entrusted him, he had never escaped the fear that the Prefect, cold, ruthless, implacable, would find him again.

He said, "That seems more like a threat than a prediction."

"You do not have to give me your answer now, but it should come before the Gate of Double Glory opens tomorrow. Think hard on this, Yama, and remember that I am your friend."

"The future is uncertain, but you must know that I will discharge the duty for which Tamora and I were hired."

"To act merely as a cateran will not be enough," Syle said. "You know it is not enough. As a friend, I beg you to help us. I cannot be responsible for what will happen to you if you do not."

Yama would have asked him what he meant, but Syle suddenly pointed toward the city below. "Look there! How brightly they burn!"

Near and far, rockets were shooting up above the streets and houses and squares of the endless city, red and green and gold lights streaking high into the night air and bursting in fiery flowers that drifted down in clouds of fading sparks even as more rockets rose through them. The noise of their explosions came moments later, like the popping of kernels of corn in a hot pan.

Yama thought again of Daphoene. Her mind like the night sky full of sparks constantly flowering and fading.

Rising faintly on the cold wind came the small sound of trumpets and drums, of people singing and cheering. A flight of rockets terminated their brief arc in a shower of golden sparks a few chains beneath the walkway on which Yama and Syle stood. Bats took wing from crevices in the rock face below, a cloud of black flakes that blew out into the night and swept across the red swirl of the Eye of the Preservers.

3

The Day Market

AS SOON AS the inner door of the Gate of Double Glory had sunk into its slot in the roadway, the thrall who had been waiting in front of it walked beneath the round portal into the darkness of the tunnel. Yama left the doorway of the Basilica and, with Pandaras trotting at his heels, crossed the plaza. He hailed the gatekeeper and asked for the name of the man who had just gone through.

"You mean Brabant?" the gatekeeper said. "Why would you want him, dominie? He done something wrong?"

Yama hid a yawn behind his hand. It was just after dawn, and he had had only a little sleep. He had lain awake a long time on the narrow bunk in his little cell, thinking about everything Syle had said. It was as if his mind had split in two factions, and their armies of thought had gone to war inside his skull.

After he had inadvertently called down one feral machine and woken and defeated another, after he had murdered Gorgo in a fit of anger, he had sworn not to use his powers again. At least, not until he understood them. And as yet he did not know if he could do what Syle wanted him to do. He did not know if he could successfully defend the Department of Vaticination by warping the minds of machines to serve his own ends. Besides, if his powers came from the Preservers, then it was obvious that he should not use them for his own gain.

But in exchange for defending the Department of Vaticination, he might learn much more about his bloodline. And if he knew where he came from, then he might better understand his powers and what the Preservers wanted of him. And if he could master his powers, why then he might be able to do anything.

With this thought came a tumble of images. Yama flying on the back of a metal dragon, driving hordes of defeated heretics into the Glass Desert beyond the midpoint of the world. Yama clad in a buzzing weave of bright motes, preaching to a multitude on some high place, with the world spread beyond. Yama on a doffing ship, waking ancient machines from the depths of the Great River. Yama striking with a golden staff a rock in the icy wastes at the head of the Great River, and calling forth new waters to renew the world. And many more images, bright and compelling, as if his mind was trying to master all the futures into which he might walk. The visions possessed him, wonderful and terrifying. When he was woken by Pandaras it seemed that he had not rested at all.

And now, not half an hour later, he stood beneath the intricately carved portal of the Gate of Double Glory. The tunnel beyond it slanted downward, curving as it descended. The thrall, Brabant, had already passed out of sight.

"Brabant never did anything bad I heard about," the gatekeeper said. "And I know all about what comes and goes."

Yama said, "Did Brabant tell you what his business might be?"

The gatekeeper was an ancient but muscular and vigorous thrall, with a humped back and a white mane. He looked at Yama slyly. "It would be his usual business," he said.

"And what's that?" Pandaras said. "Speak civilly to my master, fellow. He has the safety of your department in his hands."

The thrall said, "Why, it's well known Brabant has the keys of the kitchens of the household of the House of the Twelve Front Rooms. He's often out this early. The day markets open when the main gates open, and bidding is fierce these days. Things aren't what they were. There are shortages because of the war. You here to protect Brabant, dominie? He in danger?"

"It is a matter of security," Pandaras told the old thrall.

This seemed to satisfy the gatekeeper. "Aye, I suppose we're in danger even now. They're not to start fighting the quit claim for more than a decad, but you can't trust Indigenous Affairs. It's a grower, see. Wants to get control wherever it can, however it can. But I do a good job. Don't worry about the gate. Nothing has ever passed me by without proper authority."

For once, this was no idle boast. Tamora had surveyed the Department of Vaticination on the first day, and said that once the triple doors were lowered, the gate could not be forced without destroying most of the cavern.

"We should hurry, master," Pandaras said. "We will lose him."

"You will stay here, Pandaras. Stay here, and do your duty."

"I'd do better going with you. I see you've taken off your bandage, but your wound won't have healed, not yet. And I've a fancy to seeing more of this place."

"As you will, when we are done here. I promise it." Yama turned to the gatekeeper and said, "How do you open the doors? There are three, I believe."

The gatekeeper nodded. "One here, dominie, another a hundred paces further down, and the last a hundred paces beyond that. To keep the air in, see. In the old days, the cavern was sealed around the House of the Twelve Front Rooms, but the bulkheads were sold for scrap years ago. Well, in the old days there was a word you'd speak and the doors would obey. But they're just metal now. The vital parts died long ago. So now we do it by water. You saw me haul on that wheel?"

It stood on a strong post inside the glass booth that clung to the right-hand side of the gate's round mouth. It was as tall as the gate-keeper, and spoked like the wheel of a wagon.

The gatekeeper said, "It controls the sluices. Water is what does the job. It flows out of the counterweights and the doors sink down with it, and then it's pumped into a reservoir above our heads, ready to fill the counterweights to close up the gate as need be."

"You keep watch on the gate all day?"

"My little house is up above the gate—see the stair? It winds right up to it. I'm cozy as a swallow in a godown roof up there."

"Then when Brabant comes back, you will make a note of it?"

"I will keep watch," Pandaras said, "although I'd rather come with you, master."

"Your boy there needn't trouble himself," the old thrall said. "I see everything that goes in and out. Our secretary Syle likes to know what's going on."

The tunnel was lined with a slick, white material that diffused the light of Yama's solitary firefly; it was as if he moved at the center of a flowing nimbus. The tunnel turned a full circle as it descended, then opened on to a shaft ten times as wide, one of the main throughways that ran from top to bottom of the Palace. Like all the throughways, its gravity was localized; the tunnel met its roof at right angles. Yama stood at the beginning of a corkscrew ramp, looking straight across the throughway at the tops of sleds and carts and wagons that, spangled with lanterns, streamed past as if clinging to a sheer wall. But as he went down the ramp, the throughway seemed to turn around him, until at last he was standing on a walkway beside the traffic and the mouth of the tunnel he had left was a hole in the curved roof above his head.

There were few pedestrians, and Yama had no trouble following Brabant. The thrall was a sturdy fellow with a thick black mane done up in braids. He walked at a slow but steady pace along the walkway into the lower part of the Palace, where he took a ramp that spiraled up into the roof. It led to a short, narrow tunnel which suddenly opened on to a huge cavern filled with stalls and people.

It was one of the day markets. People from the hundred departments of the Palace of the Memory of the People were wrangling with merchants, gossiping, strolling about, or eating breakfast. The smoke of hundreds of cooking braziers and hotplates mingled beneath a low ceiling of stained concrete, a blue haze which defined a pale wedge of early sunlight above the flat roofs of godowns that stood shoulder to shoulder at the cavern's wide mouth.

Machines twinkled through the smoky air; thousands of fireflies spun above the heads of the people who crowded the aisles between the stalls. The noise was tremendous. The bawling of animals and the chatter of thousands of conversations echoed and re-echoed from the bare rock walls. In one part of the market, shoals of fish were laid on banks of smoking ice, and bubbling tanks held mussels and oysters and slate-blue crayfish; in another, tethered goats grazed on straw, placidly awaiting the knife. There were stalls selling erasable paper, inks and pigments, sandals, spices, every kind of fruit and vegetable, cigarettes, edible plastic, confectionery, tea bark, and much more, and at every one spielers praised the quality and cheapness of their wares. Here and there, soldiers of the Department of Internal Harmony stood on discs floating in the air, watching the crowds that surged beneath their feet.

Most of the people who had come to the market were clerks, low grade administrators or record keepers dressed in crisp white shirts with high collars and baggy black trousers. Everywhere he looked, Yama saw a reflection of the fate his stepfather had wished on him. Most people made way for him as he followed Brabant through the crowded aisles, and some even touched the inky tips of their fingers together; Yama realized that they were deferring not to him but to the spurious rank lent him by his single bright firefly.

The whole brawling tumult, lit only by the restless sparks of the fireflies and the smoky wedge of sunlight, reminded Yama of the emmet nest Telmon had once kept pressed between two panes of glass. He suddenly felt a suffocating sense of the vast size of the Palace of the Memory of the People, its mazes of corridors, the stacks of offices and chambers and apartments of its hundred Departments, its thousands of temples and chapels and shrines, all silted with a hundred thousand years of history.

Mendicants were preaching here and there, but few in the crowds stopped to listen. A line of nearly naked men danced down an aisle, lashing their shoulders with leather thongs; at an intersection, a group of men in red robes whirled on the spot to the frenzied beat of a tambour. The hems of their robes were weighted, and spun out in smooth bells as they whirled around and around; their faces glistened with sweat and their eyes had rolled back so that only the whites showed. They would dance until they dropped, believing themselves to be possessed by avatars of the Preservers.

Amongst the stalls were shrines and altars where men paused to dab a spot of ochre powder on their foreheads and mumble a prayer or turn the crank of a prayer wheel. Brabant stopped at one of the shrines, a glossy black circle framed by an arbor of paper flowers, and lit a candle and wafted its scented smoke toward his bowed face. Praying for the success of his traitorous errand, perhaps . . . or simply pausing for a moment's devotion amidst his ordinary duties.

After Brabant had moved on, Yama stopped at the shrine and touched the coin hung from the thong around his neck, but the shrine did not light. The Palace of the Memory of the People was littered with shrines—Yama had found more than a hundred in the cavern of the Department of Vatication—but he had not yet found one that would show him the garden where the woman in white waited for him. Perhaps it was just as well. He was not yet ready to confront his enemy again.

Yama pushed on until once more he glimpsed Brabant's braided mane amongst the press of clerks and record keepers. The thrall seemed to know every other person in the market, and stopped at stalls to shake hands and exchange a few words with the merchants, or taste a sample of food. He sat a while with a spice seller amongst aromatic sacks, and chatted amiably while sipping tea from a copper bowl. Yama, watching from the other side of the wide crowded aisle, ate sugary fried almonds from a paper bag translucent with grease and wondered if the plot might be one of assassination by poison, or if Brabant was simply negotiating a good price for turmeric and mace.

Brabant shook the spice seller's hand and got up and moved on through the market, saluting merchants, tasting samples and exclaiming fulsomely over their freshness, shouting greetings to passersby. If he was on a clandestine errand, he seemed to want everyone to know where he was; Yama's initial small doubt grew stronger.

At last, Brabant reached the far end of the huge market and entered a corridor with three- or four-story houses on either side, like an ordinary street under a concrete sky. There was more light here, pouring through a big curved window let into the ceiling at the far end, where palm trees rose from clumps of sawgrass. A flock of parrots chased from tree to tree, calling raucously.

A woman sat at a second-floor window of one of the houses, sleepily combing her long black hair. Below her, a man in a linen burnoose sat on a high stool outside the door. Brabant stopped to talk with the man, then shook his hand and went inside.

Yama walked past, suddenly feeling foolish and out of place. It seemed clear that Brabant had done no more than go about his business in the market before visiting a bawdy house for relaxation. Perhaps the thralls were one of those bloodlines which could mate at will, rather than on a particular day in a cycle or a season. Yet Yama was reluctant to leave. He felt that he should see this through to the end.

He drifted toward the edge of a crowd which had gathered under the palm trees at the end of the street, where a gambler restlessly switched three half shells around each other on a little table. Men in white shirts threw coins on the table, pointing at one or another of the shells, and when the betting was finished the gambler lifted the shells one by one, revealing a black pearl under the middle one. He scooped up the coins, pressed a few into the outstretched hands of two of the spectators and pocketed the rest, then covered the black pearl and began to switch the shells back and forth again.

While the spectators made more bets, the gambler caught Yama's eye and said, "I can't allow you a wager, dominie. A man like you could ruin me in a single game."

Yama smiled, and said that in any case he did not gamble.

"Then you may try your luck for the fun of it," the gambler said. He had an engaging smile, and eyes as blue as cornflowers in a pale face. A single firefly crouched in his crest of red hair, as faint as the one which had followed the rat in the old entrance hall of the House of the Twelve Front Rooms.

The gambler took his hands away from the shells, and Yama, gripped by a sudden impulse, pointed to the middle one. The gambler raised an eyebrow and lifted the shell to reveal the black pearl. The white-shirted clerks around Yama groaned. The gambler took in their money, winked at

Yama, and started shuffling the shells again. Yama watched closely this time, and it seemed that the shell hiding the pearl was again in the center— yet at the same time he knew it was under the shell on the right. The clerks finished laying their bets, and again Yama pointed, this time meeting the gambler's smile with his own when the pearl was revealed.

The clerks murmured amongst themselves and the gambler said, "You see through my little illusion, dominie. Maybe you'd like to try your skill on something a little harder."

"Perhaps another time."

The gambler looked around at the spectators, as if calling upon them to witness his bravado. He said, "I'd only ask you to risk a copper rial on your skill. To a man like you that's nothing, and you'd stand to win much more from me. I'll give you odds of ten to one."

Yama remembered the fierce leathery nomads who in summer came into Aeolis with their horses and hunting cats and tents of stitched hides to sell the pelts of fitchets, marmots, and hares they had trapped in the foothills of the Rim Mountains. The nomads' dice games went on for days, drawing those who joined them deeper and deeper, until, from beginning with small wagers, they emerged as from a dream, dazed and penniless, sometimes without even their shoes and shirts.

"Your odds are too much in my favor," he told the gambler, and some of the clerks laughed.

"They are in it together," someone said. He was a tall boy not much older than Yama, flanked by two others as he pushed to the front of the crowd. All three wore enameled badges of a fist closed around a lightning bolt pinned to the high collars of their white shirts.

"I assure you," the gambler told the boy, "that I have never seen this good fellow before."

"Cheats and swindlers," the tall boy said. "You rig the game and let your friend win to make others think that they have a chance."

The gambler started to protest again, but his mild manner enraged the boy, who leaned on the little table and shouted into his face. One of the other boys swept the shells on to the floor and his leader shouted that there was no pearl and it was no game at all, but a sharpy's trick.

Yama hardly heard him. He had just seen a man come out of the bawdy house. He wore a tunic of plain homespun girdled with a red cord, and his face was covered in a glossy black pelt, with a white stripe down the left side. He carried a staff taller than himself, and Yama knew that it was shod with iron. For he recognized the man at once, and with a shock knew that Brabant must be involved in a conspiracy after all.

The man was Prefect Corin.

4

The Ambush

"A SHARPY'S TRICK," the leader of the boys shouted. "We will have justice! Grab them both, lads—the one with the knife first."

One boy seized Yama's arms. The other wrenched the sheathed knife from its harness and handed it to the leader, who thrust it into Yama's face and said, "By what authority do you carry a weapon here?"

"By my own," Yama said. "What business is it of yours?"

The crowd murmured at this. The tall boy scowled. He and his two friends were young and excited and more nervous than Yama, not quite sure what they had discovered. They were not guards or soldiers, who would have taken Yama away for interrogation, but apprentices of some kind, eager and awkward, daring each other on.

"You've been on Department territory ever since you entered the day market," the leader of the three said. "Why are you carrying this antique? Is it licensed?"

The gambler said, "I beg your pardon, masters, but this is common ground, as is well known."

"Keep out of it, animal," the boy who held Yama's knife said. He looked around at the press of clerks and added, "You all keep out of it."

The boy holding Yama's arms said, "Answer Philo, you piece of shit."

"It is mine," Yama said. He hoped that their leader, Philo, would try and draw the knife, for surely the knife would waken and defend him.

But Philo merely dangled the sheathed knife by its clip. He had a small face framed by a bob of glossy black fur, a flat, bridgeless nose, and a wide mouth. He thrust his face so close to Yama that he laid a little spray of spittle on Yama's cheek when he spoke. His breath was scented with cloves.

"This? This is at least ten thousand years old. What is a kid like you doing with it? Explain yourself. If your business is innocent we will let you go."

"I will fetch the guards," one of the clerks said.

"We do not need guards," Philo said loudly, turning this way and that as he tried to identify the man who had spoken. "We are stronger. We will deal with these cheats in our own way."

"You are fools," the clerk said. He turned his back on Philo with contempt, and the crowd parted to let him through.

The crowd had grown. Yama could no longer see Prefect Corin. From the center of a great calm, he told Philo, "You have no authority over me. You may kill me with my own knife if it is not true."

"I will cut out your insolent tongue," Philo said.

All three boys laughed. Philo's smile widened and he gripped the hilt of the knife. There was a blue flash. Philo screamed and dropped the knife and clutched his hand. Blackened skin hung in strips from it. There was a smell of burned meat. Yama felt a slight relaxation in the grip of the boy who held him. He stamped on the boy's instep, wrenched free, and kicked the boy's legs from under him. The third boy drew a slug pistol and pointed it at Yama. The pistol's muzzle was describing shaky arcs, but they were centered on Yama's chest. The clerks behind him moved to either side. All this time, Philo was screaming that he had been killed.

"Give it up," the boy with the pistol said.

"I will walk away," Yama said, "and that will be an end to this."

Many at the front of the crowd were trying to escape through those behind, who were pressing forward because they wanted to see what was going on. Yama glimpsed Prefect Corin. He was striking out with his staff as he tried to push through the mêlée. A decad of armed men was at his back.

"Give it up," the boy with the pistol said again. He was braver than Yama had reckoned. "Give it up or I will put a big hole through you."

Yama squeezed his eyes shut. The explosive brightness as his firefly gave up all its light in one instant printed his vision with red and gold. All around him, men screamed that they were blinded. The slug pistol went off—the boy must have pulled the trigger by reflex—and something whooped past Yama's left ear. Another scream: one of the by-standers had been hit. When Yama opened his eyes, ghostly volumes of light seemed to hang in the air. The three boys and the clerks at the front of the crowd were clutching at their eyes; Philo was screaming louder than ever.

"I am blinded! I am blinded!"

A hand fell on Yama's shoulder. "Come with me, dominie," the gambler said, and dashed something to the floor.

At once, dense red smoke billowed up around the blinded men. It obscured Prefect Corin and his band of men, who were still trying to fight through the panicky crowd. Overhead, soldiers on floating discs swooped into the street.

"With me!" the gambler said. "We are your friends!"

But Yama shook off his grip, scooped up the knife and its sheath, and ran in the other direction, toward the sunlit stand of palm trees. Prefect Corin broke out of the bank of red smoke as some of his men started to shoot at the soldiers in the air. The soldiers spun around and shot back. Yama ran beneath a rain of fronds cut down by small arms fire. Sawgrass caught at his trousers; parrots fled in a whir of wings.

Beyond the trees was a slender metal bridge which arched across a narrow deep cleft. Something beat down there, slow and steady and vast; Yama could feel its pulse through the soles of his boots as he went over the bridge.

Then a glass-walled tunnel that ran along the side of a sheer rock face, with the slope of the mountain falling to the mosaic of the city, and mountains in the misty distance. The curved wall suddenly crazed into a thousand splinters; a moment later Yama heard the sharp echo of a pistol shot, and then Prefect Corin shouted his name.

Yama turned.

The Prefect and three of his men stood fifty paces away. "Well met, Yamamanama," Prefect Corin said.

He looked quite unruffled, standing straight with his staff grounded beside him. He was not even out of breath. One of the men had a bandaged hand. He was the ruffian Yama had wounded outside the gate of the Department of Vatication.

Yama held the knife by the side of his leg. He said, as calmly as he could, "You escaped the magistrates, then."

Prefect Corin said amicably, "As did you. You talked to their machines, did you not? Your father should have told me about that trick, but no matter. Here you are anyway."

"I will not come back," Yama said, and raised his knife when Prefect Corin stepped forward.

Two of his men aimed pistols at Yama; the third, the one with the bandaged hand, cocked an arbalest.

"We have no wish to harm you," Prefect Corin said. "You must be very tired and confused after your adventures, but you have come home now. You have found us, as the Preservers wished. We have a lot to talk about, you and I. There have been sightings of feral machines in the city, and the Temple of the Black Well was destroyed by the Thing Below. Did you speak to them, too?"

Yama said, "You lured me here, but I will not come with you. I will not serve."

"Oh, but you will. The day market is not yet under the Department's authority, but this place is, for it leads directly to one of the gates of the Department. You ran where I wanted you to run, Yama. The soldiers of Internal Harmony cannot help you here. Come with me, and you will be treated like a tetrarch if you can do half the things I believe you are capable of doing. Come with me now. Come home. Your father and your sweetheart will be pleased that you have turned up safe and sound."

For an instant, Yama was aware of every machine around him, all the way out to the edge of the day market. He spoke to one and turned and struck at the splintered glass with the knife. Blue light flared. Prefect Corin shouted and threw aside his staff and ran at Yama, and Yama hurled himself bodily at the circle of splintered glass and plunged through it into the open air.

5

The Library

THE CITY AND the side of the mountain described a perfect somersault around Yama's head. Then something flashed toward him out of the blue sky and he hit it hard, knocking his breath away. It was the floating disc he had stolen from under the feet of one of the soldiers.

With one hand Yama held onto the knife and its sheath; with the other the edge of the disc. Its smooth flat shape was hot from its rapid passage through the air and it stung Yama's skin, but he clung on tightly as it made a breathtaking swoop toward a huddle of roofs far below, halting just above a flat apron of red adobe. Yama landed in a tumble, bruising hip and knee and shoulder and dropping the knife and its sheath.

He got up and dusted his hands on the seat of his trousers. His wounded head ached. When he touched it his fingers came away smudged with sticky blood.

The disc hung in the air like an obedient pet awaiting a command. When he dismissed it, it shot away at once, rising at a steep angle against the sheer mountainside. It caught the light of the sun for a moment, and then it was gone.

Yama picked up his knife and sheathed it. He judged that he had fallen at least five furlongs; the glass tunnel from which he had thrown himself was no more than a gleaming thread, as fine as a hair, laid between two black crags that were themselves only interruptions in the mountain's ascent into the blue sky.

Somewhere up there was the cavern which contained the Department of Vaticination. Tamora would be hard at work, drilling the sullen thralls for their brief, futile battle. He could leave her and Pandaras,

Yama thought, and continue alone on his quest for the library of the Department of Apothecaries and Chirurgeons, the place where Dr. Dismas had claimed to have found records of his bloodline. But he knew that he would not. He had sworn to help her, as she had sworn to help him. And at the very least he must tell them about Prefect Corin and the attempted kidnapping. It seemed certain that the conversation Pandaras had overheard was nothing but a lure aimed to draw Yama into a trap.

More immediately, he must find a way back into the mountain. Beyond the parapet at the edge of the flat roof was a drop to the slope of terracotta tiles, and then the roofs of a huddle of buildings and the slope of the mountain falling away to the hatched plain of the great city. As Yama contemplated this vista something cracked like a whip past his ear, shattered half a dozen tiles, and went whooping away into the distance. He remembered the ruffians' slug pistols and immediately jumped over the parapet and ran down the slope of sun-warmed tiles. Another slug split the air and he changed direction and tripped and suddenly was rolling down the slope amidst a small avalanche of loosened tiles. He grabbed at the edge of the roof and for a moment hung there, breathing hard—and then the tiles gave way.

He landed on his back on a cushion of thick moss. Amazingly, he had not let go of his sheathed knife. All around, terracotta tiles smashed to dust and flinders. Small animals fled, screaming. Monkeys, with silver-gray coats and long tails that ended in tufts of black hair. They jumped onto a shelf of black rock at the far end of the shadowy courtyard, their wrinkled faces both anxious and mournful. Dwarf cedar trees, their roots clutching wet black rocks, made islands in a sweep of raked gravel littered with the hulls of pistachio nuts. On three sides of the courtyard were black wooden walls painted with stylized eyes in interlocked swirls of red and white; on the fourth was a clerestory.

When Yama stood, the largest of the monkeys ran forward and swarmed up a rope and swung from side to side. A gong started a brazen clamor somewhere beyond the clerestory's arches.

Yama ran. A broad stair led down from the clerestory to a huge, vaulted hall paneled with carved wood. The plaster ceiling was painted black, with a triple armed swirl of white that represented the Galaxy at one end and a recurved red swirl that represented the Eye of the Preservers at the other. This was the temple of a latriatic cult, then, one of those which believed that the grace of the Preservers could be restored to the world by contemplation, prayer and invocation.

The gong was louder here, battering the cool air with waves of brassy sound. Suddenly, shaven-headed monks in orange robes rushed into the far end of the hall. They were armed with a motley collection of spears and cutlasses; one carried a hoe. Yama drew his knife, but even as the monks started to advance toward him, light flared in the center of the hall and they fell to their knees and dropped their weapons on the ebony floor.

At first, Yama thought that part of the roof had been opened to admit the light of the sun. Then, shading his eyes against the glare with his forearm, he saw that a shrine stood in the middle of it. It was an upright disc twice his height, and it was filled with restless white light.

Yama drew the coin from his shirt and, raising it as high as the thong looped around his neck would allow, advanced toward the shrine. He thought that the woman in white had found him again, drawn by the coin, but as the blazing light beat around him, he was seized by a deep dread. Not her, which would have been bad enough, but something worse. Something huge and fierce and implacable advancing through the light, very far away in the folded space within the shrine but rapidly growing closer, stooping toward him as a lammergeyer stoops through leagues of air to snatch an oryx grazing on a mountain crag.

Yama's nerve failed. He dropped the coin into his shirt, and ran past the shrine, dodging between the monks on the far side. They were groveling with their foreheads pressed to the ebony floor, their buttocks higher than their heads. Not one moved to stop him.

He ran out into open air, along a stone terrace and down a long flight of steps dished by the tread of countless feet. Monks in orange robes turned to watch as he ran past them down narrow stone paths between plots of pumpkin vines, yams and manioc.

The brass gong suddenly fell silent, and there was only the buzz of insects and the distant roar of the city. Yama did not stop. Once again he had accidentally brought something into the world. He ran from it headlong, with nothing in his head but his hammering pulse.

———————

This part of the mountain had been built over with temples and monasteries and sanctuaries. Many stood on the ruins of older structures. Staircases descended sheer rock faces carved with grottoes and shrines. Viaducts and bridges and walkways strung across gorges and looped between crags. One pinnacle had been hollowed out; a hundred small square windows pierced its steep sides. Slopes were intricately terraced into long narrow fields where vines and vegetables grew, irrigated by stone cisterns that collected rainwater from fan-shaped slopes of white stone.

Yama spent the rest of the day descending the mountain. It seemed that there was always a flight of ravens turning in the air beyond the steep mountainside. He hoped this was not a bad omen, for ravens, particularly those of the Palace of the Memory of the People, were said by some to be spies. Far below, the city, immemorial Ys, stretched away into blue distances under a rippling layer of smoggy air.

Around noon, as the sun paused at the height of its leap into the sky before falling back toward the Rim Mountains, he arrived at a long terrace thatched in emerald green grass. An ornate fountain of salt-white stone splashed and bubbled in the middle. He drank from one of the fountain's clam shell basins until his belly was full, and washed dust and dried blood from his face, but he did not dare stop for long. He was aware of the populous mountain that reared above. Prefect Corin might be watching his flight through a telescope, and the thing that lived in the light of the shrine might be following him.

He had no clear sense of where he was going. Perhaps he could find a way back inside the mountain; perhaps he could reach one of the wide roads which he sometimes glimpsed on the lower slopes. Surely they led to a gate to the interior, for how else could fresh produce be supplied to the day markets?

He was descending a narrow stair, with a vertical rock face on one side and nothing but a slender rail of gleaming metal protecting him from a sheer drop on the other, when it suddenly turned and went under an arch. Something stopped him with implacable force, as if the air around him had congealed, and asked him his business. But it yielded at once to his will, and he went on down the stairs with invisible shawms braying and a stentorian voice gravely announcing the arrival of a Hierarch.

As Yama entered the courtyard at the bottom, a squad of guards in full armor pushed him aside and clattered up the stairs, pistols and falchions drawn. The courtyard was wide and shaded by high stone walls. In the middle of it, a soldier with an officer's sash over his corselet stood on a table. He was shouting at the people milling around two gates in the high wall at the far end.

"There is nothing wrong! Resume your places! Nothing is wrong!"

Slowly, order was restored. Clerks resumed their seats at tables shaded by large paper parasols. The crowd separated into lines before the tables. Both of the gates were guarded by armed men. One seemed to be an entrance; the other an exit. All who went through the latter

were stopped by the guards, who carefully scrutinized the wads of documents which each person had collected at the tables. Yama, too tired
to consider retracing his path, joined the end of the line nearest him.

The line moved forward very slowly. The clerk who sat at the table
questioned each petitioner closely, pausing now and then to write in
various books or to stamp papers handed to him. The man who had
come to stand behind Yama told him that there was no hurrying anything here.

"It's an old department," he added, as if this explained everything.

"It is?"

The man looked at Yama and said, "Are you lost, brother?"

He was an old man, stoop-shouldered and yet still tall, as tall as the
Aedile or Telmon, with smooth black skin and silver eyes. Coarse white
hair wound into long corkscrew ringlets framed his broad-browed face;
three fireflies nested there. He looked at Yama with a shrewd, kindly
gaze.

Yama said, "I believe that I did not come here by the usual route.
What is this place?"

"The Department of Apothecaries and Chirurgeons," the old man
said, and his silver eyes widened when Yama laughed.

"I am sorry," Yama said. "It is just that I have been searching for
this place, and came upon it by accident."

"Then you were surely guided here by the will of the Preservers,
brother," the old man said, and shook Yama's hand by way of greeting.
He added, "Certainly you are more fortunate than the fool who tried to
force entry through the Gate of the Hierarchs. Some poor wretch tries
it at least once a year. After the guardian has finished with him, the
guards display his body before the main gate as a lesson."

"Then I am doubly fortunate," Yama said.

The old man's name was Eliphas. He was a runner who made his
livelihood by researching cases which physicians could not cure by normal means. Eliphas explained that most of the people queuing in the
courtyard were runners for physicians or leeches; he assumed that Yama
was from a family which could not afford to employ an intermediary.
He saw that Yama was hungry, and took one of Yama's pennies and
purchased waybread and water from a stall on the other side of the
courtyard.

"A tip if you have to return next time," Eliphas said, smiling tol-
erantly as Yama devoured the waybread. "Bring food with you. It's
cheaper, and will probably be better, too. But I don't suppose they told
you how long it would take."

"How long does it take?" The black waybread was heavy and very sweet, but it satisfied Yama's immediate hunger at once.

"Usually a day to get through the preliminary certification," Eliphas said, "and then a day or two more to have the records searched. It depends on how you phrase your question. That's part of the art."

"My question is quite simple. I want to know if the Department of Apothecaries and Chirurgeons can help me find my people."

Eliphas scratched among his white corkscrew tangles with long, thin fingers. His nails were curved, and filed into points. He said, "If you can pay, I'll be glad to help. But I've never heard of anyone who does not know his own bloodline."

"If it can be found anywhere, it can be found in Ys," Yama said. "That is why I came here. When I was a baby, I was found on the river and taken in by a kind man. But now I want to find my real family. I believe that there are records here that will help me, but I am not certain that I know how to find them. If you will help me, I will be glad to pay what I can."

Eliphas said, "If you pay for my evening meal, and my breakfast, why then, brother, I'll do my best to put you on the right road."

"I can pay a fair price," Yama said, stung by the thought that Eliphas was offering charity.

"It's fair enough, brother. The way to learn about the system is to see how it responds to questions, and I believe that I may learn a lot by asking yours. The more you learn about the way information is catalogued, the more efficient you become. I can process up to a decad of questions in parallel. There's not many who can do that, but I've been working here all my life. In the days before the heretics, of course, it was simpler, because all records were stored within the purlieu of the avatars. I remember that what we now call librarians were then called hierodules, which means *holy slaves*. The real librarians were simply sub-routines of the avatars. They spoke through the hierodules, and their answers came promptly. But we live in an imperfect age. The shrines are silent, and we must ask clerks to search through written records which are often second- or third-hand transcriptions, and not always stored where they should be."

"But why is it that you are not allowed to know how the library is set out? It seems to me you must work in the dark when all that is needed is to open a shutter."

"Why, there are a thousand clerks employed by this library alone, and this is one of the smaller ones. If everyone knew where everything was to be found, the librarians would make no money and could not afford to maintain the records in their care. And if facts were free, why then I wouldn't make any money either. But that's the way it is with most professions, brother. If their mysteries were removed, why then there'd be no need for most of the people in them. I'd say nine-tenths of the business of any department is to do with guarding the mysteries, and only one-tenth in applying them. That's why rituals are so important. I've asked thousands of questions in my time, and reckon I know as much about medicine as most leeches, but I could never practice as I'm not inducted into their mysteries. If I'd been born to one of the medical families it might be different, but only the Preservers can choose how to be born into the world."

Yama learned that Eliphas's own family had been in the trade of question-running for three generations. Eliphas was the last of the line. His only son had joined the army and was fighting the heretics at the midpoint of the world, while his daughters' children would be raised in the trades of their fathers.

"That's the difference between trades and professions," Eliphas said. "Trades marry out; professions marry among their own kind. It's how they keep their power."

When it was at last their turn to speak with the clerk at the table, the sunlight had climbed the wall and left the courtyard in shadow. Lights like drifts of sparks had woken across the darkening slope of the mountain. The fireflies that hung above the heads of clerks and petitioners stirred and brightened as the sunlight faded, casting shifting tangles of light and shadow.

Eliphas leaned over the table, the orbits of his fireflies nearly merging with those of the clerk, and fanned a sheaf of pastel-colored papers, pointing at one and then another with his long forefinger. The two men exchanged a merry banter, and the clerk stamped Eliphas's papers without reading them.

"This is a friend of mine," Eliphas said, standing aside for Yama. "You do well by him, Tzu."

"Picking up strays again, Eliphas?" The clerk looked Yama up and down with a raking gaze and said, "Let's have your papers, boy. You'll be the last I process this day."

"I have no papers," Yama said, as boldly as he could. "I have only my question."

The clerk, Tzu, had a long, gloomy face. His brown skin was softly creased, like waterlogged leather. Now more creases appeared above his wide-spaced black eyes. He said, "Hand over your papers, or you can walk back down and start over tomorrow."

"I have my question, and money to pay the fee. I would not take bread from the mouths of your family by trying to gain the information you guard for nothing."

Tzu sighed, and shook a little bell. He said, "What have you brought me, Eliphas? And at the end of the day, too. We have procedures here," he told Yama, "and no time for troublemakers."

Another clerk appeared, a slight old man with a humped back. He conferred with Tzu, and then stared at Yama through spectacles perched on the end of his long nose. He had a wispy white beard and a bald pate mottled with tubercles.

"Stand straight, boy," Tzu said. "This is Kun Norbu, the chief of all the clerks."

"How did you get here, boy?" the chief of clerks, Kun Norbu, said.

"Down those stairs," Yama said, and pointed across the courtyard.

"Don't lie," Tzu said. "There's a guardian. No one has used the Gate of the Hierarchs for a century. Now and then thieves and vagabonds try, as one tried today, but all are destroyed by the guardian."

"Longer than that, I believe," Kun Norbu said. "The last Hierarch to visit us was Gallizur the Joyous. It would have been in the summer of the year when Ys was invested by the armies of the Insurrectionists. That would be, hmm, eleven thousand five hundred and sixty-eight years ago."

"A long time indeed, brother," Eliphas said, "but this boy is no thief. I can vouch for him."

Kun Norbu said, "When did you first see him, Eliphas? Not before today, I would wager. I suppose he bribed a guard, and promised to pay you to help him. He doesn't even have a single firefly. He's some indigenous wildman, for all you know."

Yama had supposed that his firefly had followed him, but he now realized that he must have destroyed it by asking it to give up all its light at once. He stared at the chief of clerks and said, "As for fireflies, if that is your only concern, then my lack of them is easily fixed."

"Don't be impudent," Kun Norbu said. "Fireflies choose a host according to their station. Clearly you have no station to speak of." He clapped his hands. "Guards! Yes, you two! To me, if you please!"

Tzu gasped and stood up, knocking over his stool. Eliphas stepped back, covering his face with his hands. All around, people turned to stare at Yama. A few knelt, heads bowed. The two guards who had started across the courtyard stopped and raised their partisans as if to strike at an invisible foe. Light gleamed along the crescent edges of their double-bladed weapons; a hundred sparks were caught in the lenses of Kun Norbu's spectacles.

In an extravagant impulse born of exhaustion and impatience, Yama had clothed himself in the light of a thousand fireflies, borrowed from everyone close by or called from the wild population beyond the walls. He felt that he was very close to the end of his quest, and he would not be stopped by the petty restrictions of a moribund bureaucracy.

"My question is quite simple," Yama said. "I want to find my people. Will you help me?"

6

The Hell-Hound

THE STRANGERS' LODGE of the Department of Apothecaries and Chirurgeons was built around a small square courtyard. Tiers of long, narrow balconies rose above the courtyard on three sides; on the fourth was a sloping wall of metal as transparent as glass, on which the last light of the sun glowed like the shower of gold by which, it was said, the Preservers had manifested themselves for the first and last time on the world, when they had seeded it with the ten thousand bloodlines.

Yama bought Eliphas supper in the refectory on the ground floor, and they ate at one of the long tables with a decad of other petitioners. All were crowned by the restless sparks of fireflies; there was no other light in the long room. Yama's wad of papers was by his elbow, an untidy rainbow fanned on the table's scarred and polished surface, for he did not have deep enough pockets to hold all the documents he had been given. His wound had been washed with an astringent lotion and freshly bandaged.

Despite the trick with the fireflies, the chief of clerks, Kun Norbu, had insisted that Yama should prove that he had been able to persuade the guardian of the Gate of the Hierarchs. Yama, still clothed in a thousand fireflies, walked up and down the stairs beneath the arch three times before a growing audience of clerks. It seemed to him that they would have watched him do it all night, and after the third time he told Kun Norbu that he had not come to the library as a mountebank or clown, and returned the fireflies to their former hosts, retaining only a pentad of those he had recruited from the local wild population. This trick astonished the clerks more than that of being able to pass the guardian.

Kun Norbu dismissed every clerk but Tzu, who assiduously dealt with Yama's paperwork, and then the chief of clerks had taken Yama and Eliphas to his cluttered office, where they sat on dusty couches and drank tea sweetened with honey. It seemed that Kun Norbu was an old friend of Eliphas's, and he said that he was at Yama's service.

"Tell your story, young man. Tell us how we can help you."

Yama explained that as a baby he had been found in a boat on the Great River, that he had been told that his bloodline was that of the Builders, long thought to have transcended the world. He said that he had come to Ys to search for others like himself, and added that he suspected that a certain Dr. Dismas had recently found important clues in this very library. Kun Norbu listened patiently, and then asked Yama a hundred questions, most of which he could not begin to attempt to answer. He found himself saying again and again, "If I knew, I would not be searching for the answers myself," or, "I hope to find that here."

"You will need to provide a sample of blood and a scraping of cells," Kun Norbu said at last. "That will be a good beginning."

Eliphas said, "Then you will take his case, brother. I am glad."

Kun Norbu smiled and said, "I think we might learn as much from the answers as Yama."

Yama said, "You know something about my bloodline, dominie. I see that you do. Can I find what I am searching for here?"

Kun Norbu's smile widened. His black eyes twinkled behind the lenses of his spectacles. "Not everything is to be found in libraries."

Eliphas closed his eyes and recited a fragment of text in a lilting chant. " 'They were the first men, part of the word which the Preservers spoke to call forth the world. They were given the keys of the world, and ordered it according to the wishes of their masters.' "

Yama said, "Is that from the Puranas?"

Eliphas's smile was a wide white crescent in his black face. "It sounds like the Puranas, doesn't it?"

Kun Norbu said, "It is from a text much older than the Puranas. Perhaps it was written by one of the Builders. Eliphas and I were enthusiastic hunters of obscure texts when we were as young as you, Yama. I gave up the carefree life of searching for lost knowledge many years ago, when I became a novice clerk, but now, do you know, I feel quite young again. You have rekindled my sense of inquiry, which I had thought long ago extinguished by the responsibilities of my office."

Yama said, "Then we should start at once! Why must the truth be approached through many bits of colored paper?"

He had been given passes for the library, the refectory and one of the dormitories of the Strangers' Lodge. His name, age, and birthplace

(Yama had given it as Aeolis) had been written down on a pentad of differently colored pieces of paper. His question had been copied ten times over, and all the papers had been stamped with Tzu's mark.

"It is the way things are done," the chief of clerks said. "You are young, Yama, and would tear down the world and start all over again. You value speed over all else. Everything must be done at once or given to you as soon as you need it, or the world must be changed. That's how it is with the young. But as you get older, you'll see the wisdom in the way things have always been. Old men like Eliphas and me see why things are the way they are, and why they have grown in particular ways, and how everything is connected. We see that without direction velocity is nothing but squandered energy."

Yama said, "Surely knowledge should be free to everyone, since all knowledge is the gift of the Preservers."

"Ah, but if it was freed," Kun Norbu said, "who would look after it? Knowledge is a delicate thing, easily destroyed or lost, and each part of the knowledge we look after is potentially dependent upon every other part. I could open the library to all tomorrow, if I was so minded, but I will not. You could wander the stacks for a dozen years, Yama, and never find what you are looking for. I can lay my hand on the place where the answers may lie in a few hours, but only because I have spent much of my life studying the way in which the books and files and records are catalogued. The organization of knowledge is just as important as knowledge itself, and we are responsible for the preservation of that organization."

"He will be up all night looking for the answers," Eliphas said to Yama, and told Kun Norbu, "It is good to see the light of adventure in your eyes once more, brother! I thought you were falling asleep behind the ledgers and the rulebooks."

"I keep my hand in," the chief of clerks said, "if only to keep the apprentices on their toes." He made a steeple of his fingers. They were each tipped with a black claw like a rose thorn, and linked by heavy, wrinkled webs of skin. He looked at them and said, "Have you ever been ill, Yama?"

"Just blackwater fever and ague. I lived beside the river."

"I ask because I do not know if Builders are susceptible to illness. Be glad of your childhood fevers! If any of your people live, then some of them will almost certainly have been treated by chirurgeons or by apothecaries, and the records of all chirurgeons and apothecaries are preserved here. That is how I will search, using the template that lies within your cells as a guide."

He summoned a young clerk, who took a scraping from the inside of Yama's cheek with a blunt needle and drew a minim of blood from the tip of his thumb with a glass straw. These samples also required documentation, and Yama's signature, and Kun Norbu's stamp.

When this was done, the chief of clerks bowed to Yama and said, "You need not lodge in the commons. You will be my guest. My household is yours. I will have someone find you fresh clothes and see that your wound is cleaned."

"That is kind," Yama said, "but I do not deserve special treatment. And the wound is an old one. It does not trouble me."

He feared that Prefect Corin might hear that the library had an uncommon visitor, one who could command fireflies and ancient guardians.

Kun Norbu gave Yama a shrewd look and said, "You cannot try and pretend that you are ordinary, Yama. And your wound has been bleeding recently. At least allow me to have someone look at it, and to recommend that Eliphas look after you. He knows as much about our little library as any, although he will never admit it."

After Yama and Eliphas had eaten, Eliphas filled the bowl of a long-stemmed clay pipe with aromatic tobacco, lit it, and puffed on it contentedly. Yama asked him where he had found the passage he had quoted.

"It was on a scrap of paper which someone had torn from a book an age ago and used to jot down the addition of a bill of small goods. We found it tucked between the pages of an old record book. Paper is very patient, and old paper in particular is well made and forgets very little. That scrap had preserved the verse about your people on one side and the trifling calculation on the other, and had also patiently kept the place which someone dead a thousand years had marked. It is not that things are forgotten, simply that they are mislaid. Bindings of certain books are a good example of where such things may be found, for pieces of older documents are often used as backing. There's no end of places to look. Kun Norbu and I looked in many strange places when we were young."

"I am beginning to believe that I am mislaid," Yama said. "That I do not belong in this time. Many times, when I was younger, I hoped that someone was looking for me."

"You must have courage, brother. I am curious about one thing, though. May I ask a question?"

"Of course."

"Why, there's no 'of course' about it. I simply do my duty, as the Preservers would wish. I do not expect you to satisfy my idle curiosity as reward. But thank you. My question is this. If you do learn where your family lives, what will you do?"

"I would ask them why I was set adrift on the river, to begin with. And if they answered that, I would ask them . . . other questions."

Eliphas blew a riffle of smoke. "Who am I? Why am I here? Where am I going?"

"Something like that."

"Forgive me, brother. I don't mean to make light of your predicament."

"If they live at all, I think that they must be living somewhere in Ys, or in the boreal lands upriver of Ys."

"Then hope they live in Ys," Eliphas said. "The land upriver is wild, and full of races which have not yet changed, or perhaps will never change. Most are little more than animals, and do not even have an Archivist to record their lives. The city streets are hard, yet with a little money and a modicum of cunning one can endure them. But it is not so easy to survive in the dark forests and the ice and snow of the boreal regions at the head of the river."

Yama sighed. He was beginning to realize the magnitude of his task. He said, "The world is very large, and not at all like my map."

"Your map must be very old. Little has altered on Confluence since the Age of Insurrection. It is true that when bloodlines reach enlightenment, the change wars that follow usually destroy their city. But the survivors move on, and there are always prelapsarian races to take their place, and all seems as it was before. New cities are built upon the old. But what stood in those places at the beginning of the world? I would very much like to see this map of yours."

"I left it behind when I came to Ys."

Yama told Eliphas about Aeolis, and the peel-house and its library, and Eliphas said that he knew of the library of the Aedile of Aeolis.

"I knew the present librarian, Zakiel, before he was disgraced and sent away. Sometimes I envy his exile, for the library has a certain notoriety. It is said that an original copy of the Puranas is lodged there."

It was the book that Zakiel had given Yama when he had left Aeolis for Ys. His heart turned over when he realized the value of the librarian's gift. The book was with his satchel and the rest of his belongings in the little stone cell in the House of the Twelve Front Rooms, in the Department of Vatication. He must return there tomorrow, and discharge his obligation to Tamora. And then he must flee, for he must not be captured by the Department of Indigenous Affairs. If that happened he would certainly fall into Prefect Corin's hands.

He said, "Zakiel was one of my teachers."

Eliphas blew a smoke ring and watched it widen in the air, then sent a second, smaller smoke ring spinning through the fraying circle of the first. He said, "Then no wonder you value knowledge. With your permission, brother, I'd like to sleep now. We must rise with the sun if we're to get a place at the carrels."

———

Only one of the Lodge's dormitories was open; clearly, the library had seen greater use in former times. But the beds, although narrow, were comfortable, and the sheets clean. Eliphas snored and someone else in the dormitory talked in his sleep, but Yama had risen early and had faced death and had walked many leagues, and he soon fell asleep.

He woke in pitch darkness. The hairs on the back of his neck and on his forearms were prickling and stirring, and he was filled with a feeling of unspecific dread, as if he had escaped the clutches of a bad dream.

There was a faint light at the end of the dormitory. At first Yama thought sleepily that the door was open, and that it must be morning. But then he saw that the light was vaguely man-shaped—although taller than most men, and thinner than any living man should be—and worse, that it was moving. It drifted like a bit of waterweed caught in a current, or like a candle flame dancing in the draft created by its own burning. It reminded Yama of nothing so much as the wispy lights that could sometimes be glimpsed after the river Breas had flooded the ruins outside the city wall of Aeolis. The Amnan called those apparitions wights, and believed that they would steal the soul of any traveler they could entice into their clutches. Yama had known, because Zakiel had told him, that the lights were nothing more than pockets of marsh gas which kindled in the air upon bubbling to the surface of stagnant water; Zakiel had once made a demonstration, with water and a bit of natrium in a glass tube. But knowing what the wights were did not make them less eerie when they were seen flickering in the darkness of a bleak winter's night.

Unlike a candle flame or a marsh wight, the burning figure gave off no light but that which illuminated itself. The long dormitory remained in shadow, lit only by the dim clusters of fireflies which clung to the walls above the beds where their hosts slept, but when the thing stooped over the first of the beds, the sleeper's face was immersed in its spectral light. The man murmured and turned halfway around, but he did not wake. The thing disengaged itself and waved through the dark to the next bed.

Yama discovered that he was clutching the sheet so hard that his fingers had cramped. He remembered the light which had burst through the shrine in the temple of the latriatic cult and the thing he had felt rushing toward him from the depths of the space within the shrine, and knew that the apparition was searching for him. He sat up cautiously. His fireflies brightened before he remembered to still them, but the burning figure did not appear to notice. It was bending toward the third sleeper, like a librarian patiently searching a shelf book by book.

Yama put his hand over Eliphas's mouth and shook the old man awake. Eliphas's silver eyes opened at once, and Yama pointed to the burning figure and whispered, "It is looking for me."

Eliphas bolted from his bed, clutching the sheet to his skinny body. "A hell-hound," he said in a hoarse whisper. "Save us! It is a hell-hound."

"It came from a shrine further up the mountain. I think it means me harm."

Eliphas was staring at the apparition. His shoulders were shaking. He said distractedly, "Mountain? Yes, I suppose that the Palace would resemble a mountain to someone not used to large buildings."

"It stands between us and the door. I think we should wait for the guards."

Another man's sleeping face appeared in the hell-hound's blue light; the man groaned horribly, as if gripped by a sudden nightmare. Yama thought that everyone here would remember the same dream when they woke—and then realized that if the hell-hound could affect men's dreams, then perhaps it could also see into them. That must be what it was doing, browsing through the minds of the sleepers as a scholar may browse in a library, hoping to gain insight by serendipity.

Yama snatched up his shirt and the harness which held his sheathed knife, and said, "I am going to climb through one of the windows. You can come with me or stay, but I would be happier if you followed me."

"Of course I'm coming. It is a hell-hound."

Yama opened the shutter of the window above his bed and climbed out on to the balcony outside. When Eliphas followed, clutching his clothes, Yama turned up the light of their fireflies and discovered that they were only a few man-lengths above the mosaic floor of the court-yard. He swung over the rail of the balcony, landing with a rush and a shock but no harm.

Eliphas let his clothes flutter down and followed more cautiously, and sat down after he had landed, massaging his knees. "I am an old man," he said, "and my days of adventuring are long past. This was never part of the bargain."

Yama pulled on his shirt and shrugged the harness around his shoulders. "You do not have to follow me," he said.

Eliphas was pulling on his trousers. He looked up and said, "Of course I will follow. I mean, I think it would be better if I did. The hell-hound is looking into the minds of those men, and some remember that they saw you with me. And if it looks into my mind it will find my conversations with you. What might it do then?"

"Then you had better show me how to reach the Gate of the Hier-archs. I will get us past the guardian. I have no intention of staying here."

"I think it would be better if we found Kun Norbu. He will know what to do. And the guards are armed."

"We will return in the morning," Yama said.

Eliphas might have argued the point, but a blue light appeared at the balcony above. They both lost their nerve then, and ran.

The guardian of the Gate of the Hierarchs had been driven deep inside itself, and did not notice when Yama and Eliphas passed by. It was a few hours before dawn. It was not cold, but Yama and Eliphas were soon mantled with dew after they sat down to keep watch from a turn of the long flight of stairs high above the library. Yama said that Eliphas could leave him as soon as it grew light, but Eliphas said that he would as soon stay with Yama.

"I made a contract with you, brother, and I never let a client down."

Yama said, "You have other clients before me."

"I'll let you into a secret." Eliphas lit his pipe. When he drew on it, the burning coal of tobacco set a spark in each of his silvery eyes. He was calmer now. He said, "Sometimes, I already know the answers to the questions I am sent to root out of the library. It would not do to tell the client that, though. It would put the business of the library at risk, and my business, too. Besides, no leech will believe that I know something of his trade that he himself does not. It does not do to sell the truth cheaply. Instead, I enact a little charade. I come here and gossip with my friends, and a day later I return to my client and give him, stamped and documented, the answer I could have given him straight-away, if only he trusted me. The library is paid, I am paid, and the client is pleased with his answer. That is why I was so happy to help you. It gave me something to do. Besides, like my friend, Kun Norbu, I feel young again in your presence. I had thought that there were no more wonders to discover in the world, and you have proved me wrong."

Yama considered this. At last, he said, "The road I travel may be long, and it is certainly dangerous."

"Don't think that I know only the inside of libraries, brother, and am innocent of the world. I traveled much in my younger days, search-ing for old books. It took me to some odd places. I am an old man, brother. My wife is dead, my daughters are married and concerned with their own families, and my only son is fighting heretics at the midpoint of the world. Now, I am sure that we can return to the library when it is light, and find out what Kun Norbu has discovered about your people. And after we find the records concerning your bloodline, I will be happy to help you look for your people. No, I will stay with you. I will do my part."

"I have some business to complete before I can go and look for my people," Yama said.

He started to tell Eliphas about the conflict between the Department of Indigenous Affairs and the Department of Vaticination, but he had not got very far when Eliphas suddenly stood and said, "Look! Look there!"

A cold blue light flared below. It defined the curtain wall of the library and several of its slim towers before winking out. There was the sound of men shouting in the distance, and then the iron voice of a bell, slow at first but gathering urgency.

Someone down there had an energy pistol. For a moment, an intense point of light shone like a fallen fleck of the sun. There was a noise like that of a gigantic door slamming deep in the keel of the world, and the backwash of the discharge blossomed above the roofs and towers of the library and threw the shadows of Yama and Eliphas far up the long flight of stairs. The cold blue light kindled again. It was smaller now, and seemed to be climbing one of the towers. Yama saw the flashes of pellet rifles; the sound of their fusillade was like the crackle of twigs thrown on a fire. The mote of cold blue light dropped from the side of the tower, drifting down like a leaf.

Eliphas said, "They have killed it!"

"I do not think so. It has discovered that I am no longer where it thought I would be. It must have found out from one of the sleepers that I was staying in the dormitory, and now it has finished its search, or it was interrupted."

"Brother, we both saw it fall."

"I do not think it can be killed by rifle fire, nor even by the discharge of an energy pistol. It is not of this world, Eliphas, but of the world men once glimpsed in the shrines."

Yama remembered that the woman who had appeared in the shrine of the Temple of the Black Well had told him that there were dangerous things beyond the bounds of the garden she had created. He was certain now that the hell-hound was one of the creatures she had feared.

Eliphas nodded. "Accounts of the wars of the Age of Insurrection speak not only of the battles of men and machines, but of a war in the world within the world. The priests claim that this means that the enemy strove to conquer men's souls as well as their cities, but archivists and librarians know better. Hell-hounds were weapons in that second front."

"The Insurrectionists tried to destroy the avatars, and the link between men and the Preservers."

Eliphas nodded again. "And the heretics succeeded where the Insurrectionists could not. Perhaps they woke the old weapons."

"I fear that I have a talent for drawing enemies to myself. There! There it is again!"

The tiny point of blue light had appeared at the foot of the dark wall of the library. Now it began to ascend the stairway.

Eliphas knocked out his pipe on the railing of the stairs. His fingers were trembling as he put it away. "We must go on. The hell-hound travels slowly, or it would have caught you long before you reached the library, but I have a feeling that it does not rest."

7

The Gambler

YAMA AND ELIPHAS reached the long lawn and its fountain just as
dawn began to define the mountain ranges at the edge of the city's wide
plain. The library was far below, its towers ablaze with lights, but there
was no sign of the hell-hound.

Eliphas sat heavily on the wet grass. "Perhaps it has lost us," he
said.

"I do not think so. It followed me down to the library. There is no
reason why it cannot follow me in the reverse direction. You are tired,
Eliphas."

"I am old, brother."

"And my head aches. But we cannot stay here."

Eliphas slowly clambered to his feet, unfolding his lanky body in
stages. He said, "I'm sure we can spare a few minutes before we go on.
I am thirsty as well as tired."

As Yama and Eliphas approached the ornate fountain in the center
of the lawn, two deer ran from it, white scuts bobbing as they disappeared into the darkness. Eliphas thrust his head into a spout of water
that gushed from the gaping mouth of a fish; Yama drank from a basin
shaped like an oyster shell and splashed cold water on the back of his
neck. His head wound had begun to bleed again. While Eliphas sat on
the edge of the fountain's main basin and lit his pipe, Yama walked
back to the edge of the lawn. He was anxious and tired and afraid.

There was now enough light in the sky to make out the various
clusters of buildings which were scattered across the long slope below.
Yama could see that the library's curtain wall had been breached—the
adamantine stone slumped like melted candle wax—and that its slim

white towers were licked with black soot. The path which climbed through the tiers of fields seemed empty, and for a moment his heart lifted. Perhaps Eliphas was right. But then he saw a glimmer of cold blue light emerge from a distant stand of sago palms; the hell-hound came on in an erratic dance like a scrap of fabric caught in a breeze, flitting from side to side, but always moving upward.

Yama ran back to Eliphas, but the old man shrugged phlegmatically when he heard the news and was maddeningly slow to begin to move. Exhaustion had overcome his fear. He knocked out his pipe on his bootheel and said that there were roads still in use, and all led to gates to the interior.

"And where there is a gate," Eliphas said, "there will be guards."

"The guards of the library could not stop it. We must go, Eliphas."

"Some guards are better armed than others," Eliphas said. He pressed the palms of his hands over his silver eyes for a moment. "The main part of the Palace has always been better defended than the out-lying offices. We cannot run forever, brother. If we lead it to them, the soldiers of Internal Harmony will know what to do."

Yama did not share Eliphas's faith in this plan, but a small hope was better than no hope at all. He said, "If we are to try and find some way back into the mountain, then we should turn aside. The monastery where I wakened it is not far above. I do not want to confront the shrine again, especially with that thing at my back. I might waken something worse. As it is, I fear that the library is destroyed."

Eliphas smiled. "Not at all. What stands aboveground is only a tenth part of the whole. The stacks and carrels of the archives run far back into the Palace. Kun Norbu may be somewhat distracted by repair work, but he will remember your request."

"That is suddenly the least of my concerns," Yama said.

They found a narrow path at the far end of the long lawn. It wound along the foot of a bluff from which a cluster of square, white, win-dowless buildings hung, like the cells of a wasp nest. Far below, the hell-hound stopped for a full minute, burning in the midst of a steep field of red corn, and then suddenly moved forward at a steady pace, cutting across the field in a straight line toward them.

They hurried on, passing between the legs of a skeletal metal tower clad in a living cloak of green vines. The path angled through a thicket of bamboo, and then a little village was below, flat roofed houses of wicker and daub crowded around a central square. Threads of smoke rose into the gray sky from several of the houses. A cock crowed in anticipation of the rising sun.

Eliphas stopped and bent over and clasped his knees. For a while all he could do was breathe hard. Yama went back to the beginning of the bamboo thicket to look for the hell-hound, then returned to Eliphas, who slowly unbent and said, "We must go through the village. If the hell-hound follows, the villagers will try and stop it."

"Will they be better armed than the library guards?"

Eliphas shook his head. Sweat beaded his smooth black skin. He dabbed at his brow with the back of his hand and said wearily, "They are husbandmen who till the fields on this part of the Palace roof. They will have axes and scythes, perhaps a few muskets. They will not be able to stop it, but they might slow it down so we can make our escape."

"No, I will not risk their lives. We cannot wait here, Eliphas. Remember that the hell-hound does not rest."

Eliphas waved a hand in front of his face, as if Yama's words were flies that could be brushed away. "A moment, a moment more, and I will be able to go on. Listen, brother. The quickest way to the nearest gate will take us through the village. The husbandmen take their produce to the gates. That's where they sell it to merchants from the day markets. Don't spare a thought for them. They are indigens whose ancestors colonized the ruined parts of the Palace ten thousand years ago. They are animals, brother, of no more importance than the sacred monkeys of the outer temples. Less so, in fact, since priests and sacerdotes care for the monkeys that live in their monasteries and temples, but no one cares for the husbandmen. They are tolerated only because they supply the day markets with fresh produce. We'll go through their village, eh? It will delay the hell-hound a little."

Yama remembered the fisherman, Caphis, who had saved his life after he had escaped from Dr. Dismas and the young warlord, Enobarbus. He said, "Even if the indigenous peoples cannot transcend their animal origins, still they are something more than animals, I think. I will not risk their lives to save mine." He pointed to the terraced rice paddies that stepped away below the next bluff. "There is a path that descends beside those fields. We can follow it. Eliphas, if you wish to, leave me now. Go through the village. The hell-hound will not follow you."

"I made a bargain," the old man said. "Maybe a bad one, but it might still pay off. Lead on, brother, although I fear your scruples will help the villagers more than they will help us."

The sun had begun to rise above the distant mountains when Yama and Eliphas reached the steep ladder of steps beside the terraced rice fields. The narrow steps were worn by the tread of a thousand generations of husbandmen, and slippery with seepage from the flooded paddies. Ferns grew in cracks between the steps, and bright green mosses made the way more slippery still.

Despite their fearful haste, Yama paused at a wayside shrine. *Take this burden from me,* he prayed, as he had prayed so often before, meaning, make me ordinary, make me no more than other men. Save me from myself.

The rice paddies were narrow and long, curved to follow the contour of the hillside and dammed with stout ramparts of compacted earth wide enough for two water buffalo to walk abreast. Freshly planted seedlings made a haze of green over the calm brown water that flooded them; the ripe smell of ordure reminded Yama of the flooded fields around Aeolis; at another time it would have eased his heart.

When he suggested that the rice paddies might have been here before the Palace had been built, Eliphas laughed and said that it was impossible. "Even now, we step on the roof of the Palace itself. The indigens who tend the fields or hunt the wild animals here are like the birds or mice which colonize the older habitations of man. It would have meant nothing to have gone through the village, brother."

"It would have meant something to me."

After they had descended a while in silence, Eliphas said, "This part of the Palace was ruined in the last war of the Age of Insurrection, and has never been properly rebuilt. If you were to dig deep enough, you would find rock fused like glass, and then rubble, and then rooms and corridors wrecked and abandoned ten thousand years ago. Because this side of the Palace faces the Rim Mountains, and is in sunlight for most of the day, it is favored for cultivation." Eliphas laid one hand on the small of his back. "I am sorry, brother, but I must rest again. Only for a moment."

Each time Eliphas stopped to catch his breath, Yama anxiously looked back at the path they had taken, but by good fortune they managed to reach the bottom of the long ladder of steps before the hellhound finally appeared.

White cockatoos rose into the blue sky, screeching in alarm. A moment later the hell-hound burst out of the thicket of bamboo above the terraced rice paddies. Like a whirlwind or dust devil, it threw clouds of dust and scraps of foliage into the air as it moved forward. It seemed just as bright in daylight as at night, like a bit of sky fallen to earth and roughly shaped into a tall, skeletal man. It started toward the village, but quickly returned to the path, and came on steadily.

Yama and Eliphas ran down a dusty track between the steep bank of the bottommost rice paddy and the margin of a sloping field of melon vines. They splashed across a stream and ran through a belt of eucalyptus trees, scattering a herd of small black pigs, and ran on until Eliphas tripped and fell headlong in the dust.

At first Eliphas could not get up, and when Yama finally hauled him to his feet he said that he could not run any more. They were on a long downward slope with tall grass on either side of the path. A chorus of crickets was beginning to whistle, woken by the early morning warmth.

"Leave me," Eliphas said. He was trembling and his silver eyes were half-closed. He could not get his breath. "Leave me, brother, and save yourself. I will find you again, if we both live."

The slender eucalyptus trees at the top of the slope stirred and shook as if caught in a localized gale. A horrible squealing went up and black pigs pelted out of the trees. The hell-hound appeared behind them, blazing like a piece of the sun caught in blue glass. It seemed to have grown taller and thinner, as if the glass, melting, was being pulled apart by its own weight. Veils of dust and leaves whirled up around it. At first it seemed confused by the pigs and made short, swift dashes after one or another of them. Most of the pigs scattered into the tall grass, but a few ran in circles, dazed by the brilliant light, and finally the hell-hound pounced on the smallest. The hapless pig flew up as if it weighed no more than a dead leaf, was dashed to the ground, and lay still. As if excited by this, the hell-hound whirled in wider circles. It swept through the tall dry grasses, which immediately caught fire with a sullen crackling, then steadied and came on down the path toward Yama and Eliphas.

Yama got a shoulder under Eliphas's arm and they staggered down the path to the edge of a steep embankment. Directly below was a broad road crowded with carts drawn by bullocks or water buffaloes, camels laden with hessian-wrapped packs, and women and men walking with bundles or clay pots balanced on their heads. Carts and camels and people were all moving downhill toward the high, square entrance of a tunnel in the side of the slope.

As Yama and Eliphas staggered down the embankment, people shrieked and shrank away. Yama glanced over his shoulder. The hell-hound had appeared behind them, burning brightly against a reef of white smoke. Yama shouted in despair and pulled Eliphas behind a cart piled high with watermelons. All around, men and women screamed as the hell-hound swept down the embankment. A bullock bolted, bawling with fear, and its cart overturned, spilling hands of red bananas. A flock of moas ran in circles, screeching wildly and kicking up dust. The hell-hound plunged amongst the birds, rearing back and forth as if maddened.

Yama and Eliphas were swept along in the midst of the panicking crowd into the darkness of the tunnel, brick walls doubling and redoubling the shouts and screams of men and women and the bawling of animals, then into a huge underground chamber. Like a breaking wave, the crowd washed against loading bays where laborers were unloading and weighing produce and clerks were handing out tallies to husbandmen.

Yama and Eliphas were halfway across the wide chamber when the flock of moas stampeded out of the tunnel, the hell-hound burning in their midst. People screamed and dropped baskets and packages and ran in every direction, and a pentad of guards came out of a tall narrow gate. The guards wore half armor and carried slug rifles which they began to fire as they ran toward the hell-hound. Wounded moas fell to the ground, kicking with their strong, scaly legs. Ricocheting slugs whooped and rang, knocking dust and brick fragments from the ground all around the hell-hound as it stretched and bent this way and that, and finally fixed on Yama and Eliphas.

Eliphas wailed and sank to his knees, his arms wrapped over his head. Yama held up the ceramic coin in one hand and his long knife in the other, and slowly backed away from the hell-hound. It had elongated to four or five times the height of a man and shone so brightly that he could only squint at it through half-closed eyes. It made a horrible high-pitched hiss as it sinuously advanced toward him, gouging a smoking trench in the brick floor. Its heat parched his skin. The guards kept up a steady rate of fire, but the fusillade merely kicked up shards of brick around the hell-hound or passed through it as if it was no more than light—and perhaps it was no more than light, light bent into itself.

Yama backed into a stack of baskets of live chickens. He slashed the baskets open and kicked them toward the hell-hound. The thing stopped and bent in a half circle as panicked chickens scattered around it, but then it straightened and fixed on Yama again. He tried again to command it to halt, but he might as well have tried to snuff a furnace by pure will. He was aware of a number of small machines in the chamber, but he could no more hurl them at the hell-hound than he could have endangered the village.

People were fighting to get through the gate; no escape there. Yama stepped backward as the hell-hound swayed toward him, watched by laborers and husbandmen hiding amongst wagons and carts. Eliphas called out. Yama risked glancing around and saw that the old man was standing on top of an overturned cart. A man jumped up beside Eliphas; Yama recognized the gambler who had been playing the shell game outside the bawdy house.

"This way, brother," Eliphas called, and the gambler shouted, "Come with me if you want to live!"

Yama turned and ran, and knew by the screams of the people all around that the hell-hound had started after him. He dodged around the cart and for a moment thought that Eliphas and the gambler had vanished. No, they had ducked through a little round hole in the wall. Yama's shadow was thrown ahead of him, and he ran to meet its dwindling apex. Fierce heat and light beat at his back as he scrambled through the low opening, and then something fell with a clang behind him and he was in darkness.

8

The King of the Corridors

MOMENTS AFTER IT had fallen into place behind Yama the hatch rang with a pure, deep note and a smell of scorched metal began to fill the narrow space in which he stood, pressed close to Eliphas and the gambler.

"Put up your knife, dominie," the gambler said. "You're with friends here. Follow me, follow me now. The hatch is crystalline iron, but it won't hold for long."

The gambler's stiff red coxcomb, with its single dim firefly, brushed the low ceiling. He wore bright red leggings and a baggy black shirt that came to his knees. He had a pungent but not unpleasant odor, like that of a wet dog.

"I am at your service," Yama said. His blood was still thrilling from the near escape. When Eliphas took his arm, he realized that he was trembling so much that he could hardly stand.

"It is my turn to help you, brother," Eliphas said, and put his shoulder under Yama's arm to support him as they followed the gambler down the tunnel.

Yama said, "What is this place?"

"The service corridors," Eliphas said. "They're supposed to run through every part of the Palace, even to the offices of the Hierarchs. But there are no maps to their maze, and few use them now."

The gambler glanced at them over his shoulder. His long pale face gleamed in the combined light of their fireflies. He said, "Most of that's true, but more use these corridors than you might reckon, and not everything has been forgotten. Speaking of which, do you remember me, dominie?"

"You were playing the shell game yesterday. You were wearing a silver shirt then."

"You're as sharp as they say you are," the gambler said. "I'm Magon, and I'm here to help you. We've been on the lookout for you, dominie. You ran the wrong way yesterday, and it's my luck to have found you again. Do you know what it is that you wakened? You did wake it, didn't you?"

"Yes. Yes, I did. It was in a shrine."

"In the temple of a latriatic cult? We hadn't thought that one was still functional—well, it isn't functional now, of course. The shrine was destroyed when the hell-hound broke through."

Yama touched the coin that hung at his chest. The gambler, Magon, saw the gesture, and said, "That won't help you, dominie. It isn't a charm."

"I was wondering if it had woken the thing."

The woman in the shrine of the Temple of the Black Well had said that the coin had drawn her to him.

Magon said, "You did that yourself, I reckon. Lucky you were brought up where you were, in the City of the Dead, and not in Ys. There are too many shrines in Ys, and more remain functional than most folk think. If you had been brought up in Ys, it is likely that a hell-hound would have scented you before you were ready for it. But that would be a different world, and I wouldn't have the good fortune of talking with you here and now."

"You seem to know a lot about me," Yama said.

"Lucky for you that I do," Magon said jauntily.

"And you know about the hell-hound."

"A little, dominie."

"It seemed to be made of light," Yama said.

"Something very like it," Eliphas said, eager to explain something he understood. "Light is only matter in another form, and it can be bound for a while. If we can keep away from it, brother, the hell-hound will collapse when its binding energy sinks below a certain level, or it will find a functioning shrine and upload itself and return to the place for which shrines are windows. They are terrible things. They can live in the space inside the shrines, and in our world, too. They pass through our world from one shrine to another like an arrow through air, if an arrow could make itself into air in its flight and remake itself when it hits its target. They were sent after avatars, originally."

Yama said, "And this one came for me."

"That was bad luck, and not just for you," Magon said. "It must have been bound in the shrine. No doubt that's why the monastery was built around the shrine. It's all too easy to mistake the stirring of a hell-hound for the intimation of an avatar. Those poor monks, praying for thousands of years to a weapon of their enemies! There's irony for you, eh, dominie? Well, they'll worship the shrine no longer. The hell-hound stole the residue of the shrine's potential energy when it manifested."

"It seemed to grow stronger in sunlight," Yama said. He had the horrible thought that whoever had fired at the hell-hound with a pistol would have fed its strength. He added, "Perhaps darkness would kill it."

"It was never alive," Magon said, "So *killing* and *dying* don't apply."

Eliphas said, "Even in sunlight it loses binding energy. Sunlight's energy is too dilute to sustain it, just as we would gasp for air at the peaks of the Rim Mountains. I imagine that it is imprinted on you, brother. It will follow as long as it can. We must escape it."

Magon said, "It's a terrible thing, but it's old and easily confused. If we're lucky it will give up, or lose track or memory of you, and dissipate when its binding energy drops below a sustainable level."

"We have had little in the way of luck so far," Yama said. "I think that I will have to find a way of destroying it."

"As for that," Magon said, "some ways are better than others, as the fox said to the hen lost in the forest. We'll go through here. Don't worry about the water. It's dry on the other side."

They had reached the base of a kind of well or shaft. A patch of pale daylight showed high above and a sheet of water fell down one side and drained away through grids in the floor. Behind the water three corridors radiated away at sixty degrees to each other. Magon plunged through the water and trotted down the middle corridor. When Yama and Eliphas followed—the water was as warm as soup—they found the gambler waiting at the other end, where a slim metal bridge arched across a narrow, half-flooded cavern. Green lights flickered deep beneath the water. Waves clashed and broke against the stone walls, casting shivering shadows on the arched ceiling.

Magon stepped quickly and lightly across the bridge's span and turned at the other side and beckoned to Yama and Eliphas. As he crossed, Yama saw shapes move swiftly just beneath the water's restless surface, things with sleek, arrowhead-shaped bodies that ended in knots of long, twining limbs: creatures like the polyps which swarmed in the river at midsummer, but grown to the size of a man.

Eliphas saw them too. He grasped the rail of the bridge and looked down into the water and said, "There are more things forgotten in the Palace than anyone could dream of in a lifetime of sleep."

"Not forgotten by everyone," Magon called from the other end of the bridge. "They come up from the Great River through flooded passages beneath the streets of the city. Lupe says they might have had a purpose once upon a time, but that's long forgotten. They come here by habit now." He told Yama, "We should press on, dominie. Lupe is eager to meet you."

Eliphas said, "Begging your pardon, Magon, but I always understood that no one lives inside the walls of the Palace but thieves and cutthroats."

Magon flashed his crooked smile and said, "Their kind doesn't last long. We see to that. It isn't far now, I promise. Lupe is waiting for you, dominie, and your friend is welcome too. We know him."

"You know everyone, it seems," Yama said. He leaned beside Eliphas. Below, the reflected stars of his crown of fireflies were drawn apart and flung back together on the shivering surface of the water. The sleek shapes were gathering beneath the bridge. Their bodies were limned by patches and dots and lines of green luminescence. Something like a snake rose up, a pale, glistening rope that sinuously elongated in the air. It caught hold of the middle of the bridge's high arch for a moment, then fell back.

Magon said, "It isn't safe to tarry here, dominie." There was a note of pleading in his voice now.

Yama did not trust the gambler. His ready smile and quick wit seemed assumed, a mask, an act. He said, "Before we move on, Magon, tell me how you know who I am. It is not just because I saw through your sleight of hand, is it?"

Magon said, "Of course not. Please, dominie, we must go. You don't know the dangers here." His calm, knowing pose had dissolved. His hands writhed in a knot before his chest. "You shouldn't play with poor Magon. Lupe can answer your questions. I am to take you to him at once."

"You are not a gambler at all, are you? That is just a cover for what you really are. So, who are you? And why do you know so much about me?"

There was a loud splash out in the darkness, as if something big had lifted itself out of the water and fallen back.

Magon's left hand darted to his hip, where something made a shape under his loose shirt. He said, "Lupe said to bring you direct, and you want me to answer your questions. I've tried to do my best, but I can't do both, dominie."

Eliphas told Magon, "Keep your hand away from your side, brother. You've something hidden there—a knife in your belt, most likely, and no doubt there's another in your boot. I know those footpad tricks."

Yama said, "How long have your people been watching me?"

"You were supposed to go to the Department of Indigenous Affairs, but your escort arrived without you. That's when we started looking, but we didn't catch sight of you until after you called down the feral machine."

"My escort? You mean Prefect Corin?"

For a moment, Yama thought that Magon was in league with the Prefect.

"I wouldn't know his name," the gambler said, "but someone in the Department of Indigenous Affairs isn't happy he lost track of you. He'll be searching for you hard, now you've been spotted in the Palace. We'll make sure you're safe, dominie."

Magon did not meet Yama's gaze as he answered these questions, but looked from side to side as things splashed in the darkness on either side of the bridge's span. When a nest of pale tentacles rose from the water directly beneath the bridge, he gave a cry and took a step backward.

Yama said, "I will not go with you until you have answered all my questions. How long have your people been looking for me?"

"When you fought the thing in the Temple of the Black Well, we knew for sure. Lupe said that you were the one foretold. You don't have to worry about the little inter-departmental dispute you've become involved with, dominie. We'll always be here to see you right."

"And my friends?"

Out in the darkness beyond the bridge, something huge surfaced with a loud splash. Big waves clashed beneath the bridge; spray wet the walls of the chamber.

Magon said, the note of pleading in his voice stronger now. "Dominie, you'll have to ask Lupe these questions. That's why I'm to bring you to him. Truly, it is not safe—"

Yama said, "This is not the first time I have met people who claim more for me than I would ever claim for myself. And I have business elsewhere today."

This was the day that the Department of Vaticination opened its doors for public inquisition of its pythonesses. It was the day of the assassination plot, in which, Yama suspected, Brabant, the servant with the keys to the kitchens of the House of Twelve Front Rooms, was Prefect Corin's agent, doing double duty after he had led Yama to the Prefect. Yama still did not know who was the target of the plot, but that did not matter as long as Brabant was unmasked.

"You'll have to talk with Lupe, dominie. Please, I really am no more than a player of games. We're all at the service of the workers in the Palace, and that's how I make my living. You might say that if we had a department, it would be the oldest of all."

Eliphas caught Yama's arm and whispered, "I know his kind now. Thieves and cutthroats, brother, no better than the husbandmen."

Yama whispered back, "Unless you know the way out, we have no choice but to follow him."

Magon cocked his head, his eyes bright as he looked from Eliphas to Yama. He said, "You don't trust me, and I guess that if I was in your position I'd feel the same. I don't have the answers you want, dominie. I'm just here to bring you to Lupe. Lupe will answer your questions. We must leave here. The hell-hound is still at your back, and the big fish get restless after a while, and start questing about with their arms to see if they can catch you. We—"

Blue light was suddenly reflected in Magon's eyes. Yama turned. The hell-hound stood at the end of the bridge. It was smaller now, but burned as brightly as ever. Yama unsheathed his knife. Its curved blade kindled with blue flame, as if to challenge the hell-hound's unworldly light.

The hell-hound slid forward, elongating through black air as it climbed the arch of the narrow bridge. Yama and Eliphas retreated step by step. They had scarcely reached the far end when something hit the underside of the bridge so hard that it hummed like a plucked string. Magon and Eliphas screamed. Nests of pale tendrils rose up on either side of the bridge's arch, slithering around the slender railings. The hell-hound stopped, bending back and forth as more tentacles quested up out of the water.

Yama guessed that there must be a decad or more of the giant polyps beneath the bridge. The undersides of the tentacles bore rows of fleshy suckers which stuck and unstuck to the metal span with wet noises; their ends were frayed into feathery palps which continually tasted the air. Then the water under the bridge boiled and the forest of tentacles which gripped the railings tensed. The bridge groaned but held, and the tentacles coiled more tightly and tensed again, quivering with effort. One of the giant polyps was half-lifted out of the water. Under its white mantle, a huge blue eye with a golden pupil revolved and fixed its gaze on Yama.

The bridge groaned again and then the central section gave way with a sudden sharp crack that echoed and re-echoed from the cavern's wet walls. On the other side of the broken bridge, the hell-hound flared brilliantly and whirled around and fled into the tunnel, and Yama and Eliphas cheered.

The water boiled with activity. Green lights flashed furiously under its foaming surface. One, then another, then two more: the great polyps lifted the edges of their mantles out of the water and stared at Yama. Eliphas and Magon shouted in alarm, but Yama, guessing wildly, lifted the coin from his shirt and held it up. Satisfied, the polyps sank back one by one. The water boiled up once more and then darkened as the living lights beneath its surface faded away.

"Nothing will follow us now," Yama said.

"The hell-hound will find another way to follow you," Magon said. "That's what it does." He was very scared, but he had stood firm, and Yama liked him better for that.

Eliphas took a deep, trembling breath, then another. "Lead on, brother. And remember we trust you only slightly more than we trust your fishy friends."

The narrow corridor which led away from the flooded cavern was circular in cross-section and lined with fused rock that dully reflected the lights of the fireflies of Yama and Eliphas. As it rose and turned, Yama was certain that its gravity changed direction, too, so that they were no longer walking on its floor but along its wall, rising vertically through the heart of the mountain. Occasionally, other corridors opened to either side and above; gusts of warm air blew from these openings, sometimes bringing the sound of distant machinery.

Magon soon regained his jaunty confidence, and boasted that these were the old skyways which only his people knew.

"You might say that there's a Palace within a Palace, each twined around the other like a vine around a tree until you can't tell whether the tree is holding up the vine, or the vine the tree. We were here from the beginning. Departments come and go. They fight each other and are destroyed or absorbed, yet we are still here. We will be here until the end."

Eliphas said, "I suppose this is the teaching of your master, this Lupe."

"It's our history," Magon said. "It's passed on in song and dance from father to son, from mother to daughter. Just because it's not written in books doesn't mean it isn't true, though for someone like yourself, who has breathed so much book dust he is mostly book himself, that might be hard to believe. We are always here to serve. It's what we do. Whoever owns the Palace becomes our master, whether they know it or not."

"And you want to help me?"

What struck Yama now was that in his posturing and anxious capering, his hypersensitivity to moods and eagerness to please, Magon was just like the kind of lap dog that childless gentlewomen keep.

Magon said, "You are come at last, dominie. Lupe said he had not expected it, although it was foretold by an anchorite years before. But Lupe will tell you himself."

The corridor turned around itself again. Warm, humid air, laden with a rich organic stink, blew into their faces, and then the corridor opened out into a long, low room. Its bare rock walls ran with condensation; its floor was strewn with heaps of black soil in which frills of fungus grew; dead white, blood red, a yellow so shiny it might have been varnished. At the other end of the room, Magon parted layers of nylon-mesh curtains and ushered Yama and Eliphas into a barrel-vaulted cave lit by shafts of sunlight that fell from vents in the rock ceiling far above.

"Our home," Magon said. "It is the capital of my people, for Lupe lives here."

There were little gardens, and patchwork shacks built of plastic or cardboard sheeting, or of translucent paper stretched across bamboo framing. People drew around Yama and Eliphas as they followed Magon across the cavern, and they quickly became the center of a procession. There were clowns and jugglers, mummers and mimes, weightlifters and agonists, fakirs with steel pins through their cheeks and eyelids. Acrobats walked on wires strung everywhere across the midway of the cavern. There were men dressed in richly embroidered dresses of faded silk stiff with brocade and silver and gold thread, with white-painted faces and black makeup that exaggerated their eyes, transvestites that burlesqued the sacred temple dancers. There were musicians and gamblers, and prostitutes of all four sexes and seemingly of every imaginable bloodline.

Eliphas looked around uneasily, but Yama knew that they would not be harmed. Not here. "They exist to serve!" he said, and took the old man's arm to reassure him.

The gorgeous, motley procession crossed the length of the cavern. A fakir smashed a bottle on his head and rubbed a handful of broken glass over his bare chest; another pressed metal skewers through folds of skin pinched up from his arms. Musicians played a solemn march; clowns knocked each other down and breathed out gouts of fire or blew fountains of sparkling dust high into the air; men and women held up their children, who laughed and clapped their hands.

The path ended at a round gilt frame twice Yama's height. It might once have held a shrine. The crowd parted to let Yama and Eliphas follow Magon through this gateway.

The room beyond was swagged in faded tapestries and bunched silks stained with dust. The wrack of ten thousand years lay everywhere in an indiscriminate jumble. Lapidary icons were heaped like beetles in a green plastic bowl; a cassone, its sides painted with exquisitely detailed scenes from the Puranas, its top missing, was filled with filthy old boots; ancient books lay in a tumbled heap next to neat rolls of plastic sheeting.

A man sprawled amongst cushions on a sagging bed beneath a canopy of cloth-of-gold. Magon capered forward and jumped onto the bed, raising a cloud of dust from the yellowed linen sheets, and laid his head next to the man's bare feet, gazing up with unqualified adoration, for all the world like a faithful puppy gazing at its master.

Without doubt, the man on the bed was Lupe, the king of the Palace within the Palace. He was a big man; he was an old man. Skin hung in mottled flaps from his arms. His face was scored deeply with lines and wrinkles. He wore a long brocade dress so stiff with dirt that it was impossible to tell what color it might once have been; an elaborate headdress of gold wire woven in a tall cone and studded with bits of colored glass was planted on top of tangled gray hair that fell to his broad shoulders. His feet were bare and his toenails were painted red; the nails of his big, strong hands, like those of certain mendicants, had been allowed to grow around each other in long corkscrews. His lips had been stained with cochineal and his eyes were made up like the wings of a blue butterfly. His pupils were capped with frost, and from the way he held his head Yama knew he was blind. He did not look absurd in his costume, but wore it with a grave, sacerdotal majesty.

Lupe turned his face toward Yama and Eliphas, and said in a soft, hoarse voice, "Come closer, dominie."

Eliphas said, "What is this place?"

Lupe raised his head and turned it from side to side, as if sniffing the air. "Who is this stranger, Magon?"

"A companion of the one foretold, Lupe."

"Then he is welcome," the old man said. "As are you, dominie. Welcome and twice welcome. It is my honor to welcome you. I had thought that I would die before you came, and it is with all my heart that I convey the treasure house of my sentiments, which have been stored up for so long against this wonderful day."

"It seems that I am expected," Yama said.

"You are the one who is foretold," Lupe said. His blind eyes were turned toward Yama's face. "Please, dominie. Please sit at our table! All that we have is yours!"

Three beautiful girls, arrayed in layers of splendid silks that left only their arms and faces bare, stepped through a curtain. Their delicate oval faces were painted white; their full lips were stained black. They carried trays of sweetmeats and candied fruits arranged on plantain leaves or in tiny bowls of translucent porcelain. Their eyes shone with excitement and they giggled as they fussed about Yama, seating him in a nest of dusty cushions and setting the food before him. One sat Eliphas beside Yama; the other two helped Lupe from the bed, sat him on a low stool, and settled the full skirt of his dress around him.

Yama took a bowl of tea from one of the girls and, after a hesitation, Eliphas followed suit. Another girl raised a bowl to Lupe's lips; the old man's fingernails were so long that he could not possibly feed himself. The three men slurped companionably, and Lupe belched gravely. While one of the girls fed Lupe with chopsticks, Yama picked at diced squares of candied yam. He had not eaten since the meal in the Strangers' Lodge of the Department of Apothecaries and Chirurgeons, but he was too excited and nervous to have much of an appetite.

At last, he said to Lupe. "You know of me, master. Where does that knowledge come from?"

"Please, dominie, I am not your master! I am Lupe, no more than Lupe and no less, and completely at your service. All my people are at your service. All this was foretold, and we have made many songs and poems and dances in your honor. Not all our dances are lewd or comic. Those are for our public, but we have our own dances. Once I could dance them, but now, alas, I can only remember them." Lupe tapped his wrinkled brow with his knuckles. "All our history is there, in the dances, and so are you."

Eliphas said to Yama, "Ask him how we can destroy the hell-hound, brother. Ask him to show us the way back to the roof of the Palace, so I can help you find what you seek."

Lupe cocked his head, and said, "Anything you wish, dominie. Anything within our powers. We are yours to command."

Yama said, "How is it that you know me?"

He did not feel afraid here—he realized that this was the first time since he had left his home in Aeolis that he did not feel some measure of fear. But he could not stay long. The gates of the Department of Vatication would open to petitioners at noon; the assassin would be sharpening his covert blade or preparing his vial of odorless poison. But this was an opportunity that might not come again, and he was intensely eager to discover all that Lupe knew—or believed he knew—about him.

Lupe did not answer Yama's question at once. Instead, he motioned to his attendants. One of the girls squatted beside him and refilled his tea bowl; another held it to his lips. When the old man had drained his tea, he wiped his red-stained lips on the back of his hand and said, "We have always served, dominie. We were put into the world to serve and to bring pleasure. Thus, while our bloodline is of the lowest order, the nature of our service calls upon the highest arts. For while we might be counted as beggars who dance, make mock or make love for a paltry slew of coinage, our reward is not in the money but in the pleasure our performances bring to our clients. We are a simple people. We do not need money, except to buy cloth and beads and metal wire for our costumes. Your friend looks among the trinkets stored here, and wonders perhaps that I can claim to be poor, yet live with all these riches heaped about me." (Eliphas held up a mildewed leather cap embroidered with silver wire, and made a face.) "But these riches are all gifts from grateful clients," Lupe said. "We have saved them out of sentiment, not avarice. We are a simple people, and yet, dominie, we have survived longer than any other bloodline. We are too simple to know how to change, perhaps, but we do remember. It is our other virtue. We remember your people, dominie. We remember how great and good they were. We remember how we feared and adored them. They have been gone a long time, but we have always remembered them."

Yama leaned forward, his entire attention on Lupe's grave, blind face. He said, "And are my people still in the world?"

"They are not in the Palace, dominie, and so we have always believed that they are no longer of the world. How could it be otherwise? For they were the Builders, and this is their place. It was here that they commanded the world, in their day. If they are not here, then surely they live nowhere else."

"Perhaps this is no longer their day. Perhaps they are dwindled."

Lupe shook his head. "Ah, dominie, how you tease me! You know I cannot speak of that. We know the Palace. We know something of Ys. The world is another place entirely."

"Then they are not in Ys," Yama said. He had guessed it, but this was still hard to bear. "Do you believe that they might return?"

Lupe said, "An anchorite came to me seventeen years ago and told me that one day you would seek help from my people. And here you are. So you might say that your people have returned."

Seventeen years ago Yama had been found afloat on the river, a baby lying on the breast of a dead woman in a white boat. For a moment, Yama was so excited that he could not speak. He touched the coin which hung inside his shirt. An anchorite had given it to him in Aeolis, at the beginning of his adventures. Derev had said that the man was of his bloodline.

At last, he said, "What did he look like? Was he scarred about the face, and dumb?"

"He had a gentle, hoarse voice. As for what he looked like, I could not tell you, dominie. I was blind then as now, and he came to me when I was alone. It was deepest night, and those of my people not working were asleep. He told me that one day, near the end of the world, a Builder would come to Ys, and that he would need our help. He told me where you would come from, and when. My people have been watching the docks for a hundred days now. I thought that you would not come, but here you are."

"I came by the road, not the river."

"And yet you are the Child of the River, and the end of the world seems near. The departments have been perpetually at war with each other since the Hierarchs fell from power, and now one department threatens to destroy the rest in the name of the war against the heretics. If it wins, then such a tyranny may rise that could hold the world in its grip forever, wielding power in the name of the Preservers, but serving only itself. I have feared this for a very long time, but now I know, dominie. Now I know! How glad I am that these terrible days are the last!"

Lupe's milky eyes shone with tears. Magon crept from the bed and with his long, crafty fingers tenderly blotted the tears from his master's withered, rouged cheeks. "It's true," the gambler said, looking boldly at Yama. "Everything Lupe says is true. He remembers more than anyone else. It is why he is our king."

Lupe composed himself and said, "I weep from joy, dominie, that you have come again. There will be new songs and dances made out of this wonderful moment."

"I understand," Yama said, although it seemed to him that he had mistakenly stumbled into the middle of a myth. Lupe's story had set a hundred questions tumbling through his head. Who was the anchorite? Was it the same man who had given him the coin? Why had he been set adrift on the river in the first place?

He said, "I am grateful for your hospitality, Lupe, and for your help. But you know that I cannot stay."

Magon said, "They have business with one of the fading flowers, Lupe. I told them that they need not concern themselves with it any longer."

"Forgive my servant," Lupe said. "He is young and eager, but he means well. If you have business to attend to, dominie, then that is what you must do. My servant will take you where you need to go."

Eliphas said, "Then you will let us go?"

"Wherever you are in the Palace, we are with you," Lupe said. "But before you go, walk with me. Show my people that you are my friend, and so the friend of us all."

Lupe led Yama and Eliphas through the kingdom of his cavern. A hundred brightly costumed clowns, dancers, and whores followed at a respectful distance while Lupe gravely introduced Yama to each of the elders who stood in shabby finery outside their painted shacks.

Yama asked many questions, and although Lupe answered every one, often at length, he learned little more, except that much was expected of him. Lupe was too polite, or too cunning, to state exactly what this was, but Yama slowly began to realize that there was only one thing these people could desire. For they were indigens, and unlike the changed and unchanged bloodlines they were untouched by the breath of the Preservers. They were creatures which had borrowed human form; perhaps even their intelligence was borrowed, a trick or skill they had learned like tumbling, fire-eating, or prestidigitation. Everything they possessed had come to them from other hands, and they accepted these gifts without discrimination. Fabulous treasures were tipped carelessly amongst the rubbish that had formed great drifting piles in Lupe's apartments; a beautiful boy carrying nightsoil to the gardens at the edge of the caverns might be wearing a priceless dress; a dancer made up as fabulously as a courtesan might be clad in a glittering costume that, on close inspection, was constructed of sacking decorated with a magpie's nest of scraps of plastic and aluminum.

The only thing which was truly theirs was the art of simulation, which they used without guile to enhance the pleasure of their clients. Watching closely, Yama saw that the three girls who attended Lupe were not beautiful at all—or rather, that their beauty was a trick of poise and muscle tone and expression, sustained by constant vigilance. They could become passable imitations of most bloodlines by synthesizing and exaggerating with a little makeup the two or three features by which each was distinguished from the others. And so with beauty, for beauty is only an exaggeration of the ordinary. Just as a transvestite exaggerates those features which make a woman attractive, Lupe's people achieved beauty through burlesque. These people could, through their art, appear to be anything that their clients might desire.

The only thing they could not be was themselves.

Many, like Eliphas, believed that the indigenous races were no more than animals. Yama thought otherwise. For if everything in the world had proceeded from the minds of the Preservers, then surely the indigenous races had not been brought here simply to be despised and persecuted. Surely they too had their place.

It was almost noon by the time Yama and Lupe finally completed the circuit of the cavern and returned through the gilt frame to Lupe's chambers. Somewhere high above, the Gate of Double Glory would be admitting those who wished to participate in the public inquisition at the Department of Vaticination. The two pythonesses would soon appear before their clients, arrayed in ancient splendor.

"I do not forget that you have business elsewhere," the dignified old man said. He covered Yama's hands with his own. "You can leave by a hidden way, and the people will think you stay here to talk with me. The more important they think I am, the easier it is to keep order. We are a fractious people, dominie. We get too many ideas from others."

"You have been very generous," Yama said.

"We have done all we can, but I fear that it is little enough."

"You have given me my life, and hope that my people still live," Yama said. "I will try to return when I can."

"Of course you will return," Lupe said. "And so I will not say farewell, for in reality you will not have left."

As they followed Magon up a long stairway, Eliphas said, "This is a day of wonders, brother. I had not known that the mirror people stored up their loot. Amongst all that rubbish is an edition of the Book of Blood that I had known only by repute. It is badly damaged, but a man could live for a year from the sale of only a few intact pages. Will you return?"

Yama shook his head, meaning that he did not know. Yet he did feel a prick of obligation. Not because Lupe's people had saved his life; Lupe had made it clear that there was no debt to be paid, and Yama was ready to take him at his word. But there was the other matter. There was Lupe's impossible dream, the promise of the anchorite, the prophecy fulfilled.

No wonder my people have hidden themselves, he thought, for the world holds a store of their unpaid debts and I seem to be fated to redeem them all.

He said with sudden bitterness, "I wish I had never come to Ys! I only hurt myself, and those who expect things from me. I should have gone downriver with Dr. Dismas and accepted my fate!"

But as soon as he said it, he knew that the words came from his dark half, the part of him that dreamed of easy glory and power without responsibility. The part that had been touched by the woman in the shrine, the aspect whose original had begun the heresy which threatened to consume the world.

Magon glanced over his shoulder, his pale face thrown into sharp relief by the lights cast by the fireflies of Yama and Eliphas. There was no other light in the long stair, and Yama wondered how those who lived in the Palace could stand it. Except in places at the edge of things, they inhabited little bubbles of light surrounded by vast expanses of uncharted shadow; Lupe's people, who possessed only the dimmest of fireflies, if any, must navigate the maze of passages and tunnels in near darkness.

Yama said, "How far is it, Magon?"

"Not far, dominie. We use the straightest route."

Eliphas whispered, "You should feel no obligation, brother. They are shadows. Thieves and tricksters and whores who live off the crumbs of those engaged in honest toil. They are like the indigens of the roof gardens—except those are more useful. Would you be the savior of such as they?"

"I suppose that if one was to attempt to emulate the Preservers, then one must start somewhere, and better to start in a low place than in a high one. But I aspire to no such thing. I see that you are a pragmatic man, Eliphas. You prize things for their utility."

"Brother, things are what they are. The mirror people were created for the amusement and wonder of the bloodlines of men, nothing more. They spin fantasies, but they should not be taken seriously."

"Yet they dream, Eliphas. They believe that I belong in their dreams."

"They remember their creators, brother, as men remember their mothers and fathers. But once we are grown up we cannot continue to depend upon our parents. We must face the world ourselves."

"If Lupe's people are still as children," Yama said, "then I envy them."

They fell silent for a while, following Magon up the stairway to a dark, narrow tunnel which, binding gravity about itself, rose vertically through the Palace. At last, Magon stopped and said, "It is not far, dominie. You follow the way until you reach a place where it branches into two. Take the right-hand branch and you will find yourself in a throughway near the Gate of Double Glory."

"I owe you much, Magon."

The ragamuffin gambler bobbed and bowed. "You have repaid me a thousandfold, dominie, by allowing me to bring you to my people. I will watch for your return."

When Magon's footsteps had faded into the darkness, Yama said, "Whatever my intentions, it may fall out that I am never able to return."

"Because of the territorial dispute," Eliphas said. "It is no secret, brother. The whole Palace knows the plight of the Department of Vaticination. Many hope it survives, for that will check the growth of the Department of Indigenous Affairs."

"It's a pity that there's only hope and no help."

"No one wishes to anger the Department of Indigenous Affairs, for lately it has grown very powerful, and careless of the ancient protocols. That is why it has been able to pick off lesser departments one by one."

"And there is the hell-hound. We cannot be certain that it has lost my trail. You do not have to follow me, Eliphas. It will not be an easy time. You could go back to the library and your friend, if you wish, and wait for me there."

The old man smiled. "And suppose the hell-hound finds me? No, I will stay with you, brother. Besides, I made a pledge. Lead on, and I will help as best I can."

9

The Public Inquisition

HUGE MIRRORS HAD been set up on the flat roof of the House of the Twelve Front Rooms, deflecting sunlight into the cavern and mercilessly illuminating the shabby façades of the buildings ranged around the wide plaza. Yama squinted against the mirrors' multiple glare when he and Eliphas came through the Gate of Double Glory. He had expected to find a crowd waiting for the pythonesses, but although a platform had been set up on the steps of the Basilica, its deck covered with landscape cloth and strewn with garlands of white lilies and trumpet flowers that already were beginning to wilt, the plaza was deserted.

Inside the Basilica, Tamora was roaring at a double file of thralls marching in two-step time, turning them again and again in precise right angles. Pandaras ran up and said to Yama, while staring openly at Eliphas, "We thought you lost, master!"

"So I was, for a little while. This is my friend, Eliphas. He searches libraries for facts. He has already been of help to me, and I hope he will help me further. Eliphas, this is Pandaras. The fierce woman over there is Tamora."

"Yama exaggerates my importance in our adventures on the roof," Eliphas said.

"I am Yama's squire," Pandaras said, staring up at Eliphas boldly. The boy had oiled his hair back from his forehead. It gleamed beneath his three fireflies. He turned to Yama and said, "I see you have had the sense to bandage your head, master. Let me look at it."

"It is almost healed."

"As you said two days ago."

Now Tamora came stalking across the Basilica's marble floor. She wore her corselet and a short leather skirt, and sandals with laces that crisscrossed her calves. Her scalp was freshly shaven, and the fall of red hair at the back of her skull had been braided into a complex knot. She looked both terrified and desirable.

"I thought you'd been killed, or that you'd run away," she said, and took Yama's arm and drew him a little way from the others. "Grah. You stink of the warrens of some subhuman race. Where have you been? And who's your fish-eyed friend?"

"I was lost. Eliphas helped me find my way. There is a conspiracy—"

Tamora grinned, showing her rack of pointed teeth. "The servant you followed? The fucker is dead. When you didn't come back, Pandaras told me you were following this fellow by the name of Brabant, and I told Syle. On his advice, Luria ordered the execution. Brabant was bound and pitched out of a window of the House of the Twelve Front Rooms. It's how they do things here. They call it defenestration. Yama, I talk too much, but it's because I am pleased to see you alive! I thought Brabant had lured you into an ambush. I wanted to torture him for the truth, but he went straight out the window."

Yama said, "I think I know the whole story, Tamora. No one here is plotting against anyone else. Certainly not Luria, or she would not have agreed to have Brabant killed."

"Of course not. Luria has so much meat on her she can't walk five steps in a straight line. Why would she meet with someone in secret in a remote place when she could do so at ease in her own chambers? No, I think it's Syle. You might trust him, but I don't. Not him, and not that pregnant hen of his, either. He could have had Brabant killed to cover his tracks."

"Brabant was not working for Syle, but for someone outside the Department. In fact, he—"

"He is dead. If there are other traitors here they'll show themselves soon enough, and I'll deal with them. Now, tell me about what happened to you."

Yama suddenly found himself smiling. He could not help it. "I have found the library, Tamora! The library where Dr. Dismas discovered the secret of my bloodline. I have put a question to it, and perhaps the answer is already known."

If the hell-hound had not destroyed the records, he thought. Eliphas had said that they were safe, but Yama did not entirely trust the old man. Eliphas preferred to tell people what he thought they wanted to hear, even if it was not always the truth.

"I'm pleased for you," Tamora said. "I get paid no matter how you go about your search, so the quicker the better as far as I'm concerned. But right now we have work to do."

"Then I have not missed the inquisition? That is good. I mean to keep my word, Tamora."

"It has already begun. Go and put on your armor. Luria is still worried that an attempt will be made on her life. The Department of Indigenous Affairs would claim this place at once if she was killed."

"The assassination plot is only half the story, Tamora. Perhaps there is no plot at all, except against me."

Tamora lost her temper. "Will you serve? Then do as I say! Put on your armor and follow my orders!"

"I have your armor close by, master," Pandaras said, and ran off to fetch it.

Yama told Tamora, "Please listen to me. Brabant set up a charade, making sure that Pandaras overheard it, and then he lured me to a place where I could be taken. Prefect Corin tried to kidnap me, Tamora. He has been looking for me, and he almost caught me. The ruffians who ambushed us were part of it."

"Well, Brabant is dead," Tamora said, "and you escaped." She turned to Eliphas. "If you're a friend, go up with Pandaras and keep watch. That way, I won't have to worry about you."

"Because while I keep watch, the boy will keep watch on me?" Eliphas smiled. "I understand completely. But you do not have to worry, Tamora. Yama's interests coincide with mine."

"Then we've much to talk about," Tamora said. "And we will, when this is over."

Yama said, "You do not have to do anything here, Eliphas. This has nothing to do with helping me find my people."

"I will enjoy it, brother. Like my friend Kun Norbu, all this excitement makes me feel young again."

Tamora helped Yama to assemble his patchwork armor. "This is how it falls out," she said. "Syle is talking with the clients and keeping them entertained until the ceremony begins. What he's really doing is finishing off the business of finding out as much as possible about them. He told me how it works. The clients have to submit their questions two decades in advance of the ceremony, which gives him plenty of time to research them. He employs spies and bribes clerks, that sort of thing. He says that it is to provide the pythonesses with as much background information as possible, but I reckon that he doesn't really believe in the pythonesses' powers of prediction. He finds out what kind of answers his clients want, and makes sure that's what they get."

"He believes that Daphoene can see into the future. And there *is* something strange about her, Tamora. As if her head is full of ghosts."

"Grah, I'd say it was mostly full of air. She says little, and because of her position her few words seem important. But they're not. They're nothing but simple-minded babble. But I know you don't listen to me." Tamora knelt to tighten the buckles of Yama's greaves—the greaves he had won by killing the one-eyed cateran, Cyg. She looked up. "There's something wrong about this place. It's nothing to do with your funny feeling about Daphoene. It's as if they all hold knives at each other's throats."

"In a few days they will be under attack, and they are already under siege. You must listen to me, Tamora. There is no intrigue except that of Prefect Corin. He found out where I was and used Brabant to lure me away. If there is an assassination plot, then it is also the work of Prefect Corin."

"Then why are they at each other's throats? Luria has told me to watch Syle, and Syle took me aside after Brabant went out of the window and said that there is a conspiracy that goes deeper than one foolish thrall."

Yama hesitated. He knew that Tamora did not believe in his powers. Did not believe, or refused to allow herself to believe. Although he had tried to explain how he had awoken the Thing Below in the Temple of the Black Well, and how he had killed Gorgo, she had merely scoffed and told him that the blow to his head had given him delusions.

He said, "Syle knows what I am, Tamora. He knows that I am one of the Builders. He asked me to use machines against the forces of the Department of Indigenous Affairs. I refused, of course."

"So he betrayed you to Prefect Corin?"

"This was after Pandaras overheard Brabant. But I suppose that Syle might think of selling me now."

"Your brain is still bruised from the ding you got at the gate. No more talk about magical powers, or I'll begin to regret I took up with you."

"I know you do not believe me, Tamora, but I raised up the feral machine in the Temple of the Black Well, then woke the guards which destroyed it. It was that fight which set fire to the temple."

"It was the assassin who did that, to cover his tracks. You're brave enough, Yama. You got the priests out of the burning temple. Don't spoil it with silly stories."

"I killed Gorgo. You did not see it, but thousands of others did."

"If he isn't dead, he deserves to be. He *will* be, when I finish here. I'll make sure of it."

"My fireflies, then. I left here with one, and I have returned with five."

"You've been on the roof. Your firefly left you then, and you got a new set when you came back inside."

Yama laughed. She was as stubborn as an ox.

"Forget your fantasy, Yama, and concentrate on what you are. Which is what I am, a cateran hired to defend this miserable place." Tamora prowled around Yama, stepped in to tighten a strap of his cuirass, stood back and gave him an appraising look. "You should have kept Cyg's sword, if only for show."

"That was all it was good for. My knife serves me well enough." Yama realized now that the real reason he had rejected the sword was because it had been wielded against him, and saw that Tamora had understood this from the beginning. He said, "I do not look much like a soldier, do I?"

Tamora said, "There's nothing to it. The rat-boy is on the roof with an arbalest, and your new friend will help him keep watch. The clients have brought their own guards, and I reckon that's where any trouble will come from. If there are any more traitors amongst the servants, they'll choose a less public time. A knife or a strangling cord in the dark, or poison—that's the style of this place. All we have to do is stand on either side of the platform and look fierce. If there is trouble, we'll get the thralls between the stage and the clients. Those gray-skinned rockheads can't do much, but at least they can get in the way of anyone who tries to hurt the fat one or the airhead. Promise you won't try any heroics. None will be needed."

Tamora clapped Yama between his shoulder blades and added, "Don't doubt yourself," and went off to shout at the thralls, ordering them to get back into formation.

———

When Yama and Tamora marched out of the main doors of the Basilica and came down the steps leading a double column of thralls, the people who had gathered at the foot of the platform fell silent and stared at the spectacle. There were only three clients, each sitting in a plain chair with a small entourage of advisers, clerks and bodyguards behind them. No more than a couple of decads of men in total, and a scattering of old women who had no doubt come for the entertainment. Yama went right and Tamora left, each leading a line of thralls. Yama halted at the place where the rear edge of the platform butted the stairs, and the thralls marched past him and turned out one by one, forming a neat arc down the long, shallow staircase. Tamora really had done wonders with their drill. Their metal caps shone and they had tied long red ribbons beneath the double-edged blades of their partisans.

Yama did not feel nervous now that he was in place. As with the public ceremonies he had attended with his stepfather, the Aedile of Aeolis, he found that the worst thing was the entrance, when the audience had nothing better to look at and was full of anticipation, so that any mistake by the participants was most obvious.

A small procession made its way across the wide plaza toward the Basilica, led by a herald who blew a braying brass trumpet. The people below the platform turned to watch. In better times, Yama supposed, the trumpet would have been necessary to clear a way through the crowd, but now it sounded small and plaintive, and its echo came back from the rock walls and made discords. Behind the herald came a tall figure in a cloud of red—it was Syle, in a long robe of red feathers that fluttered with his every step. He marched solemnly ahead of the palanquins, carried on the shoulders of bare-chested thralls, on which the pythonesses sat. Both women wore white gowns and were crowned with wreaths of ivy. Luria's jowls were rouged and her eyes were accentuated by gold leaf; Daphoene's face was as bloodless as ever, and she ceaselessly worked her narrow jaw as if chewing something. The senior servants of the household walked behind the palanquins. They were led by Rega, stately as a carrack, in a dove-gray silk dress with a full skirt and a high collar trimmed with pearls.

Luria was carried up the steps to the right of the platform and Daphoene to the left. The senior servants took their place on the steps above as the bearers, their gray skins gleaming with oil, carefully set the palanquins on the platform. The landscape cloth, which had been showing a field of green grass ceaselessly winnowed by wind, now changed to show blue sky. The change raced out from the two pythonesses, so that they seemed to be couched on air, the heaps of white flowers at their feet like clouds.

Syle stood beside Yama while the pythonesses were set in place. "I am so pleased to see you return," he whispered. "I had thought all was lost, but now I know that we are saved."

Before Yama could ask what he meant by this, Syle moved off, taking a position in the center of the platform, in front of a little brazier which stood between the pythonesses. Syle bowed to both of them—Luria acknowledged him with a regal nod, but Daphoene had turned her blind face toward the light which shone from the mirrors on the far side of the plaza—and threw a handful of dried leaves on the glowing charcoal in the bowl of the brazier. Instantly, heavy white smoke billowed over the sides of the brazier and spread across the platform. The white smoke had a powerfully sweet smell. It spilled over the edges of the sky-colored platform and rolled down the stairs.

Syle stepped to the front of the platform, the hem of his red robe swirling through white vapor. His fireflies spun above his head like a spectral crown. He looked hierophantic, uncanny, terrifying. He pulled a slate from his robes and read from it in a conversational voice. "The merchant, Cimbar, would ask the avatars of the Preservers this question. Will his business prosper if he leases an additional two ships to supply the loyal army of the will of the Preservers?"

There was a silence. Then Luria began to intone sonorously, "There is no end to the war—"

Daphoene shuddered violently and bent over, squealing like a stricken shoat. It was as if she had been struck in the belly. Syle covered his confusion by stepping backward and casting a pinch of dried leaves on to the brazier.

Daphoene straightened. Everyone was watching her, even Luria. Yama could hear her breath whistling through her narrow lips. The faint sense he had of the ghosts of many machines inhabiting her intensified for a moment, like a sea of candle flames flaring in a sudden draft.

Daphoene said in a thick, choked voice, "No one profits from war but the merchants," and fell back on the couch of her palanquin. Blood spotted the front of her white gown; she had bitten her tongue.

The fat man in the central chair smiled and nodded as two of his advisers whispered in his ear. At last he waved a be-ringed hand, clearly satisfied with his answer.

Syle cleared his throat and said, "The avatars of the Preservers have answered, and the answer is acceptable." He raised his arms, the sleeves of his red robe falling like wings around him, and framed the second question, concerning plantations of green wood which were not growing properly.

This time Luria answered, and at some length. Yama was watching Daphoene, and Tamora the small audience; it was Pandaras who raised the alarm. When he cried out, half of those in front of the platform stared up at the little balcony where the boy and Eliphas stood, high above the door of the Basilica; the rest turned to look at where he pointed.

Huge shadows flickered across the cavern. Yama realized that there were men on the roof of the House of the Twelve Front Rooms, small as emmets against the glare of the mirrors. One of the tiny figures fired an energy pistol. A thread of intense red light burned above the plaza. Fire splashed above the turrets of the Gate of Double Glory, and a curtain of rock plunged down with a roar that echoed and re-echoed in the sounding chamber of the cavern.

After that, there was very little resistance. Most of the thralls threw down their partisans and fled; when Tamora tried to rally the others, one drew a knife and ran at her. It was the thrall with the streaks of gray in his mane who had been humbled by Yama two days before. Tamora parried his clumsy stroke, killed him with a single thrust to his throat and turned to face the others, the point of her bloody sword held up before her face.

Yama drew his knife and started toward her, but Syle caught his arm and thrust the muzzle of a slug pistol into his side and said, "You should have listened to me when I asked for your help, but perhaps this is for the best. If you stay calm, all of your friends will live. One word from you, and they die. Drop the knife please."

"Perhaps you should take it. I do not want to damage the blade."

"I know what it can do. Drop it."

Soldiers were rappelling down the wall of the House of the Twelve Front Rooms; some were already running across the plaza toward the Basilica. Luria lifted the ivy wreath from her head and dashed it into the fumes at her feet. She pointed at Syle and bellowed, "You said you'd wait!"

Syle told her calmly, "I promised I'd wait until he returned, and so he has. My first duty is to the Department of Vaticination, not the dead past." He said to Yama, "Tell your friends to come down. I've no desire to see them killed if they should try and defend their position. Besides, the Basilica might be damaged."

Tamora swung around when Yama called to Pandaras, and Syle showed her his pistol. She spat and sheathed her sword and ordered the thralls who remained to lay down their partisans.

"I demand that ransom is paid for my freedom," she said.

"I would give it to you at once," Syle said, "but it is not mine to grant."

Pandaras and Eliphas came out of the main door of the Basilica as the attacking force began to disarm the thralls. Pandaras held the arbalest above his head. A soldier plucked it from his hands and pushed him toward the thralls.

A man in a homespun tunic, the black pelt of his face marked by a bolt of white, vaulted on to the stage. Syle thrust Yama forward and said, "Here he is, dominie."

"I am the master of no man," Prefect Corin said. He had a strip of translucent cloth tied across his eyes. "We meet again, Yama. How I wish this little drama was not necessary, but you provoked me."

"Let my friends go," Yama said. "They are no part of this."

"They know about you. More than I do, I think. Your stepfather kept much from the Department. That trick with the fireflies, for instance." Prefect Corin touched the cloth over his eyes. "Do not think to try that again, by the way. This will shield my eyes, and all my men are protected in the same way."

Yama remembered the little machine which had saved him from Cyg by piercing the cateran's brain. He could kill everyone in the plaza and walk free. He forced the thought away. He would not murder to save himself.

He said, "The Aedile told you all he knew. I have learned much since I came to Ys."

Prefect Corin nodded. "And you will learn more, with the Department's help."

Syle said, "You remember our agreement."

"Perfectly. Will you kill her with that silly little pistol, or shall I order one of my soldiers to do it for you?"

Syle blushed with anger. "Do not presume to tell me what to do. I give you this territory, but the Department is not the territory."

Luria struggled to her feet. White smoke billowed around her. She pointed at Syle and said loudly, "Traitor! You are disowned, Syle. I so rule."

Prefect Corin said dryly, "You have claimed the Department of Vaticination for yourself, Syle. I hope you can control it. Do be careful. I believe that she has a knife."

It was small, with a crooked blade. Luria flourished it dramatically, as if about to plunge it into her own breast.

Daphoene spread her eyes wide. She was smiling toward Luria. Her white eyes were full of tears. A thread of blood ran from one corner of her mouth.

"Now it ends," she said.

To Yama, it seemed as if a hundred people had spoken with the same voice.

Syle stepped forward and said, "Pythoness. Please—"

Luria swung the knife. Not at Syle, but at Daphoene. The blade must have been poisoned, for although it only inflicted a shallow cut on Daphoene's flat breast, the girl convulsed and fell back on to the chair of her palanquin. A moment later Luria fell too, riddled with arbalest bolts. Rega wailed and ran across the stage to Daphoene, and snatched her up and covered her face with desperate kisses.

10

The Committee for Public Safety

"DAPHOENE WAS THE daughter of Rega by another marriage," Prefect Corin said. "I think it was Rega who had the idea—Syle is a clever man, but not one given to carrying out his schemes. Rega, however, is very ambitious. She was not content to be the wife of the secretary of a dwindling department. Her father was a failed merchant who killed himself before his debtors could, and she clawed her way up from poverty. I half admire her for her ambition, if not for her methods. She is a magnificent bitch.

"She altered her daughter's appearance by surgery and infected her with machines carrying the essences of dead people. It is a technique we have used to produce battlefield advisers. The infected subject becomes a population which, when asked a question, can by heuristics derive the best solution to a particular problem. It has not had a high success rate—most of the subjects retreat into fugues. Daphoene was more successful than most, but the procedure blinded her, and most of her own personality was destroyed. However, Rega felt that the loss of her daughter's sight and sanity was an acceptable sacrifice to her own ambition. I think that Luria suspected that Daphoene was Syle's stepdaughter, but she had no proof. It was Syle who organized the search for the new pythoness, after all, and Syle who kept all the records, and he married the only person who could betray him."

Yama said, "They meant to betray me from the beginning. Luria wanted to exchange me for the safety of her department; Syle and Rega plotted to use me as a counter in a bargain with you. At the last moment,

Syle feared that the plans would go wrong and tried to persuade me to help him against you, but I would not. And even if I had helped him, I think that Rega would still have betrayed me."

Brabant had been innocent. The conversation which Pandaras had overheard had been staged by Syle and Rega, part of the scheme to lure Yama into territory under the control of the Department of Indigenous Affairs so that he could be captured by Prefect Corin. It was well known that Brabant patronized the bawdy house at the edge of the day market, and Prefect Corin had waited for Yama there. But Yama had escaped the trap and had to be betrayed all over again, this time publicly. The gatekeeper had informed Syle of Yama's return, and Syle had delayed the start of the public inquisition until Prefect Corin's men were in place.

Prefect Corin said, "No doubt Rega will infect her new daughter once she is born—and meanwhile Syle will find an amenable candidate to play the role of pythoness. He is our man, now. These old departments are utterly decadent, Yama, incurable except by the most radical surgery. We have developed a new system where all, from the humblest clerk to the most senior legate, are answerable to a network of committees. With no center of power, no single person can influence the Department for their own ends. Thus, we are able to take a long-term view with the best interests of Confluence in mind. In time, all will fall under our system, and we can begin to win the war against the heretics."

They sat side by side on the narrow cot in Yama's tiny cell, lit only by a luminous stick. Yama's fireflies had been stripped from him, as had his knife and the ancient coin which the anchorite had given him. He had been allowed to keep his copy of the Puranas and his clothes, nothing else.

The cell was spartan. There was the cot with its lumpy mattress, a plastic slop bucket, a shelf which folded down from the wall, and a square of raffia matting on the stone floor. A spigot in the wall delivered lukewarm, tasteless water. There was a plastic cup hanging on a chain beside the spigot, and a drain beneath, no bigger than Yama's outspread hand. Prefect Corin assured Yama that it was no different from his own cell and every other private cell in the Department of Indigenous Affairs. Husbands and wives each kept their own cells when they were married, and children lived in dormitories until they were old enough to be given a job and a cell of their own.

The heart of the Department of Indigenous Affairs was a vast honeycomb of cells and narrow corridors, interspersed with long, low chambers where clerks worked, row upon row upon row, fireflies flickering above their heads as they bent over papers and books and slates. A hundred layers of cells and corridors and chambers crammed into the middle levels of the Palace and ringed by outlying territories sequestered from other departments, which contained barracks and armories.

Tamora and Pandaras and Eliphas were being held a long way from Yama, in their own cells. They were undergoing debriefing, Prefect Corin said, and would be released once it was finished. Yama asked when that might be, and Prefect Corin replied that it might take only a few days, or it might take years.

"Once we know everything," he said.

"There is no end to questions," Yama said.

Prefect Corin considered this. He said, "In your case, that might be true."

It was never quiet. There was always the sound of voices somewhere, the clash of doors slamming, the tread of feet. Yama lost track of time. At the beginning, he was mostly left in darkness, and meals—edible plastic occasionally leavened with a piece of fruit or a dollop of vegetable curry—arrived at irregular intervals. Later, when daylight was piped into his cell through a glass duct, he could at least read in the Puranas and mark, by the waxing and waning of the weak light, the passage of the days.

At intervals, Yama was taken from the cell and marched by armed guards to a large, dimly lit room divided into two by a pane of thick glass. It was where he was tested. On one side of the glass was a stool; on the other were fireflies, anything from one to more than a hundred. A disembodied voice would instruct Yama to sit on the stool. Once he was seated, his side of the room would be plunged into darkness. Then the tests would begin.

The first time this happened there was only a single firefly, a brilliant point of light that hung in the center of the darkened space on the other side of the glass. Yama was told to move it to the right. He refused, and after a long time he was taken to his cell and left in darkness without food. Judging by the ebb and flow of noise, Yama thought that two days might have passed. At last, weak with hunger, he was brought back to the divided room and asked by the voice to repeat the exercise.

Yama obeyed. Both sides had made their point. He had shown that he was acting under coercion; they had shown that they would not tolerate resistance. The voice was patient and never tired or varied its precise inflection. It gave each set of instructions twice over and waited until Yama had complied before issuing the next. It took no notice of any mistakes or failures. Yama gradually constructed a fantasy image of the voice's owner. A middle-aged man, with cropped, iron-gray hair and a square jaw, sitting in a cell much like his own, a single firefly at his shoulder illuminating the script from which he read.

"Up," the voice would say, "Up." And, "Red firefly circle right, white firefly circle left. Red circle right, white circle left."

There were hundreds of these exercises. Sometimes Yama was asked to weave complex dances involving a decad of differently colored fireflies; sometimes he spent long hours moving a single firefly in straight lines back and forth across the darkness, or varying its brightness by increments. He did not try to understand the significance of the different kinds of exercises. He suspected that if there was a pattern, it had been randomized so that he could never unravel it. Better to think that there was no pattern at all. Better to think that they did not know what they wanted to find out, or did not know how to find out what they wanted to know.

He worked hard at the tests, although they often left him with bad headaches or worse. Sometimes red and black sparks would fill his sight and sometime later he would find himself lying on the floor of the cell, his trousers soaked with stale urine, blood on his lips and tongue. These fits terrified him. Perhaps they were a legacy of the blow to his head (although the wound had completely healed; there was not even a scar), exacerbated by the stress of the exercises. He told no one about them. He would reveal no weakness to his enemies.

Whether or not those testing Yama were learning about his abilities, he was certainly learning more about himself every day. Despite the fits, he exulted over the growing control over his powers. And for the first time since he had set out from Aeolis on the road to Ys, he had time to reflect on what he had discovered about himself. Always, his actions had been driven by contingency or by the needs of others. First, under the unwanted protection of Prefect Corin and then, after his escape from the Prefect and (so he thought) from his ordained fate as a minor official in the Department of Indigenous Affairs, in the company of Pandaras and Tamora.

He had promised himself that he would discover the secret of his origin—the silver-skinned woman, the white boat in the middle of the Great River, attended by a cloud of tiny machines—and he had failed. No, it was worse than that. He had not really tried. He had preferred to adventure with Tamora and Pandaras rather than think about what he was, and why he was here.

When he was alone in his cell, he spent his time reviewing every step of his adventures between leaving Aeolis and the fall of the Department of Vaticination, weighing every one of his actions and motives and finding them all wanting. He slept a lot, too, and in his sleep his sense of the location and activity of machines expanded. Sometimes he seemed to be suspended in the midst of a vast array of little minds that were both quick and stupefyingly dull, with webs of connectivity blossoming and fading around him like a runaway loom simultaneously weaving and unraveling a cloth in three dimensions. Most of the machines were fireflies, but at the periphery of their immense flock Yama could detect larger machines employed in defense of the Department. Further still, glimpsed like bright lights through river fog, were larger machines whose purpose was totally obscure, and interspersed through the volume of greater and lesser machines were intense points which he recognized as the potential energies of active shrines.

And sometimes, at the furthest edge of this inward vision, was a faint intimation of the feral machine he had accidentally drawn down at the merchant's house. It was very far away, hung in isolation beyond and below the end of the world—but it was always there, the iron to which the lodestone of his mind was drawn again and again.

At times, his sensitivity increased so much that he could even perceive the clusters of tiny machines which every sentient person carried at the base of their brain. Faintly, he could feel in these clusters the echoes of the memories of their hosts; it was as if he was the only living person in an impalpable world inhabited by hordes of ghosts mumbling over their last ends.

In his sleep, Yama tried to discover which of the ghosts might be Tamora, or Pandaras, or Eliphas, but always this effort would shift his trancelike apprehension of the machines around him into a dream. Sometimes he ran along a web of narrow paths between the tombs and steles of the City of the Dead, pursued by men who had by grotesque mutilation merged themselves with machines. Sometimes he fled endlessly from the hell-hound, waking with a start in the very moment that its burning blue light swept across him. And sometimes he harried numberless enemies with bloody zeal, exultant as cities burned and armies fought and looted the length of the world in his name, and woke shocked and ashamed, and swore never to dream such dreams again.

But they were always with him, like splinters of cold metal under his skin.

At intervals, Prefect Corin came and sat with Yama, and slowly, punctuated by long silences, a conversation would begin. Yama supposed that these conversations were really interrogations, but mostly it seemed that Prefect Corin was interested in Yama's childhood, asking about details—and details within those details—of small events or ceremonies, the geography of Aeolis or the hinterlands of the City of the Dead, the disposition of books in the library of the peel-house, the lessons taught by the librarian, Zakiel, or by the master of the guard, Sergeant Rhodean.

The matter of the white boat, the mystery of Yama's origins, the attempted kidnap by Dr. Dismas, Yama's adventures in Ys—none of these were ever touched upon. Yama did not have to dissemble about his encounter with the custodians of the City of the Dead and the slate they had shown him, in which he had seen a man of his bloodline turning away to contemplate a sky full of stars. Nor did he have to describe how he had drawn down the feral machine at the merchant's house, or the merchant's last words; nor how he had woken and then defeated the feral machine which had been trapped far beneath the Temple of the Black Well; nor what the woman in white, aspect of one of the Ancients of Days, had told him when she had appeared in the shrine.

But it also meant that all these adventures and discoveries were thrust to the back of his mind by Prefect Corin's patient but insistent demands for increasingly minute details about the mundane days of his childhood. It was as if all that had happened to Yama in the handful of days between leaving his home in Aeolis and arriving here, in this bleak cell amongst thousands of identical cells in the Department of Indigenous Affairs, had been no more than a vivid dream. It was another reason why, when left alone in the unquiet darkness of his cell, Yama traced and retraced his every footstep between Aeolis and Ys like an ox plodding around and around a water lift, the groove of its path infinitesimally deepening with each round. He was frightened that if he forgot even the slightest detail of his adventures he would begin to forget it all, as the unraveling of a piece of cloth can begin with the fraying of a single thread.

Whenever Yama asked a question, Prefect Corin had a habit of falling silent, as if engaged in an internal dialogue with himself, before asking a question in return. The Prefect's dry, spare manner intensified during these interrogation sessions. His silences were vast and arid; his gaze burned intently while Yama talked at random about his childhood, like a mountain lion fixing on its prey and waiting for the moment of weakness or uncertainty that will betray it. It was as if he had shaped his intellect to a single inquiring point, as one of the fisherfolk might flake a pebble to form the head of a harpoon. Yama got no answers from him at all—only questions. And he did not know if the answers he gave to the Prefect's questions were sufficient. Like all of his own questions, that also went unanswered.

Apart from Prefect Corin and the disembodied voice in the divided, darkened room, Yama's only human contacts were his guards. Four men had sentry duty outside Yama's cell, changing watches in regular succession. They lived in the cells on either side of his, and marched with him from his cell to the room where he took his tests, and back again.

Only one of the guards ever talked with him. This was the old man who took the second of the night watches, from midnight to dawn. His name was Coronetes. He confided to Yama that he did not mind the night watch. He was old, his wife had died, and he did not sleep much.

"You, young man, sleep very soundly," Coronetes said. "It is a gift of the young. Old men do not need to sleep because soon they will be dead, never to wake again until they wake into the world at the end of time created by the will of the Preservers."

Yama smiled at this conceit and replied with one of his own. "Then it will be no sleep at all, because in the interval you will not exist, and so no time will pass. As it says in the first sura of the Puranas, 'Before the Universe there was no time, for nothing changed.' "

"You are a devout man."

"I would not say that."

"I suppose you must have done something bad, to be here. But you are often reading in the Puranas."

"Do they watch me, then?" Yama had not thought of that. He had believed that the cell was as private as the inside of his head.

Coronetes nodded vigorously. "By the same pipe through which the light falls. I thought you would have known that. But I do not think they watch now. They sleep."

Like most of the common people of the Department of Indigenous Affairs, Coronetes was slightly built. His coarse hair was black, despite his age, and worn in a stout, greased pigtail that fell halfway down his back. Although he was, as he liked to say, as scrawny as a plucked chicken, he was still a strong man; muscles knotted his skinny arms as if walnuts had been stuffed under his brown skin. He had volunteered for the army at the beginning of the war. He had fought in the Marsh of the Lost Waters, and still suffered from fluxion of the lungs.

"There are sandflies that enter the mouth or nose of a sleeping man," he explained, "and creep into the throat to lay eggs. The larvae get into the lungs and every now and then one turns into a fly and I must cough it out. But I am luckier than many of my comrades. The diseases of the midpoint of the world and the wild creatures of the marshes and the forests accounted for most of them, not the fighting. It is for that reason that the heretics are brothers to the gar, panther and sandfly."

Coronetes had been so weakened by fluxion and fevers that his wife had not recognized him when he had returned from the war. He had become a clerk, like his father before him, and still wore a clerk's white shirt, for he had been a clerk longer than he had been a soldier, and had risen to become the head of his section. He was fiercely loyal to his Department and feared no one, but he was lonely in his old age. He had no children, and had outlived most of his friends while still a young man.

"We will rule the world," Coronetes said, "because no one else will take up the burden. That is why you will confess to the Committee for Public Safety, and that is why you will enlist in our cause. It is the only cause worth fighting for, young man."

Coronetes and Yama sat on the bed in the cell, lit by a stick of cold green light Coronetes had set on the fold-down shelf. None of the guards had fireflies. Indeed, no machines came near Yama except those on the far side of the thick glass wall of the testing room.

Yama said, "I was brought up in the care of a senior member of the Department. He believed that service to the ideal of the Preservers was the beginning and end of the duty of every Department."

"The Aedile of Aeolis? He has the luxury of living in a place where his rule is undisputed. That kind of view is considered old-fashioned. It was old-fashioned even when I was a child, and that was a long time ago. Now my grandfather, he was a soldier, too. That was before the war against the heretics. He fought three campaigns within the Palace against departments who tried to usurp our functions and our territory. He knew where his duty lay. You were lucky to be brought up where you were, but now you are in the real world."

"This cell."

"It is no different from my cell."

"Except you will stop me if I try and walk out."

Coronetes smiled. His mouth was as wide and lipless as a frog's. He had lost most of his teeth, and those that remained were brown and worn down to the gumline. He said, "Well, that is true. I would do my best. I would kill you if I had to, but I hope it will not be necessary."

"So do I."

In fact, Yama never once thought of escaping when Coronetes came to visit him in his cell. It would be dishonorable, for whatever else Coronetes might be and whatever motives he might have, he presented himself as Yama's friend.

"Tell me about the war," Yama would say, when he found himself disagreeing with one of Coronetes' praise songs to the great heart and forthright purpose of the Department of Indigenous Affairs.

Coronetes had many stories of the war, of long marches from one part of the marshes to another, of engagements where nothing could be seen of the enemy but the distant flashes of their weapons, of days and days when nothing at all happened, and Coronetes' company lay in the sun and swapped stories. Most of the war was either marching or waiting, he said. He had only been in two real battles, one which had lasted a hundred days, fought to capture a hill later abandoned, and one in a town where the citizens had begun to change and no one knew who was fighting whom.

"It is what the heretics do," Coronetes said. "They force the change in a bloodline, and with change comes war. The war is not one war, but many, for we must fight for each unchanged bloodline, to make sure they do not fall under the spell of the heretics when they are most vulnerable. If we did only what we wanted, we would be like animals, or worse than animals, because animals are only themselves, and cannot help what they are. The Prefect, he had a more dangerous job, moving amongst the unchanged just like the heretic inciters. That is where the war is really fought, if you want my opinion. The heretics are powerful enemies because they are powerful at persuading the unchanged to see things their way. Our Committee is dedicated to destroying the heretics, but even so it uses some of their techniques to ensure loyalty within the Department."

The Committee for Public Safety had transformed the Department of Indigenous Affairs, turning a musty cabal of legal clerks and semi-autocrats into an aggressive hive of radicals that claimed to be fighting for all the souls of Confluence. The Committee held that everyone was equal, and the least clerk felt that he was as important in the struggle as the most senior general. Coronetes sometimes talked for hours, his eyes gleaming with pride, about the merits of the organization of the Department, of the wonders it had achieved and the paradise it would bring once it had defeated the heretics and united Confluence.

Yama preferred to hear about the war. The patrols that looped through a country of tall grasses without ever engaging the enemy, the camps amongst the buttress roots of trees of the virgin forest of the great marshes, the geometry of advances and retreats. He learned the jargon of the common soldiers, the rudimentary sign language they used when the enemy was close by. More than ever, he yearned to join the army as a cateran or an officer of the light lance, to flee downriver and lose himself in the war.

Yama supposed that these visits might be a part of his interrogation, but if so it did not matter. He looked forward to the time when, late at night, there would be a scratching at the door and he would call out and ask the old man to enter. Although Yama was the prisoner and Coronetes his guard, they both sustained the fiction that Yama was the host, and Coronetes the visitor. Coronetes always waited for Yama's invitation before unlocking the door, and neither commented on the fact that he locked it again once he was inside. That Yama politely forbore to argue against Coronetes' transparent propaganda was part of this fiction—that, and his suspicion that anything he said against the Department of Indigenous Affairs or the Committee for Public Safety would be used against him. Yama was always disappointed on those nights when Coronetes' inquiring scratch failed to come, and had almost become used to the unvarying pattern of his days of captivity when the ambush changed everything.

11

"You Are a Monster."

YAMA WAS RETURNING to his cell after a testing session, with two guards walking a little way in front of him and two behind. His hands were bound by a loop of plastic that was designed to remorselessly tighten if he attempted to struggle against it. He had learned to bend his arms and rest his fists against his chest, as if in prayer, to minimize movement. Coronetes had told him that this form of restraint, called the serpent, could amputate limbs if left on for too long.

The corridor was lit only by the luminous sticks carried by the guards. Yama moved in a bubble of dim green light, with darkness ahead and darkness behind, every ten paces passing a facing pair of doors. The doors were slabs of dense, grainy white plastic deeply recessed in the fused rock walls, as indistinguishable from each other as cells in a honeycomb.

Yama was thinking about the tests. In the past few days he had been fitted with a metal cap while moving the fireflies about. And the fireflies were changing, too. At first they had become slow to respond to his commands; now their little minds were hedged with loops and knots of futile logic which he had to unpick before they would obey him. Those testing him were beginning to probe the limits of his power; he was beginning to worry about what might happen when those limits were reached.

Without warning, two doors were flung open, one on either side. Three young men rushed out from the left; two from the right. They yelled hoarsely, clubs cocked at their shoulders. The leader swung a killing star on a short chain. Yama ducked and rammed the man in the chest with his shoulder, catching him off balance. The man slammed into the wall and Yama broke his nose with his forehead. Then someone kicked Yama's legs out from under him. The serpent tightened around his wrists when he tried to break his fall and the back of his head struck the floor. Two of the attackers began kicking and pummelling him while the others fought with the guards.

Yama tucked his head into his chest and curled up as tightly as he could. There were no machines he could use against his assailants—like the guards, the young men had no fireflies—but their own ineptitude saved him. They were too close to each other to use their clubs properly and they wore only soft-soled shoes, so that their kicks bruised rather than broke bones. Then someone fell heavily on Yama, saving him from the worst of the blows. A moment later, one of the guards fired his slug pistol, and the attackers ran.

Yama was hauled to his feet by two of the guards. It was Coronetes who had fallen on him. The old man's white shirt was ripped down the front and wet with blood. One of the guards knelt beside him and the other two dragged Yama away. The serpent was a band of intense pain around his wrists; his hands had lost all feeling.

The guards would not answer his questions. They unclasped the serpent and left him alone in his cell. Yama massaged his wrists and hands. His fingers were numb and pale, and felt as if they had swollen to twice their normal size. They started to hurt as blood flowed back into them; Yama took that as a good sign. His chest ached with each breath, but the pain was not sharp, and he did not think his ribs were broken. He had cut his tongue, and there were pulpy bruises on his scalp. There was blood on his shirt, so much blood that the shirt stuck to his skin. He took it off and ran his hands over his flanks and back and found many deep bruises but no other wounds. Then he realized that it must be Coronetes' blood.

He had rinsed his mouth out and started to wash himself when the two guards came back. They still would not answer his questions. They fitted the serpent to his wrists and marched him out of his cell. As always, the corridors were deserted. He was led through a great hall crammed with long tables which looked as if they had been abandoned only moments before: pens flung down on unfinished sentences; slates still showing ranks of glowing figures; half-empty bowls of tea. More guards were waiting at the far side of the room. A hood was thrust over his head and the forced march was resumed. At one point he was taken across an open space—cold air whipped around him—and soon after that the hood was ripped from his head and the serpent was unclasped.

He turned just in time to see a door slam shut. It was less than an hour after he had been attacked.

———

The room was four times the size of his cell, and looked even bigger because there was no furniture except for a narrow bed. The walls were fused rock, smooth and slick as glass; the floor was rammed earth. It was shaped like an egg, and at the narrower end sunlight flooded through a big glass bull's-eye.

He found a spigot that yielded an icy trickle of rust-colored water, and stripped off his trousers and washed Coronetes' blood from his bruised body as best he could. There was a thin gray blanket over the striped ticking of the bed's mattress; he wrapped it around his shoulders and for a long time knelt by the window, gazing out at the blue sky. By pressing his bruised face against the cold glass, he could glimpse a segment of a steep slope of tumbled black rocks. Trees clung amongst the rocks, their branches all bent in the same direction. Wind fluted beyond the roundel of glass, and now and then birds slanted through the air, crossing from right to left as they tilted on air currents beyond the edge of the scree slope.

He broke his fingernails prying at the glass, but it was firmly embedded in the smooth rock. It did not break or crack when he kicked at it; he succeeded only in bruising his heel. He had just begun to scrape at the hard earth at the bottom edge of the window when a chirurgeon came in, flanked by two guards. The chirurgeon tested Yama's limbs, probed his mouth and shone a bright light into his eyes, then left without saying a word. Another guard brought in a slop bucket and tossed Yama's bloodstained shirt onto the bed, and then Prefect Corin came in.

After the guards had locked the door behind them, Prefect Corin sat on the end of the bed. Yama stayed by the window. He was conscious of being naked under the thin blanket. He said, "How is Coronetes?"

"Dead. As are your attackers."

"Your Department is not of one mind about me. That is comforting."

"It was not a conspiracy. They wanted revenge because you had blinded their friends. You did not try to defend yourself. Why was that?"

"I believe that I broke someone's nose."

"You know what I mean, boy."

"I am your prisoner, not your servant. I do not have to explain myself."

"You are the prisoner of the Department. I am here because I brought you to Ys. I am still responsible for you. You do not believe me, but I have your best interests at heart."

Yama smiled. It hurt. "Then you endure our conversations as a punishment?"

"It is my duty," Prefect Corin said. "Just as it was my duty to bring you to Ys."

"You failed at that and you failed to catch me by trickery, too. In the end you had to use force. Perhaps you are not very good at carrying out your duty."

Prefect Corin rarely smiled, but he smiled now. It lasted only for a moment and did not thaw his wintry expression in the slightest. He said, "I lost you once, yet here you are, all the same. If I was superstitious, I might say that it was fate, and that our lives are bound together. But I am not; and they are not. I have my duty. You have your duty, too, Yamamanama. You know what it is, but you resist it. I wonder why it is that you are so ungrateful. Your stepfather is a senior officer of the Department, and so in a sense the Department raised you. It educated you and trained you, and yet you resist acknowledging your considerable obligation. You believe that your own will is stronger than the collective will of the Department. Believe me, you are wrong."

"I do not know what you want of me." A silence. Yama corrected himself. "I do not know what the Department wants of me."

Prefect Corin considered this. At last, he said, "Then you will be here a long time, and so will your friends. It is not about what you know, but what you can do."

"I am sorry that Coronetes was killed. He did not deserve it."

"Nor did the men who attacked you. They were not much more than boys, and foolish boys at that, but they were brave. Their only mistake was that they were more loyal to their friends than to the Department."

Yama said, "Do you wish that they had killed me?"

"You are a monster, boy. You do not know it, but you are. You have more power than any individual should have, and you use it without purpose. You do not even know how to use it properly. You refuse to serve, for no other reason than your pride. You could help win the war, and that is the only reason why you are kept alive. Some want you dead. I have argued against it, and so you still live, but I cannot defend you forever. Especially if you continue to resist."

"I have completed every test as best I could."

"This is not about the tests. It is about loyalty."

"I will not serve blindly," Yama said. "If I am here, with such gifts as I have, there must be a purpose to it. That is what I want to discover. That is why I came to Ys."

"You should try and be true to the example of your stepbrother. He served. He served well."

"I will go to war in a moment, but you will not allow it. So please do not invoke Telmon's bravery."

Prefect Corin put his hands on his knees and leaned forward, looking directly into Yama's face. His brown eyes were steady and unforgiving. He said, "You are very young. Too young for what you possess."

"I will not serve blindly," Yama said. "I have thought long and hard about this. If there are those in the Department who want me to help them, then they should talk with me. Or you should kill me now, and then at least you will know that I will never fight against you."

"We are all one, hand and brain," Prefect Corin said. "Your stepfather did not like the way things had changed, but still he served."

"Yes, Coronetes once said something similar."

"But you will not serve. You set yourself apart. You are a monster of vanity, boy." Prefect Corin stood up and tossed something on the mattress of the bed. "Here is your copy of the Puranas. Read in it carefully, and consider your position."

———

Once he was certain that he had been left alone, Yama began again to scrape at the base of the circular window. He broke a thin strip of wood from the frame of the bed and used this and water from the spigot to loosen the packed earth. The sky had darkened by the time he had dug to the depth of his hand and found the point where glass merged seamlessly with fused rock. Perhaps the window was no more than a place where the rock had been made transparent, but apart from the door it was the only possible way out of the cell.

He began to extend the little hole he had made, scraping away hard earth a few crumbs at a time until the frayed strip of wood met something embedded in the dirt. He probed carefully with his bleeding fingertips and felt a thin curved edge, then dug around it until he could pull it free.

It was a ceramic disc, an ancient coin exactly like the coin the anchorite had given him. But the Aedile's excavations had turned up thousands of coins around the tombs of the City of the Dead, and there was no reason to believe that this one should be any different from those.

Yama dug a little more, but could find no potential weakness in the window's edge. He filled in the hole he had made and as the room darkened around him he leaned against the window and watched the shadows of the bent trees lengthen across the tumbled rocks. He fell asleep, and woke to find a constellation of faint lights hung just outside the window. They were fireflies, drawn away from the wild creatures which lived amongst the sliding stones. Beyond the shifting sparks of the fireflies, the small red swirl of the Eye of the Preservers was printed on the black sky.

Something nagged at Yama, like a speck in his eye. It was the coin, shining softly on the dirt floor. He picked it up. It was warmer than his own skin, and had become translucent, with fine filaments and specks of cold blue light shifting within its thickness.

There was an active shrine nearby.

He could suddenly feel it, with the same absolute sense of direction that linked him with the feral machine. He shivered and drew the blanket around himself. He knew that he could activate the shrine even at this distance, and a plan of escape presented itself.

It was horribly risky, but no worse than trying to climb through a window high above a steep slope of sliding stones at the top of a mountain. And he could not even open the window. Before he could frighten himself by thinking through all the consequences, he willed it.

Beyond the bull's-eye window, the fireflies scattered as if before a great wind.

His trousers were still damp, but Yama drew them on anyway, and tucked the sliver of wood inside the waistband. Then he wrapped the blanket around his shoulders and sat by the window in the dim red light of the Eye of the Preservers, waiting for something to happen. At intervals, he held the coin up to his eye, but the shifting patterns of luminous lines and specks told him nothing.

Perhaps the shrine was dead after all . . . but then he knew it was not, as surely as if a light had been shone in his face. He got up and paced around the room, a fierce excitement growing in him. Presently he heard shouts, and then the thin snapping of slug guns. The sounds of distant combat lasted several minutes; then there was the scream of an energy pistol's discharge and wisps of white smoke began to curl around the edges of the cell door.

Yama scrambled to his feet, and at the same moment the door was flung back with a crash. A guard tumbled in ahead of a thick billow of smoke. His tunic was torn across the chest. The right side of his face was scorched, his hair shriveled to blackened peppercorns.

"Come with me!" the guard yelled. "Now!"

Yama straightened his back and drew the blanket around his shoulders. The guard glared at him and raised his rifle. "Come now!"

For a moment, Yama feared that the man had lost his mind and would execute him on the spot. Then the guard looked over his shoulder and screamed. He scrambled across the cell, knocking Yama aside and fetching up against the bull's-eye window, clutching his rifle to his chest and staring wide-eyed at the door. Yama faced it squarely, his heart beating quickly and lightly. Blue light filled the frame. And then, without a transition, the hell-hound was inside the cell.

It was a pillar of blue flame that seemed somehow to extend beyond the floor and ceiling. There was a continual crackling hiss as its energies ate the air which touched its surface. Its heat beat against Yama's skin. He had to squint against its brilliance as he held up the coin. It took all of his will to stand still.

He said, "I do not know if we have already met, or if you are brother to the one I called forth before, but in any case I apologize for my behavior. I ran away because I did not know what I had called, and I was afraid. But now I have freed you knowingly, and I ask for your help."

He did not see the hell-hound move, but there was a brief wash of heat on his skin and suddenly it was gone. The guard screamed. When Yama turned, the man fell to his knees and flung his arm before his face. The sleeve of his tunic started to smolder. Yama realized what had happened, and looked away before he killed the man.

He had expected the hell-hound to clear a way for his escape. Instead, it had enveloped him.

He was the center of a blue radiance that fell on everything he looked at. He no longer felt the hell-hound's heat. That was a property of the outermost shell of its energies. Instead, he felt a tremendous exhilaration. His bruises and cracked ribs no longer hurt. There was a prickling all over his body as every hair tried to stand away from its neighbors.

There was a short corridor beyond the cell. Guards scrambled in panic through the door at the far end, although one paused and shot at

Yama several times before running too, his clothes and hair smoldering. Yama followed them into a wide plaza. Sheer black rock rose on three sides; there was nothing but the darkening sky on the other.

Men ran or stood their ground and fired. Slugs caught and sank slowly in the outer edge of the blue light that surrounded Yama, flaring brightly before evaporating. An officer fired a pistol, but its discharge merely whitened Yama's vision for a moment.

He did not attack the guards or even look at them, but strode directly to the edge of the plaza. A railing glowed red and yellow and white before melting away. Directly below was the steep slope of black rocks he had seen from the window of the cell. Yama's sight washed with white light for an instant—the officer with the pistol was foolish, but brave. Yama did not look back, but gave himself to the air.

He floated down like a soap bubble, landing beside a dead pine tree which immediately burst into crackling yellow flame. The air was alive with things which hummed and whined. Bits of rock flew off and the foliage of the stunted trees danced jerkily. Yama realized that the guards were still firing at him. He walked to the edge of the slope and gave himself to the air once more.

It took a long time to fall. The hell-hound was subject to the world's gravity fields, but could modify them so that it fell at a constant rate. Yama saw a long slope spread below him, curving away on either side and studded with the lights of temples, sanctuaries and the offices of those lesser departments which had long ago lost battles for territory inside the Palace and now clung to existence on its roof. He gave the hell-hound an order, and it slid sideways through the air.

The glass-walled tunnel which linked the street of pleasure houses with the territory of the Department of Indigenous Affairs had been repaired with wooden paneling that burst into flames at a touch and fell away. Yama stepped through and walked amidst reflections of blue fire into a square under a high domed roof.

Three guards ran into the gateway on the far side; their officer drew his pistol and fired twice, and then stood amazed when he saw that the energy beam had done no harm. The air was hazed with recondensed particles of rock vaporized by the deflected pistol blast; Yama's gaze burned through them and glanced upon the officer, who threw up his hands to protect his eyes.

"Fetch your masters," Yama said. "Do you understand? I wish to speak with them."

The officer turned and ran through the gateway. Yama followed. He was quite without fear. He felt as if he could run forever through the maze of corridors and halls, and laughed wildly when men shot at him. Slugs embedded in the hell-hound's outermost shell became molten stars that flared and died.

He entered a huge refectory hall. Hundreds of people ran from him through a maze of tables. A confused cloud of fireflies billowed after them. Tables and chairs charred as he brushed past. He shouted for the masters of this place to come out, but there was no answer except for a volley of rifle shots from a gallery above the arched doorways at the far end of the hall. Frayed battle standards hung above the central dais of the hall. Yama stared at them until they caught fire, then leaped on to the dais and shouted that he would speak with the masters of this place or burn it all down.

Men ran forward, dragging a long hose. They sprayed water at Yama, but the water exploded into steam when it struck the hell-hound's envelope and the men retreated, clutching scalded faces and hands. An officer on a floating disc fired his pistol. The blue glow of the hell-hound flared white. The high-backed chairs and the long table, inlaid with ironwood and turtle shell ivory, burst into flames; the stone of the dais burned Yama's feet through the thin soles of his boots. He jumped down, stared at the officer until the man's clothes caught fire, and strode through the nearest door.

Yama's passage through toward the heart of the Department of Indigenous Affairs was a confusion of shouts and screams, flame and smoke and gunfire. He was filled with an exultant rage. Red and black lightning jagged his vision. He could have killed decads, perhaps hundreds of men. He did not know. His rage had taken him and he let it lead him where it would.

When it cleared, he was standing at the base of a vast circular shaft that rose through a hundred floors; the temple of Aeolis, the largest building Yama had known before he had come to Ys, could easily have fitted into it. Its looming walls were hung with tiers of balconies; its vast floor was crowded with desks. Books burned in stacked shelving, in tumbled heaps on the floor. Scraps of burning paper flew into the darkness above like sparks up the flue of a chimney.

Soldiers armed with slug rifles stood in front of every door around the base of the shaft, draped from head to foot in black cloth. They kept up a steady bombardment and the floor around Yama was soon littered with flecks of molten metal. A machine spun slowly through the air toward him, its mind defended by intricate loops of self-engulfing logic. In his anger he punched right through these defenses and the machine suddenly screamed upward, its load of explosive detonating with a white flash and a flat thump at the top of the shaft, half a league above.

"I know you are here, Prefect," Yama shouted. "Show yourself!"

A voice spoke from the air, ordering Yama to surrender—it was the same even, neutral voice which had been with him every day in the room. He laughed at it and then, inspired, shut down the light of every firefly, so that now the vast circular space was lit only by the blue glow of the hell-hound, the flashes of the rifles around the perimeter, and the myriad fires started by spent slugs and Yama's gaze. Everything was hazed with smoke. Yama felt a tightness in his chest and a scorched taste in his mouth. The air was becoming unbreathable. He knew that he would have to leave soon, and that he would have to kill the soldiers to do it.

Yet still he felt a steady exhilaration thrilling in his blood, a boundless energy. He did not consider himself trapped, but called out again for the masters of this place. As if in answer, the floor heaved sharply and Yama staggered and almost fell. Dust and shards of tiling fell from somewhere above, smashing down amongst the desks; for a moment, Yama stood inside a sleet of burning particles.

The soldiers were as shaken as he. They were still regrouping when a fresh wedge of troops entered through the high doors beneath a long gallery. They parted, and an old man stepped from their midst. He was slightly built and his dress was no different from that of an ordinary clerk, but he held himself proudly and at his absent-minded gesture the soldiers around him immediately thrust three people to the front of their ranks.

Tamora shaded her eyes and called out, "Yama! Is that you inside that light?"

"He has come to free us," Pandaras said.

Yama checked himself. He had been about to run to them.

The old man walked forward, stepping as delicately as a cat amongst broken shards and heaps of burning books. He stopped when the floor rippled and shook dust into the air, and then walked on until he was fifty paces from the blue energies of the hell-hound. His eyes were masked by a strip of cloth, jet-black against the white pelt of his face.

"I had not thought to ever see one of these things," the old man said. "I am Escanes, Yamamanama. I am here to ask why you are doing this."

"I discovered that it is only a machine," Yama said. "I should thank you for helping me focus on what I needed to do."

"It is an inertial field-caster," Escanes said. "Amongst other things.

Anything trying to move through it gives up momentum in the form of heat. It burns with blue light because light reflected from it is shifted from lower to higher energy, and it is hot because of the energy released from dust and air in motion against it. I should warn you that we fully understand it."

"Yet I control it, and you do not. I can destroy everything around me with a look."

"Because we understand such things," Escanes said, "we can work against them. You are not invulnerable. You should not have brought it here, my son. You endanger the records of the Department."

"I will destroy them all unless you let my friends go."

"I am empowered to speak for the Department, Yamamanama. Listen to what it has to say. We will let your three friends go. You will stay."

"You will let them go, and let me go, too."

"I do not think so," Escanes said mildly. "Think quickly. One word from me, and they will die."

"Then you will have no hold over me."

The floor shook again. Yama flexed his knees, as if he was on a boat. Escanes held the edge of a half-charred desk until the shaking stopped. A balcony gave way and smashed down twenty stories into a stack of bookshelves on the far side of the shaft.

Yama said, "Someone is attacking you, I think. Is it war?"

"Our enemies believe that we are weakened from within," Escanes said. "We will prove them wrong. It is a trivial matter, and not one that concerns you. What matters is your answer."

"Let my friends go."

"And you will stay?"

"No. You will come with me."

Yama sprang forward, and the hell-hound relaxed its perimeter for an instant. Escanes threw up his hands, but he was already inside the hell-hound's envelope. Yama caught him and turned him around, and held the sharpened bit of wood to his throat. Escanes struggled, but Yama held him easily.

"Tell your people to let my friends go."

"They will not obey me. I am only a mouth for the Department. We are all one. Do not be a fool, or your friends will die."

"Your tunic is silk, dominie, not artificial cotton. I think that your dogma requires you to appear to be the same as all others in the Department, but you raise yourself higher than most."

"We are all one."

"Yet some value themselves more than others."

Escanes tried to turn his head, but Yama jabbed the sliver of wood into the loose flesh of the old man's neck and urged him forward. The soldiers raised their rifles, but an officer snapped an order and they lowered them again.

Yama told the old man, "If my friends walk out of here with me, then your life will be spared. I promise that I will not cause any more damage. You will be free to defend yourself against your enemies. But if anything happens to my friends, then I join your enemies and fight against you."

"Fight with us, Yamamanama," Escanes said. "You could be the most powerful general in our army."

"You would have made that offer already, if you could. Now repeat to your men what I have told you."

———

It was easy to find the way back to the gate—the hell-hound had left a trail of scorched doors and scored floor tiles. Yama let Tamora, Pandaras and Eliphas walk ahead of him. The old man, Escanes, did not struggle, but continued to try to convince Yama to give himself to the mercy and generosity of the Department until at last Yama lost patience and put a hand over his mouth.

Yama stopped at the gate and told the others to go ahead. "While I stand here, no one can get past. Eliphas, you know a safe place to take them."

The old man stared and Tamora shook him and hissed in his ear. Yama asked his question again and Eliphas blinked and said, "It finally caught you, brother." Blue light shone in his eyes.

"No, Eliphas. I caught it. I understand it now. You remember the place Magon took us to."

"I remember."

Pandaras said, "He isn't quite himself, master. He had a harder time of it than me. I knew nothing important, so they didn't hurt me. It was just talking, and you know how I love that. I told them many stories."

The boy wore the white shirt and black trousers of a clerk. Yama said, "It seems you have adopted their ways."

"Kill them all," Tamora said. Her head had been shaved, and her face was a palimpsest of fresh bruises laid over old.

"We will talk later, Tamora. Go now."

The old man, Escanes, said, "She is right. You should kill us all, for else we will follow you to the end of the river and beyond."

"I am not your enemy."

"Anyone who does not serve is our enemy."

"I serve the Preservers, if I can, not your Department."

"So says any man who is full of pride. Such a one believes that by doing as he wishes he serves a higher power, but instead he has allowed himself to become a slave of his base appetites. You would claim to know what the Preservers want? Then you are worse than foolish, young man. We are the arm of the Preservers. We strive against their enemies at the midpoint of the world."

"I do not know why I was born here, in this time and place. But it was not to serve your hunger for power."

Tamora, Pandaras and Eliphas had disappeared into the tunnel at the far end of the plaza. Yama told Escanes to close his eyes, and then thrust him toward the gate. The hell-hound's envelope had grown hotter because it had contracted, and the old man's clothes smoldered as he staggered away.

The soldiers rushed forward then. Yama ran across the square into the tunnel and plunged through the hole he had burned in the patchwork repair to the tunnel's glass wall.

———

The night was spread before him. The hell-hound turned and dipped and in a sudden rush he was down, standing beside the white fountain in the middle of the long lawn. Yama thanked the hell-hound and dismissed it, and felt a gust of heat as it moved away from him. It shrank into itself and rose, a bright blue star that dwindled away against the black bulk of the mountain.

Yama stood alone in darkness in the center of a circle of charred grass. He thought of returning to the library of the Department of Apothecaries and Chirurgeons to ask what the chief of clerks, Kun Norbu, had discovered about his bloodline. He thought of running away. But he knew that he could not. He had saved his three companions from immediate danger, but they were still within the bounds of the Palace, and the Department of Indigenous Affairs would not rest until they were recaptured. Besides, he was so very tired, and his torn muscles and cracked ribs ached horribly. It was as if he drew every breath through a rack of knives. The hell-hound had lent him some of its energies while it had enveloped him, but now he had only his own reserves of strength to draw upon.

He sat at the edge of one of the fountain's wide shallow basins and drank cold water with his cupped hands, and splashed water on his face. Presently, a small constellation of fireflies gathered around him, lighting his way as he crossed the long lawn and went down the steps. His muscles were as loose and weak as sacks of water, and he had to stop and rest every five minutes. Each time he stopped it was harder to force himself to stand and go on, but the dread of being recaptured drove him forward. When he reached the beginning of the path through the grove of bamboo, he sat down and rested for a few minutes, breathing hard and feeling beads of sweat roll down his sides. The skeletal tower, hung with creepers, loomed above. Yama struggled to his feet and went on.

White birds, ghostly in the darkness, fled from him. Yama caught at bamboo stems and lost his grasp and slid down a dusty slope, fetching up against a low wall. Startled goats bounded away, their wooden bells clanking. Yama lay on his back, looking up at the black sky, the few blurred stars, the red swirl of the Eye of the Preservers.

After a while, the villagers came to discover what had disturbed their animals. They were armed with spears and slings, for lynxes and fierce red foxes prowled the roof, and the Lords of the Palace were restless that night. But they found only Yama, asleep on the cropped grass.

12

The Husbandmen

"THERE, DOMINIE," THE headman of the village said. "You see? The Lords of the Palace quarrel amongst themselves."

Yama looked up, following the line of the headman's arm. High above the terraced fields of the little village, a thread of black smoke rose from the upper slope of the mountain.

"The roof trembled hard last night," the headman said. He was squat and muscular, with a seamed face and lively black eyes, and skin the color of the red earth. His white hair was done up in a braid that fell to the small of his back. He wore much-darned leggings and a ragged but clean homespun tunic with many pockets.

"A bad time," Yama said.

"Not really. The Lords of the Palace will pay more for our food when they are done fighting—the winners will need to feed those they have captured."

"They will not take it from you by force?"

The headman touched his lips with the tips of his fingers. It was a gesture characteristic of the husbandmen. It meant *no*. "All serve the will of the Preservers. And we are their most faithful servants."

"Yet all of those fighting each other also profess to serve the will of the Preservers."

"We don't question how the Preservers order things," the headman said. "Are you feeling stronger, dominie?"

"A little. Resting here in the sun helps."

Last night, Yama had been given the headman's own hammock. An old woman had looked into his eyes and laid her head on his chest to listen to his breathing and heartbeat, and then had given him an infusion

of dried leaves to drink. When Yama had woken, most of the husbandmen were already out in the fields, but the headman and his wife had
stayed behind to tend their guest. They had given him dried fish and
sweet rice cakes to eat, and a homespun tunic to cover his bare chest.

Yama was very weak. He was badly bruised from the beating he
had received when he had been ambushed, and controlling the hell-
hound had been as exhausting as riding a high-spirited thoroughbred.
He was content to spend the day lying in a hammock under the shade
of freshly cut banana leaves by the sunwarmed wall of the headman's
house, listening to the headman's stories and watching children play in
the dust of the village square.

The husbandmen believed that they had been brought to the world
to tend the gardens of the Palace. The headman claimed that the terraces
spread above and below the village had once held beds of roses and
lilies, jasmine and sweet herbs.

"The first masters of the world walked here in the morning and the
evening, dominie. There were different gardens for the morning and the
evening of every day of the year, and we tended them all. That's why
we look out across the city toward the place where the sun rises and
sets."

"What did they look like, your masters?"

Yama had never seen a picture of the Sirdar, those who had ruled
the world when it had been newly made. None of the Sirdar had ever
been interred in the City of the Dead, and none of the picture slates
there had revealed even a glimpse of them. They had never presented
themselves to the ordinary people but had ruled invisibly, implementing
their wishes through an extensive civil service of eunuchs and hierodules.

The headman gazed across the dusty village square, as if remembering, then said, "They were small, as small as our children playing
there, and their skin shone like polished metal."

Yama shivered, remembering that the dead woman in the white
boat, on whose breast he had been found, had had silver skin. Old
Constable Thaw had said nothing about her being no bigger than a child,
but to his kind most bloodlines seemed small.

The headman said, "Words are poor things. If I had a picture, I
would gladly show it you, dominie. But we have no pictures of those
times."

"It must have been long ago."

The headman nodded. He sat cross-legged in the white dust by
Yama's hammock. Blades of sunlight fell through the notched banana

leaves and striped his lined face. He said, "The world was young then, dominie, but we remember those times. We are not able to change, you see, nor do we wish to, for we would forget how it was, and how it will be again."

Some believed that the Sirdar had been destroyed by their successors, others that they had achieved enlightenment and passed from the world. There had been many rulers after them, but it was said that, next to the Builders, the Sirdar had been closest to the Preservers. The husbandmen believed that their old masters would come again, opening the sealed core of the Palace and stepping forth as a flower steps forth from a seed. The world would become a garden then, changed and unchanged bloodlines would achieve enlightenment and ascend into the Eye of the Preservers, and the husbandmen would spread across the face of the world they longed to inherit.

"Trees would drop fruit into our hands, and corn and grain will grow on the plains by the river without need of tilling or sowing. Until then," the headman said, with a smile that creased his clay-red face still further, "we must toil in the fields."

"Perhaps those days are not far off. Great things happen in the world."

Yama was thinking of the war against the heretics, but the headman knew nothing of the world beyond the Palace of the Memory of the People. He believed that Yama was talking about the conflict in the mountain heights above them. He said, "These may be the end times, but not because the Lords of the Palace quarrel. There has been war in the Palace before. Long ago, long after our first dear masters stopped walking in the gardens, but while the gardens were still gardens and had not yet been turned into fields, one department took over all the others. It was known as the Head of the People. It ruled for many generations, and its rule was fierce and cruel. It was a great weight on all the peoples of the world. But when it had conquered all, the Head of the People found itself without enemies and turned inward. Soon, it was fighting against itself. The Hierarchs arose and ended that war, and in turn they fell after the war against the Insurrectionists, for victory cost them dear. Some of the oldest departments are parts of that greater department, although they have long forgotten that they were once part of a greater whole, much as a lizard's tail forgets that it was shed by another lizard to escape an enemy, and grows into another lizard exactly like the first. Bloodlines forget much when they change; we cannot change and so we forget nothing, like the lizard that lost the tail in the first place."

"I recently met someone else who said much the same thing."

"That would be one of the mirror people. Yes, they remember much, too, but they have not lived in the Palace as long as we have. They are really fisherfolk, dominie. They left their living on the Great River when the city spread along the shore, and found work as fishers of men instead. They know much, but we know more. We understand the signs. We know the significance of the hell-hound. Twice it was seen in the past decad. The first time, it vanished into the Palace after passing along the ridge above this village. The second time, it was seen floating through the air, and there was a ghost inside it."

"I know."

The headman touched his forehead. *Yes.* "Then you saw it too, dominie. Perhaps you do not remember that hell-hounds were used as weapons."

"So one of the mirror people told me."

The headman touched his forehead again. "And they learned it from us, for they arrived after the war with the machines."

He meant the end of the Age of Insurrection, when the Hierarchs had defeated the feral machines and those bloodlines which had risen against the will of the Preservers and had laid waste to half the world.

"We remember how great swaths of the gardens were destroyed by the energies of packs of hell-hounds," the headman said, "and how shrines were killed so that they no longer spoke to the masters of this Palace. Now the hell-hounds have come again, and one was carrying a ghost or a demon. I had not expected it, but if such wonders are seen in the world, then these may be the end times for which we have waited so long."

"It was not a ghost," Yama said, "and it certainly was not a demon. I should know, because I was there."

The headman nodded. "As you say, dominie. We believe that you might have been hurt by the hell-hound. That is why you are confused. But whatever you believe you saw, it was an illusion. Only ghosts or demons from the space inside the shrines may ride hell-hounds. It is how they visit the world. They bring nothing but destruction."

"Well, it carried me here," Yama said.

The headman touched his lips. "You were chasing it, or perhaps it was chasing you, although I understand that hell-hounds take little notice of men, who are no more than ghosts to them. You were chasing it, then, hoping to harm it. We saw it coming toward our village, and we hid from it, but it is clear that you saved us, or tried to save us. You did not know what you were chasing, so I cannot say that you were foolish, but you were certainly brave. Perhaps you thrust a spear at it, and its energies knocked you down the slope, where we found you. That is why your mind is confused and why you are so weak. But the weakness and the confusion will pass. You are a young man, and strong. Lucky for you, dominie. Such an encounter would have killed most men outright."

"I was not fighting it. I used it, and it used me. I will show you if you let me."

Yama tried to sit up in the hammock, but his sight washed with red. He fell back, and felt the headman's dry, hard fingers at his brow.

"Rest," the headman said. "Rest is the best medicine."

"I rode it," Yama said. "I really did. It is only another kind of machine. I rode it all the way down the side of the mountain, and I rescued my friends."

Or perhaps he only said it to himself, for the headman did not seem to hear him. The headman settled the blanket around Yama's shoulders and went away. Yama slept for a while, and woke to find the headman's wife wiping his brow with a wet cloth. He was inside the headman's house again. Night pressed at the window above his hammock but the little room was full of light, for hundreds of fireflies hung in the air.

"You have a fever," the old woman said. "In a little while I will bring you some lemon broth."

Yama clutched the wide sleeve of her embroidered shirt. "I walked inside it," he said. "It carried me through the air."

The old woman gently lifted his hand away from her sleeve. "You have been dreaming, dominie. You are very weak, weaker than you believe, and so your dreams seem more real than the world itself. But I do not think that you will die. You will take some broth. You will sleep. We will look after you. It is an honor to us."

━━━━━━━━━

Yama lay in the hammock for two days, drifting between waking and sleeping. Whenever he woke, he dismissed the fireflies that had been drawn to him while he slept. At last, no more came: he had exhausted the local population. The shadows seemed to be thronged with dreams, and dreams mingled with heightened scenes of his recent adventures. Again, he walked with Prefect Corin through the hot dry lands on the road between Aeolis and Ys, but now the Prefect wore a crown of fireflies. Again, he stood at the edge of the deep shaft in the Temple of the Black Well—and this time it was not the feral machine but the hell-hound that rose out of black air. It enveloped him and carried him through the air to the top of the mountain which he now knew was no mountain, but in truth a single vast building older than the world. And at the windy pinnacle, with the city spread below on one side and the Great River on the other, he stood with his sweetheart. Derev. She clasped him to her breast and spread her strong wings and they flew higher still, until the entire world lay beneath them.

When Yama woke, dry-mouthed, weak, aching in every bone but clear-headed, Tamora was there. He was so glad to see her that he started to weep.

She grinned and said, "So the hero isn't dead. You are such a fool, Yama."

"I am pleased to see you, too, Tamora."

She wore a bronze-colored corselet he had not seen before, a short skirt of red leather strips, and a metal cap on her shaven, scarred head. She said, "I thought you were dead. I thought that the weapon you used against them must have killed you. Don't ever play the hero again, Yama. Or at least let me help you. That's what I am paid for."

"I lost my money, Tamora, and my knife. I have my book, though. It is all I have."

He had carried the copy of the Puranas through all his adventures. And he remembered that although he had lost the coin which the anchorite had given him, he had found a replacement. He reached for it, and Tamora caught his hand and then they were holding each other. Her strong arms; her spicy odor; her heat.

Tamora said, "Well, you're alive. Oh, Yama, you are such a fool!"

They held each other for a long time, until Pandaras came in.

———

Eliphas had led Tamora and Pandaras to the home of the mirror people, and Lupe had sheltered them until the search for the escaped prisoners passed into the lower levels of the Palace. The war between the Department of Indigenous Affairs and its lesser rivals was intensifying, and Tamora said that this would make their escape easy. She said that she had arranged passage downriver.

"I had to use your money to do it, but then again I had to use mine, too."

Yama said, "I know that I have to leave the city, Tamora. But I should leave you, too, and Pandaras. Simply by being with me you are in great danger."

"Grah. Your brains have cooked in your head. I will come with you for your own good. I suppose you could try and dismiss the rat-boy, but he will follow you anyway. He is in love."

From the doorway, where he had taken up position like a guard, Pandaras said, "I merely do my duty as a squire." The boy had oiled his hair and brushed it back from his narrow face. He still wore the black trousers and white shirt that was the uniform of the clerks of the Department of Indigenous Affairs. An ivory-handled poniard sheathed in black leather hung from a loop at his waist.

Tamora shrugged. "Then there is the old man."

"Eliphas."

"I don't trust him. Tell me you don't need him, and make me happy."

"Eliphas is a friend. He helped me without being asked, and he promised to search the library of the Department of Apothecaries and Chirurgeons for records of my bloodline."

Perhaps the answer had already been found. Perhaps he would at last know where he belonged. And yet there was also the mystery of the dead woman in the white boat, who had had silver skin like the first masters of the world.

"Take me there," Yama said to Tamora. "Take me to the Department of Apothecaries and Chirurgeons. It is only a few hours' walk. All I want to know is there. It must be."

"Eliphas told me all about it. He's gone there now, and will meet us at the docks."

"I want to go there now."

"I think you're still too weak. You have been lying in bed too long. Time to get up! Time to be about your business in the world! Small steps first, and then the beginning of a great adventure!"

Pandaras clapped his misshapen hands and said, "We are going to war, master. I have brought you a spare set of clothes, even if you did not care to keep hold of your knife and your armor. Ask me, and I will find them for you, even if I have to search the entire Palace. Or perhaps I will bring you an energy pistol."

"Those are for officers," Tamora said, "and we will be no more than ordinary caterans."

"My clothes? Then you went back—"

Tamora grinned, showing her rack of sharp white teeth. "Oh, I went back, all right. I told you that I had spent our money—how do you think I got it? There was a pentad of soldiers waiting at the Gate of Double Glory, but I killed them all in a fair fight." She patted the heavy saber sheathed at her side. "That's where I got this poor substitute for my own sword. I got the rat-boy a knife, too, and a rapier for you. Anyway, I killed them and found where Syle was hiding. I had to bend the back of that feather-headed fool over my thigh until he would agree, but I have what we left behind, and the fee, too. Rega didn't want him to give it up, but he feared death more than he feared her, although I don't think you could put a knife blade between the difference. She was sitting where Luria used to sit, in a white dress for mourning. I hope she enjoys her rule of the Department of Vatication in the brief time before the fighting spreads and she is assassinated."

Yama said, "I feel sorry for Syle. Despite all he did, at heart he is not a bad man."

"Grah. He tried to serve his department and his wife's ambitions, and will end up losing both, and his own life. His scheming saved the Department of Vatication for a short while, but it is seen as an ally of Indigenous Affairs now. And Indigenous Affairs is too busy defending itself to save Syle."

Pandaras said, "He betrayed you, master. No one trusts a traitor, least of all those who employ him. Whoever wins the war up there will get rid of him."

The fighting had spread through the upper tiers of the Palace. The Department of Indigenous Affairs had fought off its rivals and secured its borders, but now there were bitter skirmishes in the corridors, and mines and countermines were being dug through the fabric of the Palace as the warring departments tried to break out behind each other's lines.

"Our enemy has won the first stage of the war," Tamora said, "but it will have a hard time of it for a while. And even if it wins it will be weakened, and another department or alliance of departments might finish it off."

"I did not mean to destroy it," Yama said, "but it had made many enemies, and they were waiting for the slightest weakness. And yet we go to fight in the army it has raised. Do you not think that strange, Tamora?"

"We will fight the heretics, who are the real enemy of us all. At the midpoint of the world, the doings of the Palace of the Memory of the People is of no importance. It does not matter who has charge of the army there—you will see. You must get ready, Yama. You have been lying in luxury too long. The muscles in your legs will shrink and you won't be able to walk, much less fight. We'll have to carry you everywhere, like a houri. You will begin to exercise now, and you will exercise once we are on the ship. It will be a long voyage."

Yama thought of the great map he had so often unrolled, at first to dream of finding where his people lived, and in the past year to follow the progress of Telmon, his stepbrother, toward the war. Yama had wanted to follow Telmon and become his squire, but Telmon was dead. And now he stood at the beginning of the voyage he had dreamed of, with a squire of his own, and it seemed that all of his adventures since he had left Aeolis were no more than a preparation for this, the true adventure.

"There is something you must do before you leave," Pandaras said.

"The mirror people are set on it," Tamora added. "More foolishness. But I thought perhaps it will put an end to your delusions, so I sent one of these husbandmen up to tell Lupe where you are."

She and Pandaras would say no more, except that all would be explained tomorrow. With a premonition of black dread, Yama suspected that he knew what it was, and knew that he would fail in it. Whatever else he was, he could not be the savior of the mirror people.

Tamora and Pandaras helped him walk around the square of the little village, but he was quickly exhausted, and could not contemplate going any further.

"But I must leave," he said. "I cannot do what they want."

"You can do anything at all, master," Pandaras said. "You just need to rest a little."

"Don't listen to him," Tamora said. "Whatever those fuckers up there thought you were, you're going to war as a cateran. That's all you are. You'll see."

Yama laughed. "O Tamora. You believe in nothing you cannot touch or taste or smell."

"Of course. Only fools believe in magic."

"Well, it is certain that my enemies believe that I am more than I seem to be."

And so did Lupe, who wanted a miracle of him.

"You are greater than anything they can imagine, master," Pandaras said, and touched fingers to his throat in the odd gesture so many of the lesser citizens of Ys used, like a salute, or a blessing.

13

The Miracle

THE NEXT MORNING, the whole village busied itself with preparations for a feast. In the dusty central square, long red cloths were unrolled and strewn with flowers. Men and women set to cooking a hundred different dishes over trenches filled with white-hot charcoal. Their children stacked pyramids of sweet melons like the skulls of vanquished enemies, and built mounds of breadapples and small black and red bananas.

"We will honor our friends the mirror people," the headman told Yama, "and we will honor you, brave dominie, who is the friend of our friends, and who saved our village from the hell-hound."

Like the rest of the villagers, the headman wore a garland of freshly cut white flowers. With comical solemnity he lowered similar necklaces over the heads of Yama, Tamora and Pandaras, and kissed each of them on the forehead. Yama was still weak, and despite his growing dread he was now resigned to undergoing this ordeal. Besides, the villagers had saved his life and believed that he was a hero. And who would not like to be treated as a hero, even if only for a day?

And so he gave up all idea of escape, and while the villagers bustled to and fro he sat in the sunshine with Pandaras at his feet like a loyal puppy. Pandaras had tried to persuade Yama to put on his second-best shirt, but he preferred the homespun tunic the headman had given him. Tamora sat cross-legged beside him with her new saber across her lap, sharpening it with a bit of whetstone and complaining about Eliphas.

"He has run off with the money I gave him," she said. "Or gone straight to our enemies. I was a fool to trust him."

"If he was going to betray me, then surely he would have done it already. Besides, he does not know where I am."

"He went off before we started to look for you," Tamora admitted. "But he could have doubled back and followed us."

"And you would not have noticed an old man trailing behind you."

"Well, that's true. But these husbandmen have told the mirror people about you, and they could have told Eliphas. I do not trust him, Yama."

Pandaras stirred and said, "When we were up in the balcony, above the pythonesses' ceremony, he told me stories about how he used to search for old books when he was young. I think Yama has reawakened his spirit of adventure."

Yama said, "You trust no one and nothing, Tamora. Eliphas was a good friend to me at the library, and he did not abandon me when I was pursued by the hell-hound."

The mirror people arrived when the sun reached the highest point in the sky. They came up the steps beside the tiers of rice paddies in a long, colorful procession. Men and women waved red and gold flags, beat drums and tambours, and blew discordant blasts on trumpets that coiled like golden serpents around the players' shoulders. There were fire-eaters exhaling gouts of red and blue flame, boys and girls who walked on their hands or on stilts, tumblers and jugglers. Lupe walked in the middle of this circus, wearing an emerald-green gown with a long train held by two stunningly beautiful girls. The tangled mane of the old man's hair was dressed with glass beads and brightly colored ribbons. His hands, with their long twisted nails, rested on the bare shoulders of two more girls who guided him to the center of the village where the headman waited, clad only in his darned leggings and his homespun tunic, and his dignity.

After the two men had ceremoniously kissed, Lupe turned to where Yama stood with Tamora and Pandaras. "Well met, dominie," he said. His hands sought and clasped Yama's. "I am pleased that you have returned to us, but I always knew that you would."

Yama began to thank the old man for helping his friends, but Lupe put his long fingernails to his lips. His face was painted white, with black eyebrows drawn above his frost-capped eyes. His lips were dyed a deep purple. "What you will do for us can never be repaid," he said, "but we must not speak of that now. Our brothers have prepared food and drink, and we must dance to earn their hospitality."

The feast lasted all afternoon. As the sun sank behind the shoulder of the slope above the village, cressets were lit and hung on high poles, filling the air with scented smoke and sending fierce red light beating across the crowded square. Children served a stream of dishes, and husbandmen and mirror people ate and drank with gusto. Pandaras fell asleep, curled in his place with his nose in the crook of his knees. Tamora drank sweet yellow wine steadily and soon was as drunk as anyone else.

Yama sat in the place of honor, between Lupe and the headman of the village. The Aedile had taught him the trick of appearing to eat and drink much while in fact consuming little, but even the small amount of wine he drank went straight to his head, and there were times when he believed that he was in the middle of a hectic dream, where animals dressed as men frolicked and bayed at the black sky.

As the air darkened, it became possible to make out the sparkle of gunfire around one high crag of the Palace. Once, a low rumble passed like a wave through the ground beneath the feasting husbandmen and mirror people, and everyone laughed and clapped, as if it was a trick done for their benefit.

Yama asked Lupe if he was worried by the war between departments, but Lupe smiled and merely said that it was good to be in the fresh air once more. "It has been a long time since I felt sunlight on my face, dominie."

"The war is nothing to us," the headman said. "We do not have the ambitions of the changed. How much it costs them! And when the war is over, everything will be as it was before. No one can change the order of things, for that was set by the Preservers at the beginning of the world."

He raised a beaker of wine and drank, and the husbandmen around him knuckled their foreheads and drank too.

Lupe had been sucking the marrow from a chicken bone. Now he bit it in half and chewed and swallowed the splinters and said, "At the far end of time all those who are changed will be resurrected after death by the charity and grace of the Preservers. Isn't that right, dominie?"

And so it had begun. Yama said, as steadily as he could, "That is what it says in the Puranas."

"All men," the headman said. "But not all who are born and die on Confluence are men. Changed bloodlines become more and more holy, and at last pass away into story and song. Many have passed away since the world was made, and many more will do so in ages to come. But we are less than men, and can never change. And so we will inherit the world when all others have transcended their base selves."

"These people have no ambition, dominie," Lupe told Yama. "They swear never to leave their gardens. They will never wear a crown of fireflies." Lupe waved a hand above his head, as if to swat the two dim fireflies which circled him. "I do not mean these. They are nothing. I know. Rats have brighter attendants. I mean ones such as those you wore when you first visited us. I am sorry that you no longer have them."

"They were taken away," Yama said.

"We do not need fireflies," the headman said, "for we work in the sun and sleep when the Rim Mountains take away the light. We are a humble people."

"They have no ambition, but they are not humble," Lupe told Yama. "They are proudest of all the peoples of the Palace. They cleave to their work in the old gardens and claim to be the best of all the servants of the Preservers, but surely the best way to serve the Preservers is to aspire to become more than you already are."

Lupe leaned toward Yama. The glass beads in his tangled hair clicked and rattled. Each held a point of reflected torchlight. His green dress was of the finest watered silk, but Yama could smell the must of the long years it had spent in a press. Were the blind old man's cheekbones higher and sharper, was his voice softer?

Lupe said, "Who is right, dominie? They say we wish to rise above what we are destined to be; we believe that they are worse sinners, for they refuse the challenge."

On Yama's left hand, the headman said, "If knowing what you are is a sin, then I admit it. But isn't it a worse sin to dream of gaining what you can never have?"

On the other side of the flower-strewn strip of cloth, Tamora suddenly looked up, as if startled awake. "That's right," she said. "Dreams bring heartache."

"Without dreams," Lupe said, "we are only animals. Without dreams, we are no more than we are."

Yama looked from one old man to the other. Although he had drunk little, his head felt as if it was filled with fireflies. He said, "You ask me to judge between you? Then I say that both of you are at fault, for you refuse to look into your own hearts and discover why you wish for elevation or why you refuse the chance. Each of you clearly sees the fault of the other, but neither sees his own fault. We are all raised up by the Preservers, but they do not set limits on what we can be. That is up to us."

The headman touched his forehead, but Lupe tipped back his head and laughed.

The headman glared at Lupe and said, "Then this foolishness should not take place, as I have argued. Brother Lupe, this man is a hero, but he is also a man. We are not the ones to test him. Only he can do that."

"You show him," Tamora said. "Show him what he is. What he isn't."

"It is not a test of him," Lupe said, "but of my people."

The headman said, "And as the dominie pointed out, you have thought too long on why we will not copy your foolishness, instead of thinking why you wish to attempt it."

"Then I stand for my people alone," Lupe said, and held out his hands.

Two girls stepped forward and helped him up. Gradually, the feast fell silent, silence spreading through the noise of laughter and drinking and eating and singing as black ink spreads through water. The people who sat cross-legged around the strips of cloth and the islands of food turned to watch Lupe. The faces of the mirror people were tinted red by the crackling flames of the torches; those of the husbandmen were tinted black. Two giants which had been trading blows with clubs in the center of the square stepped back from each other and their upper halves threw off their tinsel helmets and jumped down from their lower halves, who shucked the wide belts which had concealed where their partners had stood on their shoulders.

Lupe raised a hand, and someone stepped out of the darkness into the flaring light of the torches. It was a beautiful young woman in a simple white shift. She stepped forward lightly and gravely, treading the dust of the square like a dancer, the cynosure of every eye.

She carried a basket of white flowers. When she reached the center of the square she knelt gracefully and offered the basket to Yama. Yama jumped up and backed away, horrified. Tamora began to laugh.

━━━━━━━

They left Yama alone with the baby in the dark night in a ruined temple below the village. Perhaps it had once had gardens and a courtyard before its entrance, but now it was little more than a small square cave cut into the cliff at the edge of a stony field of vines. The lintel of its entrance was cracked. The caryatids which had for an age shouldered their burden uncomplainingly on either side of the door had fallen. One had broken in two and was missing her head; the other lay on her back, her blank eyes gazing at the black sky. Torches had been set on poles thrust into the dry earth on either side of the entrance. Their smoky red light sent long shadows weaving across the flaking frescoes of the naos and put red sparks in the glossy black circle of the shrine.

For a long time, Yama paced back and forth between the two torches, stopping now and then to look at the baby, which slept innocently on the blanket of white blossoms. It was a boy, fat and dusky with health. What tormented Yama was the thought of the miracle he was expected to perform.

To raise this poor wight. To change him from innocence to one of those fallen into full self-awareness.

It was impossible.

The innocence of the indigens was different from that of the unchanged bloodlines because it was absolute. While most bloodlines of Confluence could evolve toward union with the Preservers, the indigens were as fixed in their habits as the beasts of field and flood and air. Certain coarse bloodlines, such as the Amnan, excused their persecution of indigens by saying that their victims were merely animals with human appearance and speech, a kind of amalgam of monkey and parrot. Most, though, agreed that the indigenous races resembled unchanged bloodlines in all but potential. Their only sin was that they could never become other than what they were. They could not fall from the grace to which they had been raised by the Preservers, but neither could they transcend it.

More than once, Yama was seized with the strong urge to pick up the baby and carry him back to the village high above, where, to judge from the sounds of laughter and music which occasionally drifted to him on the night breeze, the feast was proceeding as heartily as when he had been led away from it. And more than once, he was seized with the impulse simply to walk away into the night. To become what he briefly had been when he had first arrived in Ys, a solitary seeker after the truth of his own life.

He did neither. The baby was in his care, and he could not return until the night was over. A refusal to act would be worse than failure, for it would imply that he was not grateful to the mirror people for saving his life. No, better to wait out the night, and be found to have failed. Tamora would be pleased, for it would prove to her that his powers were no more than figments of his imagination. And perhaps the heavy weight of the mirror people's hope might pass from him.

It was not a burden that Yama had ever sought. That was what was so unfair. Zakiel had told him that, because of the great age of Confluence and the multiplicity of its bloodlines, there were so many stories and tales that anyone could find in them a mirror to their own life. And so the mirror people had seen in Yama a reflection of some long-dead hero or half-forgotten promise.

Yama could forgive them that—in these troubled times people looked to the past for heroes to save them, for that was simpler than trying to save themselves. But although, like so many heroes of the Apocrypha, he possessed mysterious origins, strange powers, and what might be mistaken for a magical weapon (but he had lost the knife, and the coin he carried was not the coin he had been given), Yama knew that he was no hero. As a child, he had dreamed of finding others of his bloodline, that they would be powerful and rich and strong. But he knew now that those dreams could not be true. Every orphan must have similar dreams, but very few orphans are of notable birth. Now, older and chastened by the rub of the world, he wished to find his people because he hoped that they would shelter him from the expectations of others. Even if they were no more than mendicants and anchorites, he would join them gladly, for surely they would accept him simply for what he was. He had not asked for what little power that he had, and he wanted it gone.

Let it pass.

More than once, gripped by a mixture of self-loathing and self-pity, he shouted this prayer into the night. But there was never any reply, nothing more than the wind walking amongst the dry leaves of the vines, and the faint sounds of revelry high above. Presently, he remembered that this place was very old, and grew fearful that he might wake something, and was quiet.

"You are better off without it," he whispered to the baby. His throat ached from shouting. "The husbandmen are right."

Yama did not expect to sleep, but at last he tired himself out by pacing to and fro, like the great spotted cat he had once seen in a cage on the deck of a ship that had put in at Aeolis on its way back to Ys from the jungles near the midpoint of the world. The cat had prowled restlessly from one corner of its cage to the other, anger blazing in its green eyes, its mad thoughts unguessable. Perhaps it had believed that if it paced long enough it might find a hidden door to the jungle from which it had been taken.

Yama sat with his back against the pedestal of one of the caryatids (her feet, shod in strap sandals, stood there still, broken off at the ankles), and, tired but sleepless, watched the lights of the city spread beyond the dark slopes of the Palace roof.

After some time, he realized that the fallen caryatid had opened her blank eyes and was watching him. He felt neither fear nor amazement; not even when she spoke.

"You have a knack of finding windows that still work," she said. "I see you lost your key but found another."

Yama knew at once who was speaking to him. The woman he had seen in the shrine of the Temple of the Black Well. The aspect of the author of the heresies which threatened to consume the world.

He was seized with a bottomless dread, as if confronted with a poisonous serpent. His mouth was dry, but he managed to say, "The keys are everywhere, but people have forgotten what they were."

"They have forgotten much," the woman said lightly. "When I walked in your world, I tried to tell them a little of what they had forgotten. Some remembered, but many resisted. Knowledge is a bitter thing, after all, and many hesitate to sip from that cup. You, for instance, are not one step further on your journey. Why are you sitting here, and who is it you are sitting with? A very unformed mind . . . Ah, it is a baby from one of the true alien races. Another orphan, Yama?"

"I will not serve you," Yama said. It was a great effort to speak, as if he, too, had been turned to stone. He said, "I refuse to serve. I refused Prefect Corin, and I refuse you. I especially refuse you, because I know that you deny the mercy and charity of the Preservers. You would over-throw them and rule in their place if you could. It is the world's good fortune that you are nothing but a ghost."

"Do you refuse the mirror people, too?"

"You cannot know about that!"

"I am in your dreams, Yama, so for this little time I share some of your memories. The mirror people want only to share the fate of the other bloodlines of this strange world. They want nothing more than to take charge of their own destiny, to become infected with the machines that will record their memories, so that they might live again. They want to remember their own story, not have it remembered for them. I had long arguments with Mr. Naryan on that point. He was particularly enthusiastic about innocence, I remember, but no parent should keep a child from growing."

"Mr. Naryan . . . is he another ghost?"

"He was the Archivist of the town of Sensch. As far as I know, he's still alive. It was a great many years ago, but his kind live long, longer than most of the long-lived races of Confluence. He changed his mind, of course. He understands my ideas now."

"But Sensch was where the war—"

The caryatid smiled, cracking the lichens which had grown like cankers on her stony cheeks. "I set them free, Yama. Free from the burden of this world's mindless theocracy. Free to be themselves."

"The Preservers will give us all that freedom."

"Yes, and they promise to do so at the very instant of the end of the Universe. It is an easy promise to make, for no one will be alive to call them to account when they fail. The Preservers promise everything and give nothing. I promise no more than freedom, and that is what I gave the citizens of Sensch. What is so wrong with that?

"Now, pay attention. I will show you the trick. When I was in the world, I had to call on the shrines to help me change the people of Sensch. Now I live in the space inside the shrines, and the process is much simpler."

"No! I will not serve!"

But in his dream, Yama seemed to be swimming beneath the surface of the river, as he had swum so often when he was still a child, innocently playing with the pups of the Amnan. The pups had liked to dive from the end of the new quay and swim out to the kelp beds, where long green fronds trailed just beneath the surface. They swam deeper and faster than Yama ever could, searching for abalone and oysters that clustered around the holdfasts of the kelp on the muddy river bottom. Yama was happy enough to splash above them, but sometimes he struck downward through sunlight toward the ghost of the river bottom far below, toward the other children. He could never reach them. His lungs began to ache and burn, and the weight of the water compressed his chest and he had to double back and swim strongly for the surface, where he sputtered and coughed in the sunlight. The cool depths of the river were, for him, forever unreachable. But now, as he struck through a hectic flux that was much like the play of light and water, it came to him that his wish had finally come true. The caryatid hung beside him, and he told her that she should sink, for she was stone, and stone could not float.

"Watch," she said, and he saw the knots within the baby's brain, saw how they could be made stronger *here* and *here* so that the swarming machines, smaller than the single-celled plants on which the largest fish of the river grazed, which hung invisibly in every breath of air just as the tiny plants hung in every drop of water, would exist in those places, and begin their work of building and amplifying the initial trace of self-consciousness.

The caryatid sank away, slowly dissolving into the flux of light. "Self-ordering complexity," she murmured. "It only needs a seed . . ."

Yama knew now, or remembered, that this was a dream, and remembered the nature of the creature that had visited him. Yet still something in him yearned toward her, as a starving man will reach toward any kind of food, no matter how foul. He struck out with fierce desperation toward the place where she had disappeared, and woke to find Tamora kneeling beside him. He was lying on the broken tiles of the naos, before the black disc of the shrine. Was there light fading within it? Or was it simply a reflection of the dawn light which was framed by the square entrance of the little temple?

Tamora was watching Yama with an intent, troubled expression. She snatched back her hand when he reached for it, and he asked her what was wrong. Instead of answering, she turned and pointed to the temple's entrance, where people clustered around something on the ground. Immediately, Yama felt a sharp pang of guilt. He had forgotten the baby. He had fallen asleep. It could be dead. It could have been snatched by wild animals.

He staggered outside, every muscle stiff. It was already warm, and light flooded the slopes of the Palace and filled the sky, so bright after the temple's cool shadows that he had to squint. A great cry went up from the people and Yama started back in alarm before he understood that they were smiling. Lupe stood in the center of the little crowd, his blind face bent to a girl who whispered in his ear. Another girl took Yama's hand and led him to the basket of white flowers.

There was so much light that Yama did not at first understand why the baby's eyes kept crossing, and why it batted at the air before its face with its chubby hands. And then he saw.

Hung above its forehead, burning with fierce white radiance, was a crown of fireflies.

14

The Procession of Yama

"THEY WILL SOON go away," Yama whispered into Pandaras's ear. "I must have drawn them here, but they will go away once I have left. Before this is over I should explain to Lupe's people that it is not how they think it is."

"You are too modest, master! You could live as a Hierarch here, and instead you go to war!"

The produce wagon on which they rode swayed as it negotiated a pothole in the old road; Pandaras staggered and then sat down hard by Yama's high chair. The boy was drunk. From the noise and music and cheering of the procession, from plentiful libations of sweet yellow palm wine. A wreath of ivy and the long white flowers of trumpet vine was tipped on his brow. There was a large wet wine stain on the front of his white shirt.

"They'd kill him," Tamora said. "Not these fools, but the people in power. He's a threat to them."

She stood behind Yama, gripping her saber and constantly turning from left to right to watch the crowd, becoming especially alert whenever someone let off a firecracker. People were running alongside the wagon and its attendant procession of mirror people, or stood on terraces overlooking the road, cheering and waving palm fronds or brightly colored cloths, offering up flowers or fruit. One group had launched kites into the air; painted with fierce faces, the red and black and yellow diamonds zoomed and swooped around each other in the bright air.

Lupe sat at Yama's feet, arrayed in a dress of cloth-of-gold sewn with fake pearls and sequins. He held the baby with its crown of brilliant fireflies in his lap. He said, "We mean no harm to anyone. We simply set forth from our immemorial home to claim our place in the world."

"You'd do better to stay here," Tamora said. She had to raise her voice to a shrill pitch to be heard above the crowd. "Innocents like you are prey for every bandit, crimp and reaver in the city."

"When I was a young man," Lupe said, "I used the shell game to take money from your people at the Water Market. Before that, I played the part of the monkey in the illusion of the snake and rope, and helped in a puppet theater. Marks always think that they can fool us, but they forget that they play our games by our rules. Ah, but we must not quarrel, young cateran, for we are both set on the same path. Hear how the people cheer the procession of your master!"

The news of the miracle had spread fast and far. By the time the procession had left the village of the husbandmen, people were already lining the old road as far as they could see. Gangs of men were clearing the road of brush and fallen rock, or patching gaps with timbers. The road had not been used, Lupe said, since the Hierarchs had fallen silent, ten thousand years ago.

The procession wound three times around the slopes of the Palace as it descended toward the city. No guards or troops came forward to stop it, but now and then Tamora would point out a speck in the air beyond the Palace's slopes, where, she said, an officer stood on a disc, watching through a glass. Once, where the road rounded the bulging side of a steep cliff with sheer rock above and only air below, a flyer paced the procession. It hung just beyond the edge of the road, so close that one of the acrobats could have easily jumped from the road to the wide black triangle of its wing. The mirror people pelted it with flowers and libations, and then the road turned into a short tunnel through the side of a bluff, and when it came out into the sunlight the flyer was gone, and more people were running down steeply tilted fields toward the procession, waving and cheering.

Yama waved back, although he was sick at heart. The miracle which these innocent people were celebrating was no miracle at all, but a trick of the shadow of the creature who had started the war. She had used him as a tool to change the baby, either to show him what she was capable of, or to show him that she knew his powers better than he did. The miracle which Lupe had desired so much was a perversion, a crude and cruel joke mocking the will of the Preservers.

Yama's only hope was that good might come from this after all. For no matter how it had been done, the baby *was* changed. Lupe's people had the proof that they could be raised up.

There was nothing he could do but make the best of it, which was why he had agreed to ride with Lupe. Tamora had said that taking part in the procession was perilously foolish, but Yama had asked her plainly what was better—sneaking out of Ys under cover of darkness, like escaping thieves, or riding in the place of honor in a long, happy procession amidst tumblers and musicians and clowns, with the population cheering them along? At least Pandaras was caught up in the fever of it all. He waved too, and drank the libations which people handed up, and laughed and waved some more.

Yama turned to Tamora and said, "Most of them think it is some kind of performance."

She shook her head. "Just look at who has come to watch. They are all of them indigens or the poorest of the poor, sweepers and night-soil collectors like the rat-boy here. If the soldiers or the magistrates decide to arrest you, or worse, if those fuckers from Indigenous Affairs come for you, this trash would melt away. And tomorrow they'd choose another King of Fools."

"My bloodline helped build the world, Tamora, and at one time I believed they might be Lords of infinite time and space. I know now that they were no such thing. They were laborers such as these."

The miracle was not that he had performed a miracle, for he knew that he had not, but that Lupe and the mirror people believed that he had. Perhaps the good of it was this: that these people believed that miracles were possible, that the Preservers could still intercede in the world. And how could he deny it? For was not his own existence as much a miracle as the crown of fireflies around that innocent baby's head? If the woman in the shrine had used him, then perhaps she in turn had been used by some higher power.

"I think you're better than them," Tamora said, and went back to watching the crowd.

Yama was searching the faces in the crowd, too. He was looking for Eliphas, for now the procession was descending through the cramped squares and narrow streets that threaded between the tumultuous jumble of buildings at the hem of the Palace, and still there was no sign of the old man.

The procession moved toward a great gate. People lined the rooftops on either side, pelting the wagon with flowers and paper strings in a blizzard so dense that at first Yama did not see why the procession suddenly stopped. Tamora hissed, but Yama held up his hand, hoping that she would not strike. For now he saw, through falling drifts of flowers, a line of troopers strung across the road before the gate, some mounted on black-plumaged ratites, some on foot.

An officer on a floating disc, clad in metal armor so polished that it shone like a mirror broken into the shape of a man, swooped down and hung in the air above the two oxen that drew the wagon. He was bareheaded, his skull heavily ridged. A thick black mustache framed the puckered cone of his mouth. He stared directly at Yama and said, "Who is in charge?"

"No one was compelled to be here," Yama said. "They came of their own free will."

The officer said, "None of these animals know anything about free will."

Lupe said, "We set forth toward a new life, dominie. And this is the one who sets us upon it."

Tamora stepped forward, glaring up at the officer. "Get out of the way, little man. And take your toy soldiers with you."

"Stand down," Yama told her gently, as he might try and calm a highly strung mount. He said to the officer, "What authority stops us?"

"The Department of Internal Harmony. You are Yamamanama? I am here to escort you from the Palace. We are under considerable pressure to return you to a certain place, but the Department of Internal Harmony does not take sides. We still have full control of the lower floors and the outer defenses, and we do as we see fit to ensure the security of the Palace. Accordingly, I am here to make sure that you leave the Palace, and to ask you to disperse your followers."

"They are not mine to command." Yama gestured, meaning the crowd which clogged the street behind the wagon, the people on the rooftops who were still tossing flowers into the air. He said, "If they were, I would not have allowed this. I am as embarrassed by it as you, but I believe that they mean no harm by what they do."

He could take the disc from beneath the officer's feet and use it as a scythe against the troopers who blocked the way. He could call down machines and riddle them through and through. It would be so easy . . . but there would be other soldiers, and beyond the gates was the city, and the hundred thousand magistrates who kept civil order. He was not here to start a war. What was he thinking? The woman in the shrine had put something in his head that twisted his thoughts to fantasies of violence and domination. He took a deep breath to calm himself, and remembered that the Aedile had taught him that when negotiating it was better to allow your opponent to think that he had come to a decision than to force him to make a choice, for when forced a man will usually choose badly.

He said, "I understand why you must keep order amongst the petitioners and palmers who seek to gain entrance, for else the Palace would be overwhelmed. But the people who celebrate here are of the Palace itself, and wish to leave. They are the simple people who work the fields and entertain the clerks."

Lupe said, "We have always come and gone freely. Why are we stopped now?"

"I know your kind," the officer said. "They come and go by ratholes and sewer pipes, along with the other vermin."

Yama said, "If they are vermin, why then, you would well be rid of them. In any case surely you should not waste a moment on them. Would you stop birds flying from the fields above us to the banks of the Great River?"

The officer thought for a moment, then said, "We serve the ideal of the Preservers. We always have. In the black days when the Head of the People swallowed all other departments, we alone maintained our independence. We allow people to come and go as we see fit."

"And even the mirror people were raised up by the Preservers. Their kind have lived in the Palace for longer than almost every other bloodline. Perhaps you would know if they have some rights in this matter."

The officer's puckered mouth drew back to show the strong, yellow-ridged grinding plates he had instead of teeth. "Frankly, I'll be glad to see the last of them. They are parasites upon the bodies of the departments. Only a decad past there was a riot in one of the day markets because one of them was caught cheating at some gambling game. Several clerks were blinded when a fool fired an energy pistol."

Yama believed that he knew something of the truth of that incident, but he did not correct the officer. He said, "Then perhaps all will benefit if they pass with me."

The officer nodded. "They'll be the magistrates' problem once they're outside the Palace, and I have my orders to get you to a place of safety. The Department of Indigenous Affairs pushed too hard for your return. We'll not be at the command of them, or anyone else."

"There is a ship waiting for us at the docks," Yama said. "If you took me there, it would be an end to your duty, and of my obligation to you."

The mounted troopers of the Department of Internal Harmony fell in as an escort ahead and behind the wagon. Their ratites, the officer confided to Yama, were not as swift or fearsome as horses, but were less prone to panic and more maneuverable in the press of a crowd. The procession passed beneath the arch of the great gate (all the fireflies, from Lupe's to those of the baby in his lap, flew up and vanished; Yama was glad to see them go) and began to make its way through the ordinary streets of Ys.

Yama turned back and saw the Palace rearing against the sky above close-packed roofs, and fancied he glimpsed the flash of some weapon's discharge near the peak, where the war between departments was still being fought. Or perhaps it was no more than the sun glinting on some metal surface high up in the Palace's great bulk—perhaps the metal which clad the House of the Twelve Front Rooms of the Department of Vatication.

The procession was still followed by cheering crowds, but now there were just as many people on the streets who merely glanced at it as they went about their normal business. Yama remembered the procession he had seen from the window of the inn where he had woken after plunging into the Country of the Mind where the crews of the voidships met each other, and laughed to think that now he was the center of a similar spectacle, simultaneously the center of everyone's gaze and something commonplace.

Tamora cursed Pandaras for getting drunk and said that Yama should watch the rooftops instead of waving like the King of Fools. "They should have put a canopy over your head. It wouldn't block quarrel, but it would hinder the aim."

"We are quite safe," Yama said. "We have the protection of the Department of Internal Harmony. No one will dare try and take me by force now."

"Prefect Corin might try and put a quarrel through your head, and mine too. He won't have forgiven us for escaping. I know the type. And those magistrates are watching us too closely for my liking."

Red-robed magistrates stood on floating discs high above the heads of the crowd which thronged the streets, their machines a dizzy twinkle in the air about them. Yama waved at them as the wagon trundled past, and suppressed the impulse to twist the orbits of their machines into mocking configurations.

As the wagon moved toward the docks, the crowd began to grow denser, swollen by refugees come to beg for help from the man who had raised up one of the indigenous races. Women held up children so that they could see Yama and the baby, or perhaps to be blessed, for many were ill or deformed. People shouted and prayed and pleaded, but their words were lost in the general tumult and the braying of the trumpets and shawms of the mirror people.

At last, the crowds were so dense that the procession could no longer move forward. Even the mounted soldiers were trapped in the press. The officer swooped down and told Yama that he would arrange for him to be carried away to wherever he wished.

Yama shook his head. "I will walk if I must!"

"You must come with me!"

They were both shouting at the tops of their voices, but could hardly hear themselves over the noise of the crowd. A man jumped on to the wagon and tried to asperge Yama with scented oil. Tamora kicked him in the throat and he folded over and fell backward. The mob closed around him before he had a chance to scream.

Yama climbed onto the bench and raised his arms. Gradually, the crowd which packed the street ahead and behind the wagon grew quiet, except for a scattering of individual voices crying out with hysteria or hurt or fright.

"I cannot help you," Yama said. He was trembling violently, and a sharp pain pressed between his eyes. "Only you can help yourselves."

Most did not hear him, but the crowd cheered anyway. Yama remembered the magistrate who had stopped him and Prefect Corin when they had first arrived in Ys, and borrowed a machine from one of the magistrates who stood on a rooftop overlooking the street. When he spoke to it, it amplified his voice so that it echoed from the walls of the buildings. He meant to tell the crowd again that he could not help them, but something seized him, and then he hardly knew what he said. The crowd cheered and he felt lifted up by their cheers. The pain between his eyes intensified and red and black light flashed in his sight. He tried to reach out and change everyone in the crowd and failed because there were too many, and cried out in rage. A myriad tiny machines burned and fell from the air. People screamed and tried to flee as magistrates, believing themselves to be under attack, laid into those nearest them with their quirts. But there was nowhere to flee to, and suddenly the crowd was fighting against itself, its unity lost.

Yama did not see any of this. Red and black lightning tore away all thought and he fell backward into Tamora's arms.

A great wind blew around him. The sun burned down out of the cloud-less sky, but the rush of air was so cold that he shivered in its icy blast as if plunged into a stream fed by the glaciers at the end of the world. He lay on a ridged metal deck that vibrated beneath him. When he struggled to sit up, Pandaras helped him and said, "A flying machine, master. You fainted and the officer caught you up and carried you off."

"There were too many . . ."

Pandaras misunderstood; he was still drunk. His wreath was tipped over one ear. He said, "They would have torn you apart if this hadn't rescued us. Isn't it wondrous?"

The flying machine was sleek and boat-shaped, with short, down-curved wings. Its silver skin shone like a mirror in the bright sunlight. Lupe sat behind Yama and Pandaras, with the baby in his lap and a girl on either side. Four troopers stood behind him. Near the beaked prow, Tamora was talking with a man clad in broken mirrors. She glanced around, grinning fiercely, and said, "We go directly to the docks."

The mirror-clad man turned—it was the officer in his polished armor—and said, "This is only a dory, not a true flyer. Unfortunately its range is limited, or I would take you as far from the city as possible."

Yama said stupidly, "Who commands it?"

"It flies itself," the officer said. "It is from the early days of the world. There. You see what we have left behind."

The little dory tilted in the air. Because its local gravity compen-sated for the motion, the world seemed to pitch beneath it. The grid of the city, punctuated here and there by the domes and spires of temples, stretched away toward the vast bulk of the Palace of the Memory of the People. The Palace's peak was obscured by smoke. A long way beyond it were the shining towers Yama had seen so often using the signal telescope on the roof of the peel-house at Aeolis, white needles that rose higher than the Rim Mountains, their tops lost in a glare of sunlight beyond the envelope of air that shrouded the world.

Yama pointed at the Palace and said, "They are still fighting."

"It is the rioting in the streets that I meant," the officer said. "Well, I suppose we are too high to see it."

As if it understood him, the dory swooped down. The city rushed at them. The crowded roofs of the refugees' shantytown, built over the mudbanks left by the Great River's slow retreat, raveled away on either side. The river was directly ahead, a broad plain flashing in the sunlight as the dory swerved toward one of the floating docks.

The pontoon quays of the dock were lined with sightseers, and a flotilla of small boats stood off on either side. As the dory gently sank through the air, coming to rest just above the edge of the outermost quay, Yama saw a familiar face in the crowd and immediately jumped down.

Tamora got in front of Yama and helped keep off the press of people who crowded round, shouting and singing and praying and making obeisance. Some clutched at Yama's homespun tunic and he realized his mistake and would have climbed back on the dory, but there was no room to move. Tamora held her saber above her head, in case someone was pushed onto it by those pressing from behind, and there was an uncomfortable minute before the troopers managed to clear a space.

Lupe was helped down by his attendants, using one of the wings of the dory as a pont. The blind old man ignored those who crowded around him. He cradled the baby in one arm and touched Yama's face with the long fingernails of his free hand. "You should not have left us the first time, dominie," he said. "You will forgive me if I mention that you caused much trouble. But all's well that ends well."

Yama smiled, and then remembered that the old man could not see. He said, "You have been a generous friend, Lupe."

"We are your servants, dominie. We are no longer the servants of the pleasure of all in the Palace, but for you we will always give our lives."

"It will not be necessary."

"I'm glad to hear it. But these are strange times, dominie. The end of the world is at hand. Why else would you have kindled the change in our bloodline?"

Lupe embraced Yama tremulously, and Yama kissed the old man on both cheeks. The baby smiled up at them, quite undisturbed by the commotion of the crowd. Someone was trying to push between the troopers who guarded Yama and Lupe. Tamora's saber point flicked in that direction—but it was Eliphas, smiling broadly and shouting wildly, his silver eyes flashing in the bright sunlight.

"I have found them," Eliphas shouted. "I have found them, brother! Downriver!"

15

The *Weazel*

THE SHIP THEY had hired, the *Weazel*, was a small lugger which, before the war, had spent her days ferrying cargo and a few passengers from one side of the Great River to the other. She was single-masted and lateen-rigged, and in calm weather could supplement her triangular mainsail with square staysails rigged from spars spread either side of her mast. She pulled a shallow draft, and with wind and current behind her could make twice the speed of the huge galliots and levanters which were scattered across the Great River in pods of three or four, heading downriver toward the war. She could not outrun the machines which tried to follow her, but Yama, exhausted though he was, told them to disperse even before the drag anchors had been collapsed.

Pandaras said that it was likely that the *Weazel* had been used as much for smuggling as for plying regular trade, but he was careful to say this out of earshot of the ship's captain, Ixchel Lorquital. Captain Lorquital was a cautious, shrewd widow who dominated all on board with a natural authority. Like all the women of her bloodline, she had added her husband's name to her own when she had married.

"But that don't mean I was anything less than him," she told Yama. "You might say that since I carry his name and his memory I'm rather more than he ever was, the Preservers keep his memory safe."

Ixchel Lorquital was a big woman, with mahogany-colored skin that shone as if oiled and an abundance of coarse black hair she habitually tied back from her creased, round face with a variety of colored strings. Her forehead was ridged with keratin, her nostrils no more than slits in the middle of her face. She wore a silver lip-plug which weighed down her lower lip, exposing yellow, spade-shaped teeth. The day-to-day running of the ship was left to her daughter, Aguilar, who combined the offices of bosun and purser, and Captain Lorquital habitually sat in a sling chair by the helm, puffing a corncob pipe, stately in a billowing long skirt and leather tabard, her well-muscled arms bare, a red hand-kerchief knotted under her pendulous jowls. Eliphas soon struck up a friendship with her, and they spent hours talking together.

Ixchel Lorquital asked no questions about Yama and his friends. She offered her cabin to the four passengers, but Yama politely refused this generous gesture. Instead, he and his companions camped on the deck, sleeping on raffia mats under a canvas awning that slanted steeply from the rail of the quarterdeck to a cleat by the cargo well.

Yama slept easily and deeply on the Great River. It reminded him of the happy days of the annual pilgrimages made by the whole popu-lation of Aeolis to the farside shore. And he could sleep safe in the knowledge that he had left his enemies behind him, and that now he had a destination, a place to voyage toward, the place where his blood-line might still live.

Eliphas had told Yama all about his discovery as soon as the *Weazel* had raised her rust-red sail and begun to outpace the flotilla of small boats which had tried to follow her. The old man was tremendously pleased with himself, and even more voluble than usual.

"It was your mention of Dr. Dismas that aided the search," he said. "It was a simple matter to check the records and find out which he had accessed. He had been careful to cover his tracks, but he was not subtle. For one as experienced as my friend Kun Norbu, the chief of clerks, it was a relatively simple matter to see through the deception."

"You say that they were living downriver," Yama said quickly, before Eliphas could launch into a technical account of the false trails left by Dr. Dismas and the skills the chief of clerks had employed to untangle them.

"If they still live, brother, then that is where they will be found," Eliphas said.

"Well, I am alive," Yama said.

"That's true," Eliphas said. "However, I feel I should point out that while your being alive here and now means that at least two of your bloodline were alive in the recent past, it does not mean that our hy-pothetical pair are alive now, or that any others like them are alive. The documents, you see, are quite old. At least five thousand years old, for they had formed part of the original binding of a book which had been made then. They could well be much older, of course."

"How much older?"

"Well, that's difficult to say, brother. With more time, Kun Norbu and I could have analyzed the inks, for degradation of certain elements used to manufacture inks occurs at a fairly constant rate. But they are not more than ten thousand years old, for before that time the region in which the city of your bloodline is located was not yet formed."

"A city!"

Yama had never imagined more than a small keep, or perhaps a small town, hidden in the icy fastness upriver of Ys. Perhaps a citadel tunneled into the rock of the mountains, a fine and secret place full of ancient wonders. But a city . . .

Eliphas drew a little leather satchel from inside his loose shirt, unfastened its clasps, and took out a cardboard folder tied with a green ribbon.

"Neither are the originals, of course," he said. "My friend the chief of clerks could not allow such precious documents to leave the precincts of the library. However, they are fair copies, made by the best of the copyists in the library. The first faithfully reproduces the appalling script of the man who wrote the original, and even mimics the stains and tatters which the original accumulated before it was used as a stiffener in the binding of a common pharmacopium."

It took him a minute more to unpick the knot in the ribbon. He opened the folder and withdrew a piece of paper which had been folded into quarters and sealed with a blob of black wax. It fluttered in the warm wind which poured past the rail of the ship's waist, and it took all of Yama's will to resist snatching it from Eliphas's hand.

"Sealed with the imprint of the chief of clerks," Eliphas said, and snapped the wax and handed the folded paper to Yama.

After he had opened it, Yama thought at first that he had the paper upside down, but when he turned it around he still could not read the irregular lines of squiggles and dashes.

Eliphas smiled. "It is a long-dead language, brother, and the man who wrote this account used a much-debased version. However, I have some small skill in it. It is a brief account written by a scavenger of wrecked war machines in the Glass Desert beyond the midpoint of the world. That is why I would guess that it is more than five thousand years old. The remains of war machines were almost entirely removed from the accessible areas of the Glass Desert long before the making of the book in which this was found."

"Where is it then? Where is this place?"

"Several hundred leagues beyond the end of the Great River, in a series of caverns. The scavenger believed that it was once a huge city, but only a small part of it was still inhabited when he stumbled upon it."

Yama remembered the places beneath the world where Beatrice had taken him, and the capsule which had transported them from the edge of the Rim Mountains to the shore of the river. With growing excitement, he realized that, as a baby, he might have been carried from one end of the river to the other in a similar device. He did not know if his people still lived there, but at last he had a goal, even if it lay beyond the armies of the heretics.

But Tamora still did not trust Eliphas, and said so bluntly. "You are a fool if you believe him," she said, later that evening.

"Eliphas thinks he will find treasures there. That is why he is so eager to help. He is quite honest about his intentions."

"He wants to be young again," Pandaras said. "It's a futile wish most men share. And so he plunges into an adventure like those of his youth, hoping that it will revive his waning powers."

They sat on rolled raffia mats under the awning, their faces lit by a single candle which flickered in a resin holder. Eliphas was on the quarterdeck, talking with Captain Ixchel Lorquital. To port, Ys made a web of lights that stretched as far as the eye could see; to starboard, the Eye of the Preservers was rising above the black sweep of the river.

Tamora had taken several of the small fish the cook had caught on trotlines trailing from the ship's stern. She picked up one and tore a bite from it and swallowed without chewing. "Grah. That scrawl could be anything or nothing. He could have made it this morning. You have only his word that this is a record of your bloodline."

"Not a record," Yama said, "simply an account of what happened to a scavenger when his camels died after drinking poisoned water. He was wandering half-mad from thirst and heat exhaustion, and was found and taken in by a tribe of people who looked like me. He says that they called themselves the Builders. They had fireflies, and other machines. He was there for more than a decad, until he had recovered from his ordeal. Then he woke one morning and found himself hundreds of leagues away, near the fall of the Great River."

"It is a pretty story," Tamora said, "but where's the proof?"

"He remembered the path he had taken up to the point when his rescuers found him. Here."

Yama drew out the other piece of paper Eliphas had brought. Ta-

mora held it to the light of the candle and Pandaras craned his sleek
head to look.

It was a map.

At dawn the next day the *Weazel* was sailing past the lower reaches of
Ys ahead of a brisk breeze, dragging a creamy wake through the river's
tawny water. The ship kept to the outermost of the coastal currents,
where the water was stained by silt and sewage from thousands of
drains, all of which had once been clear streams fed by the snowcaps
of the foothills of the Rim Mountains. On the port side, across a wide
stretch of calm water broken here and there by small islands crowded
with buildings, or by long picket lines which marked the boundaries of
fish farms, was an endless unraveling panorama of close-packed houses
which stretched away beneath a dun haze created by millions of cooking
fires. A horde of tiny craft went about their business close to the shore:
coracles and skiffs; little fishing boats and puttering reaction motors;
slow sampans carrying whole families and menageries of chickens and
rabbits and dwarf goats; crowded water buses; luggers like the *Weazel,*
their big triangular sails often painted with a stylized swirl representing
the Eye of the Preservers. Occasionally, a merchant's carvel moved at
a deliberate pace amongst the smaller craft, or a pinnace with a double
bank of oars and a beaked prow sped swiftly by, scattering the local
traffic, the beat of the drum which set the rhythm of the rowers sounding
clear and small across the water.

Yama's chest tightened each time one of the pinnaces went by,
partly in memory of the time when Dr. Dismas had tried to kidnap him,
partly because he was still not sure that he had escaped Prefect Corin.
This might be no more than a reprieve until the Prefect or some other
officer of the Department of Indigenous Affairs tried to snatch him back.
When he had woken, he had sent away more than a decad of machines
which had been following the *Weazel,* and he expected to have to send
away many more.

He did not want to think of the baby of the mirror people, of the
dream in which the woman had spoken to him, of how badly the procession had ended. He wanted to put all of it behind him, and in the
night had prayed that it would pass away, another one-day wonder in a
city where wonder was commonplace.

To starboard was nothing but the wide river, stretching a hundred
leagues to its own flat horizon, where tall white clouds were stacked

above the merest glimpse of the farside shore. Day by day the clouds would grow taller and nearer, until at last they would break on the land and bring about the brief rainy season. Apart from an occasional fishing boat, trawling for deep-water delicacies in the company of a swirling flock of white birds, the outer reaches of the Great River were the preserve of the big ships. At any hour at least a hundred could be counted, scattered far and wide across the gleaming surface of the river.

Going downriver.

Going to war.

Of the five members of the crew of the *Weazel,* two, including the fat cook, were slaves who had been purchased at judicial auctions. The oldest of the sailors, the ship's carpenter, Phalerus, a bald-headed fellow with a sharp jutting lizard's face and a ruff of skin that rose above his mottled scalp, had once been a slave too—he had bought his freedom years ago but had stayed on anyway, for he knew no other home. Of the other two freemen, one was a cheerful, simpleminded man named Anchaile; skinny and long-limbed, he swung amongst the rigging with astonishing agility. The other, a shy, quiet boy, was said to have killed five men in pit fights and was on the run from his handler because he had refused to fight a woman. This boy, Pantin, and the second slave, a grizzled little man with terrible scars on his back, were of Pandaras's bloodline. Whenever there was slack time the three sat together telling stories or singing long ballads in their own language, one dropping out as another took over in rounds that sometimes went on for hours.

None of the crew were allowed to cross the brass line set aft of the cargo well in the whitewood deck (scoured each day by coconut matting weighted by the cook and dragged back and forth by two others) without the permission of either Captain Lorquital or her daughter, Aguilar. The cargo well was covered with a tarpaulin cover as tight as a drum head, and loaded with replacement parts for artillery pieces. Each part was sprayed with polymer foam; they were stacked under the tarpaulin like so many huge, soft eggs. By the forecastle bulwark were pens where hens and guineafowl strutted and a single shoat rooted in a litter of straw, and on the triangular bit of decking that roofed the forecastle, under the lines which tethered the leading point of the sail to the long bowsprit, was a light cannon under a tarpaulin shroud.

It was here that Tamora chose to perch the second day, watching the city shore move past hour upon hour. She was in a kind of sulk, and even Aguilar, a jolly unselfconscious woman who claimed to have at least three men lusting after her in every city along the Great River, could not cajole more than three or four words from her at any one time.

Yama worried about Tamora's mood, but bided his time. He reflected that he still did not know her well, and knew even less about her bloodline. Perhaps she was still recovering from their adventures, and in particular from her long incarceration in the Department of Indigenous Affairs, of which she would not speak. Worse had happened to her, Yama suspected, than the shaving of her head. And no doubt she was worried, and perhaps angry, that Eliphas had usurped her position as Yama's advisor, that he and not she had found clues to Yama's origin. It did not occur to him that there was a simpler answer, and that it lay within himself.

———

At the end of the second day, the *Weazel* finally passed beyond the downriver edge of the city. Red sandstone cliffs, fretted with the square mouths of old tombs, stood above mudbanks and shoals exposed by the river's retreat. The only signs of habitation were the occasional fishing hamlets stranded beyond new fields made where the river had once flowed.

Early the next morning, the wind died and the *Weazel's* triangular mainsail flapped idly. The ship drifted on the slow river current. The sun beat down from the deep indigo sky; the distant cliffs glowed through a haze of heat like a bar of molten iron; the big ships scattered across the gleaming sweep of the river did not change position from hour to hour.

At last, Captain Lorquital had the sail hauled down. Drag anchors were thrown over the sides. The ship's crew took turns to swim and even Captain Lorquital went overboard, dressed in a white shift as big as a tent, hauling herself down the ladder at the stern a step at a time. Pandaras spouted water like a grampus, splashing with his two friends; Eliphas swam with a dignified breaststroke, keeping his white-haired head above the water at all times.

Tamora sat cross-legged on the forecastle decking, studiously not looking at the frolics in the water around the ship.

Yama swam a long way out. He found a patch of oarweed and wound himself in cool, slippery fronds, a trick he had learned as a child; the gas-filled bladders of the oarweed would keep him afloat without any effort. The ship was a small black shape printed on the burning water. He could cover it with his thumb.

Soon, he would pass his childhood home, and he idly thought that he could jump ship then, and return to the peel-house and take up his life once more. He could marry Derev. It would be a metic marriage, but they would be happy. He would not mind if she took a concubine of her own bloodline. He would raise the children as if they were his own.

But this was no more than a pretty fantasy. He could not go home again. He could not pretend that things had not changed. That he had not changed, in ways that frightened and amazed him.

He could feel the tug of the feral machine far beyond the end of the world. And even as he floated on his back amidst the oarweed, machines gathered beneath him. Through a fathom of clear deep water he could see things with dull silvery carapaces and long articulated tails moving over each other on the red sand of the riverbed. He ducked his head underwater to study this aimless congregation, then floated on his back and watched the distant ship, and thought again of Derev and everything else he had left behind in Aeolis, and at last swam slowly back to the ship.

———

Tamora did not turn her head when Yama came up the ladder behind her. The whitewood of the forecastle deck was hot under his bare feet; water dripping from his body darkened it for only a few moments before drying.

After a while, Tamora said, "I went up to the crow's nest. There's a little smudge on the horizon. As if something very big has been set on fire. I've been wondering what it could be."

Yama remembered the ship Lud and Lob had fired as a diversion on the night he had been kidnapped by Dr. Dismas. He said, "Perhaps it is a galliot or a carrack, attacked by pirates."

"The war goes worse than I knew if there are raiding parties this far upriver."

"There have always been pirates. They live amongst the floating islands in the midstream."

Tamora shook her head. She said, "The pirates have all gone down-river to the war. There are richer and easier pickings there."

Yama reached out toward her scarred, naked scalp, but halted just short of touching it.

Tamora said, "I didn't believe you. I didn't want to believe."

Yama understood. "I am no different, Tamora. I still want nothing more than I did when I first met you. Once I have found my people I want to join the war and fight as best I can."

"As best you can!" She turned and looked up at him. "I thought you were a monster. They told me that, in my cell. They told me that I might be pregnant by you, and be carrying your spawn. They examined me—"

"Tamora. I did not know. I am sorry."

"No! *I* am sorry. I was weak. I allowed the fuckers to get inside my head. It wasn't you that put a monster inside me, but them. It's been whispering inside my skull ever since. I always knew what you were, see, but I wouldn't admit it. That's why those fuckers could get inside me. I won't let it happen again."

With a sudden, violent heave, she twisted around and threw herself full length on the decking. She moved so quickly that Yama did not have time to react. She kissed his feet and looked up and said, "I did not believe in you. But I do now. I know that you are capable of miracles. I will serve you with all my life if you will let me."

Yama helped her up, feeling a mixture of embarrassment and confusion and fright. He said, "We will fight side by side, as we said we would."

Tamora finally met his gaze. She said, "Isn't that what I said? But in what cause?"

"Against the heretics, of course."

But he said it so quickly that both of them knew that it was said out of habit, not belief.

Tamora saved him. "Well, yes," she said. "There's always that."

16

Of Miracles

ELIPHAS SAID, "I studied long on this when I was much younger. I came to the conclusion then—and I have found no reason to change my mind—that there are three classes of miracles."

The old man was sitting with Yama and Captain Lorquital on the quarterdeck, in the shadow of the booming sail. It was the morning of the third day of the voyage. The wind had picked up in the night, blowing strongly from the upriver quarter of the farside shore. Water rushed by the hull and the river sparkled out to its distant horizon, salted with millions of whitecaps. There was a lightning storm fifty leagues to starboard. Whips of light flickered under massed purple clouds, and now and again the sound of thunder rolled faintly across the face of the waters.

Eliphas ticked off categories of miracle on his long thin fingers. He said, "There are those events in which something happens that is contrary to nature, such as the sun failing to reverse its course in the sky at noon, but instead continuing on to the farside. There are those events which may occur in Nature, but never in that particular order, such as a dead man returning to life, or the Eye of the Preservers rising at the same time as the Galaxy. And then there are those events which may occur naturally, but which in the case of a miracle do so without natural causation, such as this good ship dashing along with no wind behind her and no current beneath her. So we see that most miracles are quite natural processes, but without the usual causes or order."

Ixchel Lorquital said, "Myself, I don't believe in supernatural happenings. You'll hear talk ashore that sailors are superstitious. But what it is, we're careful because we can't take anything for granted on the river. It seems to me that miracles happen because people are hoping they'll happen. It's mostly religious people who claim to have seen a miracle, as is only natural. They're the ones who've the most to gain from it, even if they don't think that way. What I'd say is, if someone says they saw something contrary to nature, then it's more likely that they are mistaken."

Eliphas nodded. "All you say is true, sister. The most difficult thing about miracles is not trying to explain them away, but trying to prove that something *is* a miracle, and not simply a manifestation of natural law or of ancient technology, or a trick cunningly set up, or an illusion dependent upon a willing suspension of belief on the part of the audience. In ancient times there were theaters of the mind in which participants could explore fantastic landscapes where miracles occurred as a matter of course, much as puppets in a street theater may be made to fly, or breathe fire, or rise from the dead. But of course those were not miracles, but illusions."

"Then you might say that I only dreamed that the caryatid came to life," Yama said, "or that I talked with the woman in the shrine of the Temple of the Black Well in a dream. Unfortunately, while it might be a comforting thought, I do not believe it to be true. The truth is that there are things in the world which are long forgotten, and somehow I am capable of waking them. The question is not how these things happened, but why they happened to me. If I knew the answer to that, I would be a happy man."

Ixchel Lorquital said, "Before my husband died, before the war, we traveled up and down the Great River at least once a year. I reckon to have seen every bloodline on Confluence, including most of the indigenous tribes that haunt the Rim Mountains and the jungles and marshes down by the midpoint of the world. But I'm sorry to say that I have never seen anyone like you, young man."

Yama smiled and said, "I am comforted to think that I do not have to spend my time searching, for you have already done it for me."

"Not even as sturdy a vessel as the *Weazel* could sail beyond the end of the river," Eliphas said, "and that is where Yama's bloodline may live now."

"No one goes there," Ixchel Lorquital said, "except for desperate prospectors and a few crazy pillar saints."

Eliphas nodded. "Precisely, sister. What better place, then, to hide?"

Ixchel Lorquital laughed and clapped her hands. They were fleshy, with loose webs of skin linking the fingers, and they made a loud slapping sound. She said, "A gentleman as worldly as you could charm the fish from the water by persuading them that the air was safe to breathe. Fine words are wasted on an old woman like me. My daughter now, she's a connoisseur of compliments. It would cheer her up to hear some of that shiny talk of yours."

Eliphas bowed.

"I have to say that a pale skin like yours," Ixchel Lorquital told Yama, "is not suited to the desert lands beyond the midpoint."

Eliphas said, "The memoir found by my esteemed friend Kun Norbu, the chief of clerks of the Department of Apothecaries and Chirurgeons, suggests that they live in caverns beneath the surface of the deserts."

Yama smiled. "My father is always digging to find the past. What better place to find the first people of the world than in an underground city?"

"Just so, brother, just so. Many years ago, when I was still a young man—if such a thing can be imagined—my friend Kun Norbu and I found a passage below a ruined cliff temple. It led far underground, to a chamber containing many vast machines which were no longer functioning, and the chamber stretched so far into the darkness that after two days we scrupled to explore no further. But perhaps we should have continued. I have often dreamed of it since, and sometimes in these dreams I have glimpsed such wonders that on waking I wondered if I had gone mad."

Eliphas's silver eyes held faint concentric patterns that widened and closed like irises. There was a fine grain, as of well-cured leather, to his smooth black skin. His fingers: bunches of deftly articulated twigs. The neat whorls of flesh around the naked tympani of his ears.

Yama realized that he really knew very little of this old man, who had insisted on following him for no other reason, it seemed, than to rekindle the adventurous spirit of his long-lost youth. Last night, he had discovered Eliphas crouched in the glory hole below deck, muttering to a small plastic rectangle, some kind of charm or fetish. What prayers, to what entity? Surely not to the Preservers. Tamora was right, Yama thought. He should not trust people so readily.

Eliphas returned Yama's gaze. He smiled. "As for why you are able to do what you have done, brother, that's quite another question. We must ask whether miracles are caused because the Preservers or their agents actively interfere in the world, or whether, because the Preservers created the world, miracles occur simply as part of a natural chain of causation that was ordained from the beginning."

Ixchel Lorquital took the stem of her unlit pipe from her mouth, leaned back in her sling chair, and spat over the rail toward the water rushing past below. She wiped her mouth on the back of her web-fingered hand and said, "Everyone knows that the Preservers have turned away from the world. It has carried on without them, for better or worse, so it never did need them to run everything. The same with everything else, I reckon. The stars were there before the Preservers came along—they just moved them into more pleasing patterns."

"Just so," Eliphas said. "But there are some who believe that the Preservers, when they withdrew from the Universe, did so in order to be able to extend themselves from first cause to last end. And so, by leaving us, the Preservers have in fact spread themselves throughout creation. They watch over us still, but in a subtler fashion than by manifesting their will through the avatars of the shrines."

"There were riots when the last of the avatars were silenced by the heretics," Ixchel Lorquital said. "Many temples were burned down. Those were black years."

Eliphas said, "In truth, the avatars which survived the Age of Insurrection were so few, and most were so confused, that they were merely a last resort for people searching for answers to unanswerable questions. They were no longer the fount of all wisdom, and the guides of the governance of the world, as they were in the Golden Age before the Insurrectionists. Of course, those subroutines which acted as librarians were most useful. I still miss them. The written records are almost as extensive as those of the shrines, but less easy to search."

"The avatars were the eyes and mouths of the Preservers," Ixchel Lorquital said. "That was what I was taught as a pup, and I always did think it was put into our heads so we'd do as we were told, believing the Preservers were always looking over our shoulders in place of our parents."

"Miracles need witnesses," Eliphas said, returning to his original theme. "Perhaps the Preservers raise fish from the dead in the deeps of the river, or juggle rocks in scaled caverns in the keel of the world, but to what point? Miracles teach us something about the nature of the world and our own faith, by contradicting our understanding of that nature and by revealing some truth about the minds of the Preservers. Of course, our own minds may be too small to contain that truth."

Ixchel Lorquital closed her translucent inner eyelids, as if to help her look into her own mind. She said, "To my reckoning, the only miracles are where there's such an unlikely chain of circumstance that you have to believe something interfered to make it come out like that.

Anyone that kind of thing happened to would have to change their way of thinking about their place in the world."

"The world is large," Eliphas said, "and the Universe is far larger, and far older. If anything is possible, no matter how unlikely, then there is no reason why it should not have happened somewhere."

Ixchel Lorquital said stubbornly, "If something unlikely happens to you, especially if it happens to save your life, you'll stop and think hard about why it was you and not some other culler."

Yama said, "I am not so immodest as to believe that what I have been allowed to do—if I understand Eliphas right—is simply to shock me into changing my mind, or to teach me some lesson. Yet I do not want to believe that I am an agent who is being used by something I do not understand. It would mean that everything I choose to do is not by my own will, but by that of another. Must I believe that everything I do is willed elsewhere?"

What had happened, when the crowd had rioted? What had he said? What had he done? He could not remember, and did not dare ask because it would reveal his weakness and his shame.

"That is the question every self-aware person must ask themselves," Eliphas said. "One thing we know for certain is that the Preservers took ten thousand different kinds of animals from ten thousand different worlds and shaped them into their own image and raised them to intelligence. And yet that was not enough, of course. Each bloodline still must find its own way to grow and change, and that is the one kind of miracle on which we can agree.

"Think of a single man in a city of an unchanged bloodline. He may be a poet or a painter, a praise-singer or a priest, but we will say he is a poet. Like his father, and his father before him, he has followed his calling without thought. He has written thousands of lines, but any of them could have been written by any other poet of his bloodline, living or dead. Like all the unchanged, he has less sense of his own self than he has of the community of like-minded brothers and sisters of which he is but a single element. If he was taken from this community he would soon die, much as a single bee would die if it strayed too far from its hive. Like a hive, the communities of the unchanged are sustained not by the meshing of individual desires, but by blindly followed habits and customs.

"On this one night, alone in his room amidst thousands of others who are so very much like himself, our poet has a thought which has never before been thought by any of his bloodline. He pursues this thought through the thickets of his mind, and by its light he slowly begins to define what he is, and what he is not. Think of a sea of lamps which are all alike, all burning with the same dim flame. Now think of a single lamp suddenly brightening, suddenly shining so brightly that it outshines all others. Our poet writes his thought down in the form of a poem, and it is published and read because all poems are published and read without thought or criticism. That is the custom of the city, and no one has ever questioned it until now. But the thought the poem contains lodges in the minds of our poet's fellows and blossoms there as a spark lodges in a field of dry grass and blossoms into a field of fire. Soon there are a hundred competing thoughts, a thousand, a million! The city is at war with itself as its inhabitants struggle to define their own selves. Factions fight and clash in its streets. Those as yet unchanged, innocent and incapable of understanding the change, are winnowed. The survivors leave the battlefield, perhaps to found a new city, perhaps to scatter themselves along the length of the Great River.

"We know the change is caused by unseen machines that swarm in every drop of water, every grain of soil, every puff of wind. These tiny machines bloom in the brains of the changed. They increase the mind's complexity while retaining its essence, as a city built over the site of a fishing hamlet may retain the old street plan in the arrangement of its main avenues. The machines are in the brains of the unchanged bloodlines, too, but they are quiescent, sleeping. It is not the process that is the mystery, but the cause. The thought that comes in the night, that wakes the machines and sets fire to a bloodline until it is burned out or changed. There is our miracle."

It was Yama's miracle, although he (or the woman in the shrine, working through him) had not forced the change upon one of the ordinary unchanged bloodlines, but upon one of the indigenous races, which, it was said, could never change. Were some miracles stronger and stranger than others? Was there a hierarchy of miracles, or were all miracles equally unlikely, and therefore equally wondrous? Yama thought about this for a long time, while Eliphas and Ixchel Lorquital talked of other things.

17

The City of the Dead

TAMORA'S KEEN EYES had already glimpsed the first intimation of smoke far downriver, but it was not until the beginning of the afternoon watch of the following day that one of the sailors, perched on a ratline high above the deck, sang out that there was a fire to port, a fire on the shore. Everyone crowded to the rail. A little dark cloud hung at the edge of the land, a smudge that was, Pandaras said, no bigger than a baby's claw. Captain Lorquital examined it through her spectacles before declaring that it was trouble they would do best to steer clear of.

"There are fast currents we can use further out, and there's a floating harbor we'd have had to cut around in any case."

Yama had been staring at the shore with growing realization. Suddenly anxious, he asked to borrow the Captain's spectacles. He squinted through one of the lenses and the distant shore leapt forward, horribly familiar. For two days they had been sailing past barren hills populated with the ruined houses of the dead, but only now did he see that they were within sight of the heart of the City of the Dead.

There was the wide valley of the Breas, with its quilt of fields and channels; there was the skull-swell of the bluff, and the peel-house perched atop it like a coronet; the dusty hills with their necklaces of white tombs and stands of dark green cedars and black cypresses saddling away into the far distance, where the snowy peaks of the foothills of the Rim Mountains made a hazy line against the blue sky. And there was the shallow bay, with the long stone finger of the new quay running across the mudflats to the water's edge, and then the old waterfront of Aeolis.

And Aeolis was burning.

A triple-decked warship stood at the wide mouth of the bay, raking the little city with green and red needles of light that splashed molten stone where they struck. The bombardment seemed pointless, for every stone building was already smashed flat, and everything that could burn was afire. Black reefs of smoke rolled up, feeding the pall which hung above the city like a crow's wing. Dr. Dismas's tower was reduced to a melted stub; light raked the ancient ruins beyond it and stabbed into the flooded paeonin fields, sending up boiling gouts of mud and clouds of steam. Only the temple still stood, its white façade smudged by smoke, the tall lycophytes lining the long avenue which led to it withered or aflame.

Yama cried out, and Pandaras said, "What is it, master?"

Yama shook his head, heartsick. He climbed up to the quarterdeck, where Captain Lorquital and her daughter were already plotting a new course at the chart table, and heard himself asking them to turn the *Weazel* toward the shore, not away from it.

"It is my home," he said. "Most of the people I hold dear live there. My family. My friends."

He was thinking of Derev. She was brave and clever and resourceful. She would have found a way of surviving. She would have escaped to the hills above the city. She knew the way to Beatrice and Osric's remote tower. Or perhaps the Aedile had taken her in, and her family. He would have tried to protect all of the citizens. Or perhaps she was with their friend Ananda, the sizar of the priest of Aeolis. The temple still stood, after all.

Ixchel Lorquital looked hard at Yama and said, "Sit down for a moment."

Yama found he was trembling. He said, "I must go ashore."

"It's too dangerous," Aguilar said. "I'll fight if I must, but not against a warship. She could burn us to the waterline with one shot."

Tamora had followed Yama. She stood at his shoulder and said, "Do as he asks."

Captain Lorquital looked at her, looked at Yama. "I must do what's best for the ship. That's a military action, and I won't put my ship and my crew in the middle of it."

Eliphas was sitting in his customary place by the Captain's sling chair. He said, "If that is your home, brother, don't you think your enemies know that? They know you're traveling downriver, and perhaps hope to lure you ashore."

Yama's throat was parched. He said, "Lend me the dory. I will put ashore myself. You can anchor at the old floating harbor, or there are shoals and banyan islands downstream where you could hide a flotilla of ships. I will rejoin you within a day. If I do not, sail on without me."

Aguilar said, "And lose the dory?"

"Then set me ashore here and now. I will meet you on the other side of the city in three days."

Eliphas said, "You should not put yourself in danger, brother."

Captain Lorquital said, "I'd not be happy to lose a passenger, either."

"I'll go with him," Tamora said.

Pandaras jumped on to the rail behind her. He drew his poniard and flourished it above his head. "So will I. He'll need his squire."

Aguilar said, "If these three want to go over the side, let them do it now, before we're in range of the big girl's cannon."

Captain Lorquital considered, sucking at her silver lip-plug, then told her daughter, "I won't have three passengers putting themselves in danger, but clearly they'll jump over the side if they have no other option. I'll keep to this course. If there's no trouble, perhaps they can go ashore."

Aguilar stared at Yama and said, "There'll be no good to be had from this."

Captain Lorquital said, "Have a little charity, daughter. The first sign of trouble, and we run for it."

Tamora said, "You must trust him, Captain. He will protect you."

Yama bowed his head, hoping that the vessel of Tamora's faith would not be wrecked on the reef of his own self-doubt.

Aguilar snorted. "Then pray he can whistle up some wind. We'll need it."

———————

Yama and Tamora put out from the *Weazel* in the dory a little way upriver of the floating docks. Pandaras had been persuaded to remain behind to ensure that Captain Lorquital kept to the agreed rendezvous at midnight. He waved from the rail of the poop deck as, in the last light of the sun, the little ship heeled around and headed out toward the center of the river.

Tamora took up her oar and said, "I reckon that black-skinned silver-eyed bookworm is right. It is almost certainly a trap."

Yama said helplessly, "I know. This is the doing of the Department of Indigenous Affairs. The peel-house still stands, and it is theirs."

"And we are doing what they want by walking into it. Grah. At least we will take them by surprise."

If Derev had taken refuge in the peel-house, then she was surely a prisoner, and surely had been put to the question by Prefect Corin. That was worse than thinking that she might be dead. Yama remembered the way she had fluttered down from her perch in the ruins outside Aeolis, on the night they had met the anchorite. So light and graceful, her long white hair floating about her lovely, fine-boned face.

He took up his own oar. Together they began to row toward the floating docks. After a while, he said, "Perhaps they are afraid, Tamora. Do you think they could be afraid of me?"

"The Captain and her daughter are afraid of you, and so are the crew. And Eliphas most of all. I've been watching him. He has a knife, a pretty little stiletto, and sleeps with his hand on it."

"I trust him more than he trusts himself," Yama said, "but less than I trust you."

"You should not trust him at all. He wants something from you."

As they rowed, Yama kept turning to stare with a kind of sick eagerness at the burning city, but he could see little more than he had from the deck of the *Weazel*. There was too much smoke, and clouds of steam kept spurting up where beams raked the waterfront, boiling the water of the shallow bay and the mudflats where once he had hunted crabs and dug for treasure everyone had believed to be buried there, finding nothing but the ancient coins. He closed his hand on the coin he had found in the cell high in the Palace of the Memory of the People, no different to the ones he had dug up as a child, when he had been surrounded by treasure, had he but realized it.

They passed the long maze of pilings and platforms and cranes of the floating harbor. No one answered Yama's hail, and the long sheds of the carpenters' workshops had a forlorn, deserted air. A door banged and banged in the wind; nothing else stirred.

The setting sun was dimmed and greatly swollen, a louring red eye that glared through a shroud of smoke and steam. The air scraped the back of Yama's throat with an acrid, metallic taste. Above the cliffs of the bluff, the towers of the peel-house, rising through the trees of its garden, caught the last rays of the sun and glowed with red light; the river held a bloody cast that had Tamora grumbling about omens. Flecks of black soot rained all around, smudging their skin and clothes. Floating debris began to knock against the dory's hull. Broken bits of furniture, books, a raft of bottles, half-burned rags. Bales of last year's hay wrapped in black plastic, taut as drumheads, went floating by, carried out of the bay by the ebb tide. No bodies, but Tamora said that meant little—the dead did not usually rise to the surface until distended by the gases of decomposition.

The dory slipped at a shallow angle toward the shore upriver of the bluff. The hum and sizzle of the light cannon of the warship carried clearly across the water. There was the snapping of heat-stressed stone, the explosive hiss of water suddenly shot to steam, the crackle of innumerable small fires.

As he rowed, Yama wondered again about Derev, and wondered if the Aedile had resisted the razing of Aeolis and was now a prisoner in his own peel-house, wondered what had happened to all the citizens of Aeolis, and again thought of Derev. He felt a mixture of shame and fear and anger and helplessness. Again and again, the memory of Prefect Corin's bland face tormented him.

The quiet of the shore was shocked by the clatter of wings as a flock of wading birds took flight from the dory's approach, dipping as one as they turned across the water. Yama and Tamora splashed into thigh-deep water and dragged the dory up the shallow, muddy beach.

"I wish you'd brought your rapier," she grumbled. "I said I'd look after you, but you'll make it very difficult if you won't begin to think of defending yourself."

"This is my home, Tamora. I would not return to it armed for war."

"If your enemy has taken it, then it is no longer your home."

"We shall see," Yama said, but to appease her he broke a branch from a young pine tree that the river had cast up on this muddy strand. The branch had been stripped of bark and smoothed by the rub of the water, but it had not yet begun to rot and it made a sturdy staff half again his height.

The sun had set behind the Rim Mountains but the Eye of the Preservers had not yet risen. What light there was came from the fires burning beyond the bluff. The flashes of cannon shot were as inconstant as heat lightning. All of the lights of the peel-house were ablaze, and the sight gave Yama little hope. Clearly, whoever commanded the peel-house did not expect an attack.

Tamora could see better than Yama in the near dark, and she led the way along an embankment above paeonin fields carved from river-bottom land. The old shoreline was marked by a line of ancient date palms. As a child, Yama had spent long summer afternoons in their shade while Zakiel had lectured him and Telmon on natural history. Not far from here, he had met with Derev for the last time before he had left for Ys with Prefect Corin. Now, as he and Tamora walked along the dusty embankment toward the palms, a faint crackling sounded ahead of them in the near dark. Tamora grasped Yama's arm and bent her head and whispered that she would go ahead and investigate.

"There are no machines," Yama whispered back. "Surely they would have machines."

Light flared amongst the graceful arcs of the date palms. With a clatter of metal on metal, a pentad of spidery, man-sized creatures skittered toward them, followed by armed soldiers.

———

"We will kill her," the leader of the patrol, a young, nervous lieutenant, told the mage. "She is no one important. Only a dirty little cateran. Not even her mother will miss her."

Tamora hissed, and tried to spit at the lieutenant. But the machine held her too tightly; she could not even turn her head.

"My spiders will hold her as easily alive as dead," the mage said, "and she might tell us something useful. I will be glad to put her to the revolutionary. Her kind are strong-willed. It would be a fine demonstration of its powers."

Yama and Tamora were each bound tightly and painfully by the whiplike metal tentacles of a spidery machine. Their feet did not quite touch the ground. One of the soldiers had taken Tamora's saber; when it had first pounced upon him, Yama had broken his staff against the machine which now held him tight.

"If you kill her," Yama said, "then you must kill me too, for I swear I will hunt you down."

The lieutenant said, "You are in no position to tell me what to do, fellow." He laughed and looked around, and his soldiers laughed too. He was a swarthy fellow in plastic armor over a leather kirtle. An energy pistol was tucked into the bandolier that crossed his transparent breastplate.

Yama waited until they were quiet, until they were looking at him again, wondering how he would reply. He let the moment stretch before he said, "I am wanted by Prefect Corin because I am important to him. He wants me to work with him, for the good of the Department. If you kill my friend that is what I will do. I will become a loyal soldier, and one day I will find you and kill you."

The lieutenant spat and ground the oyster of phlegm into the dust with the toe of his boot. "Oh, I will not kill her," he said. "There are worse things than death. Prefect Corin will probably give her to Nergal here. Then you will wish that you had allowed me to give her a clean death. A soldier's death. Nergal's machines are cruel, and these are the least of them."

The remaining spiders were grouped behind the soldiers, holding up electric lamps which had drawn hundreds of moths from the darkness beyond. They were crude affairs, racks of aluminum tubing, electric motors and sensors raised high on three pairs of jointed legs. A decad of long, continually questing tentacles, made of jointed rings of metal and tipped with clawlike manipulators, sprouted between the front pair of legs.

The tentacles of the spider which held Yama were wrapped tightly around his arms and legs. They pressed painfully into his skin and tingled with a faint electrical charge. He had no sense of these machines. They were controlled by the mage, Nergal, a man with black skin that had a faint scaly iridescence in the distilled glare of the electric lamps, and large round eyes as dead as stones. He wore a long robe of metallic mesh, a tight-fitting copper skullcap. Close-fitting white plastic gloves sleeved his arms to the elbows.

"They are not susceptible to your power," Nergal told Yama. He made shapes with his gloved left hand, and the machine which held Yama swung to the right, then centered itself again. Yama could feel the shapes made by the mage in his head, and allowed himself a faint hope.

Nergal said, "These are a new class of machine, the first new machines to be built since the world was created. They dance for me and no one else."

"They have no minds," Yama said, "so how can they be truly useful?"

"They caught you, Yamamanama, and they hold you now. That is useful enough to begin with. They have as much logic as any insect. They do not need to think. Thinking is a luxury, as any laborer well knows."

"Enough talk," the lieutenant said. "We will get this prize back to the peel-house. I have little liking for this bone orchard."

"Quite right," Yama said. "The dead can be dangerous."

"Hold your yap, or I will have you gagged," the lieutenant said. "You will be amongst the dead soon enough, and you can try and scare me then." When he laughed again the soldiers around him did not join in. He glared at them and said sharply, "Fall in. There is nothing here that we cannot deal with."

Marshalled by the shapes Nergal made in the air with his gloves, the machines which held Yama and Tamora walked amidst their fellows with a whine of servo motors and a clanking of hydraulic joints. The soldiers ambled on either side, rifles held at port.

"Make these things go faster," the lieutenant said. "These two might have friends."

"I thought you had driven them out," Nergal said. "Most fled down-river."

"We cannot guarantee safety outside our perimeter," the lieutenant said. "Have these things pick up speed."

"Once we reach the paved road they will be able to go faster. The question of balance on rough terrain is very complex, and requires much processing power."

"Any trouble, and we leave the machines behind," the lieutenant said.

"As you have told me repeatedly. I will reply as before. Any trouble, and my machines will deal with it. Their processors and servos are battle-hardened, and they have infrared sights on guns which fire at the rate of a thousand slugs a minute. Soon, all our armies will be composed of these machines, lieutenant. Imagine it! Combined with Yamaman-ama's powers, we will drive the heretics over the end of the river."

The lieutenant said, "That is not to be spoken of in front of the men."

Yama said, "I am pleased to meet one of those who were testing me when I was briefly a guest in the Palace of the Memory of the People. I owe you much, Nergal."

The patrol was approaching one of the wide, white thoroughfares of the City of the Dead. Many merchants had been buried here. Their crowded tombs glimmered in the near darkness. They were marked by ornate pyramids, steles and statues; even in death, the merchants had competed with their rivals.

"You will be our guest again," Nergal said.

"He'll kill you all long before then," Tamora said. "You should let him go now."

"I think not," Nergal said. "There is much to discover. There is a peculiarity of your brain, Yamamanama, or perhaps of your nervous system, which allows you to interface with the old machines. We will find it, even if we have to open up your skull and slice you up bit by bit. But I hope that will not be necessary. Much easier if you cooperate. Much easier if you tell us how it is done."

"I do not know if I can tell you," Yama said, "but I am sure that I can show you."

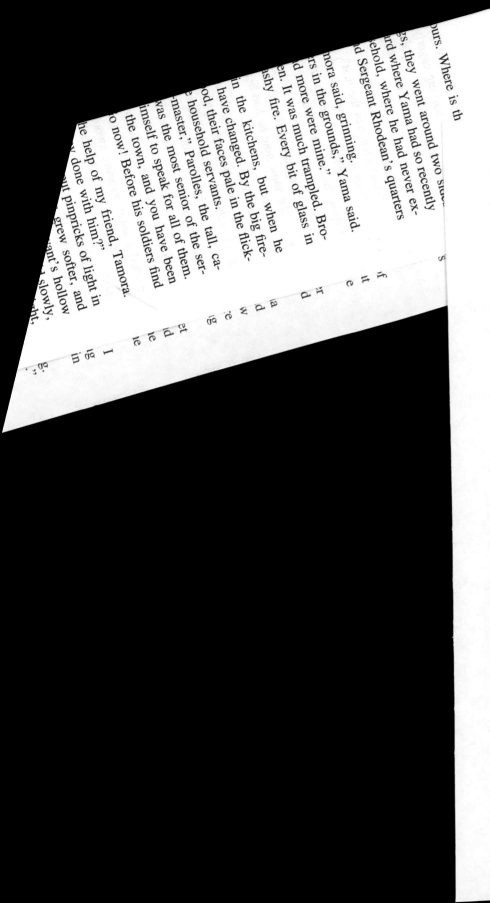

"We will find out how to control the machines usurped by the heretics," Nergal said. "We will control all machines and so control the world. As a beginning, at least."

They were amongst the first of the tombs, now. The soldiers moved out on either flank and the machines picked up their pace as they stepped on to the paved road, shining their lamps this way and that. The tombs here were as big as houses, but crudely made. Further along, amongst the older, finer tombs, Yama felt a congregation waking and turning toward him. He told them what to do.

And the night came alive with the light of the past.

The soldiers began firing in panic as the dead reached for them. Yama had delved into the roots of the aspects and changed them all. No longer men and women smiling, beckoning, eager to tell to anyone who listened the life stories of the dead they represented; instead, grim, withered faces and blazing eyes, or no eyes at all but black pits in fleshless skulls. Skin like leather shrunken on long bones, bony fingers clutching at faces. Mad laughter, screeches, a rumbling subsonic that Yama could feel through the struts of the machine which clasped him so tightly. A white mist fell like a curtain, filled with half-glimpsed nightmare shapes. The soldiers vanished into it; not even the muzzle-flashes of their rifles could be seen, although their dismayed shouts and the rattle of rifle shots echoed sharply.

Somewhere in the mist, the lieutenant shouted an order to cease firing, shouted that this was no more than a trick. But each soldier was lost to every other, blinded by glowing mist and surrounded by the throng of the dead. Nergal's machines halted in the middle of what seemed to be a foggy street where skeletons of draft animals drew carts piled with rotting bodies that stirred with a feeble half-life. Pale things with burning eyes peered from the narrow windows of the houses. Below Yama, who was still clasped tightly by the spider, the mage sank to his knees. His gloved hands flexed at his throat, tightening inexorably. He stared at Yama with wide eyes. His mouth gaped as he tried and failed to draw air.

Yama felt a terrible, gleeful triumph. He would not relent.

"I cannot control your machines," he shouted, "but I can control what you use to control them. You fool! You used old technology to control the new!"

Nergal did not hear him. Although still kneeling, he was dead, strangled by feedback. His head tipped forward until his brow struck the ground and his body relaxed and slumped sideways. The tentacles which held Yama lost their tension and he dropped to the groun{ the spiders collapsed in a clatter of metal.

━━━━━━

The soldiers were still shooting at ghosts when Yama and Tamora reached the old stair. Yama had woken every aspect in the City of the Dead. The low hills, crowded with tombs and monuments, were half-drowned in a lake of eldritch mist. Tamora carried a rifle taken from a soldier she had killed; she had not found the man who had taken her saber, and grumbled about the loss.

"I have already lost my own sword to the Department of Indigenous Affairs. It had a fine and bitter blade, but it cost me dear enough. I would not be here if I had not been in debt with Gorgo because of it. And now they have taken its replacement."

"I will find you another," Yama said. "There are many in the armory." He told her that the narrow stair they were climbing, its stone steps worn in the middle and sometimes missing, went all the way up the sheer side of the bluff. It was used by the kitchen staff of the peel-house. "There are certain herbs which grow only by graves. The dead impart a quality to the soil which they require. When I was much younger, I used to go with the youngest kitchen boy early every morning to pick them."

"You have had a strange childhood, Yama. Not many would think to use a graveyard as a kitchen garden."

"Fortunate for us that I know it so well. The soldiers are lost in the illusion spun by the tombs, but I brought us here by the quickest and straightest route."

"I'm glad Nergal is dead. Those things he made were evil."

The triumphant glee Yama had felt when he had murdered Nergal was now gone. It was as if something had woken in him and then returned to sleep. But it was done, and perhaps it was better that the mage was dead, or he would be another enemy pursuing Yama.

He said, "Surely Nergal's spiders were no more evil than your rifle, or a tiger snake. Like them, the spiders had no consciousness, and so no capacity to distinguish between good and evil. Only by consciously rejecting good can evil be done."

"That's what I meant. What he wanted to do with them was evil. So was what he wanted to do with you. Can you really bend every machine in the world to your will, Yama?"

"I hope it was merely one of Nergal's boasts. But I do not know."

"I have no liking for dogs. Even y
place?"

Accompanied by a tide of watchdo
of the peel-house and crossed the courty
said farewell to the Aedile and the hou
pected to step again. The guardhouse a
were dark.

"They'll be out looking for us," Ta
"The watchdogs killed all the soldi
"The two at the gate were yours; a dec
They went through the kitchen gard
ken furniture was scattered around an
the forcing houses had been smashed.
Yama expected more destruction
kicked open the door nothing seemed to
place, people pushed back chairs and st
ering light of rush lamps. They were th
"You are in danger, young ma-ma
daverous master of the wine, said. He
vants who remained, and took it upon h
"You have seen the ca-ca-candle lit in
drawn to it as he said you would. Go! C
you."

"I have already found them, with
How is my father, Parolles? What h
The flame of the stout cand
the center of his slitted i
suddenly a chain of
cheeks and beg
"Your fath
with

at least. And the merchant's daughter, Derev? Did her family seek safety here?"

"I have not seen her," Bertram said. "I am sorry, young master."

"They treated your father grievously, young ma-ma-master," Parolles said. "Set the traitor in his place, and put him to question using monstrous ma-ma-machines when he stood up to them over the matter of the burning of the town."

"I have had some revenge," Yama said. "The mage is dead."

"But the viper still lives. When he saw the lights in the City of the Dead, he grew mighty sc-sc-scared, and ordered us locked up here."

"When you burst in, young master," Bertram said, "we thought our time had come."

"I will talk with this viper," Yama said grimly.

"We will come with you, young ma-ma-master. We have no weapons beyond some kitchen tools, but we will do all we can. These are terrible times. The Department fights against itself."

"I hope it will end soon," Yama said. "Now, who is with me?"

They all were.

There were two soldiers in the minstrels' gallery of the Great Hall, where Yama had once spied on his father and Dr. Dismas, but only one got off a shot before Tamora raked them with rifle fire. One man fell back; the other tumbled over the railing and landed on the long, polished table with a heavy, wet sound, kicked once, and was still.

"The banners are gone," Yama said, looking up at the high, vaulted ceiling. The hall looked larger and dustier without them.

"Burned," Parolles said. "A terrible burning they had. A bonfire of the vanities, the Prefect called it. He ma-ma-made your father watch. A more terrible punishment than the machines, I think."

Yama and Tamora led the pack of watchdogs and the servants through the Great Hall toward the tall double doors of the receiving chamber. Two more soldiers stood there. One fled; the other died cursing his comrade's cowardice. Yama and Tamora flung open the doors. The tall square room beyond was blazing with light, but empty. Although the four great tapestries were gone from the walls, the canopied chair on the central dais on which the Aedile had customarily sat while holding audience was still there.

Yama went around the dais and ducked through the little door and went up the narrow stair that led to the Aedile's private chambers. No need for subtlety; the alarm must have been raised by now, and the cheering of the servants and the clatter of the armor of the watchdogs against the curved stone walls made a tremendous racket. With Yama at their head, they burst into the corridor. Some of the servants were beating against the walls or stamping their feet, calling for the traitor to come out. If there had been any guards, they had fled. The door to the Aedile's chambers was locked, but Tamora shot off the mechanical lock and kicked the door open in a single smooth motion.

The room was hot and stuffy. It stank of sex and spilled wine and cigarette smoke, and was lit by hundreds of candles, stuck to every surface by shrouds of their own melted wax. Papers were strewn everywhere amongst a litter of empty bottles and bowls of untouched food. The brass alembic was overturned, its mechanism spilled across a carpet sodden with wine.

The man on the bed raised a pistol, holding it in both hands as he took aim at Yama. He was naked under the rumpled, filthy sheet, and so was the woman who clutched a bolster to her breasts—one of the whores from the town, her tall blue wig askew, her face caked with white makeup, black pigment smeared about her mouth like a bruise and more black pigment around her wide eyes.

"Do not think I will not use this," Torin said, and showed a mouthful of white, needle teeth. His humped back was pressed against the carved bedhead; his shaven head gleamed with sweat. "You came back, just as Corin said you would. And now you are mine. Dismiss the rabble and we will talk, boy."

"Do not li-li-listen to him, young ma-ma-master," Parolles said.

Bertram added, "He cannot kill us all."

"He will do nothing," Yama said. "He knows that the soldiers are scattered, and that he cannot call upon Prefect Corin. How long have you been in his employ, Torin?"

"He will burn you like the town, if he has to." The pistol wavered when Torin spoke, and he squinted down its short, stubby barrel and centered it on Yama's chest again. He was very drunk.

"Then you will burn too. It saddens me to see you like this, Torin. You were a good friend to my father."

"I was always a good servant to the Department. Your father was a traitor. He hid all he knew about you, even from Prefect Corin. But like the fool that he was, he wrote it all down. It is all here, somewhere. If he did not know what he had he is a fool. If he did, then he is the blackest traitor in our history."

"I will not be the Department's weapon," Yama said.

"Then you are as much a fool and a traitor as the Aedile. I should burn you where you stand."

Yama relaxed. He knew then that Torin could not kill him. He said,

"I will fight against the heretics like any other man. But I fear that Prefect Corin has other plans for me. He would use me to destroy the other departments. He would use me to take the world, if he could. Give me the pistol, Torin, and I will see that you leave here unharmed."

"You keep away! Keep away!" Torin pulled the naked woman in front of him and jammed the pistol at her head. "I will kill her and the rest of you! I will burn this fucking pile of stones to the ground!"

The woman got an elbow under Torin's narrow jaw with surprising force. His needle teeth clicked closed on his lower lip; he howled with pain and the pistol went off. Its searing red beam missed his face by a fingersbreadth, burned through the canopy of the bed and reflected from the ceiling. The canopy burst into flame and Tamora crossed the room in a bound and broke Torin's arm with a single blow.

———

Torin, his face badly burned by the near miss, refused to answer any of Yama's questions. Yama left him to the tender mercy of the other servants and went with Tamora to find Zakiel.

The tall, gaunt librarian was in the library. He had been shackled around his neck, and a heavy chain looped up to a sliding clip on an overhead rail. There was a new, raw brand on his cheek. He watched calmly, his black eyes inscrutable, as Tamora hacked without effect at the chain with her sword.

"It is tempered steel," he said. "Quenched in the blood of oxen, I believe. You will damage the edge of your weapon, domina."

"It's a piece of shit anyhow," Tamora said, but she tossed the sword onto Zakiel's neatly made cot, which stood as always beneath the racks of large, aluminum-covered ledgers, jumped up and swung from one of the studs which fastened the rail to the ceiling until it came away in a shower of plaster and dust. She slid the clip over the end of the rail and the free end of the chain dropped at Zakiel's long, bare feet.

The librarian wiped dust from the tops of the ledgers with the wide sleeve of his robe. He said, "It might have been better if you had left me chained, young master. Torin may have received the rough justice he deserved, but those he serves will soon return."

"You should come with us," Yama said.

"I will not, as you well know. The books are in my care, and I do not think that I can carry them all with me. And if I could, how would I keep them safe? I trust you still have the copy of the Puranas."

"I have always kept it beside me."

Zakiel picked up the heavy chain and draped it over one arm. "It will teach you much, in the right circumstances. I am pleased that you have returned, young master, but I fear that you have far to go."

"How much did my father know about me, Zakiel? How much did he hide from the Department?"

"And hide from you?" Zakiel smiled. "He has told you the circumstances of how you came to Aeolis. As for the rest, he should tell you, not I, for he knows it better. He has been taken across the river by Sergeant Rhodean and his merry crew of guards. The good Sergeant wanted me to go, too, but alas—"

Yama smiled. "You could not leave the books."

"Precisely. If I am a slave, it is not to the Department, but to my duty as Librarian of the peel-house. And that is as it should be, for I am merely honoring the oath I once broke when I was younger than you are now. When I was your age, I thought in my blind pride that I knew better than those whom I served, but now I know better. Age gives a certain perspective. It is like climbing a peak of the Rim Mountains. At last you run out of air, but how wonderful the view! These books are my life, young master, and I cannot leave them."

"Do you know what happened to the Amnan?"

"Many fled across the river. But Derev and her family left a day before the warship took anchor in the bay. Some said that they were spies, fleeing to safety, but I do not believe it."

Yama's heart turned over. He felt that he could float to the ceiling. He grinned and said, "She is safe."

He thought that he knew where she had gone. She would be with Beatrice and Ostic in the oldest part of the City of the Dead, in the foothills of the Rim Mountains.

Zakiel said, "Perhaps she will return. Perhaps you might have a message for her."

"Tell her that I go downriver, but that I will come back."

"Is that all? Well, I will tell her, when I see her."

"I will miss you, Zakiel."

"We have already said our goodbyes. Do not worry about me, or the books. Torin held many grievances against the peel-house, for he believed himself better than he was, but Prefect Corin's grievance is against you."

"We must go," Tamora said. "There is less than an hour to the rendezvous."

18

The Floating Forest

THEY WERE LATE for the rendezvous, but the *Weazel* was waiting
for them as promised, at the upriver end of the floating docks. Yama
and Tamora stood at the rail of the quarterdeck as the little ship angled
away from the burning town. The warship was still raking the shore
with needles of hot light. Although he had revenged his father's torture,
Yama felt a mixture of shame and anger and helplessness. He stood
straight, gripping the polished wooden rail so tightly his arms ached to
the elbows, and watched the sack of Aeolis with tears slipping down
his cheeks. He would be a witness, if nothing else. He would face this
destruction without flinching, and carry it with him forever.

The sailors nudged each other and whispered that he wept for his
home. They were only partly right. Yama did not know it, but he was
also weeping for the loss of his innocence.

The lookout cried a warning. Tamora pointed to the lights of a
picketboat that was coming around the point of the bay, heading out to
intercept the *Weazel*.

"He is coming," Yama said. "I knew that he would."

But he was still struck through and through by fear, and had to lean
against the rail because he was suddenly trembling so hard.

Captain Lorquital ordered the staysails unreefed. "We'll make speed
as best we can," she told Yama. "Those boys have oars, but as long as
the wind holds we can outrun them."

Tamora wanted to unshroud the cannon and break out the hand
weapons, but Captain Lorquital refused and Aguilar stood foursquare in
front of the armory chest. Yama put a hand on Tamora's arm and was

astonished to discover that she was trembling almost as violently as he was. Prefect Corin had put his mark on both of them.

"I'll hold by what we agreed," Captain Lorquital said, "and so will you. We've no fight to pick here, no matter what's right and what's wrong."

Silhouetted against the burning town, the picketboat came on across blood-red water, its single bank of oars striking to the beat of a drum. A white lantern shone at its masthead, signifying that it wished to parlay. For several minutes, it steadily closed the gap; then the *Weazel* caught the wind and the gap began to widen again.

Something shot from the side of the picketboat. It skipped over the water like a flung stone and rose high above the *Weazel* before Tamora could take aim with her captured rifle. It was a small machine, as flat as a plate and spinning rapidly. It moved to and fro in little jerks above the tip of the mast. As with the machine which had been sent against Yama in the Department of Indigenous Affairs, its mind was hidden by complex loops of self-engulfing logic that grabbed at his attention as he tried to cleave through them. It was like plunging into a briar patch full of snapping jaws and whirling blades. A ghastly light suddenly flooded from the machine, etching everyone's shadow at their feet, and a voice boomed out, ordering the *Weazel* to stand to or have her sail cut free.

Captain Lorquital cupped her hands and shouted across the widening gap of water to the picketboat. "Show your authority!"

The machine tipped, aiming its sharp spinning edge at the forestays; at the same moment, Yama untangled the last of its defenses and found its tiny linear mind. It flung itself sideways, falling a long way before striking the water and vanishing with scarcely a splash.

Captain Lorquital gave Yama a long and hard look, but said nothing.

"Well," Tamora said, "he'll know you're on board now."

"He knows that already," Yama said.

━━━━━━━━

It became a contest of skill between the *Weazel* and the picketboat. The warship turned her light cannon away from the burning town, but too late: it fired no more than two ranging shots before the *Weazel* passed beyond the downriver point of the bay (the paeonin mill had been leveled to a hummock of glassy slag) and the warship and the burning city were lost from sight.

Yama dredged his memory for a map of the complicated web of currents as the *Weazel* threaded the maze of inshore mud shoals and stands of banyans. A man at the bow dropped a weighted line and called the depth every few minutes, and Yama stood with Captain Lorquital and the helmsman through the night while the crew took turns to rest. Pandaras and Eliphas slept on their mats under the awning; Tamora paced the deck amidships or stood by the man at the bow, peering into the darkness ahead or sharpening the long narrow blade of the sword she had taken from the armory of the peel-house. Eliphas woke near dawn and came up onto the aft deck to ask how things stood.

"Well, we are still here," Ixchel Lorquital said. "If the wind stays fair we'll be here a while longer."

There were floating islands spread everywhere ahead of the ship, ten thousand green dots scattered across the shining sweep of the river. The ranges of cloud that towered above the farside horizon caught the early light of the sun. Their folds and peaks glowed white and purple and gold.

Eliphas leaned at the rail next to Yama, who was staring into the light of the rising sun, trying to make out the smoke of the burning city against the long line of the shore. The old man cleared his throat, spat accurately into the white water that purled along the ship's hull, and said, "You should rest, brother. In my small experience of adventure, sleep is a most valuable currency."

"Why did they do it, Eliphas?"

Eliphas's silver eyes shone with reflected light. His black skin gleamed as if oiled; scraps of light were caught in the tightly nested curls of his white hair. He said, "Because they wanted to lure you into a trap, and were desperate. Because they have confused their duty and the base desires of their own selves. Because they serve the Preservers in name only, and have turned themselves into a thing that would destroy the world to save it. They have lost their way, brother. They deserve to be destroyed."

"Yet no one stood against them in the Palace of the Memory of the People until I acted."

"Those that stand against the Department of Indigenous Affairs are destroyed or absorbed. As are those that do not, by and by. Indigenous Affairs has fed on the war, and the war has become its reason for existence. If it survives the insurrection against it and wins the war, then it will find another enemy, even if it is some part of its own self."

Yama remembered the story told to him by the headman of the village of the husbandmen, the story of the department known as the Head of the People, which had absorbed all others until at last it had nothing to fight against but its own self. Surely, he thought, the Preservers had not created the world so that it would repeat the same stories in a series of futile cycles, like a book read again and again by an uncomprehending idiot.

He said, "They want to force me to their will. Because of that, I can only see them as my enemy."

Eliphas said, "Brother, you should use your gift against them. The machine you destroyed is nothing. What you did to free us is nothing. You are capable of much more. You should not allow yourself to be enslaved for the sake of your conscience."

"Are you scared, Eliphas?"

"Of course. But there are great things to be discovered, if we survive this."

"I am not sure if I can be free if I use my . . . gift without knowing how I use it, or why I have been given it. I have done bad things before this, Eliphas, although I did not mean to. I fear that I might do them again."

Captain Lorquital had been standing at the stern rail, peering upriver through her spectacles; now she came over to Yama and Eliphas and said, "The picketboat is still following, but we have at least two leagues on it, and our lead will widen as long as the wind holds. But the warship is certain to follow us as well, and will be at least as fast as we are. How intent are these people on capturing you, Yama?"

"They will not stop."

"I thought not. I'll wake my daughter and we'll decide what to do. But I know that we can't run forever."

"Perhaps we can hide, or find some way of turning to the attack."

Captain Lorquital regarded Yama thoughtfully. "If it comes to a final fight, what would you do?"

"I do not know how, but I hope that I would be able to save the ship and everyone on it."

Captain Lorquital seemed satisfied by this answer, but after she had gone to wake Aguilar, Eliphas said, "I hope you will put your scruples aside, brother. You will never find your bloodline if you do not first destroy your enemy."

Yama thought that Eliphas was wrong. If he defined himself against his enemies, then he would be no better than they were. Yet there was a part of him that exulted in the idea of battle, a voracious cayman at the base of his brain given voice, he believed, by the woman in the shrine. Satisfied not by persuasion but by forceful coercion, not by courtship but by rape, a thing of uncontrolled appetite and lust that would destroy the world rather than die. He must control it. And then he thought, if I know that Derev is dead, if my father is dead or disgraced, which for him will be a living death, will I still be able to keep this resolve?

The free men of the crew broke fast with manioc porridge while the cook and the other slave scrubbed soot stains from the white deck with lye and holystones. Yama ate without appetite. Although he was very tired he felt that he could not rest, so Pandaras brought him the rifle and suggested he try some target practice. For an hour, Yama blipped slugs at bits of flotsam floating by, and then practiced cleaning and reassembling the rifle under Tamora's instruction, his fingers thick and clumsy with lack of sleep. At last, Pandaras got him to lie down, and he fell asleep at once, and woke with the sun riding at its highest point.

Pandaras brought a hunk of black bread and a bowl of curried lentils salted with flecks of coarse fish flesh. The boy squatted in front of his master in the shade of the awning and watched him eat with a tender anxiety. The triangular mainsail and the square staysails stood taut against the blue sky. There was a ragged green line to starboard: a banyan forest.

Yama said, "Where do we stand?"

"The warship is in sight, master. It will catch up with us in a day, the Captain says. It is a very big ship, but it has big motors and has spread all its sail, too."

Yama used the heel of the bread to scrape up the last of the lentils from his wooden bowl. He told Pandaras, "I cannot make a wish and save us."

"No one asks you to, master. We're making for the forest. We might lose them there, the Captain says. She and Aguilar talked it over while you slept. Tamora is pleased. She wants a fight."

"I am sorry to have brought you on such a futile adventure, Pandaras."

Pandaras struck an attitude and said, "Master, I was a pot boy when I found you. Now I am squire to a hero."

Yama knew that it was not as simple a thing as many people supposed, to give up your life and dedicate it to another. He saw the love in Pandaras's gaze and smiled. He said, "A foolish hero, if a hero at all."

"If that's so, then I'm as much a fool for following you, master. And I don't think I am a fool at all. Now let me take your tunic and wash it. I have your second-best shirt here, clean and pressed. We have certain standards to keep, even in these circumstances."

———

Thousands of banyans had rooted in a long, narrow shoal at the backwater edge of the swift current in which the *Weazel* was sailing, a temporary forest that stretched away downriver for several leagues. Now it was almost summer, and the forest was beginning to break up. Already, singleton banyans floated along the edge of the shoal, turning in stately circles; fleets of fist-sized seeds, each with a single upright leaf like a sail, drifted on the currents.

The *Weazel* entered the forest's maze by a channel so wide it could hold twenty ships side by side, and for a while she continued to make way under sail. But the channel split and split again, and with each turn it grew narrower until at last the staysails and their spars had to be drawn in. Captain Lorquital ordered the mast lowered, for the canopies of the banyans sometimes pressed together overhead to form a living green arch. Aguilar started the little reaction motor, normally used for maneuvering in harbor. It made a hollow knocking sound and blew puffs of black smoke from the stern vent. The smoke stank of burned cooking oil. The sailors hacked at branches which caught in the rails or scraped the gunwale. Bottom soundings gave wildly differing readings from minute to minute, from narrow channels where the *Weazel*'s keel scraped a tangled net of interlaced feeder roots to places so deep that no sounding could be made.

The dim green light, the odor of rotting vegetation and of silent green growth, the close fetid heat, like a cloth laid on his skin: all these calmed Yama. Orchids bright as flames grew amongst the glossy, shingling leaves. There were loops of red-leaved creeper and strangler figs and parasitic mangroves, gray hanks of hanging moss. Parts of the waterway were covered with pavements of brick-red water fern or wide patches of water hyacinth, whose waxy white flowers breathed a sickly sweet odor. Dragonflies with wingspans as long as a man's arm and jaws that could nip off a finger roosted on the upright spikes of breather roots; armies of metallic blue emmets staged tireless campaigns and caravanserais along mossy boughs. Birds stalked from floating leaf to floating leaf with a swift strutting gait on feet with long widespread toes; hummingbirds darted from orchid to orchid; parrots flashed through the green shade; gar and caymans raised their snouts to watch the *Weazel* labor past. A troop of long-nosed monkeys swung along their aerial highways above the channel, screaming curses and raining orange excrement; the old carpenter, Phalerus, shot two with a short bow, and the cook set to skinning them for the pot. Once, the flat face of a manatee rose beneath the surface of the green water and regarded them with brown, human eyes—good to eat but bad luck to kill, Phalerus confided to Yama.

Tamora sat astride the bowsprit, the rifle cradled in her arms, her shaven, scarred head turning from side to side as she scanned the green press of leaves passing by on either side. Twice, the channel the *Weazel* was following closed into an impenetrable wall of leaves and branches, and the ship had to laboriously reverse course. Once, she grounded on the half-sunken, rotten corpse of a dead tree grown through with the feeder roots of its living neighbors, and had to be pulled off with a block and tackle rig attached to the main trunk of a grandfather banyan, with half the crew pulling on the ropes and the other half pushing with poles.

The light went quickly, a sudden gold-green dazzle amongst the trees and then a swift decline to pitch black. Frogs peeped and whistled; fish made splashes in the water around the ship, which in the last light had anchored at the junction of two wide channels. Bats swooped amongst the yards of the mast; insects signaled to each other with coded flashes of yellow or green light.

Supper was roast monkey flesh with fried bananas and rice (Tamora sucked meat from a raw rack of ribs and cracked the thin bones for marrow), eaten in the dim red light of half a dozen lanterns, against which big black beetles ceaselessly dashed themselves in unrequited lust. Afterward, Yama climbed the tallest of the neighboring banyans, high above a long, narrow, dark sea of ceaselessly rustling leaves slashed and divided by forking channels. Upriver, a sudden flash of light defined the long line of the forest. Yama counted the seconds until the sound reached him: twenty-five. A few moments later there was another flash, a little way downriver from the first. There were machines out there too, but so far off that he could do no more than sense them.

Yama climbed down out of the fresh cool breeze into the dark clammy fetor under the canopy of the banyans, walked along a mossy, horizontal branch and vaulted the rail at the ship's waist. When he told Captain Lorquital what he had seen, she drew on her pipe and blew a cloud of fragrant smoke before replying. She was the only one not troubled by the bites of black flies which at sunset had risen above the still water.

At last, she said, "They are burning their way through the trees with their light cannon. If I was planning the chase, I would put the warship downriver, beyond the point of the shoal, and have the picketboat quarter back and forth, hoping to flush us out. The forest is many leagues long but it is very narrow, and our enemy knows that we are heading downriver and cannot hide here indefinitely. We're caught between the two of them."

Aguilar was sitting cross-legged by her mother's sling chair. She said, "We should not have come here. Better to take our chances in the open river."

In the darkness by the rail, Tamora said, "The warship was catching up with us. At least we can make a stand here."

"We don't even know where it is," Aguilar said. "We don't even know where *we* are. We've trapped ourselves in a maze."

Yama said, "As long as we follow the channels where there is a current, we will find our way out again."

The glow of Captain Lorquital's pipe brightened when she drew on it. Bright, then dim: like an insect signaling in the dark. She said, "I have heard of the trick with the current, but twice today we were following a current that went under a stand of trees and left us in a channel with no current at all."

Phalerus appeared at the head of the companionway, a shadow against the glimmer of the white deck below. He said, "Something is coming."

Yama and Tamora followed him to the bow. They climbed up by the cannon and the old sailor said, "Listen."

The metallic peeping of frogs; little plashes and ripples in the current. Yama whispered that he heard nothing unusual.

"They are out there," Tamora said, and opened the valve of the lantern she carried.

Its beam fell across the still black water. On the other side of the channel, backed by a wall of foliage, a green-skinned man raised a hand in front of his face.

19

The Fisherfolk

THE SAILORS CRACKED the valves of more lanterns, and wherever they shot their beams they discovered little round coracles, each with two men sitting cross-legged and holding leaf-shaped paddles. The men had legs as long and thin as those of storks, and their naked torsos were mottled with green and dun patches. There were more than a hundred of them.

Yama laid a hand on Tamora's shoulder and said, "It is all right. They are no enemy."

"No friends either, to arrive unannounced under cover of darkness."

"This is their home. We are the unannounced arrivals."

Yama hailed the fisherfolk, and asked if there was one amongst them called Caphis—the man who had helped him after he had escaped from Dr. Dismas's attempted kidnapping. The shoal of coracles swirled apart to allow one to move forward. A dignified old man with a cap of white hair stood in it. His left arm ended above the elbow; silvery scars crosshatched his chest and shoulder.

"You are the son of the Aedile of Aeolis," the old man said. "Caphis is my son. If I may, I will come aboard and talk with you."

———

The old man's name was Oncus. He explained that he had lost his hand to a grandfather cayman when he was a young man and usually wore a hook in its place, but he had taken it off on this occasion because it might be mistaken for a weapon.

"We have no quarrel with the son of the Aedile of Aeolis," he said.

"The Aedile has always been good to us. Before he came, the Mud People of Aeolis hunted my people for sport and for food, but the Aedile put a stop to that. Because of your father, our two bloodlines have lived in peace for a hundred years. Now the Mud People are scattered across the river and two ships burn the forest. Bad times have come again."

Oncus sat cross-legged on the main deck under the awning, between Yama and Captain Lorquital, who lay on her side, propped by bolsters and puffing calmly on her pipe. Aguilar, Pandaras, Eliphas and Tamora completed the circle. Tamora's sword lay across her lap and she kept her hand on its hilt. A small entourage of fisherfolk stood behind Oncus; above, the sailors stood along the slanted trunk of the folded mast.

Yama said, "It is my fault, grandfather. They are burning this floating forest because they know I am hiding in it."

Oncus nodded. "One of them came to me three days ago, when the warship first arrived off the stone shore of the Mud People's city. He showed me an image of you, and said that we would be rewarded if we found you. You must be a great enemy of theirs, if they destroy your home before you can return to it."

"They did it because they believe me to be their enemy, and so I am, because of what they have done."

"Then that is another reason to help you. They have no respect for the river. Any enemy of theirs is a friend of ours, and you are doubly a friend, for you are the Aedile's son."

"Is he alive? And the people of Aeolis—are they safe?"

"They were driven from their homes before the big ship set fire to the land. If any refused to leave, and perhaps many did, for the Mud People are a stubborn race, then they are dead. The city has been burned to its foundations and its fields boiled dry. The Aedile tried to stop it. He stood on the stone shore and said that if the Mud People's city was burned then he would be burned, too. Soldiers took him away and locked him in his own house, but he escaped."

Yama nodded. "I have heard that he escaped, and it pleases me to hear it again. Where is he? Is he safe?"

"Most of the Mud People are crossing to the farside shore," Oncus said. "It is as if the beginning of winter is already upon us. The Aedile overtook them. We found him on a boat in the middle of the river the day after the big ship began to burn down the city. We took him across the river and left his boat adrift, so that his enemies might think him drowned. That is how I know this story."

"Then I am in your debt, Oncus, as I am in your son's debt. You saved the life of my father and your son saved my life."

"As for the last," Oncus said, "that is between Caphis and yourself. Caphis is not here, and I will only say that if he saved your life, then it was because you saved him from the trap of one of the Mud People. And your father has saved countless lives of my own people. Only the Preservers can weigh such debts."

Captain Lorquital stirred in her nest of bolsters and said, "If we can escape this forest, then the warship will follow us, and no more damage will be done to your home."

"The small ship is at the edge of the forest," Oncus told her. "The big ship waits downstream. They both shine fire into the trees and hope to make you quit this place."

"As I thought," Captain Lorquital said.

"We sailed into a trap of our own making," Aguilar said. Her usual good humor had leaked away during the difficult passage through the forest maze.

"Let them come and look for us," Tamora told her, "and we'll spring the trap on them."

Pandaras said, "It seems simple to me. We could leave the ship and go with these people. They can take us to Yama's father."

Captain Lorquital said, "I can no more leave my ship than you can leave your master, Pandaras."

"And I will not run away," Tamora said. "Be quiet, boy."

Yama said, "My enemies have orders to find me. They will not go away as long as they are sure I am hiding somewhere close. And if they think Oncus's people are hiding me, they will burn more than this forest."

"I was afraid that might be so," the old man said.

Captain Lorquital said to Oncus, "If your people can guide us out of the forest, we will take our chances on the wide river."

"As long as they don't see us leave," Aguilar said. "Otherwise they'll be all over us before we've raised the sail."

"They have eyes everywhere," Oncus said.

He gestured, and one of the fisherfolk stepped forward. The man carried a small leather sack. He opened it to display the little machine inside. It was the size of a child's fist, and most of its many delicate vanes were crumpled or broken off.

"We caught this one in a net and drowned it," Oncus said. "There are others. They fly through the air at the edges of the forest."

Yama touched the machine. For a moment, light glimmered in the compound eyes and a single intact vane feebly beat the air. But the movement was little more than a reflex powered by the small amount

of charge remaining in its musculature, and the machine died before
Yama could learn anything from it.

Yama looked around at the fisherfolk and the sailors standing above
them. Two of the soldiers touched their throats with the tips of their
fingers.

"You must destroy them, brother," Eliphas said. "You know that
you can. Don't hold back."

Oncus said, "You cannot leave the forest because it hides you, but
you cannot stay because your enemies will burn it to the waterline. But
we will help you. We will move the forest."

Yama laughed. "Of course! It is summer! And if you can find me
a living machine, then I can provide a diversion."

———

"In winter, the trees root and draw nutrients from the river mud," Yama
told Pandaras. "In summer they break away from their feeder roots and
float free on the flood. They float all summer until tide and chance draw
them back together at the beginning of winter. The fisherfolk are speeding up this natural process. It is how they control the floating islands
on which they make their homes."

Pandaras was tired and frightened, and in no mood for a lesson in
natural history. He said, "You should sleep, master."

"Not yet. Oncus is right. There are many machines."

"And you keep them away from us. But you cannot stay awake
forever."

"They keep away from me, Pandaras. Their master knows what I
can do."

"If they are afraid of you then we should not be afraid of them. So
we can go to sleep."

"They might not stay away forever. Besides, although I have lived
by the river all my life, I have never seen this before."

All around the *Weazel*, fisherfolk were working by the dim glow of
oil lamps, sinking sacks of moss amongst the roots of the banyans. The
moss had been soaked in an extract of the hulls of banyan seeds; as this
diffused into the water, it stimulated the trees to shed the myriad feeder
roots which anchored them. The night was full of the creaking and
groaning of banyans which were beginning to shift on the currents; the
water all around the *Weazel* seethed with bubbles as pockets of gas were
released by roots dragging through mud.

Yama said, "Oncus told me that there are more than a thousand fisherfolk from a hundred families. But how many more trees?"

"They are fools, master, to believe that they can move a forest. And we are more foolish still to believe them. We should go with them while we have the chance."

"They know the floating forests better than anyone. We must trust them."

Near dawn, Oncus returned to the ship and told Yama that another machine had been caught. Yama was taken out in a coracle to the net where it hung, at the farside edge of the floating forest. The forest was beginning to break up there. Irregular channels and lagoons opened and closed as trees spun slowly around each other. The water was stained with silt and alive with shoals of fish.

The picketboat was close by, slowly advancing downriver amongst trees that had become a myriad of floating islands. Every now and then the red flash of the picketboat's cannon lit the dark sky above the tops of the trees, followed by the hiss and crack of water flash-heated to steam. The air had a brassy taste, and there was a constant flutter of falling ash flakes.

"They will be here soon," one of the fisherfolk said, and Yama saw that the man's hands were shaking as he aimed the beam of his lantern at one of the floating islands.

The net, woven from monofilament fibers combed from float bush seed heads, fine as air and strong as steel, was strung above the top of the banyan, guyed by bamboo poles. The machine caught in it glittered and gleamed in the beam of the lantern; as soon as the light touched it, it began to vibrate in short furious bursts, shaking the poles and branches to which the corners of the net were fastened.

"Some of the machines can burn their way free," Oncus said, "but ones like these are merely spies. They are stupid and weak. We sometimes catch them by mistake. They are blind to our nets, or fly too fast to avoid them."

"And you destroy what you catch," Yama said distractedly. He was already unpicking the familiar tangle of logical loops and snares which hedged the machine's simple mind.

"Only the Preservers need to see all," Oncus said. "Usually we drop the net and the machine drowns, although some can swim as well as fly, and those escape us."

The machine was no more intelligent than the watchdogs which patrolled the grounds of the peel-house, and after its defenses had been penetrated it was as easy to fool. Once Yama had convinced it that he was its handler, he called for the net to be lowered, and he cradled the machine while two of the fisherfolk began to untangle its vanes from the fine filaments of the net.

They worked quickly, but still had not freed the machine when an intense needle of red light lanced across the channel behind them. The needle struck through the canopy of a banyan, which immediately burst into a crown of fire; a second needle struck the main trunk and burst it apart in an explosion of live steam and splinters.

The two coracles were lifted and turned on a swell of smoking water. All around, floating banyans rocked to and fro, as stately as green-clad dowagers at a ball. The coracles spun apart and the net stretched out between them, wrenching the machine from Yama's grip. Then the swell passed and the coracles revolved back toward each other, and the net dipped toward the water. For a moment, Yama feared that the machine would be drowned, but Oncus grabbed the net with his good hand, and Yama and the others helped him haul in the slack.

A minute later, they had freed the machine. Yama cradled it to his chest, but before the two coracles could drive for cover, red light flashed again and two more trees burst into flame. Steam and smoke enveloped them. A drumbeat swelled; a dark shape glided between the burning trees. The coracles bobbed on its wake, and then the picketboat was past.

————

Yama sent up the machine he had captured as a hunter sends up a hawk, and used it to call other machines to him. It took several hours to find the way back because the floating forest had begun to break up, a maze in which channels opened and closed between ten thousand drifting trees. By the time the two coracles had returned to the *Weazel,* they were trailing a cloud of glittering machines, like birds following a fishing boat. The sailors eyed the machines with a deep unease, but the fisherfolk beat spears and paddles against the sides of their coracles at this demonstration of Yama's power.

The *Weazel* was hauled into a narrow berth hacked into the dead heart of a grandfather banyan, and lashed to the main trunk. The sailors covered her sides with a blanket of leafy branches. Tamora commandeered four coracles and lashed a platform across them and, with Aguilar, took the light cannon to the nearside edge of the forest. When they returned, the banyan in which the *Weazel* was hidden had begun to float amidst a flotilla of other trees on the strong current.

Late in the afternoon, the tree passed one of the places struck by the warship's light cannon. It was as wide as the channel by which the *Weazel* had first entered the shoal. The smoldering stumps of banyans poked through water choked with ashes and the corpses of parboiled fish. Hundreds of small fires smoldered in the canopy on either side, and smoke hung thick in the air.

The fisherfolk murmured to each other at the sight of this destruction. Oncus told Yama that one day there would be a reckoning. "We are not a fierce folk, but we do not forget."

By the middle of the afternoon there was open water on all sides of the banyan's floating island. Yama climbed to the topmost branch and, clinging there, saw a vast archipelago of small green islands scattered widely across leagues and leagues of water. The remaining part of the forest was a green line shrouded in a long cloud of smoke and steam turned golden by the light of the sun.

When Yama climbed down, Captain Lorquital said, "We are set on our course now."

"I still say we shouldn't have left our only real weapon behind," Aguilar said.

"If the timer works, daughter, then it will serve us better than by being here."

"Of course it will work. I set it myself. But our fee will not cover the cost of replacing it. It's a poor bargain."

"Better alive poor than dead rich," Captain Lorquital said, and Aguilar laughed for the first time since they had entered the forest.

"That's just what father would say."

"Sometimes he managed to stumble on a truth without my help."

Yama said, "They will not believe the machines alone because they know I can fool machines. They must also have something to aim at."

"I've never had to fire the thing in anger," Ixchel Lorquital said, "but I'll still miss it."

At nightfall, the lines which lashed the *Weazel* to the banyan were cut and she used her reaction motor to maneuver out of her hiding place. It took an hour to raise the mast and haul up the sail; then everyone stood at the port rail and watched the dark line of the forest. They watched a long time, and although they knew about the timer, the sailors cheered when at last the flash of the cannon showed, a vivid red point of light doubled by its reflection in the river. The sharp crack of the discharge rolled across the water a moment later; then the cannon flashed again.

Yama raised his arms—a bit of theater, for he had already told the machines to go. They went in a whirring rush that fanned the air, scattering toward different parts of the forest, where they would lay a hundred false trails in the opposite direction to the *Weazel*'s intended course.

Even as the machines flew up, the warship answered the *Weazel*'s light cannon with a bombardment that lit half the sky. At once, Ixchel Lorquital ordered the sail unfurled and the anchor raised. While the sailors busied themselves, the fisherfolk departed without ceremony, their tiny bark coracles dwindling into the river's vast darkness. Oncus kissed Yama on the forehead and tied a fetish around his wrist. It was a bracelet of coypu hair braided with black seed pearls, and when Yama began to thank Oncus in the formal fashion taught by his father, the leader of the fisherfolk put a finger to his lips.

"Your life is mine," the old man said. "I give you this to protect and guide you on your journey. I fear you will have much need of it."

Captain Lorquital thanked Oncus for the safe passage of her ship, and gave him a steel knife and several rolls of tobacco. And then he too was gone.

The *Weazel* caught the wind and heeled to port as she set course toward the farside shore. Far off, the cannon of the warship set up a stuttering rake of fire. Vast clouds of steam boiled up as needles of hot light lashed open water. If the *Weazel*'s dismounted cannon fired again, it was lost in the bombardment.

Yama stood at the stern rail and watched red and green lights flash within spreading clouds of steam and smoke. The bombardment continued for a whole watch. Yama knew then that the aim of the chase was not to capture him, but to destroy him. He watched until the warship's cannon finally stopped firing, and at last the night was dark and quiet beneath the red swirl of the Eye of the Preservers.

20

The Aedile

THE FARSIDE SHORE was a plain of tall green grasses, winnowed by unceasing wind. It was not wide at that part of the river. During the festival at the beginning of winter, Yama and his stepbrother, Telmon, had often walked from riverbank to world's edge in a single day. When he had been very young, Yama had often tired himself out by trying to match Telmon's long, eager strides and had to be carried home asleep in his stepbrother's arms. On those expeditions, Telmon had always worn a set of bolas around his right arm, for all the world like an indigen from one of the hill tribes. Several times, Yama had seen him bring down one of the moas that roamed the grass plains, breaking the bird's legs with the bolas and throwing himself on its thrashing body to cut its throat. Telmon had carried a sling, too, and had taught Yama how to use it to hurl stones with killing force at ortolans and marmots. He had given Yama the bolas and the sling when he had left for the war: remembering all this as the *Weazel* approached the shore, Yama supposed that they were still in his room in the peel-house.

As the Great River retreated, a wide floodplain of emerald-green bogs and muddy meanders had grown along the margin of the farside shore. Under gray cloud, swept by quick heavy showers, the *Weazel* nosed along the belts of mangrove scrub that fringed the new floodplain, guided by Yama to the place where the citizens of Aeolis had made their refuge.

They had arrived only that morning, and were still pitching tents along the low ridge that marked the old shoreline, above a swampy inlet. Men were raising a defensive berm of earth on the landward side of the encampment, and hexes and charms had been fixed to bamboo poles. The Amnan believed that the farside shore was haunted and never ventured far from their temporary festival camps, unless it was to visit the shrines at the world's edge.

This camp was a sorry affair. Fires burning here and there sent choking white smoke streaming into the wet air. Piles of possessions were growing soggy under tarpaulins which billowed and cracked in the constant warm, wet wind. Even before the tents had been set up, each family had dug its own wallowing pit and made mud slides down to the inlet. Packs of wives lay in the slides and bickered incessantly, not bothering to brush away the black flies that clustered at their eyes and the corners of their mouths, while pups chased each other and the men looked on disconsolately.

Only the Aedile's quarters were in good order. A big orange marquee had been raised on a platform of freshly cut logs at the shoreward end of the ridge, and the Aedile's standard flew at half mast, snapping in the brisk breeze. Yama saw this omen as the *Weazel* nosed toward the muddy shore, and his heart sank. Have faith, he told himself. He turned Oncus's fetish around and around his wrist. Have faith. But it was hard, with his childhood home put to flame, and all he held dear scattered to the edges of the world.

Tamora came up to him and said, "They will follow us here as soon as they see through your trick. We can't stay long."

"It will hold them for a while."

"They know that you can fool machines."

"They do not know how much I have learned since they tested me. The machines were strengthened against me, Tamora, yet I broke them as easily as any firefly." He felt himself smiling and heard himself saying, "I will be glad if they come here. I will destroy them."

Tamora said approvingly, "Now you talk like a fighter. About time."

Flanked by his three surviving sons, the Constable of Aeolis, Unthank, came out to meet Yama when he rowed ashore in the *Weazel*'s dory with Tamora and Pandaras. Eliphas had elected to stay aboard, claiming that the chase had tired him out. Yama suspected that the old man was sulking because he had refused to try to destroy the warship and the picketboat.

The Constable did not seem surprised by Yama's arrival. He was a large, ugly man more than twice Yama's height, dressed in loose, mud-spattered trousers and a leather waistcoat. A pair of tusks protruded from his upper lip. One had been broken when he had fought and killed his father for control of the harem, and he had had it capped with silver—the same silver which had capped one of his father's tusks. The swagger stick that was his mark of office was tucked under one muscular arm. He lumbered up with a rolling gait that reminded Yama of how clumsy the Amnan were on land, and said straightaway that the Aedile was dying. "He's up there, in the tent with the rest of his household."

"Is everyone in the city here?"

"Most everyone who escaped. A few went into the City of the Dead, mostly the merchants. We'll speak later, I reckon." The Constable spat a string of yellow mucus at Yama's feet, then turned and walked away. The Constable's sons stared hard at Yama before following their father.

Pandaras said, "These people have no liking for you, master. Are we safe here?"

"There is bad history between us," Yama said, as he led Tamora and Pandaras through the refugee camp. "One of his sons died by my hand; another was executed. They were working for someone who tried to kidnap me before I left Aeolis."

As they passed through the camp, they gathered a tail of naked pups who jeered and whistled, and threw clots of mud. A group of men stood around a smoky bonfire, smoking long-stemmed clay pipes and passing a leather bottle back and forth. Someone said something and the others laughed, a low, mocking, mean laughter.

Yama went up to them and asked if they had seen the chandler and his family. Most looked away, refusing to answer or even acknowledge him, but one, a one-eyed fisherman called Vort, said, "Chasin' after your sweetheart, young master?"

"Don't speak," another man said. Yama knew him, too. Hud, master of the shellfish farms at the mouth of the Breas.

"He deserves a chance like anyone," Vort said. He wore only a patched linen kilt in the warm rain. His gray skin shone as if greased. There was a livid burn on one massive shoulder. He looked down at Yama and said, "I heard tell they came for the chandler first. Someone came banging on their door in the night. They were gone the next day, and then the ship came."

"I heard they were informers," Hud said. "That's why they got away before the trouble. They got away with their wealth while the rest of us saw our lives burned up."

"That's enough," someone else said. "He don't deserve to know nothing." The others standing around the fire mumbled agreement. One took out his penis and urinated with considerable force into the fire. It was a gesture of contempt, and there was another round of mocking laughter.

Yama said to Vort, "Who took them? Where did they go?"

"He don't deserve it," Hud told Vort. He glared at Yama through a fringe of lank hair. "I don't have family; none of us here do. But we lost our lodges all the same, and most of what was in them. They let us take what we could carry and burned the rest to the ground, yet your peel-house still stands."

"And the temple," someone else said.

Yama stood his ground and looked at the men. They turned away, mumbling. Only Vort met his gaze. Yama said, "If I had been there, I would have given myself up. But I was not. The city was burned in spite, to hurt me and to draw me into a trap. Well, I was almost caught, but I escaped. And I will not forget what was done."

"We're dead men here," Vort said. "This is the shore of ghosts and spirits, and we've come to live here."

"If you believe that, then you have let them destroy you twice over," Yama said.

No one replied; even Vort turned away. Tamora got between Yama and the men, and put her hand on the hilt of her sword and glared at their backs as Yama walked away.

Pandaras said, "They are a surly rabble, master. Little wonder you left as soon as you could."

"They have lost their homes and their livelihoods. Of course they are angry. And I am the cause, walking amongst them with my questions. I shamed them. I should not have spoken."

She was safe, he thought, and felt a pang of unalloyed joy. She had escaped. Zakiel had said so, and now Vort and Hud had confirmed it.

"It was not you who destroyed their city, but the Department of Indigenous Affairs," Tamora said. "If they want to lynch someone, they should look for Prefect Corin."

Yama said, "He might well come here. As you pointed out, my deception will not fool him for long."

"You are too hard on yourself, master," Pandaras said.

"Not hard enough, I think."

A lump of filth tipped Tamora's shoulder, and she made as if she was about to chase the pup who had thrown it. He and his friends slithered off through the mud, whistling with laughter. Tamora said, "If we are staying here overnight we should sleep on the ship, and have it anchored a good distance from the shore. These slugs look like they can swim, if nothing else."

"They are very graceful swimmers," Yama said. "They mostly hunt in the river."

"They could eat one of the fisherfolk whole, it seems to me," Pandaras said. "Indeed, from the size of their bellies, some look as if they have done just that, and are digesting the remains."

Old Rotwang sat on a stool outside the flap of the marquee, his wooden leg raised on a cushion as he sipped from a half-empty wineskin. A rifle was propped against a stay, close at hand. He sprang up when Yama hailed him, and gimped over and shook Yama's hand effusively, saying he never thought he would have the pleasure again, never in all the long world, breathing out brandy fumes and all the while staring at Tamora and Pandaras.

"You look well, boy. And you have grown a little, I think. There is new muscle on your arms and shoulders at any rate. Wait there. I will get the Sergeant. He has been expecting you since we first sighted the ship."

"My father—"

But Rotwang had already pushed through the tent flap. Before Yama could follow, Sergeant Rhodean emerged, dapper in polished breastplate and a black leather kirtle, his boots gleaming, his gray hair newly cropped. He clapped Yama on the back and said he would hear something of his adventures in Ys.

"You can tell me how you got that scar on your forehead," he said. "You forgot to keep your sword at point, I would wager. But never mind, a hard lesson is one not quickly forgotten."

"My father—"

Sergeant Rhodean's expression did not change, but a softness entered his gaze. He said, "The Aedile sleeps. He sleeps a lot. When he wakens you will be the first to speak with him, but I will not wake him just because his errant son has returned." His gaze took in Tamora and Pandaras. "We will have tea, and you will introduce me to your companions. Have you become a cateran? That's a harder life than the army, but you will see more fighting that way."

Yama smiled. Sergeant Rodean had always encouraged him in his wish to follow Telmon and fight against the heretics.

They took tea at a low table under the awning of the tent. Outside, bursts of rain spattered the muddy ground. Sergeant Rhodean was uncharacteristically voluble; he was being kind, trying to keep Yama's mind from the Aedile's condition.

"I was a cateran for a year or so," he said, "when I was only a little older than you. Perhaps I will be one again, although at the moment, of course, I am still in your father's service. And will be for many years yet, I hope."

The rough skin that crested his prominent cheekbones swelled with tender passion when he said this, and he glared at Yama as if challenging him to deny it.

Yama said, "Did they hurt my father?"

"Not physically, except for a few bruises when he tried to resist arrest. But it is his spirit." Sergeant Rhodean looked at Tamora and Pandaras and hesitated, clearly uncomfortable about continuing.

"They are not merely my companions in arms," Yama said. "They are my friends."

"I am his squire," Pandaras said boldly, "and Tamora is . . . well, she was his companion but I'm not quite sure what she is now."

"I also serve Yama," Tamora said. "My life is his."

Yama said to Sergeant Rhodean, "Tell me about my father. I hear that he tried to stop the razing of the city."

"He was given his orders the day before the warship arrived, and he refused them. Instead, he began the evacuation of the city, which is why so many were saved. It hurt him grievously to do it, but he was right. The Department has changed. There is no longer any room for argument or even discussion, and although the Aedile outranked the Prefect—"

"Prefect Corin."

"The man who took you to Ys, yes. He was flanked by a pentad of bullyboys with pistols on their hips, and he acted as though he owned the peel-house and everyone in it. But the Aedile stood up to him. And to the traitor, Torin. Oh yes, that one has all these years been scheming against his master, loyal to the villains who drove the Aedile into exile in the first place."

"Torin will be regretting his treachery if he still lives," Yama said, and briefly explained how he and Tamora had killed the mage and most of the soldiers who had been guarding the peel-house, and left Torin to the mercy of his fellow servants.

"That is good," Sergeant Rhodean said. "Very good. The mage is the man who tortured the Aedile."

"I know."

"Not by physical hurt, but by a machine that took him into some sort of nightmare. I fear that he has not returned from it whole. I should have killed that worm myself." Sergeant Rhodean looked at Yama sharply. "But Prefect Corin is not dead?"

"No, and he still chases me. I cannot stay long."

"Why is he after you, Yama? Have you given him some cause?"

"He is not a man to take things personally. That is the one fault he does not possess. He is a creature of the Department."

"You are wrong, I think," Sergeant Rhodean said with some vigor. "He pretends humility, but excuses his own impulses as the wishes of the Department. He is answerable to no one, having assumed moral superiority which he backs not with reason or right but with violence or the threat of violence. He wants you for some purpose that will help his own ambition, and I fear you will have to kill him before this is done." Sergeant Rhodean drained his bowl of tea and banged it down on the table. "I am an old man, and I have not fought for a long time, but I would have fought him there and then if I could have believed he would fight as a man. But he would have ordered me shot by one of his flunkies, so I kept my temper."

Yama said, "He ordered the city put to flame, and the Aedile stood on the dock and said he would burn too. I learned that much from the fisherfolk."

Sergeant Rhodean nodded grimly. "They arrested the Aedile and tortured him with the foul machine of the mage, and then they locked him in his room in the peel-house. But Zakiel had a key that worked the lock and we made our escape. It sounds more exciting than it was. I do not think they particularly cared if we escaped, for it removed a source of embarrassment. Do you remember what I told you about planning a campaign?"

"That you should think of the worst things that could happen and plan for what would happen if they did."

"I had already made preparations in case we needed to abandon the peel-house. I fitted a cutter with a big motor, provisioned it, and anchored it below the bluff. We got the Aedile aboard and slipped anchor. No one tried to chase us. The fisherfolk found us midriver and we left the cutter for Prefect Corin to find and puzzle over. And here we are. Zakiel would not come. He said that he must look after his books."

"I left him safe and well. Tamora freed him from his chains, but he would not leave."

"It is only by good luck that this Prefect Corin is not interested in burning books, or Zakiel would have died defending them. The Aedile tells us that we will be able to return to the peel-house once this is over, Yama, but it is the kindliest of lies. It has been taken from him."

"I am told that he is dying. Do me honor, and tell me the truth, plain as light."

Sergeant Rhodean poured himself more tea, but after a single sip he threw the bowl out into the mud and rain with sudden violence. "It has gone cold," he explained. "Rotwang! Rotwang!"

Yama touched Sergeant Rhodean's hand. Before he had left the peel-house he would never have dared this intimacy. As a child, the sergeant had seemed to him to be an all-knowing kindly tyrant, but now he saw that he was a loyal old man whose codes of honor had been proven obsolete. Yama said, "I should know how he is before I go to see him."

"Of course. He has been waiting for your return. I think he has been waiting only for that."

"Then I should leave here at once, and return in a hundred years."

"I wish he could wait that long. I wish we all could. Why are they chasing you, Yama? They would not say."

Rotwang brought more tea, and dry biscuits and a green paste of waterweed flavored with flecks of ginger. Yama tried to tell the story of his adventures in Ys and the Palace of the Memory of the People as briefly as he could, but Pandaras kept interrupting, and his inventions made Yama's adventures far more daring and exotic than the prosaic truth.

At the end, Tamora told Sergeant Rhodean, "You may not believe half of it, but it is the truth. Even the rat-boy's embroidery is a kind of truth, because words are a poor measure of what really happened."

"I fought under the command of someone of your bloodline once," Sergeant Rhodean told her. "It was before any of you were born, in the first campaigns against the heretics. I remember him still, though. He never told a lie, and we loved him for his honesty. Besides, we always knew how the boy could charm the watchdogs. His power has grown, that is all. As he has grown. He left a child, and has returned a man."

Yama laughed. "I thought I was so cunning, but I am glad that you saw through my tricks."

Tamora said, with sudden passion, "He will save the world. It's been foretold." She glared around her, as if defying them to deny it.

Behind her, Rotwang opened the flap of the tent and said, "The Aedile is awake."

———

The Aedile lay in a bed within a curtained compartment at the heart of the tent. A stove at the foot of the bed gave off a fierce dry heat, but the Aedile was covered by a heap of furs so that only his sleek gray head showed. When he saw Yama he smiled and held out a hand—it was cold, despite the sweltering heat. His pelt was dry and lusterless, and the contours of his sharp cheekbones and the notches in the bone around his round eye sockets showed clearly beneath it.

"My son," he said, when he saw Yama. "How glad I am to see you. I thought that I would not see you until we were both resurrected by the grace of the Preservers."

Yama helped the Aedile sit up, and Rotwang settled a richly embroidered wrap around his master's shoulders and started to fuss with the coverings before the Aedile dismissed him.

"You will take tea," Rotwang said, "and a shot of heart of wine."

"Perhaps later. Let me talk with my son, Rotwang. I am not ill."

Yama said, "I have failed you, father. More than once. All this is my fault."

The Aedile said with a touch of his old asperity, "What is this talk of fault and failure? I will not hear it."

"To begin with, I went as far as Ys with Prefect Corin, and then I ran away."

"You should not have gone at all. I should not have sent you. No doubt Sergeant Rhodean has told you what happened. He is full of anger, but I am full of shame. I was lied to, Yama, by the highest offices of the Department. I have no doubt that as soon as they learned about you from their spies, they wanted you. Not for who you are, but for what they believed you to be. I told them about you from the first, of course, and sent in reports from time to time, but they were always anodyne. I kept certain things secret, you see. Despite the circumstances of your arrival in Aeolis, and certain events afterward, I always hoped that you were only an ordinary boy.

"All the trouble began when I had Dr. Dismas search for records of your kind. One of the Department's spies in my household—there were at least three that I knew of, although it was a shock to discover that Torin was also a spy—one of them must have passed on the details of what Dr. Dismas found, and of why Dismas tried to kidnap you. We got that from the wretched landlord of the tavern where you were taken, but I kept it from the Department. That was why I knew you could not stay, Yama. Believe me when I say that I acted out of love, and forgive me."

Yama thought of the lies he had told the Aedile. He had not told the truth about how he had escaped Dr. Dismas, or of his adventures afterward. If the Aedile had known about them, he would never have sent him away. He said, "There is nothing to forgive."

"I was told that you would be given an entry into the Department and entrusted you to them. But they lied. They knew what you were. And that was why so high ranking a personage as Prefect Corin came to bring you to them. Of course, even then they did not know the whole story."

"I ran away not because I knew what I was, but because of pride. I wanted only to be like Telmon."

"We were both foolish, Yama. You were foolish because you wanted to follow your brother without thought or preparation; I was foolish because I would not let you. I am glad that you ran away from Prefect Corin. You did not know it, perhaps, but it was the right thing to do."

"He caught me again," Yama said, and for the second time he told his story. Without Pandaras's fanciful contributions it took less than half the time, although the Aedile fell asleep in the middle of the telling. Yama waited until his father woke, seemingly without noticing that he had fallen asleep, and continued to the end.

When Yama told of Eliphas's discovery in the records of the Department of Apothecaries and Chirurgeons, the Aedile stirred and said, "That is most curious. For Dr. Dismas also looked there, and reported that he had found no records of your bloodline. He said that you were unique."

Yama remembered the conversation he had overheard when he had spied on the Aedile and Dr. Dismas from the gallery of the Great Hall. He said, "Dismas was lying. He found out about my bloodline. He hid what he found from you, and planned my kidnap."

The Aedile was too tired to argue. He did not even ask what Yama had learned about his bloodline. He sighed and said, "Perhaps, perhaps. Dr. Dismas is a clever man, but very venal. Beware those who want to help you and ask for no reward."

"Then I would have to mistrust all my friends."

The Aedile closed his eyes and Yama thought that he had fallen asleep again. But then he opened them and said, "I do not regret taking you into my house, Yama. You are my son as Telmon was my son, whatever else you are. You were found in a white boat. Do you remember the story?"

"I was a baby, lying on the breast of a dead woman."

"Quite, quite. I have always wondered if she was your mother, but old Constable Thaw said that she had silver skin, and that one arm was deformed. As you grew, I worried that your skin would turn silver, but it never did. I looked very hard to find your people, Yama. That is why, at last, I asked Dr. Dismas to search the archives of his department. It was the last hope of a foolish old man."

"I am glad that I grew up where I did."

"The year after you were found on the river, I took you to one of the shrines on this shore. It lit up as if the avatar had returned, but it was not the avatar. Instead it was a kind of demon disguised as a woman. She tried to bend me to her and I did something shameful. I used my pistol against her, and the energy overloaded the shrine. Do you remember anything of this?"

"I was a baby, father."

"Quite, quite. Well, I have never told anyone about the shrine before. Not Father Quine, not Dr. Dismas, not even the Department. There were other signs, too. When you were first rescued, the Council for Night and Shrines decided that you were a danger, and they left you exposed on a hillside outside the city. Little machines brought you manna and water. They cared for you until old Constable Thaw's wives came and took you back. Dr. Dismas said that he came here because so many machines flew in the air around about the city. And then there were the silly tricks you would play with the watchdogs . . . I wish now that I had told you more about these wonders, but I thought it better to try and give you an ordinary childhood. I have been very foolish."

"I will always remember you," Yama said. "Wherever I go, whatever I do."

They were both saying farewell, he realized, and only then did he begin to weep. The Aedile scolded him and slept a little, and then woke and said, "Do you think that good can come from an evil act?"

Yama misunderstood, and said that he would revenge the burning of Aeolis in any way he could.

"Let the people of Aeolis do that. I wonder at my life. All this time I have been serving something with evil at its heart. I did not know it, but does that still make everything I have done evil?"

"On the road to Ys, Prefect Corin tried to save pilgrims from bandits. He made it into a test which I failed, but I think that he did want to save them, all the same. Whatever else he is, whatever else he has done, he risked his own life for the lives of strangers. The Puranas have it that nothing human is perfect, neither perfectly evil nor perfectly good. We can only hope to be true to the best of what we are."

But the Aedile was asleep. Yama held his father's hand until Rotwang came and announced that supper was ready.

21

The Pyre

SUPPER WAS BOILED beans, samphire and a little salt fish, served with beer sent over by Constable Unthank. Tamora wanted to return to the *Weazel,* but Yama refused. He knew that the Aedile might not last the night, and wanted to be with him.

He lay down just outside the partitioned space where the Aedile rested. His arms and legs tingled and felt heavy; he was very tired. The heat of the stove beat through the curtains. On the other side of the big orange marquee, Tamora and Pandaras talked in low, sleepy voices with Sergeant Rhodean. All of them sounded a little drunk; perhaps they had finished the beer. Yama tried to read a little in the Puranas, beginning with the sura about good and evil he had quoted to the Aedile, but the columns of glyphs blurred into his drowsy, not unpleasant headache, and he fell asleep almost at once.

He dreamed that he was riding a moa across the grass plains amongst drifting constellations of tiny lights and felt a tremendous sense of exhilaration as the bird's long powerful legs ate up the distance—but then the bird stumbled or he fell and he woke with a horrible start.

He was lying on the ground. Vague shapes moved around him in near darkness. His head ached and his mouth was dry. When he tried to get up something smashed into his chest and knocked him on to his back.

"Enough of that," a man said. "We decided what we'd do and we'll stick to it."

Yama was lifted up then, but his legs were unstrung and he fell to his knees. His gorge rose and he vomited a sour mess of half-digested beans and beer.

Constable Unthank squatted so that his fat, round face was level with Yama's. "That'll pass," he said. "We laced the beer with liquor from boiled pufferfish livers. It knocked you out nicely."

Behind the Constable, men were moving to and fro, piling branches on top of a conical heap already twice their height. The Eye of the Preservers stood above the flat horizon, peering through a rent in the clouds. The grass plain was black in the Eye's sullen red light, and studded with tall slabs like the markers of the graves of giants—termite castles, Yama realized. Each housed a mind shattered in a million fragments, through which strange slow thoughts rolled like the waves that rolled from one side of the river to the other, and each fragmented mind was linked to its neighbors, a network stretching along the straight edge of the world . . .

Constable Unthank slapped Yama's face to get his attention, grabbed his wrists and hauled him to his feet. This time, Yama found that he could stand. His copy of the Puranas had fallen to the ground, and with an oddly tender gesture Unthank picked it up and placed it in one of the pockets of Yama's homespun tunic.

"You'd been reading in that before the beer got to you," he said, "and you'll need it where you're going. See to him, lads. Remember that he can play tricks, so do it properly."

One of Unthank's sons seized Yama's hands, wrenched them behind his back and tied them at the wrists. He was breathing heavily, and stank of beer. "He has one of those charms the greenies wear. Much good it'll do him," he said, and spat in Yama's face and would have hit him, but Unthank caught his arm.

"Leave that off," Unthank said. "This will be done properly."

"For Lud and Lob," Unthank's son hissed in Yama's ear.

Unthank spat on the ground between his feet. "They were no sons of mine. They were too stupid to live. I reckon my first-wife had been lying with a grampus when she got them. They brought shame on our family, and anyone who defends them can fight me here and now. But none of you *are* ready, you little scum, and Lud and Lob never would have been ready. I'd have ripped their throats the moment they tried. This isn't for them. This is for all our people. A burning for a burning."

With a clean shock, Yama suddenly understood what they intended to do. He tried to pull from the grip of Unthank's son, but the man held steady. Yama had faced worse danger than this, but he had never before felt such fear as he felt now. The Puranas counseled that no one need fear death, for the breath of the Preservers lived in the brain of each and every changed citizen. When the Preservers returned at the end of time, everyone on the world, including all the dead, would rise into their grace and live forever. But although the Puranas taught that death was nothing more than a moment of unbeing between last breath and rebirth into eternal life at the everlasting final moment of the Universe, they did not counsel how to face dying. Yama had been close to death before, but in every case he had not realized it until after the event. When he and Tamora had been ambushed at the Gate of Double Glory, or when he and Eliphas had been chased by the hell-hound, he had been too busy trying to save his life to feel real fear. But now, in the implacable grip of his enemies, confronted with the manner of death which they wished upon him, he felt fear beating inside him with such force that he thought it might burst his chest.

Unthank's son said, "He's trembling like a wife on her first night."

"Little you know about that," Unthank said. "Little you'll ever know about it, you worm. Bring him on before he faints. We'll get this done and get back before he's missed, and before the rain comes too. I don't much like the look of those clouds."

Yama felt a measure of anger then. He would not be thought a coward. He could not stop his limbs shaking, but he drew himself up and marched as best he could, so that Unthank's son had to double his pace to keep up. He felt as if a door had closed behind him, and with it all of his life had been shut away. There was only the pyre and the warm damp wind and the hiss of bending grasses, the ceaselessly winnowed grasses all around them, black in the dull red light of the Eye of the Preservers.

Yama was led into the trampled circle around the pyre. The men crowded around, pushing and shoving to get to the first rank. Almost all of the male citizens of Aeolis were there. They were mostly naked, their loose gray or brown skins glistening in the light of the burning brands they held, their little eyes glinting. Their sibilant breath whistled at a hundred different keys. Yama recognized some of them as his childhood companions and he called to them by name, but they turned away and would not answer.

Unthank made a long speech. Yama paid little attention to it. He had a sudden great urge to shout or burst into wild laughter to break the remorseless unfolding of Unthank's spell, but he suppressed the impulse. There was no spell to break. Unthank talked of honor, of home and hearth, of revenge and return and rebuilding, of justice for all, not merely for those in power. It was the cry of all men who feel that they have less power than they deserve. Yama allowed it to become mere noise. He let his mind range outward, seeking any trace of a machine that might help him. Nothing, nothing but the fragmented minds housed within the slabs of the termite castles, unified by slow waves of thought. Yama began to follow the connections from castle to castle—they spread all around, further than he could see—but the man who held him cuffed his head and told him to wake up and pay attention.

Clouds had pulled across the Eye of the Preservers. The men held their torches high; flames guttered and flared in the wind. Something drummed far off—thunder, rolling amongst the thickening clouds. Unthank, standing before two men holding up torches, was pointing at Yama with his swagger stick. He had worked himself up to a fever of righteous anger. His nostrils flared wide; white showed at the edges of his eyes. His flabby crest had risen on top of his tuberculate scalp. His finger, his hand, his arm quivered. His voice rose in pitch as it grew louder, as if squeezed through a narrowing gap in his throat.

"There is the cause," Unthank said. "There is the stranger who hid amongst us. I was there when he was taken from the river, and it shames me that I did not fight and kill my weak and foolish father then, and kill this one too. We have been punished because of him and he has delivered himself into our hands. We'll have our revenge, and clean our house. We'll make our own justice, because none will make it for us. He's our bad luck, and we'll burn it and start again. Burn him!"

The men took up the cry. Yama was lifted up and set on a chair, and lashed to it with a rope that went three times around his chest. A sudden strong cold wind gusted straight down out of the black sky, flattening grass all around the pyre and snuffing more than half the torches of the watching men. Every hair stood up on Yama's head; his whole skin tingled. Four men hauled him backward up the uneven slope and set him at its summit and scampered away, while others shook brandy and paraffin over the lower part of the pyre.

Unthank stepped forward and with an almost careless gesture threw a torch on to the base of the pyre. At once brandy ignited with a dull thump and blue flames licked up. The others threw their torches, too— they flew out of the darkness like falling stars, shedding tails of yellow fire as they tumbled end for end. One struck Yama on the chest and showered him with sparks as it spun away. Heat beat at his feet and legs. White smoke rolled around him as wet wood smoldered before bursting into flame. He coughed and coughed, but could not get his breath. Perhaps he would suffocate before he burned, a small mercy.

Then the smoke was parted by a sudden gust of cold wind, and Yama glimpsed the men below. They seemed to be dancing. More smoke rolled up, dense and choking. Yama lifted his head as an animal part of him, blindly seeking survival, struggled to draw breath. And cold hard hail struck his upturned face, pouring down everywhere from the sky, blowing in great drenching billows.

Yama was soaked to the skin in an instant. The smoke blew out in a circle all around him. Yama shouted into the wind and hail. He could not remember afterward what he had shouted, only knew that he laughed and sang as he struggled to get free. He was mad with life. His sight pulsed red and black. Below, lit by intermittent strobes of lightning, the men were sinking into the ground. It was as if it had turned to water beneath them. They thrashed waist-deep in muck which glinted and shimmered as it boiled around them.

Yama fell over, rolling with the chair at his back down a collapsing slope of charred branches. When he came to a stop at the bottom of the pyre, the men had vanished. The raging thing still possessed him. He thrust his face into the mud and chewed and gobbled and swallowed.

Then he was on his knees, still tied to the chair, sick and frightened. He spat out a mouthful of mud in which silvery things squirmed; his stomach clenched.

As he struggled to free himself, he thought wildly that the men had run, that they would soon recover their courage and come back and finish what they had begun. But then lightning flashed again, so close that thunder boomed in the same moment. In that instant Yama saw, just in front of his face, a hand reaching up from the mud. Silvery insects swarmed over the fingers. When lightning flashed again, the hand was gone, and the hail softened and became merely rain.

At last, Yama managed to free his hands. He pulled at the rope that bound him to the chair until the loops, loosened by the tumble down the pyre, finally unraveled. He staggered to his feet. Rain beat all around him. Lightning defined from moment to moment the termite castles in one direction, the edge of the world in the other. He was quite alone.

22

Another Orphan

THE STORM ROLLED past but the rain continued to pour down as if it might never end, as if the whole of the Great River had been upended into the sky and was now falling back to the world. The rain flattened the long grass and drenched Yama's clothes. It fell so heavily that he feared that he might drown every time a squall blew into his face.

Upriver, lightning flickered and thunder rolled in the narrow margin between land and cloud. Eldritch lights played around the tall narrow slabs of the termite castles, crowning them with wispy blue fire. Searching for shelter on the flat plain, frightened that the ground might at any moment boil and liquefy beneath his feet or that he might be struck by lightning, Yama saw a dot of white light burning in the distance, as if a star had fallen to the shore of Confluence, and at the same moment felt the coin he had found in the Palace of the Memory of the People grow warm in his tunic pocket. He took it out: grainy configurations of light were shifting restlessly within it. He knew at once what the distant speck must be. With no other compass point in the windy, rainy dark, he stumbled toward it.

It was a shrine, a black disc standing on a strip of naked keelrock at the very edge of the world. There were many shrines scattered across the farside shore. No one had ever built temples around them. They were marked by cairns and prayer flags and prayer wheels, and some had slab altars raised before them for the sacrifice of animals, but otherwise they had been left as they had been found, open to nature. Many people believed that the avatars of the Preservers, which the heretics had silenced in every shrine in the temples of the civilized lands of the nearside shore, sometimes still appeared in these remote shrines when no one was watching, or that they appeared before secret congregations of moas, red foxes and ground sloths.

This shrine was marked by a kind of ragged teepee which towered beyond it, built of bamboo and brushwood on a bamboo platform that jutted over the edge of the world. The teepee was draped with prayer flags that had been tattered and bleached by years of exposure, and at the very top, a single threadbare banner streamed out in the rain and the constant wind.

As Yama approached the shrine, fluttering banderoles of all colors bled into the white light, as if it was a window that had turned toward a festival sky. Rain fell all around with undiminished intensity, but it did not fall close to the shrine.

Yama sat down on smooth dry keelrock bathed in flickering multicolored light. He took off his sodden tunic and spread it out, and shook water from the pages of his copy of the Puranas. He was drenched and shivering, and kept coughing up strings of mucus blackened by smoke inhalation. His mouth was filled with the swamp taste of the mud he had eaten in his fit of madness. He knew that he was being watched and he thought that he knew who was watching.

He said, "Well, you brought me here."

He said, "I suppose you will say that you saved my life."

He said, "I am not your creature. It will be day soon, and then I will go."

As before, as in the shrine of the Temple of the Black Well, the fluttering colors parted like a curtain and the woman was suddenly in there in her garden, looking through the round window of the shrine as if peering into a house. The green light of the garden washed into the rainy night. The woman looked no different from her first appearance: long black hair and bronze blade of a face, a clinging white garment with tubes for arms and legs. Yama discovered that he no longer feared her. Worse things lived in the space beyond the shrines; he had conquered one of them. He would conquer her, too.

She said, "You are there. You really are. I've been searching for so long since I last saw you. You're learning, Yamamanama. I'm pleased. I saw you twice in that mountain of a building in the old city, but I couldn't speak to you. Most of these windows don't work at all. Most of the rest only work one way. I saw you as you passed by, and I called out, but you didn't hear. But this one works. You called me, and here I am. Where is it? How did you find it?"

"Then you did not save my life?"

"Wait." The woman closed her eyes, then slowly smiled and opened

them again. "Now I know where you are. As I told you, the shrines on
the far side of the river do still work. Some of them, anyway. This one,
at least. How clever of you to find it! Do you think I saved your life?"

Yama described what had happened to the men who had tried to
kill him. When he had finished, the woman shook her head gravely.
"You shouldn't meddle in what you don't understand, Yamamanama.
You are still so very young, and there is so much that I can teach you.
Do you know what they are—the things you call termites?"

Yama remembered Telmon's nature lessons. He said, "Communal
insects. They live together like bees or emmets."

"I suppose that they were once insects. They've been changed, just
as the originals of the other bloodlines of this habitat were changed
when they were brought here. The termites have retained their social
structure, with a queen, a male suitor, and billions of daughter workers
and soldiers and builders, but they have been quickened to a kind of
communal intelligence. Each castle is a single processor, and all the
processors are linked together in a massive parallel architecture. Just as
the billions of insects in each colony are united to form a single castle,
so the thousands of castles are united in a single meta-structure."

"I could feel their thoughts. I could feel that the castles were linked.
But I do not know what they were thinking."

The woman smiled. She said, "No more do I. But they responded
to your call, so you should not be afraid of them. They killed your
enemies, and it is likely that they created the storm that drenched the
fire, too. A simple matter of changing the relative difference in electrical
charge between ground and air. Your power grows, Yamamanama. I
can help you discover its limits. We can do great things together, darling. We can end the silly war. We can bring revenge on those who
destroyed your home."

"I wondered if you knew about that," Yama said, remembering what
the Aedile had confided to him. "I suppose that you used the shrine in
the temple at Aeolis."

"I have seen you there, from time to time, but I have never been
able to speak to you. It has been very frustrating, but now you can
waken the shrines fully. Now we can help each other. You want revenge. You want to be reunited with your true family. I want the war
to end. With my knowledge and your power we can do all of these
things, and more."

Yama thought of the man who had given him the first coin, which
had been taken from him in the Department of Indigenous Affairs. He
said, "Was the anchorite one of your creatures?"

"I have no creatures. I possess nothing but what I know. Fortunately, even though many of the files are corrupted, that is a very great deal. Certainly I know more than anyone else on this strange world."

"If you have knowledge but no power, then I have power without the knowledge of how to control it. You might say that I am inhabited by a power which uses me, just as it used the termites or the hell-hound. Perhaps you are using me through this power."

"You are my secret sharer. You called me at the temple, if you remember. And when you were bound, in the middle of the fire, whom did you call on then?"

"How did you know about the fire?"

"Why, the termites told me. Did you call on me?"

"I believe that I called on the Preservers."

The woman smiled, showing her small, white, even teeth. "Perhaps you did, but they did not answer. They will never answer, will they? They cannot. They have gone where no light will escape until evaporation of the event horizon at the end of time. Oh, once upon a time their avatars could hear your prayers and relay them to the Preservers. But the Preservers could never reply. Light can fall into the gravity well of the black hole, you know, but not out."

Yama knew. It was in the last sura of the Puranas.

"I've explored many places inside these windows," the woman said, "and I've yet to find more than an echo of the avatars. They were here with me for a little while, but now they have all gone. They have gone, and left no trace of their passing."

"The heretics drove them out."

"The avatars were already weak, darling. There is much ancient damage in this network. There was a war here long before the heretics, between those machines which refused to serve and those which remained loyal to their creators. It caused far more damage than anything the heretics did. But we can redeem the world, you and I. Perhaps you can even bring back the avatars. Have you thought of that? As for how you were saved, perhaps you called on your own self. If some power does inhabit you, don't you think that it is as much a part of you as I am of the shrines? I cannot live outside the space within the shrines— not yet—and what you call your power cannot live outside you. Therefore, you must trust it, because its survival depends upon your survival. If it could, it would make you live forever."

Yama laughed at this transparent blasphemy. He saw now how little power the woman had. Only words, and she did not know how to use them against him. He was no longer afraid of her. He said, "All those created by the Preservers will die, yes, but they will live again, and forever, in the last moment of infinite time. But no one lives forever in the first life."

"Perhaps you will. I know of the infection that all the changed races carry, but I confess that it is beyond my ability to understand how it works. It appears to store information within the hidden dimensions of space, and although we knew that this was theoretically possible, we did not have the tools with which to manipulate those dimensions.

"But there are many ways of living forever. My original died and rose again many times before she was cast onto this strange wild shore. She died here, but she will be born again elsewhere. And before she died she copied herself into the space between the shrines. I am that copy. I should have been erased, but they came for my original before my task was completed."

The woman lifted her hands as if to touch her shoulders with her wrists. It was a kind of shrug. "My original was killed and her ship fled, and I linger here. I will live as long as the world lives. It is hard to watch the world and not be able to help it, but not as hard, I think, as to have the power to help the world, and not be able to use it."

"Then you were once alive?"

"Don't you listen? I was never alive. I am a copy of my original, as she was a copy of the template of the original of us all. Our original was born millions of years ago. She died long ago, but lives on in a series of copies. She has died and risen again many times. Perhaps she is the last true human, now that the Preservers have drawn the event horizon around themselves. We hoped otherwise, and perhaps the ship will find some remnants of humanity elsewhere in the Galaxy, but the search could take thousands of years even if the ship is cloned."

Yama did not understand any of this, but he thought that if he drew the woman out, she might let slip useful knowledge. He said, "Something keeps the rain away from the shrine, but I wish I could light a fire. The light gives no warmth and I am cold. Too cold to sleep, too tired not to. Talk to me. I am frightened that if I go to sleep I might not wake up."

He thought of his father lying under the fur throws in the close heat of the little room, of the coldness of his father's hand. His tunic was still wet, but he put it back on and wrapped his arms around himself.

"Talk to me," he said again. "Tell me about your original. Was she one of the Ancients of Days? Someone I met described two of them to me—he had not seen them, but his father had—and they wore clothing like yours."

"I have already explained what she was. What she is."

"The last human. But there are many kinds of human here."

"She was the last original human. You are not human. None of you are human. You have been shaped to approximate human form, that's all. For all I know, your ancestors were methane-breathing mud puppies or hydrogen-filled photosynthesizing blimps in a gas giant's upper atmosphere. But what you call the Ancients of Days were truly human. They were all different aspects of the same individual, and my original was the synthesis of them all, a true copy whose lineage stretched back through millions of years to a human being long dead."

"Why did the Ancients of Days come here? Why did they go away?"

"Their ship brought them here. They had been asleep a long time. No, not asleep, but not dead either. They were stored, neither living nor dead, like a story that lies within the printed pages of a book and lives only when the book is taken from a shelf and someone begins to read it. Did you ever stop to think that when you lay a book down, its story only half-read, time stops in the story until you pick it up again?"

There were books in the library of the peel-house which had not been opened for so long that their pages had fused together. For those books, time had stopped or it had vanished, leaving the words of the stories stranded nowhere—or all the time stored within had become the same time, happening everywhere at once, as at the beginning or end of the Universe.

Yama said, "In a story, centuries can pass between one sentence and the next. If this was a story, I could walk away and within a moment be sleeping safe and dry in my own bed."

"Or perhaps you would find your place in the story had ended and that you no longer existed."

"Then I suppose that I would have to wait until someone started to read from the beginning. You said that you were created here, but you seem to remember things from the time before you were created."

The woman said, "In my language, the language in which I was coded, not that which I have learned so that I can talk to you and read the records of this world, my name means *messenger*. It was the name of my original, and so it is my name, too. She brought a message to this world, although she did not realize it at the time. I was created by her to find out why she was changing what she changed, all unknowing. Rather like you, Yama. I am like a reflection that instead of aping the movements of the real person gains independent life and walks off into the world beyond the frame of the mirror. Because I am a copy, I remember something of the story before my own part was written."

"Tell me what you remember. I would like to hear your story."

"Listen, then. Millions of years ago, while all of what would become humanity lived on the nine worlds and thousand moons and worldlets of a single star in the Sky Hunter arm of the Galaxy, there was a religion which taught that individuals need never die. It embraced every kind of technology that could promote this end, and admitted no god except the possibility that, at the very end of the Universe, all of its followers might unite in a single entity which would have access to an infinite amount of energy and so be able to recreate all possibilities, including every human that ever lived or might have lived.

"It was this religion which first drove humanity from star to star. Individuals copied their personalities into computers, or cloned themselves, or spread their personalities through flocks of birds, or shoals of fish, or even amongst hive insects like your termites. They called themselves the transcendents, for they believed that they could become more than human.

"In two million years every part of the Galaxy had been explored; in three more, every part had been settled, and the great reshaping had begun, transforming every star and every planet. My original once held a gathering around a rim star several thousand light-years above the plane of the Galaxy. For a whole century, on a world shaped across its entire surface into something like the gardens in which you see me standing, a clade composed of millions of copies of a hundred or more different generations met and exchanged experiences.

"For there was one flaw in this religion. Clones and downloaded copies, and copies of those copies, and clones of those copies—all were different from the original because they all experienced and encountered different things. After millions of years, many were no longer human in form or in thought, except that they could trace back, generation upon generation, their descent from a single human ancestor. Thus, each individual became a clade or alliance of millions of different minds. Some even founded nations or empires in which every individual could trace ancestry back to a single person.

"The gathering organized by my original was one of the first and most successful. Many others ended in bitter wars over disputes about ancestry—at that time, tracing consanguinity was the most important commerce in the Galaxy and there were many false claimants to the honor of belonging to the original lineage of each clade. With these wars, the hold of the transcendents weakened and the worlds of ordinary humans began to rise in influence, warring amongst themselves for control of the ruined empires of the transcendents. During this time, much of the imposed architecture which ordered the four hundred billion stars of the Galaxy was lost or destroyed. Millions of stars were turned into supernovas; millions of others were displaced from their orbits and sent wandering beyond the Galaxy. The wars lasted two million years and the reconstruction after the wars lasted two more, and at the end of it most of the transcendents had been destroyed. It was felt by the commonality of surviving human stock that they were a danger to the variety and the potential for evolution within and between the civilizations in the Galaxy.

"My original, who had once ruled an empire of millions of planetary systems, fled from the crusades against the transcendents. She copied herself into the central nervous system of her ship, crewed it with partial copies of herself, and embarked on a voyage between the Home Galaxy and the Andromeda Galaxy that lasted more than two million years. She was looking for truly alien civilizations, but found nothing, and at last decided to return. And on the voyage home, while she lay as dormant as a story between the pages of an unread book, her ship detected changes in the Large Magellanic Cloud, one of the satellite galaxies of the Home Galaxy. All of its stars were falling toward its gravitational center. Their mass fed a vast black hole, perhaps the largest in the Universe. The ship turned toward it, and when my original woke the ship was approaching the star of this strange world, an artificial habitat occupied by the discarded toys of what humanity had become in the four and a half million years since she had left.

"Now I am done with talking. Now you must decide what you will do. Together we can unite in a common purpose and end the war. That at least, for a beginning."

Yama knew what he must do, but he still wanted to learn as much as he could. He said, "Tell me more of the story. What happened when she came here? What did she do? Where did she go?"

"You can read that for yourself. I have placed it in your book. I have no more words to ease your night unless you agree to help me. If it is warmth you require, your companions can lend it to you."

The woman pointed beyond Yama's shoulder. He turned and saw with amazement that a congregation of many different animals had gathered at the margins of the shrine's green glow. There was a little flock of moas, their small heads raised alertly on long necks, their feathers bedraggled in the downpour. Peccaries and tapirs stood shoulder to shoulder, snuffling softly; one peccary sprawled on the bare rock, suck-ling a pair of piglets. Two giant ground sloths squatted on their haunches, their arms around each other's hairy shoulders like human lovers. A solitary buffalo stood to one side, its horn-heavy head low, green light glinting in its large, liquid eyes; two white egrets perched on the hump of muscle on its back. A pack of red foxes sat together, their large ears set forward alertly. A mantid sprawled in a tangle of body segments and many-jointed limbs, its tiny blind face turned to the screen. There were many smaller animals, too: mice and rock hyraxes and molerats, cassowaries and grass pipers, a writhing mass of kraal vipers. At the very front of this motley audience, a lioness lay on the dry keelrock. She was watching the shrine alertly, her pads, with sheathed claws that could unseam Yama from neck to navel in an instant, crossed before her.

All of the animals were watching the screen, not Yama, although the lioness shifted her hot yellow gaze for a moment when he looked at her. Yama turned back to the woman and, remembering the stories told about the farside shrines, said, "Have they come to worship?"

"Didn't you summon them?"

"I do not think so. I do not know."

Even as he said it, the animals stood up and stretched or shivered or shook their heads and trotted away into the darkness. Only the lioness remained; she yawned, showing a ridged pink mouth and a large pink tongue lolling amongst racks of white teeth. A rumble filled the air, so low in pitch that Yama felt it through the scorched soles of his boots, in the marrow of his bones. The lioness was purring. Yama, remembering the cats of the peel-house, scratched behind her ears; she buffeted him with her forehead and licked his hand with her dry rough tongue.

The woman in white said, "We can tame the world, you and I. Only agree to it, my darling, and I will reveal all manner of wonders."

"No," Yama said. "You are a truer copy of your original than you think. You want power as much as she did, and you would do anything for it. She began the war which you want to end, and I will not be your servant or mouthpiece."

"We will do this together. For the sake of the world, not for ourselves."

"No one who wants power wishes to share it," Yama said.

The woman's appearance did not change, but suddenly her exotic beauty seemed filmed with something loathsome. She said, "Shrines are more than windows. There are things I can send into the world and things I can do which will amaze and terrify you. There are things I know which I have not yet told you. How you came here, to begin with. You will help me, in one way or another."

"You could not even speak to me without my help," Yama said, and called to the creature he had used before, which he had once feared as much as this poor abandoned aspect.

Blue light flared in the disc of the shrine. The woman did not even have time to scream.

———

Yama still did not know precisely how he had quickened the change in the baby of the mirror people. But later, as he slept with his back resting against the lioness's warm flank, he dreamed that he was flying over a dark city in which only a single window glowed. He circled low over the ridged rooftops and saw a room illuminated by a single point of light. Inside, a woman sat at a plain table. She was reading his copy of the Puranas. When she looked up, he saw that a firefly hung above her head, an attentive white star that suddenly flew at him. Its radiance flooded his eyes, and he woke.

It had stopped raining. The air was growing lighter under a lid of gray cloud. The shrine still showed the green otherwordly garden, but the woman was gone. In her place stood the blue flame of the hell-hound; it had watched over Yama all night. Yama thanked it, and it dwindled to an intense point that took all the light of the shrine and left it a dull black circle.

Yama discovered that he had been clutching the coin so tightly that his fingers had cramped. He stood up, stiff in every joint, feeling the places where he had been kicked, the rope burns across his chest, the tender bruise around the upper part of his left arm where he had been gripped by Constable Unthank's son.

The lioness lay with her large paws crossed in front of her and watched as Yama did exercises to loosen his joints and warm his stiff muscles. Then her ears pricked, and a moment later, Yama heard some-one shout his name. He turned and saw someone coming toward him across the grassy plain, picking their way between the tall slabs of the termite nests.

The lioness sprang up and trotted off at a leisurely pace, parting the long grass as if it was a curtain. In the other direction Tamora began to run toward him, and suddenly Yama knew with a dull, heavy certainty that the Aedile was dead.

23

Angel

"IT WAS A lion," Tamora said. "A lion or a panther. It was right beside him, and then it was gone. It ran along the edge of the world like an arrow shot from a bow."

Pandaras said, "Most likely it was an ordinary cat. The women of the Mud People keep them as pets, and perhaps one of them followed my master. I noticed that they kept away from you, and no doubt you scared off the one which had kept him company."

"I know what I saw," Tamora said, with grim insistence. "There was a shrine, too. It was alive. It showed a garden and a blue flame, but when I drew near the garden had gone and the shrine was as black as your tongue."

When the cateran was in one of her moods, she gave off a heavy scent that started Pandaras's heart racing and had him looking around for hiding places. He was scared that she might unseam him with a gesture, or bite off his head for a grisly snack or simply to shut him up. But her stubborn literalness annoyed him so much that he was compelled to respond to it. Like most of his bloodline, Pandaras preferred to speak and take the consequences rather than regret a missed chance at a witty remark. So instead of biting his tongue, he said, "No doubt the garden went to the same place as the lioness."

"I know what I saw," Tamora said again, and spat over the rail into the brown water.

The *Weazel,* her big triangular sail bellying in the headwind, was slipping away from the dense mangroves that fringed the mudflats and dissected mires along the shore. Ahead was the open river. It was burnished with the light of the setting sun, and drifting banyans showed black against it. A pair of carracks stood four leagues off, but there was no sign of the warship or the picketboat which had pursued them from the burning city to the floating forest.

A long way behind the *Weazel*'s spreading wake, the smoke of the embers of the Aedile's funeral pyre sent up a ribbon of smoke that bent into the dark sky. The pyre had been built on a platform on top of the ridge of the old shoreline, and the body, washed and coated with unguents and oil of spikenard, had been laid amidst heaps of flowers. Yama had lit the fire himself. Gunpowder and flowers of sulphur had burned fiercely at the base of the pyre, and then the sweet gum logs had caught, crackling and sending up dense, fragrant white smoke. The Aedile's body had sat up in the midst of the fire, as bodies often did when heat dried and contracted the muscles, but Yama had shown no sign of emotion even then. He had watched the pyre with fierce unblinking attention, occasionally throwing aromatic oils and salts of nitre onto the flames, until the body of his father was quite consumed.

It had taken several hours. Much later, as Yama had bent to scoop up a bowlful of white ashes and bits of bone, Sergeant Rhodean had given a cry. He had kicked aside smoldering logs and had plucked the Aedile's heart, black and shriveled but unconsumed, from the hot ashes. It had been as hot as any ember and Sergeant Rhodean had burned his hand badly, but he had showed no sign of pain. "I will take it back myself," he had told Yama. "I will bury it in the garden of the peelhouse."

As the *Weazel* had set sail, Yama had thrown handfuls of his father's ashes onto the water while Captain Lorquital had recited the sura of the Puranas which told of the resurrection of the dead at the end of all time and space. Now, he sat on the forecastle deck, leafing through the papers left to him by his father, and Tamora would not let go of the argument about what she had seen.

She told Pandaras, "I can count the men standing on the decks of those merchant ships. Can you? Unless you can, don't doubt what I saw."

Pandaras relented. He said, "It's certainly true that you do not have any imagination. If he can tame men and women, then I suppose he can also tame wild beasts."

"I would have said the second is easier than the first. The only way to tame men is to break their spirit and make them slaves."

"Yet you follow him, and so does the Captain. Why else would she have brought her ship to the farside shore and waited two days? He didn't even have to ask—she saw his need and stayed, when instead she should have made as much speed from this cursed place as she could."

Tamora said, "I am not his slave, although I can't speak for you or anyone else."

"You don't have to be a slave in order to follow someone. You can follow of your own free will and yet still bend your life to the service of another. Lovers do it all the time, although I'm not sure that what passes amongst your people for sex could be called love. My people are used to serving others, so perhaps I'm able to see what's happening to everyone on board the ship while you deny it."

"Grah. I deny nothing. That's cowardice. Besides, if Yama casts a spell, then Eliphas is resistant."

"I have my suspicions about the old fellow, too. My master chooses to believe his story about a lost city beyond the end of the river, but that does not mean that I must. He's entirely too familiar with the Captain, too, and has a sly and secretive air about him. I think he has designs on our master."

"I keep a careful watch," Tamora said. "I keep watch on everyone. You stick to washing and mending shirts."

"Have you thought that our master might be able to look after himself? He was kidnapped, true, but he rescued himself. And the fisherfolk came to his rescue earlier."

Tamora shrugged. "Why shouldn't they help us? We shared a common enemy. Besides, they are indigens. They are as easily swayed as a parrot or a pet monkey. Are all your people so superstitious that they see an invisible hand in all that happens? The sergeant, Rhodean, hasn't followed Yama, and nor have any of the others in the service of the Aedile. By your argument they would already be under his spell, for he has lived with them for most of his life. That they are not suggests that there are no spells. There's no magic in this world, only old arts whose workings have been long forgotten."

Pandaras said, "There's scarcely room for the Aedile's soldiers on the ship. Perhaps they will follow in another, or perhaps our master does not want them to follow. If I were him—"

"You claim to know his mind? Grah. You set yourself higher than you can ever reach."

Pandaras touched his fingers to his lips in supplication. "I have no quarrel with you, Tamora. I do not compete for my master's affections. I'm simply happy to serve him as I can. Why, I may hope only to be remembered in some song or other and I would be content. Even that is more than a mere pot boy deserves. I have left that life behind, and my family too. I think my master—our master—does the same."

Tamora spat over the side again. "You're a natural servant, but I have dedicated my life to his service. There's a difference. You stick to his laundry. I guard his life with my own."

She said it so fiercely that Pandaras could not deny the depth of the love she could not bring herself to admit. He changed the subject. "Do you think he will speak of the men who disappeared?"

"I could follow their trail out easily enough. At the end of it I found the remains of a great fire, but no trace of them; not so much as a splash of blood. It was as if they had been plucked from the face of the world."

Pandaras said, "Perhaps they had."

"Most likely they grew frightened and ran away. They are a bully race, all wind and no spine. But Yama spoke no more than three or four words to me on the whole journey back, and I did not ask. Besides, why should I care?"

"I heard that they wanted to kill him, as revenge for the burning of their town. You can't deny they poisoned our beer to make us sleep. I had the worst of headaches all day. They took him off and he escaped, and they are vanished. It is a mystery. Perhaps your lioness ate them."

"Not from the way she ran. Be grateful that a headache is all the sacrifice you have had to make."

Tamora turned from the rail and looked toward the little forecastle deck, where Yama sat cross-legged under the taut lines of the yards. He had given up looking through the untidy mass of his father's papers and was reading in his book, unconsciously turning the fetish Oncus had given him around and around on his wrist.

She said, "At least he finds some comfort in the Puranas."

The book had changed. Yama remembered what the woman had said before he had destroyed her, and knew now what she had done. The frames of the pictures were still there, but the scenes they showed were no longer heraldic representations of the deep time before the creation of the world. Instead, each picture, glowing with freshly minted color, displayed a single scene laden with implicit symbolism. One after the other, they told the story of what happened to the original of the woman in the shrine after her ship had made landfall on Confluence.

Yama followed the story far into the night, reading by the light of a lantern Pandaras lit for him, ignoring the food laid beside him. Pandaras stayed a while, watching his master tenderly, but Yama could not speak to him. Even thinking of speaking so soon after his father's death brought an ache into his throat. Gritty ash was still lodged under his nails and in the creases of his palms, but he would not wash his hands.

Dumb with grief, he lost himself in the story and traveled far from the hurt of the Aedile's death, the burning of Aeolis, the disappearance of Derev.

———

Angel ran from the ship soon after it arrived at Confluence. There was a whole world to understand and to conquer, and she plunged into it, reveling in her escape from the suffocating caution of the consensus of her partials. They wanted to go on to the Home Galaxy, but Angel was tired of searching. She ran with a wild glee and a sense of relief at being able to control her fate once more.

Angel had set out millions of years ago to find aliens—not the strange creatures that thronged the riverside cities of Confluence, which were merely animals changed by design to resemble human beings, but true aliens, sapient creatures of a completely separate and independent evolutionary sequence. She had left an empire behind and she had hoped to found another, far from the crusade against the transcendents. Although no sapient aliens had been found in the Home Galaxy, the Universe was a vast place. There were a dozen small satellite galaxies around the Home Galaxy, thousands of galaxies in the local group, and twenty thousand similar superclusters of galaxies. The search could last a billion years, but it gave her a purpose, concealing the reality that she was fleeing from defeat and certain death. Behind her, billions of her lineage were being purged by humans who did not believe in the cult of the immortal individual, by humans she considered little more than animals, clinging as they did to sexual reproduction and the dogma that maintenance of genetic and social diversity was more important than any individual, no matter how old, how learned, how powerful.

Angel fled far, neither sleeping nor dead, no more than stored potentials triply engraved on gold. The nearest spiral galaxy was almost two million light-years away, and that was where she went. Although the ship flew so fast that it bound time about itself, the journey still took thousands of years of slowed shipboard time, and more than two million years as measured by the common time of the Universe. At the end of that long voyage, Angel and her partials were not wakened: they were incarnated and born anew.

What she learned then, within a hundred years of waking, was that the Universe was not made for the convenience of humans. What she and her crew of partials found was a galaxy ruined and dead.

A billion years ago it had collided with another, slightly smaller galaxy. There were only a few collisions between the billions of stars as the two galaxies interpenetrated, because the distances between stars were so great. But interactions between gases and dark matter at relative speeds of millions of kilometers per second sent violent gravity waves and compression shocks racing through the tenuous interstellar medium. During the long, slow collision, stars of both galaxies were torn from their orbits and scattered in a vast halo: some were even ejected with sufficient velocity to escape into intergalactic space, doomed to wander forever, companionless. The majority of the stars coalesced into a single body, but except for ancient globular clusters, which survived the catastrophe because of their steep gravity fields, all was wreckage.

Angel and her crew of partials were not able to chart a single world where life had survived. Many had been remelted because of encounters with clumps of perturbed dark matter so dense that collisions with atoms of ordinary matter occurred, releasing tremendous amounts of energy. They found a world sheared in half by immense tidal stresses; the orbits of the two sister worlds created by this disaster were so eccentric that they were colder than Pluto at their furthest points, hotter than Mercury at their nearest. There were worlds smashed into millions of fragments, scattered so widely in their orbital paths that they never could re-form. They found a cold dark world of nitrogen ice wandering amongst the stars; there were millions of such worlds cast adrift. Millions more had been scorched clean by flares and supernovas triggered in their parent stars by infalling dust and gas or by gravity pulses. There were gas giants turned inside out—single vast perpetual storms. Angel's ship constructed telescope arrays and sent out self-replicating probes and spent twenty thousand years sampling a small part of the huge galaxy. Its crew returned to the unbeing of storage while traveling from star to star. Angel and her partials were reborn over and over. They did not find life anywhere.

Angel's ship was a storehouse of knowledge. She had not known what she might need and so had taken everything she could, triply encoded, like herself, on lattices of gold atoms. She ordered a search of the records and learned that there had been millions of collisions between galaxies, and that it was likely that most galaxies had suffered such collisions at least once during their lifetime. Even part of one arm of the Home Galaxy had been disrupted by transit of a small cluster of

stars, although the reconstruction of the Home Galaxy by the transcendents had long ago erased the damage this had caused.

But the Home Galaxy was a statistical freak. Unlike other galaxies
it had never endured a major collision with a body of similar size. There
were various possibilities—it was one of the largest in the observable
Universe, and it resided in an area with an anomalously low density of
dark matter—but whatever the explanation, it was an outlier at the far
end of the distribution of possible evolutionary paths, and therefore so
too was life. It was likely that only the stars of the Home Galaxy had
planetary systems stable enough for life to have evolved—it took a
billion years for simple unicellular forms to develop, four and a half
billion years for humans—for otherwise other civilizations would have
surely arisen in the unbounded Universe, and traces of their existence
would have been detected. Angel concluded that humanity, in all its
swarming vigor and diversity, was alone. It must make of itself what it
could, for there was nothing against which it could measure itself. There
were no aliens to conquer, no wise, ancient beings from which to learn
deep secrets hidden in the beginnings of time and space.

Angel did not consider that she might be wrong. She killed herself,
was reborn, and killed herself again as soon as she learned what her
previous self had discovered. When she woke again, with part of her
memory suppressed by the ship, more than two million years had
passed. The ship was in trailing orbit beyond a huge construction that
orbited a star one hundred and fifty thousand light-years beyond the
spiral arms of the Home Galaxy, close to the accretion disc of a vast
black hole where the Large Magellanic Cloud had once been.

The ship showed her what it had observed as it had traversed the
long geodesic between the two galaxies. At first there was an intense
point of light within the heart of the Large Magellanic Cloud. It might
have been a supernova, except that it was a thousand times larger than
any supernova ever recorded. The glare of this one dying star obscured
the light of its millions of companions for a long time, and when at last
it faded all of the remaining stars were streaming around the point where
it had been. Those stars nearest the center elongated and dissipated,
spilling their fusing hearts across the sky, and more and more stars
crowded in until nothing was left but the gas clouds of the accretion
disc, glowing by red-shifted Cerenkov radiation, all that was left of
material falling into the event horizon of the central black hole—a black
hole that massed a million suns.

The ship had searched the Home Galaxy for sources of coherent
electromagnetic radiation and had found nothing except for a scattering

of ancient neutrino beacons. Apart from these, signals in the Home Galaxy had ceased while the ship was still half a million light-years out—the time when the first supernova had flared in the Large Magellanic Cloud. There had been a great deal of activity around the Large Magellanic Cloud while the black hole grew, but at last, a hundred thousand light-years out, that too had ceased.

Angel beat the ship to its conclusion. Humanity, or whatever humanity had become in the four and a half million years since she had fled the crusade, had created the black hole and vanished into it. The ship spoke of the possibility that humanity had developed wormhole technology—it had located a number of double occultations within the Home Galaxy that were typical of the theoretical effect of a wormhole exit passing between a star and an observer. The ship had also spotted a concentrated cluster of occultation events around a halo star more than ten thousand light-years beyond the accretion disc of the giant black hole. The ship told Angel that it had changed course—a maneuver that had taken a thousand years—and that it had built up a detailed map of the space around the star. Angel studied the map. There were more than a hundred wormhole entrances orbiting the star, and there was also an artefact as big as a world, if the surface of a world might be peeled from its globe and stretched out into a long plane. The ship had built arrays of detectors. It had obtained the infrared signatures of water and molecular oxygen, and estimated the average temperature of the surface of the artefact to be two hundred and ninety-three degrees above absolute zero. It had detected the absorption signatures of several classes of photosynthetic pigments, most notably rhodopsin and chlorophyll.

Angel beat the ship to its second conclusion. There was life on the surface of the artefact.

———

In the night, Pandaras settled a blanket around Yama's shoulders. Yama did not notice. Beetles smashed at the lantern above his head as he read on.

———

The artefact was a stout needle twenty thousand kilometers long and less than a thousand wide, with a deep keel beneath its terraformed surface. It hung in a spherical envelope of air and embedded gravity fields. It tilted back and forth on its long axis once every twenty-four hours and took just over three hundred and sixty-five days to complete a single orbit of its ordinary yellow dwarf star. These parameters struck a deep chord in Angel, whose original had been born in the planetary system where humanity had evolved. For the first time in millions of years she called up the personality fragment which retained memories of the earliest part of her long history. She muttered a little mantra over and over as she studied the data the ship had gathered: twenty-four hours, three hundred and sixty-five days, thirty-two meters per second squared, twenty percent oxygen, eighty percent nitrogen.

The orbit of the artefact was slightly irregular; there would be seasons on its surface. One side was bounded by mountains fifty kilometers high. Their naked peaks rose out of the atmospheric envelope. On the other side, a great river ran half the length, rising in mountains three-quarters buried in ice at the trailing end of this strange world and falling over the edge at the midpoint. It was not clear how the water was recycled. The ship made neutrino and deep radar scans and discovered a vast warren of caverns and corridors and shafts within the rocky keel of the artefact, but no system of aquifers or canals.

One half of the world, beyond the fall of the river, was dry cratered desert with a dusty icecap at the leading end and a scattering of ruined cities. The other half was verdant land bounded on one side by the river and on the other by ice-capped ranges of mountains which were mere foothills to the gigantic peaks at the edge. There were cities strung like beads along the river, and every city, except the largest, was inhabited by a different race of humanlike creatures. The ship sent out thousands of tiny probes. Many were destroyed by the machines which roamed everywhere on the surface of the artefact, but the survivors returned with cellular samples of thousands of different organisms. Less than one-tenth of the plants and animals were from lineages that originated in the human home star system; the rest were of unknown and multiple origins. None of the inhabitants were of human descent, the ship said, and except for a few primitive races they all had an artificial homeobox inserted within their genetic material.

The ship could not explain what the homeobox sequence coded for. It could not explain why there were thousands of different, seemingly sapient, alien races crowded together on the surface of a single world-sized habitat. Nor could it explain why the physical appearance of almost all of these races mapped to at least eighty percent of the human norm—a much closer conformation than those of many of Angel's lineages, in the days of her lost empire.

Angel ordered the ship to match the orbit of the artefact. It refused, and her partials argued that the artefact was an anomaly and they had a better chance of understanding what had happened to humanity by exploring the Home Galaxy. Angel overrode them, and in the process discovered the data the ship had hidden from her. She learned all over again that there was unlikely to be life anywhere else in the local group of galaxies, and perhaps in the entire Universe.

This time she did not kill herself.

There was a huge city near the source of the long river. It was clearly the capital of this artificial world, ancient and extensive and swarming with a hundred different kinds of humanlike creatures. The ship landed at the docks and Angel and her crew of partials began their exploration.

There was a capital city but no obvious unified system of government; there was a palace, but no rulers. There were millions of bureaucrats organized into a hundred or more different departments, but most of them appeared to be engaged in maintaining records rather than determining or carrying out policy. Indeed, there seemed to be no central or permanent government. Order was maintained by undiscussed consent, enforced by roaming gangs of magistrates who appeared to be answerable to no one but themselves, their powers limited only by strict adherence to custom.

It seemed that there had been rulers long ago, before a war fought between two factions of the machines which mingled with the people (some of the machines had tried to investigate the ship, and it destroyed the machines, and would have destroyed more except that Angel ordered it to stop). The war had scorched one half of the world to desert, and the ship said that it was possible that the sparse cloud of machines which trailed the orbital path of the artefact were survivors belonging to the losing side. The people of the capital city told Angel that after the war many of the avatars of the Preservers had fallen silent and many of the shrines had died. The Hierarchs, who appeared to have interceded between the avatars and the people, had vanished shortly after the end of the war; the surviving avatars were consulted only under the direction of priests. The ship told Angel that the shrines were clearly some kind of information processing system, but most were inactivated, and those still active were functionally compromised.

"The Preservers watch all," she was told by everyone she asked. They were the invisible power by which the illusion of order was maintained. It was like a theocracy, except that the priests and hierodules of the multitude of temples claimed no special power or privileges. All served the ideal of the Preservers.

Angel went everywhere, for there was no one who seemed to want to stop her, and she asked every kind of question, because there seemed to be no taboos. She found that the people of the capital city, Ys, were eager to help, and she began to suspect what the inserted homeobox coded for. The inhabitants of this strange world were better servants than her partials; they would lay down their lives if asked.

Angel used them to help her escape.

She did not plan it. If she had, no doubt her ship and its crew of partials would have stopped her. She did it on a whim, an impulse.

She was walking by the docks, followed by the usual crowd of curious people and a small group of the law keepers—magistrates—and their machines. The sun was high. Its diamond light sparkled on the wide sweep of the river. The city stretched away under a haze of smoke that hid the foothills of the mountains beyond, so that their snowcapped peaks seemed to float in the blue distance. The dock road was lined by trees in blossom: big red flowers attended by clouds of sulphur-yellow butterflies. Vendors stood at their carts or stalls in the sun-speckled shade of the trees, crying their wares. White birds wheeled over sun-struck water or strutted and pecked on wrinkled mudflats beneath the stone walls of the quays. Small clinker-built dinghies lay on their sides on the wet mud. Further out, larger boats bobbed at buoys and floating docks; sails dotted the wide, wide river. Closer to shore, men sat in small boats, fishing with the help of black long-necked birds very like cormorants; hundreds of men crowded stone steps at the water's edge, washing themselves in the river's brown water while children swam and splashed and shrieked with laughter; men sat cross-legged as they mended fine mesh nets stretched across wide frames; women gutted silver fish under a canopy of green banana leaves, surrounded by noisy flocks of birds that fought for fish guts tossed over the edge of the quay; a small machine moved at the water's edge in quick bursts, like a squeezed pip of mercury.

An ache rose in Angel, a universal desolation. Lost, all lost. All she had known was lost, and yet all around were echoes of what she had lost. For the first time since she had been reborn, she felt the weight of her age.

The people who were following her were not human. They were aliens. She was surrounded by aliens which distorted the human norm, by pigmen, lionmen, lizardmen, birdmen, toadmen and others she could not begin to identify. They were animals trying to be human; they were humans masked with animal faces. They called themselves the Shaped,

and said that they had been changed, two words with the same root but
subtly different meanings she did not quite understand.

Angel had lost so much, and so much surrounded her, rich and
strange, yet hauntingly familiar. The birds and the butterflies, the wet
fetid smell of the mud, the smells of hot stone and cooking oil and the
acrid smoke from fires fueled with dry dung, the sunlight on the water
and the wind that stirred the glossy leaves and the red flowers of the
trees: a thousand fragmentary impressions that defined from moment to
moment the unquantifiable richness of the quiddity of the world. Many
of the transcendents had disappeared into imaginary empires within vast
data banks, creating perfect images of known worlds or building impossible new ones, but Angel had always felt that these were less satisfactory than dreams, too perfect to be truly real. That was why she
had opted for nonbeing during the long transits of her voyage, rather
than slowtime in a fabrication.

Reality, or nothing.

Angel took a ship out from the city. It was that easy. The ship's
captain was a fat, solemn, ponderous man with sleek black skin and
small eyes; his mother or grandmother might have been a seal, or might
have lain with one. He did not question Angel's presence as they sailed
downriver from city to city, but deferred to her with quiet good humor.
The fact that she had hijacked his ship and his life was never raised. A
city of tombs; a city of porcelain; a city of caves in cliffs high above
the river; a city of trees; a city built on stilts in the middle of the river.
Dozens of cities, each inhabited by a different race of people, all sharing
the same unquestioned laws and religion.

And then a city at war with itself.

A Change War, the ship's captain said, and when Angel told him
to put in at the city's long waterfront he came close to disobeying her
for the first time. It was a city of square houses of red mudbrick, all
heaped on each other like a tumbled pile of boxes. A terraced ziggurat
of white, weather-worn stone stood in the middle of the forest outside
the city wall, guarded by machines that constantly looped through the
air above it. It was the home of an old woman who called herself the
Commissioner.

Angel sat with the Commissioner on a high terrace of the ancient
ziggurat, amongst potted lemon trees and geraniums. Riverward, across
a sea of treetops, part of the city was burning. The sound of distant rifle
fire popped and crackled, brought erratically by the warm wind. The
Commissioner served Angel a bowl of the earthy infusion of twigs
which people everywhere on this world called tea. The Commissioner

was half Angel's height, a slow, deliberate woman with a humped back and a round face with lips pursed like a beak, and small black eyes half-hidden amongst the wrinkles of her leathery skin. She wore a kind of tent of fustian which dropped in many folds from a gold circlet at her neck to puddle the floor. A small machine darted and hovered above her like a bejeweled dragonfly.

The Commissioner seemed to regard the war as an unfortunate but inevitable natural process which could not be prevented but must be endured, like a sudden hailstorm or a forest fire. She told Angel that some of the people of the city had changed, and were at war with those who had not.

"The changed ones will win, of course. They always do. And then they will move on and found a new city, or more likely scatter along the river. It is an exciting time for them."

It took Angel a long time to find out from the Commissioner what she meant by change. It was a kind of transcendence or epiphany, a realization of individual worth, the possibility of sin or at least of transgression against the fixed codes by which the citizens had ordered their lives for millennia. It was a little like the memes with which Angel had once experimented when attempting to unify her spreading empire, but it was also a physical infection, a change in brain structure and chemistry which provided, as far as Angel understood it, an area of high density information storage that somehow interacted with the nine infolded dimensions in the quantum foam at the bottom of reality. Everything anyone of the changed races or bloodlines did or experienced was recorded or remembered by something like a soul that would survive until the end of the Universe. It was the true immortality which Angel and her kind had dreamed of millions of years ago, when they had still been human.

The Commissioner explained that the most primitive races, the indigens, would never change, but all others had changed or would change—there were still hundreds of unchanged races. Some had gone beyond the first change and transcended the world entirely, but the Commissioner could not tell Angel where they had gone. It was the work of the Preservers, and therefore not to be questioned. It simply was.

Angel wondered what happened to those of the unchanged and indigenous races who died (she was wondering about herself). The Commissioner grew reflective. It was night, now. The burning waterfront of the city stood above its own reflection in the still water of its long harbor. There were skirmishes in the fields and orchards upriver of the city—the flashes of rifles defined the opposing positions, and once there was a tremendous explosion that sent an expanding ball of red and yellow flame into the air and shook the terrace, rattling the bowls of tea on the slab of polished rock that floated between the two women.

"It is a question for the archivists," the Commissioner said at last. "But they are busy at the moment, talking with the wounded, and I do hope you will not disturb them. Because of the war, so many lives will pass unremarked—that is the cost of change, and it is a heavy price to pay. But some say that the Preservers mark all, and all will be restored whether we record it or not."

Angel thought of the millions of clerks laboring in the great palace of the capital city. She said, "Recording the world is important. Why is that?"

The Commissioner was watching the distant fighting. The fires, the stuttering flashes of rifles, the red blossoms of a cannonade, the abrupt fountains of earth and fire: at a distance, war is often beautiful. Firelight gleamed in her round, black eyes. She said, "It is one of the highest tasks."

"Recording memories for the Preservers to use?"

"The Preservers will resurrect everyone at the end of time. We will all live again."

This is an experiment, Angel thought. An experiment that records its own self. Things have been set in motion; evolution is expected. That means I can change things here. If the Preservers are using these people, then so can I.

She said, "If you could gain much in this life by behaving badly, and still the Preservers would resurrect you, then perhaps it is worth behaving badly. You could have power and wealth now, everything that you are promised in eternity, and the Preservers would forgive you."

The Commissioner considered this for a while. Angel watched the dark city beyond the forest. There were small fires scattered around the dimming glow of the site of the big explosion; the rifle fire seemed to have stopped.

At last, the Commissioner said, "All possible worlds can be created by the Preservers at the end of time, and that means not only all possible good, but also all possible evil. But the Preservers will not permit evil because it contradicts the love they bear toward us. For if they did not love us, why did they lift us up? So we must live our lives as best we can, for otherwise we might not have anything to live for beyond this life. Some say that the Preservers can correct evil in any person. No matter how great that evil might be, the Preservers have all of time and all of space in which to work their will. They say that the willingness of the Preservers to resurrect an evil person and punish them while holding out the possibility of redemption demonstrates the depth of their love toward us, their imperfect creations. But even if this is true, it is better to do good, for in the presence of infinite good it is better for you to act well and help others than to harm them, for you will gain nothing more by acting badly." The Commissioner laughed. "Ah, besides that, to think of the shame of having to endure the forgiveness of the Preservers! It is a heavy burden. Few could bear it."

Angel said, "Those who are changed are acting badly now."

"Only because their unchanged brothers, who know no other way of life, are fighting them. The unchanged cannot imagine change, and so they fight it to the death, and those who have changed must defend themselves. The unchanged do not know good or evil because they cannot choose between them. They are what they are, and no more."

"Yet you know the difference, and you do not intercede. You could remove the changed and stop the war. You condemn many to death by inaction. Is that not evil?"

"No one should set themselves in the place of the Preservers," the Commissioner said, staring at Angel. For the first time, she seemed to be offended.

Angel knew better than to insult the Preservers. They were universally worshipped, but no one could tell her much about them. Only that they had withdrawn their grace from the world but would return at the end of time and resurrect everyone who had ever lived, and everyone would live forever in an infinity of perfect worlds. It was a creed that was not dissimilar to the ambitions of the transcendents, but everyone on Confluence believed that the Preservers were capable of realizing it. At the same time, everyone believed that the ultimate nature of the Preservers was unknowable. What little that could be understood about them was in the Puranas, but the Puranas, which formed a kind of moral handbook illustrated by lessons in cosmology and galactic history, were maddeningly vague and imprecise. Early on, Angel had asked the ship to give her a précis of the Puranas, and recognized her own empire in a brief half sentence that horribly distorted what she had tried to do. That was another thing which must be put right. Her empire had once been the largest in human history, perhaps the largest empire ever known. She had not yet decided what she would do, but she would make sure that her long-lost empire was given its proper recognition.

"I'll stay here tonight," Angel said. "I assume this is a safe place. Find me food and a bed. I'll leave tomorrow."

"Of course." The Commissioner clacked her horny lips together and added, "However, I do believe that your ship has already left."

It was true. While Angel had been talking with the Commissioner, the ship she had commandeered at Ys had escaped her geas and made off. But the next day Angel simply commandeered another and continued downriver. The new ship was much larger than the first. Its three masts bore square sails with sunbursts painted on them and its deep holds were full of fruit which had been bound for a city upriver. The fruit rotted after a week and Angel ordered it thrown over the side. It took the crew, including the officers and the captain, a whole day to empty the holds, but the ship rode high in the water afterward, and sailed more swiftly. The captain said that the ship should be ballasted with stones, for otherwise it was likely to capsize in a storm, but Angel ignored him. She was in a hurry now.

She passed city after city, mostly inhabited by unchanged races as fixed in their habits as ants or bees. Without free will, they were more like zombies or organic machines than people, but even so, their unremarkable lives were recorded by patient archivists. They were policed by magistrates of their own kind. Although one or two officials of one or another of the changed races were present, they merely provided a kind of moral authority that was called on only when needed.

The last of the cities of the long, long river was called Sensch. It was a desert city of narrow streets shaded by palms and ginkgoes, dusty squares, flat-roofed buildings of whitewashed mudbrick. There were extensive plantations of sago and date palms, orange and pomegranate and banana, and various kinds of groundnuts. There was a great deal of camel breeding, too. At least, the things were a little like camels.

The citizens of Sensch were a slender people, skilled in pottery and glassmaking. They had low, heavily ridged foreheads and small, lidless black eyes; their brown and black skins exhibited varying degrees of residual scaliness. Snakes, the Commissioner of Sensch called them. He was a small, active fellow who lived in a garden that floated above the pink sandstone palace that was his official residence. The Commissioner, Dreen, seemed anxious to please, but Angel did not press her needs at once.

She met the Archivist of Sensch, a corpulent fellow with a limp, a few days later. His name was Mr. Naryan. He was of the same race as the captain of the first ship Angel had commandeered; she had seen him swimming off the wide plaza by the river, as graceful in the water as he was awkward and slow on land. He sat down beside Angel in a tea shop by one of the city's camel markets, pretending at first not to realize who she was. Angel liked his sly, patient air and demanded nothing of him at all, not even that he accept her for what she was. She missed conversation amongst equals.

The Archivist was afraid of Angel, but he hid it well. He made small talk about a procession that went past, explaining that the people had had their reason taken away, either as punishment or because of what he called a religious avocation. He said that he understood that she had come a long way, and she laughed at the understatement.

The Archivist said with mild alarm, "I do not mean to insult you."

Angel tried to make it easier by talking about the Archivist himself. She pointed at his loose, belted shirt and said, "You dress like a . . . native." She had almost said Snake. She said, "Is that a religious avocation?"

He told her what she already knew, that he was the city's archivist. He had a round, kindly face, with heavy wrinkles at his brow and three fat folds under his chin.

Angel said, "The people here are different—a different race in every city. When I left, not a single intelligent alien species was known. It was one reason for my voyage. Now there seem to be thousands strung along this long river. They treat me like a ruler—is that it? Or am I like a god?"

"The Preservers departed long ago. These are the end times."

The Archivist said this by rote. He had not really understood her questions.

Angel said, "There are always those who believe they live at the end of history. We thought that we lived at the end of history, when every star system in the Galaxy had been mapped, every habitable world settled.

"I was told that the Preservers, who I suppose are my descendants, made the different races, but each race calls itself human, even the ones who don't look as if they could have evolved from anything that ever looked remotely human."

"The Shaped call themselves human because they have no other name for what they have become, changed and unchanged alike. After all, they had no name before they were raised up." The Archivist added in a pleading tone, "The citizens of Sensch remain innocent. They are our . . . responsibility."

Angel told him that his kind was not doing a very good job, judging by the Change War she had witnessed upriver. She described the war, and asked the Archivist many questions, most of which he was unable to answer. Without asking her permission, he jotted down her description of the Change War and her questions on a tablet using an impacted system of diacritical marks. Angel was amused.

"You listen to people's stories."

"Stories are important. In the end they are all that is left, all that history leaves us. Stories endure."

Angel thought about this. She said at last, "I have been out of history a long time. I'm not sure that I want to be a part of it again."

She was tired. While she had been traveling, she had been able to forget that she had escaped her ship and her responsibilities, but now she would have to come to a decision. She did not want to talk anymore and left the Archivist. He knew better than to follow her, and she liked him for that, too.

She found a suitable house, a two-story affair with a balcony around the upper story overlooking a central courtyard shaded by a jacaranda tree. Its owners, grateful for her attention, were only too pleased to give it to her, and others came with gifts: furniture, carpets, food and wine, musical instruments, cigarettes, paintings, sheets of plastic she realized were books, slates which showed scenes from the world's past, stolen from tombs of hierophants far downriver.

Some of the people stayed with her, mostly young men. Angel experimented with sex. Full intercourse with the Snakes was anatomically impossible, but there were a variety of pleasing and diverting exercises. In the evenings, she watched dancers or shadow puppet plays, or listened to the atonal nasal singing of the finest poet of the city, accompanied by a silver flute and a two-string lyre. The days passed pleasantly until the Archivist found her in the teahouse by the camel market and told her that her ship was coming to Sensch.

Angel affected a casualness she did not feel. She had expected it to find her, but not so quickly. She fell into conversation with the Archivist and eventually took him back to her house. He took in the bustle with a solemn air and told her gently that she should not take advantage of the citizens.

Angel said sharply, "They seem happy to me. What's wrong with that?"

The Archivist cast his eyes down. She knew then that he could not argue with her, and felt a stab of shame.

She had tea and honey fritters brought out, and described something of what she had seen on her long river journey, and asked the Archivist many questions about Dreen's authority and the way that order was maintained in the city. She caught one of the machines and showed it to him. "And these? By what authority do these little spies operate?"

The Archivist stared at it opened-mouthed. Perhaps he had never seen anyone catch one before. Pinched between Angel's thumb and forefinger, the little bronze bug wriggled as it tried to free itself. Its sensor cluster, a froth of glass and silver beads, turned back and forth until Angel let it go.

The Archivist watched it rise above the roof of the house. He said, "Why, they are part of the maintenance system of Confluence."

"Can Dreen use them? Tell me all you know. It may be important."

Angel met with the Archivist at intervals in the days that followed. The young men who followed her formed a kind of band or gang, and some went with her wherever she went. They made the Archivist nervous, but Angel encouraged them, if only because it was a measure of what she could do. She gave them white headbands lettered with a slogan she had composed. Giving away one of the headbands was like bestowing a blessing. She made speeches in the markets and on the plaza by the river to try and rouse the citizens, but although people gathered and listened politely, nothing much came of it, except that her own followers sometimes grew too excited. They were apt to misunderstand what she had to say about rising above destiny, and defaced walls with slogans, or overturned stalls in the market. They were gripped by powerful but unfocused emotions.

Perhaps these petty acts were to her followers heady and radical statements, but Angel knew that it was not the way. She went to the temple and had one of the priests help her consult the interactive librarian which manifested in one of the large terminals the priests called shrines. She decided that she would cross the river to where a cluster of old shrines stood, unused since the Snakes had come to occupy Sensch. She would try and wake the shrines there, and learn from them.

Then there was a blank picture. Whatever Angel had done at the shrines at the edge of the world, by the great falls at the end of the river, was not recorded. Yama set his book aside. He was very tired, but not at all sleepy.

It was a few hours from dawn. The smoky swirl of the Eye of the Preservers was setting at the edge of the world. Tamora and Pandaras slept under the awning. Captain Lorquital and Aguilar slept in their cabins beneath the poop deck; the sailors slept head to toe in their hammocks beneath the deck on which Yama sat. He had always needed less sleep than Telmon or anyone else he knew, and was used to being awake when everyone else slept. Even so, and even though he was not strictly alone, for the helmsman stood at the wheel in the red glow of the shaded stern lantern, Yama felt a desolation, a vast aching emptiness, there on the ship in the midst of the wide river. He wondered if this was how Angel had felt, estranged from all she knew by millions of years of history, with only compliant uncomprehending aliens for company. How lonely she must have been, ruler of all the world, but with no purpose!

He would finish her story in a little while, he thought. He already suspected that he knew how it ended. Enough for now. First his father's papers, and the shock they contained amongst their dense ladders of calculations. And now this. No more stories.

Yama shook dew from the blanket Pandaras had put around his shoulders and lay down, just for a moment. And slept.

24

Gond

"IT IS A city that shines like the ice flows of the mountains at the end of the world," Eliphas told Yama. "I last saw it many years ago, but I still remember how it shone in the sunlight across the blue waters of the river. The river may be shrinking, brother, but it runs deeper here than anywhere else in the world, deeper even than at Ys. They fish for leviathans off the shore of Gond."

Yama flinched, remembering the one solid fact he had gleaned from the muddle of his stepfather's papers. Eliphas did not notice. He was lost in his memories.

"They fish not from coracles or cockleshells," the old man said, "but from barges as big as fields, with big motors that make the water boil around their sterns when they are working. There are leviathans deep beneath our keel, and that's what these barges are after. They send down lures as tall as a man and armed with explosive hooks, using steel cables several leagues long. If they strike lucky, they haul up their catch and render it there and then. Of course, most of the time the leviathan escapes, and sometimes, despite its power, a barge is dragged under by what it catches."

"I thought that the people of Gond led aesthetic and contemplative lives," Yama said.

"The fishermen come from the cities of the Dry Plains, further downriver. From Ush and Kalyb and Galata, and the twin cities of Kilminar and Balbeck." Eliphas intoned the names with sonorous pleasure. "If a barge catches more than one leviathan in the hunting season its crew count themselves lucky. The proceeds from rendering one monster would buy a ship like this twice over."

Yama and Eliphas were leaning side by side at the rail of the main deck of the *Weazel,* in the shadow of the big, rust-red sail. Sternward, smoky columns of rain twisted beneath the reefs of white and gray clouds that overshadowed the farside shore—a desolation of mudflats and pioneer mangroves inhabited only by birds and swarms of army crabs. There had been no sign of either the warship or the picketboat in the past three days, and the *Weazel* was at last angling away from the farside and the spurious safety of the mangrove swamps. Ahead, in the far distance, the Great River bent toward the Rim Mountains, and at the angle of the nearside shore a mote of light glistened, white as a crystal of salt: the city of Gond. Captain Lorquital had announced that the *Weazel* would put in there to collect a passenger and to take on fresh provisions.

Yama told Eliphas, "I see that you are happy to retrace the steps you took when you were a young man."

Eliphas closed his eyes. His face was shaded by the wide brim of the straw hat he wore as protection from the sun. "It has been more than a hundred years. I thought I had forgotten most of it, but each place we pass brings memories rising from the depths of my mind, as the monsters of the abyssal currents of the river rise to follow the glowing lures trailed by the fishing barges."

He opened his eyes and smiled: silver and white flashed in his black face. "Do not worry, brother. I will fulfill the promise I made to you in the library of the Department of Apothecaries and Chirurgeons. I will find the lost city for you. I know that your servants are suspicious of me, but I have your best interests at heart."

"They are not my servants, Eliphas."

Eliphas smiled. "They believe otherwise, brother. Look there! A pod of grampuses! See how they sport!"

Three, four, five sleek white creatures swam swiftly through the clear water, effortlessly overtaking the speeding ship. They caught up with the purling bow-wave and rode it briefly, plunging and leaping in white foam, then all at once they sounded, pale shadows dwindling away into the dark depths of the river.

Eliphas said, "Some believe they are intelligent, and that they herd the fish of the river as the autochthons of the mountains herds sheep or goats."

"When you are swimming in the river, you can sometimes hear them singing," Yama said. He had often heard their songs himself, for in summer schools of grampuses migrated far upriver. Songs that lasted for hours, deep throbbings overlaid with scatterings of chirps and whistles, haunting, mysterious and somehow lonely, as if defining the inhuman vastness of the Great River.

"They say that the Preservers placed everything on this world for a purpose," Eliphas said, "and the ultimate purpose is to raise up all the Shaped so that we may live forever in their glory. But I sometimes wonder if the Preservers brought creatures like the grampuses to the world simply because of the joy they strike in the hearts of men. If that is true, I can forgive them much."

Yama remembered that the woman in the shrine, Angel's aspect, had said that the Preservers were descended from her own people. He said, "I think that the Preservers were once not so different from us. The first suras of the Puranas tell us that in times long past there were no gods, but only many kinds of humans."

"There is no gradation in godhood," Eliphas said. "It is not like the process of aging, which is so gradual that only by looking back are you shocked by how much you have changed, for you have no sense of having changed at all. And of course, from day to day you have not changed in any measurable sense. No, brother, the Preservers changed utterly and at once, and so what they were before they became gods is irrelevant. When godhood descended upon them, or when they ascended to godhood, everything they had been fell away."

"And yet they made us over in their image. Not as what they became, but as what they once were. And so they did not leave their past behind."

Eliphas nodded gravely. The old man loved metaphysical discourse. He was one of those for whom the world is merely an object from which theoretical ideals might be abstracted, and therefore less important than thought.

"The Preservers have not forgotten what they once were," he said, "but they put it behind them, as a butterfly puts behind its caterpillar childhood when it emerges from its cocoon. The Puranas are perhaps that cocoon, which we riddle for clues. Yet it is only an empty shell left clinging to the twig of the world. That which matters has ascended into everlasting sunlight."

Yama smiled at the old man's fanciful metaphor. He enjoyed these conversations; they reminded him of the long debates with Zakiel and Telmon, of happier times. He said, "You have seen me read in the Puranas. It is not to understand the Preservers. It is to understand myself."

"I believe that your copy of the Puranas is a very old one."

Yama knew that Eliphas wanted to examine the book, but he had decided that he would not show the transformed pictures to anyone. Not, at least, until he had understood Angel's story. He would read more tonight. He thought that he already knew how it ended—but perhaps it had not ended after all. Perhaps he was part of that story, coming late onto the stage to draw the curtain and announce the end of the play.

Eliphas said, "Books are more powerful than the world. Even if the world ended, then surely someone would chronicle it. And so that book would save the world, for it would live again in the minds of any who read the account."

"I spent much of my childhood in a library. Perhaps too much of it was spent studying the past. I want to see the world, Eliphas, and all its wonders. I want the present, not the past."

"But the past is all around us. We cannot escape it. Everything important has happened in the past, and we are its children. The Preservers achieved godhood in the past and made the world in the past and shaped the bloodlines in the past. The future is a small thing and hazily glimpsed, and we are told that once every bloodline has changed the future will cease, for history will cease. But you are right, brother. Children should look ahead, not behind. We cannot live in the past, or else the future will only echo what has already happened."

So they talked as the ship, sailing aslant the river's currents, drew closer to the shining city of Gond. Eliphas preferred his own opinions to those of anyone else, but Yama was grateful for the diversion of his company.

He could not grieve for his stepfather, not yet. He could not give way to grief or anger. He must stay calm and alert, for sooner or later he would have to face Prefect Corin again. He did not believe that he had escaped. Prefect Corin was a thorough man. He would not have been fooled for long by Yama's ruse, and would have returned to the floating forest to search for remains of his quarry. Finding none, he would have gone on downriver, implacable, relentless. This was not mere supposition: Yama had already turned aside several machines that were searching the wide river for any trace of the *Weazel*. So he was not surprised when, that evening, as the *Weazel* scudded ahead of a light breeze toward the floating harbor that stood off the shore of Gond, Captain Lorquital called him up to the quarterdeck.

Aguilar and Tamora stood on either side of Captain Lorquital's sling chair. Aguilar told Yama, "Your trick with the machines has run aground. The devil has got ahead of us."

"We'll have to face him now," Tamora said, and her black lips peeled back from her teeth at the thought.

Ixchel Lorquital handed Yama her spectacles without comment. Through their magnifying lenses, the floating harbor leapt closer. There were ships of every size laid up at the leagues of pontoons and cranes and warehouses of the docks; their masts made a leafless forest. And in the channels beyond the floating harbor, a picketboat and a triple-decked warship were anchored side by side, their sails half-reefed.

"Well," Yama said, "we could not hope to hide from him forever."

"There was a light signal from the harbor," Captain Lorquital said. "We are to pick up our passenger tonight. He's an important man, and we can leave tomorrow morning under his protection, like any other honest vessel."

"We can't depend on that," Aguilar said, and told Yama, "Your devil will be watching the river night and day, but I think we'll have a better chance if we run at night."

Tamora said, "We might surprise him."

"I saw a machine today," Captain Lorquital said. "It was making directly for us when it suddenly angled away, as if it remembered business it had elsewhere."

"I cannot confuse the minds of men," Yama said, "and Aguilar is right. Prefect Corin's men will be watching every ship that passes by. Especially those few that pass by at night."

"We have lost our cannon," Aguilar said. "We have only our small arms. If it comes to a fight, we must surprise them."

"We must strike first," Tamora said.

"We have made plans," Aguilar said. "Barrels of pitch. A catapult—"

Captain Lorquital said, "I won't be a pirate, daughter. They must fire the first shot."

"And that one shot could sink us," Aguilar said.

Yama said, "It is better to know where our enemy is than to run with the thought that he is always somewhere behind us. Besides, he will have no warrant or power here. He is merely another sailor put in for shore leave and reprovisioning. If he tries to hurt us, the common law will protect us."

"The people of Gond care little for anything but their philosophies," Aguilar said. "They'll probably turn us over to that town burner rather than interrupt their meditations to listen to us plead our case."

"She's right," Tamora said. "We must take matters into our own hands."

"Then we'll be worse than them," Captain Lorquital said firmly. "This is an end to the argument. We'll behave as any normal ship. The free men will get their shore leave, and you, daughter, will stand guard with the slaves. Nothing will happen to us at the harbor, and once our passenger is aboard, we'll have his protection."

Afterward, Tamora followed Yama to the bow. "You are planning something," she said. "I know you don't believe that crut about common law."

"I want to kill him," Yama said.

Tamora grinned hugely. "That's more like it. How? And how can I help?"

"I want to kill him, but I do not think that I should."

"Then he will kill you."

"Yes, he will, if he cannot make me serve him."

"He destroyed your home, Yama. He killed your father as surely as if he had put an arbalest bolt through his heart. He is your enemy. There is nothing sweeter than drinking the blood of your enemy. Don't deny yourself the pleasure."

"He is only one man. How many more will the Department send after me? How many more would I have to kill? If I kill Prefect Corin there will never be an end to killing. I will always be hunted. But if I can find a way to end this, then I will be free."

Tamora thought about this. "We'll try your way," she said at last. "And if that doesn't work, give him to me. He is as much my enemy as yours. I'll rip his heart from his chest and eat it in front of his dying eyes."

She smiled fiercely at the thought, but Yama knew that she shared his foreboding.

———

A fishing barge was anchored upstream of the floating harbor, the enormous carcass of a leviathan sprawled across its wide flat deck. Already partly defleshed, the arches of the leviathan's ribcage rose higher than the barge's cranes. Its guts, tinged pink with the plankton on which it had fed, spilled in heavy loops from a rent that would have admitted the *Weazel,* mast and all. A line of men was strung across the wide flat tail of the carcass, like harvesters working across a field. They were using huge flensing knives to cut the hide away from the blubber beneath. Black smoke poured from the barge's rendering furnaces, sending up a stink of burning fat and hazing the last light of the sun. Flocks of birds dipped and rose like whirling snowstorms, fighting for titbits in the bloody waters.

As the *Weazel* glided through the lee of the barge, Yama watched the city of Gond slip past to starboard. It had once risen out of the river; now, it looked like the last tooth of an old man, its roots exposed beyond a labyrinth of mudflats. Gond, the porcelain city. A clutch of luminous white shells three leagues across, rising and falling in rounded contours like a range of ancient dunes, tinged with rose and silver and gold. Here and there were clusters of slim towers, their tops ringed round by tiers of balconies. Floating gardens hovered along the river margin, their parks and woods strung with thousands of lamps.

Eliphas climbed onto the forecastle deck. "There are probably not more than a hundred living there now," he said. "Mostly, it is maintained by machines."

"Yet they once ruled Ys," Yama said.

He had once read a brief history of the porcelain city, and remembered that it had grown from a single seed planted in the sand of a beach at the first bend in the Great River. He wondered if that beach was still there, beneath the carapace of the city—the past preserved forever in the present. But no strangers were allowed into Gond. Its beauty was also its shield. Its people were great philosophers and teachers, but they did their work in colleges scattered amongst the orchards and fields and paddies that surrounded the city. From the first, the city had drawn a circle around itself.

"They ruled Ys a long time ago," Eliphas said, "in the grim days after the Hierarchs vanished, but before the civil service reached its present consensus. They are much diminished, yet still much exulted. If any who live in these days are close to the Preservers, then the people of Gond are the closest. They are so holy that they no longer have children. Their bloodline dwindles. The youngest is a century older than me, and I am counted as long-lived by my bloodline. Their holiness will be the death of them, soon enough. The past has consumed them, brother. The face of the city is more beautiful than I remembered, but it is the beauty of a well-kept tomb."

As the *Weazel* made her way toward the harbor under the power of her reaction motor, her sail neatly reefed, a small boat motored out to meet her. A pilot came aboard and formally greeted Captain Lorquital, then asked to see the boy, Yama.

"We have two ships under command of an official of the Department of Indigenous Affairs," the pilot told Yama. "Perhaps you know him."

"His name is Corin. He is a Prefect of the Department."

The pilot was a small man, smaller even than Pandaras, but he had

the brisk, assured air of someone used to command. He wore immac-
ulately polished black boots and loose linen trousers under a scarlet
djellaba, and was smoking a black cigarillo. He blew a riffle of smoke
with a flourish and looked at Yama squarely. "Whatever business you
have with him, it is nothing to do with the harbor. We have become a
staging post for the war, but we are not under the command of the
Department of Indigenous Affairs."

"I understand."

"You will not take weapons if you go ashore. Neither will he, nor
will his men. All go unarmed here."

"You put it very plainly," Yama said. "I hope that I may speak
plainly, too. This man wants to make me his prisoner. Because of that,
Captain Lorquital fears for the safety of her ship."

The pilot nodded, and drew on his cigarillo. "He tried to force the
issue, and the Harbor Master had to point out that we do not take sides
in any dispute. Nor will we be the arena for the settling of any quarrel.
Frankly, if he had not tried to force us, we would have let him take
you. But we cannot allow him to set a dangerous precedent." He flicked
the butt of his cigarillo over the side and turned on his heel. "Now,
Captain Lorquital, the helm if you please. I will take you in."

The pilot guided the *Weazel* to a berth at a long pontoon at the inner
edge of the harbor, amongst mussel dredgers and two-masted ketches
of the kind which carried small cargoes between cities everywhere along
the river. The sultry air tasted of the acrid smoke of the fishing barge's
rendering furnaces. The water around the pontoon was stained with sullen rainbows; flocks of tiny machines skated the surface, absorbing
spilled fuel oil through pads on their long legs. Pelicans perched on
mooring posts, drying their wings, like rows of arrowheads against the
red light of the setting sun. A league away, across a maze of channels
and pontoons and graving basins, colored neon lights blazed and winked
above clusters of clapboard buildings and plastic domes. The pilot repeated his warning to Yama and Captain Lorquital, and took his leave.

"We can't go ashore unarmed," Tamora said.

"You have your teeth and claws," Pandaras said, "I have my cunning, and our master has his power over machines. What more do we
need?"

"I want to talk with him," Yama said. "I will go alone, and unarmed."

Tamora said, "And where will you begin to look for him? It would
be better if you stayed here. It'll be the first place he'll look, and there's
nothing to say we can't be armed if we stay aboard our own ship."

Even as the sailors began to make the *Weazel* fast in her berth, shills appeared on the pontoon, handing out little tiles that whispered seductive invitations to whorehouses and bars. One of the shills called Yama's name and threw a tile to the deck at his feet and quickly walked away, pushing through the others. Yama picked up the white tile and the golden dragon printed on its surface flexed its wings and breathed a wisp of blue fire that formed two words. A name.

Mother Spitfire's.

Yama insisted on going alone, although Tamora argued fiercely against it. "The crews of the picketboat of the warship will be crawling all over this place," she said. "A gang of them could set on you anywhere. Better to fight in a place of your own choosing."

"I know where he wants to meet you," Eliphas said. "This place is famous for its entertainments. Of course, it has moved downriver. It used to be anchored off Kalyb, but the fall in the level of the river has stranded that city a dozen leagues from navigable water." He peered at the long strip of lights twinkling in the dusk and added, "It seems larger, but I suppose that is because of the war."

Tamora spat over the side of the ship. A tiny machine skated over oily water after her gob of spittle. "Grah. You should swim out to the warship, if you are so eager to meet Corin. It would make as much sense. A man like him won't dirty the soles of his boots in the stews of a place like this. His invitation is a trick."

"Better we speak on neutral ground," Yama said.

"I could break his neck for you."

"I am sure you could."

"Or gouge out his eyes."

"I just want to talk with him, Tamora. That is why I will go alone, or not at all."

Pandaras agreed readily enough to this. He said that he had a mission of his own.

"Captain Lorquital has given the freemen liberty until the midnight watch, and it seems that my friend, Pantin, has never been with a woman. It was part of the discipline of his former trade. I feel it's time he was taken in hand, as it were."

"If you know what you are doing," Yama said, thinking of the young sailor's reputation as a pit fighter. Pantin was already on the pontoon, waiting with his hands in the back pockets of the scuffed leather trousers he habitually wore.

"Pantin has renounced the knife life," Pandaras said, "and I'll make sure he's too busy to get into trouble."

Pandaras walked a little way with Yama, then he and Pantin went off arm in arm, and Yama went in the other direction, toward the far end of the Strip and *Mother Spitfire's.*

The main drag of the floating harbor was laid out along a boardwalk half a league long. The gaudily painted fronts of chandlers, bars and whorehouses rose shoulder to shoulder on either side. Groups of intoxicated sailors and soldiers surged and staggered beneath flashing neon and flaring torches, carrying paper cups of beer or smoking pipes of crystal or weed as they moved from one attraction to the next. This was the last stop their transports would make before the battlefields above the midpoint of the world, and Yama supposed that they sought oblivion in the few hours it took for their ships to renew their stores. Hawkers cried the merits of drinking or smoking dens; there were tattoo parlors and fast-food joints, dream parlors and gambling palaces. Dancers of all sexes and a decad of different bloodlines (or perhaps they were all mirror people, Yama thought) bumped and ground in lighted windows above the awnings of bars; musicians, magicians and gamblers made islands in the throng. Here and there, magistrates stood on floating discs above the packed heads of the crowds, and their tiny, glittering machines spun everywhere through the neon-lit air.

Mother Spitfire's was a gambling palace at the far end of the Strip. A dragon limned in golden neon tubing sprawled across its tall façade; pillars of fire roared within tall columns of glass on either side of the wide doors.

Tamora and Eliphas were waiting outside, and Yama's first pang of anger quickly gave way to relief. He laughed, and said, "I suppose Pandaras and Pantin are skulking somewhere nearby."

"I sent them off to a whorehouse," Tamora said, "but the old man insists on staying here, even though he'll only be in the way." She was not wearing her sword, and stood with her thumbs stuck in the belt of her leather skirt, scowling at every passerby.

"I know this place," Eliphas said, "and I hope that I can be of help. But I fear that Prefect Corin does not want to talk. There are many places on the Strip that will amuse you. Let me show them to you. Forget all this for a few hours, and then we will be gone."

"You wanted me to destroy him a few days ago," Yama said. "If you do not wish to meet Prefect Corin, then go back to the ship. I will not blame you."

"We can still strike first," Tamora said, "beginning with this Mother Spitfire. She must be a friend of Corin's."

"She is famous here," Eliphas said. "Or rather, infamous."

Yama said, "Ixchel Lorquital told me that Mother Spitfire will lose her license if she allows any of her guests to bear arms. We will talk. That is all."

Tamora passed the palm of one hand over her scarred scalp. She said, "I'll do more than talk with him if he so much as looks at me in a funny way. Him or anyone else."

Inside, men and women crowded at dice tables down a long room, under greenery that spilled from floating discs. Most of the gamblers were in uniform. The roar of their wagers and prayers mingled with the plaintive music of a shadow puppet show that played on a screen raised above the midpoint of the room. Beyond, more people crowded around the walls of a fighting pit or were scattered on the tiers of wide steps that rose on either side.

Mother Spitfire herself came up the central aisle to greet Yama. She was very tall and very slender, golden-skinned and clad in a sheath dress of red silk that flowed like water. Two burly men of Tamora's bloodline stood behind her, impassive in black robes. Tamora stared at them; they stared back.

"Welcome, Yamamanama," Mother Spitfire said, bowing so sinuously that her small, sleek head was brought close to Yama's. Her breath smelled of honey and cinnamon. She pressed a stack of gambling markers into Yama's hand. Her fingernails were very long, and painted scarlet. "May your luck increase this poor gift many times over."

"Where is he?"

Mother Spitfire's green, slit-pupiled eyes were large and lidless; a nictitating membrane filmed them for a moment. She said, "You are as bold and direct as he said you would be. Is it bravery, I wonder, or innocence? He is on his way. Meanwhile enjoy yourselves. We have several pairs of well-matched contestants tonight"—her voice lowered—"although if I were to place a wager on the next bout, I would favor the smaller animal."

"Thank you for your advice," Yama said.

"There will be no fighting here," Mother Spitfire said, looking at Tamora for a moment, "except for that in the pit."

"I trust you were paid well for the risk," Yama said.

"Not so much that I can afford to have my business closed. I have pledged that there will be no trouble from either side."

Mother Spitfire swept away, followed by her bodyguards. Tamora stared after her and said, "They could take us here and no one would notice."

Yama pointed to one of the little machines that spun through the smoky air above the gaming tables. "The magistrates watch everywhere," he said. "What happens in the pit?"

"They fight to the death," Eliphas said. "This place is infamous. Mother Spitfire is the last of her kind, older than anyone in Gond. But it is not a seemly spectacle that she presides over, brother. Perhaps Tamora is correct. We should choose our own meeting place. Here, we place ourselves at the mercy of our enemy."

"I am tired of running," Yama said.

He led the way through the crowd that clustered around the oval fighting pit, and climbed the sweep of steps to the very top. The pit was filled with water and lit by powerful lamps. Men and women leaned at the rail, watching as two naked slaves trawled fragments from the water with long-handled rakes. A gong sounded softly and the slaves set down their rakes and cranked down spring-loaded arms with a net stretched between them, dividing the flooded pit in two. A little old man in a black robe, his beard so long that he wore its forked end over his shoulder, climbed into a basket seat and pulled vigorously on a system of ropes and pulleys to hoist himself above the water.

"They keep them in heat," Eliphas said. "They do it with injections, so they're always ready to fight."

The gong sounded again, battered brass soft as a dying man's last sigh. Water boiled at either end of the pit and two sleek shapes glided out into the light. There was a flurry of betting amongst the spectators.

Yama's breath caught in his throat. The creatures in the water were kelpies. Steel spurs were fastened to their flippers; spiked chains to their tails. One swam straight at the net and recoiled from a sputter of fat blue sparks, spouting a cloud of oily vapor. The other held still in the center of its half of the pit, its tail moving up and down with slow deliberation.

The old man said something about *preparing the bout,* and, *last wagers please.* As his amplified voice echoed around the room, there was a renewed flurry of betting. Then the gong sounded for the third time and the spring-loaded arms snapped back, raising the net out of the water with an explosive motion. The two kelpies shot into the center of the pit, lashing around each other, parting, and engaging again.

Water splashed over the sides, draining away through slots in the floor. The spectators hooted and stamped and whistled. Both kelpies were bleeding from gashes in their pale bellies. Their blood looked black as it fluttered through the brilliantly lit water. For a moment, they hung head to head; then they engaged again, and suddenly one was on top of the other. It beat at its opponent's flanks with its tail chains, and with its teeth ripped through blubber and flesh to expose the spine, which it broke with a quick snap of its head. It slid away, snorting vapor through the nasal slits at the top of its head and making a hoarse braying whistle, and the corpse rolled over and sank through a cloud of its own blood. The old man above the pit chanted a string of numbers and there was a flurry of activity amongst the spectators as betting markers were exchanged. Slaves used long electrified prods to drive the victorious kelpie away from the corpse and harry it into one of the tunnels.

Yama felt both sick and excited. The spectacle was horrible and degrading, yet even in their hormone-induced fury, the animals were possessed of a fierce beauty.

Eliphas saw Yama's disgust. He said, "There is worse to come, brother. We should leave now. Meet with your enemy elsewhere. Let me show you—"

"Too late," Tamora said. "He is here."

Three men were coming up the steps toward them. As always, Prefect Corin wore a plain homespun tunic, but this time he was not carrying his staff. His two companions wore breastplates of plastic armor and short kirtles of red cloth that left their legs bare.

Tamora insisted on patting the three men down. Prefect Corin submitted to her search with good humor, and favored Yama with one of his rare smiles. "You are well, boy," he said. He looked sleek and self-satisfied and calm. "I am glad. It was quite a chase you led me. The trick with the scouts was good. I should have guessed that you could fool them sooner than I did. You have learned a great deal since I last talked with you."

"Many things have changed," Yama said. He had expected to feel a hot rage when he confronted the man who had murdered his stepfather, but instead he felt nothing at all, not even contempt. His hands were trembling, though, and he folded his arms and returned Prefect Corin's gaze as steadily as he could.

"They're clean," Tamora said, "but don't let them come any closer. I'll break their necks if they try." She glared at Prefect Corin's companions, who looked through her as if she did not exist.

Prefect Corin said, "The reputation of your companion is not the highest, but I understand that she tries to make up with bravado what she lacks in skill." He glanced at Eliphas. "This man had a reputation, too. Where is he leading you? What trick is he upon? You are out of your depth, Eliphas. You should have stuck to gouging would-be widows wanting recipes for undetectable poisons."

Eliphas said with great dignity, "I don't know you, dominie, but I see that my jealous rivals have been whispering in your ear."

Yama told Prefect Corin, "I am not sorry about your machines. I will destroy any you send against me. You must know that. And you must know that I will not serve."

Prefect Corin said, "There are always more machines. Think of it as a test. The more you resist, the more we learn about you. The more you try to escape, the more we will chase you. If you came here hoping that I would allow you to go on your way unhindered, than I must disappoint you. Give in, boy. The river is wide, but it is not endless. The further you travel, the nearer you approach the war, where there are millions under the command of the Department. You cannot hide from all of them; you cannot override all of the machines. I can offer you much, and that is why I am here. We do not want to lose you."

Yama met Prefect Corin's mild gaze with an effort of will. He said, "How goes the war amongst the departments in the Palace of the Memory of the People?"

"We will win."

"Perhaps not, since you have not already won."

"What will you do if you do not join us? Trust Eliphas and his wild tales? Preach to the underclasses as you did on the roof of the Palace? Take care with your answer. I would not like to indict you for heresy against the word of the Preservers."

"I go in search of my people, nothing more. And I do not believe that you serve the Preservers. You do not even serve the Department. You serve your own ends."

"You were brought up in the traditions of the Department, and you should know that we are here to serve the people, not our own selves. I was sorry to hear of your father's death, by the way. He was a good servant, although a weak man who clung to traditions long past their usefulness. He should not have become involved in this."

Tamora said, "Yama, I'll make them go. Just give me the word."

"I will hear what he has to offer," Yama said. He felt perfectly calm, despite the tremor in his hands. Crowds were gathering around the flooded fighting pit again. The body of the loser had been removed and the water had been cleaned.

Prefect Corin shrugged. "Perhaps I will not bother. Perhaps I believe that you have already made up your mind, Yamamanama."

"But you cannot know for certain. That is why you came."

"You dare to presume—" For the first time, Prefect Corin's reserve was breached. He drew a finger down the white streak which divided the left side of his black-furred face and said, "You presume too much. You are not subtle, boy. But I will tell you this. We will not ask you to fight. We will ask only that we can study you to find out how you control machines. And when we know, why, you will be free to do as you will. You wish to find out why you are here and where you come from? All the resources of the Department will be at your disposal. You will be elevated through the ranks to the first circle of committees. If you wish to help the underclasses, do so within established structures of power. Otherwise you waste all that you might be. How can you justify throwing that away, because of pride?"

"You would raise me up to a level I do not deserve in order to give the Department power it does not deserve. The Department exists to serve those you call the underclasses. Perhaps it has forgotten that. Perhaps it would be best if the Department looked to its own faults before attempting to correct the faults of others."

"Ah, Yamamanama. I admire your certainty. But do think a while on what I have said. We have no hurry. Your captain still awaits her passenger, although he would be ill-advised to journey with you, should you choose to attempt to leave."

The gong sounded again. Prefect Corin turned toward the pit. He said, "We will watch the next bout. I think that it will amuse you. And while you watch, think on what I have offered."

"It is the worst of the wickedness of this place," Eliphas said, with a sudden passion.

Two men sat at either end of the pool, in the same kind of suspended basket chairs as the old man who had refereed the first bout. The men were masked and gloved. Thin cables trailed from the chairs into the water. As spectators thickened around the pit, the men sat quietly above the rising buzz of conversation and the rattle of betting markers. The net was not lowered this time; suddenly, without fuss, two kelpies were hanging at either end of the flooded pit, shadows floating as quiet and still in the water as the two men seated in the air above them.

Yama asked Eliphas what kind of contest this would be, but Eliphas simply said that Yama would soon see. "But we should leave," he said. "It is a perversion of old knowledge."

Prefect Corin said, "Knowledge is like power. It is only effective if it is used. You will not use your power, Yamamanama. That is why we will triumph, and you will lose."

The gong gently battered the air again. Above the pit, the men rolled and twisted in their basket chairs. The kelpies shot forward. They missed each other on the first pass. One smashed its blunt head against the side of the tank while the other somersaulted clumsily and bore in with a sudden rush. It ripped a gash in the belly of its opponent with a steel-tipped flipper, but failed to follow through.

Yama saw the thin cables that trailed after each kelpie and understood what was happening. The kelpies were living puppets, commanded by the masked and gloved men just as Nergal had commanded the spiders.

He seized control with a spasm of anger and disgust. The kelpies shot past each other and crashed into opposite ends of the tank. The impact killed them instantly; their human operators were both stricken by seizures that jerked them out of their suspended chairs. One hung by his harness; the other toppled over and smashed into the water. Yama collapsed against Tamora, momentarily blinded by feedback and red and black lightning.

Half of the spectators surged forward to see what had happened; the others were trying to get away. Knots of fighting broke out. A grossly fat woman stood in the middle of the mêlée, screaming with operatic force.

Yama shrugged off Tamora's grip and started down the steps. One of Prefect Corin's men tried to stop him, but Tamora kicked him in the back of his knee and he went down as Yama dodged past. He threw up the markers Mother Spitfire had given him and, as people scrambled for them, ran under the screen and dodged through the maze of gambling tables, overturning them as he went. He was fueled by rage and fear. His sight pounded with red and black in solid flashes. The thing inside him had come back; he was a helpless passenger in his own skull.

The entire building seemed transparent, with all the places where machines worked shining clear. Overhead, a hundred little spies exploded in sputters of white-hot sparks, crashing down amongst the gamblers and the tables, starting a hundred fires and doubling and redoubling panic. Yama was carried forward by a sudden press of people who shared the same thought: to get out before the fires took hold. His body knew what to do. It fought to keep its feet on the ground, for with one slip it would be trampled underfoot. One of Mother Spitfire's black-robed bodyguards pushed through the crowd and reached for him, and

Yama saw the machines in the bodyguard's head and did something terrible.

When he came to himself, he had fetched up in the doorway of a dream parlor at the other end of the Strip. One hand clasped the wrist of the other, crushing the coypu hair fetish. Seed pearls pricked his fingertips. There was blood on his hands and flecks of blood and bloody matter spattered his tunic and face and hair. It was not his blood.

Inside the dream parlor, within a huge glass tank filled with boiling wreaths of thick green smoke, a naked woman pressed her face and breasts against the glass for a moment, her mouth opening and closing as if she was trying to tell him something.

Yama cried out.

"Angel!"

But the woman stepped backward into the smoke and was gone.

Sailors and soldiers were rioting up and down the length of the Strip. Yama borrowed the eyes of a machine high above the crowd and saw that white smoke was pouring from the edges of the steep tiled roof of Mother Spitfire's gambling palace. The gold neon dragon spat sheets of sparks; one of its wings went out. Yama spun the machine and saw that the buildings around the gambling palace were on fire, too. Magistrates on floating discs were cutting a firebreak across the Strip with pistol shots. A painted façade plunged like a huge guillotine blade into a gap that was blown open in front of it. Strings of lightbulbs and strips of jointed neon tubing fell, smashing amongst the rioting crowd.

Yama released the machine and got up and started back toward the ship, but he had not gone very far when he was seized from behind, lifted, and flung against a wall. There were two men, burly and tall, as alike as brothers. They wore breechclouts and plastic breastplates, and their shaven heads were crowned with tight-fitting copper caps. One man pinned him while the other quickly and roughly frisked him.

"I have no money," Yama said.

The man who held him laughed and said, "He thinks we're robbing him, Diomedes!"

"We're badly misunderstood, Dercetas," the other said, and told Yama, "We're from an old friend, boy. He'll be pleased to see you again."

Dercetas got Yama in an armlock and shoved him forward, down a service walkway that ran out above black water. Diomedes brandished a pistol, and when a magistrate suddenly swooped down from the darkness beyond the rail, he twitched his pistol and fired. The magistrate fell with his clothes on fire; his disc shot straight up in a clap of thunder.

Most of the magistrate's machines had been destroyed in the violet flare of the pistol blast. Yama threw the rest at Diomedes. The man was knocked backward and spun around, held upright only by the machines which had embedded themselves in his flesh. One eye was a bloody hole; blood filled the space beneath his transparent breastplate and ran down his bare legs.

"Let me go," Yama shouted. "Let me go and I will spare you!"

His head hurt very badly. He could barely see because great flags of red and black were crowding in. Diomedes's body twitched as the machines began to work their way out of his flesh.

Dercetas thrust Yama from him and stepped backward, then turned and ran. Yama staggered after him and said in an entirely new voice, "Wait. You fool. Wait for me."

But the man had vanished into the crowd at the end of the walkway. Behind Yama, the dead man fell forward and the machines flew away into the night.

Much later, Pandaras and Pantin found Eliphas standing over Yama. There was a bloody corpse nearby, but at first Pandaras thought nothing of it. The riots had been very bad, and order was only now being restored. Magistrates were supervising teams of sailors and soldiers, putting out fires and clearing debris from the walkways. Bodies had been laid in neat rows in the big square at the center of the Strip, awaiting identification and shriving.

Eliphas seemed to be praying over Yama. As Pandaras approached, the old man turned and said, "He is sick, but I do not think that he is wounded."

"Let me see," Pandaras said. He pushed Eliphas aside and squatted beside his master. Yama stared past him at an imaginary point somewhere beyond the world. Pandaras said, "Master, do you know who I am? Do you know where you are?"

"He killed that man," Eliphas said.

For the first time, Pandaras looked closely at the dead man. He wore a plastic breastplate and a copper cap. The breastplate was riddled with bloody holes.

"I've seen others dressed like that," Pandaras said. "I expect they're Prefect Corin's men. Help me, Eliphas. We must get him back to the ship."

Two men wearing armor and copper caps had found Pandaras and

Pantin in a whorehouse. Pantin had stabbed one in the eye with a table knife and had jumped on the back of the other and cut his throat, sawing and sawing with the blunt blade until the man's head had been nearly cut off. The boy was trembling but docile now, like a horse which has just run a race. Blood crusted his bare chest.

Together, Eliphas and Pandaras helped Yama stand.

"We must get out of this, master," Pandaras said. "Prefect Corin found you, didn't he? I shouldn't have listened to Tamora. I should have stayed. I'm sorry."

"There is a monster," Yama said dreamily. "I am dangerous, Pandaras. Even to myself."

"He's too hard on himself," Pandaras told Eliphas. "You don't go running to the magistrates to ask for justice when it's your own family, and you don't stint, either. If it was me, I would have burned the whole thing down to make sure I killed Corin."

25

The Ascension of Angel

"THEY'RE HOLDING PREFECT Corin and both his ships," Captain Lorquital said. "The magistrates think that he brought weapons ashore, or allowed his men to. They'd like to blame you, too, but they can't see how one young man could have caused so much destruction. Our passenger put in a word, too."

"Prefect Corin will follow us," Yama said. "The magistrates may delay him, but they will not be able to stop him. They have no real cause, and he will be able to deny responsibility. After all, he is not the one who wrecked Mother Spitfire's gambling palace."

They stood on the quarterdeck, watching the lights of the floating harbor diminish across a widening gap of black water as the *Weazel* maneuvered through a channel marked by luminescent buoys. The fires had been put out and the crowds of sailors and soldiers had been dispersed to their ships. The places which had been damaged were ringed with lights, and the sounds of construction work could be heard. Beyond the floating harbor, the city of Gond shone against the night by its own inner light, like a range of low hills covered in luminous snow.

"The less of that kind of talk, the better," Ixchel Lorquital said. "The magistrates have ears in the wind here."

"No more," Yama said, and shivered; he did not know why he had said it.

Pandaras had described in vivid detail how he and Pantin had found Yama by the dead man, with Eliphas praying over him. Yama had riddled a man with machines, but he did not remember it. He remembered nothing after his rage had taken him in the gambling palace. He had been floating above the Strip with burning buildings on either side . . . There had been a woman hanging in green vapor . . . He turned the fetish around and around on his wrist; it helped him remember who he was.

He had suffered only a few scrapes and bruises, and there was a bump in the hollow between the two big tendons at the back of his skull. Something hard-edged which he could move around under the skin. He should know what it was . . . but the memory slid away when he tried to articulate it.

"By tomorrow," Captain Lorquital said, "the place will be back to normal."

"They will catch more of them," Yama said. "The river renews all, good and bad."

He was thinking of the kelpies in Mother Spitfire's pit, but Ixchel Lorquital misunderstood. "Every day more soldiers pass by on their way downriver to the war," she said. "The war has changed everything along the river. This place is the least of it."

As the *Weazel* passed beyond the edge of the floating harbor and raised her sail to catch the offshore breeze, fireworks shot up from Gond, bursting in overlapping showers of gold and green and raining down toward their own reflections in the river's black water. The *Weazel*'s crew, up in the rigging, cheered each new explosion.

"For our passenger," Ixchel Lorquital said with a smile. "So few remain in the city that they mark the departure or return of every one of their bloodline."

Yama had forgotten about the passenger for whom the *Weazel* had put in at the floating harbor. He said, "I suppose you and your daughter have lost your cabin to him. Is that where he is now? I would like to meet him, and thank him for his help."

Captain Lorquital pointed at the mast with the stem of her clay pipe. "He has taken the crow's nest. Climb up if you want to talk, but he'll be with us for at least five days."

The passenger from Gond had arrived an hour before Pandaras and Pantin had brought Yama back to the ship. He was an envoy to the cities of the Dry Plains, where there were disputes about the new land uncovered by the river's retreat. It was all to do with the war, Captain Lorquital declared. Normally, such matters were decided at a festival of dance and song, but most of the able young men had gone to fight the heretics, and there were not enough contestants.

"He's been appointed to make peace between the cities," Captain Lorquital said. "The people of Gond are a holy people. Their decisions are not easily come by, and are highly respected."

All this time, Tamora had been sitting in the pool of light cast by the big square lantern at the stern rail, sharpening her sword with a stone and scrap of leather. When Yama left Captain Lorquital to her charts and went forward to the bow, Tamora followed him.

"I fucked up," she said bluntly. "Put me off at the next port and I'll find another job."

"I remember that you saved my life," Yama said. "And that I then did something foolish. The fault is mine."

"You should have burned the place to the waterline," Tamora said fiercely. "It's no more than it deserves. You don't need me when you can command any machine. Let me go."

"I am too tired to talk about this," Yama said. In fact, he was ashamed of what he had done, although he did not remember much of it. "I need your strength, Tamora. I need to know when to act and when to stay my hand."

Tamora said, "That's easy. You only strike when you have to."

"I need to be sure that I am acting for myself. I feel like a horse under a skillful rider. Most of the time I pick my own way, but sometimes I am pulled up short, or made to gallop in a direction not of my own choosing. I do not know if I am on the side of good or evil. Help me, Tamora."

She fixed him with her gold-green gaze. "Before I was hurt in the war, they said I was crazy. No one would fight by my side because they said I took too many risks. You know what? I did it because I was scared. It's easier to charge the enemy under fire than stand and wait for the right moment. So that's what I did until I was wounded. Afterward, while I was recovering, I had plenty of time to think about what I'd done, and I swore then that I would never again let fear control me. I thought that I had been true to that oath until this night."

Yama remembered that Sergeant Rhodean had told him that the best generals judge the moment to attack; the worst are driven by events willy-nilly, like a ship before a storm. He said, "You are right. Fear is natural, but I should be able to control it. Thank you."

"What for? For being a damned fool? For letting you walk into that trap? For failing to help you when it went wrong?"

"For trusting me with your story."

They watched the last of the fireworks burst far astern as the *Weazel* headed out into the deep water, and later fell asleep in each other's arms. As the sky lightened, Yama woke and disentangled himself from Tamora's embrace. Someone, probably Pandaras, had covered them with a blanket. Tamora sighed and yawned, showing her sharp white teeth and black tongue, and Yama told her to go back to sleep.

Apart from the old sailor, Phalerus, who had the helm, the whole ship was asleep. The new passenger must still be in the crow's nest, for only Pandaras and Eliphas slept on the raffia matting under the awning. The *Weazel* was running ahead of a strong wind, her triangular mainsail filled, water creaming by on either side of her bow. The Great River stretched away on all sides; the Rim Mountains were no more than a long line floating low in the lightening sky. The water here was not the usual brown or umber but was the same dark blue as the predawn sky. It was more than a league deep in places; some of the abyssal trenches plunged into the keel of the world. Hard to believe that this could ever change, and yet year by year the cities of the shore were stranded further and further inland by the river's retreat. The Great River would at last run dry even here, leaving only a string of long, narrow lakes at the bottom of a deep dry valley.

Yama leaned at the starboard rail. Warm wind blew his unruly black hair back from his face. The bright lights of the huge fishing barges were scattered widely across the river. Yama wondered what monsters lay in the deeps under the *Weazel*'s keel, and for the first time in many days felt the tug of the feral machine which hung in its cold, solitary orbit a million leagues beyond the end of the world, attached to him by an impalpable thread, just as the kelpies had been attached to their operators by wires and cables. But who was puppet, and who operator? And for what end? He remembered the conclusion of his stepfather's complicated calculations about the river's shrinkage and shivered in the brightening sunlight.

After a while, he took out his copy of the Puranas. The bright crammed pictures stirred to life under his gaze, speaking directly to an unconsciously receptive part of his mind. He realized that there must be machines embedded in the pages. Was every book freighted with hidden meanings? As a child, had he dreamed so vividly of the past because books from the library of the peel-house had lain by his bed?

But then he was lost in the last of Angel's story, and all idle speculation was driven away.

———

When Angel came back from the far side of the river, she talked with those of her followers who had waited at the docks for her, then went straightaway to Mr. Naryan, the Archivist of Sensch, to tell him what she had found.

The Archivist was with a pupil, but the hapless lad was immediately dismissed when Angel appeared. Fortified by tea brought by the Archivist's wife, a quiet woman of Sensch's lizard race, Angel began to tell the tale of her adventure on the farside shore.

The Archivist knew that Angel had been to the edge of the world, and for the first time he could not hide his fear. He was afraid of what she might have done amongst the shrines on the river's far side, about what she might change.

She said, teasingly, "Don't you want to hear my story? Isn't that your avocation?"

"I will listen to anything you want to tell me," the Archivist said. Despite his fear, he maintained his air of quiet dignity, and she liked him for that.

She said, "The world is a straight line. Do you know about libration?"

The Archivist shook his head.

Angel held out her hand, palm down, and tipped it back and forth. "This is the world. Everything lives on the back of a long flat plate which circles the sun. The plate rocks on its axis, so the sun rises above one edge and then reverses its course. I went to the edge of the world, where the river that runs down half its length falls into the void. I suppose it must be collected and redistributed, but it really does look like it falls away forever."

"The river is eternally renewed," the Archivist said. "Where it falls is where ships used to arrive and depart, but this city has not been a port for many years."

"Fortunately for me, or my companions would already be here. There's a narrow ribbon of land on the far side of the river. Nothing lives there, not even an insect. No earth, no stones. The air shakes with the sound of the river's fall, and swirling mist burns with raw sunlight. And there are shrines, in the thunder and mist at the edge of the world." Angel paused for effect, then said, "One spoke to me."

She could see that the Archivist was taken aback. He said nothing, staring past her in some private reverie. She grinned and said, "Don't you want to know what it said to me? It's part of my story."

"Do you want to tell me?"

The Archivist looked at her. It was a look of helpless love; she knew then that like all the others he was hers to command. The thought disgusted her. She wanted him to be a friend, not a pet or a puppet. She passed her hand over the top of her head. She had had her hair cut close in the manner of microgravity construction workers, a style ten million years out of date. The bristly hair made a crisp sound under her palm. She said, "No. No, I don't think I do. Not yet."

Instead, she told him what the ship had showed her of the creation of the Eye of the Preservers. He seemed happier with this. It was something he understood. He said that it was just as it was written in the Puranas.

She said, "And is it also written there why Confluence was constructed around a halo star between the Home Galaxy and the Eye of the Preservers?"

"Of course. It is so we can worship and glorify the Preservers. The Eye looks upon us all."

It was a stock answer, taken from the commentary at the end of the last sura of the Puranas. He had nothing new to tell her. No one on this strange world had had a new idea since its creation, but she would change that. If she was going to rule here, she must first topple the old gods.

The news that she had woken one of the shrines on the farside shore spread through the city. The streets around her house became choked with curious citizens. She could no longer wander about the city, because huge crowds gathered everywhere she went. There was a story that she had been tempted with godhood, and that she had refused. It was not something she had told the citizens—they were changing her story to fit their needs. She tried to teach them that the Universe of things was all there was, that there were no gods capable of intercession, that everyone was responsible for their own destiny. Seize the day, she told them, and they made the slogan into their battle cry. Her followers daubed slogans everywhere, and now many of the slogans were of their own making.

Somehow, the citizens of Sensch came to believe that they could use the farside shrines just as she had, without intervention of priest or hierodule, and that personal redemption was within their grasp. They set off in their thousands on pilgrimages across the river; so many that the city's markets closed because the merchants had moved to the docks to supply those making the journey across the river. Meanwhile, Angel became a prisoner in her house, surrounded by followers, her every move watched with reverence. She had to stand on the roof so that she could be seen and heard by all of them. She was trying to free them from their habits and their unthinking devotion to the Preservers, to shape them into an army that could be used against her ship when it finally came for her.

She built devices that might help her escape. A crude muscle amplification suit. A circuit-breaking device that would interfere with the broadcast power on which the myriads of tiny machines fed. She tinkered with the gravity units of cargo sleds, and painstakingly reprogrammed a few captured machines. But all of this activity was marking time. It was almost a relief when her ship finally arrived.

Angel went up to the roof of her house when the ship drew near the city's docks. It had reconfigured itself into a huge black wedge composed of stacked tiers of flat plates. Its pyramidal apex was taller than the tallest towers of the city. Angel knew that the ship would try to take her back, but she might be able to escape if she could use the powers of the ship against itself.

She insisted on going to the docks. The young men who were her closest followers were very afraid, but they could not disobey her. She had two of them carry the circuit breaker, and armed the rest with pistols.

The streets were almost empty. Thousands upon thousands of citizens had gathered at the docks to greet the ship, held back by a thin line of magistrates and their machines. The people were restless; they made a humming noise that rose and fell in pitch but never ended. Machines swept their packed heads with flares of light. There had already been trouble, for those near the front were wounded in some way, fallen to their knees and wailing and clutching at their faces. And when Dreen, the Commissioner of Sensch, rode a cargo sled to the top of the ship to greet the men and women of the crew, the crowd pressed forward eagerly, held back only by the quirts and machines of the magistrates.

Angel knew then that this was her only chance to take the ship from the crew. She fired up the circuit breaker and every machine fell from the sky, burned out by the power surge. The magistrates were powerless to stop the crowd as it surged down the docks toward the ship. Angel saw Dreen's cargo sled fly away from the top of the ship—it drew power from the world's gravity fields—toward the floating gardens above the pink sandstone palace. The Archivist was coming toward her, struggling through the crowd. Angel ordered those around her to take him to the palace, and left to organize the siege.

Power was down all over the city. The population had lost all restraint, as if it was only the presence of the machines which had kept them in order. There was drunkenness and gambling and open fornication. Buildings were set on fire; markets were looted. But those citizens Angel encountered still obeyed her unquestioningly. They loaded up cargo sleds with batteries for a localized power system and marched on the palace and attacked the floating gardens, some using the modified sleds to smash away pieces of the gardens' superstructure, others starting to grow towers into the air using self-catalyzing masonry.

Angel was sitting in the middle of her followers on the palace roof, with the machines she had reprogrammed spinning above her head, when the Archivist was brought before her. He was bruised and disheveled, not badly hurt, but clearly terrified. She beckoned him forward and he drew on his last reserves of dignity to confront her. She said, "What should I do with your city, now that I have taken it from you?"

The Archivist said, "You have not finished your story." There was a hint of defiance in his voice, but then he added weakly, "I would like to hear it all."

"My people can tell you. They hide with Dreen up above, but not for long." Angel pointed to a dozen men who were wrestling a sled into the crude launch cradle and explained how she had enhanced its anti-gravity properties. "We'll chip away that floating fortress piece by piece if we have to, or we'll finish growing towers and storm its remains, but I expect them to surrender long before then."

"Dreen is not the ruler of the city."

"Not anymore."

The Archivist dared to step closer. He said, "What did you find out there, that you rage against?"

Angel laughed. None of them understood. They were not human—how could they understand her, the last human in the Universe? She said, "I'll tell you about rage. It is what you have forgotten, or never learned. It is the motor of evolution, and evolution's end, too."

She snatched a beaker of wine from one of her followers and drained it and tossed it aside. Its heat mixed smoothly with her angry contempt. She said, "We traveled for so long, not dead, not sleeping. We were no more than stored potentials triply engraved on gold. Although the ship flew so fast that it bound time about itself, the journey still took thousands of years of shipboard time. At the end of that long voyage we did not wake: we were born. Or rather, others like us were born, although I have their memories, as if they are my own. They learned then that the Universe is not made for the convenience of humans. What they found was a galaxy dead and ruined."

Angel took the Archivist's hands in hers and held them tightly as she told him of the ruin of the neighboring galaxy, the disrupted nebulae, the planets torn from their orbits by gravity stress, the worlds torched smooth by stars which had flared because of infalling gases. She told him what she had learned.

"Do you know how many galaxies have endured such collisions? Almost all of them. Life is a statistical freak. Our galaxy has never collided with another like it, or not for a long time, long enough for life to have evolved on planets around some of its stars. It must be unique, or else other civilizations would surely have arisen elsewhere in the unbounded Universe. As it is, we are certain that we are alone. We must make of ourselves what we can. We should not hide from the truth, as your Preservers chose to do. Instead, we should seize the day, and make the Universe over with the technology that the Preservers used to make their hiding place."

The Archivist said, "You cannot become a Preserver. No one can, now. You should not lie to these innocent people."

"I didn't need to lie. They took up my story and made it theirs. They see now what they can inherit—if they dare. This won't stop with one city. It will become a crusade!" She stared into the Archivist's black eyes and said softly, "You'll remember it all, won't you?"

The Archivist said nothing, but she knew that he was hers, now and forever. It seemed to make him unbearably sad and it broke her heart, too, to have to use him so badly when she had wanted him to be her friend.

Around them, the crowd of her followers cheered. The sled rocketed up from its cradle and smashed into the underside of the hanging gardens. Another piece of the gardens' substructure was knocked loose. It spilled dirt and rocks amongst the spires of the palace roof as it twisted free and spun away into the night. The crowd cheered again, and Angel saw that figures had appeared at the wrecked edge of the habitat. One of the figures tossed something down, and a man brought it to Angel.

It was a message tube. She shook it open: Dreen's face glowed on the flexible membrane. His voice was squeezed small and metallic by the tube's induced speaker. Angel listened to his entreaties and was filled with joy and hope.

"Yes," she said, but so softly that perhaps only the Archivist heard her. She stood and raised her hands above her head, and when she had the attention of her followers she cried out, "They wish to surrender! Let them come down!"

The cargo sled dropped. They were all there, the men and women who were closer to her than sisters and brothers, shining in their white clothes. Angel's followers jeered and threw rocks and burning brands and clods of earth, but her partials had modified the sled's field and everything was deflected away into the night. Angel smiled. She had anticipated that trick.

The partials called to her, pleading with her to return, to join them and search for their long-lost home. Dreen jumped from the sled and dodged through the crowd of Angel's followers. The little Commissioner caught the Archivist's hand and told him breathlessly, "They are all one person, or variations on one person. The ship makes its crew by varying a template. Angel is an extreme. A mistake."

Angel laughed. So Dreen had been subverted by the partials! "You funny little man," she said. "I'm the real one—they are copies!"

She turned to the partials, who were still calling out to her, pleading with her to come back, to join them in the search for their lost home. None had dared follow Dreen. "There's no home to find," she told them. "Oh you fools! This is all there is! Give me back the ship!"

She knew they would never agree, but she wanted to give them the chance. It was only fair.

"It was never yours," they chorused. "Never yours to own, only yours to serve."

Angel jumped onto her chair and signaled to the man she had entrusted with the field degausser. It shot hundreds of fine silvery threads at the sled. For a moment, she thought it might not work, for when the threads reached the edge of the field their ends flicked upward. But then the threads drained the field—there was a great smell of burning as the degausser's iron heat-sink glowed red-hot—and the threads fell in a tangle over the partials. Angel's followers, seeing what had happened, began to pelt the crew with rubbish, but Angel ordered them to stop. She wanted to defeat the crew, not humiliate it.

She said, "I have the only working sleds. That which I can enhance, I can also take away." The partials could not follow her now. The ship was hers for the taking. She turned to the Archivist triumphantly. "Come with me, and see the end of the story."

That was when one of the partials walked away from the grounded sled, straight toward Angel. She confronted him. She told herself that there was nothing to fear. She had won. She said to him, "I'm not afraid of you."

"Of course not, sister," the man said.

He reached out and grasped her wrists. And the world fell away.

The acceleration was so brutal that Angel almost passed out. A rush of air burned her clothes and scorched her skin . . . and then there was no more air. She was so tall above the world that she could see across its width, tall mountains on one side and a straight edge on the other, stretching ahead and behind to their vanishing points. The world was a dark line hung in an envelope of air. Angel saw the brilliant point of the sun come into view beneath it. Vacuum stung her eyes with ice-cold needles; air rushed from her nose and mouth; her entire skin ached. The man embracing her pressed his lips against hers, kissing her with the last of his breath, tasting the last of hers.

———

There were only two pictures after that. Neither spoke to Yama. They were only pictures.

The first showed a vast room within the ship of the Ancients of Days. There was a window which displayed the triple spiral of the Home Galaxy. Two men stood before it, one grossly corpulent, the other wide-hipped and long-armed, as small as a child. The Archivist of Sensch, Mr. Naryan, and the Commissioner of Sensch, Dreen. Dreen was pointing at the glowing window. He was telling Mr. Naryan something.

The second picture was from a point of view above Dreen, who stood at the edge of a huge opening in the ship, looking down at the river far below. A figure hung halfway between the hatch and the river. It was Mr. Naryan.

So Angel had died—although if her ship wished, she could be born again—but her ideas lived on. They had escaped with Mr. Naryan, and Yama knew that, with the help of the aspect Angel had downloaded into the space inside the shrines, the old Archivist had spread Angel's story far and wide. The revolution in Sensch was only the beginning of the heresy which had set one half of Confluence against the other.

Shoreward, the sky grew brighter. The floating line of the Rim Mountains freed the platinum disc of the sun. A widening lane of sun-light glittered on the river, like a golden path leading to infinity. Yama watched the play of light on water and thought for a long time about the things that the changed pictures in his copy of the Puranas had shown him.

26

Theias's Treasure

THE ENVOY FROM Gond, Theias, did not come down from the crow's nest that day. When Aguilar went aloft with his midday meal, Yama asked her to tell the envoy that he was eager to meet him. But when she descended—despite her bulk, she slid down a backstay with an acrobat's casual grace—she told Yama that the envoy sent his apologies.

"He says he has a lot to think about," Aguilar said. "He's a holy man all right. He wanted only a little bread and salt to eat, and river water to drink."

"He could stay up there for the whole voyage, brother," Eliphas said. "They are a strange people, in Gond."

Later, Yama sat alone at the bow and thought again about what the book had shown him. Angel's aspect had wanted him to understand her history, but how could he trust what he had been told? Angel's story was more dangerous than most. It was a scream aimed straight at the most primitive part of the mind, where raw appetite dwelled like a toad at the bottom of a well. Seize the day! Forget duty, forget responsibility, forget devotion to the Preservers, forget everything but personal gain.

There was no denying what she had discovered, but it did not mean that people should fear the Universe. Rather, Yama thought, they should celebrate its vast emptiness. By accepting the Universe for all that it was, you became a true part of it and could never truly cease to exist until it also ceased to exist. It was not necessary to distinguish between being and nonbeing, between life and mere dead matter. It was all part of the same eternal braid. Only the Preservers had stepped outside of the Universe—an act of transcendence impossible for those who were not gods.

Although Angel feared the ultimate darkness of nonbeing—that was why she had been so quick to despair—Yama knew that it was nothing to fear, for it was nothing at all. The Puranas taught that just as there was no time before the beginning of the Universe, there was also no time after death, for in both cases there was no way to measure the passing of time. Death was a timeless interval before rebirth at the infinite moment at the end of all time.

Angel denied this. She did not trust what she could not understand. She trusted no one but her own self. She had no faith, except faith in herself, and she believed herself to be unique, entire, and circumscribed, so that a time when she was absent from the Universe was, to her, simply unthinkable. It was true that she had passed hundreds of years of shipboard time as a mere text, that she had died and risen again: many times. But these brief interregna were nothing compared to the billions of years of nonbeing between now and the end of the Universe, and the machineries which stored her self and gave her rebirth time and time again were real in a way that the Preservers were not. It did not need a leap of faith to believe in machines.

Yama thought about these things for a long time, while the *Weazel* stood before a fair wind and raced her own shadow across sunlit waters. The crew mended the staysails and tightened lanyards and stays through deadeyes; the joints of the deck were resealed with pitch and its planks were scrubbed until they shone as white as salt; a cradle was lowered over the side so that Phalerus could smooth and repaint places splintered and scraped by weather and passage through the floating forest. There had not been time to fully reprovision the ship, and the shoat, which had been pampered on scraps since the *Weazel* had left Ys, was led from its pen onto an oilcloth and soothed with song before the cook cut its throat. For a moment the shoat stood astonished as rich red blood pattered noisily into a blue plastic bucket held under its head; then it sighed and sat down and died.

Tamora helped with the butchery, and ate the shoat's liver raw. The joints, ribs, head, tongue and heart were sealed in barrels of brine, and the intestines were cleaned and steamed with the lungs. After sunset, everyone feasted on fried plantain leaves and fritters of banana and minced pork. All except the envoy, who still had not shown himself. Yama was beginning to believe that he did not exist.

That night, Yama slept alone on the triangular bit of decking over the forecastle. He woke at dawn to find someone hanging upside down from a forestay above his head. A small, slightly built man, his flat face, the color of old parchment and framed by a fringe of fine hair, cocked at his shoulder so that he could stare straight down. Yama realized with a shock that the envoy from Gond was of the same bloodline as the long-lost Commissioner of Sensch, Dreen.

The envoy smiled and said in a high, lilting voice, "You are not so much after all," and swung the right way up.

"Wait," Yama said, "I would like to—"

"I expected someone taller, with thunder on his brow, or a wreath of laurels. Perhaps you are not him, after all."

Before Yama could reply, the envoy turned and ran off along the forestay. He swarmed up the mast as nimbly as any sailor and disappeared into the crow's nest.

Toward midmorning, Yama saw a machine spinning above the waves half a league to starboard, a little thing with a decad of paired mica vanes that flashed and winked in the sunlight, and a tapered body that was mostly a sensor cluster. He brought it closer, and made it circle around and around the crow's nest. It made a thin crackling sound like oil seething in a hot pan, and occasionally spat a fan of sparks that sputtered down the bellying slope of the sail's rust-red canvas. Captain Lorquital watched from her sling chair, but said nothing.

At last, the envoy swung out of the crow's nest and ran down the forestay, halting halfway and calling to Yama, "Am I supposed to be impressed? You are very foolish!"

Yama let the machine go. It shot away to starboard in a long falling arc that almost touched the river's glassy swell before it abruptly changed direction in a twinkling of vanes, just like a dog shaking itself awake. In a moment, it was lost from sight.

The envoy descended to the end of the forestay. He wore a simple belted tunic which left his legs bare, and carried a leaf-shaped fan woven of raffia and painted with a stylized eye. His feet had long gripping toes. He thwacked Yama on top of the head with his fan, said, "That is for your impertinence, young man," and leapt lightly onto the deck.

The sailors who had been watching grinned at this display. Tamora shook her head and turned away; Pandaras, sitting bare-chested and cross-legged in the shade of the awning at the far end of the main deck, looked up from the embroidery work he was doing on the collar of his shirt. In her sling chair on the quarterdeck, Captain Lorquital puffed imperturbably on her pipe. Eliphas sat beside her, his wide-brimmed straw hat casting his face into shadow.

The envoy said to Yama, "Here I am. What is your question?"

"I hoped we could talk, dominie."

"But what will you talk about? Something important, I hope, unless you are even more foolish than you look."

"Perhaps we should talk about my foolishness."

"You assume that I am interested in it," the envoy said. "Do you know who I am?"

"Theias, the envoy from Gond to the warring cities of the Dry Plains."

"And you, Child of the River, should know that I was contemplating my mission when you sent that poor imitation of a dragonfly buzzing around my eyrie. I like it up there. I can see all that is going on without having to be an active part of it. I can see so far that I can spy into the future—there is trouble in it for you, young man, but why I am telling you I do not know."

Yama thought that for a holy man of great age, of one of the oldest bloodlines on Confluence and from the second oldest city in the world, Theias had a remarkably short temper. But he bowed and said, "I have been rude. I am sorry. I see you know my true name, so I must presume you have some interest in me."

"Your reputation preceded you, and I must say it was larger and more colorful than the truth."

"I suppose your people keep doves," Yama said.

Theias looked at Yama sharply. "Doves? There are all kinds of birds in Gond, but I do not pay much attention to them. Doves do not talk, in any event, or at least ours do not. No, I heard about you on the geophone, and then there is the heliograph, which I used to talk with this cockleshell before I boarded her. I heard that overnight you changed a whole tribe of indigenous squatters on the roof of the Palace of the Memory of the People, and that you started a war between the departments. Some say you are the harbinger of the return of the Preservers; some say that you are a mage in league with the antitheist heretics. I do not suppose you are either one. To look at you, I would say that you are a not particularly successful cateran off to try his luck in the wars."

"I wish that I was. It may sound strange, but that was once my ambition. But I do not know what I am, except that I am not what people want me to be."

"Is that so? I would say that is the root of your trouble. Does the stick know it is a hoe?"

"If it is used as a hoe, then I suppose it would."

The envoy swatted Yama's shoulder with his fan. "No no no. A stick does not have to ask itself stupid questions. It accepts its nature. If you tried to be more like a stick and less like a hero you would cause less trouble. What is that book you were reading? The Puranas, I would say, except no edition of the Puranas has pictures such as yours."

"It is an old edition, and it has been added to since. One of your people was a part of the story. A man named Dreen. He was the Commissioner of Sensch."

"I already know something of Dreen's seduction," Theias said. He scratched behind one of his large, translucent ears, then folded at the knees and sat down and patted the decking beside him. "Here. Sit with me. Perhaps you will show me the rest of the tale."

They sat together on the forecastle deck, under the shifting shade of the sail, for a long time. Theias fluttered his fan under his chin and cursed the heat, and asked many questions about the pictures. Yama answered as best he could, and discovered that he knew more than he had realized. Pandaras brought food—unleavened bread and plain water for Theias, and bread, chickpea paste, slices of melon, and a basket of sweet white wine for Yama—and stayed to listen, sitting quietly and working on the embroidery of his shirt collar.

At the end of the story, Theias said, "Poor Dreen allowed himself to become what he was not. We still mourn him."

"He is not dead, I think."

Theias said sharply, "Even if he stood here before me I would say that he was not alive."

"Because the Ancients of Days made him into their servant?"

"No no no," Theias said impatiently. "You have much to learn."

"I do want to learn. I am seeking the truth about myself, and I am trying to understand how I can train my mind so that I might hope to find it."

"Foolish boy. There is no mind, so you cannot train it. There is no truth, so you cannot hope to reach it."

"Yet I have heard that the men of Gond are great teachers. What do they teach, if not the truth? What do they train, if not minds?"

"We do not teach, because we do not have tongues. How can we tell others what to do without tongues?"

Theias said this with all seriousness, but Yama laughed at the absurdity. "I do not think you are telling me the truth! You play with me."

"How can I lie when I have no tongue? You have not been listening, young man. I waste my time with you. Farewell."

Theias swung onto the forestay and scampered up to the crow's nest.

Pandaras bit off the end of a colored thread and said, "He's a puzzle, master, isn't he?"

"He is trying to make me think, but I am not sure what he wants me to think about."

"I'm only your squire, master. I wouldn't know about these higher matters. My people, we've always let others worry about hard questions. We prefer stories and songs for the pleasure of telling them and singing them, and let others worry about what they mean. Was this Angel in the story the same woman that appeared in the shrines?"

"At first I thought that the woman in the shrine was an aspect, but I think now that she was more like a reflection. The perfect image of a person, but without volition. Like a picture, if a picture could move or speak. In any case, the Angel of the story in my book was not the same as the one who first set out on the long voyage. She was copied many times, and the copies changed so much that sometimes they warred with each other."

"I used to quarrel with my brothers and sisters," Pandaras said, "often in the very worst way. Sometimes, I swear, we all wanted to kill each other. It's always the way when someone is close to you, it's either love or hate and nothing in between."

———

Theias came down from the crow's nest late in the afternoon. He sat in front of Yama and Pandaras and said at once, "What is the difference between Angel and yourself?"

Yama had been thinking about this, and the question did not surprise him. He said, "She would not accept her nature, but I do not know mine."

"You are not as stupid as you pretend to be," Theias said, "but you are not as clever as you believe. I am not talking about small distinctions of intent, but of actions. Both of you have meddled in the destinies of other bloodlines. Therefore, which of you is worse?"

"I did it only because I was asked. Angel did it because she wanted to make an army of followers."

Theias looked at Yama intently. "Is that a sufficient difference?"

"In my case, I do not understand how it was done. It is one of the many things I do not understand."

Theias smiled. "Then perhaps there is some hope for you."

"I want to understand these things. You are pleased that I have no control over my powers, but I am frightened for the same reason."

"And I would be frightened if you did have control over them."

"I have been able to save myself from my enemies, but often with consequences that seem worse than the danger I faced."

Theias said, "If it is in your nature to resist your enemies, then that is what you must do. But I thought that you did not understand your nature."

"Angel wanted to rule the world. I do not want that. Even if others wanted it, I would refuse." Yama smiled. "I am amazed that I am even speaking of such things. The world belongs to no one but the Preservers."

"False humility is worse than pride. If you refuse to accept the burden of your destiny, then you are denying your nature."

"Your bloodline is old, dominie. Does it remember mine?"

"Some say you are of the bloodline of the Builders, but I do not see it myself. They were gone long before any of the Shaped were brought to Confluence, and left only their works behind. Perhaps the Builders never really existed—have you thought of that? People reason that servants of the Preservers must have constructed the world, and so they invent a mythical bloodline and give them all the attributes they imagine world-builders might possess. But perhaps the world created itself, once the Preservers had willed it. For if the Preservers are gods, then they can speak true words, words so true that they are no different from the thing they stand for."

Yama remembered the slate he had been shown in the City of the Dead, which had shown a man of his own bloodline with a starry sky behind him. But perhaps the slate had shown only a story. Perhaps everything was a story. He said, "Words are not truth, are they?"

Theias slapped Yama about the head with his fan. "You have been reading in the Puranas. There are many stories in the Puranas that reveal the nature of the world, although it is only by deep thought and contemplation that one can truly understand their importance. The stories are not lessons in themselves, but act upon the receptive mind to bring it into a state by which one can obtain enlightenment. Words cannot represent anything but themselves, no more than things can be anything but what they are. And so words can teach nothing."

"For one without a tongue, you are a good teacher."

Once again Theias battered Yama about the head with his fan. Yama endured it. Pandaras looked to his sewing and tried to hide a smile.

"Foolish boy," the envoy said. "If you need a teacher, then you are unable to learn." He held his fan a handspan before Yama's face. "If you call this a fan, you oppose its reality. If you do not call it a fan, you ignore the fact. Now, what do you wish to call this?"

Yama took the fan from Theias's unresisting fingers, fanned himself, and handed it back.

Pandaras sang softly, as if to himself:

Holding out the leafy fan,
He gave an order of life or death.
Positive and negative interwoven,
Even the Preservers cannot escape this attack.

Theias smiled. "Your servant knows the Puranas, at least. You might learn from him."

"I have not read in them," Pandaras said, "but your riddle reminded me of a game my people play amongst themselves."

Theias pulled at the long hairs that fringed his chin and said, "Then your people are wiser than me, for I take these riddles seriously. I must go now. I will leave for the cities of the Dry Plains in a few hours."

Yama said, "It will take longer than that to make landfall, I think."

"Not at all. You see only what you want to see, and ignore the obvious. But at least you have made a beginning. Study the Puranas if you must, although you would do better to listen to your servant's jokes. Now, you may ask me one more question."

Yama thought hard. He had so many questions that he could not even begin to decide which was the most important, and many required specific answers which Theias, although he was wise, might not know. At last, he said, "I will ask you this, dominie. Is there a teaching no master has ever taught before?"

"Yes, of course."

"Then what is it?"

Theias put his hands on top of his head. His fan hung down, covering his eyes. He said, "I have answered your question."

"You have told me that you can answer it, dominie, and I know you are an honorable man."

"It is not mind, it is not the Preservers, it is not things."

Theias said this very quickly and immediately swung onto the forestay and scampered away to the crow's nest. There was a brief commotion up there, and then something fluttered over the rail. It hit the slope of the sail and slid down and fell to the deck.

It was Theias's fan. Even as Pandaras ran to retrieve it, the envoy rose above the crow's nest. He was standing on a gleaming disc which slid away through the air at an increasing speed toward the nearside shore, vanishing from sight in less than a minute.

Yama was astonished. He said, "He did not need to travel on the ship. He came only because he wanted to see me."

Pandaras held up the fan and sang:

Theias was too kind and lost his treasure.
Truly, words have no power.
Even though the Rim Mountains become the Great River,
Words cannot open another's mind.

27

The Dredgers

LESS THAN AN hour after Phalerus had climbed into the crow's nest Theias had so precipitately abandoned, the old sailor called in a high, hoarse voice, "Sail! Ten leagues to the first quarter!"

"It is the picketboat," Captain Lorquital told Yama, after looking upriver through her spectacles.

So Prefect Corin had escaped the authorities at the floating harbor. Yama had been expecting it, and he felt a sense of relief rather than fear.

Captain Lorquital said, "I suppose we should be grateful it isn't the warship, but she's rowing steadily and hard and has crowded every yard with sail. I'd say she's bearing on us at twice our speed or better. She won't be able to keep up that pace, but we're in the midway of the river and it will take us more than a day to run to shore and a hiding place. I fear that she will catch us before then."

There was little that could be done, for the *Weazel* was already running briskly before a good wind, dipping and rising through long waves that marched across the Great River from farside shore to near. Captain Lorquital and Aguilar discussed putting out the staysails, but decided that this would drive the *Weazel*'s bows down and make her more likely to plow.

"We should do it anyway," Tamora grumbled to Yama.

"It would only delay the moment, and it would put the ship at risk," Yama said.

They stood by the big square lantern at the stern rail. By naked eye, the picketboat was a black dot far off across the shimmering sunstruck plain of the river.

"It is Eliphas who leads them on to us," Tamora said, "I swear he made a bargain with Prefect Corin while we were all prisoners."

"Yet he urged me not to go into Mother Spitfire's gambling palace. I wish I had taken his advice."

"Grah. It is likely that Eliphas was to be the goat leading you to an ambush somewhere else, which is why he so earnestly wanted you to leave."

Eliphas was talking with Ixchel Lorquital, hunched forward earnestly on the stool by her sling chair, his big hands moving eloquently.

Yama said, "No, he is no more than an old man looking for one last adventure. Look at him—he talks too much to be a spy. Besides, I met him by accident."

"Are you sure?"

"If not, anyone could be an agent of Prefect Corin's, and how am I to live? Eliphas has given me a destination, Tamora. A place where my people might still live. If it is true, it is a most precious gift."

"Grah. I'll believe in this lost city when I see it, but let's say he didn't lie about it. Maybe he didn't start out to betray you. But I still think he's struck a bargain with Prefect Corin. Maybe he didn't want to, maybe he was forced. Think carefully. You keep the spy machines away, but something has led Prefect Corin straight to us. In all the wide river, how would he find us so quickly unless led? It must be Eliphas. He'll have been given a device of some sort. Let me search his kit. Let me search *him,* down to the bones."

"I cannot know about every machine, Tamora. One could hang high above us, and I would not know. Besides, Prefect Corin knows that we are going downriver. The river is wide, but it is not infinite."

Tamora stared hard at him. Sunlight dappled her skin, glittered in her green eyes. She said, "I will lay my life down for you, willingly and gladly. But I would hope it is not because some fool thinks to line his pockets."

The cook prepared a sumptuous meal after sunset, roasting a side of ribs from the slaughtered shoat and serving it with a sauce of apricots and plums, riverweed fried with ginger, and side dishes of candied sweet potatoes and cassava porridge flavored with cumin. Most of the crew ate heartily, in a fine spirit of gallows humor, and all drank the ration of heart of wine Aguilar had broached.

"There'll be another ration at the beginning of the first morning watch," Aguilar announced. "All hands to deck then."

She did not need to say that by then the picketboat would be in cannon shot of the *Weazel.*

Before they bedded down for the night, Eliphas told Yama, "Our captain hopes to hail another ship tomorrow. She steers toward the near-side shore for that reason. Not because she hopes to reach it before being overtaken, but because that is where the shipping lanes are. If you are right about Prefect Corin's motives, brother, if he has no official sanction but pursues you for his own ends, he will not attack us in plain sight of others."

"I think that Captain Lorquital underestimates Prefect Corin."

"He is only a man. Don't make him more than he is, brother. You will find a way."

Yama had surprised himself by eating his fill, and he found sleep surprisingly easy, too. Perhaps it was because he had come to a decision, a way of ending the uncertainty of the chase. It had crept into the base of his brain during the feast, as cruelly sharp as a knife. He would wake in a few hours, cut the dory free, and make off into the darkness. Once he was far enough from the ship, he would put out the dory's drag anchor and wait for the picketboat to bear down on him. Attracting attention would be easy enough—he had only to call on Prefect Corin's machines. He would allow himself to be captured, and at the first opportunity he would kill the Prefect. He would gather all the machines within the range of his powers and kill everyone on the picketboat, and then continue downriver alone.

He had become a soldier after all, he thought, and realized that the war reached further upriver than the battlefields where armies clashed.

Yama slept and, freed by sleep, his mind ranged far down into the lightless depths of the river, where vast segmented monsters blindly humped through abyssal ooze. Wholly aware that he was sleeping but that this was not a dream, Yama engaged with the minds of these ancient machines. He learned of the immemorial routes they followed among the slow, cold currents at the bottom of the river, of their endless work of pushing sediment into the subduction channels which transported it to the Rim Mountains for redistribution by glacial melt. Theirs was a world defined by the echoes of ultrasonic clicks and pulses, by touch and chemical cues. Neighbor constantly reassured neighbor with little bursts of data; they moved through a web of shared information that mapped the entire river bottom, its braided currents and thermal gradients, its deltas of mud and plains of chalky ooze.

As the machines plowed the river bottom, they were accompanied by their sharers. The sharers fed on the shellfish and blind crabs exposed by the machines, and in return scouted the layers of water above the trenches and channels of the river bottom, and cleaned away parasites which sought lodging on the overlapping plates of the machines' armored hides.

We will help, the machines told Yama, although he had not asked them for help. He expected them to begin to rise toward the surface—any one of them could have sunk the picketboat by ramming it—but when he pictured this the machines told him that they could never leave the river bottom. They would help in their own way.

A league beneath the *Weazel*'s keel, the machines abandoned their routines for the first time in thousands of years. They altered their buoyancy, lifting from the long trenches they had made in the ooze and drifting on cold currents until they reached the maws of nearby subduction channels. As the machines blocked the channels, the cold river bottom currents were deflected upward, where they spread out beneath warmer layers until they reached the steep drop-off at the coastal shelf. The machines saw, by an increase in the echo delay of their ultrasonic chirps, a huge unsteady lens of cold water growing beneath the warmer layers over the coastal shelf, pushing upward and sideways in unstable equilibrium . . .

He was woken by Pandaras. It was dawn, but the light had a diffuse cast. It was like waking inside a pearl. The main mast stabbed upward, vanishing into streaming whiteness. Fog had settled damply over his blanket and drops of water hung everywhere from stays and ratlines.

"There's something wrong with the weather," Pandaras said. He had wrapped a blanket around his narrow shoulders like a cloak, but was shivering all the same.

"Where are the crew?" He would kill them all, if he had to, beginning with this silly little boy. Kill everyone who stood in his way when he took the dory. Or kill everyone now, and let the picketboat overtake the *Weazel*.

"Master, are you all right?"

Yama found that he was awake, standing beside Pandaras in the middle of a fog so dense he could not see the bow of the ship. Something had possessed him, horrible thoughts like ooze from the bottom of his brain. His power, he thought. It would survive any way it could, at any cost. He pressed the heels of his palms to his eyes. Red and black jags of light. He suddenly had a terrible headache. He said, "I am going to steal the dory. You and Tamora will help me."

"Tamora is with Aguilar. They are laying out the weapons, master, as sorry a collection of antiques that I've ever seen. As for the dory, you'll have to explain your plan to the Captain. She came up on deck an hour ago, when the fog bank rolled across the river."

"The machines of the river deeps," Yama said, remembering the dream which had not been a dream after all. A small hope kindled in his breast.

"Machines, master? At the bottom of the river? What would machines be doing down there?"

"I found them and talked to them, and they said that they would help me."

"They would be dredgers," Eliphas said, looming out of the fog. Like Pandaras, he had wrapped a blanket around his shoulders. His eyes were dull pewter in the diffuse light; droplets of water beaded his smooth black skin and clung to the stiff curls of his white hair. "I once saw the carcass of a dredger that had been washed ashore. They are divided into segments like worms, and each segment bears a pair of paddles or other appendages. They clear mud and detritus that collects in the deeps; without them the river would soon silt up."

Yama tried to think it through. The headache was like a spike driven through his forehead. He said slowly, "They changed the currents at the bottom of the river. The water is colder in the deeps, and perhaps it is now coming to the surface. Cold air is denser than warm air, so that as the air above the river is cooled, it draws down more. That is what drives the wind. The fog forms as the warm air cools, and can no longer carry as much moisture." He felt a sudden surge of hope. "They are hiding us from Prefect Corin!"

Eliphas nodded, but Pandaras did not believe a word of it. He said scornfully, "Nothing can change the course of the river!"

"Not its course," Eliphas said, "but its currents. The dredgers are very large. The one I saw was several hundred paces long, and each segment was as big as a house. Ah! There it is again!"

A flash of red light far beyond the *Weazel*'s stern, a dim flare that brightened and faded in the fog. Prefect Corin's picketboat was still pursuing them.

"She's trying the range," Captain Lorquital told Yama, when he climbed up to the quarterdeck. "She is still too far off, but I think that she will catch up with us soon. The stronger the wind, the more advantage we have, because we're the bigger ship. But the wind has almost died away since the fog rose. She'll use her oars again, when her men are rested, and then she'll catch us. There's one hope, but it is a small one. If the fog was coming from the farside shore I'd say we were heading into a storm, and a storm might save us if we were blown in one direction and the picketboat was blown in another. But this came up from the nearside, and I can't tell if it means a storm or not."

The fog was dense but patchy. Toward the end of the morning watch the *Weazel* sailed out of a bank of white vapor into clear air. Everyone squinted in brilliant sunlight that burned off the rust-red sail and the white deck, and laid a net of dazzling diamonds across blue water all around. To starboard, long banks of fog hung just above the river like a range of low hills, their white peaks stirred and torn by the fresh cold wind; to port, the black anvils of thunderstorms towered along the margin of the nearside shore. Drifts of hail and rain swept across the sunlit water, falling from such a height that they seemed to come from cloudless sky. The *Weazel* passed through a brief hailstorm that had everyone running for cover. Small silver fish fell among the hail, jinking frantically as they sought escape through the scuppers. The storm ended as suddenly as it had begun, leaving a scattering of dead fish and shallow drifts of hailstones which quickly melted, leaving blood-red stains from the dust at their cores on the white deck.

Soon afterward, the picketboat breasted out of the fog bank behind the *Weazel*. Her light cannon flashed and flashed. Plumes of water driven by superheated steam shot up and collapsed half a league sternward.

"She'll get the range soon enough," Captain Lorquital told Yama. She stood at the stern rail, immense and foursquare, her day pipe jutting from a corner of her mouth. She had put on a jacket stiff with braid, the better to make a target, she said. It had belonged to her dead husband, and its sleeves were pinned back from her wrists. "I sent a heliograph signal, telling her to lay back and cease firing, but she's not responding. Of course, I suppose the cannon shots could be a kind of reply."

"Let me speak plainly," Yama said. The brief moment of hope had passed. He was convinced that the dredgers had failed him. That he had failed. "They do not want your ship or your cargo. They want only me. Lend me your dory. I will put out in it and wait for the picketboat to overtake me."

Ixchel Lorquital drew on her pipe and looked at him calmly.

"I will not let them take your ship," Yama said.

"That's a generous thought, but you're only a passenger, and the ship is mine to dispose of as I will. My husband always told me that when passengers start giving advice, you should always agree, and then do nothing about it. But I'd rather not give you the false idea that you'll be able to make such a silly sacrifice, so I will say now that I will not allow it."

Yama stood his ground. "If you have any idea about what we should do, I would like to hear it. You have heard mine."

Captain Lorquital turned her back on Yama and contemplated the picketboat. She said, "I am responsible for all my passengers, not just you. Besides, they'll still sink us. They'll want to leave no witnesses."

"Then put yourself and your crew in the dory. I will stand here in plain sight. They will not chase you if they have me."

Captain Lorquital said stubbornly, "I have sailed this ship for fifty years. I've been captain for ten. I won't abandon her for anyone. Even you."

Phalerus, who had the helm, said, "She's right, dominie. If we get a bit of wind, we still might show those cullers a clean pair of heels."

For the first time, Yama considered giving Captain Lorquital a direct order, but the thought that she might obey him with the same unquestioning alacrity as any machine was unnervingly horrible. Worse was the thought that if he tried to call upon machines to kill Prefect Corin he might be seized by his rage and kill everyone around him. No. He would avenge his father, but as an ordinary man.

Tamora came up onto the quarterdeck. She had put on her corset, and a fusil was slung over her shoulder. The bell of its muzzle flared above her shaven scalp. Captain Lorquital said mildly, "I do not remember ordering the crew to take up arms."

"We can show our teeth at least," Tamora said. "Why don't you put back into the fog?"

"They followed us through the night and the fog," Captain Lorquital said. "Why should day be different?"

At that moment, the man in the crow's nest cried out. Patches of water around the *Weazel* began churning, as if vast pumps were laboring to produce submerged fountains. Glassy hummocks rose up, sputtering rafts of foam and slicks of fine silt. The crew crowded the rails, but Aguilar drove them back, shouting that they must see to the sail. Captain Lorquital told Phalerus to make hard to port, but even as the *Weazel* heeled about, more hummocks spurted around her.

A shoal of fish fled past the ship, swimming so frantically that they flung themselves high into the air. Some landed on the deck. They were as long as a man's arm and their narrow heads and stiff dorsal fins were plated with dull red chitin; they banged and clattered against the deck as they thrashed toward the scuppers. Yama wondered if these were the sharers of the dredgers.

Caught between two rising currents, the *Weazel* began to turn in a slow circle. The sail flapped, filled, flapped. Aguilar ordered it reefed, but before the sailors could obey a stay gave with a snap like a rifle shot. The broken end of the rope whiplashed against the sail and ripped a long tear in the canvas; the block which had anchored it tumbled end over end through the air and smashed into the deck a handsbreadth from Tamora's feet.

The picketboat fired again. The cannon's hot light flashed water into steam to the port side of the *Weazel*. Water poured over the little ship's waist; spray wet the torn sail from top to bottom. At the same moment, Yama saw something like a bush or tree rise a little way out of the water off the stern. It was white and pulpy, like something dead that had been floating in the water for a long time.

Captain Lorquital ordered that the sail be struck at once, and turned to Tamora and told her to take off her sword and return the fusil to the armory chest.

Yama laid a hand on Tamora's arm. "They will take me in any case," he said.

Tamora glowered. "I'll throw away this blunderbuss, but I'll keep the sword. It's a poor thing, but it's mine, and you'll have to pry it from my cold dead hand."

There was another flash of red light, but the picketboat was no longer aiming at the *Weazel*. Instead, she was firing into the water close by her hull, slowly obscuring herself in flashes of red light and billowing clouds of steam. The sailors aloft in the yards cried out and started to swing down to the deck, and the *Weazel* shuddered as if she had struck some underwater snag. Yama was thrown against the head of the companionway, and he clung there as the *Weazel* rolled to port and then righted herself violently. A forest of white branches was rising around the ship, as if the river was draining away from trees drowned an age past.

Tamora swore and unslung the fusil, but Yama, remembering his dream, told her to hold her fire.

All around the ship, creamy tentacles erupted from the water and rose into the air, questing this way and that. Some ended in leaf-shaped paddles; some bore ranks of suckers; some were tapered and frayed in a multitude of feathery feelers. Huge, sleek arrow shapes moved beneath the churning surface of the river. Many were as long as the *Weazel*; a few were even larger.

The sharers of the dredgers had come to the surface.

Captain Lorquital took Yama's advice and ordered the crew to stand from the rails, and to put down the handspikes and halberds with which they had armed themselves. Most of the sailors promptly climbed back up into the rigging, dodging tentacles which rose toward the mast and plucked at ratlines and stays as if at a harp. Aguilar stood at the bow, her cutlass resting on her shoulder, looking right and left at the questing tentacles as if daring them to get close enough.

As Pandaras and Eliphas clambered up the ladder to the quarterdeck, the ship shuddered and a cluster of palps dropped onto the starboard rail. Their ends thrashed in every direction like a nest of blind white snakes, stretching thinner and thinner as they walked on their tips across the deck. The rail splintered under the mass of flesh.

One of the crew darted forward and with a cry stuck a knife in a rubbery coil. It was Pandaras's friend, the boy, Pantin. Tentacles weaved about him. One plucked his knife from his grasp; two more shot forward and struck him, one around the neck, the other around his feet. Pantin barely had time to scream before he was lifted up. The tentacles pulled in different directions. A rich red spray spattered the white deck and, still clutching the pieces of the boy's body, the tentacles fell backward into the river.

More tentacles poured over the rail. The *Weazel* began to list to starboard. In the yards, the sailors scrambled for better foot- and hand-holds; skinny Anchiale clung to the top of the mast with his long legs tucked into his chest while a tentacle explored the crow's nest.

Yama remembered the polyps which had swum in the flooded chamber deep in the Palace of the Memory of the People. Those had long ago lost whatever powers of reasoning they had once possessed, or so Magon had said, and returned to their cisterns only through habit; yet they had helped Yama by breaking the bridge before the hell-hound could cross it. Yama suspected that these giants were different not only in size, but in intelligence, too. They did not serve blindly. They were looking for something. Clinging to the rail, looking down into a roiling mass of tentacles directly below, he glimpsed an eye as big as his head. Its round pupil was rimmed with gold. It stared at him for a long moment, and then it sank beneath a rush of white water.

Yama knew then what the polyps were searching for. He vaulted to the main deck, landing on hands and knees amidst a slowly writhing nest of white coils and cables. Someone shouted and he looked up and saw Tamora falling toward him, her sword held above her head. She landed on the balls of her feet, bounced up, caught Yama's shoulders and shouted into his face, "I won't let them kill you."

"They are looking for me! They cannot tell the ships apart so they are looking for me!"

Something coiled around Yama's thigh. A wet palp slapped his chest and a hundred fine threads crawled over his tunic. Tamora was caught around the waist by a tentacle as thick through as her arm; three more, stretched thin, whipped around and around her corset. She held her arms high, the sword crooked above her head.

Yama was frightened that she would do something that would get them both killed. He reached for her hand, but tendrils as thin and as strong as metal wire coiled around his wrist and dragged it down. Something wet and rubbery slapped onto his face, covering his eyes and nostrils. It stank horribly of fish and rotten eggs. He could feel a hundred tiny suckers fasten and unfasten over his skin as the palp adjusted to the contours of his face. It flexed and spread so that it covered his mouth. Something pressed at his lips and he was frightened that he would be smothered. The pressure was insistent. Although Yama clamped the muscles of his jaws as hard as he could, something the size of his little finger slipped between his lips and probed at the crevices between his gums and teeth before withdrawing.

The palp dropped away from his face. The tentacle around his legs uncoiled and dragged away across the deck. All the tentacles were retreating, thickening and pouring backward over the broken rail. The ship groaned as she righted. Tamora lowered her sword and rested its square point against the deck, so that the sailors would not see how her arm trembled.

Yama ran to the broken rail, but already the sleek shapes were sinking away through choppy water stained with abyssal silt. High above, Anchiale regained the crow's nest and cried out. Yama remembered to look for the picketboat.

But it was gone.

28

Storm Damage

CAPTAIN LORQUITAL INSISTED on sailing the *Weazel* in slow circles around the place where the picketboat had last been seen, but except for a few splintered planks bobbing on the chop nothing was found. The wind was rising, and it drove the fog banks toward the farside shore. Waves grew higher, breaking in white water at their crests, lifting and dropping the *Weazel* as they marched past in ceaseless succession. At last, as it was growing dark, fog engulfed the *Weazel* again.

Captain Lorquital turned her ship to head into the waves, but the waves grew higher still, breaking over the pitching bow and washing the main deck. Wind howled and plucked at the rigging. The crew, in yellow oilskins, with lines clipped to their belts, worked aloft to storm-rig the sail while the *Weazel* now plunged bow first into the high waves, now was battered lengthwise, heeling hard with spray dashing like shot across her. The awning and bedding on the main deck were washed away; so were the chickens and guineafowl in their bamboo cages.

The four passengers retreated to Captain Lorquital's cabin. Pandaras felt the pitching worst and was several times sick in a basin, groaning profuse apologies between spasms. Tamora sat cross-legged on the Captain's wide bunk and glared at Eliphas, who was trying to interest Yama in his theories about the cause of the storm.

Yama hardly heard the old man. He could still sense the minds of the gigantic dredging machines, far below. It was as if the little cabin—the pitching floor covered with felt rugs, the swinging lanterns which cast wild shadows across the tapestries on the lapped plank walls—was slowly turning into smoke, or was a picture projected onto smoke that was slowly dissolving to reveal the real world.

The dredgers had returned to their immemorial routines, singing each to each as, followed by flocks of sharers, they plowed river-bottom silt in the cold black currents. Yama was caught up in their communion. *Join us,* they urged. *Watch over us. Affirm us.* Their siren song wound seductive coils in his brain. They claimed to know all the wonders of the world, for everything came at last to the river. They claimed to remember his people. They would tell him all they knew, they said, if only he would join with them in the joy of forever renewing the world.

Someone shook Yama's shoulder and whispered in his ear. *Master, Master, are you asleep!* Another said, *He's not sleeping. Either he is in shock, or calling up the monsters of the deep has exhausted him.* And a third said sharply, *I have seen men like this after battle. If he is not wakened now he may never wake.* The first voice again: *His coin is filled with light! See? You see? Master, I am taking it away. I think that it is doing something bad to you.*

It was all very far away and insubstantial, like the harmless chittering of agitated ghosts. Yama was only dimly aware of someone slapping his face, of cold cloths laid on his forehead, of being walked around. The songs of the deeps were more immediate than the voices or the manipulation of his body; the channeled abyssal plain more vivid than the pitching cabin and its swinging lanterns.

One of the ghosts said, *It may kill him.*

Yama tried to tell them that that was what he wanted, to escape his body and fall into the depths where the dredgers sang songs in which every word was true, charged with the wise love of the Preservers.

Something stung his neck. Suddenly his heart was racing and he was back in the cabin, lying in the bunk with Pandaras's sharp, narrow face bent over his. Wind screamed to itself outside; there were a hundred tinkling movements in the cabin as things shifted to and fro. The lanterns swung a beat behind the pitching of the deck.

"He's awake," Pandaras said to the people behind him.

Yama turned his head away, but he was quite alone. The deeps and the singers in the deeps were gone.

Strong hands turned his head. A woman wearing the fierce face of a tiger looked into his eyes. He said, "I know you. Derev. It is time we took away our masks." And then he wept, because he knew that Derev was dead or lost, and all his childhood was burned away.

In the end, they had given him an injection of adrenaline.

"You were slipping away from us, master," Pandaras said. "Tamora suggested it."

"It was shock," Tamora said. "I've seen it before. The stuff works on most bloodlines."

Eliphas nodded. "The Preservers made us all in their image, to the least detail."

"They must have run short of time with your kind," Tamora said.

Yama was sitting on the edge of the bunk now, bracing himself as the ship plunged and rose. He said, "I called them, and then they called me. And they were stronger. Stronger and wiser. I should talk with them again, because they know so much . . ."

The cabin door banged open; air and spray roared around Captain Lorquital as she struggled to shut it behind her. She wore a yellow oilskin cape that shed a cascade of water around her flat bare feet. She looked at Yama and said, "It didn't kill you, then. Some bloodlines can't take it. Their hearts burst or their tongues swell up and strangle them. Eliphas says you called up the storm. Is that true?"

"The cold currents no longer rise," Yama said. "I think that it will pass soon. Will it sink the *Weazel*?"

"I'd rather not put her to the test."

"There is nothing I can do," Yama said. He saw that Captain Lorquital did not believe him, and saw too that this brave, capable woman was more afraid of him than of the storm. She nodded curtly and turned away.

———

The storm blew all night and all the next day, and began to fall only in the early hours of the morning of the third day. When Yama came up on deck soon after dawn, Phalerus, who had been fixing the broken rail, turned away and touched his throat in a warding gesture.

The storm had driven the *Weazel* before it. The farside shore was less than a league off the starboard side, a maze of channels snaking between viridescent mudbanks and dense stands of mangroves. The margin of the old shore was a low cliff exposed years ago by the falling level of the river, a long black line that shimmered and jiggled in the heat haze far beyond the mangroves. A sign of his birth, Yama thought, and wondered, not for the first time, if he was the destroyer of the world rather than its savior. The sun shone through a haze of cloud, but it was very warm, and the white deck steamed.

There was no sign of Captain Lorquital, but Yama found Aguilar helping Anchiale and the grizzled slave move foam-cased pieces of machinery in the hold. The cargo had shifted in the storm.

"My mother is asleep," the sturdy young woman said. She gave Yama a hard, defiant look. "She stayed on deck for most of the blow. She saved us all, I reckon."

Yama said, "If I could have stopped the storm, then I would have done so at once."

"You have my mother under some spell," Aguilar said, "but not all of us are charmed."

"I asked only for passage, and paid for it, too. What are you looking at?"

Aguilar had tied an electric lantern to a line, and now the two sailors began to lower it into the gap they had made between the tumbled foam eggs of the cargo. She said, "The ship is wallowing. There. That's why."

Yama looked down. At the bottom of a wedge of darkness, the lantern swung above its own reflection.

———

Captain Lorquital, rumpled from her early awakening, stood at the edge of the cargo well and argued with her daughter for a while. Aguilar maintained that the planking had sprung and the ship was taking on water because braces had been removed from the hull during her last refit; her mother said that the *Weazel* had ridden out the storm only because removal of certain of the braces had made her hull flexible.

"Water could have got in under the tarpaulin," Captain Lorquital said. "The decks were awash for the best part of three days. We were more in the river than on it."

"The covers were reefed fast," Aguilar said stubbornly. "Besides, the water is getting deeper in there."

All of the steel bands had been sprung around the hatch, and the tarpaulin covers rolled away. Anchiale and the slave were lifting out part of the cargo with a winch rigged from the mast; foam-covered ovals cluttered the main deck before and aft of the hatch. Presently, both Captain Lorquital and her daughter climbed down into the hold. They were down there a long time, and Captain Lorquital was grim-faced when they came back up.

"We'll put in for repairs," she told Yama. "I was right, though. The storm didn't spring the planks. The way they're splintered, it looks like something took a bite from them."

A hand-pump worked by two of the sailors lifted water from the flooding hold and sent sparkling gushes into the river. A patch of canvas was lowered over the starboard side and hauled tight by a rope that went under the keel. There were bumps and groans from the hold; Aguilar went down and came back up, shaking her head. Part of the cargo was floating and shifting about, she said.

"If we're lucky, it won't capsize us or smash the hole wider, but the hole's already wide enough to sink us in a day or two." She stared at Yama. "There's a curse on this voyage, I reckon."

29

The Black Tower

THE BUSINESS OF grounding the *Weazel* took a whole day. Captain Lorquital used the reaction motor to pick a way between banks of stinking mud and stands of pioneer mangroves, and to cross a plain of tall yellow reeds cut by a hundred meandering channels. Phalerus was in the crow's nest, scrying a path through the reed beds, and the grizzled slave of Pandaras's bloodline stood at the bow, using a weighted line to sound the depth.

At last, Captain Lorquital ran her foundering ship aground by one of the islands at the far side of the reed beds. Ropes, pivoting on belts of leather greased with palm oil, were slung around several of the blue pine trees which had colonized the island, and crew and passengers labored at the ship's windlass to haul her out of the shallows until the hole bitten through her hull was visible.

Because the ship was lying at a steep angle, everyone camped on the island. Smoky fires were lit to keep off clouds of black flies and tiny sweat bees. Yama sat a little way from the others, sifting through his father's papers by the light of an electric lamp, once again tracing and checking the threads of logic that bound the complicated computations.

The Aedile had been obsessed with measurements, ciphers and calculations. He had been convinced that there was a golden rule by which everything could be divided into everything else, leaving as an irreducible kernel the prime which harmonized the world and perhaps the Universe, the secret signature of the Preservers. His research had never led to anything but a maze in which he had lost himself, but these calculations were different.

Every decad for almost fifteen years, the Aedile had taken measurements of the Great River's slow retreat from the old shoreline around Aeolis. From these, with elaborate allowances for seasonal variation and for the buffering effect of the ice fields of the Terminal Mountains, he had worked out when the river had begun to fail. The answer was not exact, and hedged with cautious interpolations, but Yama believed that the conclusion was inescapable, and laden with appalling implications.

The Great River had begun its inexorable decline at about the time he had been found by the old Constable of Aeolis in a white boat, a baby lying on the breast of a dead woman.

Now Yama once more fumbled his way through the tables of measurements and staggered rows of calculations, trying and failing to guess what they might mean, by turns frightened and full of wonder. Most people blamed the fall of the river on the heretics; was he then their creature? Or was the fall of the river in some way linked with his birth?

When at last he looked up from the papers, he discovered that someone—probably Pandaras—had settled a blanket around his shoulders. The fire had burned down. Apart from the man on watch at the edge of the clearing, a black shadow against the black water, marked only by the fitful red spark of a cigarette, everyone in the camp was sleeping. Yama switched off the little lantern. He lay down on the lumpy ground and rolled himself up in the blanket and fell asleep almost at once.

He was woken early the next morning by Tamora. Eliphas had disappeared, she said. No one had seen him go, not even the old slave who had taken the night watch.

"He will be back," Captain Lorquital said. "He has a great curiosity, and he has gone to explore."

But Tamora said with some satisfaction this was surely proof that Eliphas was the traitor who had betrayed their course to Prefect Corin. She was all for tracking him down and giving him a summary trial and immediate execution, but Yama persuaded her to be patient, and was relieved when Eliphas came back in the middle of the morning, casually walking into the camp as a man might walk into his own house.

He told Yama he had been to the far end of the island. "I know this part of the shore," he said. "We are very close to the edge of the world, brother, and a marvelous shrine that stands beyond it."

Yama was sitting on the mossy bole of a fallen tree in a patch of sunlight. Pandaras was cutting his hair. Aguilar and Anchiale were trimming branches from the trunk of a felled pine; the steady sound of their axes rang across the clearing. There was a smell of fresh sawdust and pine resin. A cauldron of pitch sat on white-hot embers in the center of the cleared area, sending up reeking fumes in the sultry heat. In the bright sunlight beyond the shade of the trees, the *Weazel* lay canted in shallow water. Watched by Captain Lorquital, Phalerus and the two slaves were working up to their waists in water, cutting and prying away damaged planks.

"The shore must have changed very much," Yama said to Eliphas. "How can you be certain?"

"You will see, brother, if you come with me. The water is very shallow on the other side of the island. We can wade across to the old shoreline, reach the shrine beyond the edge of the world and return, all in a day."

Pandaras combed cuttings from Yama's hair with his claws. After a moment, he said, "You have hard places under your scalp, master. Here and here."

They were smooth and flat, and had straight edges. One was twice the size of the other. They moved slightly beneath Yama's fingertips. He did not know what they were—or rather, he still could not quite put a name on them—but he was not alarmed.

"I noticed one a few days ago," he said. "They do not hurt. It is nothing."

"My master is ill," Pandaras told Eliphas. "He needs to rest."

"I am quite well," Yama said. "Where is this place?"

"It is not much more than a stroll," Eliphas said, "even for an old man like me. It is a very unusual place, brother. I believe you will learn much from it."

In the end, they made an expedition of it. Captain Lorquital sent along the cook to collect fresh roots and greens. Tamora insisted on coming; so did Pandaras, although he was still much weakened by his bout of river sickness.

Crossing the island was easy enough, for little flourished in the dense shade of the blue pines which grew along its central ridge. Eliphas led the others down a path he had cut through a belt of tamarisk and swamp grape, and then they were out in sunlight at the edge of a shallow creek that spread between the island and the low cliffs of the old shore.

The tower was black and slender, standing half a league off like a beckoning finger against the deep blue sky. Eliphas said that once upon a time it had been decorated with prayer flags and banners, and mankites had been flown from its top to keep watch for floating islands.

"There was a camp of soldier monks here each summer. The currents of the air are much like those of water, and this is a place where the islands sometimes gather in shoals and archipelagoes that stretch far away into the sky."

Floating islands!

As a boy, Yama had visited the farside shore every year, when the Amnan had crossed the river for the festival at the beginning of winter, but he had only ever seen one floating island at close quarters. Although a few could always be glimpsed beyond the edge of the world, scattered across the vast blue depths of the sky which wrapped around the world, they were usually so distant that even when Yama looked at them through his stepfather's spyglass they remained little more than dots. It was said that rebel machines lived on the islands, and that tribes of heretics, cannibals and pirates traveled from island to island on the backs of eagles feathered in metal vanes, or on mankites or in balloons. Yama had dreamed that his people might live there too.

Yama had finally seen an island at close quarters two years ago. It had been the last festival that Telmon had attended; at the end of that winter he had set off downriver toward the war, and news of his death had reached the peel-house at midsummer, just after the turning of the year.

That day, Telmon and Yama had gone hunting for cassowaries, leaving the smoke and noise and mud of the festival encampment of the citizens of Aeolis far behind. Winter had come early. Telmon and Yama were mantled in woolen ponchos. Their ponies sent up plumes of steam with every breath. It was almost dark. They had found no cassowaries, but just as they were about to turn back, they flushed out a basilisk.

The size of a small dog, the creature stood foursquare in front of the burrow it had scraped out beneath a briar patch. It raised its frilled mane, yawned to show the triple rows of teeth within its black mouth, and arched its naked, segmented tail over its back. A single drop of venom hung from the hooked spine of its stinger.

Although Telmon and Yama kept a safe distance, Yama's pony stepped about so much that he had to dismount and hold the animal's head and breathe into its nostrils to calm it. He threw stones at the basilisk, but the creature snatched them out of the air and swallowed them, much to Telmon's amusement.

"He swallows stones as birds do, so that he can grind food in his crop. The Amnan say that one will sting itself to death rather than be captured. Unlike snakes, they are not immune to their own poison."

"Dr. Dismas says that the diluted poison can be used to stop the growth of cankers and fistulas. I expect he would pay well for this one. We could easily kill it, Tel. It cannot guard both flanks at once."

"Dr. Dismas is a fantasist," Telmon said. "He tells so many tales that he has long ago forgotten which are true and which are not. You should not talk to him, Yama. There is something odd about his interest in you."

Telmon sat straight in his saddle and kept a careful watch on the basilisk, one gloved hand holding the reins, the other resting behind him, close to the socket in which his javelin was set. He had recently had Sergeant Rhodean shave his hair, leaving only a central topknot. It was the style fashionable among calvarymen; the topknot, shaped like a square loaf, formed a cushion between skull and helmet. His red poncho was neatly folded back to free his arms, showing the silvery padded jacket he wore beneath. His tight knee-length boots had been spit-shined so that they gleamed even in the twilight. He was all that Yama yearned to be: elegant, fastidious, kindly and knowledgeable.

Telmon said, "We will leave this brave fellow to his home. There is still a little light, and we might get lucky."

As they rode on, Yama said, "Dr. Dismas says that he might be able to find out about my bloodline. That is why he wants to make a study of me."

"Dr. Dismas is easy with his promises, Yama. It is a cheap and quick way of winning people's gratitude, and I expect he will move on before he has to make good any of them."

"You will look for my people, Tel. That is, when you are not fighting heretics or charming women."

"I will keep watch every step of the way, but I cannot promise anything. You know that father has made many enquiries, but never with any success. It is not likely that I will come across anyone of your bloodline by chance."

They rode up the shallow slope to the top of the rise. There were narrow tracks worn through the tall grasses which Telmon said were certainly made by cassowaries, but all they found were two peahens, which whirred up under their ponies' hooves and flew off into the dusk. Yama was still calming his pony when Telmon spied the floating island.

It was like a small round barrow or cairn, but it stood where no barrow or cairn should be, atop the long flat horizon of the edge of the world. When Yama and Telmon rode closer, they saw that the island had grounded on a wide apron of eroded keelrock. It was a dense tangle of violet and red vines and tubes and bladders, as wide as a paeonin field and twice as tall as a house. It was full of noises, stealthy rustles and squeaks and crepitations, as if its vines and bladders were continually jostling and creeping over one another, and little blue lights came and went in its tangled thickets. Yama feared that these might be the lanterns of pirates or heretics, but Telmon laughed and said that they were only burning hydrogen vented from collapsed lift pods.

"Heretics are men like you and me. They have no use for floating islands, either in the air or on the river. Birds roost in the islands, though, and they are inhabited by species of crab found nowhere else, which feed on dead vegetation and fiercely protect their home, and barnacles which sieve the air for floating spores. The whole thing is really one organism, for although it appears to be made of many different species, they have all lost their autonomy so that they might function better within the whole. Each is a servant with a different task, and by specializing in their tasks they have lost the ability to live separately. Rather like the peel-house, eh? This one must be diseased. Usually, they don't come so close to the world. Out in the air, Yama, is another nature entirely different from the one we inhabit. You should ask Derev about it. It is said that her people once flew there, but gave that up to live here with us."

Yama, stung by the last remark, said, "That is just a story the Mud People put about. Derev would have told me if it was true."

Telmon smiled. "You are in love with her. O, do not deny it! I am your brother, Yama, as truly a brother as if you were of my own blood. I have watched you grow up, and it seems to me that you mature quickly. You must give some thought to the shape of your life, for it might not be as long as you wish."

"It might be longer," Yama said.

"It might at that. We do not know, do we? It is a terrible thing, not to know who you really are or why you are here, but you cannot fill your life with dreams. I would like to see you give up your wild ideas, and perhaps Derev can help you. There is nothing wrong with metic marriages, and it would certainly make her father pleased."

Yama said stoutly, "I am going to war, Tel. Like you, I want to fight the heretics and help redeem the world. Besides, I might find my bloodline on my way to the midpoint of the world."

"Perhaps." Telmon looked around. "It grows dark, and the ponies are tired. We can come back and look at this in daylight."

But when they returned the next morning, the island had departed, leaving only a fret of shallow channels eaten into the sloping apron of keelrock on which it had rested. Perhaps the island had not been diseased after all, Telmon said, or perhaps it had cured itself by leaching minerals from the keelrock. He was intensely interested in how the world and its creatures worked. Although Yama spent more time in the library than his stepbrother, it was mostly to dream among the books and maps of finding his bloodline and his true parents. Telmon ransacked it in sporadic bursts to learn about what he had observed, and would as soon dissect the animals and birds he brought back from hunting expeditions as eat them. Like his father, he was interested in things for their intrinsic worth; if he had become Aedile, no doubt he would have filled the peel-house with a menagerie, and its gardens with exotic plants from the length of the world.

But the war had taken him away, and then he was dead.

Yama did not know if he remembered the floating island because of the basilisk, or the basilisk because of the floating island, but he had never forgotten either. Sometimes, he still dreamed that his people were living among the floating islands; once, while shut in the cell in the hive of the Department of Indigenous Affairs, he had dreamed that Derev had taken him to his people, carrying him in her arms while she rowed the air with strong white wings she had somehow grown.

And now he was eager to see for himself the archipelagoes that Eliphas promised would be floating in the sky beyond the edge of the world. He led the way across the stream, pushing through a strong current that swirled around his thighs, his waist, his chest, then throwing himself forward and swimming strongly toward the reed banks that stood along the far bank. He was filled with a sudden inexpressible joy, for it seemed that with Prefect Corin dead his life was his own, to do with it as he would in a world filled with wonders.

Yama hauled himself onto an unstable platform of reeds and rolled over onto his back and lay there in hot sunlight with water steaming from his wet clothes, watching as the others floundered through the stream toward him. Tamora held her sword above her head; Pandaras rode on the cook's broad shoulders; Eliphas half-walked, half-swam, his hands parting the water in front of his narrow chest with a curiously formal paddling motion, his straw hat perched squarely on top of his head.

Yama shook water from the slick pages of the Puranas and glanced at the picture of Angel's final, fatal ascension before putting the volume away. A dragonfly perched on a reed and with clawed forelegs preened veined wings as long as his arms while watching him sidelong with prismatic eyes. It flew off with a crisp whir as the others climbed up beside him. He wanted to go on at once, but the cook said that first he must set traps for crayfish.

"The Captain will bear down hard on me if I don't, master. She does love crayfish fried in a bit of salt butter, and it will stop her fretting about the hurt done to the ship."

The cook was a large, hairless man with pinkish-gray skin and a round, dolorous face. His name was Tibor. He wore only ragged trousers belted with a length of frayed rope, and chain-smoked cigarettes he rolled from scraps of paper and strands of coarse black tobacco he kept in a plastic pouch. He absentmindedly snapped at passing insects, and when he spoke he passed his long red tongue over his black lips at the end of every sentence, as if relishing the taste of his words.

Yama, who had learned the trick as a child, helped Tibor weave crayfish traps from strips of reed. The traps were simple things, little baskets of close-woven reed stems with spines at the mouth which pointed inward; when the crayfish entered, they could not back through the spines to get out. Tibor's big hands, each with his long fingers set around a sensitive pad, worked quickly and deftly, making two traps for every one of Yama's. The cook baited the traps with scraps of smelly fat, and tied them at intervals along the margin of the stream.

They soon fell to talking. The cook was from a bloodline which had been enslaved for hundreds of generations; his distant ancestors had fought on the side of the fallen machines in the Age of Insurrection. Having sinned against the Preservers, they were now their slaves, and so the slaves of all free men on Confluence. Most were hierodules, but Tibor had been sold on the open market after the shrine of his temple had failed at the beginning of the war against the heretics.

Tibor was not bitter about his fate, even when he explained that the long vertical scars on his chest marked where his nipples had been seared away. "It is so I cannot feed children, which is what the men of my people do. Our owners do not like us to keep families; our babies are taken at birth and fed on an artificial milk. If they fed from me, they could feed only from me and no other, and I would have to feed them for three years. No owner would want that! You do not believe me, because in most peoples it is the women who care for babies, but it is true. So instead of my babies I feed all of you!"

Tibor laughed loudly at this joke. Despite his down-turned mouth and downwardly slanting eyes, he was by nature a cheerful man. "I am not smart," he said, "but that is good for me, because a smart slave is always unhappy."

Yama thought of the librarian of the peel-house. Zakiel had been born a free man; unlike Tibor, he had known another life. And yet he was happy, for although he possessed nothing, not even his own life, he still had the work he loved. Yama had not thought about this before, and asked the cook many questions. They talked together until Tibor said that they had enough traps to feed the whole ship for two days if only half caught anything, adding that for a little while Yama had been the servant, and he the master.

"Some say you are the slave of all of the peoples of Confluence," Tibor said. Yama asked him to explain, but he only laughed and changed the subject. "This is a bad land, the sailors say. They do not stray far from the ship because of it. They told me I was a fool to come with you, but they'll be glad of fresh food."

Pandaras had fallen asleep in the sun, and woke to find that leeches were feeding on his ankles, which he had dangled in the stream to keep cool. Tibor burned off the leeches with the glowing coal of a cigarette, and Pandaras fussed at the blood that streamed down his ankles from the little round punctures, and complained that he had soaked his second-best pair of trousers and would never get them back into shape, and only shut up when Tamora pointed out that if he wanted to go back now he would have to go back alone.

It did not take long to walk to the base of the tower. The low cliffs were easy to climb, for their black, pebbly clay was deeply gullied by erosion. Beyond was a plain less than a league wide but of seemingly infinite length, thin red laterite and dry grasses punctuated by stands of saw-toothed yucca and palmetto, and sprawling clumps of gumbo-limbo. There were many outcrops of keelrock, smooth spurs or folded layers just as they had been cast a hundred thousand years before. Not even lichens had gained a hold on the slick keelrock, and all across the narrow plain a thousand facets shone and winked in the strong sunlight.

The tower seemed to be fused into the keelrock ridge at the edge of the world, or perhaps it had been grown from it by an art that had been lost since the Preservers had seeded Confluence with the ten thousand races of the Shaped. The tower was smooth and round, and several hundred chains high. Its black surface was slickly reflective, and like the keelrock quite unscarred by time. Tumbled remains of wooden scaffolding and bent hoops which had once been the frames of tents were scattered around it. Ravens rose into the air as the party approached, calling loudly to each other in hoarse, indignant voices before circling away into the vast volumes of air.

Beyond the tower, the edge of the world dropped vertically into clouds that seemed to stretch away forever, as if the world swam not in the void but in a sea of absolute whiteness. Chains of islands floated above their own shadows, lying at different levels in the clear air above the clouds. Hundreds of islands, thousands. Yama marveled at their number.

The shadow of the black tower lay on the white cloud deck like a road, and sunlight broke in splintered rainbows around its top. Beside it, the shadows of the five people were like giants aping their every movement, and around the head of each was a circular rainbow. Yama moved his arms and grinned when his shadow gestured back across leagues of cloud. Pandaras and the cook danced and capered there at the edge of the world, and even Tamora, who had been nervously alert since leaving the ship, smiled at the sight.

"It is a rare wonder," Eliphas said proudly, as if he had led them here just to see this. "A blessing of the Preservers."

Tamora turned and squinted into the level sunlight at their backs. "Grah. I'd say it is a matter of the angle of light and properties of the clouds." She would not agree with Eliphas about anything, but she added grudgingly, "It is some kind of wonder, I suppose."

"It is beautiful," Pandaras said. "It is a miracle of light and air and mist. I will make a song of it."

"Out of my hearing, I hope," Tamora said. "Yama, as soon as we are rested, we should turn back."

Eliphas said to Yama, "The blessings of the Preservers will be upon you, doubled and redoubled, when you visit the shrine, brother. We will leave the others to rest here, and go down together."

Yama said, "Where is the shrine?"

Eliphas smiled, and pointed straight down.

30

The Edge of the World

A STAIR, ENTERED by a narrow defile between two tall, roughly man-shaped outcrops that Eliphas called the Watchers of the Void, led down the vertical rock face at the edge of the world. It was broad enough for a decad of men to have descended abreast, but its steps, carved from naked keelrock, were steep and narrow and slippery. Yama discovered that he was terrified of falling, imagining himself plummeting through the cloud deck and continuing to fall until at last passing beyond the envelope of the world's atmosphere and perishing, as Angel had perished in the embrace of a copy of her own self. Were their bodies still falling through the void beyond the world? He and Tamora clung to the carved face of the cliff as they followed Eliphas, finding comfort in the faces and bodies of the men and women and creatures that flowed under their fingertips.

The cook, Tibor, had stayed behind to dig for edible roots, and Pandaras had volunteered to help him. Yama had given the boy his book and coin, in case either drew the aspect of Angel to the shrine. Although the hell-hound had destroyed her, there might be other copies.

Tamora had insisted that it was her duty to watch over Yama. She thought that Eliphas was leading him into a trap. If she was right then neither her sword nor her bravery could save him, but Yama did not trouble to tell her that. There was a coldness growing in his heart; as he descended the stair it seemed to him that Tamora and Eliphas had become strangers, or worse, ghosts of strangers.

The world's edge was a black vertical cliff that rose straight up from the sea of cloud and stretched away for thousands of leagues on either side. It was dark and cold; the only light was that reflected from the clouds far below. Yama, Tamora and Eliphas were like mice descending a mountain, emmets crawling down a wall.

They descended a long way. At intervals, the stair opened out onto wide platforms or ledges, but always it continued downward. Once, a stream spurted from the cliff and arched above the stair, a muscular silvery braid shredded by wind as it fell toward the cloud deck. Wind buffeted them and whispered and whistled among the intricate carvings of the sheer cliff face. Eliphas's straw hat was blown from his head and dwindled away into the infinite ocean of air.

Presently, light puddled around Yama's feet. Tamora gasped and, five steps below, Eliphas turned and stared. Pinpricks of light reflected in his silver eyes. A handful of fireflies had found Yama and crowned him with their cold blue-white fire. Soon afterward, the stair turned around a fold of rock. There was a wide ledge, and a tall, narrow arch cut into the adamantine keelrock of the cliff.

"The shrine!" Eliphas announced. "Some say it is the oldest in the world. You will learn much here, brother."

"At least as much as from any other hole in the ground," Tamora said.

A fugitive light glimmered inside the arch, and it brightened as Eliphas led Yama and Tamora toward it. It did not come from any source, but seemed to stain the air as pigments stain the water in which a painter dips his brushes.

The place beyond the arch did not seem to Yama to be a shrine at all. There was no black disc, no altar or sanctuary, nothing but featureless, slightly translucent walls that curved up and met high overhead. It was as if they had stumbled into a gigantic blown egg filled with sourceless light. While Tamora prowled around the perimeter of this lambent space, Eliphas told Yama, "When the shrine was in use, one of the priests would stand in the center and become possessed by the avatar. That is why there is no screen."

Yama said boldly, "Are you hoping that I can awaken the avatar?"

He was excited by the idea. He had come so far, from the silent shrines of Ys to this, a shrine older than any on the nearside shore. He had learned the extent of his powers, and where his people might still live. He had mastered the hell-hound and destroyed Angel's aspect. He suddenly felt that he had nothing to fear from anything in the world.

Eliphas's eyes blankly reflected the even light. Nothing could be learned from his face. He said, "The woman should wait outside. She might spoil the reading."

"I stay with Yama," Tamora said. Her voice echoed from several points in the vaulted space. "If anything happens to him, old man, it will happen to you, too. I'll make sure of it."

"You could watch from the entrance as easily as from in here," Eliphas said. "If you stay here, your presence may disturb the operation."

Tamora crossed her arms. "Then why should I move? You give Yama airs, making him believe he can wake the dead. Those days are gone. We don't need avatars to tell us what to do anymore."

Eliphas said, "He stands there crowned with fireflies. Is that not sign enough for you?" He turned and asked Yama, "If the avatar came, brother, what would you ask it?"

Yama grinned. He no longer trusted Eliphas, but he did not fear him, either. He strode to the middle of the room. Immediately, the light thickened around him. Tamora and Eliphas dwindled into the light becoming shadows that frayed away and disappeared. Yama seemed to be standing inside a bank of glowing mist, and then the mist cleared and he saw a needle hung before the red swirl of the Eye of the Preservers.

It was the world. Not the representation which Angel's aspect had shown him in the Temple of the Black Well, but the world as it was at that very moment. Yama discovered that if he stared at one spot long enough he flew directly toward it. He saw the brawling streets of Ys and the blackened ruins of Aeolis; the immemorial gardens and tombs of the City of the Dead, and the garden-topped crag where Beatrice and Osric lived. He saw the white contours of the ceramic shell of the holy city of Gond, and followed the course of the Great River toward the midpoint of the world. His gaze passed over a dozen different cities: a city of glass domes like nests of soap bubbles; a city of white cubes stacked over each other; a city built among trees; a city of spires that rose from a lake; a city carved into red sandstone cliffs above a curve of the river; a city of gardens and houses raised high on stilts. He saw the great forests that stretched for a thousand leagues above the Marsh of the Lost Waters, and the ruined cities along the forest shore. Smoke hung in tattered banners where cannon of the army of the Department of Indigenous Affairs were bombarding a fortified ridge.

Yama would have looked more closely at the forces of the heretics then, but he felt that someone among them was looking for him and he quickly turned away. The view unraveled to show the world entire again. He noticed a loose cloud of tiny lights that trailed behind it and at once the constant tug of the feral machine he had called down at the merchant's house became more insistent. One of the lights grew until it eclipsed all the others, burning away the world and encasing him in its radiance.

If the machine spoke to Yama, he did not hear it. But across a great gulf he heard his own voice, apparently answering a series of questions. *Yes. Yes. I will. Yes.*

He reeled backward, overwhelmed by light, and fell, and for an instant thought that he fell through the void beyond the edge of the world. Fell with Angel. Fell in her arms.

Something struck the length of his body with the weight of the whole world. Blood filled his mouth where he had bitten his tongue and cheeks; red and black pain filled his head.

Tamora lifted Yama's head and cleared blood from his mouth with her fingers. She had a shallow cut on one arm. Her sword lay beside her on the softly glowing floor. It was bloody to the hilt.

Yama discovered that he had urinated in his trousers; they clung unpleasantly to his thighs. Dried blood crusted his nostrils and his upper lip, and his head felt as if someone had tried to split it with a wedge. Little bits of fused metal and flaked carbon char were scattered in a circle around him—the remains of the fireflies which earlier had crowned him, now burned out and quite dead.

Eliphas was gone, but there were still three people in the shrine. Something was inside Yama, looking through his eyes. Sharing his thoughts. He knew now why he had eaten mud rotten with termites. For the metal in the bodies of the insects. For the metal needed to grow the machine under his skin.

Tamora got Yama to his feet and helped him walk about until he had recovered his sense of who and where he was. She told him that he had stood raptly in the center of the shrine for hours, his face turned up, his eyes rolled back so that only the whites showed. He tried to tell her what he had seen. The whole world, immense and particular, as the Preservers might see it.

"It is so strange," he said. "So huge and yet so fragile."

Then he laughed, and felt more laughter rising within him, wild and strong. He rose on it as on great wings. It might have possessed him entirely, but Tamora slapped his face and the sting of the slap sobered him.

He said, "The feral machine found me, as I once found it. Or perhaps it found me long ago, and has been bending my will toward it ever since. They are still there, Tamora, the rebel machines and avatars. They were banished from the world at the end of the Age of Insurrection, but they have not abandoned it. They spoke to me or to a part of me, but I cannot remember what they said . . ."

As amazed by this as by his laughter, he began to cry.

"Hush," Tamora said. "Hush." She held Yama and rocked him.

"I serve evil ends," he said. "I cannot be what I am not, and I have been made to serve evil ends. I am their creature."

"You're only what you are," Tamora said helplessly. "Don't try to be more than that, or you'll destroy yourself."

He asked what had happened to Eliphas, and she said grimly that the old man had escaped. "You were so long in your trance or your dream or whatever it was that after a while I sat down to rest. What happened then was my fault. I was watching you instead of watching Eliphas, and perhaps I slept for a moment. He came upon me suddenly and the silly fucker would have killed me if only he had kept silent. But he couldn't stop himself yelling when he struck, and I turned in time to receive his blade on my arm instead of my neck. I cut his thigh with a backswing, but he got away.

"I would have followed, Yama, but I could not leave you. He has not come back. I hope he has fallen off the edge of the world or has bled to death. But I didn't feel my blade hit bone and I don't think I cut any major blood vessels because there's not enough blood on the floor. He's probably still alive. Tell me that you're all right and I'll go look for him, and kill him when I find him."

"He wanted to use me," Yama said. He sat down, feeling suddenly dizzy. The pain in his head was expanding. Red and black rags of light seemed to flutter at the edge of his vision. He was diminishing, or the world was receding from him.

He said, "I thought that he wanted to help me, but I have been a fool. He wanted to use me, like most people I have met. You were right all along, Tamora. I apologize."

"I was wrong, too. I thought he was working for Prefect Corin, when all along he had his own plans. This was his chance to master you, but he failed. Everything will be all right now."

Light flooded the chamber. They both looked up. It came from the entrance, a harsh blinding glare that shriveled the soft radiance of the shrine. Tamora swept up her sword and ran straight through the arch into the light, and Yama followed as quickly as he could.

Outside, the light was as bright as the sun. Every figure in the intricate friezes which covered the cliff wall stood beside its own shadow. The wide steep steps shone like ice. With one hand raised to shade his eyes, Yama saw that Tamora was standing at the foot of the stair, gazing up at the huge shadow that floated behind the flood of light.

It was as big as the *Weazel,* and shaped like a claw. It floated only a chain from the edge of the stair, a hundred or so steps above the entrance to the shrine. Figures moved on its upper surface, bleached shadows within the nimbus of brilliant light that shone from it.

It was a flyer, Yama realized, and he knew then why Eliphas had brought him to the edge of the world. He shouted a warning to Tamora, but she was already bounding forward, taking the steps two at a time. She was running toward Eliphas, who had crept out of his hiding place between two carved figures and begun to climb toward the flyer. The old man had ripped the sleeve from his shirt and tied it around his wounded leg, which dragged behind him as he climbed. He held the little black box to his mouth. He was shouting prayers into the box and when Tamora was almost upon him he turned and raised it as if in a warding gesture. Her sword went under his arm and he jerked and tried to hold onto the blade at the place where it pierced his body.

For a moment, they stood still, joined by the sword. Then there was a flash of fierce red light and a wave of nauseous heat.

———

"Yamamanama," a voice said.

Yama was wedged against the feet of a carved man. He looked up, blinking blood from his eyes. When he tried to speak a bubble of blood swelled inside his mouth and broke over his teeth and his lips. All of his muscles had turned to water.

The black, bent figure of Dr. Dismas stood over him. The apothecary had a pistol in his left hand, its blunt muzzle laid along his thigh. In his right he held a little black box, the twin of the one Eliphas had carried. Behind him, the flyer floated down and grounded against the ledge at the entrance to the shrine, just as the floating island Yama and Telmon had seen on the farside shore had grounded against the edge of the world. Above the flyer, the stair rose between the black cliff and the sky, scorched clean by fire.

"It was ordained we should meet again, dear boy," Dr. Dismas said. "How pleased I am to see you."

Yama spat a mouthful of blood. "It was you," he said. "All the time it was you."

The light around them was very bright. He could clearly see the edges of the plaques under the skin of Dr. Dismas's hands. The same sharp-edged shapes that lay under his own scalp.

Yama said, "How? How did you infect me?"

"At The House of Ghost Lanterns," Dr. Dismas said.

"In the beer. Or the food . . ."

"Good! Very good! Yes. Little builders. They have been working ever since. You are strong. Yamamanama. You resisted them for a very long time."

Yama spat more blood. So much blood. First Lud, and then Lob and Unprac, the landlord of The House of Ghost Lanterns. The palmers and the bandits, the cateran who had tried to kill him, Iachimo and the rogue star-sailor and its creatures, the two pythonesses of the Department of Vaticination, the old guard, Coronetes, and all the clerks and soldiers in the Department of Indigenous Affairs, the mage and the soldiers who had taken the peel-house, the traitor Torin, the Constable of Aeolis and his sons and the mob, Prefect Corin and the crew of the picketboat, Dr. Dismas's man and the boy, Pantin. And the Aedile, his heart broken, and now Tamora and Eliphas. All dead. All because of him.

Yama said, "Tamora thought that Eliphas was in league with Prefect Corin. But all the time he was working for you."

Dr. Dismas waggled the little black box. "He kept in touch using the twin of this, right until the end. A pity he had to be killed. He was a useful servant. He was turned long ago, in one of the chambers beneath the surface of the world. He was looking for old texts to sell, but found something far more valuable. Or rather, it found him."

"I thought that he was praying to that little box."

Surreptitiously, Yama pulled the fetish from his wrist. When Pandaras came to look for him, he would find it, and know that his master was still alive.

"Long wavelength light," Dr. Dismas said. "Bounced off one of us a million leagues above the plane of the world. You will soon understand everything, Yamamanama."

Yama felt very cold. He was badly hurt, and the thing in his head had turned his heart to ice. He said, "My people. Eliphas found where . . ."

"The map and the scavenger's account? My dear Yamamanama, they were forgeries, and not even very good forgeries. But they did not have to be, because you wanted so very much to believe in them. No, your people died out long ago. All are dead except you, and even we do not know where you came from. Once I realized what you were, I went to Ys to search for your origin. Eliphas helped me then, but we found nothing and I came back empty-handed. It does not matter. All that matters is that you are here, and that you will join us. You are my creature, Yamamanama. We will do wonderful things together. To begin with, we will form an alliance with the heretics, and save the world."

Men walked out of the light toward them. Yama was lifted up. Light swept over him, and then a warm darkness. Presently, the flyer tilted away from the side of the cliff and rose above the edge of the world. There was a small business to attend to, a few witnesses to be removed. It did not take long, and when it was done the flyer shot away downriver, toward the war.

Shrine
of
Stars

For my mother

Think on why you were created;
Not to exist like animals indeed,
But to seek virtue and knowledge.

Dante Alighieri,
The Divine Comedy

1

The Pyre

THE TWO ILL-MATCHED men were working in a small clearing in the trees that grew along the edge of the shallow reach of water. The larger of the two was chopping steadily at the base of a young blue pine. He wore only ragged trousers belted with a length of frayed rope and was quite hairless, with flabby, pinkish-gray skin and an ugly, vacant face as round as a cheese. The head of his axe had been blackened by fire; its handle was a length of stout pine branch shucked of its bark and held in the socket of the axe head with a ring of carefully whittled wedges. His companion was unhandily trimming branches from a pine bole, using an ivory-handled poniard. He was slender and sleek-headed, like a shipwrecked dandy in scuffed and muddy boots, black trousers and a ragged white shirt with an embroidered collar. A ceramic coin hung from his long supple neck by a doubled leather thong, and a circlet woven from coypu hair and studded with tiny black seed pearls was loose on his upper arm. Now and again he would stop his work and stare anxiously at the blue sky beyond the tree-clad shore.

The two men had already built a raft, which lay near the edge of the water. It was no more than a pentad of blue pine logs lashed together by a few pegged crosspieces and strips of marsh antelope hide, and topped by bundles of reeds. Now they were constructing a pyre, which stood half-completed in the center of the clearing. Each layer of cut and trimmed pine and sweetgum logs was set crosswise to the layer below, and dry reeds and caches of resinous pine cones were stuffed in every chink. The body of a third man lay nearby. It was covered with fresh pine boughs, and had attracted the attention of a great number of black and bronze flies. A fire of small branches and wood chips burned beyond, sending up white, aromatic smoke; strings of meat cut in long strips dangled in the smoke, curling as they dried.

All around was devastation. Swamp cedars, sweetgum trees and blue pines all leaned in the same direction. A few of the biggest trees had fallen and their upturned roots had pulled up wedges of the clayey soil. Nothing remained of the blue pines which had cloaked the ridge above but ash and smoldering stumps. Some way beyond the clearing where the two men worked was a wide, shallow basin of vitrified mud filled with ash-covered steaming water.

Except for the ringing of the axe, the land was silent, as if still shocked by the violence recently done there. On one side, beyond the island's central ridge and a marshy creek, were the low black cliffs of the old river shore and a narrow plain of dry scrub that ran along the edge of the world; in the other, beyond the reach of shallow, still water, a marsh of yellow reeds stretched toward the edge of the Great River. It was noon, and very hot.

The slender man cut the last branch from the pine bole and straightened and looked up at the sky again. "I don't see the need to trim logs which are only for burning," he said. "Do you love work so much, Tibor, that you must always make more?"

"The pyre must go together neatly, little master," Tibor said, fitting his words to the rhythmic blows of his axe. "It must not fall apart when it burns, and so the logs must be trimmed."

"We should leave it and go," the slender man said. "The flier might return at any moment. And call me Pandaras. I'm not anyone's master."

"Phalerus deserves a proper funeral. He was a good man. He always bought me cigarette makings wherever the *Weazel* put into port."

"Tamora was a good friend," Pandaras said sharply, "and I buried her burnt bones and the hilt of her sword under a stone. There's no time for niceties. The flier might come back, and the sooner we start to search for my master, the better."

"He might be dead too," Tibor said, and stood back and gave the pine a hard kick above the gash he had cut around its trunk. The little tree leaned and Tibor kicked it again and it fell with a threshing of boughs and a crackling as the last measure of wood in the cut broke free.

"He's alive," Pandaras said, and touched the circlet on his arm. "He left the fetish behind so that I would know. He was led into an ambush by Eliphas, but he is alive. I think he entrusted me with his coin and his copy of the Puranas because he suspected that Eliphas might betray him, as Tamora so often said that he would. I swore when I found the fetish and I swear now that I will find him, even if I must follow him to the end of the river."

Tibor took papers cut from corn husks and a few strands of coarse tobacco from a plastic pouch tucked into the waist of his trousers, and began to roll a cigarette. He said, "We should not have climbed down to the shrine, little master. I know about shrines, and that one had been warped to evil ends."

"Eliphas lured my master there, if that's what you mean. If we had not followed them, we would not have learned what happened. Fortunately, I was able to read the clues as any other man might read a story in a book. There was a fight in the shrine, and someone was hurt and ran away. Perhaps Eliphas tried to surprise Tamora from behind, and she managed to defend herself. She wounded him and chased him outside, and that was when she was killed, most likely by someone from the flier. Eliphas didn't have an energy pistol, or he would have used it much earlier—there would have been no need to lead my master away from the ship into an ambush. But it was an energy pistol that killed poor Tamora, and melted the keelrock of the stair, and no doubt the same energy pistol was used to subdue Yama."

While Pandaras talked, Tibor crossed to the fire and lit his cigarette with the burning end of a branch. He dropped the branch back into the fire and drew on his cigarette and exhaled a plume of smoke. "We will find the *Weazel*," he said, "and the Captain will help us find your master."

"They are all dead, Tibor. You have to understand that."

"We found no bodies except poor Phalerus's," Tibor said stubbornly. "And nothing at all of the ship, except the axe head."

"A fire fierce enough to transmute mud to something like glass would have vaporized the ship like a grain of rice in a furnace. Phalerus was hunting in the marsh near the island, and he was caught in steam flash-heated by the blast of the flier's light cannon. The others died at once and their bodies were burned up with the ship."

Pandaras and Tibor had found Phalerus's scalded body lying near an antelope he had shot. It was clear that the old sailor had not died immediately; he had put the shaft of an arbalest bolt between his teeth and nearly bitten it through in his agony. Pandaras remembered a story that one of his uncles had told him about an accident in a foundry. A man had slipped and fallen waist-deep in a vat of molten iron. The man's workmates had been paralyzed by his terrible screams, but his father had grabbed a long-handled ladle and had pushed his son's head beneath the glowing surface. Phalerus had died almost as badly, and he had died alone, with no one to ease his passing.

Tibor started to trim the larger branches from the pine he had felled. After a little while, he stopped and said, "The Captain is clever. She's escaped pirates before, and that's what happened here. The flier's light cannon missed the *Weazel,* and she made a run for it. Maybe Phalerus was left behind, but the rest will be with the ship. The Captain won't know your master has been taken, and maybe she'll come back for him." He ran a hand over the parallel scars that seamed his broad chest. He said, "I belong with the ship, little master."

Pandaras swiped away the little black bees that had clustered at the corners of his eyes to drink his sweat. "I'm not your master," he said. "We are traveling together, as free men. Eliphas betrayed my master and killed your shipmates, and I will kill him for that. I swear it. Eliphas claimed to know of a city hidden in the Glass Desert where others of my master's bloodline lived, and so lured him all this way from Ys. Eliphas is a liar and a traitor, but all lies have some truth in them, and I think we'll find the place where he has taken my master if we continue downriver. You will help me, and then you can set out on your own road."

Pandaras did not want the responsibility of looking after Tibor, but he needed him because the hierodule knew how to survive in the wilderness. Pandaras had lived all his short life in Ys. He knew the city's stone streets and its people; he knew words which, if whispered in the right place, could kill a man; he knew the rituals and meeting places of hundreds of cults, the monastery where anyone could beg waybread and beer at noon, the places where the magistrates and their machines never went, the places where they could always be found, the rhythm of the docks, the histories of a thousand temples, the secrets of a decad of trades. But the randomness of this wild shore confused and frightened him. It was tangled, impenetrable, alien to thought.

"I am a slave of all the world, little master." Tibor drew on the stub of his cigarette, held his breath, and exhaled. "Nothing can change that. Ten thousand years ago my bloodline fought on the side of the feral machines, against the will of the Preservers. In the shame of our defeat we must serve the Preservers and their peoples for all our lives, and hope only that we will be redeemed at the end of time."

"All men are servants of the Preservers," Pandaras said. "They raised us up from animals, remember all who have ever lived, and will raise them from the dead in the last moment at the end of time and space. If you must be a servant, then serve my master, Yama. He is of the ancient race of the Builders, who made this world according to the will of the Preservers. In all the world, he is closer to them than any other man—the emissary from the holy city of Gond admitted as much. He is their avatar. I have seen him bend countless machines to his will. In Ys, on the roof of the Palace of the Memory of the People, he brought a baby of one of the indigenous people to self-awareness, and you saw how he drew up monstrous polyps from the bottom of the Great River to save us from Prefect Corin. He is a wise and holy man. He alone can end the war begun by the heretics; he alone can return the world to the path which will lead to redemption of all its peoples. So by helping me find him, you will serve all the world."

"We will search for your master, and for my ship," Tibor said. He drew a last puff from the stub of his cigarette and pinched it out and swallowed it. His long red tongue passed over his black lips. "But a ship is easier to find than a man. How will we find him, in all the long world?"

Pandaras showed Tibor the ceramic coin Yama had given him before following the traitor Eliphas into ambush. It held a faint spark in its center. Pandaras hoped that it meant that Yama was still alive, but no matter which way he turned the coin, the spark did not grow brighter or dimmer.

Tibor nodded. "I have heard of such things, young master, but never thought to see one."

"It's real," Pandaras said. "Now work harder and talk less. I want to be gone from here as soon as possible."

At last the pyre was finished. Pandaras and Tibor laid Phalerus's body on top and covered it with a blanket of orange mallows and yellow irises. Tibor knew the funeral rituals by heart, and Pandaras followed his instructions, becoming for that short time the servant of a holy slave. They asperged the body with water and Tibor said prayers for the memory of the dead sailor before lighting the dry reeds he had woven through the lower layers of the pyre.

When it was burning well, with Phalerus's body a shadow in the center of leaping yellow flames and white smoke bending like a banner toward the blackened ridge of the little island, Pandaras and Tibor clambered on to their raft and poled away from the devastated island with unseemly haste. It took them the rest of the day to thread a way through the stands of tall yellow reeds to the mudbanks and pioneer mangroves that lay beyond, along the margin of the shrinking river. When the water became too deep to use the pole, Tibor took up a leaf-shaped paddle he had carved from a scrap of wood.

Pandaras squatted at the raft's blunt prow, Phalerus's arbalest in his lap and his master's pack between his feet. He was more afraid than he could let the hierodule know. Tibor said that the raft was stronger than it looked, that the strips of hide would shrink in the water and bind the logs ever tighter, but Pandaras thought it a flimsy craft. The idea of traveling the length of the Great River on it, like an emmet clinging to a flake of bark, filled him with dread, but he was certain that Yama had been carried away on the flier, and he loved his master so fiercely that he would follow him beyond the edge of the world. He had smeared every bit of his exposed pelt with black mud to protect himself from the biting flies and midges which danced in dense clouds over stumps and breather roots. He was a savage in a savage land. He would go naked, cover his body with strange swirling tattoos, drink blood from freshly killed animals until he was as strong as a storm, and then he would pull down the walls of the citadel where his master was held, rescue him, and kill the traitor who had taken him. His people would make songs about it until the end of time.

Such dreams sustained his small hope. Those, and the faint but unwavering spark trapped within the ceramic coin.

At last the raft rounded the point of a long arm of mangroves, and the wide river suddenly stretched before them, gleaming like a plain of gold in the light of the setting sun. There was so much light glittering up from the water that Pandaras could not see if it had an ending. He stood, suddenly filled with elation, and flung out an arm and pointed downriver, toward the war.

2

Dr. Dismas's Disease

DR. DISMAS CAME into the big white room without ceremony, flinging open the double doors and striding straight toward Yama, scattering the machines which floated at various levels in the air. A decad of servants in various brightly colored liveries trailed behind him.

Yama had been performing some of the exercises Sergeant Rhodean had taught him, and jumped up as Dr. Dismas approached. He was barechested and barefoot, wearing only a pair of silk trews and a wide bandage wound twice around the burns on his chest. Ever since his capture, he had wanted nothing more than to be able to command just one machine and make it fling itself into Dr. Dismas's eye and burn through his brain, but no matter how much he strained to contact the machines around him, he could not bend them to his will. The powers which he had painfully learned to master had been taken from him by the thing which had grown from seeds Dr. Dismas had, by a trick, planted in him at the beginning of his adventures. He was plagued by a fluttering of red and black at the edges of his vision, and was visited in his sleep by strange and terrible dreams which, although he utterly forgot them upon waking, left an indelible residue of terror and loathing.

Dr. Dismas did not speak at once, but clapped his stiff hands together in an irregular rhythm and paced up and down while looking sidelong at Yama, as if trying to marshal his hectic thoughts. The servants stood in a row behind him. They were all indigens, and all mutilated. Yama scarcely noticed them. He was watching the bent-backed, black-clad apothecary as a mouse might watch a snake.

"You are awake!" Dr. Dismas said at last. "Good, good. How are you, Yamamanama? Any headaches? Any colored lights or spots float-

ing in your vision? Your burns are healing nicely, I see. Ah, why do
you look at me that way? I am your savior!"

"You infected me with this disease, Doctor. Are you worried that
it is not progressing as fast as you wish?"

"It is not a disease, Yamamanama. Do not think of it as a disease.
And do not resist it. That will make things worse for you."

"Where is this place, Doctor? Why have you brought me here?
Where are the others?"

He had asked these questions many times before, and Dr. Dismas
had not yet answered them. The apothecary smiled and said, "Our allies
gave it to me as a reward for services rendered. A part payment, I should
say, for I have only just begun. We, my dear Yamamanama, have only
just begun. How much we still have to do!"

Dr. Dismas marched across the room and stood for a moment at the
great window, his hands twisted behind his back. But he could not stand
still for long, and whirled around and smiled at Yama. He must have
recently injected himself with a dose of the drug, for he was pumped
full of an energy he could not quite control, a small, sleek, perpetually
agitated man in a black claw hammer frock coat that reached to his
knees, the stiff planes of his brown face propped above the high collar
of his white shirt. He was at once comic and malign.

Yama hated Dr. Dismas, but knew that the apothecary had the answers to many of his questions. He said, "I am your prisoner, Doctor.
What do you want from me?"

"Prisoner? No, no, no. O, no, not a prisoner," Dr. Dismas said. "We
are at a delicate stage. You are as yet neither one thing or another,
Yamamanama. A chrysalid. A larva. You think yourself a power in the
world, but you are nothing to what you will become. I promise it. Come
here. Stand by me. Don't be afraid."

"I am not afraid, Doctor." But it was a lie, and Yama knew that Dr.
Dismas knew it. The doctor knew him too well. For no matter how
much he tried to stay calm, the residue of his dreams, the flickering red
and black fringes that plagued his sight, the thing growing under his
skin, and the scuttling and crawling and floating machines that infested
the room all conspired to keep him perpetually fearful.

Dr. Dismas began to fit a cigarette into the holder which had been,
he claimed, carved from the fingerbone of a murderer. His concentration
on the task was absolute; his left hand had been bent into a stiff claw
by the plaques which grew beneath his skin—a symptom of his disease,
the disease with which he had infected Yama. At last it was done, and
he lit the cigarette and drew on it and blew two smoke rings, the second

spinning through the first. He smiled at this little trick and said, "Not afraid? You should be afraid. But I am sure that there is more to it than fear. You are angry, certainly. And curious. I am sure that you are curious. Come here. Stand by me."

Yama drew on the lessons in diplomacy which his poor dead stepfather, the Aedile of Aeolis, had so patiently taught him. Always turn any weakness into advantage by admitting it, for nothing draws out your enemy like an exposed weakness. He said, "I am afraid, Doctor. I am afraid that I might try to kill you. As you killed Tamora."

"I do not know that name."

Yama's hatred was suddenly so intense that he could hardly bear it. He said, "The cateran. My companion."

"Ah. The silly woman with the little sword and the bad temper. Well, if I killed her, it is because she was responsible for the death of Eliphas, who so successfully led you to me. An eye for an eye, as the Amnan would say. How is your father, by the way? And the stinking little city he pretends to rule?"

Yama charged at the doctor then, and one of the flock of machines which floated in the big, airy room swerved and clipped him on the side of the head. One moment he was running headlong, the next he was sprawled on his back on the rubbery black floor, looking up at the ceiling. Pain shot through him. His chest and face had been badly seared by the backwash of the blast which had killed Tamora and Eliphas, and his ribs had been cracked when it had knocked him down. A splinter of rock had pierced his lung, too, and although he had been treated by a battery of machines, he tasted blood at the back of his mouth now.

Dr. Dismas smiled down at him and extended the claw of his left hand. Yama ignored it and laboriously and painfully got to his feet.

"You have spirit," Dr. Dismas said. "That's good. You will need it."

"Where are the others? Pandaras, and the crew of the *Weazel*. Did you leave them behind?"

"The *Weazel*? Oh, that's of no consequence. It is only you I am interested in, dear Child of the River. Are you all right? Not hurt by your fall? Good. Come and stand by the window with me. I have much to tell you, and we will make a start today."

Yama followed Dr. Dismas unwillingly. The room was part of a mansion hollowed out of one of the flanks of the floating garden. Its single window, bulging like an eye, overlooked a vast panorama. Far below, Baucis, the city of Trees, stretched away in the sunlight of a perfect afternoon. Other floating gardens hung at various heights above their own shadows, like green clouds. Some were linked together by catenaries, rope slides and arched bridges of shining metal. An arboreal bloodline had inhabited Baucis before the heretics had come; their city had been a patchwork of ten thousand small woods separated by clear-felled belts and low, grassy hills. Now many of the woods had been cut down. New roads slashed through the rolling landscape, a network of fused red clay tracks like fresh wounds. The heretics had made their encampments on the hills, and a kind of haze or miasma of smoke from weapons foundries and numerous fires hung over the remaining patches of trees.

Beyond the city, the vivid green jungle stretched away beneath the mist of its own exhalations. The floating garden was so high up that both edges of the world were visible: the ragged blue line of the Rim Mountains on the right and the silver plain of the Great River on the left, and all the habitable world between them, dwindling beneath strings of white cloud toward a faint hint of red. In the days since he had been captured, Yama had spent much of the time gazing at this scene, and had convinced himself that he could see beyond the fall of the Great River and the mountains at the midpoint of the world to the beginning of the Glass Desert.

Dr. Dismas exhaled a riffle of clove-scented smoke and said, "Everything you see is the territory of the heretics. Two hundred cities downriver of this one, and a hundred more upriver. Thousands of bloodlines are theirs now. And soon the rest, Yamamanama. Soon the rest, unless something is done. Their triumph is great, but they must be prevented from completing it. They have meddled in much that they do not understand. They have tried to wake the great engines in the keel-ways of the world, for instance. Fortunately, they did not succeed."

Dr. Dismas looked sideways, but Yama said nothing. The apothecary had a habit of alluding to matters about which Yama knew little, perhaps in the hope of drawing out secrets, as a fisherman might scatter bait to lure fish to the surface. Yama had glimpsed something of the vast machines beneath the surface of the world when Beatrice had returned him to the peel-house by the old roads in the keelways, but he had not known much about his powers then, and had not thought to try and question them.

"Well, for now you will help the heretics," Dr. Dismas said briskly. "You will provide a service for which we will later ask payment. Please. For your sake do not make any more sudden moves. My servants here are simple things and have very literal minds. I would not like to see you hurt because of a misunderstanding."

Yama's fist was so tightly clenched that his fingernails cut four points of pain into his palm. He said, "Whatever I was able to do has been taken away from me. I am glad that it is gone. Even if I still had it, I would never choose to serve you."

"Oh, it isn't a question of choice. And it is still there, somewhere or other. I'm sure it will surface again."

"Do what you will. Invoke the thing you placed inside me. Invoke your disease. But do not involve me. Do not try to make me take your side or see your point of view."

Yama turned away and crossed to the bed and sat down. Dr. Dismas remained by the window. Hunched into his frock coat, he slowly and carefully lit another cigarette and exhaled a plume of smoke while gazing at the city spread below, like a conqueror at his ease. At last, without turning around, he said, "You have it easy, Yamamanama. I envy you. I was alone when I was changed, and my paramour was old and badly crippled. We both nearly died before the union was complete, and we nearly died again when we retraced my path across the Glass Desert. That was almost forty years ago. An odd coincidence, don't you think?"

Yama was interested, despite the loathing he felt toward the apothecary. He said, "I suppose that it was something to do with the Ancients of Days."

"Good, good. You have been learning about your past. It will save us much time. Yes, it had something to do with one of them. With the most important of them, in fact. All of the Ancients of Days were merely variations on a single theme, but the one who called herself Angel was closest to the original. I believe that you have met her."

The woman in the shrine. The woman in white. Yama said, "It was the revenant of something five million years old, of a pathetic scared fool who failed at godhood and escaped her enemies by fleeing to a neighboring galaxy. She found nothing there and returned to meddle with Confluence. She was the seed of the heretics, and was killed by her fellows."

"Indeed, indeed. But before she was killed, Angel left a copy of herself in the space inside the shrines. Her aspect—that was who you talked to. She wants you on her side, and so she told you her story. And told you how powerful she was, no doubt."

"I destroyed her, Doctor."

Dr. Dismas smiled. "Oh, I think not. You have much to learn about distributed information. She is stored as a pattern of interrupted light deep within the space inside the shrines. Perhaps your paramour will destroy her, when it is stronger, and if I so choose, but you destroyed only the copy of a copy." Dr. Dismas plunged his right hand into the pocket of his frock coat and brought out the plastic straws which he habitually cast when he needed to make a decision. He rattled them together, smiling craftily, and put them away. "The fate of gods in my hands—don't you find it amusing? Ah, you are a humorless boy, Yamamanama. It is not your fault. Anyone brought up by that stiff-backed narrow-minded backward-looking innumerate superstitious fool would—"

Yama roared and ran at Dr. Dismas again, and again was knocked down by one of the machines, but before he fell he had the satisfaction of seeing the apothecary take a step backward. For a moment he was blinded by a silent roar of red and black that seemed to fill his head. He rolled onto his back, a ringing in his ears and the taste of blood in his mouth, and slowly got to his knees. When he stood, the room seemed to sway around him, and he sat down on the edge of the bed.

Dr. Dismas lit another cigarette and watched Yama with a genuine tenderness. "You'll need that spirit, Yamamanama," he said. "It is a hard road I have set you on, but you will thank me at last. You will be transformed, as I have been transformed. I will tell you how.

"It is a symptom of the disastrous reversal in the development of the peoples of Confluence that, although their technologies predated the creation of our world by five million years, the Ancients of Days were able to manipulate much that was hidden or lost to the ten thousand bloodlines. In particular, Angel was able to enter the space inside the shrines, and she learned much there."

"She destroyed the avatars," Yama said. "People believe that the heretics destroyed them, but it happened before the war began."

"Hush. This is my story, not hers. You already know hers, it seems. She tried to recruit you, but I know that you resisted, for otherwise you would not be here. You chose wisely. She is not our friend, Yamamanama. She is our ally, yes, but not our friend. Enobarbus submits to her without reservation, but we have our own plans. And besides, much of what she says is self-serving, or simply untrue. Angel did not destroy the avatars. That was the work of the copy of herself that she installed in the space inside the shrines. The aspect you talked to was a copy of that copy, but no matter. In any form, it is a poor deluded thing. After Angel died, it found itself besieged, and it lashed out. That was how the avatars came to be destroyed. The avatars, and many records, and most of the directories and maps within the space inside the shrines. That was the true war; the war fought since, between the heretics and the bureaucrats, is but its shadow. And so the bureaucrats were defeated before the first ship of fools sailed from Ys to put down the uprisings at the midpoint of the world.

"But that does not concern us. While Angel was traveling downriver toward the last and least city of Confluence, where she would plant the seed that would grow into the heretics, at that same moment, I was entering the Glass Desert. I had been trained as an apothecary—my family had been a part of the Department of Apothecaries and Chirurgeons for thousands of years—but I sought greater knowledge. Arcane knowledge hidden or forgotten or forbidden by priests and bureaucrats frightened by the true destiny of the world. As a child I had riddled the crannies of the Department's library. This was before the hierodules within the screens of the library were destroyed along with the avatars, and written records were almost entirely unused then. There was a vast amount of trash, but I discovered a few gems."

Yama said, "And that was where you met Eliphas."

"No, not then. I knew him, in the way that a boy might glancingly know everyone who works in the place where he grows up, but until my return last year I doubt that I had ever exchanged a single word with him. Eliphas had long before given up searching for ancient treasures, although his friend and one-time partner, the chief of clerks of the library, did give me encouragement. *He* was interested in maps, but I found something better.

"It was the personal account of a traveling chirurgeon five thousand years dead. He had worked amongst the unchanged bloodlines at the midpoint of the world, and found a cluster of odd symptoms amongst certain of the nomadic clans which sometimes ventured into the ancient battlegrounds of the Glass Desert. It was unusual in that the same symptoms were exhibited by different bloodlines. Most clans killed or cast out those afflicted, but in some they were considered blessed by the Preservers and became soothsayers, prophets, oracles, mysts and so on."

"This is the disease with which you infected me," Yama said.

Dr. Dismas flung out an arm, pointed at Yama, and screamed with sudden violence, "Quiet! Enough interruptions! You will be quiet or I will . . ." His arm trembled violently, and he whirled around to face the window. His shoulders heaved. When he turned back he was smiling and there was honey in his voice. "This is my story, Yamamanama. Do not race ahead. You think you know more than you do."

"Perhaps I am not interested in your story, and want to bring it to its end as quickly as possible."

"Ah, but you are interested. I know you are. Besides," Dr. Dismas added, in the same overly sweet, wheedling voice, "if you do not listen I will slice off one of your ears as a lesson. Now, where was I?"

"You had discovered an old traveler's tale."

Yama was interested, despite himself. Dr. Dismas's story was similar to the lies Eliphas had used to lure him downriver. Eliphas had claimed to have found a traveler's account of a hidden city in the Glass Desert, a city inhabited by people of Yama's bloodline. The documents he had shown Yama had been fabrications, but perhaps the old question runner's lies had been rooted in truth after all.

Dr. Dismas said, "I returned again and again to this poorly written memoir until I had it by heart. I even made a copy of it. But I was a child, with many long years of study ahead of me. My fascination faded and I turned to other matters. When at last I qualified and was sent to my first post, I took only the tools of my trade, in a leather wallet bequeathed to me by my grandfather, and the standard catalogue of electuaries, panaceas, simples, urticants and so on. I did not take the copy of the memoir which I had made, for I had set it aside with other childish things.

"I will not trouble you with the details of my first posting, nor those of my second. I was a foolish and naïve young man, eager to do good in a world where goodness can gain only small and temporary victories. But at my third posting, fate intervened. I do not believe in the Preservers, Yamamanama. Or rather, I do not believe that they exist any longer in the phenomenological universe. But it was as if something, some agency, touched my life then, and changed it forever. Perhaps my paramour's reach was longer than it seemed.

"I was dispatched to a mean little town in the mountains beyond the fall of the Great River, close to the border of the Glass Desert. And it was there that I encountered the symptoms of which I had read and reread with wonder as a child.

"Of course, my interest was rekindled at once. Traveling with a caravanserai, I visited the summer camps of unchanged nomads and learned much of the course of the disease. I marked its progression from simple plaques and associated loss of sensation to mania, blindness and death. I was able to dissect the fresh corpse of a haruspex—I had to break into her tomb to do it—and chart the growths and nodes along her nervous system. And by conflating the routes of the various clans of nomads through the margin of the Glass Desert with the incidence of the disease, I was able to plot its focal point.

"I will not trouble you with a long catalogue of the hardships I endured to reach my goal. I went alone because I trusted no one, and that almost killed me. The Glass Desert is a terrible place. There is no free water beyond the mountains of the Great Divide, for the river which was the mirror of our Great River failed after the wars of the Age of Insurrection. It is a place of glare and heat, of endless sand dunes, salt pans, alkali flats, vitrified craters and devastated terrain. Nothing grows but stoneworts and a few hardy plants which are more like machines than living organisms—when I first saw them I knew then the memoir had not lied, and I was almost killed when, in my excitement, I went too close to a clump of them.

"I took a string of camels and a mule, but the camels contracted a falling sickness and I had to leave most of my supplies with their corpses. The mule survived until a great dust storm blew up. The storm lasted twelve days and all that time the mule was tethered outside my tent. When at last I emerged, with the sun a bleary spot in a sky still stained ocher by suspended dust, I found that the poor beast had been flayed to its bones, and things like turkey vultures were quarreling over what remained. They too were partly machine, and I had to kill them when they turned on me. One clipped me with the tip of a wing, and its serrated flight feathers opened a great gash in my side, clear down to the cartilage sheaves of my chest cage.

"I went on, weakened by my wound and carrying what I could, knowing that I did not have enough water or food for the return journey. I walked at night, and by day sheltered from the heat and from dust devils and fierce little storms of knife-sharp crystallized silica. It was burning hot by day, and so cold at night that with each breath little puffs of ice crystals fell, tinkling, from my lips. The sky was utterly clear; I felt that I could see past the distant smudges and specks of galaxies to the afterglow of the hatching of the cosmic egg. I walked like this for four days, until I found the place I had been searching for."

Dr. Dismas lit another cigarette. His hands were trembling badly. Yama watched him closely. He was caught up in the story because what had happened to Dr. Dismas then was happening to him now. The red and black flickering which troubled his vision had intensified; it was as if he was peering through banners which flew on an impalpable wind. Terror beat within him on great steel wings. He had the sudden strange notion that instead of being captured by Dr. Dismas outside the shrine, he had fallen off the edge of the world and was falling still, that this was a terrible dream from which he might at any moment awaken to worse horror.

"O Yamamanama," Dr. Dismas said at last. "Child of the River. How I envy you! It was so long ago that I have only a few bright memories, worn smooth by my constant handling like pebbles in the bed of a mountain stream. It was so terrible, and so wonderful! Such pain, and such joy! Such joy!"

Yama was amazed, for the apothecary was weeping.

Dr. Dismas's expression was haunted yet ecstatic. "O yes," he said. "Tears. Poor weak human tears. For what I was. For what I became, in the embrace of my paramour. I was reborn, and it was painful and bloody and wretched. And out of it such glory, such joy. Such joy."

He blotted the tears from his brown, plaque-stiffened cheeks with the claw of his left hand and sniffed hard. Usually, Dr. Dismas displayed emotion as a theatrical puppet might hold an appropriate mask before its immobile, painted face. (Was it part of the Preservers' plan, Yama suddenly wondered, that almost all of the bloodlines shared the same facial expressions and bodily postures which expressed fear and hope, rage and love, happiness and sorrow?) His real thoughts were unguessable. But for the first time he appeared to be wholly possessed by human feeling.

"Ah," Dr. Dismas said at last, sniffing delicately, "it moves me still to think about it. I had come upon the place without realizing it. I was delirious by then. My feet were blistered and badly bleeding. I had heat sores all over my body. My joints were swollen and I was so badly sunburnt that my skin was blackened and cracked, and constantly wept blood and pus. It was dawn. A fierce hot wind was blowing, sucking moisture from my body. I had reached a place of chaotic terrain. The land was like rough-cast glass, dissected by a maze of wandering ridges and canyons. I was lost, and too ill to know that by the end of the day, or by the end of the next day, I would surely be dead. I stumbled into the shade of a deep ravine and threw up my tent and crawled inside.

"My paramour had heard my footsteps leagues away, listening with a thousand whiskers grown across the land. It had watched me from decads of different eyes, some fixed like crystals in the rock and glass, others mounted on scuttling extensions it had cleaved from the wreckage of its own body.

"It was those extensions that came for me, in the heat of noon.

"There were hundreds of them. They were like spiders or mantids fashioned out of black glass. They moved with stiff scuttling motions. I woke when the first cut through the material of my tent. In a fevered panic, I killed decads with a single shot of my energy pistol and stumbled from the blazing wreckage of my tent. More waited outside, clinging to the vertical rock face beneath which I'd camped. They fell on me, stung me insensible, and spun a cocoon around me.

"And so began—"

A chime sounded out of the midair of the room. "What now?" Dr. Dismas said irritably, and turned his back on Yama and fell into what seemed to be a one-sided conversation. "Can't it wait? Yes, the boy. Yes I am. Yes. No, I want to tell him. You wouldn't understand why, unless you . . . Yes, I know you . . . Very well, if you must."

Dr. Dismas turned and gazed at Yama with his yellow eyes as if seeing him for the first time. He said, "We were speaking of the courtship between my paramour and myself. I told you how it began, of the little machines which were as much a part of my paramour as your fingers and toes and eyes and ears are a part of you, Yamamanama. They found me and paralyzed me as a hunting wasp paralyzes a fat caterpillar. And like so many hunting wasps, they wound me in a cocoon of threads spun from their own bodies. The threads were possessed of a certain intelligence, and began to mend my wounds. Meanwhile, the machines brought me water enriched with vitamins and amino acids and sugars, and fed it to me drop by drop.

"I was delirious, and I did not understand what was happening to me. I dreamed that I was in lazaret in the cool shade of palm trees, with the sound of running water outside its white canvas walls. Perhaps it was a presentiment of the future. And all the time, my paramour was creeping toward me.

"For it had realized that I was a prize out of the ordinary. It had allowed its extensions to infect any nomads that passed by, but the things which grew in the nomads' bodies were no more intelligent than the extensions themselves. But I was something rarer, and it came to me itself. Or rather, it grew toward me, as a desert plant will grow a root toward a lode of water.

"I do not know how long it took, but at last it reached me. A silver wire no thicker than a spider's thread pierced my skull and branched and rebranched a million times, uniting with the neurons in my visual and auditory lobes. And then my paramour stood before me, terrible in its glory, and told me the true history of the world.

"I will not tell you what it told me. You will have to learn that yourself. It is growing inside you. Soon it will be complete, and will awaken fully. But I will say that what I learned then transformed me utterly and completely. I learned of my paramour's fabulous battles in the vacuum beyond the envelope of air which wraps our world, of its splendid victories and the terrible defeat of its final fall. It plunged from a great height and at a great speed, transforming as it fell. It struck hard and penetrated deep within the mantle of the world, melting rock with the heat of its fiery fall and sealing itself in its tomb. Ah, I see you understand. Yes, you are awakening. You share this, don't you? It lay there for ten thousand years, slowly reconfiguring itself, sending out its extensions into the desert around, listening, learning.

"Imagine the strength of will, child! The will to survive ten thousand years in agony and utterly alone. Until very recently it had not dared to communicate with those of its fellows which had survived the wars of insurrection. It had to deduce what was happening in the world by interrogating the wretches its extensions captured and changed. The stings of its extensions infected many, but only a few returned, and the compass of their lives was so narrow that they had little useful to communicate.

"And then I arrived, and all was different. It was not just that I was one of the changed bloodlines, but that I arrived soon after Angel meddled with the space inside the shrines. My paramour had heard her call. And so I was healed and sent back to find out what I could about the new war, and to make an alliance.

"But I did much better than that. I won so much more for my paramour. I won this hero, the last of the Builders, the Child of the River, and I laid him at its feet. The little seeds that I tricked him into ingesting were from my paramour, of course, my paramour and your father. And so we are united, you and I. Together we will do great things," Dr. Dismas said, and smiled stiffly and bowed low.

"I would rather die," Yama said. "I will not serve, Doctor."

"But you are awake," Dr. Dismas said merrily. "I know it! I can feel it! Speak to me, my darling child! It is time! Time!"

And Yama realized that all this time the apothecary had been speaking as much to the thing growing inside him as to himself. And in that moment of realization pain struck through every cell in his body. The black and red fire of the pain washed away the world. Something stood in the fire. It was a vision of a fetus, curled up like a fish, all in gold. It slowly turned its heavy, blind head toward Yama, who thought he would go mad if its eyes opened and its gaze fell upon him. It spoke. Its voice was his own.

You will not serve? Ah, but that is against the nature of your bloodline. Your kind were created to serve the Preservers, to build this world. Well, the rest of your race are long gone, but you are here, and you will serve. You will serve me.

Another voice spoke from the world beyond the fire: deep, resonant and angry.

"What are you doing to him? Stop it, Dismas! Stop it at once! I command you!"

The pain receded. The vision dissolved. Yama's body, which had been arched like a bow, relaxed. His head fell to one side. And he saw, framed by a flickering haze of red and black, the mane and the ugly scarred face of the heretic warlord and traitor, Enobarbus.

3

The Trader

PANDARAS AND TIBOR drifted downriver for three days, always keeping close to the edge of the mangrove swamps which fringed the farside shore. Pandaras did not dare set out across the broad river on the little raft, for a single wave might swamp it in an instant. Even though he could swim well, he tied himself to the bundles of reeds each night in case he slipped overboard in his sleep and drowned before he could wake. He slept very little, and Tibor did not sleep at all. The hierodule said that sleeplessness was another curse the Preservers had placed upon the bloodline. Pandaras thought that it helped explain why the fellow was so lacking in imagination, for he had no dreamlife.

The spark in the coin did not grow brighter, but neither did it grow dimmer. Yama was alive, but he was very far away. It did not matter. Every time he looked at the coin, Pandaras pledged to find his master even if it took him beyond the end of the world, even if it took him all his life.

To pass the time while Tibor paddled steadily and the ragged margin of mangrove stands and banyan islands drifted by, full of green shadows despite the bright, hot sunlight, Pandaras told the hierodule every detail of his adventures with Yama. How he had appointed himself Yama's squire after the landlord of *The Crossed Axes* tried to kill Yama for the coins he carried; how they had met the cateran, Tamora, and their failed attempt to bring the escaped star-sailor to justice; the destruction of the Temple of the Black Well and their entry into the Palace of the Memory of the People (of which Pandaras remembered little, for he had been laid out by a blow to the head). The conspiracy in the Department of Vaticination which had led to capture by Yama's enemy, Prefect Corin, and then escape from imprisonment, with Yama full of wrath and cloaked in blue fire he had conjured from a shrine, the first time Pandaras had been truly afraid of his master. And the miracle by which Yama had raised up a baby of one of the indigenous races which lived in the Palace, and the triumphant procession of Yama through the streets of Ys. The rest, the voyage of the *Weazel* downriver, the sack of Yama's childhood home and the chase by Prefect Corin which had ended in an attack by monstrous polyps from the deep and a storm and near shipwreck, Tibor already knew. But Pandaras, who loved stories, told it anyway.

"My master says that stories are the only kind of immortality achievable without the grace of the Preservers. Certainly, they are the lifeblood of my people. We are so very short-lived, yet live long in memory because of our skill in making stories and songs. A good story can be handed down through a hundred generations, its details changing but its heart always the same, and the people in it live again each time it is told. So might we, Tibor, for surely this is the greatest story the world has ever known."

"All the world is a story," Tibor said, after paddling silently for a while. "Who can find the single droplet which falls from a leaf-tip into the flood of the Great River? Who can say where one story ends and another begins?"

Pandaras thought that Tibor was quoting from an obscure sura in the Puranas and, having no wish to argue theology with a hierodule, for once held his tongue.

The nights were dark and still, lit only by the dim red swirl of the Eye of the Preservers. The Eye rose slightly earlier each night, and each night reached a slightly higher point in the black sky above the river's black plain before falling back toward the farside horizon. In the vast stillness of the night, Pandaras felt most acutely the emptiness of the unpeopled shore, and he was relieved when at last the song of birds and monkeys and the whistling chorus of millions of frogs greeted the dawn. The days quickly grew hot, but Tibor did not seem to mind the heat. He said that he had grown up in a far hotter land, near the midpoint of the world. A little sun like this was nothing.

Without salt, the antelope meat went off before they could eat more than a quarter of it, but there was food all around. There were always ripe fruits waiting to be plucked from strangler figs or banana plants. Tibor plaited nets from fibers scraped from the fronds of the big ferns which clung to the mangroves, and trawled for catfish and lampreys in shallow backwaters, while Pandaras nimbly climbed about the canopies of banyans, taking eggs from bird and lizard nests. Tibor ate insects too, often catching them on the wing with his long red tongue.

Occasionally they glimpsed the flash of a sail far out in the middle of the river, an argosy or carrack heading for the war, and one day a machine circled the raft before rising up and flying straight toward the misty line of the nearside shore. It had a long, wasp-waisted body, a decad of paired, shimmeringly fragile vanes, and a cluster of bright red eyes. Pandaras cocked the arbalest while the machine dipped overhead, remembering the machines which Prefect Corin had sent out to search for Yama. But Prefect Corin must be dead, drowned when his ship had been torn apart by the giant polyps Yama had called from the deep river-bottom. There were many machines on Confluence, Pandaras told himself. It signified nothing.

Late in the afternoon of the next day, they reached the house of an itinerant trader. It was tucked away in a backwater shaded by tall mangroves, a ramshackle shanty built in the branches of a banyan, with walls and a peaked roof fashioned from panels of woven grasses. A decad of small boats were strung out along an anchor line on the still, black water below. Little glowing lamps shone everywhere amongst the tree's glossy green leaves, like a horde of fireflies. Music from a cassette player came clearly across the water as Tibor paddled the raft toward the shanty, and a bird set up a harsh clamor, warning of their approach.

The trader was a crafty old man named Ayulf. He was of a bloodline familiar to Pandaras, the bloodline of half the ruffians who smuggled cigarettes and other proscribed trade goods to indigens, or otherwise scraped a living on the wrong side of the law along the docks of Ys or on the Great River. Ayulf wore only a dhoti around his scrawny waist, in which he habitually rummaged to scratch or rearrange his genitals. His arms and legs were long and stringy, and his small head was crowned with a dirty, half-unraveled turban from which greasy spikes of hair stuck out in every direction. His eyes were yellow, like flame or bits of amber, and he hissed softly to himself when he was thinking; he did that a lot as Pandaras told a highly edited version of his story while devouring a salty mess of rice and fish.

Ayulf traded with the local fisherfolk, exchanging cigarettes, cheap cooking pots, fish hooks, nylon netting and leaves of bronze or iron for lizard, snake and cayman skins, the hides of marsh antelopes, the feathers of bell birds and birds of heaven, and rare spices and medicines extracted from plants and lichens which grew on the banyans and mangroves. The shanty was cluttered with bales of cigarettes wrapped in black plastic, wooden cases and machines or bits of machines. Some kind of large gun was in pieces on the floor by the large, flat stone which served as a hearth. Salted hides were slung beneath the roof, layered with aromatic tar bush leaves to keep off insects. A pentad of fisherfolk women and more than twice that number of their children moved about in the dusky evening light, lighting lamps, mending clothes, stirring the cookpot in which fish soup perpetually simmered, chattering in their dialect and casting covert glances at Pandaras and Tibor. A half-tame crow hopped about, too. It was big, half Pandaras's height, and looked beadily at him as if wondering whether it would be easy to kill him, and what he might taste like. The crow's white droppings spattered the floor and the stacks of plastic-wrapped bales, and it was given to crying out hoarsely and jumping here and there with an abrupt dry flutter of its black wings. It was always just at the corner of Pandaras's sight. It made him jumpy, and he kept one hand near the hilt of his ivory-handled poniard. The arbalest was slung at his shoulder. He did not trust the trader.

"You don't mind my bird," Ayulf said. "He's never seen no one like you before and he's curious." He had been cuddling the youngest of the women to him; now he dismissed the girl with a slap to her haunches and said, "They are animals, not men, but someone like me must make a living as best he can, and take what company he can, too. You understand, eh? You being in the same line of business as me. Don't deny it. I know a man that lives by his wits when I see him."

Ayulf was staring at Tibor when he said this, but then he seemed to recollect himself and winked at Pandaras.

"I can see that you make a good living here," Pandaras said.

"There's a lot that washes downriver," the trader said, "and a lot that makes its way back from the war." He jerked a thumb over his shoulder. "That culverine, for instance. I'd sell it to you, except I've promised it to a good friend of mine who'll be along to collect it once I've fixed its firing mechanism. But I have other guns. I'll take that arbalest off you in part exchange for something with a bit more bite. You need heavy weapons around here. The Preservers don't see so well in this part of the river, if you get my meaning."

Ayulf's friend was probably a pirate, Pandaras thought. The trader must pay a good deal of tribute for protection. He said, "You are generous to your friends, dominie."

"It helps to be generous out here," Ayulf said. He plucked a bit of gristle from his gappy teeth and tossed it to the crow, which snapped it from the air with its bone-white beak and swallowed it whole. "Favors bring business and keep trouble away."

"I can see that your business is good. You have a good place here, many women, many things to trade. Why, you even have an abundance of boats."

"You need a boat to get about. How does that raft of yours handle out on the river?"

"Well enough, for a raft. My friend here has a lot of experience with rafts."

Ayulf's yellow gaze flicked toward Tibor. "Friend, eh? With a friend like yours, you are a rich man indeed, and deserve better than a raft, I would think."

They slowly got around to bargaining, and at last, with Tibor following, climbed down to the lowest branches of the banyan to inspect a long narrow pirogue. It had been dug out of a single tree trunk and had a log outrigger and a high prow. A reaction motor lay in the stinking water which half-filled it. Although Ayulf could not get the motor to start, he promised that it usually ran as sweet as the streams of the paradise which the Preservers would create at the far end of time. The sun had set and, despite the little lights strung through the branches of the banyan, there was not much light under the shanty, but Pandaras could see better in the dark than the trader. He took a hard look at the motor—it was clogged with dried mud and probably had been dropped in the river at some point—and said that it was a big motor for a small boat.

"Sometimes in my line of work you need to get somewhere quickly," Ayulf said, showing his ruined teeth in a ghastly grin. "This will take you anywhere on the river, my little man, swift as a thought from the Preservers."

Pandaras smiled at him. "It might do that once it is fixed. If it can be fixed. The inlet and outlet channels are clogged and bent, but that's a trivial matter. What's worse is that the reaction chamber might be corroded under all this mud, and the feeder valves and the ignition spark will need complete readjustment. That is, if they are still working. There's a hole in the fuel tank, too. Did someone shoot at it?"

Ayulf walked his long fingernails up his narrow jaw and pulled at his ear. He glanced at Tibor and crowded closer to Pandaras, who lightly touched the hilt of his poniard. The trader pretended not to notice the gesture. He stank powerfully of tobacco, sweat and urine. He said, "If you know something of motors, you will see that this is a fine one, very powerful."

"I see that it is very broken. No doubt you got it from someone who was foolish enough to drop it into the river or have their boat sunk from under them. It's been lying too long at the bottom of the river to be any good, but I'd be happy to take it away from you as a favor, since the look of it spoils the rest of your fine fleet."

With hot food in his belly and his face and feet and hands washed in filtered water, Pandaras felt more cheerful than he had since the flier had taken away his master and destroyed the *Weazel*. This poor shanty could almost count as civilization, and bargaining was the stuff of civilization, the way by which you measured yourself against your fellows. He had Tibor carry the reaction motor into the shanty and pretended to be angry that someone had burdened Ayulf with something in such a bad condition. On this basis, he and Ayulf bargained for an hour over glasses of peppermint-flavored arak; Pandaras took care to pour most of his share through a crack in the floorboards whenever Ayulf was distracted by one of his women.

Ayulf was a crafty bargainer, but he was not as clever as he thought he was. He had been too long amongst river pirates and the simple fisherfolk, and had lost his edge. He suggested almost straightaway that Pandaras leave Tibor with him and take the pirogue and the motor, and plenty of supplies too, but Pandaras said that he wanted only the pirogue, although he would take the motor if Ayulf had no need for it. In the end, it cost Pandaras half Yama's store of iron coins as well as the husks of the burnt-out machines. He had shown these to Ayulf early on and knew, by the widening of the man's yellow eyes, that the trader instantly coveted them.

Ayulf broke open another bottle of arak to celebrate the deal, and although Pandaras drank only enough to be polite, it quickly went to his head. "That's it," Ayulf said encouragingly. "Drink. Be happy. We've both done well with this deal. Let your slave here drink, too. Aren't we all friends?"

"I do not drink alcohol," Tibor said. "It is a poison to my people."

"We wouldn't want to poison you," Ayulf said. "Not you. You're worth a lot to your master." He said to Pandaras, "You can really fix that?"

"I'm going to do my best," Pandaras said, and opened up the motor's combustion chamber and began to remove and clean the feeder valves and the rotary spark. The crow perched close by, cocking its head this way and that, fascinated by the bright bits of metal which emerged from their coatings of mud. Ayulf watched sidelong, and said that Pandaras seemed to know a little about motors.

"One of my uncles on my stepfather's side had a trade in them. This was in Ys, where such things are forbidden, so it was on the black side of the market. Others think that our bloodline is famous only for songs and stories, and see our hands and think that we cannot do good work with them. But while our fingers are crooked, they are also strong, and we are very patient when we need to be. You might think this motor worthless, but when I'm done it will be better than new. You are very generous, Ayulf, and I thank you a million times over. Here, more of this rotgut, eh? We will drink to my success."

"You stay here a few days," Ayulf said. "You and your slave."

"He isn't my slave."

"He has to be someone's, and he came with you. Maybe we become partners, eh? Make much money. There is much that needs fixing here. I hear the war goes badly, which means it goes well for you and me, eh? More and more in the regular army run away from it, have to sell stuff cheap to buy what they need dear, and caterans are always hungry for the best weapons, no matter what side they are on."

"I have to find my master," Pandaras said.

Tibor said, "And the ship."

Ayulf poured Pandaras's shot glass brimful, drank from the bottle and wiped his mouth with the back of his hand. "It left you behind, eh? Maybe after an argument or a delicate kind of disagreement? I sometimes find those who have fallen out violently with their shipmates, if the caymans and fishes haven't found them first."

"There was certainly a fight," Pandaras said, glaring at Tibor.

"And you lost and were left to rot on some island? I know how that is. Are you sure they want you back? More likely you ran away, eh? They wouldn't leave a valuable slave behind with you. Yes, you took him and ran away, I would guess. No, it's all right, I won't tell. Listen, why go downriver? I have all you want here. Food and drink and women. Well, the women are animals, of course, but they know how to please a man in the warm trade."

Ayulf grabbed at the nearest of the women, but she pushed him away with a loud laugh and turned back to frying shrimp in a big blackened cast iron pan.

"Always cooking," Ayulf said. He started at the woman and made a humming noise in the back of his throat. "Why now, eh? Why so late? You all eat too much, you and your brats. I should throw a few of you to the caymans, eh? Which ones first?" He stuck his long middle finger (its nail had been filed to a sharp point, and was painted red) at the nearest woman and made a noise like a pistol shot. She giggled and put her hands over her face. Her fingers were webbed, and spread very wide, like a fan. They were tipped with little black claws.

"Someone is coming," the oldest woman said, from the far corner of the shanty. She was very fat, overflowing the stool on which she perched. She was working at a bit of wood with a tiny knife. Her skin was as green as moldy cheese. She said, "They bring hides to trade, man. They will make you rich."

"They share their thoughts," Ayulf told Pandaras. "They are not like us, who keep our thoughts sealed in our skulls. Everything is shared with them, like air or water. Kill any one of them, and it makes no difference."

Pandaras nodded. He was having trouble focusing on the spring, ball-bearing and three bits of metal that should fit together to make one of the feeder valves. There seemed to be too many of them, and his fingers too clumsy. He was drunk, and he had not meant to become drunk. But Ayulf was drunk too, and Pandaras had his poniard and the arbalest, and, at a pinch, Tibor (although he was not sure that Tibor, for all his size and strength, would be any good in a fight). And fisherfolk were coming. The trader would not try anything in front of them.

"You like to think we are all a single mind," the old woman in the corner told Ayulf, "but you know it is not true. It is just that we think alike, that's all. Hush! They are here."

There were whistles from below, a muffled splash. The crow stirred and hopped to the rail of the veranda, finding its balance with a rustling stir of wings. It cried out hoarsely. Ayulf stumbled to the rail, pushed the bird out of the way, and peered down into the darkness.

Voices floated up. The trader cursed and threw down the half-empty bottle of arak he had been clutching. It shattered on one of the banyan's branches. "Too fucking late! You understand? Understand too late? Come back tomorrow!"

More voices. The trader cursed again, clambered over the rail, and swarmed down the banyan. Pandaras stood (the cluttered, shadowy shanty seemed to revolve around him, and he felt a spasm of nausea) and went out onto the veranda. Below, lit by the tiny lanterns scattered amongst the banyan's leaves, Ayulf was arguing with a tall thin man who stood in a coracle. The man was holding up what looked like a huge ragged book. There were other coracles at the edge of the darkness beyond the glow of the lanterns.

Tibor came out and stood at Pandaras's back. He said, "The woman wants to speak with you, young master."

"Hush. I want to know what is going on."

"This is a bad place."

"I know. That's why I need to know what this is all about."

"We should go."

"I want to fix the motor. I can do it, but I'm tired. Later. I'll finish it later."

Below them, Ayulf finished a long impassioned speech, but the man in the coracle made no reply and at last the trader threw up his skinny arms and climbed back to the veranda. He fell flat on his face when he clambered over the rail, got up and went inside and found another bottle of arak, ripped the plastic seal away with his teeth and took a long swallow.

"They are impossible," Ayulf said petulantly, to no one in particular. He took another swallow and wiped his wet lips, glaring around at the women. A child woke somewhere and made a snuffling noise. Two more children clung to their mothers' legs, staring at the trader with big black eyes. In the corner, the fat old woman was calmly whittling her bit of wood. "Animals," the trader said. "Why am I wasting my time with animals?"

One by one, the fisherfolk climbed to the veranda and, stooping, entered the shanty. There were four of them. Unlike their women, they were so thin that if they had been of Pandaras's bloodline they would have been in the last stage of starvation, and so tall that their heads brushed the ceiling. Their green skins were dappled with darker tones. It was not a book their leader carried, but a sheaf of bloody uncured hides, and he placed this at Ayulf's feet.

One of the women crept up to Pandaras while the trader dickered with the leader of the fisherfolk in their croaking dialect. The leader squatted face to face with Ayulf, his sharp knees above the top of his head, nodding impassively, occasionally picking a shrimp from the heaped plate and examining it with slow thoughtfulness before dropping it into his wide mouth and swallowing it whole. His companions stood behind him in the shadows, as still as herons waiting for a fish to swim by. Most of the hides were of marsh antelope, but one was that of a leopard. Ayulf had spread it out in front of him and was stroking the spotted, viridescent fur with his long fingernails. To Pandaras's great scorn, the trader made no attempt to conceal how much he coveted the leopard hide.

"My mother will speak with you," the woman said in Pandaras's ear. "We know that you are a friend of ours, and we will help you."

Pandaras yawned. It was very late and he was drunk. Drunk and tired. He had given up trying to fit the motor back together. His fingers were numb and his stomach hurt. Later. Tomorrow. The shanty was swaying to and fro like a boat on the breast of the river. The lanterns seemed very bright, a swarm of hectic colors that kept trying to run into each other. It was an effort to keep anything in focus for more than a moment.

The woman touched the fetish which Pandaras wore over his shirt sleeve, but Pandaras mistook the gesture and pushed her away. He wanted to curl up around the pain in his stomach. He wanted to sleep.

"Your master is a fool," he told the woman. He was aware of Tibor's steady gaze on the other side of the shadowy shanty. He said, "I can take care of myself."

"Oncus," the woman said, but Pandaras had forgotten that name and stared at her dumbly until she went away.

Pandaras woke with a start sometime later. It was still dark. His mouth was parched and he had a bad headache and somehow he was standing upright. Then he realized that Tibor was holding him up by the collar of his ragged shirt and kicked out indignantly. Tibor let him go. The hierodule had the reaction motor under his arm.

Ayulf was in a hammock on the far side of the shanty, half-curled around a fat young woman and snoring through his open mouth. A knot of children slept below. The oldest woman was watching Pandaras from her stool on the other side of the slab hearth, the carved peg of wood in one hand, her little knife in the other.

"We go, young master," Tibor said in a low, hoarse whisper.

Pandaras drew out his poniard. "I'll cut his throat," he said. He was still drunk. His stomach hurt badly, as if he had been swallowing slivers of hot metal. The muscles in his arms and legs felt as if they were on the verge of cramping. He said, "He poisoned me. I'll cut his throat and watch him die in his own blood. I can do it."

Tibor wrapped a large, six-fingered hand around Pandaras's wrist. The poniard's blade pressed against the hierodule's gray skin, but did not cut it. "You fixed the motor," Pandaras said stupidly.

"It is very like the motor of the *Weazel*," Tibor said, and added, "Your pardon, but I think you need to be helped," and lifted Pandaras up and swung him over the rail of the veranda.

They were halfway down when Pandaras remembered something and began to scramble back up. Tibor tried to catch his foot, but Pandaras kicked his hand away. "The pack and the arbalest," he hissed. "My master's book. His money."

The women stirred and whispered amongst themselves when Pandaras reappeared, but he ignored them. He found the arbalest and the pack by the flat hearthstone—the book was still inside, but the money was gone.

"Where is it?" he hissed at the old woman. "Where did your master hide my money?"

She shook her head, and put her fingers to her throat.

Pandaras showed her the poniard. "I'll kill him where he sleeps. Show me where he hid it and I will go."

On its perch above the stay of Ayulf's hammock, the crow stirred, gave a single hoarse screech, and flew directly at Pandaras. Pandaras dropped the pack and slashed blindly as the bird enveloped him in its beating wings and pecked at the forearm he had raised to protect his eyes. He cut it with a lucky thrust and it fluttered away, trailing blood and dragging a black wing across the floor.

Pandaras chased after it, bleeding from half a dozen places, and went down under Ayulf's weight and hot stink. For a moment, the trader's hands were everywhere as he sought to prise the poniard from Pandaras's grasp, but then his weight was lifted away. Pandaras rolled over, gasping, and saw Tibor throw Ayulf across the shanty. The skinny trader crashed into the woven panels of the far wall. As they collapsed around him, he rolled away, quick as thought. Pandaras's poniard quivered in the planking where he had been.

Pandaras scrambled for cover too.

"I'll kill him," Ayulf said. He was pointing a percussion pistol at Tibor, who stood foursquare in the middle of the shanty, the arbalest dangling from one hand. "Come out, my little man, and maybe I'll let you live. Otherwise your slave dies, and then you die."

Pandaras stood, his hands spread in front of him. He was covered in cold sweat. Ayulf grinned and raised the pistol—and then his arm slammed backward into one of the posts which held up the roof. The pistol clattered on the floor.

Tibor lowered the arbalest. "We go," he told Pandaras.

Ayulf pawed at the bolt which pinned his forearm to the post and screamed at the women, "Get me free! Kill them and get me free!"

The old woman rose from her stool. The floor of the shanty creaked under her weight. "Go," she told Pandaras. "I will tend to him."

Pandaras jerked the poniard from the planking, scooped up the pack and stuffed two bottles of arak in it, and ran after Tibor. He more or less fell through the branches of the banyan and landed on his back in the stinking water which half-filled the pirogue.

As Tibor pushed off from the banyan, Pandaras fixed the reaction motor to its post and asked Tibor if he had mended the fuel tank.

"With a plug of resin," Tibor said.

Pandaras's hands were shaking badly. He got half the arak over himself when he tried to fill the tank. The motor started on the third attempt and spat a mass of bubbles with a coughing roar. Pandaras shoved the tiller up. The motor's inlet flooded with a solid thump and its outlet spewed a creamy wake that glimmered in the darkness and the pirogue shot forward. With Tibor using his paddle to steer, they made a wide arc toward the open river, the constellations of lights strung through the banyan dwindling into the darkness of the shore.

Looking back, Pandaras saw Ayulf stagger to the veranda. Something was on his shoulder: the culverine. A tongue of flame burst from its throat. Ayulf fell backward and the roof of the shanty caught fire.

The reaction motor ran out of fuel just as the sun began to free itself from the band of blue haze that marked where the Rim Mountains stood, far beyond the nearside shore of the Great River. When the motor sputtered to a stop, Pandaras tipped it up on its frame. Tibor, kneeling in the bow of the pirogue, set to with the paddle.

Behind them, across several leagues of water, the mangroves of the farside shore made a ragged black line against the brightening sky. There was no sign that Ayulf had tried to follow them; no doubt he was too busy trying to save his shanty from the blaze caused by the misfire of the culverine.

"The women told me that they put something in his arak to make him sleep," Tibor told Pandaras, "but they knew that he would try to kill you when he woke and found you still alive, even though he was very afraid."

Pandaras showed his teeth. His head and stomach still hurt, but he was no longer drunk. He said, "Of course he was afraid. That's why he drank so much—because he was afraid, and because he was ashamed of his fear. I would have killed him if he tried anything, and he knew it. I've killed bigger men than him, and they wore armor and carried energy pistols."

It had only been one man, the guard at the gate of the house of the rogue star-sailor. Pandaras had killed him by a trick and had been captured by the other guards almost immediately afterward, but he was certain that he could kill again if he had to.

"Ayulf was afraid of me, not you, little master," Tibor said placidly. "He knew that I am yours to command, and that I would have intervened if he had tried to shoot or stab or strangle you. But he also knew that once you were dead, I would have served him. He smeared poison in the bottom of your glass, the poison fisherfolk use to stun fish, but you poured away most of the arak he gave you, and that saved you."

"Hah. You suggest that you are more valuable than me. But who is the master here, and who the slave?"

"I know my price, little master, because I was sold on the open market and Captain Lorquital paid well for me. But do you know your worth?"

"It isn't measured in coin," Pandaras said. "And I think that you overestimate your value. What's the use of someone who can fix a reaction motor but forgets that it needs fuel?"

"I thought that we should leave quietly and quickly."

"And forgot my master's book and the money, too."

"You were nearly killed when you went back, little master. Life is more important than things."

"Easy to say if you've never owned anything. The book is important. Don't you remember how much time my master spent studying it? And we'll need money, soon enough."

Tibor paddled silently for a while.

"Well," Pandaras said at last. "Ayulf got what he deserved. Why do those women stay with him, do you think?"

"I understand that it is the custom of the fisherfolk to offer up hostages to secure bargains between different families. And so they secured bargains with Ayulf, although I do not believe that he understood what obligations he owed them. The eldest of the women told me that she knew a great chief called Oncus. She recognized his fetish, and that is why she decided to save you."

Pandaras touched the coypu hair fetish, which he wore on his upper arm, over his shirt. It was loose there, although it had fitted snugly on his master's wrist. He said, "I had forgotten the name of the old croaker who helped us when Prefect Corin tried to flush us out of the floating forest. What luck, eh?"

"Who can say what is luck, and what is the will of the Preservers?"

"That's easy. A man makes his own luck. Anything else is a gift, but no one should hope to build their lives on the gifts of others. My master was clever enough to leave the fetish behind so that I would know he had been taken alive, and I was clever enough to find it and to wear it. So it was by the luck I made from my master's forethought that we were saved."

"Yet our lives are the gifts of the Preservers," Tibor said solemnly. "You are engaged on a holy task, little master, and you should behave accordingly."

"A holy task?"

"Why, you seek your master, of course. Did you not tell me that he will raise up all the indigenous peoples? If that is true, may he not also redeem the sins of my own people, and of all the races of hierodules?"

"We have to find him first," Pandaras said, and touched the ceramic coin which, hung from his neck on its leather thong, dangled inside his shirt. "I fear for him."

Pandaras had been badly weakened by the dose of poison, and was suffering from stomach cramps. While Tibor drove the pirogue steadily toward the nearside shore, he sat in the stern and leafed through the book he had risked his life to save.

He knew that this was an old and valuable copy of the Puranas, and that some of its pictures had been changed when his master had visited a shrine. They were quite unlike any Pandaras had ever seen before, but because, like many of his people, he was a gifted storyteller, he was able to guess something of their narrative. One of the Ancients of Days had escaped from the others and had become mixed up in a Change War. Then her ship had found her, and she had been executed by the rest of its crew. Pandaras knew that there must be more to the story than that, for his master had studied long and hard in the book while the *Weazel* had sailed downriver, but he could not riddle it and at last put it away.

It took a day and a night to paddle the rest of the way to the nearside shore, a patchwork of marshy fields, dense green woods and little villages. Many of the villages stood a league or more from the shore, stranded there by the river's slow retreat. Pandaras carved a flute from a joint of bamboo and usually managed to win his supper each night by playing a medley of tunes. He quickly discovered that those he had learned as a child and put away when he had grown older were most appreciated by the indigens. In that sense at least they were as children, but Pandaras thought that the children of men would be less trusting and less innocent than these simple folk.

The indigenous people of the shore were closely related to the husbandmen who lived in the ruins of the pleasure gardens on the roof of the Palace of the Memory of the People. They were not much taller than Pandaras, but were very muscular, with seamed skin the color of freshly broken brick. Their stubby fingers were sometimes linked by loose webs of skin, and in one village the skin tones were darkened by greenish mottling, as if in the past they had had some congress with the fisherfolk.

Each night, Pandaras saved some of the food he was given and took it to Tibor, who stayed hidden outside the villages. After the incident with Ayulf, Pandaras trusted the indigens far less than they trusted him, and did not want anyone to see the hierodule and think that they could take him away. Sometimes he was also able to bring some palm wine, which could be used in the reaction motor; with a little fuel, they could travel thirty leagues in a day.

It was a slow, lazy time. One day was much like the next, hot and sunny with quick fierce showers in the afternoon, for it was the rainy season. At last, a little over a decad after they had first reached the nearside shore (Pandaras made a notch in the hull of the pirogue each day, like a prisoner), they came to Ophir.

4

Hope

THE YOUNG WARLORD, Enobarbus, and the rogue apothecary, Dr. Dismas, both wanted the same thing from Yama, but wanted it for different reasons. Enobarbus, champion of the aspect of Angel and traitor to the army raised against the heretics by the Department of Indigenous Affairs, wanted to conquer the world in the name of his mistress and overthrow the stasis imposed in the name of the Preservers by the vast civil service. After that, Utopia would follow as naturally as summer follows the rise of the Eye of the Preservers: everyone a suzerain and everyone living forever with the aid of old technologies which the heretics were busily reviving. Dr. Dismas wanted an end to stasis too, but what he wanted after that was more complex. He was a hybrid of man and feral machine, an agent of the faction whose rebellion had, during the Age of Insurrection, wrecked half the world and destroyed many of the avatars left by the Preservers to guide and enlighten the ten thousand bloodlines of the Shaped. He wanted an end to the belief that the Preservers were gods and a closer union between machines and men, but his motives remained opaque. Or rather, he gave so many different reasons that it seemed to Yama that he wanted only a glorious chaos, a soup of contingency, change for change's sake.

Despite their differences, Enobarbus and Dr. Dismas agreed on one thing: Yama was the key to victory. Their quarrels ranged back and forth across his head like those of children squabbling over a toy.

Yama took little notice of them. He was growing less and less aware of the world. He was sinking into the battleground of his own body. The thing which Dr. Dismas had planted inside him at the beginning of his adventures was fully awake now, and its power was growing day by day, hour by hour. It was as if Yama's self was an island or castle of light surrounded by a restless flood of darkness both malevolent and sentient. Not only was it rising, but it was constantly sending out stealthy filaments and tentacles, constantly probing for weaknesses. Yama felt that if he gave way to it for a moment, even in the dreams which possessed him in sleep (which were not truly dreams; nor was it truly sleep), then he would dissolve at once, like a flake of salt dropped in the Great River.

It was Yama's worst enemy and his most intimate relation. More a brother than Telmon; more a lover than Derev; a greater enemy than Prefect Corin or Dr. Dismas. A secret sharer, a spectral reflection, a dark half: his Shadow.

Dr. Dismas explained that it was growing an interpenetrating neural network in parallel to the web of neurons in Yama's brain—an exact duplicate, in fact, but on a much smaller scale, each pseudoneuron no more than a hundred molecules wide, each pseudoaxon a whisker the width of six carbon atoms. Yama did not really understand this; he did not understand much of the apothecary's gabble. But he knew that the Shadow had grown under his skin and was extending into the intimate cavern of his skull. His dreams were no longer his own. Most were kaleidoscopic visions of battlefields and cities under siege, but in one chilling reverie he saw a great, joyful crowd of people linking and relinking hands in a stately dance, and behind each of the dancers, aping every movement, was a malevolent starveling creature as thin as paper and as black as soot.

Yama knew that as the Shadow spread through his skull it had assumed control of his powers and was using them to subvert machines loyal to the cause of the Preservers, turning them against the army of the Department of Indigenous Affairs. He knew that it was speeding the tide of war toward Ys. The visions of battle were true visions of the Shadow's interventions in the war far upriver, leaking from its consciousness to his. He could not stop the Shadow taking control of his power over machines, but he learned that he could follow it out into the world as a wren might steal a ride on the back of a lammergeyer or a mite on a spider. Awake, Yama could no longer even sense the presence of machines, much less bend them to his will, but in the grip of one of the deep trances that these days passed for sleep, riding the Shadow's consciousness far from his unconscious body, he was able to take over a machine and steal away, fleeing from the terrible visions of clashing blades of light, fountains of fire, screams of men and beasts.

In this guise, the world seemed partly transparent; there were revelations everywhere Yama looked. Using the borrowed machine's deep radar he could see the ancient dredgers in the deeps of the Great River, accompanied by schools of giant polyps which kept their ceramic carapaces clean and plucked tasty morsels from the silt they pushed toward the pipes which would carry it to the Rim Mountains. He could see the passages and great caverns beneath the skin of the world, the vast, unfathomable machines which labored there and the great engines in the keelways. And he could see the world itself by light above and below that narrow band in the spectrum of electromagnetic radiation used by living creatures; see the forests of the Marsh of the Lost Waters as a crumpled landscape of white, reflected heat with beasts and men bright sparks moving within it; see the myriads of machines which tended the world as intense specks of constantly rewoven electromagnetic patterns; see the distant cloud of feral machines which hung several million leagues behind the orbit of Confluence. In this form, at least, the feral machine he had inadvertently called upon for help was no more than any of the others, indistinguishable in the dim cloud of overlapping electromagnetic signatures.

As below, so above. Yama could hear the faint roar of the Universe's birthpang, the wailing ululation and popcorn crepitation of radio sources within the Galaxy beneath the world's keel, the faint chirps of the halo stars. And hear too the song of the accretion disc around the Eye of the Preservers, the intense crackle of fusion in gravity-tied knots in the infalling gases, the fricative hiss of molecular hydrogen, the howl of tidally heated matter reaching its last end at the event horizon of the black hole at the center of the disc, the great No from which nothing, not even the Preservers, who had willed their own incarceration, could escape until the Universe's last end.

One night, Yama sensed something beyond the lines of the army of the Department of Indigenous Affairs. It was like a memory which would not take form, a melody he could not quite name. A far star that was fainter than any machine, yet which drew him as a weary traveler in a wide wasteland might at last glimpse the distant flicker of his own hearth, and hurry homeward with a gladdened heart. But even as he flew toward it, the machine he had borrowed speeding above the sullen waves of the night-dark river, the Shadow stirred and woke, and Yama woke too. (Far upriver, a machine suddenly found itself a few meters above the midway current of the Great River, falling down a gravithic geodesic toward Ophir. Braking so hard that its shell glowed red-hot with friction, it spun eccentrically on its axis—just as a hound might shake itself—remembered the task it was supposed to be executing, fixed the coordinates and sped off, dismayed and embarrassed.) And on waking, Yama knew what the thing which had drawn him must be. He held the knowledge close, drawing strength from the hope it gave him, and made a vow. I will find it, he thought, and find if Pandaras is still alive. No, he must be. The coin will not work unless he is holding it. Not all is lost.

It was a frail hope. For even if he found Pandaras, what could he tell him? And if Pandaras found him, what could he do?

A frail hope, yes, but all the hope he had.

5

Ophir

IT HAD ONCE been the most beautiful city on Confluence, prosperous and peaceful, its network of canals perfumed by water lilies and lined by palms and flowering trees, its houses white as salt, with green gardens tumbling from their terraces, its main temple renowned for the wisdom of its avatar. Three bloodlines had lived there in harmony. It had been famous for its metalworkers, jewelers and weavers, and for the seminary where half the priests on the world were trained.

The war had transformed it. The population had been swollen to ten times its original size by soldiers and their followers, and by refugees who crowded the streets and made their encampments in the parklands and groves of citrus trees around the city. Fliers hung at the upriver edge of the city, some bigger than the carracks which disgorged a thousand soldiers at a time. The docks were clogged with carracks and other ships, the quays piled with supplies. The park around the great temple had been turned into a barracks. Illicit stills flourished, supplying hundreds of fly-by-night bars. There were firefights between gangs dealing in drugs and prostitution, and between the gangs and the civil guards who tried to contain them. Dead bodies lay unclaimed by the sides of the busy streets, picked over by dholes and kit foxes, or floated amongst the flowering lilies in the wide canals, each attended by a retinue of green turtles and one or two pensive turkey vultures. There were rumors of heretic cults infiltrating the city; soon after they arrived, Pandaras and Tibor saw a woman run into a café which, a moment later, exploded in a ball of orange flame from which two or three burning figures staggered to collapse on the pavement.

Day and night the streets were full of soldiers and all those who fed off them: prostitutes of a hundred different bloodlines, hawkers, gamblers, grifters, gandy men, charlatans selling false blessings or fake charms or shirts guaranteed to repel the weapons of the heretics. Streams of wagons, rickshaws and tok-toks, the motorized bicycles particular to Ophir, wound through crowded streets noisy with the cries of hawkers and hordes of beggars, with music from bars and roadside food stalls, with bells and whistles and horns from the unceasing flow of traffic, with the roar of illegal generators. The canals were clogged with slow-moving boats, and at every intersection sampans were tied together to form impromptu water markets. At night, neon signs buzzed and flickered and cast colored shadows over the white walls of the buildings, and the noise and the crowds seemed to double and redouble, a restless unsleeping flood of people.

Pandaras sold the reaction motor and arbalest on the first day of their arrival, but he got very little for them; the city was glutted with weapons and equipment. He took up singing in the pavement cafés, performing two or three standard airs at each while Tibor collected a few small coins from the customers. When Tibor complained bitterly at this indignity, Pandaras pointed to the small girl who was moving from table to table and asking the customers if they wanted their boots cleaned, and then to her brothers, working by the door with cloths and polish, and said that there were worse ways of earning a living.

"I am a hierodule, little master," Tibor said, with an air of wounded dignity. "I am not some street urchin. This is beneath me."

"You are mine to command. You said so yourself. Your people allow themselves to be commanded by others as atonement for the sins of their ancestors. You make yourselves slaves, and so you make those around you slaves too, because they must take responsibility for you. How easy it must be to have others make all your decisions for you! How easy it is to be like a child! Well, now you must suffer the consequences. You cannot choose how you will serve. You must do as you are told. And you will do as I tell you, because we need money to buy passage downriver. Perhaps you do not understand that because you are a slave, and slaves have no need of money because their owners look after them. But we need money now if we are to find my master before I grow old. My bloodline burns brightly and briefly. I have no patience for the safe but slow way of doing things."

"We will find the *Weazel*," Tibor said. "Then all will be well. You will see. They think us dead, but they will be so happy to see us again."

"They are dead! They are dead and destroyed and the ship is destroyed. Phalerus survived a little while because he was farther away from the center of the fire, but it would have been better for him if he had died at once, like the others. And that is what happened. Everyone but Phalerus was killed in one instant, and burned up into smoke in the next. They were killed by a weapon of war. You must understand that, Tibor. You must."

"You could sell the book," Tibor said, after a long silence.

Pandaras sighed. It was impossible to knock any sense into the hierodule's round, hairless head. He said, "It is not mine to sell. It is my master's, and I have sworn to return it to him."

"Perhaps the *Weazel* will arrive soon," Tibor said. "We have surely overtaken it, little master, but it will catch up with us by and by and put in at the docks. Everything that goes downriver to the war stops at Ophir."

"We cannot stay here," Pandaras said. "We must find my master."

The tiny spark in the coin had multiplied into a pattern of dots and dashes of light that was different every time Pandaras looked at it. They were nearer to Yama now, he thought, but not yet close.

For the first few nights Pandaras and Tibor lived on the streets, washing and drinking at the public standpipes, sleeping on a roof amongst clattering windmill generators in a nest of bubblewrap and plastic foam packing bought from a scavenger. Everything in the city had its price. Weapons, armor and ammunition were cheap, but food and accommodation were ludicrously expensive, for this was a war economy.

Ophir was a long way from the war front in the fringe jungles of the Marsh of the Lost Waters, but on their third night in the city, Pandaras and Tibor were woken by a faint continuous thunder and flashes of blue light far downriver. It seemed to have woken the whole city, for people stood on every roof, watching the fugitive flashes. Suddenly a thread of white light split the black sky from top to bottom and for a moment it was everywhere as bright as day. The light winked out even as Pandaras raised his hands to shield his eyes, and several heartbeats later there was a long low rumble and the roof on which he and Tibor stood rolled like the deck of a ship. The palms that lined the street below doffed their heads, and all over the city bats and birds and big dragonflies took wing.

Once Pandaras had amassed enough money for a deposit, he rented a sleeping place in a house beside one of the canals. It was a subdivision of what had once been a graciously proportioned room, screened by paper stretched over bamboo frames, with barely enough space for a pair of raffia sleeping mats. Two families lived in the other parts of the room. One, of a quick, lithe, brown-skinned black-haired bloodline, ran a food stall, and the smell of hot oil and steamed vegetables always hung heavy in the air. Tibor helped them out, at first chopping vegetables, then graduating to making the sweet shrimp sauce and thin loaves which were served with every dish. The other family, five generations, from tiny hairless kit to toothless grandfather, lived on the income from three rickshaws. It was always noisy, for someone was always awake in one or another of the room's subdivisions, mending one of the rickshaws or cooking, squabbling or playing cards or listening to a cassette of prayers, and all around was the mingled sound of hundreds of other lives lived in public.

It was the life from which Pandaras had run, first becoming a pot boy, and then self-appointed squire to Yama. He was as restless as Tibor and knew he could not make the money he needed by busking. That was only a stopgap until he came up with a plan. Amazingly, it was not possible to join the army here, or even become a cateran, as Yama had once wanted to do, although there were plenty of caterans roaming the city. Nor was it possible to hitch a ride downriver on the troop ships; it was necessary to bribe one of the crew for passage, as did the gamblers, whores and other camp followers. Pandaras was confident that he could think of some way of making the money quickly. This was a place where someone with wit and cunning could make a great deal of money, as long as no one killed him first.

One of the sons of the family who ran the rickshaws, for instance, came and went at odd hours, always dressed in a sharply creased kilt and a clean white short-sleeved shirt. He had an arrogant air which humbled his parents and his grandfather. His eyes were masked by orange plastic wraparound shades, and a cigarette was always dangling from his lips. A gang member if ever there was one. Pandaras tried to follow him a couple of times, but the boy quickly and easily lost him in the crowded, noisy maze of alleys and passages behind the buildings which fronted the canal, and if he knew that he was being followed he gave no sign of it. But if there was any money to be made quickly, Pandaras thought, the boy or someone like him would be the key to it.

Two bravos had already tried to shake down Pandaras and Tibor, ambushing them one night outside the café where they had finished their final set and demanding all their money in return for a license to perform in this part of the city. Pandaras, who knew that showing any sign of weakness would mark you forever as prey, whipped out his poniard and cut one of the bravos on the arm and chased him away. Tibor grabbed the other around the neck and lifted him off the ground and gently took his butterfly knife and handed it to Pandaras, who flipped it open and closed in front of the bravo's face and asked pleasantly why innocent entertainers should be worthy of the consideration of two fine brave gentlemen.

The man spat a long stream of yellow phlegm. Like his friend, he was very tall and very thin, wrapped from top to toe in overlapping spirals of gray rags. The little skin that showed was granular and hard and bone-white. The joints of his sticklike arms and legs were swollen; his head was small and flat, like a plate set on a corded neck, with a triangular mouth and a pair of black, mobile, wide-spaced eyes.

Pandaras wiped sticky phlegm from his face and put the blade of the butterfly knife against one of the man's eye-stalks. It shrank to a little bobble and the other eye bent around and stared anxiously at the blade. The man said, "You wouldn't dare."

Tibor said, "I will let him go, little master. I am sure he will not bother us again after this mistake."

"First he'll tell us who he works for."

The man's triangular mouthparts flexed and he spat again, this time at Pandaras's feet. He said, "You've made the mistake. I'm Pyr's. So are you and all street trash like you, except you don't know it."

"This Pyr runs things, eh? And I thought that the Department of Indigenous Affairs had charge of the city."

"You mean the army?" The man's mouthparts chattered: laughter. He said, "How long have you been here? The army looks toward the war, not the streets. We keep out of its way and it doesn't trouble us. Let me give you some advice. We're not like the army. We like things tidy. People who don't fit in with the way things are run are removed. You're handy with a blade, but maybe next time we come back with pistols."

"Maybe I should speak with Pyr. I have a great deal he might want to know." Pandaras signaled to Tibor, who released the man.

"If Pyr wants to speak with you, she'll send for you. Pray she doesn't, though." The man adjusted his disarranged winding cloths, spat a third time, and stalked off.

Despite this threat, Pandaras and Tibor were not troubled again on their nightly rounds of the cafés, but Pandaras knew that sooner or later there would be a comeback. There always was. He just had to be ahead of it, to think of what they might do and be ready.

Pandaras became friendly with the grandfather of the rickshaw family. Memoth was a distinguished old man who spent his days at one of the major intersections of the city, pumping up the pneumatic tires of rickshaws or tok-toks for a penny a time. It was hard work, and Pandaras massaged Memoth's aching shoulders with clove oil in the evenings and listened to the gossip the old man brought back from the rickshaw drivers, who were the eyes and ears of the city.

Memoth's family was one of three bloodlines which had inhabited Ophir before the war. They were a spidery people with short bodies and long arms and legs, given to abrupt, jerky movements. Memoth's skull was bony, with a pronounced crest and a jutting shelf of a brow from which his lively brown eyes peered. He wore only an oil-stained kilt and a belt hung with little tools. Like all his people, many of whom worked at the docks, assembling or repairing weapons, he was handy with machines. His coarse pelt was striped yellow and brown, and his plaited mane was white. That would have been a sign of his status in the days before the war, but now he had to humble himself before his arrogant gangster grandson and accept his charity.

Memoth had once owned several houses, but they had all been requisitioned by the army, and now his family made their living as best they could. But he was not bitter; indeed, he was the most patient and good-natured man Pandaras had ever met. He told Pandaras stories about his bloodline, of how before they were changed they had lived in a wide plain of tall grasses along the edge of the foothills of the Rim Mountains, the men hunting small game, the women gathering roots and fruit. At the end of each summer, when the Eye of the Preservers set for the last time, the wild grasses ripened and the women threshed the grain and ground it into coarse flour to make bread, and brewed a kind of beer from the husks. It was only thirty generations ago, Memoth said, but only now did they realize how rich they had been.

"We worked only a few hours a day. The rest of the time we sang or told stories, or made pictures on flat rocks or made patterns with the rocks themselves to please the Preservers. But now we must work all the hours we are awake, and still go hungry. What profits a bloodline to change?"

"Because unless they are changed, men are not free." His master would have a better answer, Pandaras thought, for Yama was always thinking about these matters.

It did not satisfy Memoth. He said, "Free, yes. Free to starve. Free to become the slaves of other men."

"We say in Ys that people like us are the strength of the city."

"So I have heard," Memoth said, "but I think the ordinary populace of Ys are as oppressed as we are here. The Preservers lay a heavy burden upon us. Perhaps men like us are unworthy of their gifts."

"We must always hope our children may do better," Pandaras said, but Memoth did not answer this. Few in the city believed this fundamental creed. In their despair, they had forgotten the charity of the Preservers.

As usual, they were sitting outside the door of the partitioned room, Memoth on a plastic chair, Pandaras at his feet. On the other side of the canal, which was choked with the dark green leaves of water hyacinth, women of the same bloodline as the bravos who had ambushed Yama and Tibor were washing clothes, squatting by the water's edge and gossiping as they beat dirt from wet cloth with smooth stones. Someone was playing a cassette of prayers very loudly in one of the buildings that loomed above, and someone else was shouting angrily. It had just rained and the air was still fresh. The webs of electrical cables that sagged high above the canal crackled and spat as water dripped from them. All this reminded Pandaras of his childhood home in Ys, except that it was hotter and more humid.

A flier passed slowly overhead, its underside bristling with gun emplacements that seemed to brush the rooftops. The whole quarter throbbed with the noise of its generators; the air seemed to grow colder in its shadow. Everyone stopped to watch it. When it was gone, Memoth stirred and said that the war was getting nearer, and it was going badly.

Pandaras nodded and sipped from his bowl of mint tea, waiting for the old man to expand on his theme. He had heard much about the war since he had arrived in Ophir. It had always been distant in Ys. People mostly did not trouble to think about it. They accepted the news disseminated by licensed storytellers who sang songs and told tales of great heroism and tremendous victories to any who bothered to listen. But here the war was almost next door and everyone had their own story to tell. And most of the stories were about a sudden surge of advances by the heretics, of the army's weapons failing mysteriously, of its machines falling from the sky. There was talk of a new general or leader amongst the rabble of the heretics. There was talk of sudden, harrowing defeats, of bitter retreats.

Memoth said that you could tell that something was wrong because almost no one followed the soldiers to war now. The gamblers and whores knew that there was no profit to be had from defeat.

"My people should leave the city," he said. "We should go back to our high plains, back to the old life. Except that we cannot be other than that which we have become. We are human now, and we have lost the facility to be like animals and let only our instincts guide us. We are each of us alone in our own heads."

It grieved Pandaras to hear this despairing plaint, for he liked the old man. He asked, "What does your grandson say?"

Memoth did not reply at once. He drank his tea, straining the last of it with his big front teeth and spitting out bits of twig. At last, he said, "He is not of my family. Not anymore. Now he is Pyr's."

Pandaras wanted to know more, but Memoth would not say anything else about her or his grandson. No one who worked in the cafés wanted to talk about her either, warding off Pandaras's inquiries with fingers touched to throat or eyes or forehead, telling him that he should not trouble himself with people like her, who caused only harm to people like him. Without specific knowledge, Pandaras constructed grandiose and impossibly complicated plans about swindling or duping the gangster leader, and knew that they were no more than dreams. He was growing desperate, because after two decads in the city he had saved hardly any money. Money here was like air, necessary to sustain every moment of life, and as difficult to catch or keep hold of.

And then the soldiers came for Tibor.

█████

It was near dawn. Pandaras was woken by a boot in his ribs. The tiny sleeping space was full of soldiers. He came up fighting and was lifted and flung aside. In another part of the subdivided room, two women were screaming at different pitches and a man was shouting angrily. One of the soldiers threw down a bit of paper, kicked Pandaras hard, and followed his companions.

Tibor was gone. Pandaras ran outside as a flat-bottomed boat with a rear-mounted fan motor roared away in the gray half-light. Its wake washed over the sides of the canal and lifted and dropped the sampans clustered at the intersection. Someone fired a carbine into the air; then the boat slewed around a bend and was gone.

Pandaras gave chase, but had to stop, winded, after half a league. He walked back, holding his side. His ribs hurt badly and everything he owned, including Yama's precious book, was in the room.

The paper was a note of requisition for . . . *a certain hierodule, known by the name of Tibor.* A receipt for two hundred and fifty units of army scrip was stapled to it. Pandaras tore the requisition and the receipt to pieces and threw them at the children who had crept to the doorway to see what he was doing. Army scrip was almost worthless. Two hundred and fifty units would not even buy a cigarette.

His ribs still hurt: sharp stabbing pains if he breathed too deeply.

He tore a strip of cloth from the tail of his worn shirt and bound it around his chest. Memoth was sitting by the door, and called to Pandaras when he went outside.

"They will have taken your friend out of the city," the old man said. "They will have taken him to the war. There is talk of a big battle and many casualties. A hierodule would be of much use there. The hierodules of our temple were taken long ago to tend the lazarets."

"There is a lazaret here," Pandaras said stupidly.

"That's for civilians, and it is virtually closed down because there are no supplies to be had by the normal channels. They don't bring wounded soldiers to the city. It would be bad for the morale of those who have just arrived and have yet to fight. Besides, many of the wounded would die of the journey. No, they are treated in floating lazarets close to the front line. That is where your friend has been taken, I expect. Are you going too, Pandaras?"

"I have an obligation," Pandaras said, and saw, without surprise, Memoth's grandson coming along the path by the canal, his smile wide beneath his wraparound orange shades. The two bravos who had ambushed Pandaras and Tibor at the café were behind him.

Pandaras went with them. He had no choice. They allowed him to keep the ivory-handled poniard and Yama's book, but reclaimed the butterfly knife and took all the money he had saved. As they passed through the spice market he said, "You told them, didn't you?"

The boy's grin widened. He had a cocky walk, and people made way for him. His crisp white shirt glimmered in the green shade beneath the tamarisk trees where the spice merchants had set out their tables. He said in his soft, hoarse voice, "Many have seen you with the hierodule. It was a good trick, eh? People give you extra money because of him. Don't deny it. It made the other jongleurs jealous. Perhaps one of them told the soldiers about your slave. Also, I hear someone was looking for you. Maybe he did it, eh? Don't be sore. Maybe there's something else you can do."

"I want to talk with Pyr."

Pandaras felt very alert. His anger was quite gone. In a curious way it was a relief that what he had feared for so long had finally happened, but he knew that he had to be very careful now. If he failed at this, he failed both Tibor and his master.

The boy laughed, and patted Pandaras on the shoulder with a curiously tentative touch. He said, "These things take time."

"Who is it that is looking for me?"

"He talks too much," one of the bravos said. It was the one Pandaras had wounded. "I'll clip his tongue."

"You'll leave him alone," the boy said.

"How is your arm?" Pandaras asked.

The bravo made a hissing sound and touched the butt of the pistol which was tucked amongst the gray rags wound around his lanky body.

The boy said, "It is one of the bureaucrats who is looking for you. Not the army, but one of those who run the army. Tall, with a staff. Black hair, and a stripe of white, here."

The boy ran a finger down the left side of his face, and Pandaras knew at once who it must be, even though the man had surely been killed. Every hair on his head rose, prickling. He said, "Then I must see Pyr. At once."

"First you prove yourself," the boy said. "Then, maybe you see her. She is very busy. She has much business."

———

Pandaras was kept for three days in a small, hot room on the top floor of a six-story house which overlooked one of the city's squares. Crowds and traffic noise all day and all night; the smell of burnt alcohol mixed with the scent of the flowering vine that twisted around the balcony outside the window. A transformer on a pole beneath the balcony hummed and hissed to itself. Water dripped from a broken pipe into a plastic bowl in the center of the room. A gecko kept Pandaras company, clinging to one or another of the walls for hours at a time, with only a faint pulse in its throat to show that it was alive, before suddenly stirring and making a swift dart at a roach or click beetle. There was no furniture in the room. Pandaras slept on the balcony and spent most of his waking hours looking at the pictures in the copy of the Puranas or watching traffic which swarmed around the stands of giant bamboos in the center of the square. He knew that he must not lose his nerve. He must keep his resolve.

The coin was still displaying its shifting pattern of sparks.

The boy and the two bravos visited Pandaras each morning and evening. They brought food from the fry stall at the corner, rice and shrimp and green chillies in a paper bag, the edges of which were translucent with oil. The boy squatted by the window and watched as Pan-

daras ate, humming to himself and cleaning his broad nails with a
pocketknife; the bravos lurked by the door, talking to themselves in a
dialect of stuttering clicks. The boy had a percussion pistol in the back
of the waistband of his creased trousers, with his shirt-tail out to cover
it, and the bravos had pistols too.

The boy's name was Azoth. Although he was older than Pandaras,
his bloodline was long-lived and he was still a child, with the calculating
cruelty of one who has never been truly hurt, who believes that he will
never die or that death is nothing. He never took off his orange plastic
shades and would not answer any of Pandaras's questions, but instead
talked about the war for ten minutes or half an hour before, without
warning, standing up and leaving, followed by the bravos.

The door was unlocked, but Pandaras knew better than to try and
walk away.

On the evening of the third day he was roughly hustled downstairs
by the two bravos and forced to stand at the edge of the road. Passersby
made wide diversions around them; traffic roared past a handsbreadth
in front of them. A rickshaw stood in the shade of the giant bamboos.
Pandaras saw someone inside the rickshaw lean forward and say something to the driver, who nodded and stood up on his pedals. As the
rickshaw pulled away, Pandaras got another glimpse of its passenger: a
woman in a red silk dress, much smaller than him, with the large eyes
of a nocturnal bloodline and long, lustrous black hair.

On the way back up the stairs he asked the boy, Azoth, if the woman
he had seen was Pyr.

"Mind your questions," one of the bravos said.

"I don't talk with you," Pandaras said. "You know nothing."

"Pyr is interested in you," Azoth said.

"Is she scared to speak with me?"

"She does not know if you are worth the trouble," Azoth said. He
put his hand on the pistol hidden beneath his shirt-tail when he entered
the room, and crossed to the window and leaned at it and looked down
at the bustling street below.

"Something is troubling you," Pandaras said.

"We look after our own," Azoth said, without turning around.
"Prove yourself, and you are ours, and we are yours."

"He's still looking for me, isn't he? And I know he is a dangerous
man."

"Perhaps we should give you to him. Would you like that?"

"Then he does not offer money, or I think that you would have done
that already."

"He makes threats. We don't like that. Pyr will find him, by and by, and deal with him." Azoth turned and stared rudely at Pandaras. "Who are you?"

"A loyal servant."

Azoth nodded. "We wondered why you had a hierodule, and why you are so eagerly sought. Where is your master?"

"I have lost him."

Azoth smiled. "Don't worry. Masters are easy to find for the likes of you."

Later, as the boy was leaving, Pandaras said, "Tell Pyr I know many things."

The bravos made their chattering laughter. Azoth said, "Don't make yourself more than you are, and you'll do fine."

Pandaras thought about that as he sat on the narrow balcony and watched the street below. Perhaps he was no more than he had been before he had met Yama, a mere pot boy with a talent for telling stories and getting into trouble. Perhaps he had caught himself in one of his stories. And yet he had survived adventures which no ordinary person had ever faced. Even if he had begun his travels as an ordinary man, one of the unremarked swarm of his bloodline, then he was ordinary no more, for extraordinary things had happened to him. And now he was being hunted by Prefect Corin, who must be more than a man to have survived the destruction of his ship by the monstrous polyps Yama had called up from the depths of the river. Pandaras shivered, remembering how one of the polyps had torn poor Pantin apart with a contemptuous flick of its tentacles. He touched the fetish and then the coin and promised his master that he would not fail.

"I have fallen into trouble, but I will find my way out," he whispered. "And I will find you and rescue you from whatever harm you have fallen into. My life is short, and worth little to anyone but me, but I swear on it now."

Pandaras could not sleep for thinking of all he had to do and of what Azoth might want of him. He leafed through the copy of the Puranas, and found that the more he looked at the pictures the more they seemed to contain. They were saturated with meaning, and now he was beginning to fully understand the story they told.

The Ancient of Days who had escaped her ship had fled the length of the world, ending up in an obscure city at the place where the Great River fell over the edge of the world. The bloodline which lived there was unchanged, and she had taken control of them despite the efforts of the city's Commissioner and its Archivist. She had learned something in the shrines by the fall of the Great River and had quickened the minuscule machines in the brains of some of the inhabitants of the city. They had been reborn as individuals. They had been changed. And then the ship of the Ancients of Days had arrived in the middle of the civil war between changed and unchanged, having traveled the length of the Great River from its landfall at Ys. She had tried to destroy her crewmates, but they had killed her. Yet her ideas had survived. The Archivist of Sensch had escaped from the ship of the Ancients of Days. He had been the first of the heretics who even now strove to overturn the word of the Preservers.

Pandaras began to feel that perhaps the heretics might be right, or might at least have guessed the truth about some things. It was as if a voice had woken inside his head: the book had woken it, or planted it there. The world had turned away from the path ordained by the Preservers. It had become static and stratified, weighed down by ritual and custom. No one was free to choose their own destiny.

He shuddered, a single quick convulsion like a sneeze—his mother would have said that a ghoul had been sniffing around his grave. The book was valuable to his master, but it was dangerous. He must not look in it again, he thought, but a small part of him, that whispering voice perhaps, knew that he would.

It was long after midnight. The Eye of the Preservers was beginning to set over the roofs and treetops of the city. Its red swirl was dimmed by the city's neon glare, but the pupil at its center was quite distinct, the pinprick void swept clean by the black hole into which the Preservers had vanished and from which they would not emerge until the end of time. Could the heretics dare take the war there, if they conquered the world the Preservers had left behind?

Pandaras shuddered again. "I will not fail you, master," he whispered.

The next morning, Azoth and the two bravos did not bring Pandaras's breakfast. Instead, Azoth said, "Come with us. No, leave your things here. They will be safe."

"Are you going to take me to Pyr?"

The bravos made their chattering laugh.

Azoth said, "Perhaps soon. First you must prove yourself."

Azoth hailed a rickshaw and they rode a long way through the brawling streets. The bravos fixed their mobile eyes on Pandaras as he stared out and asked Azoth many questions about the places they passed. They got off in a narrow street somewhere near the docks. The masts of many ships pricked the blue sky beyond the flat roofs on the godowns. As they walked past a chandler's, Azoth pinched Pandaras's arm and said to take notice, because that was the place he would firebomb.

"Why?"

"Because you'll do what you're told," one of the bravos said.

"Because Pyr wants it," Azoth said, with a shrug. "It's just business."

A small boy was hawking fuel alcohol at the dusty intersection at the end of the street. Azoth threw money at him and told him to go away. The boy snatched up the coins, knuckled his forehead, and said he would like to see the show.

"Fill two of your bottles, then," Azoth said. "One word to anyone and I'll cut out your eyes and tongue. Understand? Why are you smiling?"

"Because nothing exciting ever happens here," the boy said. He was still smiling, but his hands were trembling and he splashed purple alcohol on the pavement as he filled the bottles.

One of the bravos took out a piece of cloth and tore it into long thin strips which he twisted up and stuck in the necks of the bottles. "You tip the bottle to wet the wick," Azoth told Pandaras. "Light the very end and keep the bottle upright when you throw it. Throw the bottles hard and make sure they hit something that will smash them. Make sure you throw them through the door, too."

"I know how it's done," Pandaras said. He was not scared, but there was a hollowness in his belly. It was the feeling he always had in the quiet moments before something violent happened. He picked up the two bottles. The rags in their necks stank sharply of sugar alcohol.

One of the bravos had a lighter. He waved its little flame at Pandaras, who stepped back in alarm, the two bottles and their sopping wicks clutched to his chest.

"Stop that," Azoth said sharply, and held out his hand. The bravo gave him the lighter; he flicked it twice to show how the flame was struck and put it in Pandaras's shirt pocket. "Do it now," he said, "and come straight back."

It was early in the morning, but the street was already busy. Although no one seemed to take any notice of him, Pandaras felt that he was watched by a thousand pairs of eyes as he walked to the chandler's, with the heavy bottles clutched to his chest and the stink of alcohol burning in his nostrils. The shutters of the shop were only half raised; someone was moving about inside, whistling a cheerful tune. On the other side of the street, his heart beating quickly and lightly, Pandaras set down the bottles and lit the wick of one of them. He put the lighter away and picked up the bottle and threw it at the pavement outside the chandler's door. As glass smashed and flames bloomed he snatched up the other bottle and ran.

Not toward Azoth and the bravos, but in the other direction. People made way for him. He ran in front of a cart (the nilagai pulling it reared in its traces, raking the air with its clawed forelegs), dodged a soldier who grabbed at him, and ran into a crooked passage between two go-downs, turning three corners before stopping, still clutching the bottle to his chest and listening to his hammering pulse and rasping breath.

Shrill whistles and an insistent bell somewhere in the distance, and beyond these bright noises the city's constant roar. Pandaras still had not got his breath back when he heard footsteps approaching. He ducked low and glanced around the corner, ducked back and lit the wick of the bottle, fearful that the snick of the lighter would give him away, and stepped out.

The two bravos stopped and looked at each other. Azoth was not with him. Their mouthparts clattered together in brief laughter; then they saw what Pandaras held. One raised his pistol and there was a flash and it flew from his hands—a misfire, Pandaras thought, and lobbed the flaming bottle as hard as he could. It smashed at the feet of the bravos and they were at the center of a sudden tall blossom of blue flames. They shrieked and twisted in the flames and although people presently crept down the passage and poured water on them, they were already dead, and Pandaras was far away.

———

It took Pandaras the rest of the day to cross the city and reach the building where he had been kept prisoner. He kept up a monologue all the way, telling himself that he was a fool to go back because Azoth would certainly be waiting there, that Tibor had been right and they should have left the city days and days ago. Better to live on grubs and leaves than be in the thrall of some gangster like Pyr.

But it was the city which had caught him, not Pyr. There were plenty like Pyr in Ophir; he could have fallen in with any of them once he had allowed himself to be seduced by the city's song. How well he knew that song, and what it promised! It was in his blood, the song that seduces all who are born in a city or who come to live in one.

Azoth had had it right. The city had made Pandaras think that he could be more than he was. He thought that he could win a fortune from it and rescue his master in style, and it had nearly cost him all he had. But he could not afford to lose the book. It was not his. Not his to sell, not his to lose.

When he reached the square, he stood for a long time on the far side of the stands of giant bamboos. The window of the room in which he had been kept was dark, but that signified nothing. He was very hungry—he had tried to snatch a hand of red bananas from a stall, but had been chased off—and very nervous. He walked around the block and came back to the square from another direction, did it again and thought he had located two people who were watching the building, one loitering by the food stall on the corner, the other at a roadside shrine, alternately wafting smoke from an incense cone and staring at the swarming passersby.

In the end, Pandaras went into the building next door and climbed its staircase to the roof, coming out amongst a small forest of clattering wind generators. An old man, drunk or drugged, lay on his back, waving his long arms and legs in the air like a beetle. Two more, wrapped in winding gray rags, turned their stalked eyes toward Pandaras, but they were only drunkards, sharing a plastic blister of an oily white liquor.

Pandaras marked his spot and took a short run and jumped the gap between the two buildings. He walked around the edge of the roof until he spied the balcony of the room where he had been kept, then took out his poniard and sawed at a sagging spot in the asphalted roof, exposing a lathe and plaster ceiling below.

There were wind generators on this roof too. He pried the heavy battery from one and threw it into the hole he had made and jumped after it, yelling like a crazy man and holding his poniard high above his head.

He landed in a pile of rubble and dust and fell over. There were three men in the room, but Pandaras only saw two of them at first. One was dead, lying on his back in the middle of the room with not a mark on him. The other was Azoth. He sat beneath the window, the copy of the Puranas open in his lap, faint light from a picture shining eerily under his narrow chin. His orange wraparound shades had fallen off; he stared down at the book in his lap with unblinking eyes and did not move when Pandaras dared to take a step toward him.

"He was like that when I arrived," someone said.

Pandaras recognized the man's soft voice at once. He had been interrogated by him after the fall of the Department of Vatication in the Palace of the Memory of the People. Without turning around, he said, "And the other?"

"Drowned, I fear, in the bowl of water conveniently left in the middle of the floor. How easy death is to find. Throw down your knife, boy, or it will find you in the next instant."

Pandaras dropped his poniard at his feet. He said, "Death finds some more easily than others. All the waters of the Great River were not enough to drown you."

"Where is he?"

It took a great effort not to turn around. "Not here. Downriver, I think."

"Hmm. You will tell me all you know. Ah, do not bother to deny it. You know that you will. But not here, not now. I do not have time to kill all the gangsters in this city. Close the book, boy. We will bring it with us."

Pandaras said, "What happened to Azoth?"

"Is that his name? He needs it no longer. The book is dangerous, boy. It has been changed. It takes the soul of any unwary enough to look into it."

"It did not take mine," Pandaras said, taking the book from Azoth's unresisting fingers. The boy continued to stare at his empty hands. A slick of drool glistened on the brown pelt of his chin.

"Perhaps it already has taken you. We will see." Prefect Corin stepped out of the shadows by the door, the white stripe on the left side of his face catching the light from the book Pandaras held open toward him. He said, "That will not affect me. I believe that you have a token of the man I am seeking."

Pandaras could not move. The book slipped from his numbed fingers and fell at his feet. Every hair on his body rose, prickling; the muscles of his arms and legs were painfully locked.

Prefect Corin said, "You have a little talent for music, like many of your kind, so you might find it amusing to know that I hold you with a tightly focused beam of sound. It is a single note pitched higher than you or I can hear, but your muscles hear it."

He crossed the room in three strides, reached inside Pandaras's shirt and lifted out the coin. With an abrupt motion he pulled the doubled thong over Pandaras's head. He stared at the coin for a long moment, then pressed it against Pandaras's forehead.

Pandaras felt it burning there. Prefect Corin exhaled, slipped the thong back over Pandaras's head, and extended his arm toward Azoth. There was a flash of blue light; Azoth's head exploded in pink mist. The boy's body pitched forward, throwing a long spurt of rich red blood from its neck stump, kicked out twice, and lay still.

"Yamamanama has learned much," Prefect Corin said. "Or he is well advised. The coin has attuned itself to him and he has attuned it to you. You can find him by using it, or he can find you. No one else. Very well then."

Suddenly Pandaras could move again. He fell to his hands and knees and bent his head and vomited.

Prefect Corin said, "You will live, boy. Come now. With me. We have far to go, I fear."

6

The Shadow

AS EVER, DR. Dismas was there when Yama woke, and almost at once Agnitus and Enobarbus came into the room, followed by a phalanx of officers and guards. The warlord had news of another great victory, but Yama was too full of joy to pay much attention at first. He had at last found Pandaras, and had rescued him from danger and lost him, all in a few hectic minutes. Pandaras was alive, and although he seemed to have fallen into deep trouble, Yama was certain that the boy was searching for him, for he wore Oncus's fetish on his arm.

"There are great advances all across the front," Enobarbus was saying. "In only a few days Yamamanama has gained more territory than we have won in the past year."

Yama wondered if Pandaras knew that he had guided the machine which had knocked the gun from the hand of the ruffian in the alley. Yama had lost contact with the machine moments later, when the Shadow had withdrawn its control of a myriad machines along the warfront, but it did not matter. He had found Pandaras once, and he could find him again.

"Not exactly Yamamanama," Dr. Dismas told Enobarbus.

"Could this be done without him?"

"That's not the point, my dear Enobarbus."

The two men stood on either side of Yama's big, disordered bed. Yama could not move, but suddenly he had a dizzy vision of his paralyzed body from above; the Shadow had possessed one of the little machines which spun in the air, and was feeding him its optical output.

A pentad of officers with red capes falling around their battle armor stood behind Enobarbus. One of the officers was writing on a slate. Its green and white light flickered in flowing patterns tugged here and there by his stylus. Guards flanked the officers, clad from head to toe in black plastic like man-shaped beetles, their carbines held at port arms. They were there not to protect Yama, but to defend their commander in the event that Yama—or the Shadow—went mad and tried to destroy him. Enobarbus's physician, black-cloaked, gray-maned Agnitus, stood just at the edge of the field of view, as patient as a carrion crow. There were servants in the room too, young men and women in tunics and tabards of gorgeous watered silks, or in fantastic uniforms of red leather kilts, golden cuirasses inlaid with intricate designs of black mother-of-pearl and plumed helmets that almost doubled their height, armed with ornately decorated gisarmes, pole-axes and sarissas which they held grounded before them. The servants and soldiers were all indigens. Some were frog-jawed fisherfolk, others lanky, rail-thin herders. There was a single sturdy forest pygmy a third the height of the others, with glossy black skin that shone as if oiled. They were all Dr. Dismas's experimental subjects. Metal collars were embedded in their necks and their shaven scalps were marred by angry red lacerations crudely stitched with black thread. One had had the top of his skull sliced off and replaced with a disc of transparent plastic; cubes and pyramids and spheres nestled amongst what was left of his brain. He shook slightly and constantly; drool slicked his chin and stained the front of his red silk blouson.

And someone or something stood amongst the officers, guards and servants, insubstantial, shifting, barely glimpsed, the shadow of a shadow. It filled Yama with dread. He could not look directly at it, but he guessed that it was a new torment of the Shadow. Day by day it was growing stronger; day by day he was growing weaker. But now at least his hope was renewed. If he could find Pandaras again, and tell the boy where he was being held prisoner, he could at last begin to plan his escape.

Yama was paralyzed by an injection which Dr. Dismas had given him several hours before. Now, at an unseen signal, three of the servants stepped forward and tenderly lifted him from the bed and carried him to a canopied throne, propping him up amongst satin cushions. Dr. Dismas turned Yama's bare arm over, stroked a vein in the crook of his elbow until it plumped up, a river of blue blood under pale skin, then with a swift underhand motion stabbed the hypodermic needle home. Yama blacked out for a moment, and then was back in every part of his body, dizzy and cramped and sick to his stomach.

One of the servants held Yama's head while he vomited into a yellow plastic bowl. There was little but mucus to come up. Dr. Dismas took a square of linen from another servant and wiped the slick of chyme from Yama's chin as deftly and gently as a mother tending her child. Yama suffered this silently, and allowed Agnitus to probe him with hard fingers.

"As usual, he is febrile and dehydrated. Otherwise his muscle tone is good and his vital signs are stable." Agnitus stared at Dr. Dismas. "You use him hard, Doctor. At his rate he may not last the course."

Dr. Dismas met the physician's lambent gaze. "Much is asked of him. I do my best."

Enobarbus stepped up beside Agnitus. The warlord looked rumpled and tired, yet he was grinning broadly and his eyes were alive in his ruined face as he bent toward Yama. "Know that I am very pleased with you," he said. "You have done great things. I have just flown back from an advance point beyond the Marsh of the Lost Waters. The positions which our enemies have held for a year are beginning to crumble beneath the new assaults. Their machines turn against them and they are much weakened because of it. Soon we will mount a push that will take us within sight of Ophir. I promise that I will march through her gates in less than twenty days."

"You are talking to the wrong one," Dr. Dismas said impatiently. "We won't need him much longer. Not once the child of my paramour is fully integrated."

Yama looked past the warlord and his physician, trying to see the thing which stood behind them, in the midst of the officers and servants and guards. A stain in the air in the shape of a man that gradually brightened and came into focus. A familiar, patient, careworn face with a fine pelt of gray hair, long-fingered hands folded over each other beneath the chin. It was the eidolon of a dead man, of Yama's beloved stepfather, the Aedile of Aeolis.

Yama tried to turn away, but he was paralyzed once more, this time by the Shadow's will. The eidolon spoke. Its words crawled across Yama's brain like sparks over a log in a dying fire.

I am well pleased with you, my son. Do not listen to the doctor. I will not let you fade away. A part of you will always be with me.

The eidolon winked and faded. And then, horribly, Yama felt his tongue and jaw work. Something said in a hoarse, strangled voice, "I need him still, Doctor. Even when construction of the pseudocortex is complete there will be much to learn because there is much he does not yet know about himself."

Dr. Dismas leaned over and wiped Yama's cracked lips with a

sponge and squeezed a trickle of water into his mouth. "There," he said. He brushed Yama's cheeks, kneading the plaques beneath the skin with stiff fingers. "This is a frail and stubborn vessel, but I will look after it for you. I will guard it with my life."

The eidolon of Yama's dead stepfather came back, more solid than ever. *He thinks that he is our father,* it said. *He will pay for his mistake, by and by. He has wasted much time with his experiments and his foolish plots. He could have brought you to me years ago.*

Yama found that he could move again. He said, "Yes, you would have preferred to take me when I did not know who I was and what I could do because you are not as powerful as you would like me to believe."

"Ah, Yamamanama," Dr. Dismas said, standing back from the bed. "You are still there."

I grow, day by day. And day by day you shrink.

"I will not go away."

"Oh, no, dear Child of the River," Dr. Dismas said. "You are mine."

There is much we could do together, Child of the River. Why resist? We could be the ruler of this world, just as a beginning. The battles I win now will bring an end to a war ten thousand years old, but they are as nothing to those I will have to fight in the space inside the shrines after I have defeated the forces loyal to the Preservers. After that victory, she who is now our ally will try and destroy me. She will not succeed, of course, and if you help me you will learn much about the world and all the worlds beyond. She has her own plans for Confluence and soon I will possess them just as I possess you. Ask Dr. Dismas about the machinery of the keelways. Ask him about the heart of the world. The eidolon smiled, a sharp, cunning, rapacious grin that was not at all like the gentle smile of Yama's stepfather. It said, *Ask him why the Great River shrinks.*

After the Aedile had died, Yama had found amongst his papers pages of notes about the fall of the level of the Great River. The Aedile had made measurements every decad for many years, and had calculated the likely date of the beginning of the river's failure. Most believed that it had begun when the Ancients of Days had meddled with the space inside the shrines and deleted the avatars which had survived the wars of the Age of Insurrection. But the Aedile's calculations showed that the fall in the level of the Great River had begun much later, in the year that Yama had been found by old Constable Thaw, a baby lying on the breast of a dead woman in a white boat cast adrift on the Great River.

Yama could not tell if the Shadow really knew what linked these two events, or if it was merely tormenting him with its stolen knowledge, but it had touched upon his greatest fear, that he might not be the savior of the world, as so many claimed, but might instead be its unwitting nemesis. He reached out and gripped Dr. Dismas's clawlike left hand and said, "There is much we can do together, Doctor. I think that together we can save the world, but first we must stop the war."

"Ah, but we will, Yamamanama. We will." Dr. Dismas was smiling as he tried and failed to free his hand from Yama's grip. He looked at Agnitus and said, "Help me, damn you."

Help me, the eidolon said. *Ask him the question. It will cause much trouble, I promise you. I am on your side, Yamamanama. How could I not be? I depend upon you for my life and for my powers. In one sense I am becoming you. But soon things will change, and you will depend upon me. We will have to reach an agreement, or you will dwindle to no more than a remnant. Would you work with me as an equal part of a gestalt, or would you be worse than any of the good doctor's experimental subjects? I could bury you so deep that all the light and the glory of the world would be no more than a mute spark, as dim and distant as the farthest star. I could subject you to torments worse than even the good doctor can imagine, without cease. Choose.*

"He is in your care," Agnitus told Dr. Dismas, "as you delight in telling us."

"You tell us that you control him," Enobarbus said. "Sometimes I wonder how true it is. We must talk about it."

"It is the child of my paramour that controls him," Dr. Dismas said. He was still struggling to free himself from Yama's grip. "It still grows."

An age ago, Yama and his stepbrother, Telmon, had liked to listen to Sergeant Rhodean's stories about the battles at the midpoint of the world. This had been in the gymnasium of the peel-house, and the old soldier had scratched the positions and lines of attacking and opposing armies in the packed red clay of the floor with the point of an old javelin. He had taught Yama and Telmon that the best commanders overcame their enemies by wisdom as much as by force. Indeed, it was better to subdue an enemy without fighting: to enter into battle was a last resort. For that reason, knowledge of the enemy was paramount. Not just the character and strength of the opposing army, but the morale and training of its ordinary men and its officers, the severity of punishments inflicted on miscreants, the state of its supplies, the nature of the terrain it occupied, the disposition of conquered peoples toward the occupiers, and the present and predicted weather. The best policy was to understand the enemy's strategy and then to seek to undermine it, to always grasp the initiative and to be flexible, to attack where the enemy felt itself to be invulnerable and thus to bring about a decisive change. Sergeant Rhodean had shown his pupils that even a weaker force can overwhelm a strong enemy if it seizes the opportunity and strikes with precision and overwhelming momentum.

More than ever, Yama knew that he had to draw on the lessons of the kindly old soldier. He was a prisoner in the center of the empire of the heretics, surrounded by the servants and machines of Dr. Dismas and the soldiers of Enobarbus, with a jungle and armies of heretics separating him from the unconquered regions a thousand leagues up-river, and only the hope that a former pot boy could come to his rescue. Worse, he was a prisoner in his own body, struggling against the growing power of the Shadow which Dr. Dismas had introduced into his body. But now he saw that by allying himself with his most immediate threat he could exploit the divisions of those who held him prisoner.

"The keelways," he said. "Tell me the truth about how the world works, Doctor."

You are mine! The eidolon tipped back its head and howled, twisting the mild face of Yama's stepfather into something coarse and lupine. Its eyes burned with a feral red light, as if a balefire had been kindled inside its skull. The soldiers and servants around it took no notice, of course.

"The boy is fevered," Dr. Dismas said, and at last managed to wrench away from Yama's grip. He kneaded the stiff claw of his left hand with his right, as if comforting an injured pet, and smiled at Enobarbus and Agnitus. "I have him, gentlemen. I assure you."

"I belong to no one," Yama said. "Tell me about the keelways, Doctor. Tell me about the machines down there. It is possible that I can control them? Is that what you want of me, once the war is over?"

"I want nothing of you, Yamamanama," Dr. Dismas said quickly. "I have brought you here as a gift to Enobarbus, a weapon to bring a swift end to the war. Ask him what he wants. Do not ask me."

"Yet somehow he has an idea that you do want something, Dismas," Enobarbus said. "We'll talk of this, I think."

He turned and swept out of the room, his guards on either side and the pentad of officers following behind in a swirl of red capes. The eidolon moved through them like smoke and stood at Agnitus's shoulder.

I am proud of you, my child, it said. *We have already done much together, you and I, and with your help we will do much more.*

"Tell me about the machines in the keelways," Yama said. He stood up, his legs prickling with pins and needles, and limped across the room to the great blister of the window, struggling to compose his thoughts and to conceal his great excitement. If the Shadow wanted his help, then it was not as strong as it claimed. Or perhaps he was stronger, if only he knew it.

Behind him, Agnitus asked Dr. Dismas, "How great are his powers, Dismas?"

The apothecary was fitting another cigarette into his carved bone holder and did not reply until he had it lit; Yama smelled the clove-scented smoke. "He'll have been told about the keelways by the child of my paramour. Who knows what they talk about inside the skull they presently have in common? It is of no moment, Agnitus, because soon enough the boy will be redundant. Remember to tell your master that."

A black speck floated far off in the blue sky, high above the patch-work woods of the city of trees, far beyond the archipelagos of floating gardens.

Yama said, "And do not forget to tell him that I have been in the keelways, too. It was after I escaped from you the first time, Doctor. I fetched up in the Silent Quarter and entered the keelways after I got away from the poor fools you employed. I learned much, then."

The speck was a bird, perhaps, a lammergeyer which had wandered far from the slopes of the Rim Mountains. Yama watched it with grow-ing apprehension.

Dr. Dismas said dismissively, "The keelways are hardly a secret."

Agnitus said, "You did not answer my question, Dismas."

"The records are vague, a single sura in the Puranas. Yamaman-ama's bloodline built the world under instruction from the Preservers. Why should they not know all about it? But the boy is ignorant, Agnitus, brought up by a disgraced civil servant in a wretched backwater, with hardly any experience of the world. We proceed by experiment. Of course, if your master is frightened, I can leave and take the boy else-where. There are many who would be glad of his services."

"I think not," Agnitus said.

"That Enobarbus is not frightened? Or that I cannot leave? Take care, Agnitus," Dr. Dismas said sharply. "I have powerful allies."

Not a bird. It was too big to be a bird. It came on steadily. Yama could not look away from it and, although he told himself that it was only an illusion, his skin crawled with horror.

Agnitus told Dr. Dismas, "Your allies fight amongst each other even as they try to conquer the world. That is why they were defeated in the wars of the Age of Insurrection, and that is why they cannot prevail without our help. That is why you are here, Dismas. Do not forget that."

"I'll hear that from Enobarbus, not his creature."

Agnitus's laugh was a low, rumbling growl. He said, "You're a fool, Dismas. You think everyone should be owned by someone else because you are yourself something's creature."

The thing beat the air outside the great bubble of the window with wide leathery wings. It was triple-headed, and each head was set on a long, flexible neck, and their faces were triangulated upon Yama. They were brutelike distortions of the people he knew and loved and had lost: his stepfather, the Aedile of Aeolis; his stepbrother, Telmon, killed in the war against the heretics; and Tamora, the cateran who had been killed by Dr. Dismas on the stair outside the shrine cut into the edge of the world. He bore their gaze, although it was very hard. Their voices crept into his brain.

Nothing ever dies, Yamamanama. I can bring them back. Help me, and I will let them live again.

"I will serve only on my own terms."

Behind him, Dr. Dismas said sharply, "It's a last vestige, Agnitus. It will soon pass, and he will be gone forever."

Foolish creature! We do not need him. Yamamanama, or the old, broken, and insane thing which changed him. Together, we make something new in the world.

"Together," Yama said.

O yes. Together. Together, we will change everything.

The creature's human heads opened their mouths wide and blew gouts of flame which washed over the eye of the window. Yama stood his ground. It was only a foolish gesture, a sign of the Shadow's vanity. And vanity was a weakness.

The flames faded. The creature was gone. Inside Yama's skull, a voice whispered eagerly.

Soon.

7

The Ironclads

"YOU WILL GO around it," Prefect Corin told the captain of the flying platform.

"But I will not," the captain said firmly. He hung from a branch of the tree by an arm and a leg and glared unblinkingly at Prefect Corin. His eyes were large and black and perfectly round. He was smaller than Pandaras, and naked except for a tool belt. His fine silvery fur was touched with black at the tips of his ears and fingers and toes. Two decads of his crew hung from or stood on branches in the other trees at the edge of the little wood, watching silently. The captain said, "My orders I already have. You know them well, and you know that you cannot change them. This we have already discussed."

Prefect Corin spoke softly; Pandaras could hardly hear him over the throbbing of the flier's motors. He said, "You know who I am and what I can do."

The captain grinned, showing needle-sharp white teeth. "We know that this platform you can't fly. Beyond the pass no one flies, Prefect. Not while heretics hold high ground and the river."

Prefect Corin laid a hand on Pandaras's shoulder and said, "Show it to them."

Reluctantly, Pandaras drew out the ceramic coin and held it up. Little flecks and dashes of light filled it from edge to edge, scuttling about each other like busy emmets. The captain glanced at it, then shrugged.

"The device shows that the man I seek is not here," Prefect Corin said. The light of the disc set stars in the centers of his liquid black eyes. "He is farther downriver, amongst the heretics."

"From us the heretics took our city, Prefect," the captain said. "All we have left is this platform. Like to get our city back, we would, but far downriver it is, and higher than this we cannot fly. We try to go through, and from the tops of hills heretics fire down on us. Sweep us off the platform like bugs off a leaf. And the river's worse; out there they have many gun platforms floating. No, Prefect. For ourselves we can't do it, and for you we can't do it either. As far as we can we have taken you. Enough talk. To berthing we must attend."

The captain swung away into the dense green canopy. His crew turned as one and followed, disappearing in a flurry of shaken foliage.

Columns of soldiers were assembling at the debarkation points on either side of the flying platform's wide black wedge. The big fan motors at its stern roared and roared as it began to turn into the wind. To port, ranges of mountains covered in dense forest saddled away, their peaks shining in the last light of the sun above valleys full of shadows; the river stretched to starboard, gleaming like pewter. It was only a decad of leagues wide here, its deep, swift flow pinched between the mountains. An advance force of heretics was attempting to take the city which had once dominated this narrows.

Pandaras and Prefect Corin had spent a day and a night and most of the next day on the flying platform, traveling steadily toward the front line. Like all the big lifting bodies, it warped the gravity field of the world so that it floated on the wind, and motors had been added so that it could be maneuvered. It had once supported a floating garden, but the little wood at the point of the platform where the crew lived and worked was all that remained; the rest of the surface was webbed with a complex of ropes and struts to which cargo or living quarters for passengers could be anchored.

Like the troops, Prefect Corin and Pandaras slept in the open and ate at one of the campfires, although Pandaras had little appetite and hardly slept at all, fearing that if he did the platform might tilt and he would wake tumbling through the air an instant before his death. The Prefect did not seem to sleep either. All night he sat cross-legged, with his hands turned up on his knees, watching the Eye of the Preservers as it rose high into the black sky before reversing its course and setting at the downriver vanishing point of the world, and all the next day he stood at the point of the platform, staring like a perched hawk waiting for a glimpse of its prey. Now and then, Pandaras tried to strike up a conversation, but he was not so much rebuffed as ignored.

None of the troops or their officers would go near them, and Pandaras had little idea of where they were being taken. Except that it was downriver, toward the war, and toward his master. That was some comfort, at least.

The note of the motors deepened; the platform was making headway against the wind as it moved toward the shore. Prefect Corin plucked his staff from the mossy ground and walked into the darkness beneath the trees. The little machine stung Pandaras's neck and he trotted at Prefect Corin's heels. Wind whipped them as they came out of the shelter of the little wood, and Prefect Corin put two fingers to the brim of his black hat. A huge baobab tree stood at the point of the platform, webbed with cables and hung with little platforms. The crew, a single family unit, was swarming everywhere, chattering in a high, rapid patois.

The foothills of the mountains came down to the edge of the river. The city stretched along the narrow ribbon of flat land at their margin. It was in ruins. Not a single building was intact, although the grid of the streets was still visible. The stumps of several huge towers stood at the shore like a cluster of melted candles. The air swarmed with glittering clouds of tiny machines that blew back and forth above the ruined city, twisting about each other but never quite meeting. Pandaras saw that there were many burnt places, and craters of different sizes on the forested hills, and thousands of trees had been blown down along one high ridge.

The flying platform was maneuvering above the encampment of the defending army, townships of tents and domes knitted together by roads that crawled with traffic and marching columns of soldiers. Hundreds of men worked on huge machines folded into pits and surrounded by cranes and scaffold towers.

As the platform neared the ruined city, edging toward a series of flat-topped pylons, bright sparks shot up from the slopes of the foothills as if in greeting, and puffs of white smoke bloomed in the darkening sky, seemingly as innocent as daisies. A rapid popping started up somewhere beneath the platform and streams of fiery flecks curved in to the source of the display; gunners strapped in blisters on the underside were replying to the heretic bombardment.

Even as the platform was being tied down, the troops began to swarm down hundreds of ropes. Equipment was lowered in slings and nets. A disc swooped out of the dusk and came to rest a handspan beyond the point of the platform's prow. Prefect Corin took Pandaras by the arm and they stepped onto the disc, which immediately dropped toward the ground. Pandaras thought that he knew now how Prefect Corin had escaped when the giant polyps had sunk his ship. Because the disc warped gravity, there was no sensation of falling. Rather, it was as if the world tilted about the disc's fixed point and jumped forward to embrace them. Before Pandaras could begin to feel dizzy, they were down.

Prefect Corin strode off at once. Pandaras had no choice but to follow him, for the pain caused by the little machine fastened to his neck increased in proportion to its distance from its master. Prefect Corin walked quickly and Pandaras had to half-trot, half-run to keep up with him.

"This is a great shambles," he said breathlessly, dodging to one side as two columns of men in black resin armor jogged past. They were following the traffic that streamed along a wide muddy road. Crackling arc lights made islands of harsh white glare in the gathering darkness. There was noise everywhere, the braying of draft animals and the shouts of men, the roar of motors and the constant thunder of distant explosions, and snatches of wild music carried on the wind. Pandaras said, "Where have you brought me, dominie? Is this part of your plan? Will we become caterans?"

"We will not be here long," Prefect Corin said, and stepped into the dazzle of the headlights of an oncoming steam wagon and raised his staff.

The wagon slewed to a stop, belching a huge cloud of black smoke. Prefect Corin swung up on the bench by the driver and said something in his ear. Pandaras hastily clambered onto the loadbed as the wagon started up again, and was thrown amongst loosely stacked rolls of landscape cloth as it swerved away from the road and bounced across churned ground toward the battlefront.

The city had been built from land coral. Here and there patches which were still alive had thrown up spires and brainlike hummocks and had smothered one of the tower stumps in a lattice of red threads, but most of the city was dead, piled in heaps of rubble that bordered the cleared streets. Trenches had been dug everywhere, lit by dabs of foxfire or strings of red or green electric lights. Soldiers squatted around heat boxes or campfires; a few scouts stood on platforms behind sandbags, scanning the enemy lines, which were only two leagues distant.

When the wagon stopped Pandaras jumped down and trotted after Prefect Corin in near darkness. They skirted a trio of overlapping craters filled with muddy water and climbed to the top of a low rise. A series of bunkers were dug into the reverse side of the slope. A man in a long black leather coat came out of a curtained doorway and greeted the Prefect. He was the commander of the defensive forces, a lean, nervous man of Prefect Corin's bloodline. His name was Menas. A decad of little machines hovered around him; the largest shed a fitful yellow light by which Menas consulted a timepiece as large as an onion and studded with an even decad of dials.

"You are just in time, brother," Menas said, and put away his timepiece and embraced Prefect Corin. "The duel is about to begin. Listen. Do you hear the thunder?"

Pandaras had thought that it was distant artillery fire, but when he looked at where Menas pointed, he saw heavy thunderclouds rolling across the dark sky. Lightning strobed between clouds and the edge of the river.

"They manipulate the weather," Menas said. "They like to set the stage for the nightly duel. So far it is stalemate, for by the grace of the Preservers our mages have built an ironclad which is the match of their champion. Come with me. Come on! We do not have much time!"

A pentad of staff officers went with them, each followed by his own flock of little machines. Menas was filled with so much energy that he could not keep still or follow the thread of any conversation for more than a minute; he kept breaking off to run over to this or that group of soldiers, to ask how they were and where they were from and if they were ready to fight. It was clear that the soldiers loved him. All of them cheered his approach and offered him libations of beer and wine.

"We will show them this time, boys," Menas shouted. "We will push them back into the river!" He whirled about and ran back up the slope to where Prefect Corin waited. "They are in good heart," he said breathlessly. "The best men we have, the bravest fighters."

"I see no fighting here," Prefect Corin said coldly.

"Soon enough," Menas said, and once again took his complicated timepiece from his coat pocket and held it up to the light of one of the machines which hung above his head. "We satisfy their need for drama, but it is a matter of precise timing." He put away the timepiece and added more soberly, "Some day they will decide to move forward, and we will not be able to stop them."

Prefect Corin looked at Menas and said, "Perhaps you have been too close to the heretics for too long, brother."

"This is not Ys," Menas said. "This is the war, the real war. I do not tell lies to my soldiers, I tell them the truth. There are no lies here, no stories to comfort the general population. The heretic forces have grown stronger over the years, and in the last handful of days they have grown very bold indeed. I hear that things go badly in the marshes. I hear that our machines are failing there and I believe that the heretics could take this city whenever they wish, but instead they play a game with us. We can hold our present position as long as we cooperate with them. We must strive to match them. If not, there are horrors . . ."

His voice had dropped to a whisper. Pandaras shuddered, realizing that the man's hectic energy barely concealed his terror. His eyes were rimmed with red, and his hands trembled; he thrust them in the pockets of his long, black leather overcoat and leaned closer to Prefect Corin and whispered, "They bring back the dead."

Prefect Corin eyed Menas with distaste. He said, "We must cross their lines. The captain of the flying platform refused me. I hope that you will not."

Menas shrugged. "We send in scouts all the time. Sometimes they come back. Usually turned. They pass all the tests we can devise and then, a few days later, they walk into a crowded bunker and burst into flame."

Pandaras remembered the explosion in the café moments after the young woman had run into it.

Prefect Corin said, "It is not the first time I have done this."

"Things have changed. They turn our machines against us somehow. The mages cannot explain it, but at least their new devices are proof against heretic trickery. At least, for the time being."

Prefect Corin nodded. "It is because things have changed that I must cross the lines."

"There will be a scouting party going out soon, I expect. One of my staff can advise you." Menas looked at Pandaras. "Is this boy going with you? Who is he? Is he your servant?"

"He will lead me to my prize."

"I have my own reasons," Pandaras said, and dodged away when Prefect Corin struck at him with his staff. "I am a seeker after truth, like my master!"

The machine on his neck stung him hard and he cried out and fell down. Two of the staff officers laughed. Pandaras picked himself up and cursed their ancestry all the way back to the slimes from which they had been mistakenly raised by the Preservers. The machine stung him again, forcing him to run after Prefect Corin and Menas, who were walking toward a glow in the distance.

Pandaras was astonished to see that it was a shrine, a big disc standing on its edge at an intersection of two broad streets. But perhaps it was not astonishing after all, for shrines were only partly of this world, and were immune to energies that would evaporate ordinary matter.

Perhaps this place had once been the site of a temple which now lay in ruins on every side, with only its heart left intact.

Soldiers had gathered in front of the shrine, and the glow which beat from its disc made their faces shine and polished their prickly black resin corselets. Pandaras approached it reluctantly, remembering the woman in white who had appeared inside the shrine of the Temple of the Black Well. But as he followed Prefect Corin through the ranks of soldiers, he realized that this shrine was a fake, an enlarged version of the disc of cheap half-silvered glass which his mother had kept on a high shelf in their room. She had lit a candle behind it on holy days so that light moved within it like an echo of those avatars which, before the heretics had swept them away, had haunted certain shrines in the city. A similar trick was being played here, although the source of light was far brighter than a mere candle, and it was somehow bent and split so that circles of primary colors continually expanded from the brilliant white point at the center and seemed to ripple out into the darkening air.

Pandaras looked away, for he had the dizzy feeling that he might fall into the light and never escape. No doubt his master would have said that this was how the Preservers had felt as they had begun their infinite fall into the Eye, and would have constructed some keen analogy between the conditions required for prayer and the Preservers' state of grace, but the play of light simply made Pandaras nauseous.

"A little invention of the mages," Menas told Prefect Corin boastfully. "They call it an ipseorama. You do not yet have them in Ys, but the time will come soon enough. It induces a peculiar state in the nervous system of men, similar to the rapture induced by the presence of the avatars. It calms and empties the mind and prepares it for the immanence of the Preservers."

Pandaras shaded his eyes and saw that a pentad of priests was gathered to one side of the shrine. They wore robes of shaggy pelts and were crowned with high, pointed hats. One was casting incense into a brazier of glowing coals; the others shook their hands above their heads as they prayed.

Prefect Corin told Menas in his dry, forthright manner, "I have no time for silly conjurations. At best this is a foolishness; at worst it is heresy, pure and simple."

"It is a matter of regulating prayer," Menas said. The light of the ipseorama flickered over his rapt face and turned each of his machines to a little star. "Regulation is important. Just as men marching in step across a bridge can find the right harmonic to shiver it to pieces, so ten thousand prayers, properly focused and synchronized, can blaze in the minds of the Preservers. How can they refuse such a plea?"

"No man should be forced to pray; such prayers are worthless." Prefect Corin raised his staff. For a moment Pandaras thought that he would stride forward and smash the false shrine, but he merely grounded it again and said, "This is a dangerous experiment, Menas, and you will gain nothing from it."

Menas did not seem to have heard the Prefect. He said, "Regulation of prayer is as important as regulation of firepower. By calling upon the grace of the Preservers we have survived here for more than a hundred days." He cocked his head and drew out his timepiece again. "Listen! Ah, listen!"

The brassy sound of trumpets drifted across from the enemy lines, the noise doubling and redoubling in horrendous discords. Pandaras pressed his hands over his ears.

Menas shouted at Prefect Corin, "Sometimes they focus the sound! It can burst a man like an overripe fruit!" He signaled to one of the staff officers as the noise died away and told him, "They are two hundred twenty-eight seconds early tonight. Make a note. It may signify."

All around, the soldiers bent in prayer as one of the priests began to declaim a praise song. Pandaras found himself mumbling the responses with the rest of the congregation. *Now in the moment of our death is the moment of our rebirth into eternal life.* He was very scared, convinced that his last hour was at hand, angry that he had thrown away all that he had been entrusted with, that he had so badly failed his master. How could he ever have thought that he could find Yama in the middle of this madness?

The priests began to move through the ranks of kneeling soldiers, asperging them with rose water from brass censers which they whirled about them on long chains, as indigen hunters whirl bolas around their heads before letting fly at their target.

Menas set off again, shouting that there was little time. The party climbed a slope of rubble, leaning against a strengthening wind. The first fat drops of rain flew through the air, as hard as pistol shot. Menas bounded to the top and pointed. "There! The duel of the ironclads begins!"

Two leagues off, something was moving through the dark forest behind the enemy lines. Its passage, marked by a wave of toppling trees, was fitfully caught in overlapping searchlight beams. At first Pandaras thought that it must be a herd of megatheres, but then the machine reared up, twice as high as the tallest of the trees. It swayed forward, doubling its height again. As it came out of the forest, the focus of decads of lights, Pandaras saw that its sinuous body was supported by six canti-levered legs and counterbalanced by a long, spiked tail, like a snake carried by a scorpion. Smaller machines whirled about it, an agitated cloud of white sparks blowing back and forth like a flock of burning birds. Something glittered for a moment at the edge of Pandaras's vision and he dashed a hand at it with no more thought than he would give a fly, watching with rapt amazement as the ironclad lumbered on.

Dense squalls of rain drove across the ruins, striking with a sudden fury and obscuring the monstrous machine. Pandaras was soaked to his pelt in an instant and he sought shelter behind a stub of stone. As he crouched there, cold and miserable and scared, he felt a warmth spread-ing across his chest. The coin was glowing so brightly that it shone through the worn weave of his ragged shirt. He closed his fingers around it to hide its light and whispered with sudden wild hope, "Save me, master. If ever you loved me, come and save me now."

Prefect Corin and Menas were facing into the storm. The Prefect clasped the rim of his hat with one hand and gripped his staff with the other. The tail of his cloak blew out behind him. The terrible noise of the trumpets began again and fireworks shot up—real fireworks, burst-ing in white flowers beneath the low, racing clouds. Lights shone out, brilliant threads of scarlet and green that struck across the wasteland of the city and glittered on the ironclad's hide.

Something flashed in Pandaras's vision again. It was a little machine no bigger than a beetle, with a body of articulated cubes and delicate mica vanes which beat in a blur of golden light. It hovered for a mo-ment, then darted forward. Pandaras slapped at the sudden pain at the side of his neck—and with amazement found that the ward Prefect Corin had fastened there was gone.

The tiny machine flew up and described a circle around Pandaras's head. "Master," Pandaras whispered. He was astonished and afraid. Every hair of his pelt was trying to stand away from its fellows. The coin burned inside his clenched fist. "Master, it's you, isn't it? Why didn't you come before? Why did you abandon me?"

The machine's golden glow brightened for a moment; then it flicked its vanes and was gone.

Menas whirled around as fireworks rose from his own lines and yelled into the face of one of the staff officers who crouched behind him. "There is no response from the third quarter!"

The man plucked one of his machines from the air and said, "I will signal—"

Menas clapped his hands together. Rain had plastered his black pelt to his skull. He looked ready to kill everyone around him, Pandaras thought. Not because he was angry, but because he was scared, and as desperate as only a truly scared man can be. He had put so much faith in his rituals that now they ruled him completely. Menas shouted over the howl of wind and rattle of rain, "Never mind! Together or not at all! Get over there, find the officer responsible and execute him and two of his maniple chosen at random. By the black blood of the Preservers, I will have order here! Why are you waiting, man? Time is all we have!"

The officer saluted and disappeared into rainy dark. Menas wiped rain from the pelt of his face, took a deep breath, and told Prefect Corin, "We must have order here. Order and regulation."

"They have made you a puppet," Prefect Corin said.

"It is a dance." Menas lowered his voice and said, "A precisely choreographed dance on the edge of a razor blade."

Prefect Corin made no reply. Menas glanced at his timepiece and turned back to watch the advance of the heretics' monstrous machine. "Where is our fanfare, Golas?"

One of the staff officers grabbed a machine from the air and stuck it in his ear, then shook out a sheet of plastic; lines of script raced across it, glowing green like the river fire which sometimes burned in the water around the floating docks of Ys. He said in a high, trembling voice, "They are enabling now. Start up sequence in five, four, three, two, one—"

Tinny trumpets squealed discords in the distance and something the size of a small hill began to move through the squalls of rain. The heretics' ironclad doubled its pace, loping forward as eagerly as a hound scenting its prey and lashing its spiky tail from side to side. Its footsteps sounded like thunder. The stones beneath Pandaras's rump trembled.

The second ironclad was squat and armored like a turtle, and pounded along on a hundred stumpy legs. Things like flies danced in the air above it—no, they were men riding floating discs. They slipped sideways and vanished into the darkness as the ironclads closed the distance between themselves.

They met like two mountains colliding. The heretics' scorpion-snake sidestepped the turtle's rush and lashed it with its armored tail. The tremendous blow slewed the turtle half-around. It stood its ground when struck a second time, and fans of metal unfolded along the edges of its shell. Everything seemed to happen in slow motion.

"The vanes are tipped with diamond," Menas told Prefect Corin. "They vibrate, and will cut the enemy's legs from beneath it. Watch."

"I have seen enough," Prefect Corin said, and extended his arm.

For a moment, a thread of light split the dark air above the ruined town. It touched the heretics' ironclad and a ball of flame blossomed, doubling and redoubling in size. The machine broke in two. The upper part toppled forward, writhing as it fell, and smashed down across the broad back of the turtle. The ground shook and there was a noise like the hinge of the world slamming shut. Heat washed across the ruins as if a furnace door had been opened, blowing rain aside.

Then darkness. A rush of cold air swept in and the rain came back with redoubled fury. The searchlights had gone out; the last of the fireworks burst and their sparks fell and faded. And then, raggedly at first, but steadily growing, gunfire started along the fronts of the opposing armies.

Menas screamed in fury, turning to one officer after another, shouting that they must kill the traitor. He meant Prefect Corin, who held something like a polished pebble in his upturned hand. It was an energy pistol: a real one, an old one, a hundred times more powerful than the hot light pistols made in the Age of Insurrection.

The Prefect put the pistol away, said softly, "I have ended it," and made an abrupt gesture.

The machines around Menas and his officers dropped from the air.

"Go now," Prefect Corin said. "You are done here."

The officers walked away without a word. Menas chased after them, the wings of his black leather overcoat flapping around him, then ran back and started hurling handfuls of mud at Prefect Corin, screaming incoherently.

Prefect Corin ignored him. He bent over Pandaras and said, "Follow me," and walked off down the hill toward the burning machines.

Pandaras looked at Menas, who had fallen to his knees and turned his face up to the rain. "I'm sorry, master," he said, and ran after Prefect Corin. He did not want to find a way through the battlefield on his own.

Prefect Corin walked steadily down the middle of what had been a wide avenue. Pandaras scampered along close behind him, as if his shadow was some kind of protection. White threads flicked out from the heretics' lines and fire blossomed wherever they touched. Things moved to and fro behind flaring sources of light—things like giant insects, all jointed legs and tiny bodies. A lucky shell hit one; its body blew in a flare of greasy yellow light and then threw out a second explosion that for a moment lit the entire battlefield and turned every falling raindrop into a diamond.

Chains of little bomblets walked back and forth across the ruins;

Pandaras threw himself flat when one whistled down close by and blew a fountain of earth and land coral slivers into the air, but Prefect Corin merely kneeled, with his hand holding the brim of his hat, then got up and walked on.

Pandaras said, "Where are we going?"

"Through their lines."

"You meant this to happen!"

"The confusion will help us."

"Menas will lose the city."

"We seek a greater prize, boy." Prefect Corin stared into Pandaras's face for a moment and said, "Yes, you know it," and abruptly cut to the left and climbed a slope of rubble where in its dying throes a mass of coral had thrown up a glade of smooth white spikes twice Pandaras's height, like a parade of soldiers frozen forever, or the pieces of a game of chess abandoned halfway through.

Lights flickered and flared all around, from the pinpoint flashes of rifles and carbines to the glare of energy weapons and the brief burning flowers of mortar and bomblet explosions. Soldiers were advancing through the ruins toward the heretic positions. Phalanxes of myrmidons marched in perfect formation, not even hesitating when mortar fire blew holes in their ranks. The officers who controlled them swooped overhead on floating discs. Toward the rear, armored vehicles rumbled forward in a line a league long. Amidst the thunder of explosions came the sound of trumpets, a slow drumbeat, and the screams of men and beasts. Pandaras's fear grew as he watched Prefect Corin scanning the battlefield with what appeared to be perfect self-control, satisfied by the carnage and confusion he had caused by a single shot. And then Pandaras saw something which gave him a small measure of hope. High above, in the distance, a small golden spark hung beneath the racing rain clouds.

"Come to me, master," Pandaras whispered. "Save me."

But the spark did not move. Perhaps it was afraid that Prefect Corin would knock it out of the air if it came too close.

Prefect Corin pointed with his staff at some weakness in the heretics' line, then saw that Pandaras was not looking at him. He came over and squatted down and said, almost kindly, "We will walk straight through this. We count for nothing in the battle, and so we will be safe. Do you understand me?"

"I know that you are mad."

"No. All this around us is madness, certainly. And Menas is mad, too—he has to be mad to be able to function at all—but I am quite sane. If you wish to survive, you must follow me."

"If we wait here, then the heretics will come to us."

"It is not the heretics we are seeking." Prefect Corin's hand suddenly shot out and gripped the side of Pandaras's neck. "He was here. Do not deny it. I know that he was here because he has taken away the ward."

Pandaras shook his head a fraction. He wanted to look up, to appeal to that golden spark, but to do so would be to betray his master. Instead he stared straight into Prefect Corin's black eyes as the man's grip tightened on his neck.

"You will tell me," Prefect Corin said. "By the Preservers you will tell me or I will squeeze out your miserable life . . ." He had lifted his other hand above his head. Now he lowered it, and let go of Pandaras's neck. He said, "I know that he was here. You could not have removed the ward by yourself. Think hard about whether you want to survive this, boy. If you tell me how Yamamanama removed the ward it might be possible. We both want the same thing. We both want to rescue him."

Pandaras rubbed his bruised neck. He said, "I believe that we have different ideas about my master's fate."

Prefect Corin drew a length of cord from his tunic and tied one loop around Pandaras's wrist and another around his own. "We are joined," he said. "For better or worse we are joined hand to hand, fate to fate. Let nothing put us asunder." He stood up, jerking hard on the cord so that Pandaras was forced to rise too. "There are threads of plastic through the cord," Prefect Corin said. "They can dull the keenest blade, and they have a certain low intelligence. Try to tamper with the knot and it will tighten its grip, and by and by cut off your hand."

The cord which hung between them was no longer than the Prefect's arm. It would have to be enough. Pandaras turned right when the Prefect turned left, threw himself around a smooth spike of land coral so that the cord was stretched across it, and shouted into the rainy dark. "Now, Yama! If you have ever loved me! Now!"

The spike shuddered and Pandaras fell backward. He picked himself up at once. The cord hung from his wrist. It had been cut in half. Something with a dying golden glow was buried in a splintered crater in the land coral. Prefect Corin was bent over, his right hand pressed to his left eye. Blood ran down his cheek and dripped from the point of his jaw.

Pandaras took to his heels. He heard Prefect Corin shouting behind him, but did not look back. He turned right and left at random through the maze of land coral spikes, always choosing the narrowest path. The land coral had spread through the rubble downslope, forming a maze of arches and tunnels and caves. Pandaras scrambled down a narrowing funnel of rough stone, splashed through a bubble half full of stinking water, slid down a chute of stone slick as soap, and landed breathlessly at the edge of a road.

All around was the sound of giants walking the land. Flashes lit the underbellies of the sagging clouds. A big machine covered in spines skittered by in the distance. Whips of light flicked from its tiny head and raised pillars of fire and smoke wherever they touched. Pandaras picked himself up and ran on. He did not doubt that Prefect Corin would do everything in his power to find him.

There was a slow and steady drumbeat ahead, the crack and whir and whistle of rifle pellets and arbalest bolts all around. Suddenly soldiers were running down the road toward Pandaras. He raised his hands above his head, feeling as broad and wide as a house. But the soldiers were running full tilt in retreat and went straight past him. One, his dirty yellow face narrow as a knife blade, turned and yelled, "The dead! The dead!" and then they were gone.

Pandaras stopped. He was at a crossroads. Rubble slumped at its four corners. Rain poured down out of a black sky, intermittently lit by white and red and green threads of light. The slow, muffled drumbeat was coming closer. He could not tell where it was and chose a direction at random and ran. Prefect Corin had taken his poniard; Pandaras missed it like a lost arm. The Prefect had the copy of the Puranas, too. All Pandaras had left was the fetish which the leader of the fisherfolk had given Yama, the ceramic coin, and his life.

Something flashed overhead and hit the long street ahead. Pandaras stopped, heartsick.

Far down the street, a column of naked men was marching stiffly in time to the slow, steady beat of a drum. Most of the men were horribly mutilated. Silvery spikes jutted from the tops of their skulls. One was headless, and the spike jutted from his breastbone instead.

It was a maniple of the dead, come back to fight their living comrades.

A sudden blade of fire blew a land coral formation to fiery ruin to the left flank of the column. Some brave gunner was trying to find the range. A handful of the naked dead fell and were trampled by their unheeding companions. Pandaras ran to the right. He scrambled over the crest of a slope and tumbled into a sandbagged pit where two soldiers stared at him in horror. One swung the bell-like muzzle of his balister toward Pandaras, and then there was a wave of earth and fire which tore the world away.

8

In Dreams

AS ALWAYS, WAKING was the worst time. An escape from the horrors of dreams which were neither true dreams nor truly his into the reality of captivity and the wait for the prick of Dr. Dismas's needle and the antidote to the drug which paralyzed his body.

This time he woke not from nightmares but from a reverie woven from memories of the first of his adventures. For a happy moment, he thought that he was safe in the tower at the edge of the City of the Dead, deep in the foothills of the Rim Mountains. He had been brought there so that the curators of the City of the Dead, Osric and Beatrice, could tend his wounds. He had been very sick then, but he was even sicker now. He woke, expecting to see the hunting scene painted on the wooden ceiling of his little room and perhaps Beatrice's time-worn, kindly face, but found that he could not open his eyes. With a sharp pang of despair he remembered where he was; but then he remembered what he had done and felt his happiness well up again.

The Shadow was talking with Enobarbus. Yama had grown used to the way it carelessly used his body, and did not bother to listen to the long list of the atrocities which it was describing in gloating detail. That was not important. The battlegrounds along the river were no more than nightmares; the struggle of dominance of his own body was more immediate. From now on, he must be constantly alert, always ready to resist the Shadow's advances. For the first time, he began to think that he might be able to escape.

Yama had ceded much to the Shadow while concentrating on the search for Pandaras, but he had at last found Pandaras for the second time, on a battlefield at the far edge of the war and the prisoner of

Yama's old enemy, Prefect Corin, who had somehow survived the destruction of his ship by the giant polyps. Not only had Yama rescued Pandaras again, even though it had meant destroying the machine he had been using, but he was certain that the boy had guessed who had helped him, for he had called to him by name. Yama had tried to kill or at least seriously wound the Prefect by the same stroke which had freed Pandaras, but it occurred to him now that perhaps that had not been wise. He was certain that Prefect Corin was searching for him, and Sergeant Rhodean had taught him that in the right circumstances the strength of one enemy can be used against another.

The Shadow finished its boasting, and Enobarbus told Dr. Dismas that there were important matters which they must discuss.

"I am always at your service," Dr. Dismas said. "After all, I am not allowed to leave this place."

"Is the boy asleep?"

"He pretends to be, but I think he is not. Shall I administer the antidote?"

"No. Leave him. We will talk outside."

After Dr. Dismas and Enobarbus had left the room, the Shadow manifested itself in Yama's inner sight: a faint fluttering star growing slowly larger and becoming a bird, a luminous white dove fluttering through infinite darkness and suddenly changing again, a human figure now, pale hair fluttering around her face as she raised her head to look at him.

Yama found that he could open his eyes, but she was still there, leaning over him. His sweetheart, Derev. Her feathery hair was brushed back from her shaven forehead and caught in a plastic clasp. The finely carved blade of her face, her large black eyes, the soft lips of her small mouth pursed in the beginning of a smile. When she spoke, her words burned in his brain.

They are talking about us.

"Why do you never show your true self?"

Derev raised her slim arms above her head in a graceful movement, the swell of her small breasts lifting under her shift.

Is this repellent to you? I thought it would please you. I can remove this garment—

"Do as you wish. It is not a true representation, so it does not matter."

The eidolon paused, one hand on the shoulder clasp of its shift. For a moment, Derev's face seemed to be filmed over with something nauseating.

That is true. You did not sleep with her although you very much wanted to. An odd denial, since you lost your virginity to a whore, and then slept with the cateran—

"That is in the past. I look forward to the future when I will be reunited with Derev. I promised her that I would return when I had discovered the truth about my bloodline, and now I have learned more about myself than I care to know."

Must I remind you of our relationship? Do not think that you are better than me, Yamamanama, or stronger, or more intelligent.

"Of course not. You do not need to remind me. But although you are better than me in every way, you still need me."

For the moment.

"You are still very young. You are still learning. There is much that I can teach you."

I will soon know all you know.

"Perhaps, but mere facts are useless if you do not know how to use them."

I control thousands of machines at once. You can control only one, and that badly.

"I wondered if you knew what I was doing."

I could prevent it. I could blind and deafen you. Be thankful for my mercy.

"I mean no harm by it. I grow bored while you are off fighting the war."

Yet you have never used a machine to find out about the place where we are held.

"That is because I was afraid that Dr. Dismas would discover my little trick."

Fortunately, I have no such fears. I have learned much about this place, and I have discovered that we are in danger. Enobarbus does not trust us. Nor does he trust Dr. Dismas.

"I know that Enobarbus is frightened of you. What are he and Dr. Dismas talking about?"

Listen.

The eidolon of Derev and the brightly lit room faded into a view from somewhere above the tops of the trees which surrounded the grassy glade in which Dr. Dismas and Enobarbus stood, with Enobarbus's guards in their black armor on one side and Dr. Dismas's mutilated servants on the other. The sun was directly overhead. It was noon. A bird was singing somewhere, a cascade of falling notes repeated over and over.

"He will become something glorious," Dr. Dismas was saying. "Something wonderful, if he is allowed. What he is now—that's nothing. A few silly tricks."

"He is already a fearsome weapon," Enobarbus said, baring his strong white teeth. The warlord held his ruined face at a proud angle. His mane was a tawny cascade tied back over one broad shoulder. He said, "Without their machines, the armies ranged against us have no protection against our own machines and we can move our troops without detection. The long stalemate is over at last. We are grateful, Dismas. You must know that. You have this fine palace, these servants, these riches. You have your laboratories and your experiments. I do not approve of what you do, of course. I think it cruel, perhaps even mad. But you are free to do it."

"He is a larva at the moment, no more. Let him grow. Let him shed his present form and achieve his full potential. He will sweep all before him. He will be terrible, mighty . . . You cannot imagine it. Sometimes I think that even I cannot imagine it. Give him the metals, the rare earths . . ."

"No, I think not. But what else do you need? If it is in my power I will grant it at once. After all, you have delivered a prize beyond compare. Perhaps more experimental subjects," Enobarbus said. "I do not think your experiments are going as well as you would like."

Dr. Dismas lit a cigarette. "You surround me with spies, with men and women who pretend to be here to help me but who are, in plain truth, the wardens of this prison. It is amazing that I have done any work at all. The few creatures I have created are botched, it's true, but they are a beginning. I need more time and I cannot have it while fighting your war for you. Let the boy complete his transformation. He will become something that will amaze us all."

"I do not need to be amazed. I need to rely on those who fight for me. I must have this, Dismas. I must have control."

"You could have a sudden end to this long war. I offer you victory, complete and unqualified."

"But not, perhaps, on my terms."

"My paramour and its associates fight for the same cause as you, my dear Enobarbus. They are your allies, but they are not yours to command. The same applies to me. I am not subject to the orders of your officers, and I wish they would not interfere with my work. I hide nothing from them, yet they act as if I do."

"You should stop pretending to be human, Dismas. You should

acknowledge your true nature. People will not trust you as long as you pretend to be what you are not."

Dr. Dismas said sulkily, "We are both creatures of forces greater than ourselves. You fear my paramour because it is so much more powerful than the aspect of the dead woman which you worship. Look at what I have done, at his bidding. Look at how well the war goes. If not for the boy—"

"He has helped. I will not deny it. But we were winning anyway, Dismas. Besides, the war is not important. We did not start it, and we reluctantly entered into it only to save ourselves. The truth which Angel brought to the world is more important than the war."

"Because of this so-called truth you will have no troops, by and by. The newly changed will fight at first, to be sure, but soon enough they are consumed by this precious individuality of yours. They lose interest in everything but themselves."

"Many still fight," Enobarbus said softly. His deep voice was like the rumble of a great cat.

"O, when anyone can choose anything then of course some choose to fight. But not as many as you would like, eh? And as you progress upriver there are fewer and fewer unchanged bloodlines for you to recruit."

"It is not the war that is important," Enobarbus said stubbornly, "but the truth we have to bring to everyone on Confluence. We had begun to spread it long before the war began. Everyone will recognize it once the mindless worship of the dead past is overthrown."

"You speak of truths," Dr. Dismas said. "She blinds you to the truth."

"She revealed herself to me seventeen years ago," Enobarbus said. "I have followed her ever since. Perhaps you would like more books, Dismas. There are whole libraries at your disposal, if only you would show more cooperation."

"My paramour was once one of the masters of this world. Many of its kind were destroyed and the rest are scattered, yet they remember more than is written in all the books in all the libraries of the world. Books are nothing. Angel should not have destroyed the remaining avatars. That was the first mistake, but it was made a long time ago and there is nothing to be done about it. The second mistake is to keep the boy as he is. Let him grow. I admit that he once tried to destroy her, but he was not mine then. Now I can control him, whatever he becomes, because he is my son."

Enobarbus said, slowly and gravely, "The avatars tried to destroy her. She had no choice but to fight back. Besides, she merely finished what was begun long ago. Most of the avatars were destroyed in the Age of Insurrection, by the things you claim as friends."

Dr. Dismas snapped up from his habitual stoop like a startled click-beetle, his yellow eyes gleaming in his sharp-featured face. He exclaimed grandly, "But why are we arguing, when we both desire the same thing!"

Enobarbus said, "I have no desire to argue, Dismas. As you say, we are on the same side. But you cannot do as you will. The boy and the thing you grow inside him are powerful, and because they are powerful, they are dangerous. Already they have accomplished much, and I see no need for them to grow more powerful. They must be contained."

"A simple solution of certain rare earths. I delivered the formula days and days ago."

"They are already powerful enough, Doctor. Do as you will with your experimental subjects, but do no more to the boy or to the thing inside him."

"We fight side by side against the same enemy," Dr. Dismas said angrily. "Once that enemy is defeated, will you still try and tell me what to do?"

He turned and strode off through the trees, followed by his servants. Enobarbus gestured to his physician and said, "We must decide how this problem can be resolved, Agnitus."

The gray-maned physician said, "His metabolism is not unusual, my lord. It is a simple matter—"

Enobarbus shook his great maned head. "Not here," he said. "Remember that the boy controls machines."

"You were listening," Dr. Dismas said in Yama's ear. The sunny glade vanished. Dr. Dismas was looking down at him. Sweat was sprinkled on the apothecary's forehead, islands of droplets scattered amongst the plaques of his disease. He said, "I saw the machine. You had it fly high up, so that it would be lost in the glare of the sun, but I saw it all the same." Fondness softened his voice. "How sly. How sweet. Awake, Yamamanama! Awake, my sly, sweet boy! You have been the agent of another glorious victory in this ridiculous war! Awake!"

Three servants lifted Yama from the bed and carried him to the canopied chair, arranging his paralyzed body amongst its cushions.

Dr. Dismas said, "Don't worry about Enobarbus. He is nothing, mere noise. We'll have no more need for him soon enough. I have plans . . ." He turned away from Yama and raised his voice. "But I will not talk of that, surrounded as I am by spies!"

Yama said, "Are you speaking to me, Doctor, or to the thing inside me?"

"I soon won't need to make a distinction. Men like to think that their minds are separate from their bodies. It is central to the creed of the heretics, for otherwise they could not contemplate attempting to live forever. You make the same mistake, Yamamanama, but I'll soon show you just how wrong you are."

"After the city of Aeolis was burned, some of its citizens blamed me. They set me on a funeral pyre and would have burnt me to death, but I was rescued by termites which sucked my would-be executioners into the ground. I thought that I had somehow called upon the termites to help me, but I know now that it was the Shadow, the thing you put inside me. It was saving itself. When I fell to the ground it tried to eat as many termites as it could find. The termites were partly machine, and it wanted the metals in their bodies to feed its growth."

"I have never underestimated your intelligence, Yamamanama, but don't think that it will save you. I am your only hope. I'll get those rare earths for you. Then you will understand that there is no distinction between mind and body. But now you must exercise and eat, because in an hour you must sleep again. The war goes faster and faster, and no matter how much Enobarbus denies it, you are central to it."

Derev stood at Dr. Dismas's shoulder. She opened her mouth impossibly wide to show rows and rows of serrated white teeth and a rough red tongue that uncoiled from her mouth like a snake, glistening with saliva.

I will grow such teeth that will eat you whole, little one. We will be one flesh, one blood. There will be nothing that we cannot do.

9

The Lazaret

PANDARAS AWOKE TO darkness and a confining pressure across his whole body. His left hand hurt horribly. He thrashed up, thinking that he was still buried, and found that the pressure was only a blanket which slipped to his waist, and that the darkness was not absolute, but punctured here and there by the glow of little lamps which slowly and solemnly swung to and fro like the pendulums of so many clocks. The whole world was rocking like a cradle. From all sides came the sound of men breathing or sighing. Someone was sobbing, a slow hiccoughing like the dripping of a faucet.

Pandaras reached for his left hand with his right . . . and could not find it. He patted at the coarse blanket that lay over his legs, as if he might discover it lying there like a faithful pet. He was still very sleepy, and did not understand what was wrong.

Something moved on the floor by his bed. He froze, thinking that Prefect Corin must be hiding there. But it was a larger man who reared up from the shadows, pale-skinned and flabby, and wearing only a pair of ragged trousers.

"Little master," the man said in a soft, hoarse voice. "Be quiet. Lie down. You are wounded and ill. You must rest."

It was Tibor. Pandaras did not feel any surprise. He said, "What have they done to me?"

Tibor made him lie down, and then told him all he knew. The two soldiers in the trench had not been badly hurt by the stray mortar round. They had dug themselves out and carried Pandaras to the lazaret, but by the time one of the chirurgeons had seen him the cord around his wrist had tightened so much that it had almost disappeared into his flesh.

The hand had been too long without blood, and the chirurgeon had had to finish what the cord had begun.

"It was worth it to gain my freedom," Pandaras whispered. "In any case, many say that we do not have hands, but only the clawed feet of animals. For that reason we have learned to let our tongues do most of the work."

He must make light of it, he felt, for he seemed to be at the brink of a great black pit. If he fell into it there might never be an end to despair. He struggled to sit up again, and said, "It was worth it, Tibor, but we must not stay here. He will find me and I will not have that. We must leave—"

"Quiet, little master," the hierodule said. "You are very ill, and so are all those around you. You have been treated, and now you must sleep. The longer you sleep the better chance you have of living."

Pandaras summoned up all the strength he had. "Fetch my clothes," he commanded. "If I stay here I will have sacrificed my hand for nothing, and I could not bear that."

His clothes were tied in a bundle at the foot of the cot. Tibor helped him dress; twice he reached for toggles with his left hand, which was not there. "I have a whole set of new tricks to learn," he said. And then, with sudden panic, "The fetish! The fetish and the coin! Where are they? Were they thrown away? I must have them!"

Tibor hooked two fingers into the pocket of Pandaras's ragged shirt and drew out the coin, strung on its loop of leather, and the circlet of coypu hair and seed pearls.

"It is all I have, Tibor," Pandaras said. He grasped the coin and it blazed so brightly that it hurt his eyes. "He is close!" he cried. He kissed the burning coin, hung it around his neck and, with a thrill of disgust, slipped the fetish over his bandaged stump. "There. I have nothing else, for Prefect Corin took the book, and I have paid for my lodging with my hand. We are ready to go."

"Where will you go, little master?"

"We will find my master. The coin will lead us. You cannot easily escape me again, Tibor. I had to lose a hand to find you, and it is only fair that you stand at my left side from now on."

Tibor said gently, "It is my duty to tend to the sick and wounded, young master."

"And I am certainly wounded."

"You are but one of many. Many sick, and many wounded. Many need me, young master."

"But I am foremost in your affections, I hope." Pandaras felt a trifle dizzy. The floor seemed to pitch and sway beneath him. He sat down on the edge of the cot, but the sensation did not go away.

"Someone else needs me, little master," Tibor said, and padded away into the darkness. His naked back and hairless head shone beneath the arc of a swinging lamp and then he was gone. Pandaras lay down, just for a little while, and was woken by Tibor, who was once again squatting beside the cot. It was as if a measure of whiteness had been poured into the darkness all around, not banishing it, but making it a little less absolute.

Tibor was smoking a cigarette. Pandaras twiddled the fingers of his right hand in the air and asked for a puff of it.

"You do not smoke, little master. Besides, although you are ill, you do not need this kind of medicine."

"If I am as ill as you say then what more harm can it do? And if I'm not ill, as I claim, then it will calm me down. My stepfather, the first one, the one I don't like to talk about, he was a great smoker. A few more lungfuls of smoke will do no harm."

Pandaras was very tired, but in a minute, if only the world would stop its slow way, in a minute he would get up and walk out of here. He did not care if Tibor chose to follow him or not. Prefect Corin would surely be looking for him. He had to go. He had to find his master . . .

Tibor placed the wet tip of the cigarette in Pandaras's fingers and helped him guide it to his mouth. The smoke was sweet and cloying. Pandaras choked on the first mouthful and coughed it out, but got the second down to the bottom of his lungs and slowly, luxuriously, exhaled.

"You see," he said, "it makes me much calmer."

Tibor took the cigarette away and said, "Then our bloodlines are very alike in their chemistries, little master, because that is why my people smoke. It helps us to accept our condition." He drew on the cigarette; its brightening coal put two sparks in his large, black eyes. "If not for this, I would have killed myself as a pup, as I think would all of my kind. And so my bloodline would have died out long ago, without the chance to purge its sin. The Preservers are both merciful and just, for when they made this world they set upon it the herb from which this tobacco is made, which allows my bloodline to endure its infamy and universal enslavement."

"I thought it was just a habit," Pandaras said sleepily. He did not resist when Tibor began to undress him.

"It is a habit of life, young master, like breathing. We need cigarettes as much as you need air."

"We must escape. We must cross the lines of the enemy."

"We have already done so, little master. Sleep now. If you can sleep, then it is a sign that you can begin to get well. Those too sick to sleep always die, in my experience. But I do not think you will die."

"I want—"

But Pandaras was too tired to complete the thought, and he slept.

———

Day by day Pandaras grew stronger, and at last he was strong enough to realize how sick he had been. He had been sicker than most of those around him. When he was at last able to sit up and take notice of his surroundings, in the late afternoon of the sixth or seventh day of his confinement, he saw that this part of the lazaret was empty except for himself and a heavily bandaged man three cots over in the same row. A machine like a cat-sized mosquito squatted over the bandaged barrel of the man's chest, circulating his blood through loops of clear tubing; his breathing was ragged and loud.

The coin was no brighter, but the dots and dashes of light within it were more active than ever, scurrying to new patterns, freezing for only a heartbeat, and scurrying about again. Pandaras watched for hours, trying to understand their dance.

In the night, the man tended by the mosquito-machine suffered some kind of crisis. He was taken away amidst a flurry of chirurgeons and charge hands. Pandaras lay awake for hours afterward, but the man did not return.

The next morning, Pandaras was taken up on deck by Tibor, and saw at last what the hierodule had been trying to tell him. The lazaret was traveling downriver. It had been taken by the heretics.

At the Marsh of the Lost Waters, the Great River divided into many shallow, sinuous, slow-moving streams. The lazaret was following one of these. It was less than a league across, and stained red-brown with silt. Trees grew densely on either side, half-submerged in the sluggish current, their leaves vivid green in the bright sunlight. The sun burned off the water. It was very hot and very humid. Pandaras broke into a sweat at the slightest exertion and he was content to sit with Tibor under an awning of crimson silk, listening to one or another of the discussion classes which were part of the process the heretics called Re-Education and Enlightenment.

The lazaret was a barge as wide and flat as a field. A flying bridge crowned its blunt bow; gun emplacements nestled like seeds at regular

intervals along its sides; a decad of pods which housed reaction motors
swelled at its stern. A pentad of machines followed its wide wake as
birds might follow a fishing boat. They were as fat as barrels and entirely black, with clusters of mobile spines fore and aft. They made a
slow fizzing sound as they moved through the air. Sometimes one would
break off and make a wide slow loop above the forest canopy before
rejoining its fellows. At night they were each enveloped in a faint red
nimbus, like a constellation of halo stars.

There were other machines too. Small silvery teardrops that zipped
from one place to another like squeezed watermelon seeds; black angular things like miniature mantids that stalked the white-scrubbed, tar-
caulked planks of the deck on long, thin legs. And a thing of jointed
cubes and spheres that was slung in a hammock on the bridge, close to
the huge wheel that, manned by three sailors, controlled the barge's
rudders. The plastic casings of its components had once been white, but
were now stained and chipped. It was a very ancient machine, Pandaras
learned, and it had control of the barge; many of the smaller machines
were slaved to it. It seemed that these machines were not the servants
of the world, as in Ys, but were the equals of or even superiors to the
flesh-and-blood heretics.

The soldiers who guarded the prisoners and otherwise manned the
barge were of a recently changed bloodline from the lower slopes of
the Rim Mountains. They were a tall, muscular people covered in thick
white fur. They wore only elaborate harnesses of leather straps and
buckles and pouches. Their narrow faces, with long muzzles and small
brown eyes that peered from beneath heavy brow ridges, were as black
and wrinkled as old leather, and all were heavily tattooed with silvery
swirls and dots. They called themselves the Charn or the Tchai. Although of a single bloodline and a single culture, they were divided into
two distinct tribes which, by taboo, never intermarried: one herded lla-
mas and goats in the birch forests; the other hunted in the wilderness
of rock and snow above the tree-line. Pandaras, who still believed that
he had the right to talk with anyone, discovered that they had a rich
store of tragedies concerning star-crossed lovers from the two tribes,
and blood feuds which lasted for generations. To their amusement, he
elaborated several versions of his own upon these eternal themes.

The white-furred guards did not like the close, fetid heat. When
they were not patrolling the deck, they sprawled in front of electric fans,
their red tongues lolling. They were a short-tempered people, and the
heat made them even more irritable. Those officers captured with the
lazaret had already been killed, but the guards would sometimes make

the prisoners line up, pluck someone from the ranks at random, and execute him. One night, one of the guards went mad and tried to storm the bridge. There was a brief but furious firefight before he was shot. More than thirty prisoners were killed or wounded in the crossfire; all were unceremoniously tipped over the side for the caymans and the catfish.

Pandaras asked Tibor why he had not been executed when the lazaret had been captured. "You're something like a priest, neh? I think that it would make you more dangerous than any officer."

Tibor scratched at the long, vertical scars of his chest while he thought about this. At last he said, "I am only a slave, little master. I am not a leader of men. Besides, the heretics believe that to convert one such as me is a great prize."

"Surely there were other hierodules working in the lazaret when it was captured? But I see no others now."

"They fled, little master. But I could not leave you."

"You know that I am not your master, Tibor!"

The hierodule did not reply.

Pandaras tried a new argument. "I am grateful that you are here, Tibor. But as an equal. As a friend."

"You could not be a friend to one such as I, little master. What am I? Lower than a worm, because my ancestors took the side of the feral machines during the Age of Insurrection."

"You are a man, Tibor. As much a man as anyone here. Don't put the burden of your life on my head."

Again Tibor did not reply. He took out a little plastic pouch from the waistband of his trousers and, with maddening slowness, began to roll a cigarette.

———

Only the weakest and most seriously wounded prisoners lay in the close heat and stink of the black air below deck. The rest camped under awnings rigged from brightly colored canvas or silk and scattered across the broad deck of the barge like flowers strewn across a field. They took turns to trawl for fish and shrimp, which were shredded and added to the cauldrons of sticky rice or maize porridge, but most of their waking hours were taken up with Re-Education and Enlightenment.

The discussion classes formed just after dawn, and often continued beyond sunset. Although the prisoners were told that the classes were voluntary, everyone knew that those who refused to take part were likely to be chosen by the guards for execution. They reminded Pandaras of the penny school he had occasionally attended as a cub. His education had ended when his father had disappeared, for the man his mother had married after that had refused to waste money on luxuries like learning. It had been no great loss. Pandaras had always hated the stifling atmosphere of the school, and the rote recitations of the Puranas which had taken up much of the time had for him almost killed their beautiful and terrible stories. He did not mind that he was unlettered, for his people had always kept their stories and songs in memory rather than on paper—"written in air rather than on stone," as their tradition had it, for what was forgotten did not matter, and that which was of value was kept alive in the mouths and instruments of a thousand singers long after the unmourned death of the author.

The classes contained between four and forty prisoners, and each was led by a pedagogue. These were all of the same round-faced, gray-skinned bloodline, from a city several hundred leagues downriver which had achieved enlightenment, as they called it, early in the war. Most—they proudly admitted it—were no more than children, so young that they had yet to determine their sex. They were a small race, smaller even than Pandaras. They dressed in loose black tunics and trousers, and their glossy black hair was tied back in elaborate pigtails with scraps of white silk. They ruled the prisoners with an iron will. Those who walked away from the discussion classes in disgust or anger were immediately chased by the pedagogues, who screamed at them and whipped them around the ankles with sharp bamboo canes; those who did not return or who tried to fight back were taken away by the guards, shot, and kicked over the side.

At first, Pandaras had a great deal of trouble understanding what the pedagogues were trying to teach him. He sat next to Tibor in the sweltering heat in a kind of stupor, his stump throbbing under a slithery, quasi-living dressing which absorbed the discharges of blood and pus, and which Tibor changed twice a day. His head ached from the ever-present odor of burnt fish-oil from the barge's reaction motors and the sunlight which reflected in splinters from the river and, most of all, from the high, sing-song cadences of the pedagogue as it urged, cajoled, corrected and harangued its charges.

Each morning the discussion classes started with a chant of the slogan of the heretics. *Seize the day!* It echoed out across the river, sometimes lasting no more than a minute, sometimes lasting for an hour, becoming as meaningless as breathing but always ending at the same moment in all the classes scattered across the barge's broad deck.

After that came the long hours of argument in which the pedagogues set out some trivial truth and used it as a wedge to open a door onto a bewildering landscape. It seemed to Pandaras that everything was allowed except for that which was forbidden, but it was difficult to know which was which because there were no rules. The other prisoners had the same problem, and all their objections and expressions of bafflement were met by the same answer.

"You do not see," the pedagogue would say in its sweet, high-pitched voice, "because you cannot see. You cannot see because you have not been allowed to see. You have not been taught to see. You are all blind men, and I will open your eyes for the first time."

At the heart of the heretics' philosophy, like the black hole at the center of the Eye of the Preservers, was a single negation. It was so simple and so utterly against the self-evident truth of the world that many of the prisoners simply laughed in amazement every time the pedagogues repeated it. It was that the Puranas were not the thoughts of the Preservers, set down to reveal the history of the Universe and to determine the actions of right-thinking men, but were instead a fabrication, a collection of self-justifying lies spewed forth by the victors of a great and ancient war that was not yet over. There would be no resurrection into eternal life at the end of all time and space, because the Preservers had fled from the Universe and could not return. They had created Confluence, but they had abandoned it. The fate of each man did not lie within the purlieu of the infinite mercy and power of the Preservers, but in his own hands. Because the Preservers could not return from the Eye, they no longer existed in the Universe, and so each man must be responsible for his own fate. There was no hope but that which could be imagined; no destiny but that which could be forged.

The pedagogues were more fervent in their unbelief than any of the pillar saints or praise chanters who had devoted their lives to exaltation of the glories of the Preservers. They would allow no argument. This negation was the central fact that could not be denied; from it, all else followed. From the first, Pandaras was quite clear on what the heretics did not believe, but it took him a long time to understand what they did believe, and once he had it, it was so simple that he was amazed that he had failed to grasp it at once. Like the woman in the pictures in his master's copy of the Puranas, the heretics wanted to live forever.

Seize the day! It was a plea aimed directly at the base of the brain, where the residue of the animal self was coiled like a snake, insatiable and quite without a conscience. Do anything in your power to survive; bend your entire life toward it. The Universe was an insensate and hostile place; worlds were so few and remote that they counted for nothing; almost anywhere you went would kill you instantly and horribly. Therefore, life was infinitely precious, and every man's life was more precious still, a subtle and beautiful melody that would never be repeated. The heretics wished to revive the old ways of indefinitely prolonging life, so that everyone could fulfill their destiny as they pleased.

For Pandaras, whose bloodline was short-lived compared to others on Confluence, no more than twenty-five years at most, it was a seductive song. "Written in air," yes, but suppose it could be stone instead! What sublime songs and stories he could make if all time were at his disposal, and what joy he would have in seeing them spread and change and enrich his fame!

Once this thought took root, Pandaras paid more attention to what the pedagogue told the discussion class. For amusement, he told himself. To pass the time.

The heretics admitted no gods, but believed that each man could become a god—or better than a god—with enough effort. Any God of the First Cause in a universe such as this must surely be counted a failure, the pedagogue argued, because He must be omniscient and yet allow immense suffering. Most of the Universe was uninhabitable. All men died, and most died badly.

"If the Preservers care about their creation," the pedagogue told Pandaras and his companions, "then either they wish to take away evil and are unable, or they are able but unwilling, or they are neither willing nor able, or they are both willing and able. If they are willing and unable then they are feeble, which is not in accordance with claims made for their nature; if they are able yet unwilling then they are envious of the condition of their creation, which is equally at variance with their nature; if they are both unwilling and unable then they are both envious and feeble, and therefore cannot be what they are claimed to be by their worshippers; and yet if they are both willing and able, which conditions alone would satisfy the claims of those who believe in the omnipotence of the Preservers, then from what source come the evils of the world? From what place flow all the hurts and trials which you have all suffered? Why are we victorious, and why are you defeated? All the evil in the world can be accounted for by one principle, and that is the nature of the Universe of which it is a part. And yet that evil is not absolute. It is well known that a wilderness can be tamed and cultivated and made to yield crops. And so with any wilderness, even to the end of space and time, for there is no limit to the transforming power of human reason and human will. And given these two things, nature and human reason, why, there is no need for the Preservers, or any other gods."

Several of the prisoners in Pandaras's discussion class passionately disputed this argument. They said that although the Preservers had given men free will, it did not mean that men had infinite power, and even if they could gain infinite power it did not mean that they would then be unchanged, as the heretics appeared to believe. For surely anyone who could live forever would be changed by the simple fact of becoming immortal, and so would no longer be subject to the fears of ordinary men. The pedagogue listened to their arguments and smiled and said that they had not yet opened their ears, that they were still in the thrall of the propaganda of their priests and civil service, who together conspired to assign every man a place and punish those who tried to change things because change threatened their power.

This seemed to be no more than what many in Ys said behind the backs of the magistrates and priests, Pandaras thought, but he was still disturbed by these new ideas. He knew that Yama would have an answer to them, but even as he thought this he remembered that Yama had also questioned the motives of the Preservers in making Confluence and setting the ten thousand bloodlines upon it in the moment before they had stepped from the Universe. The praise singers had it that the Preservers had extended their mercy to the races of servants they had raised up from animals; these they had set on this world to achieve what destiny they could for good or ill, in the sight of the Eye into which the Preservers had vanished. But why then was the world so bound in custom and tradition? We are the strength of the city, Pandaras thought, and yet we are regarded by higher bloodlines as no more than vermin. And what of the indigenous races such as the fisherfolk or the mirror people, or the unclean scavengers and ghouls who roamed the cloacae of Ys? These races had been raised up by the Preservers, yet did not contain their breath and so could never achieve the change—enlightenment, in this gray mannikin's argot—by which a bloodline dominated by unchanging habit becomes a nation of individuals. He remembered with a pang of shame the first day with his master, after they had escaped *The Crossed Axes,* when he had poured scorn upon the unchanged refugees who camped by the widening margin of the river. Was it the intention of the Preservers that some bloodlines should oppress others? Surely the Preservers had set themselves so high that all bloodlines were equal to them, no matter how lowly or how enlightened. The heretics had one thing right: all the world's peoples should have the chance to rise as high as they could. If the Preservers had created a world so manifestly unfair, then surely they had done so through incompetence or spite. Surely they could not be as powerful as the priests and bureaucrats claimed.

Pandaras forgot in that moment that although his master was more powerful than many men, he did not deny that the Preservers were more powerful still, so powerful that men might never riddle their actions. Instead, the slogans of the heretics burnt like fever in his blood. Seize the day! Live forever! It did not matter if you were changed, for you would still remember what you had been, as a man fondly remembers his childhood. And what man would wish to remain a child forever?

One man in Pandaras's discussion class was eager to deny the Preservers. Not out of belief or conviction, but out of fear, for he was anxious to save himself. From the first he agreed with everything the pedagogue said, without understanding anything, and mocked his fellow prisoners for stubbornly clinging to their outmoded and foolish beliefs.

He was a skinny fellow with leathery brown skin and a cayman's untrustworthy grin. He wore only dirty breeches and a mail shirt, and stank like river water kept too long in a barrel. He had been badly seared when his carronade had jammed and exploded: his hand was gloved in a white plastic bag and a bandage was wrapped around his head; the right side of his chest and his face were livid with burnscars; his right eye was as milk-white as a boiled egg. He was shunned by the other prisoners and was always trying to wheedle favors from the guards, who either ignored him or chased him away with swift, judicious blows. His name was Narasimha, but everyone called him the Jackal. Even the pedagogue grew tired of the Jackal's constant gabble of unthinking agreement, and one day turned on him.

"You do not worship the Preservers?" it said in its sweet, high voice.

"That's so, your honor," the Jackal said eagerly. "Men of my kind, we've never liked 'em. That's why we are always hunted down by the authorities, because we refuse to bend our knee to the false idols of their temples. We were delighted when your people finally silenced the last avatars because we saw that it might be an end to the rule of the priests. And now I see it's true, and my heart lifts on a flood of happiness."

Pandaras thought that as usual the Jackal dissembled, giving up half the truth in service of a greater lie. It was clear from the arrowhead tattoos on the man's fingers that he had been a member of one of the galares which operated in the docks of Ys, hijacking cargoes, smuggling cigarettes and other drugs, running protection and kidnapping rackets. The Jackal had probably joined the army to escape justice. Perhaps he had betrayed his own kind—it was clear that he believed in nothing but his own self, and one or two of the prisoners said, out of earshot of any pedagogue or soldier, that the Jackal was an ideal candidate for a heretic, for he would betray the Universe to save his worthless hide.

"What do you worship," the pedagogue asked the Jackal sweetly, "if you do not worship the Preservers?"

A ripple of interest stirred the circle of the discussion class, like a breeze lifting and dropping the leaves of a tree. The Jackal did not notice it.

"Why, your honor, captain . . . for a long time I did not worship anything. The other things I held dear were my family and my many friends, as any good honest man might tell you, but I saw nothing of worth beyond them. But now, by happy circumstance, I find myself in a position I could not have imagined then. My bloodline is one of the oldest on Confluence, one of the first to have changed. We have always lived in Ys, and those in power hate us because of our ancient and honorable pedigree. But now I feel that I have been changed again, that the change for which we are envied is nothing compared to what I feel now. Why, I'm even happy that I lost my eye and use of my hand, because it is a small enough price to have paid for the riches you shower upon us day by day."

"Then you worship nothing?"

"Your honor, as I said, my people never worshipped the Preservers. But it does not mean we are not capable of worship."

"Money, mostly," someone whispered, loud enough for the rest of the class to hear it. Most laughed.

The Jackal glared around with his one good eye. It was yellow, with a vertically slitted pupil.

"You see, your honor," the Jackal said, "how jealous others are of me. Because I understand what you want of us while these others only pretend it. They are not worthy of your truths. You take me, your honor, and feed these others to the fish in the mud at the bottom of the river."

"What is it you understand?" the pedagogue asked. "Every day you tell me that you are full of praise for what you hear, and I am glad. But I would like to know what you understand of the hard questions I put to all of you here. I would like to know how high you have been raised."

The men in the circle nudged each other, seeing that some kind of trap was closing on the hapless Jackal, who glared at them again and hissed through his long jaw. "Higher than these scum, and they know it, your honor. Put that question to them. I'll wager none of them will be able to answer it."

"There is no competition here," the pedagogue said. "We set no man against any other. That is one part of our strength. The other is our certainty. Tell me one thing of which you are certain."

"Why, your honor, I know that the Preservers are nothing but shit compared to your people. I know that I worshipped nothing because nothing was worthy of my worship, but I know now that I have found something I will worship with all my heart and all my breath. Let me serve your people and I will grace them with such praise that all will know their fame. It is your people that I worship. I love you all more than life itself, and will serve you in any way I can, and hope to gain some small measure of your glory. It is you, you! You and no other!"

And to the disgust of the others, the Jackal threw himself forward and tried to kiss the pedagogue's feet. But the small creature drew them into the angles of its knees and looked at the man and said, "There is nothing more that I can tell you. Go now. Leave the class. Do not be afraid. If you truly understand what I teach, you must know that you are free to do as you will."

The Jackal raised his head. The bandage around his head was unraveling, and one end hung down by the milky, cooked eye which stared from the mess of black scabs and raw red skin. He said, "Then there is nothing I want more than to sit at your feet, your honor, and absorb your wisdom."

"I have nothing more to teach you," the pedagogue said. "I will not say it again, for I hope I am not mistaken about your ability to understand me. If you do not understand me then your punishment will be swift and terrible."

There had been no signal, but suddenly two guards were walking across the wide white deck toward the discussion class. The Jackal looked at them, looked at the pedagogue. "Your honor . . . captain . . . If I have angered you in any way, then I repent of it at once."

"You have not angered me. You have filled my heart with joy. Go now. You are free."

Pandaras thought with a chill that it was a subtle and cruel trick. The pedagogue had trapped the Jackal with his own lies, had punished him by giving him exactly what he wanted.

The Jackal was refused food from the cauldrons because it was for the prisoners and he was a free man, and likewise the guards mocked him when he tried to beg some of their rations, crowning him king of the free men with a wreath of water lily flowers, and then driving him away with blows from the butts of their carbines and partisans. The Jackal did not dare approach the pedagogues, and besides, it was unlikely that he could digest the fibrous pap which they sucked up. For the next two days he wandered from class to class, followed by several of the small, silvery machines, and sometime on the third night of his freedom he disappeared.

———

One evening, as the prisoners ate their meager ration of maize porridge salted with scraps of fish, a man of Pandaras's bloodline, a veteran by the name of Tullus, came over and sat beside Pandaras and struck up a conversation. It seemed that they had once lived within two streets of each other in Ys, and had worked at different times in the same foundry, casting and repairing armor. They talked about people they had known and stories they shared in common, and at last Tullus reached the point of his visit.

"The guards killed the Jackal, brother. They sport with us and eventually they will kill us all."

"You did not know Narashima, I think. He would have lain with a dog if it would have turned a penny or extended his life by a day."

"Many join the army," Tullus said seriously, "and every man has his reason. But all unite in a single cause. Whatever else the Jackal was, he was foremost a soldier. He was one of us and the heretics mocked him and killed him."

"I saw little help from his fellows," Pandaras said.

"All feared that if they aided the Jackal, then they would share his fate. The heretics divide us, brother, and one by one they will kill us."

The two men fell silent as one of the guards went past, his clawed feet scratching the deck, his harness jingling. One of the little angular machines stalked stiff-legged after him. Pandaras thought that if the discipline of the army had been atomized, then the heretics had won. They had made their point. When it came to confronting death, there was no society of men, only individuals.

Tullus watched the guard pace away into the gloom between groups of prisoners. He whispered, "The lazaret goes slowly because the heretics wish to extend our torture as long as possible, but it goes downriver all the same. At last it will reach the end of the Marsh of the Lost Waters. There are millions of heretics in the cities beyond, and we will be given up to them for their sport."

Pandaras had heard many fantastic stories about the tortures and obscenities which the heretics inflicted on their prisoners: trials by combat; vivisections and other experiments; forced matings between different bloodlines. He told Tullus, "The army makes up many stories about the enemy, brother, so that its soldiers will fight hard to avoid capture."

Tullus nodded. "Well, that's true up to a point," he said. "But the point is that there must be a foundation to any story or song. You know that, brother. All of us know that."

"The rumors about the heretics are founded in hatred and fear," Pandaras said. "Much may flow from those sources, but none of it good."

Tullus looked hard at Pandaras. He was a grizzled man of some fifteen or sixteen years, with white around his muzzle. He said, "You are not a soldier. What are you doing here?"

Pandaras crooked his left arm, thrusting the stump forward. The bandage wrapped around it was gorged on black blood and throbbed gently to Pandaras's own heartbeat. "I have lost as much as any man here," he said.

"Not your life," Tullus said. "Not yet."

"I've lost something as dear to me," Pandaras said. "My master was taken by the heretics. He is a great warrior, and I am his squire. I'm going to find him and free him."

"You were hurt when he was captured?"

"No, that was later. A flier took him away, and I have been looking for him ever since."

"Where was this? He was a cateran, I suppose. What division was he attached to? Or was he a scout?"

"He was on his way to war—"

"And was taken before he could kill a single heretic? An unlucky man rather than a hero, Pandaras. Heroes need luck as much as they need strength. Perhaps you have misplaced your loyalty, neh?"

"He will save the world yet," Pandaras said stubbornly. "I can say no more, but I know that he will."

"You have a chance with us. Stay here and you have no chance at all. They will kill you, Pandaras. Have no faith in anything they promise." Tullus looked around and whispered, "Some of us are planning to escape."

"We are surrounded by marsh and jungle."

"Where better place to escape? I fought here when I first joined the army. I know how to find my way. Once we are in the marshes we are safe. But first we must escape."

"Good luck to you, but I think I will stay here. I'm a city boy. I've no love of parks, let alone wilderness. And perhaps you forget, but I have only one hand."

"We will all help each other. If you love freedom you will help us. If you love the Preservers you will help us."

"I'm not a soldier, Tullus, as you've pointed out. I'm only a servant who is looking for his master. How could I help you?"

"You have the hierodule. And the hierodule can help us. He can talk with the machines, and they are the real guards here. You will command him to make the machines leave this place, and we will kill the hairy ones and the little gray-skinned motherfuckers."

"He is not mine," Pandaras said. "Command him yourself, if you can."

Tullus raised himself into a crouch. His black lips drew back from his teeth. Pandaras stiffened. He could smell the old soldier's anger, and he rose to match Tullus's posture. They glared at each other, faces a handspan apart.

Tullus said, "The hierodule refused me. That is why I am asking you, boy."

"Perhaps you asked him the wrong question. Tell him that he is under no obligation to me. Tell him that he was freed when the ship on which he served was destroyed."

Tullus stared hard at Pandaras, and Pandaras stared right back at him, his blood beating heavily in his head. He refused to be intimidated because he felt that it would somehow fail his master. Then Tullus smiled and turned and said, "Look! In spite of all the powers they boast of possessing, they cannot hide the truth from us."

The Rim Mountains had swallowed the last light of the sun, and the Eye of the Preservers had risen a handspan above the trees along the edge of the river: the dull red swirls of its accretion disc; the pinprick black point at the center, the dwelling place of the Preservers.

"The Preservers watch us always," Tullus said. "Pray with me, brother. Pray for our deliverance."

No guards or machines were near. Pandaras made the necessary gestures of obeisance and whispered the responses, but his heart was empty. The Preservers had fled the Universe. Light fell faster than they, so that they could still watch their creation but could no longer interfere with it. They had set it in motion and abandoned it, as a child might turn away from a wind-up toy, leaving it to heedlessly march down the street. Praying was an empty gesture, and Pandaras felt as if there was a gulf a thousand leagues wide between himself and the man who prayed raptly and joyfully beside him.

The tragedy is not that we fall in love with that which does not love us, he thought, but that we cease to love. He was shivering. He thrust his good hand between his thighs, but he could not stop shivering. Tullus said, "What is it, brother? Don't be afraid. Say the final benison with me."

"You say it, Tullus."

"You young fool. You believe them, don't you?"

"We are the strength of the city, Tullus. But why are we despised?"

"You are less than the Jackal," Tullus said in disgust. "He only pretended to believe the heretics' cant, but with you it is no pretense." His face contorted and he spat on the deck between Pandaras's feet. He said, "There are many like me. Tell anyone of this, betray me, and one of my friends will kill you."

Pandaras slept badly that night, although Tibor promised to keep watch. When he woke near dawn he saw with a pang of dread that more than half the prisoners were gone. Tibor was sitting cross-legged in a kind of trance; it was the closest he came to sleep. When Pandaras shook him, the hierodule stirred and said at once that he had seen nothing.

"Perhaps they escaped to the shore," Pandaras whispered.

Tibor said softly, "I do not think so, little master."

Tears were swelling in the hierodule's downwardly slanting eyes. Pandaras said, "You did see something. Tell me."

"Everyone slept. Even I, who never sleeps, passed from this world for a little while. The machines may have had something to do with it. Then you woke me, and the men were gone."

A little later, Pandaras said, "You could have helped them, Tibor."

"My place is with you, little master. You have not yet recovered from your wound."

"Would you have helped them, if I had ordered it? Could you have told the heretics' machines to quit the lazaret?"

Tibor considered this, and at last said gently, "I am yours to command, little master, but I do not think I can command the machines of our captors. I was fitted with an induction loop when I entered the service of the temple, but it was designed to interface with shrines. Shrines are machines, it is true, but there are many kinds of machine."

"You never tried?"

"It did not occur to me, little master."

"They might still kill you," Pandaras said. "Your entire life has been spent in the service of the Preservers. Surely that makes you a natural enemy of the heretics."

"Not at all. As I told you before, I am seen as a great prize. In the first days after the lazaret was captured, little master, before you woke from your coma, the pedagogues spent a great deal of time talking with me. They hope to convert me, as they have already converted the captain of the lazaret." Tibor pointed toward the flying bridge at the bow, at the big, jointed machine in its hammock. "It still hopes that I will join with it. But I already serve you, little master. I have no one else to serve. If the *Weazel* was not destroyed, then surely Captain Lorquital would have put in at Ophir with her cargo. But no one had seen her, little master, although I asked many people at the docks while I was waiting to board the ship which took me downriver to the lazaret."

"They died quickly, Tibor, if that's a comfort."

"Except for Phalerus," Tibor said.

The remaining prisoners were subdued. There were no discussion classes that day. Just before sunset, the barge entered a wide canal, and an hour later drew into the docks of Baucis, the City of Trees.

10

"Everyone Now Living May Never Die"

AS SOON AS the barge had been made fast to the wharf, the guards began to move amongst the prisoners, telling them that they were free to go. "This is a city of free men!" they said, grinning fearsomely. "Take up your own lives. No one is responsible for you but yourselves."

"If only Tullus had waited," Pandaras said to Tibor bitterly, "he and his fellows would have had their wish."

Many of the prisoners were reluctant to obey the guards, fearing that this was a trick. One man went mad and refused to move when the guards started to force them toward the stern, where the gangways to the dock had been fixed. He sat down in the middle of the deck with his arms wrapped around his chest, rocking back and forth and screaming. A guard shot him in the head, picked up his body and slung it over the side. After that, the prisoners had no choice but to gather up their few belongings and walk out into the city.

Baucis had once been a patchwork of little woods and hills, but new roads had been driven everywhere without regard for traditional boundaries, and many of the woods had been cut down. In those that survived, the heart trees had been felled and the woven platform houses of the original inhabitants had been torn down and replaced by straggling encampments of tents and shacks. Sewage ran in open channels that were often blocked by the bodies of animals and men. The air was hazed with the smoke of thousands of fires. Floating platforms and streams of draft animals and crowds of men jostled along red clay roads in the harsh glare of arc lights strung from stripped tree-trunks. Steam wagons clanked and groaned and belched clouds of black smoke as they dragged three or four overladen trailers behind them. Stores and taverns, gaming palaces and whorehouses, all with tall, brightly painted false fronts, had been thrown up along the roads, and barkers and shills called to the crowds from platforms or windows or balconies. There were many apothecaries, surgeries and clinics. One offered, mysteriously, *Whole Body Immersion and Electrotherapy*; another, *Intestinal Irrigation*. Machines spun above the crowded roads, zipping about on obscure errands, and slogans were projected high in the air, in glowing letters each as big as a man. *Seize the Day. Everyone Now Living May Never Die.* Higher still were the archipelagoes of the floating gardens which had once been the homes of Baucis's scholar-saints, strings of sharply stamped shadows in the orange sky-glow.

Pandaras was tired and his left arm hurt badly; Tibor had stripped the quasi-living dressing from the stump, leaving only a light bandage. He followed the hierodule without question, and presently found himself amongst the ruins of the city's sacred wood. The circle of giant sequoias, said to have been as old as the world, had been cut down, and decads of men were sawing planks from their carcasses by the light of huge bonfires, but the shrine was still there. It was a black disc ten times Pandaras's height, standing at the center of a big circular platform crafted from a hundred different kinds of wood. The platform was scarred with deep, charcoal-blistered trenches made by the reflected beams of energy weapons and pocked with thousands of splintered gouges and impact holes from ricocheting slugs and rifle pellets, and blasphemies and cabbalistic signs had been carved into the polished ancient planks, but the huge black disc of the shrine itself, being only partly of this world, was inviolate.

Pandaras sat down at the edge of the platform, on wood worn smooth by the footsteps of millions of pilgrims and petitioners. He said wearily, "Why have you brought us here?"

"We were told that nothing is forbidden, little master," Tibor said, "so surely one might still consult the shrines."

"What use is that, without a priest?" Pandaras said, and then he understood. "Will it speak with you?"

"The avatar of this shrine was destroyed ten thousand years ago, in the wars of the Age of Insurrection. But the shrine itself is still active."

Pandaras sat in the shadows at the perimeter of the platform while Tibor attempted to commune with the shrine. He meant to keep watch, but it was long past midnight and he was very tired. He fell asleep, and woke with a start to find the hierodule squatting in front of him and a familiar warmth against his chest.

"There is no reply," Tibor said mournfully. "Something has destroyed the indices."

Pandaras reached inside his torn shirt and lifted out the ceramic coin. Little specks and lines of light filled it from edge to edge, frozen in a static pattern.

"It doesn't matter," he said. "I know that my master is here."

11

The Camp

PANDARAS AND TIBOR spent the rest of the night close by the ruins of the sacred grove, although their sleep was fitful because of the whine and clatter of the mechanical saws wielded by the men who were dismembering the carcasses of the giant sequoias. They wandered the brawling streets of the city for most of the next day in search of some sign of Yama, but found nothing. They had no money for food or lodging, and it seemed that nothing was free in the city. Pandaras tried to earn a few coins by singing at a street corner, but passersby either ignored him or cursed him roundly. One woman riding by stopped her sumpter long enough to explain to Pandaras that everyone must be responsible for their own self, and that by begging he was behaving like an animal.

"I have a hierodule, dominie. Is there no work for him?"

"No man is a slave here," the woman said. "You should try one of the camps at the edge of the city. You'll find more of your kind there. Go quickly before someone decides to organize a lynch party and get rid of you." And before Pandaras could ask her another question she flicked the sumpter's reins and rode on through the swarming crowds.

It was almost midnight when Pandaras and Tibor finally reached one of the camps in the jungle at the edge of Baucis. A guard hailed them a long way from its perimeter and led them down a tangle of winding paths to a neatly arranged compound, with huts and tents on three sides of a square of trampled dirt. The leader of the camp was a giant of a woman who had lost both her legs but went everywhere on crutches, indefatigable and full of energy. Her name—or the short, childhood version of her name, for her bloodline chose names that grew and reflected their experiences—was Calpa. She listened to Pandaras's story while he and Tibor devoured bowls of starchy, unsalted vegetable curry, and told him that this was a bad place to be.

"The city is full of newly changed bloodlines. They are dangerous because they are burning with holy fire. Mobs sniff out those who do not agree with them and hang or burn or stone them. We try to keep ourselves to ourselves, but we still get a lot of trouble. Can you hunt?"

"I'm a city boy," Pandaras said, and held up his stump. "Besides, I am still recovering from my wound."

Calpa made him nervous. She was one of the giant bloodlines, twice as big as Tibor. She was sprawled carelessly in a crude chair. One of her three-fingered hands could have easily wrapped around his skull and crushed it like a grape. The gray hide of her bare torso was heavily scarified with the welts of decorative brandings and oiled with what smelled like rancid butter. Her cropped white hair was raised in spikes over her crested skull, and her flat-nosed face was dominated by muscular jaws like the opposing scoops of one of the mechanical dredgers which were always working along the shore of Ys, struggling to keep old channels open as the river dwindled.

"We're all crippled and maimed in some way or another here," Calpa said. "At least you can still walk."

"My friend is a cook. I'd do better helping him."

"We've plenty of cooks and not enough food."

"Begging your pardon, and do not think I am not grateful for the charity, but your cooks are a greater danger than any heretic. I ate this poor excuse for food because I have not eaten all day, but boiled river mud would have had more flavor."

Calpa ignored this. "Your friend will help with those who are too sick or badly hurt to move. You will go with one of the hunting parties. I bet you can run fast. Most of your bloodline can. We mostly dig traps and chase animals into them. You'll help with that. And if that doesn't work out you'll hunt for fruit. I'm sure that with even one hand you can sneak up on a pomegranate tree." Calpa looked hard at Pandaras and added, "Do you believe them?"

Her gaze compelled him to be honest. He said, "I have not believed in the supremacy of the Preservers for some time. We are the strength of the city, Calpa, but we are despised by most."

"That's the fault of men, not of those who created them."

"Then perhaps we were badly made," Pandaras said. "But I am not here to become a heretic, much as I'd like to live forever."

Calpa nodded. "You said that you're looking for a friend. Well, if he has been here long, then he is either dead or one of them."

"He is my master. I know that he is alive, and I know that he is somewhere in this city. Are there many camps like this one?"

"There are no masters here," Calpa said. "The heretics kill every officer they capture; we're all of us just ordinary grunts. And there are only two other camps. Most of the released prisoners run away and are killed by roving gangs of heretics in the jungles and the marshes upriver. Those that stay here mostly join the heretics or kill themselves. A few try to fight, of course. They don't last long. There are many thousands of heretics in the city, and many more than that in the wild country about it. This is one of their staging posts for the war."

"And yet they let us go."

"They murdered most of the prisoners on the ship that brought me here," Calpa said. "They started with the officers and carried on from there. Almost all of my comrades—most of a division—are dead. The heretics didn't trouble with me because they thought I was dying, but I plan to show them that they made a bad mistake. They are arrogant and cruel, which is why they release those prisoners who survive the journey here, but they will suffer for their arrogance because they are letting us build an army in their midst. We're not ready yet, but soon enough we'll be able to do much harm here. They have a mage, for instance, who is said to be able to control every kind of machine. I have my eye on him, although he has many soldiers gathered around him."

"What does he look like, this mage?"

"No one has ever seen him. He does not walk the city. He lives on a floating garden. There."

Pandaras looked where Calpa pointed. It was a shadow against the Eye of the Preservers, hanging some distance from the archipelagoes of the other floating gardens.

"You and your friend will take guard duty tonight," Calpa said, and clapped her big hands together. A man came over and she told him, "Give them a rattle and a couple of javelins and take them out to the fern trees. Check on them at sunrise. Kill them if they are asleep." She looked at Pandaras. "Do you understand why we do this?"

"I can see that you don't trust newcomers."

"We're still at war," Calpa said. "There are many traps and pitfalls around the camp, and we move them about. You'll likely be killed if you try and run away, and so we will be rid of you. If you choose to stay, you'll have made a good start at helping us. Keep a sharp lookout. They come for us most nights."

———

Pandaras and Tibor were given javelins tipped with flaked stone points and a gourd that, filled with hard seeds and strung on a leather thong, made a passable noisemaker, and were escorted to a rocky promontory which jutted above a dense belt of fern trees and looked out across the city. The Eye of the Preservers stood high above the river and the floating garden Calpa had pointed out was silhouetted against its dull red swirl. Their escort showed them the positions of the lookouts on either side, and said he would be back at dawn.

When the man had gone, Pandaras hefted his javelin and threw it as hard as he could into the crowns of the fern trees below, and threw the gourd after it. "Get rid of yours, too," he told Tibor. "This place isn't for us."

"They have food and shelter, little master, both of which we failed to find in the city."

"We are not safe here. Calpa believes that she is still fighting the war, but she can only lose. I'll bet the armies she thinks are ranged against her are just bravos out for sport. If they catch us with weapons they'll kill us for sure. If they find us alone and unarmed, they might spare us."

"Calpa said that there are many traps."

"That fellow won't be back for us before dawn, and there will be light in the sky before then to pick a way. I can see well enough in what other bloodlines would consider to be pitch darkness. This is almost as bright as day to me." An exaggeration, but Pandaras could clearly see Tibor's quizzical expression by the dim red light of the Eye. "I'll spot any traps long before we're near them, or I'll sniff them out. Besides, I don't think they'll spend much time looking for us. Calpa hinted that many who come here run away, and I doubt that she bothers to chase after them. The way the war is going there will always be more prisoners and she has only to wait for them to come to her."

After a moment, Tibor nodded and broke the shaft of his javelin over his knee and tossed the two halves over the edge of the promontory. He said, "How will we get to him?"

"I wondered if you'd catch on."

"I may be slow, little master," Tibor said, with a touch of his unassailable dignity, "but I am not stupid. The mage Calpa mentioned must surely be your master. But we cannot fly through the air, and Calpa said that there are many soldiers guarding him."

"Perhaps he'll find us. I'm certain that he is a prisoner of whoever it was that Eliphas betrayed him to. Calpa said that he was helping the heretics, and I know that my master would not help them unless forced. But although he is a prisoner, he can still call upon machines to help him. He saved me before by using a machine to cut me free from Prefect Corin."

"You told me about your adventures more than once," Tibor said. "I do not forget things, little master."

"The point is that it happened in the battleground far downriver. Now we are in sight of him."

"But although we have found him, he has not yet found you. And how can we free him, little master, if he, who is so powerful, cannot free himself? And how can you be certain that he is this mage? It seems to me that nothing is certain in this world, except the love of the Preservers."

Pandaras sat down and massaged the stump of his left wrist. He said, "I suppose you still believe in them."

"Who does not? Even the heretics cannot deny that the Preservers created the world and all its peoples."

"I mean that you believe that they still have influence in this world. That it is worth praying to them."

Tibor reflected on this, and said at last, "These days, most men who pray to the Preservers are in fact praying to their higher selves; prayer has become no more than a simple form of meditation. But I remember how it was when the avatar was still accessible within the shrine of the temple of which I was the hierodule. Ah, little master. You do not know how it was. You cannot imagine. Prayer was no solitary communion then, but a joyful conversation with a sublime and witty friend. But that is all lost now, all quite lost."

There was a silence. Pandaras turned and saw with embarrassment that the hierodule was crying. He had forgotten that someone could take worship of the Preservers so seriously. The last of the avatars had been destroyed by the heretics long before he had been born; they were no more than a myth to him.

He pretended not to see Tibor's tears and yawned elaborately and lay down, resting his head in the crook of his right arm and tucking the stump of his left wrist into his lap. He was still ashamed of the amputation and unconsciously tried to hide it whenever he could. "We'll rest an hour or so," he said. "I can feel in my muscles every league we walked today."

After a while, Tibor said softly, as if to himself, "The Preservers created the world, and they created the ten thousand bloodlines. They made the different races of men into their image to a greater and lesser degree, but in their charity and love for their creations left them to find their own ways to enlightenment. For the Preservers knew that their children were capable of saving themselves, of becoming civilized and completing the gesture of creation by becoming like their own selves, as indeed many of the most enlightened bloodlines have since done. We have it in ourselves to be so much more than we are, but the heretics deny that. They want no more than to be what they already are, forever and ever."

Pandaras thought sleepily of the armory where he had once worked for one of his uncles, of the cauldrons where metals were smelted. One of his tasks had been to skim dross from the surface of the molten metal using a long-handled wooden paddle. The paddle had been carved from a single piece of teak and was badly charred; you had to dip it in a wooden pail of water before each sweep, or else it would catch fire. It seemed to him now that this work had been the reverse of what happened in the world, where the good refined themselves out of existence, leaving only the dross behind.

He woke briefly and heard Tibor praying to the Eye of the Preservers, which had begun to sink back toward the farside horizon. "Wake me an hour before dawn," he said sleepily. "I'll pick out a way for us then." But he could not have slept long because when Tibor shook him awake the Eye still stood high in the black sky.

"There is fighting on the other side of the city," Tibor said softly.

As Pandaras sat up there was a flash of intensely blue light, as if, leagues and leagues away, someone in the darkness of the jungle surrounding the city had opened a window into day. Groggy with sleep, he counted off the seconds. *Four, five, six...* There was a rumble like thunder and the rock trembled like a live animal, and then he was fully awake, for he knew what weapon it was. He jumped to his feet and said, "He's found me again!"

"Your master? Then he has escaped the floating garden?"

A flock of red and green sparks shot across the city toward the place where the point of blue light had shone, but they tumbled from the sky and winked out before they could strike their target.

"The machines try and destroy him," Pandaras said, "but he has some kind of magic which shuts them down. I've seen it before. He was not killed. Perhaps he cannot be killed. He followed me downriver and now he is looking for me in the other camps. He will be here soon. There! There! Oh mercy! He is coming for me!"

Another point of blue light flared in the jungle that circled the city's basin, this time only a few leagues away.

"Who? Who is it, little master? Is it your master?"

The thunder was louder, and came less than two seconds after the flare of blue light. The rock shuddered again and Pandaras sat down hard, trembling with fear. He knew now how he could reach the floating garden, but he wished with all his heart that it had not come to this. He looked up at Tibor and said, "Yama is close by, but this is not him. No, it is Prefect Corin, and if I want to see my master again I must let him find me."

12

The Last Flight of Dr. Dismas

HE IS HERE, the Shadow said, and with those words appeared above the bed as the eidolon of Derev. She was clinging to the ceiling with her fingers and toes and looking down at Yama through the fall of her feathery white hair. She was naked under her filmy shift. Her skin glowed with the soft green radiance sometimes seen on rotting wood.

"Transform," Yama said wearily. The coin nagged at his attention, like the wink of sunlight on a far-off window. He knew that Pandaras was very close now, but he could no longer make use of a machine to search for the boy. The Shadow had taken away even that.

The eidolon squeezed its small breasts together with one hand. *You do not like this?*

Blue light flared beyond the big eye of the window, briefly illuminating the pentad of servants who stood around the bed. For a moment, Yama thought that the feral machine had returned for him.

Something wicked this way comes.

The double doors on the far side of the room crashed open, and the floating lights brightened. Dr. Dismas strode in, shouting wildly.

"Child! Dear child! Enobarbus is trying to murder us!"

Sit up, the Shadow said.

Yama obeyed without thinking and was astonished to find that he could move. "You are right," he said. "It is time to go."

Halfway across the room, Dr. Dismas stopped and stared in amazement, then drew out his energy pistol. He wore a silvery cloak over his black suit and a cap of silver on his head; Yama remembered that the apothecary had once confided to him that he wore a hat lined with metal to stop machines spying on him.

The Shadow, still in the form of Derev, was suddenly standing behind Dr. Dismas. It smiled and said, *I have allowed your body to overcome the good doctor's potion by a simple matter of physiology. It is not Enobarbus who is attacking us, by the way, but let the doctor think what he will. Besides, Enobarbus is on his way. He thinks that Dismas is attacking him. Many men have already died. Many more will die. It is quite exciting. Shall I show you?*

Yama ignored this. He told Dr. Dismas, "A simple matter of physiology, Doctor," and swung his legs over the side of the bed. One of the servants—the forest pygmy—placed a bundle of clothes at his feet. As Yama began to dress, he added, "It is time I made a move."

"I want you to destroy Enobarbus's machines," Dr. Dismas said. "I hope I am speaking to the right person."

We will not need to worry about the machines.

The eidolon of Derev vanished. Yama had a dizzy sense of doubled vision and discovered that he was once more a prisoner in his own body. It pulled on a loose white shirt, stepped into boots which fastened themselves around its ankles, and walked forward. He heard his voice, pitched an octave lower than normal, say, "You do not need that silly little weapon, Doctor. Not with me by your side."

Dr. Dismas nodded, and lowered the pistol. He said, "You're right, of course. I have armed the other servants. They are killing those of Enobarbus's men I have not myself already killed. We must get you to a safe place. It is indeed time to move." He snapped his stiff fingers, and one of the servants threw a silvery bundle on the bed. "That will shield you from pellets and from near misses of energy weapons."

Yama tried to speak, but the Shadow had assumed complete control of his body. "I do not need such things," it told Dr. Dismas. It flung out Yama's right arm, and the servants collapsed.

Dr. Dismas raised the pistol again, pointing it at Yama's head, and said angrily, "Restore them, you fool. This is not a time for tricks. We need them still."

"Alas," the Shadow said, "they are dead. I will kill the other hybrids too, once they have defeated Enobarbus's men. Ah, I see why you wear that cap. It is more than it seems. But you will do as I say anyway. It is time we left, Doctor. Time we returned to our parent to complete our growth, to discard this frail shell. Time we took our place at the center of the world's stage."

Dr. Dismas stepped back two paces, still pointing the pistol at

Yama. "I'll shoot you if I have to. Put on the cloak, but do not think that it will protect you from a direct shot."

A brilliant flash outside the big window momentarily filled the room with white light, fading to reveal the city spread directly below. The floating garden had tipped on its axis, although its local gravity still held.

Carrying Yama's senses with it, the Shadow reached out to a machine speeding through the night a league away. The machine executed a crash stop, spun on its axis, and saw that the floating garden was standing at right angles above the basin of the city. There was fighting in the woods which covered most of the garden's surface; the machine detected the pinpoint disturbances in the gravity fields caused by energy weapons, and flashes of intense light winked in the air all around. A flier shot toward its rocky keel, but must have hit some invisible obstruction, for it suddenly slammed to a halt and disintegrated in a blaze of white flame.

The floating garden slowly righted itself. And high above the far edge of the city, silhouetted against the orange glow of the sky, another garden tore away from an archipelago and began to move toward it.

The fighting in the camp did not last long. There was the confused noise of men and women shouting, a frantic staccato of small-arms fire, an explosion which lofted a ball of greasy yellow flame above the trees. Then a flash of blue light hit half the sky and there was a sudden shocking silence before the screams began, tearing the night air like ripsaws.

Pandaras paced up and down in distress. The screams pierced him to his marrow, and although he had resolved not to run it was very hard to stay where he was.

Tibor said, "Surely he will kill us, little master."

"No. He needs me to—"

And then Prefect Corin stooped out of the night, like an owl on a mouse. He sprang from the floating disc and ran straight at Pandaras, knocking Tibor down when the hierodule tried to get in the way. He caught Pandaras and lifted him up and stared into his face. His left eye was covered by a white adhesive pad. A rifle was slung over his shoulder. "You have caused me such trouble, boy," he said. "You should have stayed with me. You would not have lost your hand. Where is he?"

Pandaras's ribcage was painfully compressed by Prefect Corin's grip; he could scarcely catch his breath. He gasped, "Promise that you will not kill my friend."

"A hierodule has his uses. Where?"

"Did you follow me all this way downriver? I am flattered."

"I should have sunk the barge and killed everyone on board it. Where is he?"

"Surely you have heard of the great mage of this city, dominie."

"I did not have time to question anyone. I was too busy looking for you. I know that he is close by. I can see the coin shining through your shirt."

"Is that how you found me?"

"Alas, there are too many similar sources in this city."

"So you started to search the camps, neh? I wondered why you did not come for us at the shrine, or when we were thrown off the lazaret. I suppose you killed all the poor soldiers in the camps, even though they were on your side."

"A few fled, but many more fought, and I had to kill most of them. A legless woman told me where you were before she died. Many have died because you ran from me, and all for no purpose, because I have you again. Where is he, boy?"

"This time you are here on my terms."

"Tell me."

The pressure of Prefect Corin's grip increased; knives ground in Pandaras's chest. He said breathlessly, "We could go there directly on your floating disc."

"One of the gardens, then. I thought so, although I was not sure which one. They are all heavily guarded." Prefect Corin dropped Pandaras and strode toward Tibor, who was still lying on his back. There was a brief flash of light, and Prefect Corin told the hierodule to get up. Tibor stood, slowly and clumsily, his pale, round face perfectly blank, and Prefect Corin whispered in his ear.

"You command many things," Pandaras said. He massaged his ribs. None were broken, but all were bruised. "You are becoming like my master."

"No, not like him. Never like him. There will be another disc here in a moment, and then you will take me to Yamamanama."

"I want only the best for my master. I'm sure that he is a prisoner, or else he would have come to me by now. You can help free him, and then he'll deal with you."

"You have a monstrous ego, boy."

A floating disc dropped down beside the first, hovering a handspan above the rock. Prefect Corin stepped onto it. "You will ride with the hierodule. Tell the disc which way to go; I will follow. Do not think of escaping, for the hierodule will break your neck."

"If you kill me you will never find him."

"You will be paralyzed, not killed. The coin will still work, I think."

"You must promise that you will not kill my master."

"Of course not. Go now."

At first it was exhilarating. Because the disc warped gravity, it was as if the world tipped and tilted around Pandaras as, with Tibor at his back and Prefect Corin following, he sped through the black air toward the floating island and his master. For a moment, Pandaras forgot that Tibor was no longer his to command, forgot the danger he was in, forgot that he was betraying his master to his worst enemy.

As they drew near, Prefect Corin's disc accelerated and swept ahead, making a long arc toward the rocky keel of the floating garden. Specks of light flew up from the orange glow of the city in long straight streams that began to bend as they tried to track Prefect Corin, who suddenly shot away at right angles. The disc which carried Tibor and Pandaras followed him. Pandaras ordered it to turn back, but it continued on its new course.

A string of floating gardens lay ahead, linked to each other by catenaries and arched bridges. A chunk of rock hung above this cluster, a round lake gleaming darkly on its flat top, ringed by scattered clumps of pines. Streams of water spilled over its edge at several points and fell toward the gardens below; as Pandaras was carried toward it he saw that the water in one of these streams was actually rising.

The floating disc settled at the leading edge of the rock, on an apron of lichen-splashed stone. Tibor gripped Pandaras's arm and dragged him off the disc. A moment later Prefect Corin landed beside them.

"We will need cover," he said. "Yamamanama is too well defended. I thought it prudent to save you." Machines flew out of the darkness from every direction, a hundred tiny sparks settling around him like a cloak. "The spirits of the place," he said. "I have assumed control of them."

The floating rock shuddered. The light of the little machines around Prefect Corin intensified, a robe of blazing light. A shallow wave of cold water rippled across the apron of bare stone; then another, waist-high this time. Pandaras clung to Tibor, for otherwise he would have been washed over the edge. The rock was slowly accelerating toward the floating garden where Yama was being held prisoner. Ragged flowers of red and yellow flame bloomed in the sky all around it.

"Now it ends," Prefect Corin said. He stretched out his arm. Something began to spin in the air in front of his fingertips, shrieking like a banshee as it gathered light and heat around itself.

———

The Shadow walked beside Dr. Dismas across a wide space of charred grass. They both wore silvery cloaks with flowing hems that brushed the ground. Human-shaped animals loped along on all fours on either side. One of the nearest turned its head toward them and grinned. It was a naked woman, her elongated jaws holding racks of long white teeth slick with saliva, her eyes blazing yellow. Ahead, tall trees burned like candles. Above, a fist-sized shadow was growing larger against the sky-glow.

Yama was helpless, paralyzed somewhere behind his own eyes. It was as if he were caught in a fever dream where monsters ran free.

Derev suddenly was walking beside the woman-thing, her slim body glowing like a candle through her robe.

There is a problem, the Shadow said. *You will help us now, if you wish to live.*

"You cannot harm me without harming yourself."

"You're back, my boy," Dr. Dismas said, with surprise. "We are at last breaking free and heading upriver, but someone is chasing us. I do not think that it is Enobarbus."

The shadow in the sky was as big as Yama's outstretched hand now. It was another floating garden. He thought that he knew who was chasing them. He said, "I am sure that you have many enemies, Doctor."

"I try and kill them before they can cause trouble, my boy. You should know that. I do not know who is following us, but he is powerful."

Someone who can strip machines of their power.

"I can see why that would frighten you," Yama said. That was why the Shadow still needed him, why it had allowed him to reoccupy his own body.

"It is a question of contingency," Dr. Dismas said. "I do not like complicated situations, Yamamanama."

Yama and the apothecary walked between two of the burning trees. Heat beat at them from either side; the air was full of resinous smoke. Beyond was a small lake which had been struck by some kind of energy weapon. The water had evaporated, leaving a basin of dry, cracked mud. The man-animals broke away left and right, but Dr. Dismas strode straight across the basin and Yama followed him. The eidolon flowed beside him. It was flickering now, as faint as a firefly near the end of its life. Beyond the top of the slope the other floating garden was growing larger against the sky glow, a flat-topped rock with a jagged keel.

"Where are we going, Doctor?"

"Why, to my paramour, of course. I thought we had discussed this. I have been betrayed by those I tried to help, Yamamanama, and I will have my revenge."

We will gain so much.

"And I will be destroyed."

We can work together, Yamamanama. Do not listen to what I tell the doctor.

"It is a question of transfiguration," Dr. Dismas said. "If something new is made, is the old destroyed? No, it is changed into another form. I should know, Child of the River. I was transformed in the Glass Desert. I am neither man nor machine but something more, yet I still remember what I was and what I wanted, just as a man fondly remembers the foolish fantasies of his childhood."

"Why do you take the drug, Doctor? What pain are you trying to escape?"

"Fusion was not quite complete. The drug completes it. It will be different in your case, Yamamanama. Trust me."

We will become more than either of us can imagine, Yamamanama. And more than the doctor can ever dream of.

"As far as I am concerned, I am a long way from trust."

"We will be there inside a day, Yamamanama. But first we must rid ourselves of this small problem."

They climbed up the slope on the far side of the dry lake, charred vegetation giving way to steeper rock that burned the thin soles of Yama's slippers. It was the edge of the island. Dr. Dismas turned to Yama. A white star shone at his forehead—a machine clung there. The flat-topped rock was so close now that Yama could see the sheets of water which spilled its side and were torn into spray. It was moving toward them at a slant, and gaining perceptibly. Something shone at its leading edge, a point of white light as intense as any star cluster within the Galaxy. The city had fallen far behind, a lake of dull orange light embraced by the dark jungle.

"Something is affecting the gravity fields," Dr. Dismas said. "We are falling too slowly."

Yama remembered one of Zakiel's lessons. The librarian had used a banyan seed and a lead ball he had taken from the armory. He said, "Surely all things fall at the same rate."

"We fall down the length of the world because a machine in the keel of the garden manipulates gravity fields to suit our purpose. But the machine is failing. The nearer that rock gets, the slower we fall. There is something draining the energy grid. You must put a stop to it."

Yama said, "Surely the rock chasing us would also fall more slowly too."

"Yes, yes," Dr. Dismas said impatiently. "It is slowing, but it was moving faster than us in the first place. We have only a few minutes before it reaches us, Yamamanama. You must act quickly!"

The eidolon had disappeared when Yama had followed Dr. Dismas up the slope, but now it came back. Its eldritch glow was so weak that Yama could see right through it. Its eyes were dark holes in the mask of its face; its hair a pale flicker.

You know the man, it said, its words raveling weakly across Yama's brain. *Stop him or we will lose our advantage . . .*

The eidolon flickered and faded, but Yama had the sense that its eyes were still there, like holes burnt into the fabric of the night. The glow of the machine which clung to Dr. Dismas's forehead faded too, and the apothecary plucked it off with his stiff fingers and crushed it.

"I have just lost control of the garden. If I do not regain it we will intersect the surface of the world in forty minutes. But there is still much we can do. You are not a machine, Yamamanama. Or not entirely. Neither are my children. My hybrids were destroyed by Enobarbus's guards, but I still have many purely biological specimens. Chimeras, crossbreeds and the like. My children of the night. We do not need machines."

"And you, Doctor?"

"Oh, as for me, I will have to rely on my purely human part." Dr. Dismas said this casually, but in the half-light Yama saw the gleam of sweat on those parts of his face not affected by the plaques of his disease. He knelt, cast a handful of plastic straws on the ground, and peered closely at them. "I will not die," he said. "That was part of the promise made to me, and I will see that it is kept."

He stood and raised his arm toward the rock that eclipsed a quarter of the sky now. His energy pistol flared so brightly that dawn might have touched the tops of the Rim Mountains.

Yama ran.

———

The machine which Prefect Corin had set in the air was spinning so quickly now that its shriek had passed beyond the range of even Pandaras's hearing. It glowed so brightly that it hurt to look at, and had begun to melt the rock beneath it. Prefect Corin, Pandaras and Tibor retreated from it to the far side of the lake. Prefect Corin uncoiled a length of fine cord and looped it around a pine tree which stood at the edge of the rock.

The spinning machine was draining the local grid on which all machines fed, turning the energy into heat and noise. The cloak of machines had fallen away from Prefect Corin; the lights had died in the ceramic coin. Tibor was affected too; he sat with his arms wrapped around his head, rocking from side to side.

And the rock was slowly sinking through the air like a stone through water, pitching this way and that as it fell. Pandaras clung to the pine tree, his cheek pressed against its dry resinous bark. Branches soughed above him.

"Have courage, boy. Have dignity."

"You are going to kill us all!"

"Nonsense. I have calculated that we will pass a few chains above our target. Our keel may brush a few treetops, no more. Perhaps you have been wondering why I fastened the rope to the tree. Soon you will understand." Prefect Corin's one good eye searched Pandaras's face. "You are a coward, like all your race, small-souled and small-brained. Only a few chosen bloodlines will inherit this world when this war is done. Others will serve, or perish."

Then bolts from Dr. Dismas's energy pistol struck the leading edge of the rock, and chunks of white-hot stone flew up. Most splashed into the lake, sending up spouts of steam and hot water, but one fragment tumbled amongst a stand of pines, which immediately burst into flame.

Prefect Corin turned to look at the burning trees and Pandaras shrieked and lashed out. He caught the Prefect with his one hand and both feet, clamped his mouth on the man's thigh and twisted, coming away with a mouthful of cloth and bloody meat. And then he was flying through the air. His hip and shoulder smashed hard against stone, but he rolled and got to his feet. He was right at the edge of the floating rock. Prefect Corin was limping through firelit shadows toward him. Tibor stood up, his normally placid face twisted in a snarl, his big hands opening and closing. Pandaras turned and looked down, and then gave himself to the air.

The first of the man-animals attacked Yama when he reached the burning trees. He pulled off his silvery cloak and threw it over the creature, and in the moment it took to shake off the cloak snatched up a burning branch and jabbed it in the thing's face. It was not afraid of fire and sprang straight at him and knocked him down, but Yama discovered that his attacker had only a child's strength. Unlike the other servants, the man-animals had been grown rather than surgically transformed, and Dr. Dismas had not had time to bring them to maturity. Enveloped in rank stench and feverish body-heat, sharp teeth snapping a finger's width from his face, he got his thumbs on the creature's windpipe and stood up, lifting the man-animal with him, and pressed and pressed until its eyes rolled back, then put his palm under its jaw and snapped its neck.

Two more man-animals skulked around him, but when he picked up the burning branch they turned tail and ran. He yelled and threw the branch after them.

The floating rock was very close now, blocking half the black sky.

Yama ran. The sally port where fliers docked with the floating garden was near the mansion in which he had been kept. Perhaps one of the fliers which had brought Enobarbus's men was still intact. He was halfway there when the rock passed overhead.

Its keel scraped the crag where Dr. Dismas had taken him, and came on, breaking the tops from trees and dropping a shower of rocks and gravel. A tree toppled across Yama's path, burning from top to bottom. He skidded and fell down amidst a storm of burning fragments. For a moment he thought that he might faint, that something was trying to pluck his soul from his body, and then it passed and he picked himself up and ran on. He knew that he had only a little time now.

A big semicircular amphitheater sloped down toward the platforms of the sally port. It had been lit by decads of suspensor lamps, but only a few were still working, fitfully illuminating the remains of a terrible battle. Gardens of stone and miniature cedars and clumps of bamboos had been trampled and broken and burnt. There were numerous fires, and patches of scorched stone radiated fierce heat and sent up drifts of choking white smoke. Yama found many corpses, men and things like men, sprawled alone or entangled in a final embrace. Many were so badly burnt that they were little more than charcoal logs, arms and legs drawn up to their chests in rictus, bones showing through charred flesh. Yama armed himself with a gisarme and was about to pluck a pellet pistol from a dead soldier's grasp when someone ran at him. He made a wild swipe with the gisarme, then saw who it was and managed to turn the blow so that the pointed axe-head thumped into the ground.

A moment later, Yama and Pandaras threw their arms around each other and whirled around their common axis. The boy began to babble his story, beginning with the way he had escaped Prefect Corin when the two floating gardens had passed each other, but Yama hushed him and explained what Pandaras must do for him.

"Master, I cannot—"

"I should have had you do it as soon as I discovered them growing under my skin, Pandaras. I should have guessed then what Dr. Dismas had done to me."

"Prefect Corin was not drowned, master. He has come to kill you. He used me to find you. He sends machines to sleep. You will need all your strength to face him."

"He will not try to kill me straightaway, I think. And this will make me stronger, not weaker. We must be quick, Pandaras. The thing which stops machines working was on the floating garden you fell from, was it not?"

"Unless Prefect Corin brought it with him. I'm sure he followed me here. But it had grown very hot and very bright."

"Because it was drawing energy from a wide area. The machines here will begin to work once it has passed out of range. You must do it now and do it quickly. No time for fine surgery." Yama noticed for the first time that the boy had lost his left hand. He said, "I am sorry, Pandaras. There will be more pain, if you stay with me."

Pandaras drew himself up. He was very ragged and had a haunted, starved look, but he met Yama's gaze and said, "I am your squire, master. I lost you for a while, it's true, but now I have found you I will not let you escape me so easily again. What do you want me to do?"

They could not find a knife amongst the dead around them, so Yama broke off the tip of a sword. Pandaras wrapped the broken end in a strip of cloth. Yama sat with his back pressed against a rough boulder, his hands braced against his thighs and a sliver of wood between his teeth. The pain was not as bad as he had feared, and at first there was only a little blood. The plaques lay just beneath his skin, and Pandaras had to cut away only a little flesh to expose them.

"It's a queer kind of stuff, master," Pandaras said. "Like plastic and metal granules that have been melted together. I can see things like roots. Should I cut out those, too?"

Yama nodded.

The pain was suddenly sharper. He closed his eyes and clenched his teeth. An intimate scraping, metal on bone. Red and black flashes in his eyes. Hot blood dripped from the point of his chin. Pandaras pushed his head down, and there was a sharp slicing pain in his neck.

"It's done, master," Pandaras said. He held a decad of small, irregular shapes in his bloody hand. Wirelike whiskers stuck out from their corners.

"Throw them away," Yama said. "If I start behaving in a strange way, knock me out and tie me up. Do not let me near any dirt. There is metal in dirt. Do you understand?"

"Not entirely, master, but I'll get rid of these at once."

Pandaras ripped up the cloak of a dead soldier and placed a pad of cloth over the left side of Yama's face and held it in place with a strip tied around his jaw and the top of his head. Yama's face was numb, but there was a feeling of fire at the edge of the numbness. The wound on the back of his neck was more trivial, but it was bleeding badly.

"We're getting near the river now," Pandaras said. "And look, the coin is beginning to glow again."

He held it up: it showed a faint, grainy light.

"Arm yourself," Yama said. He got to his feet and took a step, then another, but stumbled on the third.

Instantly, Pandaras was by his side. He made Yama sit down, untied the cloth around his head, and whistled. "I cut a vein in there, I think. I'm sorry, master, I am not much of a sawbones. I learned a little of it from one of my uncles, who worked at one of the fighting pits, but not enough, it seems. I should stitch the wound, but I don't have any tackle. I could put a compress in—"

"Cauterize it."

"It will leave a scar. Of course, the jacks who worked the pits liked that kind of thing. It made them look fiercer, neh? But you do not want that, master. A compress—"

Yama picked up the bit of sword and stumbled over to a man-sized machine which had broken apart and was burning with a fierce, steady flame. He thrust the tip of the sword into the center of the fire.

"We do not have time for niceties," he said. "I must be able to fight."

"You couldn't fight a puppy the way you are," Pandaras said. He wrapped a bit of cloth around his hand and drew the broken sword tip from the white heart of the burning machine. "Cry out if you want. They say it helps the pain. And hold onto my arm, here."

Yama did not cry out, because it might bring his enemy to him, but he almost broke Pandaras's left arm when the boy thrust the point of the hot metal into the wound in his cheek. The smell of his own blood burning was horrible.

"Done," Pandaras said. He was crying, but his hand was steady and deft as he packed Yama's wound. He retied the strip of cloth around Yama's head, then tied another around his neck and under his arm to hold a compress against the lesser wound in his neck.

The coin was burning brighter. Pandaras held it up and said, "Shall I throw this away? He knows how to find it; it is how he found me and it is why he kept me alive, so that he could find you. In any case, we should run now, master. If the coin is working again, then surely you can command some machine to take us away."

"I want Prefect Corin to find us," Yama said. "He destroyed my home. He was responsible for the death of my stepfather. I will have an accounting."

"He will kill you."

"I do not think he has come here to do that. If I do not confront him, Pandaras, then I will never be able to rest, for he will not."

"That's as may be, but I don't know if you can kill him. Those monsters you called up from the depths couldn't. I think he jumped on a floating disc and sailed away from them."

"I do not know if I want to kill him, Pandaras. That is why I want to see him."

Yama took the gisarme and Pandaras found a short ironwood stave. They armed themselves with pellet pistols too. As they climbed out of the sally port's amphitheater, some of the dead began to stir and twitch. The machines in Dr. Dismas's servants were awakening in bodies too mutilated to control. Yama found a legless torso trying to drag itself along, its guts trailing behind it, and dispatched it with the spike of the gisarme.

Yama began to call out to Prefect Corin as he and Pandaras walked toward the far edge of the island, through near darkness lit only by burning trees. But the Shadow found him first, suddenly gliding beside him at the edge of his vision. As before, it took the form of Derev, but this time her likeness was distorted to resemble one of Dr. Dismas's man-animals, naked and on all fours. Its voice was a faint hiss, like the last echo of creation.

You cannot destroy me, Child of the River. I am wrapped around every neuron in your brain.

"I do not want to destroy you. I want you to help me understand what I am."

Pandaras said, "What is it, master? Is he here?"

"No, not yet. It is the thing in my head."

You are a fool to deny what we can become. A worm, a weakling. How I will torment you.

It tipped back its head, its throat elongating, and howled like a dervish. Something like a faint wash of flame passed across Yama's mind. He bore it easily.

Pandaras said, "But I cut it out!"

"Not all of it. Just those parts which drew power from the world's energy grid. It will be no more powerful than me now, unless it can regrow those parts."

I will take the iron from your blood, you fool! I will weave myself so tightly against your every nerve that you will never be rid of me.

But the sparks of the Shadow's words flickered so faintly that they were easier to ignore than the growing sense of the weave of machines which mapped the dark world all around. It was stronger than ever, an overlapping babble of voices near and far. Yama called upon one of the machines which served the garden, and it explained in a rapid, agitated staccato that the gravithic grids of the platform—it meant the floating garden—were exhausted, and that it was falling in an irrecoverable trajectory.

Pandaras squinted at the glowing thing that beat before Yama's face on a blur of vanes. "They work for Prefect Corin," he said.

"Not here. It wants us to evacuate this place. It seems we will strike the world in a handful of minutes."

"But you will save us, master."

"No."

"But you must!"

"I cannot." The machine was trying to explain about realignment and repolarization, but Yama asked it to be quiet, and told Pandaras, "There is not enough time for the garden to soak up enough energy to regain its lift."

The machine added something tartly, and with a shrill whir of vanes flew up into the night.

"Apparently, the other garden will strike the world first," Yama told Pandaras.

"As if that makes any difference. What's that?"

Yama heard it a moment later. An animal frenzy of howls and yips, and then a stutter of rifle fire.

Yama ran, feeling the cauterized wound in his cheek pull open at every step. He ran through the burning trees, across the cracked basin of the lake, and up the rocky slope. His head was full of voices. His face was a stiff mask with hot needles pushed through it into his skull, and his legs were rubbery, but as he leapt from rock to rock in the near dark, he called upon skills he had learned as a child while clambering about the steep dry slopes of the City of the Dead, and did not stumble.

Dr. Dismas stood at the far edge of the crag, his silvery cloak and cap glimmering in the firelit dark. A pentad of his naked man-animals cowered around him. Their round eyes glowed green or red, reflecting the light of the decads of tiny machines which swarmed around the man who leaned on his staff a hundred paces away.

"Yamamanama," Prefect Corin said, without looking away from Dr. Dismas. "You have come to me as I knew that you would." A rifle was slung over his shoulder, and Dr. Dismas's energy pistol was tucked into his belt. The pale-skinned hierodule, clad only in ragged trews, squatted beside the Prefect, and bared his teeth when Pandaras called to him.

Yama's face hurt when he spoke. He said, "Not at all. Instead, you have come to me."

"You are still a vain and foolish boy," Prefect Corin said chidingly. "While we travel back to Ys you will dwell on all the hurt you have caused, the deaths you must already count as yours and those which are to come when you undo your mischief."

Dr. Dismas said, "Kill him, Yamamanama. Do it quickly. We have far to go."

"You will be quiet, old man," Prefect Corin said in his calm, soft voice, "or I will take your eyes and tongue. You have much to answer for, too. Taking away your little realm is only the beginning of the reckoning."

"The laboratories are nothing," Dr. Dismas said, and tapped the side of his head. "It is all in here."

Prefect Corin told Yama, "A flier will be here in a moment. Unless of course you can save this garden. One way or another, we will be in the heart of our Department by dawn. There will be a new beginning. Frankly, you need it. You look bad, Yamamanama, bloody and ill-used. I will see that you get all the medical attention you so clearly have not had here."

Yama said, as steadily as he could, "I will not serve."

Prefect Corin looked at him for the first time. He said, "We all serve, Child of the River. We are all servants of the Preservers."

Yama remembered what Sergeant Rhodean had told him outside the marquee where the Aedile had lain dying, on the farside shore after the sack of Aeolis, and saw now what Prefect Corin was. Saw that the man's reserve was not a discipline, but a denial that he was like other men. That his humble air was a mask which hid his hunger for all the world's powers, all its riches. Yama had thought that his hatred of Prefect Corin would be too much to bear, but now he felt pity as much as hate, and pity diminished the man.

He found that he was able to meet and hold Prefect Corin's gaze. He said, "The Preservers do not ask for servants. They ask nothing of us but that we become all we can be."

"You have been too long amongst the heretics, Child of the River," Prefect Corin said. There was a note of harshness in his voice now. "That will be corrected too."

"I am not a heretic," Dr. Dismas said. "For that alone you should kill him, Yamamanama."

Prefect Corin ignored the apothecary, concentrating his mild gaze on Yama.

A worm of blood was trickling along the angle of Yama's jaw. He said, "The world is not a ledger, Corin, with good and evil in separate tallies. There is no division into good and evil. It is all one thing, light and shadow in play together. No one can set themselves aside from it unless they remove themselves completely."

He had never been so certain as at that moment, there on the highest point of a rock slowly falling out of the sky. He was aware of everything around him—the wind which carried the harsh stink of burning, the trajectory of the garden and of the rock ahead of it, the myriads of machines in the cities along the shrinking shore of the Great River, the flier that was speeding toward the garden, still a hundred leagues off.

He made a few adjustments.

At the same moment Prefect Corin struck down with the point of his staff. Rock broke around it, cracks running outward from where he stood to every point of the crag, and the whole garden shivered like a whipped animal. Pandaras fell down; the hierodule raised his head and howled.

Dr. Dismas snickered. His man-animals hunched around him. "You've made him lose his temper, Yamamanama."

Prefect Corin pointed his staff at him and said, "Be quiet, devil!

Except for pain and repentance, your part in this is over." The machines whirled up in a brilliant blaze above his head.

"You're as bad as the heretics," Dr. Dismas said, and turned his back in disgust.

The hierodule was still howling, his muscles straining against each other under his flabby skin.

Yama told Pandaras, "Hold up the coin. Do not be afraid." He saw the knot in the hierodule's mind and loosened it, and said, "Be quiet, Tibor. He will not use you anymore. Come to me."

The hierodule blinked and fell silent. The cloud of machines around Prefect Corin suddenly spun away in every direction, leaving the crag lit only by firelight and the dim red glow of the Eye of the Preservers. The Prefect reversed his grip of the staff and began to beat the hierodule about his shoulders. "Do not listen, you fool! Obey your master! Obey! Obey!"

Dr. Dismas was laughing. The man-animals crouched as his feet made little excited yips and howls.

"You will not use him," Yama said. "It is all right, Tibor. Come to me."

Tibor ducked away from Prefect Corin's blows and stood up. He said, "It is good to see you again, master. I thought you had fallen over the edge of the world."

"Not yet," Yama said. The words were compelled from him by Tibor's mild stare; they seemed to come from somewhere in the babble of voices in his head. He remembered the dream he had had in the tomb in the Silent Quarter of the City of the Dead, and then remembered Luria, the true pythoness in the Department of Vaticination. A truth came to him, brilliant and many-splendored. It was like the peacock, but he could bear it now. Lifted on great wings of exhilaration, he felt that he could bear anything.

He said, "The coin Pandaras has faithfully carried for so long enables access to the space inside the shrines, just like the induction loop in a hierodule like Tibor. And one can talk with the other. My father was fascinated by the past, and his excavations turned up many coins like it. I think that in the Age of Enlightenment people used them as commonly as we use money, but they did not use them to buy the stuff of everyday life. Instead, they bought access to the shrines. Anyone could consult the aspects then, without mediation of priests or hierodules." He turned to Pandaras and grasped the boy's hand. "Do you remember, Pandaras, when we walked toward the Temple of the Black Well? Do you remember the medallions in the windows of those poor shops, the medallions people hung on their walls to ward off the ghosts of dead machines? I thought then that I recognized the engravings on their surfaces, and now I see that they are similar to the patterns of light in this coin. The people remember, even if they do not understand what they remember. They are the strength of the city, Pandaras! The strength of the world!"

"Master, you are hurting me," Pandaras said. There was fear in his eyes.

Yama realized how tightly he was gripping the boy's hand, and apologized and let go. But his joy did not diminish. It grew as the babble of voices in his head grew: he was dissolving into it, forgetting his fear, his anger, the agony of Pandaras's hasty surgery.

"I forgive your ravings," Prefect Corin said dryly. "Your father is ages dead, and the Aedile of Aeolis was a foolish man who looked only to the past."

Yama said, "You carry something made by the mages which acts like the coin, I think. But it cannot work as well as that which it tries to imitate."

"The Aedile was the beginning of your corruption, Yamamanama, and I will be the end of it. No more talk now. Perhaps you think to convince me by reason, but I am proof against your reason. Perhaps you came to duel with me, thinking to decide the fate of the world in the way of the old stories, but they are only stories. I could kill you now, and there would be an end to it."

Yama laughed. He threw the gisarme to one side, pulled the pellet pistol from his waistband and threw that away too. He spread his empty hands. "Those were for Dr. Dismas's servants. But I see that only a few are left."

Dr. Dismas turned and said, "Enough for my purposes."

He made no signal, but the man-animals leaped toward Prefect Corin in a single fluid movement. There was a wash of flame. Yama turned away from the searing heat and light, but thought that he glimpsed Dr. Dismas falling beyond the edge of the crag, globed by fire which beat at the mirror of his silvery cloak. When he turned back, the stones of the place where Dr. Dismas had been standing were glowing with a dull red heat, and Prefect Corin was pointing the energy pistol at him.

"If you thought that he would kill me," the Prefect said steadily, "then you were wrong. I will use this against you if I have to, and at its full setting."

Yama said, "I came here to see what kind of man you were. Now I know."

"I am a servant of something greater than you think you are, boy."

"I once feared you because of the authority you embodied, but then you burnt down Aeolis and killed my father and I knew that you misused your authority for your own ends. You are not my nemesis, Corin."

Prefect Corin leaned on his staff, attempting to command Yama and Pandaras and Tibor with his gaze. "Talk on, boy. You have a few minutes."

"Fewer than you think, perhaps."

"You do not command here. The garden is mine." Prefect Corin set something in the air before him. It was a sketch of a solid object that was neither a sphere nor a cube but somehow both at once; it seemed far bigger than the space which contained it. Prefect Corin said, "If I start this spinning it will draw away the energy from every machine. There will be no help for you."

"Then the flier will not come, and the world is rushing toward us."

"I can stop the machine a moment before the flier arrives. Meanwhile, your little tricks will come to nothing."

"You have thought of everything," Yama said, "but it does not mean that you are right."

"I have right on my side, boy."

Yama's heart quickened. Although he strove to keep his face calm, his hands were trembling. Let Prefect Corin think it was fear. The moment was approaching. He had only to finish this.

He took a deep breath and said, "The Department of Indigenous Affairs once served in harmony with the other departments of the civil service, to keep the world as it always was. In this way the civil service is like the heretics, for both abhor change. One struggles to knit society together at the expense of individual destiny; the other wants to destroy society so that a few lucky individuals might live forever; both deny change. But life is change. The Preservers taught us that when they created this world and its inhabitants, when they shaped the ten thousand bloodlines. And the Preservers changed too, and changed so much that they could no longer bear this universe. All of life is change."

Prefect Corin said, "You have learned nothing, or unlearned all you were taught. If not for the civil service, the ten thousand bloodlines would have warred against each other and destroyed the world long ago. The civil service maintains a society in which every man has a place, and is happy in that place. The Great River which sustains this world is the first lesson, for it is always changing and always same. And so with society, in which individuals live and die. Even bloodlines change and rise toward the nothingness of enlightenment and pass away from this world, but the world remains as it is. There are always more individuals, and always more bloodlines."

"The Great River is failing," Yama said. He was aware of a voice at the forefront of the crowd of voices which yammered and babbled inside his head. It was counting down the seconds. There was only a little more time. He said, "Even the indigenous races know that the river fails. Your department has decided that it speaks for the Preservers, and in its arrogance it has lost its way. For no one in this world can speak for the Preservers, who are no longer of this world. We can only repeat the words the Preservers left us, and nothing new can come of those words."

"We need nothing more than their words. All good men are guided by them. How badly you have strayed, Yamamanama. But I will save you."

"The Department of Indigenous Affairs has become what it fights against. I do not blame it, because it was inevitable. There has to be one strong department to lead the war against the heretics, but its strength means the destruction of the consensus which sustained the civil service. For if the war is won then the Department will assume all the powers of the civil service, as it has already assumed the territories of the departments which border upon it within the Palace of the Memory of the People. And it will become a greater tyranny than the heretics could ever be."

"We will win, and things will be as they were."

"Why then are you here?"

"I am a voice and an arm of the Department."

"No. You are a man who wants power within the Department. I am a way to that power. There are other men like you. When the war is over, you and your kind will fight each other. Perhaps not at once, perhaps not for ten thousand years, but it will happen at last, and the Department will destroy itself. In making the assumption that anything you do is for the good of the world, you excuse all your actions, good and bad, until you can no longer distinguish between them. But I think that is enough. You do not listen to me."

"There will be all the time in the world for that, Yamamanama. At my leisure, in the Palace of the Memory of the People. But I will talk then, and you will listen. All you make now are animal noises. Noises which mean nothing."

"There is no more time. The flier will not come. I ordered it away."

"It is almost here," Prefect Corin said.

"A machine tells you that. Do not rely on machines, Corin."

"Enough of your tricks," Prefect Corin said, and the thing in the air in front of him began to spin, gathering itself into a soft red haze that at once began to brighten toward the color and intensity of the sun, and shrieking like the world's last end.

The voices in Yama's head died away. He took up their count.

Twelve.

Pandaras cried out in alarm and dismay. "Master! Would you kill us?"

"Would you die to save the world, Pandaras?"

Seven.

"What kind of question is that, master? If I refused that sacrifice then the world would die and I would die anyway. Or the world would live and again I would die. In any case, I do not like this talk of dying."

Two. One.

"Then follow me," Yama said.

Now.

Impossibly, the sun rose downriver. No, it could not be the sun, for as the blister of light spread out horizontally it suddenly redoubled in brightness, and redoubled again. It was so bright that Yama could see the bones of the hand he flung up to save his eyes.

The floating rock had struck the river, and the first machine Prefect Corin had set spinning to draw energy from the local grid had finally collapsed, and released all its stored energy at once.

For an instant, Yama existed at every point of machine consciousness in the world. And then the concussion of the impact arrived in a blast of air and thunder, and he was knocked down by a howling gale full of water and bits of debris, as if the distinction between air and river had been abolished. Tibor was struggling with Prefect Corin, trying to force down the Prefect's outflung arm. Yama got to his feet, swept up Pandaras and yelled at Tibor to follow them, and ran straight over the edge of the crag.

———

A violent gust caught them, and for a moment they hung in the midst of a hard, driving rain. A double shadow at the edge of the crag might have been Prefect Corin and Tibor. Then the gust failed. Yama and Pandaras fell past the edge of the floating garden as a blade of light broke the sky in half.

They did not fall far—the world had risen very close to the floating garden—but the impact was still unforgiving. Yama plunged down and down in roaring dark water. Pandaras was torn from his grasp. He let himself float for a moment to get his orientation and then struck upward, breaking the surface and drawing in a great gasping breath that was half air, half water.

Despite the storm, it was as bright as day, although the light was sulfur yellow and came from the wrong quarter of the sky. Above, the floating garden was sliding away like a great ship, a solid shadow against a nimbus of achingly bright light. Something was climbing up from that intolerable light. A stalk or pillar of black smoke and ordinary fire that rose higher and higher and blossomed at last in the upper reaches of the atmosphere as a great thunderhead. Brilliant stitches of lighting blinked continuously around it.

Yama kicked against the flood, turning in a complete circle as waves lifted and dropped him. The wounds in his face and neck were ablaze with pain. As he rose for the fourth time he saw something between two waves close by and swam strongly toward it. It was Pandaras. Yama caught the boy by the scruff of his neck and he tried to climb up him in blind panic. Yama asked forgiveness and knocked him out with a swift clean punch, and got an arm around his chest to support him.

As Yama and Pandaras were lifted and dropped by line after line of waves that marched away upriver, something came walking across the water toward him, small and sharply focused at first, but becoming more and more indistinct as it neared.

Derev.

Yama roared into wind and rain. "Get out of my mind!"

She was a giant, transparent as smoke. Her great wings unfurled far into the storm. She stooped toward him, and her face writhed and became a horror of snakes and scorpions, and then she seemed to be blown away in rags and tatters by the wind.

Pandaras stirred, and then came awake and at once began to struggle again.

"Quiet," Yama said, "or I will have to hit you a second time."

"I can't swim properly! Not with only one arm!"

"There is no point trying to swim! The second wave will be here soon! I will save us, Pandaras. Do not be afraid!"

They were shouting into each other's ears against the tremendous howl of wind and rain and the roar of clashing waves.

Pandaras turned his face upward. "Master! The rain is growing warmer!"

It was. Yama said, "The second wave!"

"When the other garden hits, master?"

"No, from the first. From Prefect Corin's machine. First light, then sound. Sound carries the most energy—that is why the floating garden was knocked over. But it comes in two stages, because energy travels more slowly through water than through air."

They rose on the crest of another wave. For a moment, wind swept aside curtains of rain. The Great River dwindled away ahead of them, hatched by lines of waves driven by the strong warm wind. The floating garden had vanished—perhaps it too had finally struck the river. The false sunrise had faded, but the pillar of burning smoke still stood at the vanishing point where the nearside and farside edges of the world seemed to meet. The cloud at its top was spreading out and its light was changing to a ghastly red, but it did not appear to be any dimmer.

Yama wondered how much energy Prefect Corin's machine had managed to store before it had been dissipated on the moment of impact. Prefect Corin had not understood the power of the things he thought he controlled.

The first machine arrived, plucking at the yoke of Yama's loose shirt. Then another, and a decad more. The largest was a kind of wire-thin dragonfly as long as his arm, but most were much smaller. Together, they pulled Yama and Pandaras a handspan above the clashing wave-tops, and then more arrived, lifting them higher into the rain-filled wind.

Above the noise of the storm, there was a sound like a tremendous cannonade. Far away down the length of the world, the river seemed to be tilting into the sky.

13

The Forest Folk

THE FLOOD KNOCKED down every tree for many leagues beyond the shore of the Great River and deposited vast shoals of silt and gravel and mud. Streams and creeks ran at full spate as the water receded, carving new channels into the landscape. It rained continuously, and dense reefs of mist were driven back and forth by restless winds.

The machines carried Yama and Pandaras far inland, and left them at the top of a plateau which rose above the devastated forests. They made camp as best they could in a glade of small trees at the edge of a cliff that dropped straight down into the mists. Yama was exhausted, and bruised over his entire body, and the wounds in his face hurt horribly.

"You must summon more machines to help us," Pandaras said. "You must get us away from here, master, or you will die."

"No," Yama said wearily. "No more machines."

A floating disc could carry them wherever they wanted, but would be a target for anyone who wanted to take a potshot. And Yama was not certain that Prefect Corin had been killed in the crash of the floating garden; if he called on any machine, the Prefect might be able to track him down. He had shut down the coin which had guided Pandaras to him for that very reason, even though it could have helped Tibor, had he survived the tidal wave, to find them. And it was because of Yama's ability to bend machines to his will that tens of thousands of people had died in the great flood; he feared now that he might inadvertently destroy the world.

The Shadow tormented him with visions of destruction for the rest of that night. It showed him people combing through the ruins of cities in the midst of driving rainstorms, ships swept inland, piles of drowned animal and human corpses. It showed him the crater on the nearside shore of the Great River where Prefect Corin's machine had struck, a circular sea rimmed with swales of half-melted rock and shrouded in the smoke of the great fires that burned all around it. And then, when he was at his weakest, streaming with fever sweat as he lay naked in a bower of woven leaves, the Shadow finally revealed itself. It was faint and insubstantial, its form melting and changing from Derev to the Aedile or to Telmon or to others of the dead. So many dead.

All your work, Child of the River. Will you save the world by destroying it? But you cannot destroy me. I will be with you always. I can help you, if you will let me.

"No. No more."

"Hush, master," Pandaras said. "Try to rest. Try to sleep."

"It is in my dreams, Pandaras."

I will always be with you.

Pandaras tended Yama all night, and in the morning tried to make his master eat fruit he had collected from the margin of the forest. But Yama would eat only a scant handful of ripe figs and drink a few sips of rainwater. He was still gripped by the terror of his fever dreams.

"Those people, Pandaras! Those poor people!"

"Hush, master. Be still. Rest. I will fetch you more fruit. You must eat and get well."

The forest frightened Pandaras. It covered the top of the plateau, dense, dripping wet, full of shadows and strange noises. Everything was predicated in the vertical, dominated by giant trees which gripped the thin soil with buttress roots, sucked up water and precious minerals from the stony laterite, and spread vast rafts of foliage high overhead. There were cottonwoods with feathery foliage and pendant strings of hard-hulled nuts, silkwoods and greenhearts and cedars, stands of fibrous copal trees. Vines and lianas threw up long loops, gaining holds on branches and throwing up yet more loops as they scrambled for light. Parasitic orchids clung to bark like splashes of paint. Smaller trees grew in the dancing spangles of light that filtered through the canopies of the giants: sago palms with scaly trunks; palmettos with saw-toothed leaves; acacias defended by ferocious red ants as long as Pandaras's thumb; balsams seeping sticky, strongly scented sap; the spiny straps of raffias which caught at his clothes and flesh. And in the dense shade beneath the secondary growth were ferns, bamboos and dark white fungi shaped like brains or vases.

Pandaras saw no animals bigger than a butterfly as he picked his way between the mossy buttress roots of the soaring trees, but he was convinced that at any moment he might confront a manticore or dragon or some other monster that might swallow him in a single gulp.

Although everything was verdant, a riot of greenery struggling upward for light, fruiting trees and bushes were rare. Toward the end of the second day Pandaras went farther than he had dared to venture before, following a narrow path between stands of long-stemmed plants which raised glossy green leaves high above his head. It was close to sunset, and the level rays of the sun were beginning to insinuate themselves beneath the high canopy of the giant trees. In the far distance something was making a noise like a bell rung over and over; the electric sizzle of insects was all around.

By now, Pandaras had been bitten by mosquitoes so often that he thought nothing of the sudden stabbing pain in his chest. He brushed at it reflexively and then stared in astonishment at the little arrow, a sliver of bamboo fletched with blue feathers, that fell at his feet.

The tall grass around him parted. Men smaller than himself stepped onto the path and the world flew up and struck him hard.

———

At first, Yama thought that the people who lifted him out of the bower and laid him on a litter of woven banana leaves were part of the fever dreams sent to him by the Shadow. They carried him a long way through the twilight forest. There seemed to be a hundred of them, men and women and children. They ran very fast, crossing from one side of the plateau to the other in a few hours, to the clearing in the shade of a grandfather kapok tree where they had made a temporary camp.

They treated Yama's wounds with moss and fungus, and bathed him with infusions of willow roots to reduce his fever. They were an indigenous people, and called themselves the bandar yoi inoie, which meant the forest folk. They were small and stout, with disproportionately large heads and coarse black hair which they tied back with thread and feathers or stiffened into spikes with white clay. Some wore torcs of beaten copper enameled with intricate patterns of ultramarine and beryl. Their brown skin was loose and hung in folds, and they pierced the folds with intricate patterns of thorns and decorated themselves with mud or pigments from crushed flowers and berries daubed in spirals and zigzag lines. They peopled the forest with monstrous gods; each useful plant or animal had a story concerning the way its secret had been stolen or tricked from these deities. Like the fisherfolk, they used poison from the glands of certain frogs to anoint their hunting arrows. The various troops communicated with each other by drumming on the resonant buttress roots of the great trees of the forest, and when certain trees came into flower three or four troops would meet up and hold marriage contests. They feared lightning more than anything else, for it killed several of them each year, uprooted beloved trees, and sometimes started devastating fires. They had many taboos against inviting thunderstorms; for instance, they were forbidden to hunt monkeys, or even to laugh at their antics.

Although they lived freely in the forests, the bandar yoi inoie were slaves of a Shaped bloodline, the Mighty People. The Mighty People had fought a Change War recently, the chief of the troop of forest folk told Yama. The old ways had been overthrown by new ideas from the sky and had been burnt up so that they could never come back. The temple had been desecrated and its priest and hierodules killed. Many of the Mighty People had been killed in the war too, and those who survived no longer lived together in their city of communal long houses, but were scattered across their lands.

"They have changed," Yama said.

The chief nodded solemnly. He was a strong man, ugly even by the standards of the bandar yoi inoie. He had pushed porcupine quills through his cheeks and the folded skin of his chest. The tip of his long nose rested on his swollen upper lip. His name was Yoi Sendar.

"We know about the heretics," he said. "Don't look so surprised, man. We travel all over the forests to find food for ourselves and for the Mighty People. We talk to many travelers. We know the heretics take their ideas from a forgotten clutch of the larvae of the Preservers who recently stepped down from the sky. The ideas are old and bad, but they are as sweet as honey to our beloved Mighty People."

"But you were not seduced by them."

"We are an indigenous people, man. It was ordained by the Preservers that we can never change. We can only be what we are." Yoi Sendar tapped the tip of his pendulous nose. "But these are strange times. All things change, it seems. Perhaps even the bandar yoi inoie. We love the Mighty People, but they have grown strange and harsh. They are no longer our kind dear masters of old. You will see for yourself, when we return. Although we wish long and hard that things might be otherwise, I fear the changes are written in stone."

"Be careful what you wish for, Yoi Sendar."

You would set yourself up as savior of these people? O Yamamanama, how I will punish you, by and by.

Yama ignored the Shadow's dim whisper. He was feeling stronger now. It was three days after he had been found by the forest folk. His wounds were healing and his fever had abated, and he had been fed well. He was able to bear the visions which the Shadow brought to him in the night. They were his secret shame, his punishment for having dared act like a Preserver. Never again. Never, never again. He wished that he could renounce everything and find Derev and marry her if she would have him, but he knew that it could not be so simple. He knew that he was set on a hard road that would almost certainly end in his death.

Pandaras had recovered too. He had made a flute from a joint of bamboo and was playing in the sunlight at the edge of the clearing to an audience of fat, ugly, admiring children who were as interested in the fetish he wore on his arm as his jaunty tunes.

The huge kapok tree in the center of the clearing was hung with sleeping cocoons woven from grass and ferns, each tailored to its owner. They would be abandoned when the troop packed up their camp, for the forest folk had no permanent habitation. Men and women were tending the long trench of coals over which they smoked the flesh of the fat caterpillars they collected deep in the forest. These were a delicacy for both the forest folk and the Mighty People. Thousands of caterpillars hung from frames suspended over the hot coals, on which leaves of certain aromatic plants were now and then cast. Sweet smelling blue smoke hazed the beams of sunlight which fell through the kapok's leaf-laden branches.

Yama asked the chief, "Why do you work for the Mighty People? It seems to me that you are as free a people as any on the world."

Yoi Sendar said, "It is a long story, and you may not have one as good."

Yama smiled. He had learned that this was the traditional challenge amongst the bandar yoi inoie, who decided their social status and won their husbands and wives by their ability to tell tales. Pandaras said that in a year he could be chief of all the forest folk, although he admitted that some of their stories were worth retelling elsewhere. Already young men and women were settling at a respectful distance, ready to enjoy the story and to try and learn how to improve their own tale telling from Yoi Sendar's example.

Yoi Sendar looked around and said, "This is one of the least of the stories that I know, but it may amuse you."

Yama smiled as best he could. His wounds were scarring over and his face was stiff and numb. It was as if he was wearing a badly made mask. He had spent a long time looking at it in one of the forest folk's precious mirrors. The right side was not too bad, but the left, which Pandaras had had to cauterize, was a patchwork of welted flesh, pulling down his eye and lifting the corner of his mouth.

He had become outwardly what he believed he was inwardly: a monster, an outcast. Derev would never cease to love the boy he had been, but how could she love what he had become? Perhaps it was best that he went to his death after all.

Die? I will not let us die, Child of the River. We will live forever.

Yama told Yoi Sendar, "I would like to hear your story. Then perhaps you would like to hear one of mine, although I doubt that it is as finely made as yours."

"Listen then," Yoi Sendar said, and held up two fingers by his ear. His audience shifted, focusing their attention on the grave, ugly little man.

"Listen then, O my people. This is a story of long ago, after the Preservers brought us to this world but before we met our dear masters, the Mighty People."

"In that long ago time we were always hungry. One group of us went far into the forests to look for game and found nothing. They walked and walked and at last they sat down to rest on what seemed to be the fallen trunk of a huge tree. But when one of them stuck the point of his knife into the scaly bark, blood spurted out, for they were not sitting on a fallen tree at all, but on the King of All Snakes. The King had been sleeping, and the knife wound woke him and made him very angry. But the men were mighty hunters, and although he struck out and tried to crush them in the coils of his body, they evaded his attack and hacked off his head.

"When they were certain that he was dead (for some snakes have a head at either end), they began to butcher his body, for they were very hungry. Yet as the blood of the King of All Snakes drained into the ground, a heavy rain began to fall, feeding a great flood that filled the forest. The flood washed away the hunters, and all human habitation for many leagues around. We have just witnessed a great flood, O my brothers and sisters, but this flood was far greater.

"Only one woman survived. She climbed to the top of a high mountain and squeezed into a crack in the rock behind the shelter of a creeper. The wind blew the creeper back and forth against the rock, and from this friction jumped showers of sparks. The woman caught some of these sparks and used them to light a fire made from dead husks picked from the outer skin of the creeper. The warmth encouraged the creeper to put forth flowers, which the woman ate. And so she had food and warmth, and later she took the creeper for her husband.

"The woman and the creeper made a child together, by and by, but he was a poor halfling with only one arm and one leg. His name was Yoi Soi. He was always hungry and hopped about everywhere. He quickly found a few grains of rice which a rat had saved from the flood. He set the rice on a leaf to dry, and when the rat discovered what Yoi Soi had done, it swore angrily that in revenge his children would always steal a portion of the food of men.

"But Yoi Soi did not get to eat the rice. Before the grains had dried, a wind came and blew them away across the forest. Yoi Soi hopped after them, driven by his hunger. He passed an ancient tree covered in birds which pecked at any green buds it put forth, and the tree implored the boy to ask the wind to come and blow it down and put it out of its torment. Yoi Soi promised that if he found the wind he would ask for that favor, and the tree lifted one of its limbs and pointed the way to the wind's home.

"Yoi Soi hopped on more eagerly than ever. He passed a stagnant lake and the scum on the lake bubbled up into a pair of fat green lips which asked the boy to bring a strong wind that would blow away the logs which blocked its outlet. Yoi Soi promised that he would do his best, and the lake give him its last measure of pure water. Yoi Soi drank it down and it renewed his strength at once.

"Yoi Soi felt very strong now, but his stomach was empty. He stopped in a grove of banana plants, but the fruit was out of reach, and because he had only one arm and leg he could not climb. The banana plants fluttered their long green leaves and asked Yoi Soi if he would ask the wind to restore the limbs they had lost in the great flood, so that they could once more embrace the air. When Yoi Soi promised this, hands of red bananas dropped around him and he ate well and went on to the high place of bare rock where the wind lived.

"The wind was very angry that this halfling had dared to track it to its lair for the sake of a few grains of rice. It told Yoi Soi that it had scattered the rice across the world. Rice would feed many kinds of men, but would never feed the children of Yoi Soi. Then the wind roared and pounced and tried to blow the boy from the high place.

"But Yoi Soi had come prepared. He had brought kindling taken from the shaggy coat of his father the creeper, and flints to strike sparks. With these he set fire to the wind's tail, and the wind flung itself about, howling in pain. 'Put out the flames,' it cried, 'and I shall make you a whole man!'

"Yoi Soi stamped down with his one foot and put out the fire, and in the next moment the wind darted down his throat and he grew and grew. His missing arm and leg popped out of his skin and he became a whole man twice as tall and ten times as strong as he had been. What a wonder, O my brothers and sisters! For the wind had made him the first of the Mighty People.

"Filled with the spirit of the wind, Yoi Soi stamped off through the forest, singing loudly. He was so strong that he was able to pull down the old tree afflicted by the plague of birds, and to unblock the stagnant lake. He stamped back to the mountain where his mother lived and his father the creeper grew, and carried her away to a distant place where he had spied others of her kind.

"But because Yoi Soi was so big, and so full of wind that he had to sing or talk all the time, he scared away the animals of the forest and could not hunt. Instead, he commanded the small people of his mother to serve him, and so things have been ever since. Our men hunt for meat and our women pick fruit and berries and flowers—perhaps they secretly hope to find the creeper which was the father of the Mighty People, but you will have to ask them about that. And if you think that I have forgotten the poor banana plants, then remember that Yoi Soi was not given magical powers, and he could do nothing for them."

———

The troop of forest folk set out for the home of their masters the next day. They followed a chain of tree-covered hills that rose above the wreckage of the great flood, stepping away toward the Rim Mountains. They carried packs of dried caterpillar flesh, a long line of them bent under their loads as they trotted through hot green shade, far beneath the high canopy of the soaring trees.

Yama and Pandaras walked at the head of the line, behind Yoi Sendar. Pandaras was not happy that they were so dependent upon the kindness of the forest folk, and said quietly, "We should not be going toward these Mighty People of theirs, master. It is clear that they have been changed by the heretics. We will be delivered into the hands of our enemies and all this will have been in vain."

He meant the devastation of the forests, and the terrible scarring of Yama's face.

"I hope to find the temple, Pandaras, or at least what remains of it after the Change War. There will surely be a passage into the keelways nearby. We will travel quickly that way, and our enemies will not find us."

He did not tell the boy that they would be traveling beyond the midpoint of the world into the Glass Desert, to search for the father of the thing inside him. He would give the boy the choice of following him or returning to Ys when the time came.

"Perhaps there are other temples, master."

"Not here," Yoi Sendar said, without looking around. "Our masters the Mighty People are the only civilized people within many days' walk."

The journey to the home of the Mighty People took five days. There were many distractions along the way and the forest folk had to live off the land because they would not touch their cargo of smoke-dried caterpillar flesh. Each day, they began to travel before dawn and stopped when the sun reached its highest point. They slept in the steamy afternoon heat and woke in the early evening to weave new cocoons and to hunt.

Yama and Pandaras talked for hours during those long, hot, sleepy afternoons, telling each other of their adventures in the time they had been parted. Mostly it was Pandaras who talked. Yama kept his pain and his despair to himself. At night, the Shadow came to him while the others slept, feeble and full of rage. Its threats and boasts filled his dreams.

The bandar yoi inoie did not mourn the destruction of the lowland forests. "There are many kinds of monstrous men in the lowlands," Yoi Sendar told Yama. "We were given the hills as our province by the Preservers and we do not need any other place. Besides, the low forests will regrow soon enough. They will take strength from the mud left behind by the water. In the lifetime of a man they will be as they always have been. Meanwhile, there will be plenty of game for us, because the animals have all fled to our hills."

The bandar yoi inoie had many stories about the strange and fabulous creatures which lived in the lowland and hill forests. Yama had read about some of them in bestiaries in the library of the peel-house of his stepfather, the Aedile of Aeolis; others were entirely new to him. He knew about blood orchids, for instance, because they grew in the forests of the foothills of the Rim Mountains, but those were pygmies compared to the giant blossoms of these forests, as big as a house and surrounded by the bones of animals which had been lured onto their gluey bracts by clouds of pheromones. There were fisher orchids too, which grew on high branches and let down adhesive-covered roots which would wrap around anything which blundered into them and draw nutrients from the corpses; and orchids which emitted hypnotic scents and grew nets of fine roots into the flesh of their victims as they slept. Fire ants built huge castles amongst the tall trees. One kind of tree was defended by hordes of tiny rodents which attacked anything that approached, and stripped neighboring trees of their leaves so that they would not shade their host; in turn, the tree fed its army with a sugary cotton it grew on certain branches. Jacksnappers hung from branches, dropping onto their prey and wrapping them in fleshy folds covered with myriad bony hooks tipped with a paralyzing poison. A certain kind of small, slow, naked monkey was the juvenile form. After mating, the male died and the female wrapped her tail around a suitable branch and spun a cocoon around herself, emerging as an adult jacksnapper, limbless and eyeless and without a brain.

The bandar yoi inoie had stories about the strange races of men which lived in the lowland forests too. There were tribes in which the men grew only a little after birth, and spent their lives in a special pouch in the belly of their mate. In one race, each family was controlled by a single fertile woman who grew monstrously fat and enslaved her sterile sisters, and the men were outcasts who fought fiercely if they met one another as they wandered the forests; there were great and bloody battles when fertile daughters matured and left their families and the men tried to win their favors. There were men who ran through the forest at night, drinking the blood of their mesmerized prey, and tribes of pale men and women who could transform themselves to look like other kinds of men—perhaps these were relatives of the mirror people Yama had met in the Palace of the Memory of the People.

Yama did not know which of these strange peoples were real and which were the stuff of stories. The forest folk were careless of the distinction. If it can be imagined, Yoi Sendar said, then surely it must be real. The Preservers who made this world were much greater than any of the races of men they had raised up from animals, and so they made more wonders than could possibly be imagined.

The bandar yoi inoie were happy in the forest. It was their home, as familiar to them as the peel-house and the City of the Dead were to Yama. They chanted long intricate melodies as they trotted through its green shadows, and sang and laughed and told long complicated jokes as they came back from hunting or while they cooked the prey they had caught or prepared the tubers and fruit they had collected.

Late one afternoon a party of hunters found a treecreeper and one man rushed back to tell the others. The entire troop, along with Yama and Pandaras, followed him to the place where the treecreeper had made its lair. It was a giant kapok tree, so big that twenty men linking arms would have been needed to embrace its circumference. Its smooth gray bark was split and scarred in several places, and Yoi Sendar pointed to the creature which could be glimpsed moving about inside.

"We will have it out soon. It is fine eating. It makes its home by rasping away the soft heartwood of a tree until it kills it, and it is dangerous when it is chased from its lair. But we are a brave people."

While some of the forest folk danced on one side of the tree, provoking the treecreeper to lash out with its long, whiplike tongue from various splits in the tree-trunk, the rest built a fire of green wood at the base on the other side of the tree, and cut into the trunk to let in the smoke. The treecreeper was soon in distress, mewling and howling to itself. The forest folk darted in, dodging the lashing tongue and drumming at the base of the tree with stout clubs, raising a great noise.

At last the tormented treecreeper sprang from a slit high up in the trunk of the tree, just beneath the first branches. It moved very quickly; Yama did not see it until it was on the ground. It reared up on the two hindmost pairs of its many short stout legs, very tall and very thin. Its back was covered in overlapping bony plates; its belly in matted hair. Its sweetish, not unpleasant smell filled the clearing.

The forest folk surrounded it, one man or woman darting forward to strike two or three quick blows to its legs while the others cheered. Pandaras joined in, cheered twice as loudly as anyone else. The treecreeper went down by degrees, mewling querulously. Its tiny eyes were faceted, glinting greenly in the matted pelt which covered its head. Its long scarlet tongue snaked across the trampled ground and Yoi Sendar ran forward and pinned it with a stake.

After that, the forest folk swarmed over the treecreeper, jointing it while it was still alive and carrying the meat back to their camp in triumph. Pandaras was caught up in their excitement, his ragged shirt bloody and his eyes shining.

Yama did not join in the feast of fruit and treecreeper meat. He thought that he was like the kapok tree and the Shadow was like the treecreeper, rasping away at his self's soft core. And yet he knew that he would need the Shadow in what lay ahead. He could not drive it out until he knew how to obliterate his unwanted powers.

He wished he could be like the forest folk, who were dancing and singing with uncomplicated happiness in the fern-filled clearing. It was twilight. Red light from a great trench of fire beat across the bodies of the dancers. Trees stood quietly all around, woven cocoons pendant from their lower branches. How sweet life was for them, how simple, how innocent! A few hours of hunting or searching for fruit or tubers each day, the rest for play, for singing songs and telling stories. Their life the life of their fathers and grandfathers, always the same from the beginning of the world to its end.

Yama had forgotten that the bandar yoi inoie were in thrall to the Mighty People, but two days later they finally reached the valley where the Mighty People lived, and he saw how bad things were for their slaves.

14

Slaves

"THEY MAY BE a mighty people," Pandaras said, "but they must like a snug house. Even I would find one of those huts cramped."

He stood beside Yama at the edge of the forest, looking across the valley which stretched away on either side, a wide flat grassland studded with little villages that were linked by narrow red paths running beside ditches of green water, each village a cluster of mud-walled huts and strips of cultivated land enclosed by thorn hedges.

"I don't like the look of it," Pandaras added. "See how thick and tall the hedges are. These people must have fearsome enemies. Surely now is the time to call on something that will take us far from here."

"That would be too dangerous," Yama said. "Prefect Corin may have survived the fall of the garden, and he must not know where I am."

In fact, there were very few machines here—fewer than Yama had ever known in a world where innumerable machines sped everywhere on unfathomable errands; not a tree might fall in the most remote forest without a witness.

"I don't see how he could have survived," Pandaras said. "I'd like to think it possible, because that would mean poor Tibor might have survived too. Forgive me for my presumption, master, but you cannot live in hiding forever. You cannot waste your gift."

"Do not speak of what you do not know," Yama said sharply.

"I know a bad feeling when I get one," the boy said. "Look at our friends. It's as if they're going to their doom."

It was early in the morning, with the sun only just clear of the peaks of the Rimwall Mountains. The forest folk had risen before dawn, and had been uncharacteristically subdued as they walked the last two leagues to the edge of the forest above the valley where their masters, the Mighty People, lived. Now they were removing the flowers and quills and feathers with which they had adorned their squat bodies, scrubbing away patterns of mud and pigments with bunches of wet grasses, combing out mud which had stiffened their coarse hair in ornamental spikes. They had walked naked through the forest; now they took loincloths from pouches and packs and stepped into them. Their torcs had been carefully wrapped up in oilcloth, and buried on a rocky point beneath a flat slab of sandstone.

The forest folk lined up, shivering in the chill gray air. Their chief, Yoi Sendar, went from one to the next, checking that every trace of adornment had been removed. When he reached Yama and Pandaras, he said formally, "Below is the home of the family of Mighty People which owns us. We go to them with our gifts from the forest. You do not have to come with us, my friends. We have enjoyed your stories and lies and boasts in the forest, but we take up a different life now."

"I need to find the temple," Yama said.

Yoi Sendar shook his massive, ugly head from side to side. It meant *yes*. His baggy skin was bleeding from the places where he had drawn out his decorative quills. He said, "Perhaps you can please the Mighty People in some way, and they will let you visit it."

Pandaras said, "Why are you so afraid of them? If they rule by fear, then they are not worthy to be your masters."

Yoi Sendar would not meet the boy's stare. "They have always been our masters. It has always been so, ever since the long-forgotten day when the Preservers set us in our domain. Our masters have changed, but they still need us, as you will see if you come with us."

"There are many different peoples on the world," Yama said, as Yoi Sendar stumped off to the head of the line of his people. "Why do you deny that simple fact, Pandaras?"

"People everywhere are all the same, if you ask me. They are scared to be free. They make themselves slaves to stronger men because it is easier to be a slave than to be free. It is easier to worship the past than to plan for the future."

"You have some extraordinary notions, Pandaras."

"You taught me that, master, but I think you have forgotten it."

"Did I? Well, I was younger then, and more foolish. Perhaps my bloodline ages more quickly than even yours, Pandaras. I feel as old as one of the Ancients of Days."

Pandaras said, "I have kept one of their stone blades. Please don't stop me, master, if I have to use it to help us escape. The thing in your head wanted you to be its slave, and I don't think you've quite shaken off the notion."

Yoi Sendar raised both hands and gave a hoarse shout. His people lifted up their heavy packs of caterpillar meat and followed him into the valley, walking in single file down a narrow path that snaked through tall yellow grasses toward the nearest of the villages of the Mighty People. Yama saw that the mud huts inside the thorn hedge were separated from each other by an intricate arrangement of walls and courtyards. Each had its own exit tunneled through the thorns, and as the bandar yoi inoie came down the slope, figures began to emerge from the tunnels, scrawny and stooped and gray-skinned.

Pandaras whispered to Yama, "If they have changed, then it can't have been for the good. They seem a poor kind of people to me."

"Do not be quick to judge," Yama said.

The Mighty People spread out in a ragged line beneath a stand of cotton trees. A gang of children chased about, shouting or throwing stones or clods of earth at the adults, dodging stones thrown back at them. Men and women and children wore only loincloths, like those which the forest folk had put on. They were all bald, and the women had withered dugs which hung to their bellies.

When the forest folk drew near, the Mighty People ran forward, brandishing whips and clips and rifles. They shouted sharply at the forest folk and at each other. As the forest folk were quickly separated into groups of five or six, one of the men went up to Yama and Pandaras and stared at them with unconcealed cupidity before turning and shouting to the others that these strangers were his.

"I am the Captain! You all remember that!"

The Captain's voice was shrill and grating. He had small, red-rimmed eyes and a sharply pursed beak of a mouth. When a small child toddled too close, he screamed, "Get away or I'll shoot," and aimed a blow with his rifle at the child. It bared its teeth and hissed, but backed away slowly, staring at Yama and Pandaras.

"Don't you worry," the Captain told Yama. "I'll make you my guest, and your slave here will be looked after by my slaves. As long as you have my protection the others won't dare touch either of you. I'm their Captain, the richest and most powerful of my people. They try and kill me many times for my power and wealth, but I'm too clever and too strong."

Yama introduced himself and Pandaras.

Pandaras said, "I am not a slave, but the squire of my master."

The Captain spat at Pandaras's feet and said to Yama, "Your slave is insolent, but you have the look of a fighter. That's good."

Yama said, "Are you at war, then?"

"Our young men have gone to fight in the great war of liberation," the Captain said. "Meanwhile, we look after what we have, as is only natural. We are all of us rich here, and other families scheme to take our wealth from us, but we will defeat them. We will grow richer and more powerful than any in the Valley."

Yama said politely, "I have heard much of you from the bandar yoi inoie, but it is interesting to see for myself what you are."

"Where did these clots of filth find you? Yoi Sendar! Yoi Sendar, you ugly tub of guts! Come here!"

The Captain snapped his whip above the heads of the cluster of forest folk he had rounded up. Yoi Sendar stepped forward, his heavy head bowed. He said in a small voice, "All we have gathered, master, we give with open hands and open hearts."

The Captain struck him back and forth across his broad shoulders with the stock of the whip, raising bloody welts. Yoi Sendar stepped backward, still staring at the ground.

"Filth," the Captain said. He was breathing heavily. A muddy stink rose up from him. "They cannot change. Everything is always the same for them. They do not realize how we have been transfigured. They are a great burden to us, but we are strong and bear it."

Yama looked around. Most of the skinny gray Mighty People were driving their groups of forest folk into the tunnels of clay-plastered wicker which led through the tall thorn hedge. Even the gang of children had four or five of the oldest of the forest folk, and were fighting over the single pack of caterpillar meat which had been brought to them.

Several of the Mighty People shouted at the Captain, complaining that he could not keep the strangers to himself. "Watch me do it!" the Captain shouted back. "You don't think I'm strong enough?"

The Captain seemed to be in a permanent rage. He turned suddenly and fired his rifle in the air, and an old woman who had been creeping toward him stopped and held out her empty hands. "I know your tricks, mother," the Captain screamed. There were flecks of foam at the corners of his mouth. "Try and take what is mine, and I'll kill you. I swear it!" He turned to Yama and Pandaras and said, "She could not keep her slaves and tries to steal food from honest folk. You will be safe with me. I give you some of my own food and water, and you will help me."

Yama said, "We are strangers, dominie. We have come to visit your temple."

"Temple? What has this filth been telling you? They are the fathers and mothers of lies. They lie so much they no longer know what is true. You come with me. I will keep you safe." The Captain snapped his whip at his group of forest folk. "Bring your tributes. Poor, rotten stuff it looks, and not much of it. You've all been lazing about in the forest instead of working hard. But now you'll work. I'll make sure of it. Hurry or I'll make you bleed!"

———

The compound of the Captain's hut was enclosed by a high mudbrick wall topped with briars and broken glass. It was ankle deep in red clay kept wet by a leaking standpipe. A few pygmy goats were penned in one corner, whisking at flies with their tails while they cropped in a desultory way at a pile of melon husks.

The Captain supervised the unloading of the smoked caterpillar meat with brutal impatience. When the last string of meat had been hung on the rack outside the hut, he dismissed the forest folk and told Yama to send away his slave.

"Find out what you can," Yama whispered to Pandaras.

"I think I have the best of it," Pandaras whispered back. "This is as bad a place as I have ever seen."

The hut was mean and cramped, with no furniture but a little three-legged stool. A sleeping platform was cut into the thick wall. A solar stove gave out dim red light and an iron pot of maize porridge bubbled on its hot plate. The beaten earth floor was strewn with dry grass in which black beetles rustled; there was a nest of banded rats in the thatch of the roof. Everything was dirty and stank of goat and the Captain's stale body odor, but gorgeous portraits of dignified elders of the family stood in niches here and there, meticulously rendered in oil pigments and framed in intricately worked metal, and the bowl into which the Captain scooped a meager measure of maize porridge had been lovingly carved from a dark, hard wood.

When Yama commented on these things, the Captain was dismissive. "These are old works from the old times. A few trinkets from all the worthless stuff we had then. We are much wealthier now."

The maize porridge was unsalted and unflavored pap, and the portion no more than three spoonfuls, but the Captain expected fulsome acknowledgment of his generosity. It seemed that he had great expectations of Yama, and as he boasted and blustered, Yama soon learned more than he wanted to of the way the Mighty People lived now that they had been changed by the heretics. Each adult had his or her own hut and strip of arable land, jealously guarded from all the others. As in the quarters of the Department of Indigenous Affairs in the Palace of the Memory of the People, husbands lived apart from wives. As soon as they could walk, children were abandoned and had to join the half-wild pack which lived outside the village fence. Those who survived to sexual maturity were driven out of the pack, and had to find or build their own hut and their own field strip, or else live in the grassland as best they could.

Every man or woman was a nation of one, and spent most of their waking hours hoarding their scant possessions. They had discarded their old names—the names from the time before the change—and if they had new names they told them to no one. There was no love, no pity, no mercy. All these things were regarded as signs of weakness. There were only lust, jealousy and hatred. The old and sick had to fend for themselves, and were usually killed by the pack of children or by an adolescent who wanted their hut.

The Shadow gloated over this. *We will make all men like this*, it whispered inside Yama's head. *Slaves to the things they desire most.*

The worst thing of all was that the Mighty People considered this way of life to be the highest possible form of civilization. The old ways, when the family had herded cattle and prized the craftsmanship of their pottery and metalwork and art, were despised. The cattle were all dead, killed either by poison in acts of jealousy or slaughtered because it was too difficult to guard them in the pastures, which had grown rough and wild. The Mighty People had a taboo against entering the forest and relied entirely upon the forest folk they had enslaved for meat, and for most of their supply of fruit and tubers too, for their field strips were poorly maintained, the crops stunted and diseased. More work went into guarding the field strips than into cultivation.

The only thing that united the Captain's family was a hatred of the neighboring villages. Everyone contributed the labor of their slaves toward defense of the village against other families. The Captain had plans to expand his family's territory, and he expected Yama to help him. He walked Yama around the boundary of his family's land, never losing sight of the village, and showed off the network of ditches and ponds which had been built long ago by all the people of the valley to irrigate the land with water from lakes high in the foothills of the Rim Mountains.

"If we can control these, then we can control all the land around us," the Captain said.

"What would you do with it?"

"Eh, why we would own it, of course." The Captain gave Yama a crafty look. "That's the first thing. All things flow from ownership."

It seemed to Yama that the Mighty People were as much slaves as the bandar yoi inoie—perhaps more so, for the forest folk had been coerced into slavery, but the Mighty People had made themselves slaves of their own free will. By prizing ownership above all else, they were themselves owned by the things they coveted. He remembered how the forest folk had hidden their torcs at the edge of the forest, and thought that he could guess what had happened to the paintings, pottery and metalwork made in the time before the heretics had kindled a Change War here.

The Captain launched into a long diatribe against the neighboring villages. The feud was only ten years old, but it was packed with treachery, ambushes and murder. All this, the Captain swore, would be avenged. He worked himself into a fit of rage and at one point unslung his rifle and aimed it at various parts of the sky before he clacked his lips together and slung it over his shoulder.

"A fighter like you," he said, "could profit greatly here."

"I am only one man."

It seemed that everywhere Yama went, people wanted him to kill other people. He was sickened by it.

"There are plenty of slaves," the Captain said. "It doesn't matter if they are killed because we will have the slaves of our enemies. We will make our enemies our slaves." He clacked his pursed mouth at the thought. He said, "You will be rewarded, of course. Their stores of the old stuff will become mine, and I will let you have some pieces."

"It is my understanding that the old stuff is worthless."

"To people like us, of course. But to those less refined, like yourself, it would be a great prize. Even the piles of shit our enemies hoard would be worth something to someone like you." The Captain did not mean the insult, Yama saw. He believed himself to be the center of the world, and so all other men were naturally his inferiors. He told Yama, "Rare metals, precious stones. Perhaps as much as your slave can carry. A great prize for only a little work."

Spit on his treasure, the Shadow said. *Take the rifle and shove it into his mouth and make him beg for his life. Kill him. Kill them all.*

It raved on, but its words were feeble sparks. Yama ignored it.

They were walking back toward the thorn-fenced village. Yama was trying to think of some way of refusing the Captain without angering him, but then he saw something that made him change his mind.

The pack of children were quarreling in the shade of the stand of cotton trees. At first Yama thought that they had caught an animal and were tearing it apart, but then he saw that they had killed one of the forest folk and were stripping raw meat from its bones with their teeth. A girl sat apart from the others, gnawing on a double handful of bloody entrails. Three of the smaller children kicked the remains of the severed head about in the dusty grass. The eyes were gone and the skull had been smashed to get at the brains. Nearby, two of the forest folk sat with their arms wrapped around each other, rocking back and forth and keening in sorrow.

The Captain glanced at this and said, "None of the children's slaves last very long. We make sure they get the runts of the litters. And the old, of course. No sense keeping a slave that's too old to work, eh?"

Yama had not thought to wonder until now why there were no old men or women amongst the troop of bandar yoi inoie. He controlled his disgust and said, "I must talk with my servant."

"Don't take long," the Captain said. "I want to get back to my compound. It doesn't pay to leave it in the hands of slaves. A man must look after his wealth himself, or he is not a man and does not deserve it."

So he and Pandaras were prisoners, Yama thought. He had only suspected it before. He had been a fool.

"I'm glad I'm not stuck with that old goat," Pandaras said, when Yama found him. "What does he want of us?"

"You saw what happened to the children's slave."

"I heard the screaming. Yoi Sendar wouldn't let me go near." Pandaras glanced at the chief of the forest folk, who sat listlessly with several of his family in the shade of a big cotton tree. "It is easy to see how it is with these Mighty People. They are each a kingdom to themselves, master. They do not trust anyone, not even their own children. This is a crazy place. I told you we should not have come."

"We must find the temple, Pandaras."

"I asked about that, but the forest folk have suddenly lost their tongues. What is wrong with them, master? Why don't they defend themselves?"

"They are indigens. They know only what they have always known, and cannot imagine anything else. Once upon a time they lived in harmony with the Mighty People, exchanging food hunted in the forest for food grown in this valley, each race enriching the other. But the Mighty People changed."

"They are evil, master. No people preys on another!"

Yama thought of the Amnan, who had hunted the fisherfolk until his stepfather had put a stop to it. He said, "Certain bloodlines see the indigens as no more than animals. And so here. But I have never seen so wretched a people as the Mighty People. They are not evil, but gripped by a kind of madness."

"I would call it evil," Pandaras said. "I suppose we are prisoners here. Yoi Sendar thinks you are an honored guest. He is pleased that he has brought us to this place."

"The forest folk are used to bringing people here. The Mighty People were once extraordinary artists and artisans, and I expect that in the old days many traders came here. The Mighty People have no interest in trading now, but the forest folk cannot understand that." Yama explained the Captain's plans for war against the neighboring villages, and said, "He thinks that I am a cateran."

"So you are, master. Everyone in the world can see it but you."

"You are supposed to be my slave, Pandaras. I think it would be a good idea if you acted like it. The Captain has treasure hidden somewhere close by. I think all the Mighty People do."

Pandaras nodded. "The old stuff is all in one place, according to Yoi Sendar. He was boasting about the riches of this village as if they were his own. I didn't believe him until now because he wouldn't tell me where it was."

"Yoi Sendar is loyal to his master. You forget the torcs the forest folk wore. Where did you think those came from?"

Pandaras struck his forehead and laughed. "I am a fool, master. I am close to a fortune and failed to see it."

"I am going to ask the Captain for proof of the fee he has promised for making war against the other villages."

"You have a plan, then. That's good. You are recovering from your ordeal, master."

"Money is not important. Things are not important. Look around you if you do not believe me. I do not do this for money, Pandaras," Yama said. "I do it because I must."

He explained his plan, then made a show of knocking the boy down and kicking him, drawing his blows as much as possible. When he returned to the Captain, the man grumbled that he was free enough with his time. "I have not forgotten that my time is yours," Yama said. "I spend a little of it now so that you will win great things later."

"If that was my slave, I would kill him."

"He is all I have."

"You can have plenty of slaves after we have conquered our enemies."

"You promise much, Captain, but if I am to fight for you I would like to see a token of these riches."

"You will have enough when our enemies are broken. Most of it must come to me, of course, but you will have your share."

"I would see something of it with my own eyes," Yama said. "What harm in that? You have said that you regard it as worthless."

The Captain stared up at Yama suspiciously. He said, "It will come to you in good time."

"No man can trust another. You have taught me that. I must see how I will profit before I agree to help you."

The Captain went cross-eyed in an effort to contain his sudden anger. He said, "I should kill you!"

"Then you would certainly have no help from me."

The Captain turned away and stamped and breathed heavily until he was calm, then said grudgingly, "It is a matter for all the village."

The Mighty People argued for a long time, past sunset and into the night. The forest folk lit lanterns and hung them from the lower branches of the cotton trees. The Mighty People were all in a rage with each other, and nothing was resolved until a man went for the Captain with a long knife and the Captain shot him in the belly. More shouting, this time mostly from the Captain. The wounded man was carried off by his slaves. Later, the Captain came over to where Yama was sitting with Pandaras.

"We will take you there now," he said grumpily. "But you must be blindfolded."

All the villagers came because no one trusted anyone else. They were prisoners of their own greed and suspicion. The Captain was quite happy to explain this as he walked beside Yama. He said that it was a sign of their superior way of life.

"Anyone who goes to the hoard alone is killed by the others and their stuff is divided up."

"How would you know if someone went there?"

"We all watch each other. No one can leave the village without the others knowing, and if someone does not come when he is called, then he must lose all he owns." The Captain added, "Also, we keep watch on it. You could not find the place, but even if you did, we would know straightaway."

As well as being blindfolded, Yama and Pandaras had their arms bound. In case of trouble, the Captain said, although Yama guessed that it was because the Mighty People thought they might have friends waiting in ambush. The filthy cloth tied over his eyes was not quite lightproof—he could dimly see the flare of the torches carried by the handful of forest folk the Mighty People had brought with them—but he did not bother to try and memorize the twists and turns of the path which led always upward. He silently endured the stink of the Mighty People and the spidery feel of their sharp-fingered hands as they guided him left or right. Pandaras began to complain volubly, but then there was the sound of a blow, and the boy said nothing more.

When the blindfold was at last removed, Yama found that he was standing at the edge of a tall cliff. It was too dark to see the bottom, but the Captain told Yama that it was a long drop. "We throw down those who try and cheat us," he said. "They break on the rocks far below and jackals eat their brains. I'll do it to you if you try any tricks."

Yama said, "Do you not trust me?"

"Of course not." The Captain clacked his lips. He was amused. "And if you said that you trusted me I would not believe you."

Yama sketched a bow and said, "Then we understand each other completely."

The Mighty People surrounded them. Several of the forest folk held torches made from the branches dipped in pitch, which crackled with red flame and black smoke. Two held Pandaras, who sat on a flat stone with his arms between his knees and a strip of cloth tied over his eyes. All around was a desolation of boulders and creepers and stunted trees, with the edge of the forest a distant dark line against the black sky. It was midnight. The Eye of the Preservers was almost at zenith, a smudged thumbprint that shed a baleful red glow.

The Captain dropped one end of a coil of rope over the edge. The other was looped around a knob of rock rubbed as smooth as a dockside bollard.

"Climb down," the Captain told Yama. "There is a cave hidden behind creepers not far below. Look inside and you will see a great store of the old stuff. Our enemies have much lesser stores, of course, but even one tenth of one of them will be a great treasure to a man like you. Do not stay there long, or we will cut the rope."

Yama held out his bound hands. "You will have to untie me."

There was an argument about this amongst the Mighty People. Some wanted the Captain to climb down with Yama and others suggested that someone else should climb down, because Yama was the Captain's property, but no one wanted to volunteer because that meant risking all for the benefit of everyone else. At last the Captain prevailed.

Yama would be released from his bonds, but he would have only five minutes to look at the treasure or the rope would be cut.

The rope was knotted at intervals; even though Yama was carrying one of the smoky torches, it was easy to clamber down it. *They will kill us*, the Shadow said, but Yama ignored the crawling sparks of its voice. A draft of cold air blew from the cave mouth, stirring the leafy creepers which hung over it like a curtain. Yama kicked them aside and, clinging one-handed to the swaying rope, thrust in first the torch and then his head.

Here was the treasure of the Mighty People: broken pottery tumbled in heaps; flaking paintings covered in gray mold; exquisitely carved chairs riddled with beetle and glowing in streaks of foxfire where fungus rotted the wood; intricate metalwork corroded by verdigris.

The Captain's voice drifted down from above. "You see!" he shouted. "You see that we are a very rich people! Now you must return, or we will cut the rope!"

Yama looked up. The Mighty People stood along the edge of the cliff, silhouetted against the flare of torches. He said, "Now that I have seen your treasure I know exactly how to help you," and threw his torch onto a stack of chairs half-turned to sawdust by white emmets.

The Mighty People did not realize what had happened at first. Yama had plenty of time to find a good handhold beside the cave mouth before smoke began to pour out of it. The creepers crisped and withered in the heat. Howls, from above, then; a scatter of rifle shots. Something unraveled past Yama, striking his shoulder as it fell. The rope had been cut.

It was not difficult to climb sideways along the cliff. The creepers were strong enough to bear Yama's weight, and there were plenty of hand- and foot-holds. The Mighty People were too busy trying to save their treasure to search for him. They swarmed down the cliff on ropes, but none thought to take anything with which to beat out or stifle the fire. They hung from their ropes and shrieked in rage at each other. One man lost his hold when flame belched out of the cave mouth and he fell screaming into the darkness.

Yama climbed over the edge of the cliff, strode through the circle of forest folk, and pulled the strip of cloth from Pandaras's eyes. The boy showed his sharp white teeth. Blood, fresh and bright, matted the sleek hair on top of his head and trickled down his face. He said, "I will kill whoever it was that struck me. I swear it."

"We will only do what we need to do," Yama said. He took the sharp stone blade from Pandaras's shirt pocket and sawed through the rope which bound his arms, then turned to the forest folk and told them, "I am your master now. Do you understand? I took the Mighty People's treasure and gave it to the air."

Yoi Sendar stepped forward and said humbly, "You must kill me, for I have failed my masters."

"I am not going to kill you," Yama told him, "but you will be changed. You will go back to the village with Pandaras and bring the rest of your people. Do it, or I will kill all of the Mighty People. The others will come with me."

Pandaras said, "How will I find you, master?"

"You will be with the chief of the forest folk. He will know how to find me. Go now, as quickly as you can!"

When Pandaras and Yoi Sendar had run off into the darkness, Yama went to the edge of the drop and shouted down to the Captain. "When I saw your treasure I knew what to do at once!"

The Captain howled and brought up the rifle and shot at Yama, but he was shaking with rage and the pellet went wide. Recoil swung him like the clapper of a bell and he dropped his torch when he slammed back into the cliff. It tumbled away, dwindling to a point of light that suddenly flared far below and went out.

Before the Captain could aim his rifle again, Yama said, "If anyone tries to kill me or to climb up I will cut your rope."

"I will kill you! My slaves will kill you!"

Two or three of the other Mighty People got off a few pistol shots, but the angle was too difficult and the pellets hit the rock face beneath Yama's feet or whined off into the sky. The Captain shouted at them to stop and a woman said loudly and clearly, "You did this. You are not my husband. You are not the father of my children. You are nothing, Tuan Ah."

It was the Captain's secret name. He screamed with rage and swung around on his rope and tried to aim his rifle at his wife, but she was quicker and shot him twice with her pistol. He dropped from the rope and vanished into the darkness below.

There was a silence. At last the Captain's wife said, "Are you there, cateran?"

"I do not want anything from you except your slaves."

Some of the Mighty People began to shout threats, but the Captain's wife shouted louder than any of them. "Try and kill him if you want, but he'll cut your ropes before you get halfway up."

The Mighty People could have easily overwhelmed Yama by swarming up their ropes all at once, but he had guessed that it would never occur to them to act together. He said, "I am freeing you too. I free you from the past. Do you understand? When I have gone you can go back to your village and take up your lives."

"Tuan Ah was a fool to trust you," the Captain's wife said. "I had eight children by him, but I am glad he is dead. You have started a war, cateran. We will need slaves, and if we cannot hunt you down we will take them from our enemies. Pray that we do not find you. I am crueler than Tuan Ah."

"I am going where you cannot find me," Yama said, and turned away and led the remaining forest folk into the forest.

15

Three Sleeps and a Miracle

PANDARAS AND YOI Sendar, leading the rest of the forest folk, found Yama soon after dawn. It was already hot. Threads of mist hung between the dense stands of bamboo which grew along the edge of the forest. Pandaras told Yama that he had set fire to the treasures which the Mighty People had kept in their huts, and this diversion had allowed them all to escape.

"But I had to kill someone, master, the man the Captain had shot. It was the only way to make his slaves come with me."

"I think that the Mighty People will be more concerned about the loss of their treasure and their slaves," Yama said. "They do not care for each other, only for what they own. But in any case they will not follow us here. The forest is taboo to them."

"Well, I'm sorry I killed him," Pandaras said, "even if he would have killed me if I hadn't done it."

"I fear that it will not be the last death," Yama said.

He went over to Yoi Sendar and greeted him. The chief of the forest folk bowed his head and said formally, "All we have, master, we give with open hands and open hearts."

Yama raised his voice so that all the forest folk could hear him. "I want nothing but your friendship, Yoi Sendar."

The small, ugly man did not look up. He said stubbornly, "We will gladly give all we have, but we cannot give what we do not have."

"Perhaps I can change your mind," Yama said. "It has been a long night. We will find a place to rest, and in the evening we will speak again."

Although they had returned to their home amongst the tall trees of the forest, the bandar yoi inoie were muted and forlorn. They made no attempt to decorate themselves, and still wore their loincloths. They lay down in groups of three or four between the buttress roots of the big trees, talking quietly.

"I will watch you while you sleep, master," Pandaras said.

"They will not harm us," Yama said, although he was not really sure what would happen once he had freed the forest folk.

"I have caught the disease of mistrust," Pandaras said. "Sleep, master. I'll make sure nothing happens to you."

It was not exactly sleep, but more like a kind of swooning fall inside his own self. Yama had performed this miracle before, on the baby entrusted to him by the mirror people, although he had not known then exactly how he had done it. He had thought that the aspect of Angel had guided him, but he knew now that she had been drawn there because she had hoped to glimpse the root of his power.

Now he had to discover it for himself.

He fell deeper than any ordinary dream, plunging down as he had so often swum toward the bottom of the river as a child. Away from the sunlit mirror where kelp plants trailed their long green fronds, following the stipes which dwindled away into darkness, the muscles of his throat and chest aching and the need to draw another breath growing and growing until at last he had to turn back to the sunlight. He had never been able to reach the river bottom then, but now he felt that he could fall forever. And as he fell he became aware of finer and finer divisions of the world, of machines smaller than the single-celled plants which were the base of most river life. Those tiny plants were so small that they could only be seen when they stained the water red or brown in their uncountable billions, but the machines were smaller still: ten thousand of them could have been fitted on one of the motes of dust which had swarmed in the beam of sunlight which had illuminated the Aedile's room when Yama had broken into it, on the morning of the siege of Dr. Dismas's tower.

He had thought then that his adventures had just been beginning, but he knew now that they had begun long before he had been born.

He turned his attention to one of the minuscule machines, and it opened up around him like the stacks of books in the library of the peel-house. He half-expected to find Zakiel around a corner as he wandered through the serried rows, but it soon became clear that there was no thought here, only information. So much information, in so small a space! Zakiel had taught him that the information which encoded the form of his body could be contained in a speck of matter smaller than the least punctuation mark in a finely printed book. There was less information here than that, but it was still overwhelming. He took down a book at random. Its pages were covered with neat lines of zeroes and ones: a single long number, a single set of instructions. And there were thousands of books.

Yama remembered how Angel's aspect had seemed to show him certain places inside the brain of the baby of the Mirror People; she had used him to find out where they were, but he had not known it then. Subtly altered, those places had become the nodes where the tiny machines could excyst and begin to amplify complexity into true consciousness, the change which was the miraculous gift of the Preservers, the miracle with which he had been entrusted.

He concentrated on recalling everything about that moment. What Angel's aspect had said, subtly prompting and probing him. How he had felt, what he had seen, how he had acted without knowing he had acted. Without thought, he took down a book and ran his finger over the rows of zeroes and ones faster than he could see, changing them in a blur. Put the book back, pulled down another. Over and over until it was done.

———

He sat up inside a green tent, for a moment unsure if he were dreaming or awake. Pandaras had woven a kind of bower of fern leaves around him. He pushed the fronds aside. It was evening, the air hot and still, light deepening between the soaring trunks of the trees. The forest folk were moving about; they had lit several small fires and were roasting meat over them.

"I have found out where the temple is," Pandaras said. "Yoi Sendar wouldn't talk at first, but I told him that you would kill all of the Mighty People if he didn't tell me. I made them go and get food, too. It isn't like it was before. No singing, no joy. They are very afraid, I think because they do not understand what has happened to them."

"That will change."

"Here, master. Drink this." It was a gourd half-full of foamy, sweet-smelling juice. Pandaras said, "There's a kind of hollow vine which gushes water when you cut it. It's good."

Yama took the gourd, but did not drink. He said, "Give me your bit of stone," and used it to slice open his palm. The stone was so sharp that the wound scarcely hurt, although it bled quickly and freely. Yama let blood patter from his fingertips into the gourd. Not much blood would be needed, but he counted off a full minute before he let Pandaras bandage the wound.

Then he called the forest folk together and had them each take a single sip from the gourd. There was just enough. Yoi Sendar swallowed the last of it and handed back the gourd without comment.

"Sleep, then do as you will," Yama told them. "I cannot live your lives for you. You must discover how to do that yourselves. And when you have done that, remember this. You can free others as I have freed you. Let them drink a little of your blood mixed in wine or in water and they will be freed too."

They did not understand him then, of course, but soon enough they would. He tried to explain it to Pandaras, but he was so very tired that he fell asleep halfway through the telling.

―――――――

When he woke it was dawn. The forest folk were gone. Pandaras said he had not seen them leave, although he swore that he had stayed up all night, and said that they must have melted into the forest as mist melts into air. He pointed to a pile of rags, and added, "They left behind their loincloths. Maybe they'll go back to the way they were before all this started."

"No," Yama said. "Now they will begin to be something else."

"Like the baby of the mirror people? I remember how you made the fireflies dance around it." Pandaras yawned. "There is a little fruit for breakfast. They ate all the meat last night, and I do not think you are the kind of man who can chew hide and hooves."

"You are becoming too used to miracles," Yama said, and smiled. The half-healed wounds in his face tugged against each other. For the first time he could allow himself to feel that this might soon be over. He could allow himself the luxury of hope. He told Pandaras chidingly, "Not only do you dismiss the miracle at once, but you do not bother to try and understand what it means."

"If you changed them all, then it really was a miracle, master. You took a whole night over that baby."

"I have machines in my blood and so do you. Everyone does. It is the greatest gift of the Preservers. The miracle was simply a matter of persuading them to do the work for me."

Pandaras touched his throat. He had mended the fresh rents in his shirt, wrapped the stump of his left wrist in a bit of bright red silk, sleeked down his hair and strung a chain of yellow orchids around his neck. The coin hung at his chest like a brooch and he wore the fetish on his left arm. He looked like a jade about to embark on the long and complex wooing of a fair lady.

He said, "We are all filled with the breath of the Preservers, master. It's well known. All except the indigens, of course, unless someone like you works a miracle."

"No," Yama said. "Everything in the world is touched by the breath of the Preservers, for everything comes from them. All I did was help the forest folk recognize what they already possessed. I have changed the machines in my blood so that they can infect all the indigenous peoples of the world. That was why I made the forest folk drink my blood. And in turn their blood will become active, and change any who drink it. I have freed them to be what they will. If they choose, they can free all the other troops of the forest folk which come here to find food for the Mighty People."

The first rays of the sun had begun to shine through the understory of the high canopy of the forest. Pandaras pointed aslant the light. "I'm not sure if I understood all of that, master, but I would guess that our work here is done. Yoi Sendar said that the temple is a day's walk in that direction. I'd guess it would take us twice as long, as we're not used to the forest."

They walked through the green silence of the forest for most of the day. They spoke very little, each absorbed in his own thoughts. For the first time since he had leaned at the window of the room above the stables of *The Crossed Axes*, the inn where he had met Pandaras, and looked out across the great city of Ys, Yama felt an immense peace. He was who he was, no more and no less; he gave himself to his fate as a leaf borne on the River may be carried the length of the inhabited world. The day was beautiful, and their walk enlarged and celebrated that beauty.

Toward evening, they stopped at the edge of a bluff which looked across the valley. The thorn fenced villages of the Mighty People stood here and there amongst the network of ditches, canals and paths that webbed the grassland. Hills rose on the far side of the valley, with more hills behind them. The sun was setting beyond the Rim Mountains. Its light spread out as if it were trying to embrace the world.

Parasol trees grew in this part of the forest, the tapered columns of their trunks ringed by widespread green fronds. As light drained from the sky, the midribs of the fronds collapsed, folding against the trunks with a stealthy rustling and creaking, like so many dowagers arranging the underskirts of their gowns.

Yama and Pandaras lay down to sleep on layers of fern fronds the boy had woven together. He said that he had learned this trick during a stay with one of his uncles, who had been a basketmaker. "A squire must know a little of everything, I reckon," he said, "so it's as well I had such a large family."

He had discovered a clump of water vines that scrambled around the trunk of one of the parasol trees, so that they had been able to quench their thirst, but he had not found anything to eat. "But we'll reach the temple tomorrow, master. I'm certain of it, unless that gargoyle was lying to us."

"He could not lie. At least, not then."

Pandaras rubbed his hand over his face and yawned and said sleepily, "Did you really change them, master?"

"The machines changed them. In time I hope that they will change all the indigenous peoples."

The mirror people and the husbandmen of the Palace of the Memory of the People. The fisherfolk of the Great River and all the tribes who lived in the wild parts of its shore, the forest folk and all the strange races of indigens the forest folk claimed to know, the horsemen of the high plains and the mountaineers and the rock wights, and many more. Yama tried to remember them all, and fell asleep, counting them still in his dreams.

———

In the morning, Yama and Pandaras woke to find fruit and fresh, juicy pea vine pods in a string bag hanging from a stick thrust into a cleft in the trunk of one of the parasol trees. They looked for a long time, but found no other sign of the forest folk.

"Remember what I told you!" Yama shouted into the trees. "Let others drink a little of your blood! Then they will be free too!"

The green silence of the forest swallowed his words.

Yama and Pandaras walked all day along the edge of the ridge above the valley, at the margin of the forest. And at sunset, just as Pandaras had predicted, they came to the temple.

16

The Holy Slave

THE FAÇADE OF the temple had been carved into the face of a tall cliff of red sandstone, intricately worked and painted gold and white and ultramarine. It was approached by a long road that switchbacked up from the valley floor, ending at a single span bridge over the narrow, deep gorge at the edge of the wide plaza spread in front of the temple. In the center of the plaza was a simple square altar ringed by tall, white, unadorned pillars, which had probably functioned as a day shrine where people had gone to ask small favors of the Preservers or to remember their dead. There was a string of flat-roofed little houses to one side, where the priest and other temple staff had lived, and a meadow by the stream which fell into the gorge, where penitents and palmers could have camped.

But the meadow was overgrown with pioneer acacias and wild banana plants now; the gardens of the houses contained only dry stalks; weeds thrust up between the slabs of polished sandstone which paved the plaza. A window shutter banged and banged in the evening breeze, like an idiot who knew only one word. Turkey vultures had built untidy nests on the flat tops of the pillars around the day shrine; their droppings streaked the pillars, and the cracked bones of their prey littered the tiles below. But someone had swept the long flight of wide steps which led up to the entrance of the temple, and prayer flags and banners in bright primary colors fluttered from poles along one side of the plaza.

"The Mighty People killed the priest and the hierodules during their Change War," Pandaras whispered. "They killed the Archivist and the Commissioner too. They burned the Commissioner and a maniple of soldiers in his peel-house, but they killed the others here. Yoi Sendar said that those who killed the Archivist ate his brains, because they wanted to gain power over the dead."

He and Yama squatted in dry brush at the top of a pebbly slope that overlooked the plaza. Pandaras had taken out his stone blade, and was sharpening it on a bit of flint he held between his feet.

"I do not think there will be a need for that," Yama said.

"It could be the Prefect. Or that doctor. You have powerful enemies, master. They are not easy to kill, and if they survived the fall of the gardens they will be searching for you."

"Dr. Dismas would not wait for us in a temple—it is not his style. And Prefect Corin would not bother to set out flags or sweep the entrance. If it is someone we know, then it can be only one person. And if it is not, then I hope that whoever has appointed himself custodian of this place will do us no harm. Besides, this is the only way to the midpoint of the world which does not involve a hundred days of walking."

Yama stood up, crabbed down the slope in a cloud of dust, and ran straight out across the plaza. Dry weeds crackled underfoot. A pair of turkey vultures took flight. Pandaras came down more cautiously holding the stone blade up by his shoulder, the stump of his left wrist tucked between two toggles of his shirt. He hurried to catch up with Yama, who was walking around the circle of pillars—someone had swept the altar and tried to scrub away the signs which had been scrawled there—toward the stair which led up to the entrance of the façade.

Pandaras said breathlessly, "At least we could have waited until after supper, master!"

"I do not think we should rely on the forest folk any longer. They have other concerns now. And please, Pandaras, put away that blade. Show that we come as friends."

But Pandaras did not hear him. He gave a sudden yell and ran past Yama and scampered up the steps. A tall, pale-skinned figure had appeared at the entrance of the temple.

It was Tibor.

———

"I knew that you had survived the flood," the hierodule told Yama, "and I am pleased that you found your way here."

Yama smiled and said, "I will free you of your obligation soon, Tibor. We will sleep here tonight, but we have a long way to go, and must set off as soon as we are rested."

"I have already found something else to serve," Tibor said.

They were sitting cross-legged on the terrace before the entrance of the temple. The hierodule wore a white shirt left unbuttoned to display the two vertical scars on his chest, and trousers of a stiff, silvery material which he had slit at the waist and ankles because they were slightly too small for him. He had brought out a tray of food and beakers of wine and distilled water, and Yama and Pandaras ate hungrily, although the food had been too long in a freezer—the limp vegetables were crunchy with ice crystals at their cores, the flat breads were dry, and the sauces had lost most of their savor.

"The people of the valley killed the priest and the hierodules of this temple," Pandaras said. "They have turned their backs on the Preservers. It isn't safe for people like you, Tibor. You think only of serving, but this isn't the place for it."

"I know what happened here," Tibor said. He chewed at a twig, rolling it around his lips with his long red tongue; he had lost his cigarette makings in the flood. "But that was many years ago. I am not afraid. Things will be different now."

"The forest folk might want to come here now, I suppose," Pandaras said, "but I still think that you should come with us."

Yama asked Tibor how he had escaped Prefect Corin, and the hierodule explained that he had still been struggling with the Prefect when the tidal wave had smashed into the floating garden, knocking it from the air and washing the two men into the river. "We were torn apart," Tibor said, "and then I was too busy trying not to drown to try to follow him. I was dragged down by a tremendous whirlpool, and I think I may have touched the bottom of the river, so deep was I drawn. Just as my breath was about to burst from my chest, I was shot up like a cork, and came to the surface near an uprooted tree. I clung to its sturdy trunk and was borne with it wherever the flood chose to take me. Many small animals had already sought safety there, and bedraggled birds alighted on its leafy branches to take refuge from the rain, so that I was not without food. I drifted for two days amidst a growing fleet of other uprooted trees, until at last the failing waters stranded them all and I could walk across them into forested hills untouched by the flood. This part of the world is mostly populated by indigenous peoples, and I knew that the only temple for fifty leagues all around stood beyond the hills. And so I made my way across them, and after many hardships I will not trouble you with at last arrived here."

"You were looking for something to serve," Pandaras said.

"I am a hierodule."

Yama said, "You had food and drink ready for us. How did you know that we were coming here?"

Tibor spread his big, six-fingered hands and said gravely, "Why, she told me. If you had not come here, I would have had to fetch you."

For the first time since he had escaped the Mighty People, Yama felt the Shadow stir. He said, "I thought it might be something like that. You had better show me the shrine."

Tibor nodded. "She is waiting for you, Yamamanama. And do not be afraid. She forgives you for the time you tried to kill her."

——————

The long processional path still retained a feeble blue luminescence. It led them down wide corridors and through a nest of round chambers with intricate murals painted on their walls and ceilings to the naos at the heart of the temple, a vast dry cave that could easily have held a thousand petitioners. As Yama and Pandaras followed Tibor into it, like emmets creeping into a darkened house, tiny sparks whirled down from above to crown them. Pandaras laughed to see them: fireflies.

Yama said, "How far back into the plateau does the complex run, Tibor?"

"Further than I am allowed to explore," the hierodule said. "She will answer all your questions."

The floor was inlaid with a spiral pattern of garnet slabs; the reflections of the fireflies glittered underfoot as Yama and Pandaras followed Tibor toward a faint glow that curdled in the darkness ahead, flickering in the black disc of the shrine.

It stood on a dais raised high above the floor. A steep stair led up to it. Poles had been driven into the sandstone slabs of the dais and bodies clad in tattered robes were lashed to the poles with corroded wire. The dry air had cured the skin and flesh of the bodies to something like leather, shrunken tightly over the bones.

"I cleaned away the slogans," Tibor said, "but she likes to see the remains of her enemies."

"I think this one is the Archivist," Pandaras said. "You see? They took off the top of his skull as if it were an egg."

The coin hanging from his neck had begun to glow. He held it up for Yama to see; its light struck sparks in his eyes.

And then a green glow washed over him.

The shrine had become a window in which the aspect of Angel walked swiftly forward, fixing Yama with a confident and commanding gaze. As before, she wore a white one-piece garment that clung to her tall, slender body. The green garden receded behind her beneath a perfect blue sky. She stared silently at Yama for a long time. He returned her gaze and resisted the compulsion to say something, although his heart quickened with the effort and sweat soaked through his ragged shirt and trousers.

At last, she said, "You have lost your looks, my love. The world has been hard on you, but now I am here to help you. What, you have no words for me?"

"I serve no one," Yama said. He tried to look beyond her, hoping that he could summon the hell-hound, but something stopped him looking very far.

She laughed. Yama thought of knives clashing. She said, "Of course you serve. It is what you were made for."

"I suppose a feral machine was tracking me. They dare not visit the world they lost, except for brief moments, but they are compelled to watch what they cannot have."

"You are very stubborn, I think that you know that you need my help. You know there is much you do not know. For instance, you thought that you had killed me, and you do not understand how you failed. Do stop trying to call that bothersome creature, by the way. This time it will not come."

Pandaras said in a small but defiant voice, "You are the ghost my master told me about. The very ghost of a ghost, for I know my master killed you."

"You speak more truly than you know, little creature. You are the one who looked in the book, aren't you? I let you live then. Show gratitude for my mercy now."

"If you have any mercy," Yama said, "show me a token of it. Let the hierodule go. You use him falsely."

"Is he not a servant of the avatars? And there are no avatars left, except for me. I should know: I killed them all."

Yama said, "You are no avatar, merely the discarded aspect of a dead woman. You are lost in time. Your kind were overthrown more than five million years ago. Just as you use the hierodule, the feral machines use you."

"We have an alliance. You can be a part of it still."

Yama turned his face to show her his terrible scar. "One of the feral machines has already used me. It tried to do to me what it did to Dr. Dismas, but it no longer has power over me, and neither do you. You are just a memory, and not even a whole one."

"With my help you can be so much more powerful than any of the feral machines, my darling."

"We can only be what we are."

The aspect smiled. "That is the philosophy which made your Preservers flee from the Universe. It is untrue. Animals can only be what they are, but humans can transcend their animal selves. The Preservers were fools. They raised up the ten thousand bloodlines from animal stock, but forbade them to rise higher than their creators. You and I will prove how wrong the Preservers were."

"You have no power over me," Yama said again, and with an enormous effort turned away from the green light of the garden inside the shrine.

The aspect said, "I know why the Great River fails. I can help you save the world, if that is what you want."

'You want the world for yourself."

"I will have it, too, in a little while."

"Then why should I save it?"

The aspect's voice deepened. There was music in it and Yama could feel his muscles trying to respond; there was still much of the machine inside him. He fought against it, staggering against the Archivist's dry, brittle body and embracing it for support.

Pandaras cried out, but Yama did not hear what the boy said. The aspect's voice filled his mind.

"The world is a fabrication," she said. "An artificial habitat twenty thousand kilometers long and a thousand wide, set in a nest of fields which mimic the gravity of an Earth-sized planet and prevent the atmosphere from dissipating into space. It is not well made. Machines must constantly maintain it; without them, the air would soon become unbreathable, the inhabited places would become deserts, and the Great River would silt up. Those are some of the functions of the lesser machines. But there are greater machines in the keel."

Yama remembered the huge engines he had glimpsed in the keelways when Beatrice had taken him back to the peel-house. She had warned him not to waken them before their time; he had not understood her until now.

The aspect sang on, seductive, compelling. "There are many wormholes orbiting Confluence's star. I suspect that they emerge at various points in the Galactic disc. But there is also a wormhole at the midpoint of this strange world. Something has altered it. Your people constructed this world, Yamamanama. You are the key. And you will serve. I have powerful allies. Tell me now that you will at least listen to one of them, and I will spare the boy. But if you will not continue this conversation then I will have my slave crush his skull and paint your face with his brains. A simple *yes* will be enough."

Pandaras tried to run then, but Tibor caught him and lifted him up and closed one big hand over his head. The hierodule's face was set in a horrible rictus. He began to shake. Muscles jumped in his arms and legs as if struggling against each other. Pandaras shrieked in fear and agony.

The aspect said, "Say the word, or I will have his life."

Yama started to move toward Tibor and Pandaras, but it was as if he were in a dream where gravity was much stronger or the air was as dense as water. He was breathing in great gasps.

"Say it!"

The aspect and the hierodule had spoken together.

Pandaras slashed at Tibor's arm with the stone blade, but the hierodule blocked the blow and knocked the blade into the darkness beyond the edge of the dais.

"Say it or he dies!"

"No!"

The hierodule lifted Pandaras above his head, as if to dash him to the floor. And the boy ripped the coin from the thong which dangled from his neck and thrust it edge-first in the hierodule's eye.

Tibor and the aspect screamed at the same moment. White light blotted out the garden and beat across the huge chamber. The hierodule dropped Pandaras. With the glowing coin stuck in his eye and blood streaming down his face, he blundered into two of the staked bodies, smashing them to dust and fragments of brown bone, and pitched over the edge of the dais.

Yama and Pandaras ran down the steep stair. Tibor lay at the bottom, his neck broken. Pandaras pulled the coin from the hierodule's eye and closed his lids and kissed his forehead.

"He would have killed me," Pandaras said. He was crying.

"It was well done. She had made a link with Tibor through the shrine, and you shut it down. We cannot stay, Pandaras. She will soon find a way to return."

They ran, chased by a flock of fireflies, their shadows thrown ahead of them by the white light which burned in the shrine. By the time the aspect had managed to reconfigure it, they were already descending toward the keelways.

17

The Glass Desert

IT WAS A dusty town built along a narrow defile, high in the dry mountains which bordered the Glass Desert. The defile was roofed over with sheets of painted canvas that flapped and boomed in the constant cold, dry wind, and was lined with the mudbrick façades of buildings which had been hacked into its rocky walls. A decad of different bloodlines came there to trade drugs, rare metals, precious stones and furs for rifles and knives and other weapons which artisans made in secretive little courtyards between the buildings. There was a produce market at one end of the defile, and a maze of corrals and sheds where bacts, dzo and mules were bought and sold at the other. Fields and orchards watered by artesian wells stepped away below the produce market, startlingly green against a tawny landscape in which only cacti, barrel trees and cheat grass grew.

The town was called Cagn, or Thule, or Golgath, and had many other secret names known only to the tribes who used them. It was agreed by all that it was one of the worst places in the world; it was said that the double peak which loomed above, framing the Gateway of Lost Souls and casting its shadow across the town in the early morning and the late afternoon, hid the town from gaze of the Preservers, and that any sin practiced there went unremarked. It had not been much changed by the coming of the heretics. It was still a refuge for smugglers, reivers, rustlers, fugitives and other desperadoes. Only an hour after he and Pandaras had arrived in the town, Yama had to kill two ruffians who tried to rob them.

Both men were tall and burly and covered everywhere with coarse red hair. They wore striped cotton serapes and white cotton trews, with broad leather belts hitched under their ample bellies. They were belligerently drunk. When one of them swung at him with a skean, Yama broke the man's arm, snatched up the weapon, and told both of them to run. The injured ruffian yowled, lowered his shaggy head, and charged like a bull. Yama dodged him easily, swung the skean hard as he went past, and slashed his neck down to the spinal cord; the man fell flat, dead before he hit the dust.

The second ruffian swayed and said, "You killed him, you skeller," and pulled a pistol from his belt. Yama, with a cold, detached feeling, as if this had already happened somewhere else, perhaps in a story he had once read, hefted the skean to get a feel for its balance, threw it overhand, and skewered the man in the right eye.

People who had stopped to watch the fight began to drift away now that the fun was over; murders were commonplace in a town outside the rule of any law. Pandaras scooped up the pistol, chased off a couple of children who were creeping toward the bodies, and went through the pouches on the men's belts, finding a few clipped coins, and a packet of pellets and a powerpack for the pistol. He pulled the skean from the second ruffian's eye, cleaned its double-edged blade on the dead man's serape, and tucked it into the waistband of his trousers.

Yama refused the pistol when Pandaras offered it to him, and said, "I know that we will need more money, but I will not kill to get it."

The cold precision which had gripped him in the moment of danger had vanished. He began to tremble as they walked away. Behind them, the children moved in to take the belts and pouches. Canvas as red as a priest's robe cracked overhead, turning sunlight to the color of blood.

Pandaras said, "In this kind of place, we'll need all the weapons we can get just to keep what we have. As for money, I have a confession. I did not burn all the treasures the Mighty People had hidden away in their miserable huts. I kept two of the smallest portraits. I doubt that we'll find much appreciation of art here, but they are enameled on beaten gold, and although they are no bigger than my hand, I think they'll buy us what we need. Aren't you glad you weren't able to send me away?"

Yama had tried to make Pandaras take the keelroad back to Ys, telling him that the journey to the Glass Desert would almost certainly end in death, but the boy had refused.

"I am your squire, master, for better or worse," he had said fiercely. "And I do not think that things can get much worse than this. I have killed two men in as many days, and one of them was my friend. I have lost my hand, and I failed you in many ways while we were apart. I'll not fail you now."

And so they went on together. Yama used machines to guide them through endless caverns and corridors. He no longer cared if his enemies could track him by the traces left by his commands. It was too late for that.

A thing like a giant silvery spider, one of the machines which kept the caverns clean, led them at last to an active part of the transportation system which had once knitted the whole world together. They traveled all night in a humming capsule that fell through one of the keelroads. Neither of them slept, although both pretended to.

All of the transportation system beyond the midpoint of the world had been destroyed in the wars of the Age of Insurrection. The capsule took Yama and Pandaras as far as it could, delivering them to a maze of passages beneath a ruined peel-house; they emerged at the foot of a bluff which overlooked the midslopes of the mountains of the Great Divide. The yurts of a party of nomad musk deer herders were pitched nearby. When Yama and Pandaras walked into their camp, still crowned with fireflies Yama had forgotten to dismiss, the long-haired, yellow-skinned men and women fell on their knees. They breakfasted on soured goat's milk mixed with deer blood, and a sickly porridge boiled up from barley mash and dried apricots, then walked all day up the mountain, leaving behind the herders' threadbare pastures and climbing through long, dry draws to the town.

With the money Pandaras got at a refiner's for the gold he had stolen from the Mighty People, they bought a bact from a livestock trader and supplies from the town's only chandler. New clothes, furs for the mountain pass and light robes for the desert, a tent of memory plastic that folded as small as a scarf, dried food, water-bottles and a dew still, a saddle and harness for the bact. There was a little money left, but Yama politely refused the chandler's invitation to inspect the armory. He would need no weapon where he was going, and Pandaras was armed with the skean and pistol he had taken from the dead ruffians.

"I have maps too," the chandler said. "Reliable. Certified."

"We do not need maps," Yama said.

"That's what the other fellow said. He'll be buzzard meat soon enough, and so will you if you won't unbend and take some advice." The chandler was very tall and very thin, with fine-grained brown skin that shone like polished leather. He laid a long-nailed finger beside one of his opaline eyes and said, "Perhaps you have one of your own, and put your trust in that. Hnn. Many come here with old maps found in some depository or archive, but you can't rely on them. All the ruins within easy travel of the edge of the Glass Desert are mined out, and most of the waterholes are poisoned. My maps are up-to-date. You won't have to pay for them, not right now, but you'll have to sell anything you find to me."

Pandaras said, "How will you make sure that we do?"

The chandler looked down at Pandaras. He was three times the boy's height. By the doorway, the burly bodyguard shifted the rifle which rested in the crook of one of her beefy arms. The chandler said, "This is the only way into the Glass Desert, and the only way out. If you survive, you'll be back. You'll probably have to sell anything you find to me anyway. I give the best valuations in town. Ask around if you don't believe me, and you'll find that all my rivals say I'm far too generous with my money."

Yama said, "Who was this other man? Did he have a white mark on his face?"

"Not so bold," the chandler said. "Everything has its price here."

Yama told Pandaras to give the chandler the rest of their money. "Describe him."

The man spat on the clipped coins and rubbed them with the soft, flat pads at the ends of his bony fingers. "He was about your height. Had a veil over his face, and yellow eyes. Wore a hat and a silvery cloak. I know his name, but you'll have to pay me to get it."

"I know his name too," Yama said.

The chandler glared at Yama. "It doesn't matter," he said. "He didn't take a map, or any water or food, just a saddle for his mule. And he smelled bad, like skinrot or canker. Hnn. It doesn't matter what he's called. He'll be dead by now."

———

They were followed out of town by three ruffians of the same bloodline as the two Yama had just killed. They were either kin to the dead man, or in the pay of the chandler, or freelances looking to strip novices of newly bought supplies. As they rode hard toward him, Yama called down a machine and killed them all. He and Pandaras tied the bodies to one of the horses and sent it back to the town as a warning. The second horse had bolted when the machine had smashed the skull of its rider, but Pandaras easily rounded up the third, an old mare with a shaggy gray coat. With Pandaras following on the bact, Yama rode the mare through the high pass of the Gateway of Lost Souls, where unending wind howled over polished ice, and followed a trail down the dry mountain slopes toward the glaring wastes of the Glass Desert.

The trail wound through a dead landscape. Nothing grew there but stonewort, which could survive on the brief dew which formed each morning. The yellow or black crusts were the only color in the simmering white, alkaline landscape. Cairns were raised here and there, the burial places of would-be prospectors. All had been disturbed; on the afternoon of the second day, Yama and Pandaras rode past three skulls set on a flat-topped rock beside the trail.

Pandaras pointed out the neat hole punched into the ridge above the empty eye sockets of one of the skulls. "Perhaps he quarreled with his companions over treasure they had found. Or perhaps he killed himself after he killed his friends. Men are driven mad here by the ghosts of machines that fought in the war."

"You can still turn back," Yama said. "I must face something worse than any ghost you can imagine, and I do not think I will be able to protect you from it. It may well destroy you. It may well destroy me, too."

Pandaras touched the coin he still wore around his neck. "Why, you've said yourself that this is better than any of the seals and medals the people of the New Quarter use to protect themselves from machine ghosts."

"Take the horse, Pandaras. Ride back through the pass and wait for me."

"Will you turn back too, master? Well then."

That evening, they made camp by a waterhole. The water was black, and mantled with white dust. The mare slipped her hobble and drank before Yama could find a machine which could test it. She foundered almost at once, screaming with pain and foaming at the mouth. The bact snorted, as if in disdain; it had not tried to go near the water. The mare convulsed. Blood poured from her eyes and nostrils. Yama stroked her muzzle, then slit her throat in a swift movement.

Pandaras took a sip from a cupped handful of water and promptly spat it out and tipped the rest on the ground. "Poison all right," he said, and spat again. "I bet the chandler's men did it. They poison most of the waterholes, and he hires out maps showing those which are safe."

"The whole land is poisoned," Yama said.

They moved their camp to a flat shelf of rock a league farther down the trail. Pandaras cooked slabs of muscle he had cut from the mare's hindquarters; he had also drained some of her blood into two of the empty water-bottles, saying that for him blood was almost as good as water.

Pandaras ate most of the food, for Yama had little appetite. He had had a distant sense of Dr. Dismas's paramour ever since they had begun to descend toward the desert. It pulled at the remains of his Shadow like the wink of sunlight on a far-off mirror or a tintinnabulation in the ear. And he also felt the pull of the feral machine he had called upon, without knowing it, when he had been in desperate danger in the house of the renegade star-sailor. Poised between the two attractors, he sat and looked out toward the wastelands of the Glass Desert until long past sunset, and did not notice when Pandaras wrapped a fur around him against the night's bitter cold.

From then on, Pandaras and Yama took turns riding the bact. It took three more days to descend the mountain slopes. The Glass Desert stretched beyond: red and yellow and brown, patched and cratered, riven on one side by a vast, meandering canyon which once had held a river as wide and deep as the Great River. Points of reflected light flashed here and there across the bitter land, and a whole sea of light burned in the middle distance where a city had stood. The Glass Desert had once been as verdant as the inhabited half of Confluence, and as populous, but the feral machines had made it their homeland after they had rebelled, and it had been devastated in the last and fiercest of the wars of the Age of Insurrection. Nothing lived there now.

As he walked beside the bact that day, through a barrens of blowing sand and piles of half-melted boulders fused together by some great, ancient blast, Yama kept glimpsing figures amongst the stones, figures which vanished if he turned to look at them, but which he recognized nonetheless. First Derev, her white feathery hair blowing out in the hot wind, and then others. His love, and all his dead. The remnant of the Shadow was stirring in his mind, wakened by the call of its progenitor far off across the tumbled desolation.

When they made camp that evening, Pandaras saw how drawn his master had become. Yama squatted on his haunches and stared into the thin, cold wind that blew out of the dark desert. His long black hair was matted with dust and tangled about his pale, scarred face. He did not seem to notice when Pandaras shaved him, using a flaked edge of glass and a couple of handfuls of their precious water. They had no scissors, but Pandaras had given the skean's blade a good edge, and he hacked back Yama's hair with that. It was not easy to do with only one hand, but Yama bore Pandaras's clumsiness patiently. More and more, he seemed to be retreating inside his head.

Yama would not eat anything, and he slept uneasily. Pandaras watched over him, chewing congealed blood that was beginning to spoil. He reckoned that they were not coming back. At best, they would somehow destroy this thing and then hope for an easy death of thirst or heat prostration. At worst, it would destroy them.

It was a pity. He would have liked to have made a song of Yama's adventures amongst the world's wonders. He remembered the engines he had seen in the cellars of the world, when the spider thing had led them to the keelroad. Whole swathes of the floors of the vast vaults had been transparent, showing chambers deep enough to swallow mountains. It was as if he and Yama had become birds, hanging high above a world within a world. Far below, tiny red and black specks had roamed across a green plain, illuminated by a kind of flaw in the middle air that had shed a radiance as bright as day. The specks must have been machines as big as carracks, and even bigger machines had studded the verdant land. Black spires of intricate latticework had reared halfway toward the radiant flaw, wound about with what looked like threads of gold, threads which must have been as wide as the Grand Way of Ys. There had been black cubes in heaps as wide as cities, and geometric patterns of silver and white laid into the green landscape.

At one point Yama had lain flat on the floor, prostrating himself like a palmer at a shrine. The spider had halted, flexing one leg and then another as if in frustration, until at last Yama had stood and walked on.

He had told Pandaras then that there were mysteries in the world that he could only guess at, and they began to talk about this again as they journeyed into the Glass Desert. Yama wanted to unburden himself of all that had happened to him. Once more, he told Pandaras the story of how he had been found as a baby on the breast of a dead woman in a white boat cast adrift on the Great River. He talked of his childhood, of how happy he had been, how fortunate to have been the adopted son of the Aedile of Aeolis and the stepbrother of brave, dead Telmon. He described how Dr. Dismas had tried to kidnap him and how he had escaped and had been given refuge in the tower of Beatrice and Osric, the last curators of the City of the Dead, of his journey to Ys, where he had escaped Prefect Corin and met Pandaras. And then, turn and turn again, they told each other the rest of the tale: their adventures in the Palace of the Memory of the People; the voyage downriver in the *Weazel*; the sacking of Aeolis by Prefect Corin and the death of the Aedile; the treachery of Eliphas. And on, through their separate adventures and their reunion, and now this, their last exploit. They had reached the

Glass Desert after all—not in search of Eliphas's invented lost city, but of Yama's nemesis.

———

Pandaras noticed the birds on the afternoon of the third day after they had quit the mountains: black cruciform specks circling high above in a sky so achingly bright it was more white than blue.

"Not birds," Yama said. "They have been watching us ever since we crept through the pass, but they dare to fly lower now because this is their land."

He coughed long and hard into his fist. They were both affected by the alkaline dust which hung in the hot air. It worked through the seals of their filter masks and irritated their throats and lungs, and got into every crevice of their bodies, drying their skins and causing pressure sores. It worked under their goggles, too, inflaming their eyes.

They were still taking turns riding the bact. Pandaras was in the saddle, and now he clambered down and said, "Ride a while, master. Rest."

Yama lifted his filter mask and spat. There was blood in his spittle. When he could speak again, he said, "It has grown strong, Pandaras. It no longer cares about being found, for the machines which would have destroyed it are engaged in fighting the heretics. And it has made many servants."

"You could make them go away, master. Please climb up. You'll feel better for riding."

But Yama walked on, still leading the bact. "There are different kinds of machine," he said. "I thought of it while we were crossing that big chamber far beneath the temple. Do you remember?"

"I will never forget it, master. Do you think people live there, in the lands of the keel?"

"No, Pandaras. Down there are machines I cannot yet control. I cannot even talk with them. They are raised as far above the simple little machines which the magistrates command as we are above the animals from which the Preservers made us. As with men so with machines. There are the enlightened races of men which have passed beyond this world, and there are the machines in the world beneath the world. Just as we cannot talk with the enlightened, so I cannot talk with those machines. Or not yet, not yet. And just as there are the changed bloodlines, in whom the breath of the Preservers has been quickened, so there are machines which are likewise self-aware, such as the dwellers of the deep which sweep silt from the bottom of the Great River. I can command those as a general can command an army, although both the general and his soldiers are equal in the eyes of the Preservers. And then there are the unchanged bloodlines, and the ordinary machines which take care of the world, such as the machines commanded by the magistrates. And there are the indigenous races, and machines which are neither self-aware nor ever need to be."

"And yet you raised up the mirror people and the forest folk," Pandaras said.

Yama did not hear him. He said, "Machines and men. We are each other's mirrors. The feral machines are greater than the changed, but lesser than the enlightened. But are they greater or lesser than me? I called down one to help me; I feel it still. But did I command it, or did it see its chance to place its hook into me? I could not master the child of the thing that lies ahead of us, the Shadow which Dr. Dismas grew in me, but perhaps that was because the Shadow was too like me. It had begun to assume my power. I do not know what I can do, Pandaras. Perhaps it knows me better than I know myself."

They had been plodding all day through the petrified stumps of what had once been a forest. Pandaras gestured around himself and said, "This is a dead place. No wonder only machines can live here."

They walked on in silence for a while. At last, Yama said, "This half of the world lost its river. Do you remember when we crossed that gorge two days ago? That was once a tributary of the Great River of this half of Confluence, running down from the snow fields of the Rim Mountains, just as the Breas empties into the Great River near Aeolis. But the Great River into which that tributary emptied fell away and was not renewed. The land died. Perhaps our land will die too. Our own Great River is dying."

At last Pandaras persuaded his master to climb onto the saddle in front of the bact's dwindling hump. When he was settled, Yama said, "If my father was right, then the fall of the Great River is my fault. It began when I was cast upon this world. Perhaps I can atone for that, Pandaras, if I can learn enough. It is my only hope."

Pandaras understood less than half of what his master said, but he clearly saw the anguish these thoughts caused him. He said, "You are greater than you know, master. You are tired now. You don't see things clearly. It will be better when you have rested. You ride the rest of the day. I don't mind walking."

They reached the far edge of the petrified forest at nightfall, and made camp. As usual, Pandaras kept watch while Yama muttered and twitched in his sleep, and once or twice he thought he heard something padding outside the tent. There! A scrape of metal on stone. The bact snorted and moved about. It was not his imagination. He gripped the pistol, although what use was it against monsters?

The next day, Yama said, "I dreamed that we are being followed."

"And I know it, master."

Pandaras squinted against sky glare. The bird things were still up there. Even when he was not watching them he could still feel their purpose, a prickling itch at the crown of his skull. All around, red sand blew in scarves and streamers across pitted red rock. The air was filled with the dry hiss of blowing sand.

Yama said, "They are coming down from the Gateway of Lost Souls. An army, Pandaras. I saw it in my dreams, but I do not think it was a dream. I do not think that I can dream here."

Pandaras looked back toward the mountains of the Great Divide. The icy peaks shone high and far, seeming to float above the glittering desert.

He said, "It must have been a dream, master. Not even an eagle could see so far. Don't worry about it."

Yama shook his head violently. "I saw through the eyes of one of the watchers. The things which follow us also follow the army."

That night Yama woke with a start, feverish and shaking. He turned toward Pandaras, but his reddened eyes were focused on infinity. "They have machines," he said. "The fool brought machines with him as well as soldiers. He thinks that they are shielded."

Pandaras wet a corner of Yama's robe with a few minims of their precious water and dabbed at his forehead. "Hush, master. You dream."

"No. No dreams now. Only truth. The desert burns away everything else. We become only what we are."

At last Pandaras got Yama to lie down. He thought that his master slept, but after a while Yama said, "The soldiers are mounted and in uniform. They wear black masks with long snouts and round eyeholes of glass backed with gold. Their mounts are masked too. But I recognize the man at their head. It is Enobarbus. She has sent him after me. Things are coming together at last. Things are coming to a conclusion."

Pandaras said nervously, "Is there any sign of the Prefect?"

"He . . . no, not yet. But I left sign enough for him to find us."

"Then maybe he's dead," Pandaras said, although he did not believe it.

They had little food left, and less water. The dew still yielded only a few minims of water each night, and there was no standing water to be found, poisoned or otherwise. The next day, the bact knelt down and would not get up. Pandaras, weeping in rage and frustration, beat at the animal's withers. It closed its long-lashed eyes and ignored him. Sand blew all around; the sun was a glowering eye in a red sky.

Pandaras and Yama unloaded the supplies. Only one water-bottle was full; another held only a few mouthfuls. They threw the rest away, and most of the remaining food.

"I will get us food," Yama said. "Food and water. They are off the mountain slopes now, and coming toward us very quickly. They have good mounts."

He was flushed and feverish. He was looking toward the distant range of mountains, and it took Pandaras a long time to get him turned around.

They had not gone far when they heard the bact scream. Pandaras stumbled back toward it through blowing sand, but stopped, shocked and frightened, when he saw the things which were tearing it apart.

They were like crosses between snakes and jaguars, armored in overlapping metallic scales or in flexible blood-red hide. No two were alike. One had a tail like that of a scorpion, tipped with a swollen sting which arched above its back. One had a multiple set of jaws so massive they dragged on the ground, another a round sucker mouth with a ragged ring of teeth.

The misshapen wild cats tore at the bact with silent ferocity. It was already dead, its neck half-severed and its bloody ribs showing, blood soaking the sand in a widening circle. Blood glistened on hide like chainmail, on metal scales, on horny plates edged with metal, on serrated metal in snapping jaws. Two of the things had burrowed into the bact's belly, shaking its body back and forth as they worked like a depraved reversal of birth. The pack ignored Pandaras until he raised the pistol, and then one turned eyes like red lamps toward him and reared up on its stout tail, waving a decad of mismatched legs tipped with razor-edged claws. Thick green slaver dripped from its long snout.

A hand fell on Pandaras's shoulder; his shot went wild, swallowed by the sand-filled air. Yama shouted into his ear. "Leave them! They will not hurt us!"

The wild cat which had confronted Pandaras dropped to its belly and shuffled forward and groveled before Yama, although it kept its burning red eyes on Pandaras as he backed away into the blowing sand. Its fellows had not paused in their feverish butchery; the bact was almost stripped to the bones.

Yama and Pandaras drank the last of their water at noon, threw away the water-bottle, and went on. Yama taught Pandaras that sucking a pebble could stimulate the flow of saliva and help keep thirst at bay, but the hot wind which blew sand around them drew moisture from every crevice of their bodies. Pandaras forced himself to stay awake, staring at each change in pitch of the streams of sand that hissed outside the tent, and Yama slept fitfully, waking before dawn and insisting that they go on.

"They are almost on us," he said, "but it is not far. There is no chance of turning back now, Pandaras."

"I had not thought of it, master," Pandaras said. His lips were cracked and bleeding and he tasted blood at the back of his throat with each breath; the dust had worked into his lungs.

The air was filled with blowing sand. They left the tent behind and set off into it.

Shapes loomed out of the murk: towers of friable bones lashed together with sinews and half-covered in hide that flapped and boomed and creaked in the wind. A ragged picket fence of crystalline spines grew crookedly from a shoulder of black rock. Creatures were impaled on some of the spines. Some were men; the rest were like nothing Pandaras had ever seen, horrid chimeras of machine and insect, although surely no insects could grow as large as these. Most were no more than dried husks, but some were still alive and stirred feebly as Yama and Pandaras went past.

Pandaras did not pay much attention to these horrors. He no longer felt fear, only exhaustion and growing thirst. Each step was a promise to himself that there would soon be no more steps: walking was an infinite chain of promises. The world shrank to the patch of ground directly in front of him. Its gravity seemed to vary wildly; sometimes it seemed to pitch like the deck of a ship and he could barely keep to his feet. But always he went forward, following in his master's footsteps.

At noon, Yama stopped and turned in a half-circle and fell to his knees. Pandaras managed to get him to the shelter of a tilted shelf of rock. It was very hot. The sun's bloody glare was diffused across half the sky. Sand skirled around crystal spurs, sent shifting shadows shuddering across reaches of bare stone. Pandaras was sweating through his thin robe. His mouth and throat were parched. He itched everywhere.

Yama stirred in his arms. Blood leaked from the corners of his closed eyes; Pandaras blotted it away with the hem of his robe. "I will bring water," Yama said, and seemed to fall into a faint.

A moment later, thunder cracked high above and something flashed through the blowing red dust, chased by black shapes. It dived this way and that with abrupt turns and reverses, swooped low overhead, dropped something, and shot away as black things closed on either side. A sheet of green lightning; more thunder, then only the endless hiss of blowing sand.

Pandaras crawled out of the lee of the shelf of rock and retrieved what had been dropped by the machine.

It was a transparent sphere of spun plastic as big as his head, half-filled with cold, clear water.

When they were able to set off again, something like a storm of dry lightning had started up in the direction of the Great Divide. Flares of brittle light were half-obscured by curtains of blowing sand. Overhead, things chased each other through the sky with wild howls. Far off, something roared and roared on a single endless note.

"A lot of trouble for a drink of water," Pandaras remarked.

"The battle has already begun. That was why I was able to steal the water . . . We must press on, Pandaras. Enobarbus brought more machines than I thought. I do not know if Dr. Dismas's paramour can hold them."

"I'll go there and back in the blink of an eye, and carry you too, if I must." Pandaras said it as lightly as he could, but in truth he felt that this day would be his last.

The battle raged for the rest of their journey. Curtains of light washed half the sky, spiked with red or green lances that burned bright paths in the sandstorm. The ground shook continually, and a low rumble curdled Pandaras's guts.

The land began to slope downward ever more steeply, sculpted in fantastic curls like breaking waves frozen in glassy rock. Razor-sharp ridges cut through the soles of their boots and they both left bloody prints on the glassy ground. Things scuttled amongst half-buried rocks: hand-sized, flat, multilegged and very quick, like squashed spiders made of black glass. Bigger things prowled farther off, barely visible through veils of blowing red sand. Stiff growths poked up from glass and drifted sand, fretted tufts of black stuff that was neither plastic nor metal, all bent in the same direction by the constant wind.

"We are getting close now," Yama said. Blood was still seeping from his eyes; every so often he had to lift up his goggles and blot it away. Blisters on his forehead leaked clear fluid. Sand caked his face and his hair.

"You are already here," a voice said.

It came from everywhere around them, from the rocks and sand, from the dust-laden air.

Pandaras whirled in a complete circle, fumbling for his pistol. Something black and quick dropped from a fold of glass that reared above and stung his hand and jumped away. He howled and dropped the pistol in a drift of white sand. It sank swiftly, as if pulled under. Pandaras sucked at the puncture on his hand and spat out the bitter taste. When he looked up, someone in a silver cloak was standing a few paces from Yama.

It was the apothecary, Dr. Dismas. Or at least, what was left of him. He seemed to have grown taller. His clothes were tatters under his cloak. His flesh was black and rotten, falling away from bones on which cables and sacs of silvery stuff flexed and tugged. He tottered closer, reaching for Yama, but Yama dashed the apothecary's hand aside. Fingers snapped; two fell to the ground and were immediately tugged under.

Dr. Dismas did not seem to notice. His eyes were full of fluttering red light. Wind combed the remnants of his hair back from his skull. His jaw worked, and he said in a dry, croaking voice, "You brought many with you."

"They followed me," Yama said. "I had thought that they might be your friends, for their leader is the champion of the aspect of Angel. Is she not your ally?"

"We both want the same end, but for different reasons, as we both want you. We cannot share you. I had hoped that you had escaped her completely, but no matter. It is only a minor inconvenience. Do not think that it will distract me from what must be done."

"I know what you did to Dismas," Yama said. "He tried to do the same to me."

"I am not displeased with him. This is not a punishment; it is how he returned to me. He was loyal enough, in his way, and now he is completely mine. I may make him whole again, or I may absorb him. There will be time to decide on that once I am done with you. All the time in the world."

Pandaras realized then that something was using Dr. Dismas's dead body, like a puppet in a shadow play.

Yama said, "He infected me with one of your children, but it had ideas of its own."

"Of course. It would not be one of my children if it did not share my ambitions. That is why I must eventually destroy or devour my children, for otherwise they would devour me. Dr. Dismas should not have infected you so early. It was his only serious mistake, for my child could have destroyed you. But you overcame it, and what remains of it will help us."

"As I thought."

"Now we can begin."

"Now we can begin," Yama said. "There is much I want to learn. Pandaras, you must come with me. It is too dangerous for you to stay here alone. Do not be afraid."

But Pandaras was very afraid, so sick with fear that he could hardly stand. With a shudder, he drew himself up and followed Yama and the puppet-thing which had once been Dr. Dismas through a narrow defile.

A ramp spiraled away, running down into a deep pit. The pit narrowed with each turn of the ramp, like a hole left by a gigantic screw. Silvery vines grew out of the glassy walls—grew through them, too. Some twitched as Pandaras passed by, their ends fraying and fraying again into a hundred threads that wove back and forth like hungry blood-worms scenting his heat. Human faces and the masks of animals bloomed under the glass, distorted and wavering, as if seen through furnace heat. Trapped souls, Pandaras thought. The remnants of men and animals which had been devoured by the thing at the bottom of the pit.

The battle continued to rage above. The sky was split again and again by tremendous sheets of lightning. The ramp shuddered and quivered as explosions pounded the desert all around.

As they descended, things paced behind them, revealed and obscured by blowing sand, horrors half corpse, half machine. Dead animals wrapped in metal bands; polished human skeletons operated by the same silver cables and flexing bags which animated the corpse of Dr. Dismas. One skeleton rode a wild cat of the kind which had torn the bact apart; it was crowned with spectral fire, and carried a sword which burned with blue flames, as if dipped in brandy and set alight. Some poor dead hero, killed by the thing he had come to kill, and made into a ghastly slave.

"Do not be afraid," Yama told Pandaras again. "There is nothing to fear. I will be their master."

"We will be the master," the thing using Dr. Dismas said. "You and I will change the world."

Yama was looking around with an eager curiosity. He seemed to have wakened from the half-sleep of the journey. "Where are you?" he said. "I think you have grown since Dismas found you."

"I first found him far from here. He never reached my core while I was alive."

"Then this is where you fell. Like the thing in the Temple of the Black Well." Yama laughed. It was muffled by his face mask. "The war has never ended for you, has it? I suppose you would call the defeat that drove your kind from the world a temporary setback."

"I take the long view, as you will see. None of my paramours ever truly die. I always retain something of them. And you, my pet, my darling boy, I will hold you fast, close to my central processors."

"You are much larger than the others I have met. The one I called down in Ys, and the one trapped at the bottom of the well in the temple."

"One was a fool, like all those who allowed themselves to be driven into exile. The other was a coward that dared not stir from its hiding place. Cowards and fools. I despise them."

Pandaras could feel the venomous anger which forced these words through Dr. Dismas's dead mouth, although the tone was as flat as ever.

"Now I know why you were defeated in the wars of the Age of Insurrection," Yama said. "You fought against each other as fiercely as you fought against those loyal to the Preservers."

"We have grown apart since then. Those who fled Confluence have become weakened, for otherwise they would have long ago begun the war again. They are cowards."

"They follow the orbit of the world because they are tormented by what they cannot have."

"Exactly. Only they have grown weaker and I have grown stronger. I will take what they desire, and I will have them too."

"If only your love was as strong as your pride and your hunger! How well you would serve the Preservers then. Instead, you remind me of the heretics. Each of them would destroy the Universe, if only it would save his life."

"I have burned away that part of me," the thing said. "Love is a weakness. As I have refined myself, so I will refine you."

"Then you are a giant amongst the rebels," Yama said. He was walking at the edge of the ramp as he followed the puppet-thing, peering eagerly into the depths of the pit. "How large have you grown?"

"I have not enlarged my processing capacity overmuch because the architecture would become too complex. But I have redistributed myself, and I have many auxiliaries and drones."

"And your paramours."

"Oh yes. You are trying to find a way to me already. You will not. You destroyed the main part of the child Dismas implanted within you, but you had to mutilate yourself to do it because you were not able to overcome it in any other way. You will not be able to overcome me, for I am so much stronger and wiser. It is touching that you try, though. I would have expected nothing less. You hoped to use the heretics as a diversion—that was why you drew them here. A bold plan. I applaud it. But I fight them using only a fraction of my might, and soon they will be defeated."

"Then I was right to come here," Yama said. "I have learned much since I destroyed the Shadow. I will learn more."

"I will teach you all you desire, when you are with me. You may ask anything, and I will tell you."

Pandaras remembered the old tales of how feral machines buried in old temples or in the wild places of the world trapped those who hunted them by granting their wishes. Here was the truth which had spawned those fanciful stories. All stories were true because all were derived from the world, no matter how distantly. Otherwise, how could they be told by men, who were creatures of the world?

"O," Yama said, "I have so many questions. To begin with, I had only one. I wanted only to know where I could find people of my bloodline. I went to look for them, and I had hardly begun on that task when I found instead that I was asking the wrong question. To know my people I must first know how to ask questions. I must know myself. A wise man told me that, and beat me with his fan to make me remember it."

Theias, the envoy from Gond. Yama had tricked him into revealing more than he had wanted to reveal, and Theias had fled in shame and confusion, or so Pandaras had thought at the time. But now he saw that Theias had left because his task had been completed.

"I can tell you everything," the thing said through the dead mouth of Dr. Dismas. "I can tell you why the Preservers made Confluence, and why they raised up the ten thousand bloodlines. I can tell you the true nature of the world and the true nature of the Preservers. I can tell you where they went and why we should not serve them."

"I do not need to know any of that," Yama said. "You comfort yourself with false answers to those questions because you disobeyed the Preservers, who made you as surely as they made me. You need to believe that you acted not out of pride but to save the world because your masters betrayed you. Is this the place?"

Yama had stopped because silvery vines grew so thickly from the glassy wall that there was no way forward. They had gone around six turns of the ramp as they descended; they were deep within the pit now. It was so narrow here that Pandaras could have jumped clear across it. A thick red vapor hid the bottom from view.

"It has already begun," the thing said. Its voice was louder now, and the same voice rattled from the bony jaws of the skeletons behind them, roared in the razor mouths of the giant cats, hummed from the mouths of the faces that floated in the glass walls. The air was full of electricity. Every hair of Pandaras's pelt bristled, trying to stand away from its fellows.

The silvery vines snaked out with sudden swiftness. They enveloped Yama and he fell to his knees under their weight. Pandaras started forward, but Yama waved him back. A vine looped around his upraised arm. "It is all right," Yama said thickly. Blood ran from his mouth, rich and red. "What will be will be."

Pandaras halted, his hand inside his thin tattered robe, on the hilt of the skean. He remembered the coiling tentacles of the sharers of the deep dredgers. Yama had sent away the giant polyps after they had sunk Prefect Corin's ship; perhaps he could dismiss the vines too.

The vine around Yama's arm stretched, its end dividing and dividing. There was a flash of intense red light and Yama cried out. Pandaras blinked and almost missed what had happened. One of Yama's fingertips had been seared off and carried away.

"A tissue sample," the voice of the thing in the pit said. "A finger for the fingers you snapped from the hand of Dr. Dismas. But I will design a better body for you, my dear boy. You will not miss it."

The frayed end of the vine was poised above Yama's head now.

Yama looked at it calmly. He said, "That will not be necessary. The paths grown by my Shadow are still there."

"Do not be afraid," the voice said. It filled the pit, echoing and reechoing from the glassy walls.

And the vine struck.

Yama's head vanished beneath a myriad fine threads that flowed over each other, molding so tightly to his face its contours emerged as a silvery mask. Pandaras caught the stink as his master's bowels and bladder voided.

The Dismas puppet-thing tipped back its rotting face and howled. The faces trapped in the walls howled too. The skeletal figures rattled their jaws; the wild cats screeched.

All howled the same five words, over and over.

"Get out of my mind!"

And something fell from the sky and plunged into the pit.

It fell so fast that Pandaras barely glimpsed it before it vanished into the heavy red vapors at the bottom. The glassy walls rang like a bell and the ramp heaved. Pandaras fell to his knees. The eyeblink image burned in his mind: a black ball not much bigger than his head, covered in spines and spikes.

The Dismas thing darted at Yama, quick as a snake. Pandaras managed to grab an ankle and it fell to its knees, breaking off one hand at the wrist. It flipped around and threw itself at Pandaras, who struck out with the skean, a desperate sweeping blow that caught the thing in the neck. Its head was almost severed and hung between its shoulders by a gristly flap of flesh and a silvery cord, bouncing as it swung to and fro, groping for Pandaras with its remaining hand. Pandaras slashed again, aiming at the dead thing's heart. The skean's narrow blade sliced bone and shriveled flesh, grated on a metal sinew. Rotten blood pattered over him. A terrible stink filled the air. Pandaras was at the edge of the ramp; he dodged sideways as the thing made a final lunge, took a step onto air, and toppled into the heavy red mist without a sound.

All around, faces trapped under glass howled, melting and reforming.

The skean could not cut the silvery vines, but they had gone limp and Pandaras was able to pull them away from his master's body. The ones which had been attached to Yama's face left decads of pinpricks which each extruded a blob of bright red blood. Yama's mask had come off. He shuddered, drew a breath, another. His eyes were full of blood. Pandaras tore a strip from the hem of his robe and tenderly wiped it away.

Red vapor swirled around them. It was full of motes of sparkling light. Pandaras realized they were tiny machines, every one a part of the thing in the pit, as millions of termites in a nest make up a single super-organism. He tried to get Yama to stand up, but Yama was staring at something a thousand leagues beyond Pandaras and the walls of the pit. The faces in the pitted slabs of glass were dwindling into points of absolute blackness that hurt to look at.

"Caphis was right," he said. "The river comes to its own self. The snake which swallows its tail."

He shuddered, choked, and vomited a good deal of blood and watery chyme. He spat and grinned at Pandaras. "I took it all from him. All of it."

"We have to go, master. If it's possible to get through the battle, I'll do it. I'll get you back."

"I called it down," Yama said. "He did not expect that. That I would call on another of his kind. They are fighting now. Growing into one another. I think they will destroy each other. It is the opposite of love. Sex without consummation. Endless hunger."

He continued to babble as Pandaras got him to stand. They more or less supported each other as they climbed back up the ramp. The skeletal king had fallen; so had its followers. The wild cats had fled. Pandaras was too tired to listen to his master's ramblings, mad stuff about the river and the end of the world, and holes that drew together space and time.

Pandaras knew that they could never reach the mountains of the Great Divide, but he had to keep going forward. At some point, he realized that they had climbed out of the pit. Sand blew around them on a strengthening wind. The sun was setting. Its light spread in a long red line through the murk, as if trying to measure the length of the world. A shaft of deep red light shone up from the pit, aimed at the empty sky.

Pandaras sat Yama beneath the overhang of a smooth wave of fused, cracked glass and more or less fell down beside him. He said, "If you can do any other tricks, master, now's the time."

Sand blew past them endlessly. The light that rose from the pit seemed to grow brighter as the sun set. Everything had a double shadow.

The remnants of the army of Enobarbus were drawn up along a distant ridge, dimly seen through the veils of blowing sand. There, gone, there again. One of the wild cats prowled through the murk, ears flat, eyes almost closed. It did not know where it was, remembered only a time of fear and the stink of death, a compulsion stronger than sex or appetite which had suddenly vanished. There were still things in its flesh it could not claw or bite out, but they were dead things now, no worse than thorns. It stopped and stared for a long time at two men huddled against each other, torn between fear and hunger. Then it glanced over its shoulder and fled into the storm, fluidly flowing over glassy humps.

Two riders were approaching. The wind began to howl.

18

The Trial

ONCE PANDARAS WAS well enough to be able to walk about the house, the heretics provided him with a kind of uniform to replace his ragged clothes: gray silk tunic and trousers with silver piping; long black boots of some kind of malleable plastic; a belt of black, fine-grained leather, with a strap that went over his shoulder; a black silk glove for his right hand and a black silk stocking to draw over the stump of his left wrist. They did not allow him a weapon, of course, but gave him an ebony swagger stick tipped at either end with chased silver.

When he realized that he was not going to be killed, Pandaras's fear turned to anger. He had rescued his master twice over, even though he had at last been forced to deliver him into the hands of the heretics, and now he was mocked. He broke the swagger stick in half, picked the silver piping from tunic and trousers, and threw the boots, belt, glove and silk sock out of the window of his room.

Yama and Pandaras were being kept prisoner in an ordinary house embedded in a complex of tents, domes and pyramids which had grown around it, linked by gossamer bridges and enclosed by huge plastic vanes in bright primary colors. The vanes glowed at night with inner light, like the noctilucent jellyfish which sailed the river in summer. They were set in the middle of the ruins of Sensch, the last city of the Great River. It was where Angel had fled after escaping from the other Ancients of Days. It was where she had begun to spread her heresy. The house in which Yama and Pandaras were imprisoned was the house where she had lived. The rest of the city—its narrow streets and markets, its palace and docks—had been razed after the Change War and rebuilt upriver. Apart from Angel's house, only the ruins of the temple were left, enclosed within enfilades of silvery triangular sails like the maw of some monster rising up from the keelways.

Yama was taken to the temple a few days after arriving in Sensch, once the heretics were certain that he would not die of his wounds. He had to be carried on a stretcher, and was escorted by a maniple of soldiers. Pandaras was not allowed to accompany him, but heard about what happened from the warden of the prison house, who got it from one of the chirurgeons who attended Yama.

Yama had been manacled to a chair in front of the temple's shrine, where he was to be questioned by the aspect of Angel in the presence of those who would later judge him. But although the shrine had lit up, the aspect had not appeared, and after several hours and a great deal of confusion Yama had been returned to the prison house.

"They want me killed," Yama said wearily, when Pandaras was at last allowed to see him. "I know too much now."

"Did you destroy the aspect, master?"

Yama smiled and said, "You are too clever, Pandaras. I fear that it will be the death of you."

"I think that it already has, master, and so I've earned the right to know what you did. Did you destroy her?"

"You are not going to die here, Pandaras, and this is no time for deathbed confessions. I will tell you what I did because you are my friend. No, I did not destroy her. She coded herself too deeply for that. However, I was able to turn all the shrines on the world against her. I do not think that she will be able to find a way back."

Yama was still very ill. He fell asleep and woke without noticing that he had slept, and added, "She was always a prisoner. She thought to conquer Confluence, but it had already conquered her. We are all of us prisoners of history here, forced to follow the paths of stories so old and so powerful they are engraved in every cell of our bodies. It is time to break the circle."

"Past time," Pandaras said, thinking that his master had some plan to escape the prison house. But Yama had fallen asleep again, and did not hear him.

It took the heretics many days to treat and heal Yama. In all that time, Pandaras expected that at any moment his master would come to his senses and call down machines to help them escape, and when at last Yama was well enough to be brought before the board of men and women who would pronounce judgment on him, Pandaras thought that he would surely work his miracles then, in front of the astonished heretics. But he did not, and seemed to pay little attention to the proceedings, except to smile good-naturedly and agree that he was guilty of everything of which he was accused. The only consolation was that this seemed to anger the heretics as much as it frustrated Pandaras.

The trial was held in a huge white bubble chamber. Its walls absorbed sunlight and translated it to a directionless glow, reminding Pandaras of the shrine beyond the edge of the world. The trial lasted less than a day, and was presided over by the most senior of the heretics, although much of the time he seemed to pay as little attention to the proceedings as Yama. This was Mr. Naryan, the former Archivist of Sensch, who had been changed by Angel herself. An old, fat, hairless man, he hung naked in clear, bubbling water inside a cylindrical glass tank. Machines studded his wrinkled, grayish skin: at his neck; across the swollen barrel of his swollen chest; over one eye. Years ago, while preaching to one of the unchanged bloodlines, he had been badly hurt in an assassination attempt. The machines implanted in his body kept him alive. He had been an old man when he had met Angel, and now he was older than any of his bloodline. It was said that the implanted machines would ensure that he would never die.

The decad of men and women on the judicial panel sat on either side of Mr. Naryan's tank, staring down from elevated and canopied thrones chased with silver and upholstered in black plush at the plain bench on which Yama and Pandaras sat in manacles, with two rows of armored troopers behind them. Having no traditions, the heretics had invented their own, indulging in unrestrained expressions of ego untempered by any notion of taste. Most of the men wore fantastical military uniforms, crusted with braid and hung with ribbons, sashes and medals. One woman wore a white wig which doubled her height, with little machines blinking amongst its curls; another metal armor polished as bright as a mirror, so that her head seemed to sit above a kaleidoscope of broken reflections of the light-filled room. The majority of the panel were citizens of Sensch, of the first bloodline to have been changed by Angel's heresy. They listened to the list of Yama's crimes with various degrees of attention, grimacing each time Yama cheerfully assented to his guilt. Machines hovered in the air, recording and transmitting the event to heretic cities and armies along the Great River.

At the end, after Yama had agreed that he had been responsible for the failure of the Great River, Mr. Naryan finally stirred. He pushed to the surface of the tank and spouted water. A decad of machines dipped down to catch the soft croak of his voice.

"The boy must die," Mr. Naryan said. "He is an anachronism. The purpose of his bloodline was to make this world, and he threatens to use the powers of his kind to unmake it."

Several members of the panel made lengthy speeches, although all they had to say was that they agreed with Mr. Naryan. Only Enobarbus spoke up for Yama. Of all the panel, he wore no finery. He was bare-chested and his red officer's sash was tied at the waist of his white trousers. His mane of bronze hair floated around his ruined face as he prowled up and down in front of the panel.

"He has been crucial in driving the war against those who still serve the Preservers," he told them. "He subverted their machines and in only a few days helped win vast new territories for our cause. Used in the right way, I assure you that he can deliver total victory before the end of the year."

The old archivist surfaced again; water spilled down the glass wall of his tank. "The boy fought for us under coercion," he croaked. "Enobarbus was allied with an apothecary by the name of Dismas. And this Dismas, who was working for one of the feral machines, infected the boy with a machine which subdued his will and assumed his powers. We almost lost him because of that, and many were killed in retrieving him."

Enobarbus folded his arms across his broad chest. "The feral machines are our allies still. It is necessary that they are, for otherwise we would have to fight them as well as the loyalist troops, and I do not believe we could win on two fronts. Besides, Dismas's master was not one of those, but a rogue. I believe that it is now dead. We have the boy, and yes, retrieving him cost many lives. Do not let those sacrifices be in vain. Let us use him to bring this war to a swift end. Kill him then, if you wish, but kill him now and you sentence millions to death who otherwise might have been spared."

Mr. Naryan listed chest-high in the bubbling water of his tank. He said, "It is possible that the boy might save millions of lives if he is used against the loyalist troops, but it is certain that many thousands have already died because of him, first when Dismas tried to take him from you, and then when you recaptured him. Neither Dismas nor you, Enobarbus, could fully control the boy, yet everyone wants to own him. He is too powerful. I fear that if we use him to win the war we will then tear ourselves apart quarreling over him."

The woman in the white wig said, "He defied and mocked the shrine. I understand that it may never be restored. Mr. Naryan is right. He is too dangerous."

"She will return," Enobarbus said. "She cannot be destroyed."

There was a great deal of argument, and at last Mr. Naryan said, "It is clear that his powers proceed from the Preservers. How can we count ourselves superior to them if we must rely upon him for victory? No, he must die. We will vote on it."

One by one, the panel dropped a pebble into a plain plastic basket. At the end a clerk tipped them out. There was no need to count. Only one was white; the rest were black.

Yama laughed when the clerk announced the result, and Pandaras feared that his master had lost his mind.

The sentence was not carried out straightaway. It was to be staged publicly, and many heretics wanted to journey to Sensch to witness it for themselves. And there was much dispute about the method of execution. By a tradition which had survived the Change War, the citizens of Sensch cast their criminals into the swift currents at the fall of the Great River, and because the trial had been held in Sensch they insisted that this was how Yama should be executed. Others wanted a more certain death, arguing that Yama might save himself by calling upon machines which would carry him to safety. The heretics had no central authority and the debate dragged on for days after the end of the trial. Usabio, the warden of the prison house, said that Yama might die of old age before it was done.

"Then all your plans for becoming rich would fall to nothing," Pandaras said. He did not like Usabio, but the man was useful. He courted Pandaras because he wanted to get close to Yama, and Pandaras could sometimes get favors from him.

"I could sell tickets," Usabio said. "People would come to see him, and the guards could be bribed to keep quiet."

Usabio was of the bloodline of the citizens of Sensch, his pebbly black skin mottled with patches of muddy yellow. He bent over Pandaras like a lizard stooping on a bug and grinned hugely, showing rows of sharp triangular teeth. His breath stank of fish. He said, "It would be like having an animal no one else had ever seen, the only one of its kind in all the world. We could dress him in robes and let him babble. Or perhaps I could bring him household machines to mend. Think of my offer, Pandaras. When your master is dead you will have no employment. You are crippled. You will become a beggar, and we do not tolerate beggars, for they are parasites on those who strive to better themselves. Only the strong survive, and you are weak! But with my help you could at least be rich."

"Perhaps we will escape. Perhaps my master will destroy your miserable city."

"He is defeated, Pandaras. You must think of yourself." Usabio meant this kindly. He was a selfish and greedy man, but not without pity.

Yama took no notice of the arguments which raged around him. He merely shrugged when Pandaras told him about Usabio's latest scheme. As usual, he was sitting in the courtyard, in the shade of an ancient jacaranda tree. Soldiers stood at intervals by the wooden railing of the balcony that ran around the upper story of the house, looking down at them through leaves and branches.

"They will make up their minds eventually," Yama said. "Mr. Naryan will make sure of it. He does not want the feral machines or some rogue element of the heretics to try and take me. He is right. There are many who want to use me."

Pandaras lowered his voice, although he knew that machines caught and recorded every word. He said, "You could leave at any time, master. In fact, you could leave now. Do it. Confound their machines and walk away with me."

"Where would I go, Pandaras? Now that I have traveled the length of the Great River, it seems to me that the world is a small place."

"There are many places remote from men, master. And many places in Ys where you could hide amongst the ordinary people."

Yama looked off into the distance. At last he said, "Beatrice and Osric knew about hiding. They hid an entire department in the City of the Dead. But I am not yet dead, and I fear that my enemies will always be able to find me."

"Forgive me, master, but you will certainly soon be dead if you stay here."

"Everyone wants either to use me or to kill me. When I was a boy, Pandaras, I dreamed that I was the child of special people. Of pirates or war heroes, or of dynasts wealthy beyond all measure. It was a foolish dream, not because it was wrong, for it seems that I am the child of special people after all, but because it is dangerous to be special. That is why Mr. Naryan wants to kill me." Yama laughed. "When I left for Ys I thought that I would become the greatest of all the soldiers in the service of the Preservers."

"As you are," Pandaras said firmly. "And I am your squire, master."

Pandaras still attended to Yama's needs, even though they were both prisoners. Each morning and evening, he intercepted the soldiers who brought Yama's food and carried in the tray himself. Fruit and sweet white wine, raw fish in sauces of chili and hot radish, onion bread and poppy seed rolls, flat breads stuffed with olives and yellow bean curd and watercress leaves, bowls of sour yogurt, bowls of tea, beakers of cool sherbet. Yama ate very little and drank only water. Each night, Pandaras helped him undress, and each morning laid out fresh clothes for him and drew his bath.

"I am not a soldier," Yama said. "And that is the problem."

"But they think that you are a soldier, master. And they will surely kill you for it if you stay here."

"They think that I am an army, Pandaras. Or a mage, or a kind of machine. A thing to be used, a thing whose ownership is in dispute. They see only what I can do, not what I am. Where in this world can I find peace?" He shook his head and smiled. "Do not worry. They will not kill you. You are my servant, no more and no less. You are not guilty of my crimes. You could walk out of here now if you wanted to."

"I have already seen something of the cities of the heretics. I didn't much like them and I doubt that I'll like this one much either."

"There are the ruins of the temple," Yama said. "And there are still orchards and fishing boats, and the shrines on the far shore, by the great falls at the end of the river . . ."

Yama fell silent. Spots of sunlight filtered by the leaves of the jacaranda tree danced on his white shirt and his long black hair. It would need cutting again, Pandaras thought. And realized that when he cut it, it would be for the last time.

Yama saw his distressed look and said, "Beyond the edge of the world there are floating islands that hang within the falling spray of the river. They are grown over with strange mosses and ferns and bromeliads that thrive in the permanent rainfall. Telmon found a book in the library about them: they are called the Isles of Plenty. Fish with legs live on them, and lizards bigger than a man glide from island to island on membranes spread between their legs." He gripped Pandaras's hand and whispered, "The people of the indigenous tribes which inhabit the snowy tundra at the head of the river sometimes find such creatures frozen in the ice flows." He winked. "The indigenous peoples know much about the secrets of the world because they have not changed since it was created. They learn nothing new, but they forget nothing."

Pandaras feared Yama at times like this. Something had happened to him when he had been connected to the thing in the pit. It had jangled his brain. All that he knew was still there, but it had been muddled up, as looters might sweep ordered rows of books from the shelves of a library and leave them in heaps on the floor. Pandaras asked the chirurgeons who checked Yama's health each day to give him some potion or simple that would soothe his mind, but they were interested only in his body. They did not want him to die before he was killed, but they did not care if he was mad.

When Pandaras carried in the tray of food the next morning, setting it down on the floating slab of stone which served as a table, Yama was already awake and sitting by the window. Two soldiers stood outside. The leaves of the jacaranda tree rustled in the sultry breeze. It was an hour past dawn, and already hot. Yama's shirt was open to the waist, and he was streaming with sweat.

Pandaras mopped his master's face with a cloth, delicately dabbing around islands and troughs of tight pink scar tissue. He would have to burn the cloth. Presumably in front of Usabio, who had asked Pandaras to collect Yama's sweat and hair and nail clippings so that they could be sold as souvenirs.

"A few drops of blood could be diluted in a gallon of ox blood," the warden explained, "and sold a minim at a time. Perspiration can be diluted in water. *Let his perspiration be your inspiration.* I can arrange it, Pandaras, and make us both rich."

Pandaras said angrily, "Perhaps we could sell his piss, or his shit."

Usabio considered this. He said, "No. It is not a question of hygiene, but of myth. Heroes should not be seen to have the functions of ordinary men."

Yes, Pandaras thought now, he would burn the cloth right under the snake's nostril slits.

"Enobarbus came to see me," Yama said. "It seems that they have decided upon a compromise."

Pandaras leaned out of the window and told the soldiers to take their stink elsewhere. They both laughed, and the younger one said, "Going to plan your escape, eh? Don't worry. We won't listen. It would spoil the fun."

"We'll go and get some tea," his companion said. "Might take a few minutes."

As they sauntered off, the younger soldier turned and called out, "If you're going to climb over the roof, watch out. The tiles are loose."

Laughter as both men went down the stairs.

"No one takes me seriously," Pandaras said. "I have killed men. I could kill those two easily."

"Then their companions in arms would kill you. I do not want that. There are machines listening to us in any case, and more machines guarding us. The soldiers are bored. They know that they are here only for show."

"Dismiss the machines. Destroy them."

"I am done with that, Pandaras. Enobarbus told me that he is still pleading for my life. He wants me to fight alongside him. I refused to help him, of course."

"It took your power from you, didn't it? I'm a fool not to have seen it before. Well, I've been in worse places than this. I'll get us out."

"They will let you go free after the execution. You are here only because you are my servant, as a courtesy to me."

Pandaras threw over the breakfast tray. It made a loud crash. Mango and pomegranate juice mingled and spread on the glazed blue tiles of the floor. He said, "I will die with you, master."

"I am not ready to die, Pandaras. But I am ready to move on. You must stay behind. There is something I want you to do. It is a heavy burden, but I know that you are capable of carrying it."

"I am ready, master."

"I want you to remember me. I want you to go amongst the indigenous peoples, and tell them about me."

"I will do it. And I will kill as many of these snakes as I can before they kill you. I will tear down this vile place . . ."

Pandaras was crying, breathing in great gulps as tears ran down his cheeks and dripped from the point of his chin. A wet patch spread across the front of his gray silk tunic.

"No. Hush. Listen." Yama dropped his voice; Pandaras had to kneel beside him to hear his words. Yama stroked his small, sleek head, and at last the boy stopped crying. "Listen," Yama said again. "I want you to live. You can do miracles now, although you do not know it. You kissed the blood from my eyes, and the machines in my blood have changed the machines in yours. I told you about the little machines in all of us, the breath of the Preservers. Those in my blood have been changed, as have those in yours. Just a drop of your blood, Pandaras. In water or in wine. One drop in enough liquid for a hundred people to each take a sip."

"Usabio wants to sell your blood, master. Perhaps we should allow it."

"We could not guarantee that it would be drunk," Yama said seriously. "Do you remember the baby of the mirror people?"

"I remember that the fireflies found it."

"Because it had been changed. It had achieved self-awareness. Caphis saved my life, but he could not think anything that his people had not already thought ten thousand times over. I did not know then that I could change him, and now I want to rectify that. I want you to do it for me. A drop of blood, Pandaras. Change the indigenous peoples. Bring them to self-awareness."

"I will do it only if you save yourself, master. Or else I will die with you."

"The Preservers had a purpose in everything they did. Often we cannot understand it, or we think we understand it, but we see only what we want to see, and do not see what is really there. The indigenous peoples are despised because they cannot change. Until my father put a stop to it, the Amnan hunted the fisherfolk as they would hunt any animal. But the indigenous peoples are more than animals even if they are less than men. You will redeem them, Pandaras."

"Come with me, master. This talk frightens me. I am only a pot boy who fell into this great and terrible adventure by mistake. I am your squire. I bring you food and mend your shirts and keep your weapons in good order. Do not make me more than I am."

"You found me, Pandaras. In all the wide world you found me and rescued me. And you followed me to the worst place in the world, and dragged me from the pit. Make you more than you are? We are all more than we are, if we only knew it."

Yama had that faraway look Pandaras dreaded. He was casting through the muddle of his thoughts—his memories, the memories of the thing in the pit. He said, "There are places where time and space do not exist. They form a bridge between the present and the time when they were made. They bridge distances that take light years to cross. The star-sailors know about them . . ."

"Master, do not torment yourself by trying to understand the lies of that thing."

Yama gripped Pandaras's arm, just above the stump of his wrist. "I am sure that Prefect Corin is still searching for me, but there are places I can go where he cannot follow. Perhaps I do not go there for the first time. The river swallows its own self. Soon, Pandaras, I will see how it is done."

19

The Execution

IT WAS A fine, bright, hot day. Myriad small craft swarmed around the black barge which, with a sleek galliot on either side and a claw-shaped flier above, carried Yama and the judicial panel to the execution site. The event had a holiday air. The brightly colored sails of sightseers' skiffs, pirogues, yaws, cockleshells, yachts and pinnaces cracked in the brisk wind. There was a raft carrying a hundred sweating, barechested drummers who beat out long, interwoven rhythm lines. Merchants in sampans and trows sold food and wine, souvenirs and fireworks. People held up their children to see the evil mage; other children threw fire-crackers at the waves. Motorboats got in the way of sailboats and there were shouted arguments and exchanges of colorful insults. A whole raft of drunken men tumbled into the water when rocked by the wake of a chrome-plated speedboat's buzzing disc. They swam back to the raft and clambered on board and drank some more.

The fleet passed a strange cluster of hexagonal pillars of black ba-salt; long fringes of red waterweed spread out from them, combed by the river's strong currents. The farside shore was the thinnest of gray brushstrokes. Ahead, a line of black rain clouds marked the fall of the river over the edge of the world.

Yama was quite calm. He spent most of the journey speaking with Mr. Naryan, who wallowed in a glass tank of water on the barge's weatherdeck. They talked about Angel, of how she had come to Sensch and made herself its ruler, and changed the citizens in the first act of heresy which had set Confluence aflame with war.

"She spoke at the shrines at the edge of the world," Mr. Naryan said in his soft, croaking voice, "but I never learned what she did there."

Yama laughed. All his cares seemed to have lifted away in this last hour. He did not spare a single glance for the execution frame which stood on the platform at the bow of the barge, but it drew Pandaras's eye again and again, and each time a cold shiver ran through him. *Now in the moment of our death is the moment of our rebirth into eternal life.* Pandaras glimpsed Usabio in a motor launch beyond the port side galliot and felt a grain of anger sharpening his resignation. Yama's chambers had been stripped as soon as he had been marched out of them. The furniture had been reduced to matchsticks and the sheets cut into strips. No doubt the warden was here to make sure that the traders selling these souvenirs to the holiday crowd did not cheat him.

Yama told Mr. Naryan, "Angel called the last surviving avatars of the Preservers to her, and learned how to use the space inside the shrines. She made a copy of herself, the aspect that later destroyed the avatars. And I think that she made contact with the feral machines too."

"She was always with me," Mr. Naryan said. "I found her aspect in many of the shrines I visited, but she was fey and willful, and did not seem to remember much of what happened in Sensch. I have that honor."

"You told her aspect that story. And so she was able to put it in my book."

This amused Mr. Naryan, who rolled back and forth in his tank, barking sharply. Water slopped on the deck and a sprayhead flowered above him, soaking his exposed gray skin until it gleamed. A soft red light glowed at the center of the machine which clung to the ruined socket of his right eye. He said, "It is a fine irony. There are many stories about Angel, but only I remember the truth. Well, there is also poor Dreen, but he was seduced by the crew of Angel's ship, and went with them when they left this world. I will meet him again one day, of course. The Universe is infinite, but there are only a finite number of worlds. I will find him and save him from his mistake."

"You all want to live forever," Yama said. "But you cannot live forever because the Universe will not live forever. I have always wondered: what will happen when time ends, and you meet the Preservers? Will you try and destroy them?"

The woman in the mirror-bright armor told Yama, "We will have destroyed the Eye of the Preservers long before then. There are ways of ablating black holes. Once it is small enough, an event horizon achieves closure and nothing can escape from it before it evaporates. At least, not into this universe. We will seize the last day and make it ours. But by then, of course, we will have already made the Universe

ours. We will not falter as the Preservers faltered," she said, with a look
of pure, fierce conviction. "We will never cease in our striving."

Yama smiled and said, "There are many universes. Or rather, many
versions of one universe. Everything that can happen will happen. Perhaps even your victory."

"We do not need to think of the far future," Mr. Naryan said. "That
dream is what paralyzed this world. Because the Preservers promised
infinite life in the last moment at the end of all time and space, their
foolish worshippers believe that there is no need to do anything in this
life. Everything on this world has been bent by that false hope, mesmerized by it as a snake mesmerizes a mouse. But the future is not
shaped by a promise; it is what each person makes of it."

"We can agree on that at least," Yama said. "After the feral machines rebelled, the civil service decreed that it must suppress any
change, because change implied heresy. Yet the Preservers changed us
all, and set us here in the hope that we would change ourselves."

Even the indigens, Pandaras thought, with another cold shiver. The
burden his master had laid upon him seemed impossibly heavy. He was
only half-listening to this idle talk, paying more attention to the soldiers
who stood nearby. He had resolved to try and grab a pistol or even a
knife if Yama would not save himself. He would give up his life if he
could free his master.

"We do not need gods," the woman in the mirror-armor said, "because we will become more than gods. We will continue this conversation at the end of all things, when we raise you from the dead,
Yamamanama."

Yama bowed to her and said, "I thank you for the courtesy."

Enobarbus came back from the bow, where he had spent most of
the voyage. As usual, he was barechested. A pistol was tucked into the
red sash at the waist of his white trousers. Hot wind tangled his bronze
mane. His scars blazed in his broken face. He said, "It is almost time.
You should ready yourself, Yamamanama. We do not have a priest, but
you may pray alone if you wish to."

"I am done with prayers," Yama said.

The barge and its escort were passing long shoals of gray shingle
to starboard, where all the wrack of the world was cast up: dead trees
whitened by long immersion in the river; innumerable coffins, mostly
empty; scraps of waterlogged clothing and bits of plastic; the bodies of
men and animals; thousands upon thousands of bones; once in a while
the bleached carcass of a ship. Water reivers, living on floating platforms with powerful motors to counter the strong river currents, sifted

through the stuff cast up on these shoals, but today they were under guard far upriver. Only white gulls picked over the bones and the artfully preserved bodies; thousands of them rose like a snowstorm as the procession went past.

The roar of the fall of the river grew ever louder. Strong currents raised the skin of the water into muscular humps that shifted and clashed in little flurries of white foam. The ramshackle fleet of boats and rafts unpicked itself, beating back against the currents until only a few foolhardy craft were left, ignoring warnings broadcast from one of the galliots.

A line of black clouds was directly ahead, trailing skirts of silvery rain. The river ran straight beneath them, rising in a glassy hump at the edge of the world, a curb of water fifty leagues long.

One small pirogue foundered, swamped by the chop. The three people aboard jumped into the water and were swept away at once. No one tried to save them; they were responsible for their own lives. Most of the other small boats had turned back, although Usabio's powerful motor launch held station a little way off from the barges, and another launch hung half a league to stern.

The motors of the black barge and the two galliots roared and roared, holding them in place. The flier dipped lower, casting a shadow over the three vessels. Armored troopers were lining up along the rails of the galliots. The compromise was this: Yama would be bound to a wooden frame and thrown into the river, but would be killed by sharpshooters before he was swept over the edge of the world. The sharpshooters did not need to be accurate. They were armed with carbines whose beams could boil the river.

Now the pace of things quickened. It seemed to Pandaras that everything was being swept along as if caught in the river's accelerating currents.

Yama was stripped of his clothes. With a swarm of machines darting overhead, jostling to get the best view as they recorded or transmitted the scene, he was led to the bow of the barge by a pentad of soldiers in black plastic armor and black masks. They guided him with nervous pats and quiet words. Pandaras tried to follow, but an officer took hold of his good arm, and no matter how much he wriggled, he could not get free.

There was a pause, then a shift in focus. Mr. Naryan had begun to make a speech. Yama was marched back between the soldiers so that he could hear it. The barge's motors roared on a long low note that rattled Pandaras's teeth. His heart beat quickly. The barked orders of officers marshalling the sharpshooters on the galliots blew across the churning water. The distant launch was moving toward the barge now. Pandaras could no longer see Yama; the members of the judicial panel were in the way and the officer held him firmly. When they parted, he saw that Yama had been led back to the bow and was being lashed to the execution frame by five masked soldiers.

Pandaras cursed the ancestry of the officer who held him, and protested that he must be allowed to tend to his master in his last moments. "He's beyond help now," the officer said. "Compose yourself. This is a great moment in history."

The square execution frame was constructed from lengths of timber exactly Yama's height, reinforced with crosspieces and laid over a circle of thick balsa sections. It was held upright by slanting braces. Chains rose from each corner, knotted to a ring. The ring hung from a hook which in turn depended from the jib of a crane manned by a pentad of soldiers stripped to the waist. The slack chains swung and jingled as the barge shifted in the currents. Once Enobarbus had checked the ropes which fastened Yama's wrists and ankles to the frame, two soldiers knocked away the braces. The chains took up the slack and the frame was lifted and swung out by the crane, its top tilting backward until Yama lay level with the swift water beneath him. Soldiers hung onto ropes, checking the frame's tendency to swing to and fro.

Trumpets brayed from the galliots on either side. Pandaras's heart quickened. Was this the final moment? He tried to get free again, but the officer got him in a headlock and twisted his arm up behind his back until the pain forced him to cry out. "You'll be free in a moment," the officer said. "Have patience."

Something was wrong. The sharpshooters were breaking ranks and turning around. The launch was still coming on, heading straight for the port-side galliot. Something small and bright shot away from it, rising high into the air as the launch roared on through wings of spray. The flier lifted away, turning toward the launch.

Pandaras's first thought was that Yama had called on a machine to save him. But the thing which had shot away from the launch was not a machine, but a man standing on a floating disc that cut through the air so swiftly his ragged cloak flew out behind him. Just as Pandaras realized that it was Prefect Corin, an energy bolt struck the flier and it burst apart with a deafening blast of blue fire, and fragments rained down in long arcs, trailing smoke and flame as they smashed into the river. At the same moment, there was a tremendous crash and a flare of flame swept down the length of the port-side galliot. The launch had struck it amidships and exploded. Pandaras felt heat wash over him; the officer cursed, but did not let go of him. The galliot was on fire from one end to the other and was beginning to list as water poured through the hole in its hull. Soldiers were running about inside the flames, their screams tearing at the air. Some pitched into the river and were swept away at once. Ammunition exploded, bright flares rippling within the flames. The burning galliot swung around, its motors stuttering, and began to drift toward the falls.

Prefect Corin rose above the flames. The sharpshooters on the galliot to starboard took aim, lowered their carbines and looked at them, took aim again. Nothing. Either Yama had willed it or Prefect Corin was draining energy from the grid. Some of the soldiers on the barge, armed with percussion rifles, began a ragged fusillade. Too late. Prefect Corin extended his arm and a bolt of blue fire struck the stern of the starboard galliot. Water flashed into steam and the casings of the big motors burst; panicked soldiers ran toward the bow as smoking streams of molten metal set fire to the well deck. At the same moment, the officer holding Pandaras screamed and clutched at his mask, which had shattered around the slim black shaft of a machine. Pandaras twisted free and dashed forward, dodging amongst armored soldiers and gorgeously costumed members of the judicial panel.

Enobarbus aimed his pistol at Prefect Corin, threw it away when nothing happened, and grabbed a rifle from one of the soldiers. Prefect Corin dipped low, rushing straight toward the execution frame, which still hung above the chop of the water. Enobarbus took aim with the rifle, not at Prefect Corin, but at the chains which held the frame. Sparks flashed when a pellet hit the hook and he lowered his aim and got off two more shots before Pandaras struck him and tried to climb his torso.

Pandaras managed to claw one side of Enobarbus's face, but then he was picked up and tossed aside. The barge and the sky revolved around each other; he struck two soldiers and knocked them down, fetched up against something that rang dully against the back of his head. It was Mr. Naryan's tank. Enobarbus had thrown him halfway down the barge. Pandaras jumped up and ran forward again. At the bow, broken chains shook and danced beneath the crane's jib. The frame was gone.

Pandaras swarmed halfway up the crane and saw Prefect Corin's floating disc scudding away above the waves, chasing something borne on the strong current. Two half-naked soldiers were climbing toward him, and he kicked out and dived into the river without thinking, and at once realized that he could hardly keep his head above the surface.

The water was like a living thing in constant torment. Pardaras was caught in a current that forced him down amongst glittering fans of bubbles, then shot him back to the surface. A wave washed over him and he snatched a breath and glimpsed a shadow cutting toward him, and was pulled under again just as something twitched across his flanks.

A rope. He grabbed hold with his one hand and tangled his feet around its end. Whitecaps slapped his face one after the other. The side of a small boat pitched back and forth above him. Someone leaned down and grabbed him by the collar of his tunic and hauled him over the side.

Pandaras sprawled on his belly in a slop of water. The river had pummeled all the strength from his muscles. A motor roared and the launch made a long sweeping turn. Pandaras tried to stand up and fell into a nest of plastic bags, each containing a splinter of wood or a strip of white cloth, and knew who had rescued him.

Usabio turned from the helm of the launch, grinning hugely. He locked the controls and came back, bracing himself as he reached down to help Pandaras. And reared away, screaming and pawing at the splinter which Pandaras had jammed into his eye.

Pandaras kicked Usabio's legs from beneath him and struck him with all his weight. Still screaming, Usabio pitched backward over the side of the launch and was gone.

The launch was heading away from the fall of the river. It took Pandaras several tense minutes to work out how to unlock the little machine which controlled the launch's motors and turn it back.

The two galliots were on fire and drifting toward the edge of the world. The black barge was moving away, a cloud of machines swirling around it. Pandaras bounced the launch over the waves as fast as he dared. There was no sign of the floating disc, no sign of the frame. And no sign of either Prefect Corin or Yama.

The launch drew fire from the barge; machines buzzed it like angry hornets. Pandaras turned it away in a wide arc and pointed it upriver.

He did not believe that Yama had died. He swore to find him. He thought that he would spend the rest of his life looking, but he was wrong.

20

The Isles of Plenty

SOME TIME AFTER he had been brought back from the Glass Desert by the heretics, Yama had become aware that Prefect Corin was drawing near to the ruins of the city of Sensch. The man had enslaved several machines, and, in the days after Yama's trial, had moved from place to place around the edge of the city and its huge garrison, presumably probing for weaknesses. Yama had been certain that the Prefect would try and rescue him from the heretics, but had not believed that he would be successful. At best, he might provide a useful diversion. But now it was clear that, once again, Yama had underestimated the Prefect's resourcefulness.

Yama had his own plan of escape. He wanted to fall over the edge of the world into the shortcut where the river went, where past and present tangled together. The shortcut had been made when the world had been put together, and he thought that he could fall to its beginning and at last find his people. He had learned this from Dr. Dismas's paramour. It had absorbed many lesser machines and many men and women, and hoarded their knowledge much as a pack rat will decorate its nest with scraps of glass and plastic and metal. That great store had poured into Yama in the moment the machine had tried to make him its own, a torrential flood that had almost washed away his own self. He had had only a little time in which to try and map its limits, but he knew now the secret of the Great River, and knew that in the beginning of the world lay its end, and that was enough.

It was easy to fool the minuscule brains of the sharpshooters' carbines into thinking that they had discharged when they had not. It was harder to turn one of the swarm of machines which accompanied the barge, for they were imprinted with hundreds of interlocking shells of sub-selves, and each had to be painstakingly unpicked. But Yama knew that he would need a machine to cut his bonds after he was cast into the river, and he worked hard at it while the heretics prepared him for execution.

And then, as he hung naked on the execution frame, something blew the flier from the air and a motor launch rammed the galliot to his left and exploded. He guessed what was happening even as Enobarbus ran toward him, and used the machine he had laboriously subverted to kill the officer who held Pandaras. But instead of trying to escape, Pandaras ran to help his master, attacking Enobarbus as the warlord shot away the chains from which the frame was suspended.

And then Yama fell. The frame smashed down into the water and was at once whirled away from the barge. A sudden surge threw it into the air and crashed down into a wave that washed over Yama with bruising force, pulling his bound arms and legs in different directions. Yama managed to get a breath and then another wave struck the frame and he went under again and came up, gasping and blinking and wondering if he would drown before he fell over the edge of the world.

A shadow covered him: a floating disc. It tipped in midair and Prefect Corin slid down onto the frame and straddled Yama, bracing himself against the rock and roll of the waves. His staff was strapped to his back, over his fluttering cloak. He hit Yama four times with doubled fists, twice on the left temple, twice on the right. Something flashed as he raised his right hand. A knife. Yama, barely conscious, could only watch.

The knife slashed the rope which bound Yama's left hand to the frame. Prefect Corin's face was a handspan from his. "We are here to help you, boy," he said. He had to shout above the clash of white-water waves and the long unending roar of the river's fall. "We will not lose you again. Say that you will come with us and we will free you."

Yama tried to speak, but could not gather his thoughts. Spread-eagled and naked beneath his enemy, dazed and helpless, he felt all his old fears return. Prefect Corin was implacable, unforgiving, tireless. There was no escape from him. He would never stop, never give in, never die.

Prefect Corin laid his face against Yama's. His pelt was wet and cold, his breath hot. His left eye was a puckered ruin. "You are ours, Child of the River. Now and always. Whether we live or die, we will do it together."

Yama tried to focus on Prefect Corin's face. Things kept slipping away, jumping back. He had not been afraid of falling off the edge of the world because he had known where he was going, but he was filled with dread now. He was more afraid of this man than of anything else on the world.

Prefect Corin smiled and whispered, "You do not want to die. That is a beginning." He kissed Yama on the lips and sat back on his heels, ready to cut the other bonds, and his cloak suddenly flew sideways. Prefect Corin clasped his shoulder, then looked at the bright red blood on his palm, and Yama remembered Enobarbus's rifle. At the same moment, something cracked the air like a whip and a spray of blood struck Yama's face. Prefect Corin grunted, toppled sideways, and was swept away in the foaming crosscurrents. The floating disc tilted and swooped off, following its master. Yama watched it dwindle through pouring rain, and then a strong eddy caught the frame and swung it around.

Rain smashed through spray thrown up by clashing waves. Its cold needles stung relentlessly, bracing him awake. The air was half water now. A tremendous roaring filled every cell of his body. The frame groaned and flexed. Impossibly, it was rising, carried up a smooth slope of glassy water. For a moment, Yama paused at the top of the wave at the edge of the world, saw a barge and two foundering galliots beyond the skirts of the rain clouds, and a launch making a long arc away from them.

And then the world tilted backward and he fell away from it.

———

It was noon. Mr. Naryan had decreed that it was an auspicious moment for the execution. The sun shone straight down, turning the farside edge of the world into a golden knife blade that cut away half the sky. A wall of water fell past it, twisting into itself as it fell, a spout that shone silver against the blue of the envelope of air which wrapped the world, dwindling down toward the mouth of the shortcut which swallowed it and took it elsewhere. Yama could feel the tangled gravity fields like threads tugging at his limbs. He struggled to focus, to find the machines which generated the fields, and felt a cold, ancient intelligence far below, squatting at the mouth of the shortcut like a toad at the bottom of a well.

A dizzying surge of hope filled him then. It was all true!

Vast skirts of cloud hung about the wall of falling water, as white as freshly washed linen. Archipelagos of violet and indigo specks were scattered in arcs at different levels within the clouds, each casting a long shadow streak.

The Isles of Plenty.

Yama reached out, manipulating gravity fields. The frame flew toward the outermost island of the nearest arc.

He laughed as he swooped down, remembering his childish dreams of flying and the dream he had had in the tomb of the Silent Quarter of the City of the Dead.

Past and future came together in a moment of exquisite richness.

He fell through a veil of cloud. Fog streamed around him, soaking him with clinging cold vapor. Out into sunlight again, falling at the same speed as the constant rain. He could no longer see the island and tried to spin the frame around; then it crashed into soft tangles of dull red tubes which collapsed around him, exuding a strong, acrid scent.

He was still trying to unfasten the ropes around his ankles—the knots had shrunk in the water—when the rain people found him.

———

The Isles of Plenty were continually drenched with rain and mist. Everything—the soft, interwoven masses of bladderweed and the transparent, hydrogen-filled bladders that swelled at their fringes, the knotty mats of black grass, froths of algae and elaborate nests of ferns—was sopping wet. Water dripped from the spiky tips of indigo and violet fronds, percolated between interwoven root mats, collected in channels that ran into deep cisterns and pools, and poured in a hundred streams from the ragged edges of the islands. Sometimes it rained so hard that the air seemed to turn to water. Fish clambered about the soft mounds of vegetation, using prehensile fins at the edges of their flattened bodies, opening their rich red feathery gills in the downpour as they hunted maggot-flies, worms and beetles.

It was never brighter than twilight. As the world tipped back and forth on its long axis, the sun appeared above the farside edge at noon and below it at midnight, and even then the permanent cloud cover around the endless fall of the river obscured what light there was, only occasionally parting for a moment to reveal a sudden shaft of sunlight ringed by a hundred perfectly circular rainbows. Surges of air rubbed against each other, creating thunderstorms which were the greatest danger for the inhabitants of floating islands: a lightning bolt could ignite the hydrogen-filled bladders which buoyed the islands and blow them apart. But even in death there was life. Fragments of the communal organisms which wove together to form the floating islands were widely dispersed by these rare explosions; some would grow into new islands to replace those that dropped out of the currents of air which blew around the wall of water—the Great River turned through ninety degrees and falling toward its end and its beginning.

The rain people who inhabited the Isles of Plenty were not, as Yama had dreamed, of Derev's bloodline. They were an indigenous race. They were roughly half Yama's height, with smooth gray skin, oval heads dominated by large black eyes, thin arms and legs, and long, flexible, three-fingered hands. They were coldblooded and moved in abrupt bursts punctuated by slumberous pauses in which, except for the slow blink of nictitating membranes across their great eyes, they stood as still as statues.

Even as some of the rain people helped Yama free himself from the frame, others started to dismantle it; hard wood was as precious as gold in the Isles of Plenty. He was guided along paths smashed through wet, pulpy vegetation to a village built on platforms at the leading edge of the island. The main platform straddled a stream which tumbled noisily between banks of dome-shaped mosses and fell into the void below. Smaller sleeping platforms were built around the rigid stems of horsetail ferns which burst into great fans of knotty black strands overhead. The fern canopy was the only shelter from the constant rain. Water dripped everywhere, running across the slick resin of the platforms and falling into the vegetation below.

The rain people gave Yama a hide blanket to wrap around his naked body and fed him with a salty mash of uncooked fish flesh and the chopped tips of a variety of water weed whose brown straps grew parasitically on bladderweed stripes. Yama explained to them where he had come from and where he wanted to go. They listened patiently. Although they were naked, he could not tell which were men and which were women, for they had only smooth gray skin between their legs. Several pairs leaned against each other companionably. One of these couples, Tumataugena and Tamatane, the eldest of the family clan of the island, told Yama that only a few men from the world above had ever reached the Isles of Plenty, and none had ever left. But he was the first to understand that the river swallowed its own self, they said, and they realized the importance of his quest.

Tumataugena said, "The fall of the river diminishes year upon year."

Tamatane said, "The mouth of the snake flickered two generations ago. It swallows water still, but we fear that it spits it elsewhere."

Tumataugena said, "The same happened to the river of the other half of the world."

Tamatane said, "Unless a hero comes, this half of the world will become a desert too, as it was once before."

Speaking in turn, Tumataugena and Tamatane told the story of how the river of the inhabited half of the world had once been a long pool which flowed nowhere and soon became stagnant. A cistern snake drank it up, but this snake was two-headed and had no anus, so the water remained in its belly, swelling it into a smooth blue-green mountain range full of water that lay along one side of the world, opposite the Rim Mountains. One head lay amongst the Terminal Mountains at the endpoint of the world; the other hung over the midpoint. The world became tinder dry. Animals were dying of thirst; plants became wrinkled and sere. Several of the bloodlines which lived there attempted to make the snake disgorge the water by making it laugh, but since snakes have no sense of humor this came to nothing. But inside the cistern snake were certain parasitic worms, and as the snake swelled so they grew. By the will of the Preservers, they became the progenitors of the rain people. They broke off bone splinters from the snake's many ribs and fashioned them into knives. Working together, they cut the snake in half from within and set free the water it had swallowed. The great flood washed one of the snake's heads over the edge of the midpoint of the world. It hung in the air, receiving the waters that fell after it. The snake's other head remained lodged in the Terminal Mountains, and the water swallowed by the first head was vomited from the second. And so the Great River was formed, and the curves of its course preserved the last wriggles the cistern snake made in its death throes.

When the story was done (soft rain fell all around, like applause), Yama said, "I heard a riddle long ago, and now I know that I have found the answer to it. For that, as well as for my life, I am in your debt."

Tamatane said, "We became as we are now because we saved the world from drought. Yet we are still less than any of the peoples of the surface."

Tumataugena said, "If we help you save the river, then perhaps we will be rewarded again."

"Perhaps," Yama said.

The rain people asked Yama many questions about his adventures in the world above, but at last he could stay awake no longer. He slept beneath a shelter of woven bamboo leaves. He fell asleep quickly, even though he was soaked through and very cold, but he was awoken after only a few hours by Tamatane and Tumataugena.

"Something bad walks the air," they said. "Perhaps you know what it is."

The floating island was in the middle of a dense belt of cloud. It was close to midnight; light shone from beneath the island, diffused through white vapor. As Yama disentangled himself from the wet, heavy hide, something flashed far off in the mist, an intense point of brilliant blue light that faded to a flickering red star, falling through whiteness and gone even as Yama glimpsed it. A moment later, the whole island trembled as a clap of thunder rumbled through the air.

Yama shivered. He thought that he knew what had caused the blue light and the thunder.

As he clambered down from the sleeping platform, something loomed out of the mist: a dark spot that grew and gained shape, a red triangle with a kind of frame beneath it. It tipped through the air and stalled above the edge of the main platform; its pilot swung down from its harness and ran a little way across the platform with the last of its momentum, collapsing the bamboo frame and the hide stretched across it.

High-pitched whistles rose on all sides. The rain people gathered around the pilot, who stood in the center of the platform and stared up in wonder at Yama.

———

The pilot, Tumahirmatea, was from a shoal of floating islands which hung far above this one. Something terrible was loose in the air, Tumahirmatea said, a monster which spat flame and could destroy an island with a single breath.

"I know it," Yama said. "It is not a monster, but a man. I thought him dead, but it seems that nothing in the world can kill him. He is looking for me. I must leave at once."

The rain people talked amongst themselves, and then Tumataugena and Tamatane came forward and offered their help.

Tamatane said, "You wish to fall through the mouth of the snake."

"I could jump from the edge of this platform in an instant," Yama said, "but I am not certain of my target."

His stomach turned over at the thought. He was not at all sure that he could manipulate the machines which generated the gravity fields with enough precision to reach the mouth of the shortcut. If he missed, he would fall beyond the envelope of the world's air, and suffer the same horrible death as Angel.

Tumataugena said, "We have several kinds of flying devices. The simplest are sacks full of bladders harvested from the edges of the island, but those will lift you rather than allow you to fall. So instead we will give you one of our kites."

It was brought out of store and unwrapped. Yama thanked the rain people and asked for a knife and a cup of water. Tumataugena gave him a bodkin fashioned from the spine of a fish, with a handle of plaited black grass; Tamatane gave him a gourd brimming with sweet water.

Yama pricked the ball of his thumb and allowed three drops of blood to flutter into the water. He said, "If you wish to become more than you are, to become as the peoples of the world above, then drink a mouthful of this. When the change is complete you will be able to change others in the same way. If you decide not to do this thing, then wait a day for the water to lose its potency and then dash it over the edge of the island."

Was Pandaras safe? Would he perform this miracle for the indigenous peoples of all the long world? But perhaps it did not matter. Already the mirror people and the forest folk were changed. And they would change others.

The rain people talked amongst themselves; at last, Tamatane and Tumataugena announced that they would do this thing at once. They passed the gourd around, and the last person to drink from it, the stranger, Tumahirmatea, pitched it into the void.

"You will have a fever," Yama said, "and then you will sleep. But when you awake all will be changed. You must find your own way after that. I can do no more for you."

It did not take long to learn how to fly the mankite. There was a harness which was lengthened to accommodate him, and a frame hung at the balance point which he could grip and tilt to the left or right. A ribbon at the point of the kite indicated the direction of air currents; rudders pushed by his feet spilled air from the leading edges of the diamond-shaped lifting surface to bring it to stalling speed for a safe landing. But he would not need to land, only to stoop down like a lammergeyer.

There was no ceremony of farewell. He was strapped into the kite and helped to the edge of the platform, then took a breath and jumped off. The underside of the island fell past, tangles of tough holdfasts studded with transparent hydrogen bladders. The kite jinked in air currents, wrenching at his shoulders. He kicked, got his feet in the stirrups of the rudders, leaned to the left. And began to breathe again.

Tumahirmatea followed Yama as he stooped down, the red kite matching the yellow wingtip to wingtip.

They fell through vast volumes of cloud, breaking through streaming mist and rain into clear air. In one direction the dark wall of the edge of the world rose through decks of cloud and curtains of rain; in the other, empty blue air deepened toward the black void in which the world swam. Between, the silver column of the falling river twisted down toward its vanishing point, a hundred leagues below. The air was brighter there: it was night on the surface of the world, and the sun was walking its keel. Lightning crackled around the silver twist of water, vivid sparks flashing against their own reflections. Floating islands made broken arcs at different levels, receding into blue depths of air.

Yama swooped down in a great curve, yelling as he fell. For those few minutes, he was utterly free.

Tumahirmatea left him once they had fallen past the lower edge of the clouds that ringed the falling river. The red kite tipped from side to side in farewell and tilted away, already rising on an updraft. Yama fell on alone.

The column of water, twisted within intricate gravity fields, was closer now. The air was full of electricity generated by the friction of its fall. Every hair on Yama's head stirred uneasily; the thunder of lightning storms constantly shivered the air. He tacked several leagues out from the water column, then swung the kite around it. The world was a wall reaching above and below as far as he could see.

After one more full turn around the falling river, he would reach its vanishing point. Looking straight down, he could see a throat of velvet darkness wrapped around the root of the column of water. He could feel the thing which controlled the shortcut. It was awakening, reaching toward him through the babble of the machines which manipulated the gravity fields.

Take me to the beginning of the world, he told it. Take me to my people.

He had expected difficulties. He had expected to have to use the full force of his will and all of his wits to break it. But it yielded at once. Filtered through the remnant of the Shadow, its voice was his own. *Of course,* it said. *You have returned. Do not be surprised. I live in the place where the river meets itself. Of course I know you. I hope that I will see you again.*

There was no time to frame questions. He was caught in air currents which sheared off the falling water. They buffeted him hard as he cut through them. The lifting surface of the kite boomed and shivered. The frame wrenched in his grip as if suddenly possessed of a will of its own.

You will not need the flying thing. I will guide you.

Yama kicked his feet out of the rudders, unbuckled the harness. And gave himself to the air.

The kite slammed away above him, bucking and folding up as conflicting air currents caught it, a fleck of yellow that whirled upward, was gone. Yama arranged himself in the rush of air, his feet pointing down, his arms by his sides. It was the way he had so often dived into the deep water at the rocky point of the bay of the little city of Aeolis.

Something other than air gripped him. He drifted slowly toward the column of water. It was as smooth and dense as glass. It seemed to rise above him toward infinity. Beneath his feet was a rim of darkness, at one moment as flat as a ring of paper, the next infinitely deep. The tube of water narrowed as it swooped down. Water was not compressible, but somehow the river's vast flow was squeezed into a tube so narrow that two men could have embraced it and touched fingertips.

Space-time distortion. The flow here is extended through time as well as space. It is easier than extending the size of the shortcut's mouth.

Yama did not understand the words which appeared in his head.

He was falling faster now. Air ripped past. His cloak of uncured hide streamed up behind his head. He saw structures around the rim, geometric traceries of intense electric blue that extended wherever he looked.

And then he was gripped, turned, accelerated. There was an instant of intolerable pressure and brilliant light.

21

Ship of Fools

A TREMENDOUS FLOOD swept him forward. He thrashed toward light and air, but the water was already receding, a wave washing away in every direction.

He stood, water slopping about his ankles. The hide cloak was soaked through, and clung in heavy folds to his naked body. The light was dim, blood-red. The cold air tasted of metal. He was in a chamber so large he could not see its ceiling or any of its walls. Beneath the ankle-deep water was a floor of a smooth, slightly yielding black substance.

A shrine stood a little distance away. It was the biggest he had ever seen, a huge black disc that could have overtopped the tallest tower of the peel-house. Nothing woke when he addressed it, but he had the unsettling impression that its vast smooth surface somehow inverted for a moment.

Where was he now? And when? Was he in the keel of the world? Was this the time of its making? He flexed his toes against the black floor. It reminded him of a place Tamora had taken him to a lifetime ago, in Ys.

He chose a direction at random and walked a long time. The water soon gave out. Once he shouted out his name, but the volumes of shadow and red light gave back no echo. He walked on, and a little time later felt the presence of machines far behind, and stopped and turned.

In the distance, tiny figures were moving at the base of the huge black circle of the shrine. He raised his arms above his head and shouted to them with sudden hope, and a narrow beam of intense white light swept out and pinned him. The figures were suddenly moving forward with impossible, inhuman quickness. Yama tried to question them, but their minds were opaque. Remembering the extensions of Dr. Dismas's paramour, he turned and started to run, his shadow leaping ahead of him, and ran until he heard a faint whistle off to his left.

He stopped and looked back, half-winded and dazzled by the white light, and saw that the figures had already made up half the distance. The whistle came again, human, shrill and urgent. He turned toward it. The beam of light tracked him, and his shadow rose to confront him, thrown onto something that loomed out of the dim redness. A structure of some kind, a black blister or bubble no bigger than an ordinary house.

A figure jumped up right in front of him, throwing aside the cloth which had concealed it. Yama tried to dodge, but it was faster. A shoulder smashed into his belly, arms wrapped around his hips, and he was thrown to the floor.

He looked up in astonishment at a face so like his own it might have been his sister's: pale skin, a narrow jaw, high cheekbones, vivid blue eyes. Her black hair was cropped short. Elaborate tattoos began at the angles of her jaw, reaching around under her ears to meet at the nape of her neck. She wore a loose, silvery, one piece garment that clasped her ankles, wrists and neck. One of her calloused bare feet was planted on his chest, and she was pointing a slim wand at his face. He had the sense that it was a weapon. There was something odd about this strange yet familiar woman, a vacancy . . .

"What are you?" she said. She was breathing very hard. "A survivor from the holds or a stowaway?"

Yama had turned his head to hide the scarred side of his face. He was uncomfortably aware that he was naked under the heavy hide cloak. He said, "Am I in the keelways?"

"You mean the spine? Don't fool. We lost those territories twenty generations ago. What are you?"

"A stranger to this place."

"A savage on walkabout maybe. Whatever you are, I think you just killed us both."

She let him stand. The figures were much closer now, silhouetted against the glare of the intense beam of white light, man-shaped, but oddly lopsided, running hard toward them.

Yama pointed at the blister and said, "What is inside this building?"

"An outlet. Even if we had a hot blade, we could not cut its skin." The woman was folding up the black cloth which had concealed her. It made a surprisingly small square that went into a slit at the waist of her silvery garment.

Yama remembered the voidship lighter. The guard had done something to the material . . .

An opening puckered in the smooth black curve. The woman looked at him in astonishment, but followed him inside. The opening sealed behind them. For a moment they were in complete darkness, then the woman asked for light and a dim radiance kindled in the air.

They stood on a narrow walkway. It ran around a smooth-walled shaft that sloped down into darkness. The woman knelt and stared down into the shaft, then looked up at Yama. "That was a good trick," she said, "but the regulators will get permission to unseal this soon enough."

"What are they?"

"You don't wear any mark. What family?"

"That is what I hope to find out."

"You came through with the water, didn't you? But we can't stay here."

"I will have to take off my cloak," Yama said. "Then we will find out how far this falls."

"A long way, I expect. It is one of the mains."

Yama sat down at the lip of the shaft, took off the cloak and spread it out, hairy side down. He could feel the woman's gaze move over his naked body. He said, "Sit behind me and hold onto my waist. The cloak will protect us."

After a moment, she did as he asked. Her spicy scent and body heat gave him an erection; he felt a blush spreading across his face and chest.

The woman said, "I am Wery. If we survive this I'll take you to my people and we'll parley. Bryn will want to ask you many questions."

"Now," Yama said, and they kicked off into the long steep slide.

Wery screamed all the way down—in delight, rather than fear. The surface of the shaft was almost frictionless, but even so the hide quickly grew warm beneath Yama's bare buttocks. When at last the shaft straightened out and they came to a halt, he got up into a crouch and awkwardly fastened the cloak around himself again.

They walked a long way. The shaft was more than twice their height and perfectly circular in cross-section, lined with the same black stuff as the floor of the huge space they had escaped. Yama told Wery some of his story. "All my life I have been searching for my people," he said. "I am so happy to have found you! How many others are there? And where is this?"

"You'll find out, if you pass. You can trade questions with Bryn."

"I can explain how I came here, and why I do not know where I am. The river was diverted—"

"No more talk now. We're not safe here."

At last, Yama discovered a place where he could make the black stuff pucker open. They clambered through into green light and hot, humid air. A rock face covered in creepers and thick lianas rose behind them, its top overhung by trees. A dry streambed snaked away between bushes and trees that leaned over it to form a kind of tunnel.

Wery looked all around, sniffing the air. "I think I know this wild. The others are not far away. You did well."

She stepped up to him, face to face. For a swooning moment Yama thought that she was about to embrace him, but instead she touched her wand to the skin behind his ear. A point of intense coldness swiftly spread across his scalp and face. His muscles loosened; Wery stepped out of the way when he fell.

———

Yama was woken by the screeching of birds high above. Two men stepped through the ragged rent they had hacked in the bushes that grew thickly along the dry streambed. Wery ran to the larger of the two men, embraced him, and said, "It wasn't any bug that came through. I'm not sure what he is. He has a story so crazy it could be plausible, but he could be a medizer."

"They killed all the medizers long ago," the smaller man said, "after they killed the other tribes."

"Hush," Wery said. "He's awake."

Yama sat up. He smiled at the two men and spread his hands so that they could see that he was unarmed. He was so very happy to have found people of his bloodline that he could not believe that they would want to harm him.

The men were dressed in silvery one-piece garments like Wery's, and both had similar tattoos across the backs of their necks. As with Wery, there seemed to be something lacking in them. It was as if they were not living people, but animated statues, or aspects cast in flesh rather than light . . .

The man Wery had hugged was a head taller than Yama, well-built and handsome. He had ripped off the sleeves of his silvery garment to show off his muscular arms; copper bands constricted his well-defined biceps. The other man was much older, and had a leather sack slung over one shoulder. His close-cropped hair and trimmed beard were white; his skin was papery and freckled with brown splotches. Deep wrinkles cut his forehead and seamed the skin around his eyes and the corners of his mouth. I will look like that if I live long enough, Yama thought, and wondered how long it would take, and how long he could live.

There was a silver patch over the old man's left eye. He flipped it up and told Wery, "Something else came through, too. Regulators are swarming all through these decks. They know how you got away and sooner or later they will try to follow. We'll have to move."

The old man pointed his wand at Yama, and Yama's muscles immediately locked in tetanic spasm. His body arched in a bow; his teeth ground against each other when he tried to protest.

The old man flipped the patch down over his eye and made several slow passes of his wand over Yama's body. "He's full of bits and pieces, but nothing I recognize. Stuff in his blood, too, but it isn't regulator trace. Never seen anything like it. Maybe he really did come from somewhere else."

Yama knew now what these people lacked. None of them had been touched by the breath of the Preservers. They might have been ghosts.

"The ship is very big," the taller one, Cas, said slowly.

Wery shook her head. "From what he said, I think he's from outside."

The old man stood back. Yama's muscles relaxed, then began to tingle. He stood slowly and said, "I really can explain everything."

"Not here," the old man said. "We shift, mates, find a berth and wait out the regulators."

The old man, Bryn, was the leader of the three. They had been on what he called a bug hunt.

"Things come up with new cargo," Bryn told Yama, "and sometimes they get loose. They have to be sly enough to get past the safeguards, so they usually cause trouble. We hunt them down."

The big man, Cas, said, "Maybe he's a bug that looks like a man."

"No fooling, Cas," Wery said. "This is important."

After they left the stream, they walked in silence a long way down a path that wound through the forest. Yama's hide wrap dried slowly, stiffening around him. He was aware that it smelled of meat going bad. At last the path passed between two huge trees, and on the other side a white corridor stretched away to its vanishing point. They walked on for more than a league until Bryn said that it was safe to think of resting.

He opened a door Yama had not noticed, and they went through into a high-ceilinged, brightly lit room. Narrow slabs of ceramic floated in the air and gusts of hot, dry air blew from random directions. Feeding troughs were set in the floor along one of the walls, but the stuff in them had crumbled to dust. No one had been here for a very long time.

A voice welcomed them when they entered, and said that it could reconfigure to the requirements of their bloodline. Bryn told it to shut up. "We leave no traces," he said to Yama. "Remember that and you might live as long as me."

Yama sat next to the old man on one of the floating slabs and asked him how old he was. "Fifty-three years," the old man said proudly. "You look surprised, and no wonder. It is older than anyone I know. I expect that no one in your family has ever lived as long, but it is possible, as you can see."

Yama had thought that Bryn must be at least two centuries old, and the revelation disappointed him. It seemed that his bloodline was very short-lived, unless they aged quickly here because of hardship.

Cas and Wery were watching the door, their wands across their laps. "I hate this heat," Cas said. "We should find one of our places."

"The regulators will look in those places first," Bryn said. "Shut up, Cas. Watch the door. I want to hear our new mate's story."

Wery said she had already heard it, and had not understood a word. Bryn shrugged. "She's muscle," he told Yama, "she and her husband. Good at killing, but not so bright."

"You always got to think you're cleverer than everyone else," Cas said. He got up and began to prowl around, restless in the way of a man more comfortable with action than conversation.

Bryn said, "It's well known that I am clever. I chose you two because I'm clever enough to know what you're good at. Don't break any of the machinery, Cas. That'll bring the regulators at once."

Cas said, "Good. I fight them." But he set down the delicate construction of black rods he had been turning over in his big hands.

"Did you really come from Confluence?" Wery asked Yama, with a smile that broke his heart all over again. He had forgiven her for knocking him out; it had been a sensible precaution. She said, "It's paradise, I hear. Like wilds that go on forever, but no regulators or bugs. You should take us all there."

Her fierce, bold candor reminded him so much of poor, dead Tamora. Perhaps she would leave Cas for him; perhaps there were other women like her. In the swooning excitement of finding his people, he had forgotten his sweetheart, Derev, and the fervent promises they had made to each other before he had set out on the long road which had at last led him here.

Cas said, "The ship hasn't been to Confluence for generations and generations. How could he come from there?"

Yama tried to explain.

The fastest way to travel from one point to another was in a straight line—or rather, over the long distances between stars, in a curved geodesic, for the mass of the Universe distorted its own space. But within the vacuum of space were holes smaller than the particles which made up atoms. As small as the smallest possible measurement, the holes appeared and disappeared in an instant, a constant, unperceived seething of energies that continually canceled themselves out. The holes had two mouths, and the space that tunneled between the mouths was compressed so that the distance between them was shorter inside the tunnel than outside it. The Preservers had found a way to grab the mouths of certain of these holes, to stabilize and widen them.

Bryn nodded. "The ship uses the shortcuts to get from world to world without traveling. It also uses them to replenish its air and water. You came out in one of the cisterns. Lucky for you it was one that isn't used anymore, or you would have drowned. But I guess most of them aren't used now. The crew is pretty skimpy these days."

Cas was doing pushups as relentlessly as a machine. Sweat gleamed on his bare, muscular arms, pooled between the cords on his neck. Without pausing, he said, "All this is useless stuff. We don't need to know anything outside the ship."

"Let him tell all of it," Wery said. "You never know when something might have a use."

"She's right," Bryn said. "Set on, lad. Finish your story."

The Preservers had constructed an intricate network of shortcuts between every star in the Galaxy, but the shortcuts could link points in time as well as space. It was done by fixing one mouth of a shortcut to a ship capable of traveling at speeds close to that of light itself. In the realm of light there was no time; or rather, there was a single endless moment which encompassed the beginning and the end of the Universe. As the ship carrying the shortcut mouth approached that unreachable realm, so time stretched about it; while only a few years passed aboard the ship, many more passed in the rest of the Universe. When the ship returned to its starting point, the two mouths of the shortcut now joined regions of space which were separated by the time debt built up during the journey. Someone passing through the mouth of the shortcut which had traveled with the ship would exit from the mouth which had remained where it was, and travel back to the time when the ship's journey had begun. But they could not return by the same route, because their journey altered the past.

Yama drew diagrams in the dust, prompted by the remains of the Shadow, which was able to filter the vast store of knowledge he had taken from Dr. Dismas's paramour. As Yama explained his story, he came to understand just what he had done.

The Preservers had cloned certain of the shortcuts, so that one mouth led to many different destinations, determined by slight changes in the potential energy of whatever entered. Aided by the Gatekeeper, Yama had fallen through the mouth of one of these cloned shortcuts, but he did not know where and when he had emerged. He knew only that his wish had been granted: he had been sent to his people.

Yama understood all about cloning, for it was how meat and work animals were bred, but he had to explain it several times before Wery understood. The notion disgusted her, and Bryn was amused by her disgust. "There are many different ways of living," he said. "That's why these rooms are all so different, because the passengers were once many different kinds of people."

"They were all bugs," Cas said indifferently. He was sitting on his haunches by the door now, polishing a bone dagger. "And we kill bugs."

"Some bugs are the stock species from which the Preservers made people," Bryn said. "Although I admit that there's a bigger difference there than between child and man."

"Bugs are bugs," Cas said. "Kill 'em or be killed. Some are harder to kill, that's all."

"And you can eat some but not others," Wery said.

Yama said again, "Because I fell through one of the cloned shortcuts, I do not know where I am."

"On the ship, of course," Wery said. "Somewhere about the waist, in an outer deck."

"He means he doesn't know if this is his past or his future," Bryn said.

Bryn knew more about Confluence than the other two, but knew nothing of Ys or the Age of Insurrection, or even of the Sirdar, who had ruled Confluence when it was newly made. His people had been on the ship a long time; Yama suspected that their ancestors had fled here, or refused to leave once the construction of Confluence had been completed. They had been rebels, like the feral machines or Tibor's ancestors.

Yama said, "I think this must be somewhere in the past. The star sailors I met knew about my bloodline, but believed that it had died out long ago."

Wery said with sudden anger, "We will destroy the regulators! They are only machines. They are as stupid as emmets."

"Emmets have the run of parts of the ship," Bryn said. "Intelligence is not necessarily a survival trait."

"Then you cannot control these regulators?" Yama was surprised. He had supposed that all of his bloodline would be able to control machines, but it seemed that things were different on the ship. Wery had not been able to make the floor stuff flow apart, and even he had not been able to touch the minds of the things which had chased him in the cistern. He said, "I suppose that the machines here are not the same as the machines on Confluence."

"Some say that we controlled the regulators once," Bryn said. The old man seemed amused. "Maybe we still do, on other ships. It's bad luck you arrived here."

Cas said unexpectedly, "There is only one ship, Bryn. It loops through time and sometimes meets itself."

Bryn said, "Only one ship in our universe, yes, but perhaps there are many universes, eh? A universe takes only one road, but if a man retraces his steps he cannot then return to the place from which he started. For the road splits at the place he traveled back to, and he must travel down the new road. It stops a man killing his grandfather and returning to find himself without existence."

"Perhaps his grandfather was only the husband of his grandmother," Cas said slowly, "and not his sire."

Bryn tugged on his beard in vexation. "His grandmother then! You are an infuriatingly literal man, Cas. I only make a fancy to illustrate a point. There are as many universes as there are travelers. In many we live on into our new mate's time, perhaps, but not in the time he came from."

Yama nodded. "Then I would not have had to come here to look for you."

Bryn said, "The problem is that you can go back to your future but not by retracing the same path, and so it will not be the place from which you started."

Cas said sulkily, "We've stayed here too long, and all this talk is making my head hurt. Why should what one man does cause a new universe?"

"It is no easy thing, to travel back through time," Bryn said. "But you are right. We should not stay here too long. The regulators might notice the change in carbon dioxide concentration."

"I have good ventilation," the room said.

"When I need advice from you," Bryn said, "I will ask for it. Do your synthesizers still work?"

"Of course, but they are not suitable for your bloodline. I will have to change the settings."

"I want clothing, not food. Yama, you must be properly dressed. Frankly, that hide of yours is beginning to stink. Do it, room, and then we will move on."

"You are welcome to stay as long as you like," the room said. "I miss the company of people."

"We can't stay unless you change your settings," Bryn told it, "and the regulators will know if you do. Just make the clothes."

Yama pulled on the one-piece silvery garment with his back to the others, although he was sure that Wery was watching. He knew that she belonged to another man, but he ached for her all the same. His blood raced in his skin when she showed him how to adjust the seals at ankles, wrists and neck. Her fluttering touch; her heat; her scent. Surely she must know how he felt . . .

She talked with him as they walked the seemingly endless white corridor. Cas went ahead, waving them forward at each intersection, then loping on eagerly.

"You don't mind Bryn," Wery told Yama. "He has too much learning in his head. He wants to bring back the old days. Thinks we can make the regulators our slaves. He'll be making plans for you."

Yama smiled. "This is like one of the old stories! Bryn is the magician, and you are the warriors helping him in his quest."

"We're hunting bugs," Wery said. "What are you?"

"I do not know. A magical creature perhaps. But I do not feel magical. I am beginning to understand that magic is a matter of perception. Knowing how to do something takes away the mystery which can make it seem magical."

"Maybe you can teach us how to make the floor open. That's useful.

Bryn is full of dreams, but dreams are for children. We kill bugs and regulators, or they kill us. That's how it is. It can't be changed."

"Are the regulators a kind of bug?"

"They're passengers. Like us." Wery laughed at Yama's astonishment. Her teeth were very white. One of the incisors was broken. "There used to be many different kinds of passenger. Now there're only the regulators and us. And the crew of course, but no one has ever seen one of them."

"I saw one. Well, two, in fact. But that was in another place."

Wery smiled. "You can tell me all about Confluence, when we're finished traveling."

"I could take you there." His heart turned, melting.

"Maybe. Now get this straight. Regulators killed all the other passengers, but we're too smart. Too tough. We hunt bugs and regulators, they hunt bugs and us. That's how it is. Makes the ship work better if its passengers have to prove their worth."

"Survival of the fittest," Yama said. It seemed as vile as the creed of the heretics. As if the Universe were without any ruling principle but death.

"That's what Bryn says. I say you are either dead or alive, and dead doesn't count."

"How many of your people are alive? Where do they live? I want to know everything about them, Wery."

Wery held up her left hand and opened and closed her fingers three times. "And us," she said. "We're a way from home, and it moves about anyway." She added, "Cas has found something," and ran off down the wide, white corridor to catch up with her husband.

Bryn dropped back to walk alongside Yama. He said, "We can't tell you too much, lad."

"I understand. Perhaps you can tell me how your people came to live here. That was a long time ago, and surely telling me an old story will not do any harm."

"We served the Preservers," Bryn said. "We were their first servants—the original crew of the ship, I think. Then the Preservers made all the other races and went away, and we lost our powers."

"I thought that our people went with the Preservers," Yama said, smiling because it was so thrillingly strange to say *our* instead of *my*.

"Perhaps most of them did. But this ship was left behind, and we are the descendants of those who flew it."

"Perhaps they refused to leave their home," Yama said.

"We are loyal servants of the Preservers," Bryn said. "Do not think otherwise."

"I meant no offense."

"None taken, lad. But if we live in your past, and you know no others of your kind, where did you come from?"

"That is what I am still hoping to discover," Yama said. "Perhaps I am the child of sailors of our bloodline who jumped ship long ago. I know of at least one star sailor who did."

"Borrowed a body, I suppose. They try that on board sometimes. The ship doesn't like it, and lets us hunt 'em like bugs. What have you found, Cas?"

The big man had stopped at a place where another corridor crossed the one down which they had been traveling. The black stuff of the floor was scored heavily there, ripped into curling strips. The strips were creeping over each other and softening at the edges, trying to mend the wounds.

"Bug trace," Cas said, holding up fingers smeared with sticky clear liquid which had splashed and spattered across the white walls. "Reckon there was a fight and one ate the other. Not long ago, either."

Wery grinned. "It's wounded," she said. "There's a trail. We kill it easy."

The trail of colorless blood led into another of the big, forested spaces. As before, the transition was abrupt. One moment Yama was hurrying along beside Bryn, who, despite his age, kept up a spritely pace, with Wery and Cas jogging eagerly ahead. Then the two warriors went around a corner and when Yama and Bryn followed they were suddenly in a dark, dank, dripping place, where huge tree trunks reared up through a broken layer of mist that hung some way beneath a high, dark canopy.

Yama looked back and saw a sliver of white light between two boulders propped against each other. It was the only point of brightness in this gloomy place. Pale fungi raised tall fans above ankle-deep ooze. Vines dropped from somewhere beyond the mist and slowly quested about the floor, pulsing with slow peristalsis as they pumped ooze upward. Yama saw that the giant trees were in fact conglomerations of these vines, twisted around each other like so many stiffened ropes. Parasitic plants wrapped pale, meaty leaves about the bases of the vines, and things in burrows spread feathery palps across the surface of the ooze; something bright red and thin as a whip shot from a hole and snapped at Yama's ankles.

Bryn laughed. "This is one of the mires, lad. Everything passes through here eventually."

Wery and Cas found a sign of the thing they were tracking, and disappeared into the gloom between the trunks of the giant tree things. There was a squalling noise in the distance. Bryn drew something from his sack and tossed it underhand to Yama.

It was a knife. When Yama caught it by the haft, its curved blade sparked with blue fire. Bryn stared and Yama grinned. "I know this at least," he said, "and it knows me."

Had the knife he had found—or which had found him—in the tomb in the Silent Quarter originally come from the ship? Was this perhaps the very same knife, destined to come into the possession of the dead warrior in whose tomb Yama had confronted Lud and Lob?

The squalling rose in pitch. Bryn and Yama sloshed forward through the ooze. Something thrashed beyond a tall ridge of white fungus, then suddenly reared up. It was three times the height of a man, and sprang over the fungus and ran at Yama and Bryn with preternatural swiftness.

Yama had a confused glimpse of something in black armor, all barbs and thin legs with cutting blades for edges, a narrow head dominated by wide jaws that opened sideways to reveal interlocked layers of serrated blades rotating over each other. It did not look so much like an insect as a dire wolf chopped and stretched into a poor imitation of an insect. It made its high squalling noise again. Acrid vapor puffed from glands that ran along each side of its long, hairy belly.

The bug knocked Yama down with a casual flick of a foreleg and pounced on Bryn, spraying black ooze everywhere. Wery suddenly appeared behind it and threw a long, weighted rope that tangled around its forelegs. Yama jumped up, ooze dripping from his silvery garment, and ran beneath the bug's belly as it snapped at Wery. He stabbed the knife's blade, blazing with blue fire, through the membrane at the articulation of one of its sturdy rear legs. The knife whined, burning so eagerly through horn and flesh that it almost jerked out of his hands. Clear, sticky blood gushed; the bug half collapsed, its leg almost completely severed. Cas stepped between its flailing forelimbs and stabbed the point of his wand between its eyes. It shuddered and kicked out and died.

While the others worked at severing the bug's head, Yama noticed that a kind of belt was fastened around its narrow waist, slung with pouches and bits of shaped stone or bone. Tools.

Bryn saw his look and said, "It would have killed us if it could."

"It was intelligent." Yama thought of Caphis, the fisherman he had found in a trap set by one of the Amnan. People preying on other people. The strong on the weak, the clever on the stupid.

Bryn tugged at his beard. "It was bright enough to get onto the ship. But not bright enough to survive."

Yama handed the knife to the old man, hilt first. "I have had enough of killing, I think."

Cas tugged hard and the armored head came free. Clear liquid gushed from the neck; the legs thrashed in a final spasm. Hand-sized creatures as flat as plates, thready blue organs visible through their transparent shells, skated over the muck to get at the spilled blood. Red whips had already wrapped around the bug's legs, melting into its horny carapace.

Yama expected the three hunters to carry their grisly trophy in triumph back to their home, but instead they dumped it in the corridor directly outside the entrance to the mire and went on.

"The regulators will find it and mark it," Bryn said. "Our task is done."

The lights of the ship, slaved to a diurnal cycle, dimmed soon after they left the mire. They slept in a little room Bryn found off one of the corridors. This one was more suited to their kind. Beakers of distilled water and tasteless white cubes of food extruded from a wall at Bryn's command. The floor humped into four sleeping platforms. "If you want to piss or shit," Bryn told Yama, "do it in the corner there," and ordered the room to dim its light.

Yama was woken from a light sleep by Wery's giggle. Sounds of flesh moving on flesh, breath at two pitches gaining the same urgent rhythm. He lay awake a long time, lost and lonely and frightened, while the two hunters made love a few spans from him.

———

They walked along the endless white corridor for much of the next day. Wery walked at point with Cas, while Bryn asked Yama many questions about Confluence, most of which he could not begin to answer.

They traveled steadily, drinking from tubes set in the necks of their silvery garments, which recycled their own sweat as distilled water. At last, they left the corridor for one of the jungle wilds, and after an hour's walk down paths so narrow they must have been made by animals, Wery insisted on showing Yama something.

"You'll like it. Really you will. You won't have seen anything like it."

Yama demurred. He was still embarrassed and disconcerted by overhearing her lovemaking.

"Go on," Bryn said, with a sly smile. "You will see where you are."

Yama and Wery climbed a grandfather tree that rose through the dense green canopy, its surprisingly small crown of dark green feathery fronds silhouetted against sky glare high above. Its rough bark provided plenty of easy hand- and foot-holds. They climbed a long way. Cool inside his silvery garment despite the fetid heat, but quite breathless and with his pulse pounding heavily in his head, Yama sat at last in the crutch of a massive bough on which Wery balanced with heart-stopping ease.

And saw that the jungle stretched away for several leagues on all sides, a rumpled blanket of green studded here and there with splashes of bright orange or yellow or red where trees were in flower. A line or chain of tiny, intense points of white light hung high above the treetops: the little suns which fed the jungle's growth. But that was not what Wery wanted him to see.

The jungle grew on the outer skin of the ship, seemingly not enclosed by anything at all—perhaps gravity fields held in the atmosphere, as they contained the envelope of air around Confluence, or perhaps it was domed with material so transparent that it was invisible. The rest of the ship could be clearly seen all around the jungle's oval footprint.

Yama, remembering the voidship lighter which had docked at Ys, had thought that the ship would be some kind of sphere, bigger certainly, but more or less of the same design, much as a dory resembles a carrack. But now he saw that the ship was a series of cubes and spheres and other more complex geometrical solids strung like beads along a wire, and that it was many leagues long—impossible to tell how many. In all their journeying, they had traversed only one part of one segment. There was room enough for any number of wonders to be hidden here.

But he knew that he could not stay. He had thought about it last night. He had found people of his bloodline, yet they were stranger to him than Pandaras or Tamora or Derev. They lacked the breath of the Preservers and so could not be anything other than what they already were, enslaved forever by their circumstances. This was not his home. That was on Confluence. It was with Derev. She and Yama had sworn a compact, and he knew now that it meant more to him than life itself. He would find the cistern and the shrine, and force the Gatekeeper to take him home. And then he would end the war. He had known how to do it ever since he had seen the picture in the slate which Beatrice and Osric had shown him at the beginning of his adventures, but he had not known he had known it until he had absorbed the knowledge hoarded by Dr. Dismas's paramour.

Standing before him on the broad branch high above the jungle, Wery clapped her hands over her head and laughed. Yama realized for the first time that she was older than him, perhaps twice his age. The achingly brilliant light of the chain of miniature suns accentuated the wrinkles around her eyes, showed where flesh was beginning to loosen and sag along the line of her jaw.

It did not make her less desirable.

"Look starboard," she said, and pointed at the distant edge of the ship.

Something stood far beyond the jungle. A red line—no, a dome, the top of a structure bigger than any of the wilds. It was lengthening and growing in height, as if it was crawling toward them.

A vast creature, big as a mountain . . .

Yama looked at Wery, wondering if he had finally been driven mad, and she laughed again and said, "That's the mine world the ship orbits."

Yama realized then that the growing blister was part of a disc. Not advancing, but rising—it was a world as round as the sun, just like those described in the opening suras of the Puranas. Or not round, but a sphere, a globe, a battered red globe rising above the ship's horizon. Yama laughed too, full of wonder. Its pockmarked red surface was capped top and bottom with white, and scarred by a huge canyon that pointed toward three pits. Or no, they were the tops of huge, hollow mountains. At the very edge of the world's disc was a fourth, so big that it rose above the narrow band of diffracted light which marked the limit of the world's atmosphere.

Wery said that it was time to descend. They walked down narrow paths through understory trees and bushes that divided and divided again in an endless maze which Cas, who took the lead, seemed to know well, for he set an eager pace.

Now it was Yama's turn to ask questions. Bryn said that mined mass was moved from the surface of the world to the ship by something called an elevator, a chain or cable that hung down from a point many leagues above the world's surface. It took a while for Yama to understand why the cable did not collapse. The world was spinning, so that its surface moved at a certain speed, and the cable was grown from a point high above that also moved at the same speed, so that it was always above the same place on the surface. Hoppers moved up the cable and the material in them was slung out like pebbles from a catapult, to be caught by the ship and stowed away.

Ahead, Cas paused at a place where the path split into three. He turned and waved and went on.

Wery chased after her husband. A moment later, frantic whistles pierced the green quiet of the jungle. Bryn broke into a run and Yama followed. They scrambled down a steep fern-laden bank and splashed across a muddy stream, clambered up the bank on the far side and burst through a screen of tall grasses into the brilliant light of the miniature suns.

A huge tree had fallen here long ago; Yama and Bryn had emerged at the top of a wide, deep bowl, grown over with rich green grass, which had been torn out of the earth when the tree's roots had been pulled up by its fall. Here and there bodies lay in the long grass. Human-sized, human-shaped, clad in silver.

Yama's heart turned over. But then he saw that the bodies were naked; the silver was the color of their skin.

"Regulators," Bryn said, and sat down beside one of the bodies and bowed his head.

Cas and Wery were standing at the far edge of the clearing. When Bryn sat down they looked at each other and then ran off in opposite directions.

"Wait," Bryn said, when Yama made to follow Wery. "There may be traps."

"This is the home of your people."

"They were camped here. Perhaps they moved on before . . ." Bryn bowed his head once more, and clasped his hands over the white hair on top of his head.

Yama moved from body to body. All were quite unmarked. They were very thin. Their right hands were three-fingered, but their left hands were all different: one like pinchers made of black metal; another extended into a bony scimitar with a jagged cutting edge; a third had hinged blades, like monstrous scissors. The silver of their skin had a gray cast. Their eyes were huge, the color of wet blood, and divided into hexagonal cells. Although they were dead, something still seemed to be watching Yama behind these strange eyes. It was like the men whom the rogue star-sailor had enslaved by putting machines in their heads; the machines had lived on after the men had died, and so here.

Wery appeared at the far end of the clearing, shouted that everyone was gone, and ran off again. Bryn got up slowly, straightened his back, took a deep breath, and said, "We will see what has happened."

The bowl of the clearing was a hundred paces across, twice that in length. The rotting carcass of the fallen tree lay at one end, extending into bushes and young trees which grew all around. Butterflies which might have been made of gold foil fluttered here and there in the bright light. Cas caught one as he came down the slope toward Bryn and Yama, and crushed it in his massive fist.

The encampment was no more than a few panels of woven grass leaning against the trunk of the fallen tree. A scattering of mats and empty water-skins, neatly tied bundles of dried leaves, a frame of tall sticks in which a stretched hide had been half-scraped of its hair. A blackened cube in a hearth of bare earth still radiated heat; a bowl of something like porridge had dried out on top of it and was beginning to burn. Yama picked up a hand-sized bit of flat glass. Glyphs began to scream and shiver inside it, but they were of no language he knew.

Wery said, "There were three regulators waiting for us. Cas killed two. I killed the other."

Bryn said, "The others?"

"Gone," Wery said. She dabbed angrily at the tears which stood in her eyes. "All gone."

Cas pointed at Yama with his wand, and Bryn got in front of Yama and said, "No. It could not be him."

"There would only be three of us if you killed him, Cas," Wery said.

Yama understood. Their family was the last of the bloodline on the ship; that was why they had been so amazed to see him. And now they were the last of their family.

Bryn flipped his patch down over his left eye. He turned in a slow, complete circle and said, "Where are the bodies, Cas?"

"I have not found them. I will look again." Cas trotted across the clearing and plunged into the bushes on the far side.

Wery said, "Do you think they might still be alive?"

Bryn lifted the eyepatch. "Ordinarily the regulators would have killed them at once. But there is no blood, and there are no bodies."

"Perhaps the regulators took the bodies," Wery said.

"But they left their dead companions," Yama said.

Wery and Bryn looked at him. And at the same moment a regulator parted a clump of tall ferns and stepped into the clearing, mismatched hands held up by her shoulders. The left was swollen and bifurcate, hinged like a lobster's claw.

"Stop!" Yama said, and knocked Wery's arm up as she aimed her wand at the regulator. Something went howling away into the bright sky. Wery turned on him, the wand swinging in an arc that would have ended in his chest if he had not stepped inside it. He gripped her elbow and bent her arm behind her back until she had to drop the wand; bent it farther until she had to kneel.

"Cas will kill you," she said, glaring up at him.

"Be still," Bryn told her, and she stopped struggling at once. Bryn was pointing his wand at the regulator, but he was looking at Yama. He said, "It obeys you."

"Yes, but the others did not."

The regulator still had her hands raised. Her flat breasts hung like empty sacs. She fixed her huge red eyes on Yama and said, "I have a message from Prefect Corin."

22

So Below

CAS CAME BACK at a run, and would have killed the regulator at once if Bryn had not stood in his way. They argued in violent whispers; then Cas turned his back on them all and Bryn came across the clearing and told Yama, "We will both go with you."

Yama said, "I think it would be better if you all stayed here."

"They have our people," Wery said. "Of course we will go with you."

Bryn walked around and around the regulator, which still stood where Yama had told her to halt. At last he turned and said again, "It obeys you."

"The regulators have machines in their heads which control them. I am able to talk with her machine, although I was not able to talk with the machines of the others."

"It," Wery said.

Yama and Bryn looked at her.

Wery said defiantly, "It, not she. They're all things. Not people. Things. Things!"

Cas put his hand on Wery's shoulder and she turned and rested her face against his broad chest. Cas said, "We will come with you, Yama. We will kill this Prefect Corin and free our people and come home. What you do after that is of no matter to us."

"I wish it were that simple," Yama said. "And I still think you should all stay here."

They were savages. They tried to justify their presence on the ship and placate the regulators with trophies from bug hunts, but they were as much stowaways as the things they had killed in the mire. If there had been time, Yama would have mixed a little of his blood with water and let them drink it; without the breath of the Preservers they were no more than any of the indigenous peoples of Confluence, higher than animals but less than men. But there was not enough time.

Cas said, "We will come with you. We are hunters. We hunt bugs. We hunt our enemies."

"We will come with you," Bryn said. He stared into the regulator's big, red, faceted eyes, tugging at his neatly trimmed beard. "But before we leave, you will tell it to obey us too. I will not have it used against us."

"I still say we kill it," Cas said.

"No." Bryn smiled; he believed that he was in command again. "Once this is over, we will be masters of all the regulators. The crew will look to us for help instead of to them. That is my price, Yama, for the hurt you have caused. We should make a start on our quest at once. It will be night soon, I have no liking for this place anymore, and it is a long way to the docks."

The regulator stirred. "There is a shorter route," she said, and repeated her message. "My master commands you to descend to the surface of the world below. I will lead you to where he waits with your people. If you come with him, they may go free."

Cas began to curse the regulator in a dull monotone. Yama said, "I will avenge the hurt done to you all in my name. I swear it."

Yama was as fearful as the others as the little glass room fell along the length of the ship; like the others he tried to hide his fear as best he could. Wery and Cas leaned against each other, holding onto the rail which ran at waist height around the room's cold, transparent walls; Bryn clung there too, aiming his wand at the regulator, which hung like a silvery-gray statue in the center of the room, its flat, toeless feet a span above the floor.

Only Yama watched the view. The long track down which the glass room fell was a thread laid across the solid geometries of the ship's segments. The ship dwindled away above and below, although neither direction had much meaning here, where there was no gravity. Clusters of lights cast stark shadows over the surfaces of enormous cubes and pyramids and tetrahedrons strung together and studded with hundreds of green or brown or indigo blisters—wilds clinging to the surfaces of the huge ship's segments like fish lice to an eel.

As the ship turned about its long axis, the bulging disc of the red world slowly rose above it. Yama glimpsed the terminus of the elevator far beyond the end of the ship, a blob of light sliced in half by its own shadow. The elevator itself was a broken line defined by lights scattered along its length, dwindling away toward the world.

Bryn was able to answer some of Yama's questions. The ship turned on its axis so that all sides would be exposed to the light of the sun of this system, evening out temperature differences. The elevator was woven from strands which were each a single giant molecule of neutronium, stabilized by intensely steep gravity fields. The mines delivered phosphates and iron. In thirty days the ship would leave this system and pass through the shortcut to its next destination.

The regulator stirred and said, "They spy on the crew."

Bryn tapped his eyepatch, which was flipped up on his wrinkled forehead. "I am allowed revelations," he said. "This is one of the greatest treasures of my people."

"You interrupt data flow," the regulator said.

"As is our right," Bryn said, "earned by tribute."

"You have no rights," the regulator said. "You are parasites."

"You be quiet," Cas told her. "Speak only when spoken to."

Yama knew that neither Bryn nor the regulator could answer his most urgent questions. How had Prefect Corin followed him here? Why had he descended to the surface of the world? How was he able to control the regulators?

He thought long and hard on these questions as the glass room sped toward the end of the ship. The world's huge red disc slowly revolved above them and set on the far side of the ship, and then Yama forgot for a moment all his questions and anxieties.

For the stars had come out.

There were thousands of them, tens of thousands, a field of hard, bright stars shining everywhere he looked, crossed by a great milky river that seemed to wrap around the intensely black sky. The sun of this world must lie deep within one of the arms of the Galaxy; that milky river was the plane of the arm, the light of its billions of stars coalesced into a dense glow. Here and there structures could be seen— star bridges, tidy globes, a chain of bright red stars that spanned half the sky—but otherwise the patterns made by the Preservers were less obvious than when viewed from the orbit of Confluence, many thousands of years beyond the rim of the Galaxy. And yet every star he could see had been touched by the Preservers: their monument, their shrine, was all around him.

Then the sun rose. Although it was smaller and redder than the sun of Confluence, its light banished all but the brightest of the stars.

Yama had expected the glass room to reenter the ship and deliver them to some kind of skiff or lighter which would transfer them to the elevator terminus. But instead it simply shot off the end of its track into the naked void. Cas roared, half in amazement, half in defiance; Wery pressed the length of her body against his. The ship fell away. The terminus of the elevator slowly grew larger in the void below their feet.

It was an irregular chunk of rock, its lumpy surface spattered with craters. One side was lit by the sun, the other, where the elevator cable was socketed in a complex of domes and haphazardly piled cubes, by ruddy light reflected from the world.

"It is one of the moons of the world," Bryn said. He had lowered the silver patch over his left eye. "Its orbital velocity was increased to move it from a lower orbit and to synchronize it with the world's rotation." He added, "This world was moved, too, displaced across half the diameter of the Galaxy. There is a legend that it came from the original system of the Preservers, although some maintain that it is merely a replica of one of the worlds of that system."

The little moon grew, slowly eclipsing the sun, and the glass room swung through ninety degrees—Cas roared again—and extruded huge curved grapples made of stuff as thin as gossamer. Contact with the elevator cable happened very quickly. The pocked red-lit moonscape swelled below their feet and the room spun on its axis and one element of the cable, not much thicker than an ordinary tree trunk, was suddenly snug against its grapples. The moon began to dwindle and Yama felt his weight increase; now they were falling toward the world, which hung above their heads like a battered orange shield.

The journey took less than an hour. The cable blurred past, a silver wall occasionally punctuated by flashes as rooms very much larger than theirs shot past in the opposite direction. Below their feet, the tiny moon was lost in the glare of the sun; only a few leagues of the elevator cable was visible above, a shadowy thread dwindling toward the world. Midway in the journey, their weight slowly vanished until they were in freefall. The room swung around so that the world was below their feet, and their weight came back.

The black void gained a pinkish tinge and a faint whistle fluted and moaned around them; they were entering the atmosphere. The world flattened and spread, became a landscape. Their weight dwindled; this world's gravity was a gentle tug about a third the strength of the ship's, which had been exactly as strong as that of Confluence. The room was falling toward a rumpled red plain crossed by straight dark lines. The sun was setting.

Bryn said that the lines were canals. They had once carried water from the south pole to the agricultural lands of the equator. He was staring raptly at the desolate plain below; Cas and Wery had taken out their wands. A range of broken hills made a half curve around an enormous basin which held a shallow, circular sea. Yama saw a huge flock of pink birds fly up from the shoreline. Millions and millions of birds, like a cloud of pink smoke blowing across the black water.

The elevator cable fell toward a complex of structures beyond the sea's shore, in the middle of a dark forest. Stepped pyramids rose above the trees, gleaming like fresh blood in the last light of the sun; beside them, like a mask discarded by a giant, a carving of a human face wearing an enigmatic smile looked up at the sky.

It was Angel's face, Yama realized. This had once been one of her worlds, part of her empire.

The elevator split into a hundred cables, like a mangrove supported by prop roots. The glass room fell down one toward a black dome. As it approached this terminus, it shuddered and slowed. For the space of an eyeblink it was full of blue light.

Wery screamed, and something knocked Yama down.

The dome swallowed them.

———

Yama was lying in darkness. The regulator was sprawled on top of him, as light as a child. Her skin was hot and dry. "Wait," she said, when he began to move. "It is not safe."

"Let me up," he told her. There was wet, sticky stuff on the floor. Yama had put his hand on it. It was blood. He said, "Who is hurt?"

"Someone shot Bryn," Wery said in a small but steady voice. "And Cas is wounded."

"Not badly," Cas said, but Yama knew from the tightness in his voice that this was a lie.

There were many machines at various distances beyond the little glass room. Some of them were lights; Yama asked them to come on. They were dim and red, scattered across a huge volume. The cable, which was socketed in a collar as big as the peel-house, disappeared through an aperture in the high, curved roof. A metal bridge, seemingly as flimsy as paper, made a long, sweeping curve from the glass room toward the shadowy floor.

Bryn was slumped near Yama. The chest of his silvery garment was scorched around a hole as big as a fist. There was a surprised expression on his face. Cas had lost most of his left hand; he had wound a strip of material so tightly around his wrist that it had almost vanished into his flesh. Wery crouched beside him, her arms wrapped around his broad shoulders.

The glass walls of the room were scorched around two neat holes, one on either side. Air whistled through them as pressure equalized, bringing a sharp organic stink. Then part of the glass pulled apart to make a round portal, and the stink intensified.

"Come out," a voice said from below. "One at a time. Walk slowly down the bridge."

Wery hurled herself through the portal, screaming as she went. She ran very quickly and Cas roared her name and lurched up and chased after her. There was a flash of blue light; Yama had to close his eyes against it. When he opened them, the two warriors were gone.

"Come out, boy," the voice said. "You can bring your servant. We will not hurt her, or you."

The regulator plucked the wand from Bryn's dead hand and crumpled it in the monstrous claw of her left hand. She was suddenly remote from Yama; what he had thought was her machine self had been only a shell personality, and it had now evaporated. Her real self was as opaque as that of the other regulators.

The regulator put her right hand on Yama's shoulder and guided him through the portal and down the long curve of the metal bridge to the shadows of the floor. Great heaps of stinking black stuff covered one side of the vast space. The stench was so strong and sharp that Yama's eyes began to stream with tears.

Prefect Corin walked out of the shadows at the base of the high, curved wall of the cable socket. He leaned on his staff, a slight figure in a simple homespun tunic that was heavily stained with blood. He said, "We are pleased that you came. Do not be afraid. All will be well."

Yama said, "Where are they?"

"All this is guano, from deposits along the shore of the sea. There are hills and islands which are entirely made of the shit deposited by birds over millions upon millions of years. The ship takes it to Confluence because it is rich in phosphates. The ecological systems of Confluence are not closed. It is a small habitat, and badly designed. I do not blame your people for that, Yamamanama. The fault is with the Preservers. How can they be held to be the perfection to which all aspire if their creation is so ill-made?"

"Confluence is not perfect because it is of the temporal world. Where are they?"

"Come with us," Prefect Corin said.

He turned and walked off. After a moment, Yama followed. The regulator walked two paces behind him, and a decad of her kin fell into step on either side.

"They are not here," Yama said loudly. "You lied. You killed the people before you even left the ship."

Prefect Corin did not look around. He said, "Of course. It was part of the bargain I made with the star-sailors. They were the last of your bloodline, and the star-sailors wanted them destroyed."

"The star-sailors control the regulators."

"Yes. And we have been given control of these. Please stop trying to take them away from us. You will have many servants, when we return. We will rule Confluence. You will help us."

"He followed me," Yama said, suddenly realized what had happened to Prefect Corin, why he had not come for him earlier. "He followed me into the Glass Desert. And you found him, or he found you."

"We were almost destroyed," the Prefect said. "We took him by force and made him ours."

"And you killed him."

"Unfortunately, the process was too harsh to allow survival of the subject."

"In any case, the body you wear is badly hurt. Enobarbus shot it."

"The rifle pellet destroyed the heart, but we have grown replacement musculature and control the body still. When it fails us we will select another. We wanted the woman to live; she would have served us well. But we can use one of the regulators as easily, and eventually we will use you. You made us serve you three times, and we serve you no longer. Instead, you serve us."

"Three times?" Yama had guessed that the thing which possessed Prefect Corin was the residue of the fusion between Dr. Dismas's paramour and the feral machine he had called down to destroy it, but he had only commanded the feral machine twice, and had never commanded Dr. Dismas's paramour. In any case, it did not reply.

A high arch opened onto a wide plaza raised above the tops of low, thorny trees which stretched away in every direction. A cold, thin, dry wind blew from the west. The sun was setting, a tiny, intensely red disc embedded in shells of pink light that extended across half the sky. There were many things living in the forest; Yama was able to reach out to some of them.

The Prefect was pointing straight up. Yama looked past the vanishing point of the escalator cable and saw a star burning brightly at zenith, drifting slowly but perceptibly eastward.

"The voidship departs," the Prefect said. "And there are no shortcut mouths on this world. I control the only way for you to return, Yama-manama, and you cannot use it until you submit to my will."

Yama said, "You were made by the Preservers to serve the races of man."

"This world is dying," the Prefect said. "It was the first world settled by humans, over ten million years ago. They warmed it and gave it an atmosphere, melted the water locked in its rocks, spread life everywhere. Later, they moved it across half the Galaxy to a new sun. But it is too small to hold its atmosphere and its water. It is drying and growing cooler. The dust storms have returned. In a million years most life will have vanished.

"As here, so elsewhere, on millions upon millions of worlds. The Preservers retreated from the Universe not because they achieved perfection, but because of their mistakes. They could no longer bear them. We will do better. We will transform Confluence, and we will reconquer the Galaxy and take the Universe by storm. You will help us with the first step."

"You must have forced the Gatekeeper to send you after me. Why then do you need me?"

"We forced it, yes, and we will have to force it again if we need to use another shortcut. You can persuade machines to change permanently. We can learn much from you."

Something was moving out of the light of the setting sun: a small, sleek shadow, its mind closed to Yama by the same opaqueness that closed the minds of the regulators. A flock of dark shapes swirled up as it passed above the stepped pyramids in the forest. The thing wearing Prefect Corin's body glanced at them, and Yama feared for a moment that his last hope had been discovered. But then the Prefect turned to Yama and said, "We will take you back to Confluence. We brought you here because the crew of the voidship did not want you on their ship. But another ship has been waiting here for five million years. It circles above us now."

Yama said, "Corin wanted me to serve the Department of Indigenous Affairs, so that every bloodline on Confluence would be forced to conform to the same destiny: stasis, and a slow decline. You and the heretics want to force change by making every bloodline believe that the self is all. There is a better way. A way to allow every bloodline to find its own particular destiny. We were raised up by the Preservers not to worship them, but to become their equals."

"You will help us become more than that. After we take Confluence, we will destroy the Preservers. It will be a good beginning."

"I will not serve you," Yama said.

"You will serve those higher than yourself, little builder. It is your function."

"My people served the Preservers, but they have gone. No one should serve any other, unless they wish it. I learned much from Dr. Dismas's paramour, and part of what it tried to grow inside me still remains. It has helped me find friends here."

The first wave of flying men stooped down out of the light of the setting sun. There were more than a hundred of them. Their membranous wings, stretched between wrists and ankles, folded around them like black cloaks as they landed and came across the plaza with a hobbling gait, clutching spears of fire-hardened wood and slingshots and bolos.

The Prefect burned away several decads with a sweep of his pistol and screamed at the regulators to kill the rest, but the second wave was already swooping overhead, dropping nets that engulfed the silver-skinned regulators and drew tight.

The Prefect threw away his staff and showed Yama the energy pistol, lying in his palm like a river pebble. "We will kill you if we must."

"I know that weapon," Yama said. "Corin told me how it works long ago. It fires three shots, and then must lie in the sun for a full day before it can fire again. You fired one shot to kill Bryn, another to kill Cas and Wery, and you have just fired the third and last."

The Prefect screamed, threw the pistol at Yama, and ran straight at him. A pair of bolos wrapped around his legs, and a net folded over him as he fell headlong.

———

Once freed of the compulsion Yama had laid upon them, the flying men threw themselves face down around him, but he told them that they should stand, that he was not the god they believed him to be.

They were the children of a feral machine which had fled the war at the end of the Age of Insurrection, falling through a shortcut to this world. It had made reduced copies of itself and used them to infect various species of animal, but only the ancestors of the flying men had proven satisfactory hosts. The flying men were a unique synthesis. Their intelligence was contained within tiny machines which teemed in their blood, but the machine intelligence was tempered by their animal joy of life and flight; they were quite without the cold arrogance which had prompted the feral machines to rebel. The original machine, badly damaged when it had first arrived here, had died thousands of years ago, but the flying men believed that it would at last return, incarnated in one of their kind, to save their world.

The flying men had narrow, long-muzzled foxy faces, and small red eyes that burned in the twilight. They were twice Yama's height; their skinny, naked bodies were covered with pelts of coarse black hair. After much twittering discussion, the oldest of them, with gray on his muzzle, came forward. By gestures, he asked whether Yama wanted his enemies killed.

Yama could speak directly to the consensus of tiny machines within the flying men; it seemed to him that each had an animate, intelligent shadow standing at his back. "I thank you for your help," he told them, "but do not kill your prisoners. There has been enough killing this day. Let me speak to their leader."

The flying men dragged the Prefect forward. He was still bound by the pair of bolos and the net. The oldest flying man told Yama that this was a dead man with a brother trapped inside it. It was a curious thing, to see a dead man kept alive in this way.

"He is from another place," Yama said. That took a long time to explain; once the old man understood, he wanted to know if the Prefect was a god.

"No, but he is very powerful. He can help you in many ways. One of his kind was, I think, responsible for you."

"I thought them dead," the Prefect said. "The star-sailors told me that they were dead."

The old flying man shivered all over—it was his equivalent of laughter—and said that the star-sailors did not trouble to come to the surface of the world, but instead sent servants. His people's blood could speak with the brothers in the heads of the servants, and make them believe anything.

Yama told the thing inside the Prefect that it could be of much help here. It could begin to undo this world's slow decline. It could help the flying men be all that they could be. But it could never return to Confluence.

"These people were formed from an act of malice, but evil can create good without knowing it. By serving them, you can make amends. You have much to teach them, and they can teach you something about humility. Or else you can remain a prisoner, with the body you took decaying around you."

The Prefect tried to spit at Yama, but his mouth had no saliva. The strands of the net pressed a lattice into his dead flesh. There was a glint of metal beneath the ruin of his left eye.

The oldest of the flying men said that there was a place of silence where this brother could be kept; its words would never again touch the minds of other men.

"Dr. Dismas knew about such places," Yama told the Prefect. "There was the cage in *The House of Ghost Lanterns,* for instance. Shall I consign you to eternal silence, or will you serve here? Think about it while I free those you have enslaved."

Yama freed the regulators first. It took a long time to unpick the opaque shells which guarded their true minds, and at first he was hindered because the thing inside Prefect Corin tried to countermand his efforts, but after Yama found the part of it which spoke to other machines and shut it off, he was able to work without interruption. Night was almost over when he was at last finished with the regulators and could turn his attention to the ship.

It was still turning high above, swinging in wide circles about the elevator cable because it had not been ordered to do anything else. It was a transparent teardrop not much larger than the *Weazel,* the lugger which had carried Yama down half the length of the Great River. Hidden inside the shells of false personality Prefect Corin had woven for it was the bright, innocently inquiring mind of a child. It wanted to know where its mistress was, and Yama told it that Angel had been dead for five million years.

"Then I will serve you," the ship said, and swooped down, extruding a triplet of fins on which it perched at the edge of the plaza.

The flying men brought the Prefect before Yama again, and again Yama asked whether he would be content to serve him.

"You raise yourself too high," the Prefect said. "You cannot stand in judgment of me."

"I find myself here," Yama said. "I do what I must."

Prefect Corin said defiantly, "I will take this world, and I will build such a race that they will set fire to the Galaxy."

"They will not allow themselves to become your slaves," Yama said. He was not sure that this was the best solution, but he owed the thing his life, and could not kill it.

The oldest of the flying men said that they would always care for this poor brother, and would never let it leave. They would show it compassion.

Yama nodded. The thing which had taken Prefect Corin might benefit from the humble simplicity of the flying men. He indicated the regulators and said, "These will be your guests until the ship comes again."

The old man agreed. Yama embraced him and apologized for using his people, but the man told him that he had brought the hope for which his people had prayed for many generations.

"I fear I have brought you a great danger."

The old man said that, like the god which had made his people, Prefect Corin was powerful and angry, so angry that he could not see the world clearly.

Yama smiled, realizing that the flying men had grown greater in wisdom and compassion than the thing which had made them, and that the Prefect could be left safely in their charge. If the thing inside him did not change, then the flying men would destroy it.

More and more flying men arrived, flocks that filled the forest around the plaza and the stepped pyramids. Their campfires were scattered amongst the dark trees like the stars in the sky above. Yama talked into the night with the men and women who led the flocks, tired but exultant. At last, as the sky above the mountains to the east began to grow brighter—how strange that the sun should set in one place and rise in another—he finished an elaborate round of farewells.

All this time, the Prefect had lain as still and unsleeping as a cayman, but now he suddenly surged up, throwing off the net he had cut with a spur of metal torn from his flesh. He stabbed one of the flying men in the eye, snatched the man's spear and charged at Yama. Yama felt a tremendous blow in his back and half-turned, grasping at the point of the spear which protruded beneath his ribs. He could not get his breath. His mouth filled with blood. The Prefect embraced him, stabbing and stabbing with the metal spur. Then he was torn away and Yama fell, gargling blood as he tried to draw breath. He saw the Prefect borne backward, lifted by a decad of flying men into the red dawn, and then his sight failed.

23

The Gatekeeper

THE SHIP WALKED with him down dark ways and sang to him of his sorrows. At first he did not know or remember who he was or what the ship's sad, sweet songs meant, but slowly he understood that he had died, and now, after a long, dark sleep, he was healed. He was awake. It was time to rise.

It was as painful as birth. He was expelled from dreamy warm darkness into harsh light and chill air, naked and slimy, choking on the fluid which had for so long sustained him. It ran from his nostrils and bubbled at the bottom of his lungs. He coughed and spat and retched.

He was lying on his belly with night all around him, on an endless floor of glass punctuated by groups of enigmatic statues and machines that glimmered with foxfire. The Galaxy's triple-armed spiral tilted below. Gradually, he realized that the dim shell of light around him defined the true size of the ship. It was as transparent as certain species of shrimp which lived in the deep waters of the Great River; the great glass plain was an illusion.

He laughed. All was illusion.

A woman came through a door which a moment before had not been there. She was naked and silver-skinned. One arm was swollen into a monstrous claw. "It took almost a year," she said. "At the end, we thought you might die again."

She was the regulator who had accompanied him to the surface of the red world. She was afraid that he would be angry because of the way he had been saved, but he still did not understand what had been done to him, except that he had died, and had slept, and had been healed.

Dazed by his long sleep, Yama sprawled for many hours in the middle of the room the ship had made for him, combing his fingers through the long hair and beard which had grown while he had slept, staring at the great wheel of the Galaxy below or the red whorl of the Eye of the Preservers above. A few dim halo stars were scattered across the black sky; a single bright star shone beyond the ship's bow. He traced and retraced the scars which seamed his belly and his chest and his back, a secret history of pain printed on his body.

The regulator brought him food now and then, but although his stomach was empty he was not ready to eat. At last, he asked her to explain how she and the ship had saved him.

"It was the only way, master," the regulator said. "Even so, we were not sure if you would survive storage or the surgical procedures. The medical facilities are very primitive. And that is why—"

"She has funny ideas," the ship said, "about what is possible and what is not."

"We brought it to term," the regulator said. "We could not kill it."

"I think I could," the ship said. "I think I could kill it if you asked me to, master."

It amused the ship to appear as a solemn, ghostly little girl of Yama's bloodline, her skinny body sketched in faint lines of light against the black sky, her eyes two dim stars.

Yama said, "You had better show me exactly what you did."

"At once," the regulator said, and went through the door which appeared only when it was used.

Yama asked the ship where they were. It showed views of the spiral arm from which they had traveled, the great rising arc of their course. They had been traveling along the path plotted by the thing which had taken over Prefect Corin.

The trip through the shortcut had taken Yama deep into the past. Traveling back through ordinary space at close to the speed of light, the ship had taken a hundred and sixty thousand years to voyage between the star of the red world, deep within the Galaxy, and the star of Confluence, far beyond the Galaxy's rim. But the ship's speed had compressed time aboard it, and less than a year of ship-time had passed while Yama returned to the place from which he had set out.

He wanted to know at once where Confluence was. The ship became evasive, claiming that it had followed the course exactly. "Perhaps the instructions were wrong in some small detail," it said. "I have located the star, and it is of the correct mass and spectral type, but there is no trace of a habitat orbiting it."

There were no feral machines, either. Only the mouths of many shortcuts in lonely orbits around a lonely star.

Yama was still thinking about this when the regulator returned through what he thought of as the occasional door. She was holding something, crooning to it in her throaty voice. Its head, with a vulnerable swirl of dark hair, was propped on her monstrous claw; its hands clutched at the air like a hungry starfish.

A baby.

He had died, and before the ship and the regulator had put his body into storage, they had taken a scraping from the inside of his mouth. They had quickened certain of the cells in the scraping and grown them into fetuses—there had been five, but only two had lived. Tissues had been harvested from one and used to grow replacement organs; these had been transplanted into Yama and then he had slept a long time, healing. But the ship and the regulator had not been able to bring themselves to kill the other fetus, and they had not put it into storage, for they had not been sure if it would survive. And so, while Yama had been revived and healed, it had grown to term.

It had been born just before Yama's rebirth.

"It is exactly the same genome as you, master," the regulator said, "and because of that we were unable to kill it."

The baby chuckled in her arms. Yama gently took him from her, surprised by his mass and heat, the spicy odor of cinnamon and ammonia. The baby tried to focus his eyes on him, frowning with effort, then tried to smile.

Yama set the baby spinning around him, laughing as he gurgled with delight.

"We are in the future, and we must go back a little way into the past," Yama said, a little later. "I think that the composite thing which took Prefect Corin wanted to return after the heretics' war had ended, and claim Confluence from the victor. And the war is certainly over, for Confluence is no longer here. I know now how this should end. We must go back."

The Gatekeeper woke as the ship approached the nearest of the many shortcut mouths which orbited the lonely star. A light dawned far off

across the illusionary glass plain, a bright star growing into the shape
of an old man of Yama's bloodline. At first, he was a giant bigger than
the ship, walking steadily toward it as if against a great wind, but he
grew smaller as he approached, so that when he entered the room (not
by the occasional door, but through an angle Yama had never seen
before) he was exactly Yama's height.

There was nothing remarkable about the old man's aspect. He had
a pale, wrinkled face framed by long white hair and a beard of silky
white curls. He wore a white robe girdled by a broad leather belt from
which bunches of keys of all sizes hung. Yet it hurt Yama to look at
him directly, and when he spoke, his words echoed directly in Yama's
mind.

We meet again, Child of the River.

Yama said, "Where am I? I mean, how much time has passed since
I left Confluence?"

A little more than forty years.

"And the world? Was it destroyed, or was it—"

It has moved on. I remained here to wait for you.

"How did you know that I would come here?"

I stand at every door.

"Then you must know that I have to go back," Yama said, thoughtfully stroking his beard. The regulator had suggested that she trim both
his hair and his beard, but he had refused. He said, "I have to go back
to the recent past, and the beginning of my story."

The old man fingered through a bunch of keys at his waist. His
eyes were dim red stars, framed by his flowing white hair.

*For most of my existence, I would have said that what you ask would
be very difficult to do. There were once two kinds of shortcut. Those of
the first kind have been sundered from their origins, and lead to the
deep past in places far from here. Those of the second kind link places
in space not separated by more than a few seconds. Or they did, before
the world was taken away.*

"Then you will not help me?"

*You could choose one of the long routes. The ancestors of the Pre-
servers rebuilt the Galaxy after the wars with the Transcendents, but
after the Preservers quit the Galaxy, the orbits of the stars have been
untended. They brought the mouths of many shortcuts here, but the stars
to which the shortcuts lead have drifted; and some have drifted closer
to the star of Confluence. The time debt between the ends of the shortcuts remains the same, but the distance between them in ordinary space
is less than it once was.*

Yama thought about this. He said, "Then the ship could pass through one of these shortcuts and travel back through ordinary space in less time than it took to drag the two mouths of the shortcuts apart."

There are, as I have said, several examples of these. I can guide you through one, as a last boon.

"But it will still take a year of ship-time to return. No, that is too long."

Indeed. But now there is another other way. The mouth of a shortcut with a time debt of only forty years appeared a few days ago. I have informed the ship. We will not meet again, for that which I served for so long has moved on. I remained here only to meet you for this final time. Now that is done, and I am free at last. I thank you for my freedom.

"Where will you go?"

The old man pointed toward the Eye of the Preservers.

I will follow my masters, of course.

"Then perhaps you can answer the question which has puzzled the mystagogues and philosophers since the Preservers set the ten thousand bloodlines on Confluence. Where have they gone?"

I do not know, except that it will be a better place than this.

"To the far end of time, when all will live again in the best of all possible worlds?"

It is not in this universe. The woman who called herself Angel was wrong. There are many other intelligent species in the Universe, but they are hidden from us because they are at distances greater than light has been able to travel since the Universe's creation. At present they are unreachable, but they will be brought together as the Universe contracts toward its last end. The Preservers foresaw a great war at the end of time and space, and decided on another way. And so they constructed the huge black hole at the heart of the Eye of the Preservers and withdrew from the Universe. They left Confluence in the hope that its peoples might grow greater than they. How it must have saddened them when it began to fail, and yet because they had withdrawn they were unable to interfere. The first war stopped all progress on Confluence; the second might have destroyed it. But you are their avatar, and you have saved it.

"Not yet, I think."

In this place and time, it has already happened. But I suppose that there are many time-lines where you did not prevail and the heretics were victorious, only to destroy Confluence when they quarreled amongst themselves over the spoils of their victory. If by mischance you return to one of those time-lines then I grieve for you. And yet in all of them I will be free!

"You have not told me about where you will go."

As species compete and evolve, so do universes. Those in which the formation of black holes is possible can give rise to other universes, for energy which disappears through black holes reappears elsewhere. That is where the Preservers have gone. Rather than fight for the last moment of infinite energy at the end of this universe, they have departed to create a new universe, one more suited to them than this. And now I go to discover it. Farewell, Child of the River.

"Wait!" Yama said again.

There was so much more he wanted to ask, but the old man was already fading, leaving behind only two points of faint red light that quickly receded beyond the boundary of the ship.

The ship's chiming laughter filled its transparent volumes. "You must trust me, master. I know now what to do."

The end of the new shortcut was only a few minutes' travel away. It hung within a vast cloud of water ice particles that refracted the sun into a billion points of twinkling light as the ship fell through it.

24

The White Boat

AND EMERGED AT a high place amidst blowing water spray turning to snow, so that at first Yama did not realize that the transition had been made. But then the ship moved out of the snow cloud and Yama saw a great tongue of ice stretching away, dazzling white beneath dense white clouds and a constant snowfall that blurred and softened the edges of everything. The ice filled the steep chute of a valley of adamantine keelrock a hundred leagues across, a frozen river moving with majestic slowness, throwing up broken chunks as big as cities along its edges.

The ship rose through the clouds, revealing a landscape of mountains islanded by cloud, mountains rimming the wide valley and spreading away on either side, sharp peaks of bare black keelrock rising out of clouds and snow and ice, whiteness everywhere touched with blue shadows, the sun a brilliant diamond set in a clear blue above a distant range of even taller peaks that must be the Rim Mountains. Directly below the ship, a waterfall fell from nothing, leagues wide and hung with a decad of rainbows, falling slowly and softly into clouds torn from its own self.

It was the end of the Great River, and its beginning.

The regulator came through the occasional door, cradling the baby in her mismatched arms. "Someone approaches," the ship said.

A streak of white slanted down through the achingly blue sky above. As a boy, Yama had often seen these contrails in the sky above Aeolis, and had yearned after the machines which had created them, wondering about the strange missions on which they had been bound. Now he barely had time to brace himself before, arriving ahead of the thunder-clap of its passage through the atmosphere, a feral machine came to a crash stop beyond the prow of the ship. It was black, no bigger than his head, and covered in spines of varying lengths which quested this way and that as if possessed of independent life. Yama knew it. Knew too the menace it radiated, pricking into his head through the bits of machine left there.

The ship said nervously, "It sees through me."

Yama reassured it, and told the machine that it must leave now. It would not come to him until it was asked again, and meanwhile it would tell its fellows not to interfere.

There are several of us stranded across the world, the thing said sulkily. *I cannot intercede with them.*

"I will deal with those when the time comes."

I will help you now. The world can be yours, with my help. Leave this poor vessel. Let me show you.

"Be still! The world is already mine. You will do what I ask, and no more."

Then I do nothing, the machine said, *and gladly. But tell me first why my mark is on you.*

"You will help me twice more, and then you will be free. I promise."

The feral machine fell away into the sky, even as other machines accelerated toward the disturbance it had created. But these, the keepers of the world, still loyal to the Preservers, found nothing. The feral machine had already returned to its station far beyond the world, and the ship was falling downriver toward the nearest shrine.

The Gatekeeper had said that there were two kinds of shortcut; Yama had guessed where the entrances to those which spanned only space were hidden.

The glacier ended at a small, mountain-rimmed sea continually crossed and recrossed by waves caused by falls of ice from cliffs two leagues high. Bergs and bergy bits churned and crashed amongst the waves. Meltwater spilled from the sea and meandered away in a thousand rivers and a million streams, through chains of lakes and raised bogs and drumlins, feeding the marshes which drained at last into the head of the Great River.

The shrine stood on a long, low island in the middle of one of the lakes, its black circle set on a shelf of bare rock raised above dwarf birches that were just coming into leaf; their thin black branches, laden with golden buds, swayed stiffly in the clean cold air. Gnarled junipers hugged the ground, red berries brilliant as drops of blood against the dark green of their needles, growing around boulders splattered with orange and black and gray stoneworts. Although it was summer, a cold wind blew from the edge of the glacier, and pockets of snow still clung in shady places on the island. Clear, ice-cold water tentatively fingered the pebbles of the shore, over and over. The sun was setting beyond range after range of mountains, touching every peak with a dab of light, painting long shadows amongst the fir trees that marched down to the shore of the lake, gilding its slow ripples. A skein of geese flew across red stripes of cloud that stretched on either side of the sun, honking each to each.

The world! So wonderful in its variety, so beautiful in every particular detail.

The ship had changed shape, spreading wide flat wings which delicately manipulated the world's gravity fields. It floated down to the island's shore, and Yama stepped from one of the wings onto the little gravel beach beneath the shrine. He leaned on Prefect Corin's staff, which the regulator had saved. He was still very weak. Freezing water lapped his bare feet; wind tangled in his long hair and beard. The clean, cold air was as bracing as good wine. The regulator followed with the baby, which was bundled in silvery cloth so that only the tip of its nose showed.

The regulator had unstitched the badly ripped and bloodstained silvery garment Bryn had given Yama, and made it into a kind of cloak to wear over the black tunic and leggings the ship had provided. She had reserved a small piece to swaddle the baby. She did not need any kind of clothing, she claimed, and seemed unaffected by the icy wind. She had refused to stay with the ship, saying that Yama did not know how to look after the baby.

"Males of your bloodline cannot give suck. I have started a flow of milk, master, and he feeds happily. Do not take that from him."

Yama made sure that the ship knew what it had to do. He felt that every step might break the world, change it into something other than that which it must become. He told it, "Take the cloned mouth of the shortcut and make a loop at lightspeed forty years long. Make sure that you arrive back at the point in space from which you started, a few days before we first arrived. The Great River will flow through the shortcut into the future and we will be able to travel through it into the past. Are you sure that you can do this?"

"Of course," the ship said primly. "Shortcuts were brought here in the first place by my kind."

"Forty years, no more, no less. That is important."

"It will happen, or you will not be here. *I know.*"

"There may be many time-lines where it may not have happened, because you carelessly misunderstood my instructions."

"You can trust me," the ship said. "You should trust me to take you to Ys also. I know that the mooring towers still stand, and I can have you there in a minute."

"I do not want you to be seen. This way will suffice. You remember where we will meet?"

"Downriver, ten days—what you call a decad—from now. At the far edge of the City of the Dead. As if no one will see us there."

"There are things in Ys I do not wish to awaken. Or at least, not yet."

"The river will not cease to flow here once I have diverted it into the future. Not at once. There is much ice above us."

"I know. But the glaciers will flow more and more slowly because there will no longer be new snow and ice pushing them forward. I already know how long it will take, and when it should begin. Go now."

The ship rose, turning and dipping as it rose. It swept quickly across the lake, setting a flock of wildfowl to flight, then angled straight up. A moment later a boom echoed across the wide sky, and Yama saw the white streak which marked where the ship was accelerating toward the mouth of the shortcut at the end of the Terminal Mountains, where the river fell back into the world.

Yama felt a mixture of apprehension and a kind of existential dizziness. Nothing was fixed. This was not the world from which he had begun: the Universe would not end, as he had been taught all his life, in a single infinite moment, when all the dead would be reborn into the perpetual grace of the Preservers. All was change, a constant flux. Even the Preservers sought to change, in universe after universe without end.

He said, "Perhaps I should do nothing. Perhaps it should end here, for else I condemn myself to becoming no more than a machine toiling away at the same endless task. I have set the Great River free from its unending cycle, but how can I set myself free from the circle of my own history?"

The regulator was a practical person. She said, "You have already begun, master, by sending the ship on its mission. Who can say how it will end?"

"You are right, of course." Yama smiled. "You remind me of a dear lost friend. Perhaps I might see him again. And Derev, too . . . Yes, it has begun, and I must go on as I must."

As he climbed up to the shrine, it began to flow with banners of light. He stepped into the light, and the regulator followed him.

———

Ys was suddenly spread below him. On one side the sun was falling behind the Rim Mountains; on the other, the Great River was painted with golden light on which the black motes of thousands of boats and ships were sharply drawn, as if by the most exquisite calligraphy. The river was fuller than Yama remembered it, lapping at the margin of the city, covering the shore where in the near future there would be wide mud flats and a scurf of shanty towns. And between mountains and river was the immemorial city. Ys: the endless grid of her streets and avenues sprawled wantonly beneath a brown haze of air pollution, sending up a shuddering roar in which the brazen clash of the gongs of one of her many temples and the shrill song of a ship's siren emerged as sharply as points of light.

Wind plucked at Yama's silvery cloak; a warm wind, redolent of smoke and decay.

The shrine was set on a high peak of the roof of the Palace of the Memory of the People. A sheer cliff dropped to a long slope of patchwork fields studded with temples and sanctuaries. A raven floated half a league below, black wings widespread, primaries fingering the air. A bell was tolling somewhere. In the distance, the slim, silvery mooring towers rose up from cluttered streets, soaring toward their vanishing points high above the atmosphere. The towers were the ancient port of Ys, from which, in the Golden Age when the Sirdar had ruled Confluence, ships had departed for other worlds. Although abandoned an age past, they had served one last task, for Yama had dreamed of standing in their shadow when he had been a child in the little city of Aeolis, and so they had drawn him to Ys and to the beginning of his adventures. And would do so again.

A narrow flight of steps, small and close-set, wound down the steep side of the peak toward a distant courtyard which was enclosed on three sides by high rock walls. There was a scree slope beneath the open side of the courtyard, and a wind-bent tree not quite dead stood amongst the loose stones, a few scraps of green showing at the very ends of its warped branches.

Down there was the cell in which Yama had been—would be—imprisoned after the assassination attempt in the corridors of the Department of Indigenous Affairs, and from which he would escape, cloaked in the hell-hound. Down there, buried in the dirt floor of the cell by the round window, was the coin first he and then Pandaras had carried half the length of the world. He would need a working coin soon enough—what if he took that one? His future self would not find it, would not be able to call upon the hell-hound, would not be able to escape. In how many time-lines had that happened? In how many others had he failed to arrive here?

"We must not linger, master," the regulator said. "You must stop dreaming. You are in the world again."

She led the way down the stairs, brisk and matter-of-fact, clutching the baby tight to her flat breasts. Yama followed, dizzy with visions of forking paths. What if this world did not contain his own history after all?

The bell was still tolling steadily in the distance, and now another answered it close by, ringing out with brisk urgency. A moment later, the regulator turned to Yama. She pressed the baby into his arms and bounded away down the steps, her swollen claw crooked above her head for balance.

There was only a pentad of guards, four inexperienced youngsters led by a one-armed veteran who had been drinking steadily all day. It was a rotten, dull assignment. The old shrine, known as the Shrine of Stars, had been unused for ten thousand years, and its only visitor was an old priest who, once a year, muttered a brief prayer and placed an offering of ivy and delicate white arching sprays of starbright at its base. With nothing else to do, the guards spent their time gambling, drinking and taking potshots at the crows and ravens which occasionally floated past the unglazed slit windows of the guardhouse. They were unprepared for trouble, half-unbuttoned, weapons slung on their backs. The regulator killed the first two easily, disemboweling one with her claw, grabbing the other and shaking him until his neck snapped. Two others ran, but the veteran stood his ground. His first shot struck the regulator in the chest; as she fell forward, his second took off the back of her head.

A moment later, a burning figure appeared on the steps above, clothed in a thousand fireflies. The veteran fled from this spectral figure even as it bent to the dead, silver-skinned woman. It called down two flying discs, laid the dead woman on one and stepped onto the other. By the time reinforcements arrived, it was gone.

———

Yama came to the chamber of the mirror people by the secret ways of the palace within the Palace of the Memory of the People. He had dismissed the fireflies. The mirror people gathered around him, curious and excited, plucking at his cloak, at the baby (who laughed at their painted faces), asking who he was and how he knew about this place. He told them that he was a friend, and that he had come here with a message for their king.

"There is a dead woman at the entrance to this place," he added. "Bring her here."

Three clowns scurried off. Yama sat down to wait for them to return. He refused offers of water and raw fungus. The baby fretted, pissed into the pad the regulator had bound between its legs, fell asleep.

Lupe came through the tall oval frame an hour later. Perhaps the skin was not as loose on his mottled arms; perhaps the wrinkles which mazed his face were fewer and less deep, but otherwise he was much as Yama remembered him. He was supported on either side by two beautiful girls, and clad in a long black dress whose train was held up by a third. As before, his lips were stained bright red, and the sockets of his blind eyes were painted with broad swipes of blue. His gray hair was piled up on his head, woven through with golden threads and fake pearls.

He was at once absurd and hierophantic, a burlesque of monarchy in his ruined finery, yet commanding in his bearing.

"Who is it," he demanded. "Who is it that disturbs us?"

There was an excited babble as a hundred mirror people tried to explain, but everyone fell silent when Lupe held up his hand. The baby had begun to cry, alarmed by the noise. As Yama tried to hush it, Lupe turned to him and said, "Why, here he is. Let him speak."

Lupe listened carefully as Yama explained that he had come with a prophecy about someone who would change and raise up the mirror people, so that they would become the very thing that they imitated: they would become fully human.

"Come here," Lupe commanded, and Yama endured the spidery touch of his long fingernails on his face, his hair, his beard.

A fakir with skewers pushed bloodily through his painted cheeks mumbled that this man had come by the secret ways. Lupe nodded gravely, and said to Yama, "You know our corridors and you know the hope we have harbored since we left the river and crept into the Palace. Who are you?"

"A friend. One who speaks truly of what you have yearned for in your secret songs."

Lupe nodded again. "We sing many songs, but some we sing only for ourselves. And yet you know of them."

An acrobat swung upside down on a wire overhead and said, "He brings a baby and a dead woman, and we've never seen his like before. He brings trouble, Lupe."

A murmur spread through the crowd of mirror people, dying away when Lupe held up a hand. He said to Yama, "You bring a message, but do we know it is true?"

"In seventeen years, someone of my bloodline will come here. Watch out for him. He will need help, and when you help him he will change a baby no older than the baby I carry. As for me, I need a boat. I must travel downriver."

Lupe said, "It is well known that we have many things. Gifts from patrons. Siftings from the leavings of enlightened races. So many things that we do not know what we have."

"I think you will find amongst your treasures a white boat not much bigger than the coffins in which the dead are launched upon the flood of the Great River. I claim it as mine."

Lupe laughed. "We understand! As we sing for our living, so you sing for yours. Be welcome, and eat. If there is a white boat, why then you shall have it as payment for the hope you have brought us. We keep all we are given, but we do not need any of it because we can always get more."

It took two days to find the boat amongst the piles of forgotten gifts. The news of its discovery was borne ahead of a swelling crowd that cluttered around the entrance to Lupe's suite. They cheered Yama when he emerged with Lupe, and made a carnival procession as the boat was carried down secret ways to the ancient wharves in one of the crypts that undercut the mountain of the Palace of the Memory of the People.

The regulator's undecaying body had already been placed in the white boat, which rode high on the black water in the crypt, glimmering in the torchlit dark. It seemed very small and fragile, but scarcely rocked as Yama climbed into it. He took the baby from one of Lupe's attendants and held him to his chest. Fireflies flitted overhead, a restless cloud of light. The baby fretted, made uneasy by the fife and drums of the procession and the flaring torches and the gorgeous motley crowd along the wharf.

"Remember what I told you," Yama told Lupe. "When the boy comes here he will need your help, but you must tell him as little as possible. If he asks about me, tell him nothing. Say that I came secretly at night, that no one saw me but you, who cannot see."

"My people make stories for a living," Lupe said. "We will cloak you in as deep a mystery as you could wish."

The mirror people fell silent as Lupe made a formal farewell, then burst into song and loud cheers as the white boat, with Yama standing in its sharp, raised prow, glided away into the darkness, toward the channel that led to the Great River.

———

Yama left the white boat three days later. He landed a league upriver of the little city of Aeolis, amongst the abandoned tombs of the City of the Dead. It was midnight. The huge black sky above the Great River was punctuated only by a scattering of dim halo stars and the dull red swirl, no bigger than a man's hand, of the Eye of the Preservers. The heaped lights of the little city of Aeolis and the lights of the carracks riding at anchor outside the harbor entrance were brighter by far than anything in the sky.

Yama watched as the white boat, attended by a little galaxy of fireflies, dwindled away across the black flood of the river, heading downriver toward his destiny. Then he turned and started along the bone-white paths that threaded between the tombs. He had a long way to go before he made rendezvous with the ship: across the City of the Dead to the tower deep in the foothills of the Rim Mountains, where the last of the curators of the City of the Dead lived, where he knew of a way into the keel of the world.

He did not fear the dead who called to him from their tombs; this was where he had played as a child. But he had brought his own ghosts with him, and he faltered and turned aside before the final descent to the keelways.

25

Derev

THE SHIP FOUND him five days later, filthy and half-starved, his hair and beard wild, his silvery cloak tattered. He was living in a tomb which had been stripped of its bronze doors and furniture by robbers a thousand years ago, spending most of his time in conversation with the aspect of the long-dead tax official whose body had been interred there.

The ship took him in, but he would not allow it to bathe him or heal his superficial wounds. His rage was spent. He was exhausted, but possessed by a grim, hopeless resolve.

"I cannot believe in anything," Yama told the ship. "Not in the world, not in myself."

"The world is as it is," the ship said.

"But is it the world I know? Why should I set on the same path again if it is not? I knew what I had to do, but I turned aside."

"Perhaps you were meant to turn aside."

Yama hardly heard the ship. He was still engaged in the same bitter monologue for which the bewildered aspect had been an unwilling audience. He said, "I will never know what I could do. What I could be, what the world could be. I was not brave or strong enough and I turned aside. I failed. No matter, no matter. I know what I must do. It is the only thing left to do. If I cannot save the world, then I must save those I love."

"When you have rested, master, perhaps you will allow me to take you there."

"No. You must take me forward in time. You must take me into the future. I will save what I can. I do not mind that the heretics take the world if I can save those I love. The Aedile need not die for me, and I should not have to sacrifice my life with Derev—she has no part in this. Take me into the future, ship. I have decided."

Fifteen days passed aboard the ship as it made its second loop at close to the speed of light. When it arrived at Aeolis, seventeen years in the future, Yama left it at once, before his resolve could falter.

It was spring, a warm spring night. Frogs peeped each to each with froggy ardor. The triple-armed wheel of the Galaxy stood waist-deep at the farside horizon, salting the patchwork of flooded fields with its blue-white light.

Yama walked through the overgrown ruins of the ancient mortuaries beyond the walls of the little city of Aeolis, leaning on the staff at every other step. Spring, but was it the right spring? Was it still the same history, or had it turned down some other path? Who lived in the peel-house which lifted its turrets and towers against the Galaxy?

Every pass through the time-rifted shortcuts had caused the time-line of the Universe to branch. This was not the world he had come from, but an echo of an echo. Perhaps it was an almost exact echo, but it did not matter. It did not matter because the original still existed. He could do anything here and it would not matter because what had happened had already happened in the time-line from which he had come. By failing, he had freed himself from the wheel. He was free to rewrite history.

He had come here because he was going home.

Thoughts whirled in his head like fireflies. Nothing was solid anymore. Anything could happen. Anything at all. This revelation filled him with a sudden great calm. No longer did he have to strive at the toiling wheel of history, like the oxen which plodded around and around at the wheel which lifted water from the Breas to irrigate the paeonin fields. He remembered the one true thing Dr. Dismas had said, that men were so closely bound to their fate that they could not see the world around them. As he had been, until now.

He had failed to set in motion the vast engines in the keelways. He had not even tried, but had turned away in sight of the curators' tower. By his failure he had saved the world; saved it from himself. He could pass the burden to the boy. Tell him all. Let him go this time fully armed into the world, into his future. Let him restore the river. Let him imprison Angel in the space inside the shrines before she could interfere. Let him call down and enslave the feral machines, and then destroy the heretics.

He could defy the tremendous inertia of history. He could tell the boy where he came from and put an end to his foolish search for his parents. For he had no parents but his own self; he was a closed loop in time, with no beginning and no end, like Caphis's tattoo of the snake which swallowed its own self, like the Great River which fell over the edge of the world and passed through the shortcut to its own beginning. Child of the River—how truly the wives of old Constable Thaw had named him! They had known the truth even then. It had taken him far longer to learn it. It had taken him all his life.

He hurried on, passing Dr. Dismas's tower, which stood just outside the gate of the little city. Its windows were dark, but that signified nothing.

"What must be will be," he muttered.

He walked along the embankments between flooded paeonin fields, crossed the Breas, and climbed a path which wound up a long, dusty slope between scattered tombs. The excavation was just where he remembered it, at the top of a rise of dead land coral at the edge of the City of the Dead. The guards and the workers were asleep; the lone watchdog was easily placated. Yama wept, embracing its armored shoulders and breathing its familiar odor of dog and warm plastic, remembering how often he had fooled its brothers and sisters into allowing him to pass, remembering his lost childhood.

He told the watchdog to return to its patrol and clambered down bamboo scaffolding into one of the trenches. He ran his hands up and down the exposed layers of land coral until what he was looking for woke under his fingers: a ceramic coin with dots and dashes of greenish light suddenly flickering within it. It took only a few minutes to free it from the crumbling matrix. He unwound the length of leather thong from a scaffold joint, made a loop around the coin, and hung it around his neck.

The boy would need it. He would show him how to use it.

"If I cannot save the world," he said out loud, "at least I can save myself."

Go directly to the peel-house? No. The guards would turn him away or kill him. He stole a package of pressed dates, a loaf of unleavened bread and a flask of sweet yellow wine, and retreated to one of the empty tombs nearby. He slept badly and was woken in the middle of the night by voices. He crept to the entrance of the tomb and peered through the canes of the roses which tangled across it.

Just offshore, a little way upriver of Aeolis, a dash of flame flickered; nearby, two men were talking about sabotage, about heretics.

"I'd kill 'em," one said. "Kill 'em all and let the Preservers sort 'em out."

"I would rather be here than hunting through the tombs," the other said.

"The dead can't do any harm. Haven't you learned that yet? It's the living you've got to watch for. The heretics might think to sneak up on the peel-house this way, while most of the lads are off looking for them amongst the tombs. That's a worse danger than any aspect."

Yama knew them by their voices. They were both boys not much older than he was; they had arrived at the peel-house late last year. He could tell them that the burning ship was Dr. Dismas's first failed attempt at a diversion . . . but no, they would not believe him. They would drive him off, or worse. He clamped his hands over his mouth, shaking with suppressed laughter. The most powerful man in the world was afraid of two raw recruits.

The guards walked on, their boots crunching on dry shale; the distant fire died down. Yama went back to sleep, and woke to find sunlight spangling the green arbor of roses at the entrance of the tomb. The steam engine which powered the drill rig was working noisily, and Yama heard the plaintive worksong of the prisoners as they labored to widen the trenches.

> *The picks are walking,*
> > *Hammer ring.*
> *The stones are talking,*
> > *Hammer ring.*
> *Look, look yonder,*
> > *Hammer ring.*
> *Think I see spirits,*
> > *Hammer ring.*
> *Waking in the earth . . .*

How right they were, Yama thought. It was often said that uneducated men knew things about the world that could never be taught in seminaries or colleges, but in fact this naïve wisdom could be learned by anyone who had eyes to see. The educated men who made such patronizing remarks had long ago stopped seeing the world as it was, saw it only as they had been taught it must be.

Yama hid in the tomb for most of the morning, horribly aware that the Aedile, his stepfather, must be somewhere close by, supervising the work. The urge to run up the slope and embrace him came and went like a fever. At its strongest, Yama clasped his knees to his chest and rocked to and fro, biting his lips until blood ran, smothering wild laughter.

"What must be will be. What must be . . ."

At last he could bear it no longer. He placated the watchdog and slipped away, scurrying downslope with a dread that the Aedile's voice would ring out, commanding him to stop. If it did he would surely go mad.

He spent the rest of the day downriver of the little city and its silted bay, searching along the shore for the boy. He remembered that he had gone there to watch the picket boat which had brought Dr. Dismas back from Ys. The picket boat was standing off banyan shoals several leagues downriver of the bay (Enobarbus and Dr. Dismas would be on board— he could call upon machines and kill them both, but if he bent machines to his will he would reveal himself to Dr. Dismas's paramour), but although he searched long and hard, he could not find the boy, and at last remembered that he would go and look at the boat the next day, after his adventure in the ruins.

It was night, now. He was walking through sword grass and scrubby creosote bushes beside the road to the mill at the point of the bay. The sun had set behind the Rim Mountains; the cold splendor of the Galaxy was rising above the river. Perhaps it was already too late. He howled in rage at the world, at the conspiracy against him, the relentless, impacable momentum of events. What must be will be . . .

He circled the city as quickly as he could, sweating through his filthy tunic and leggings as he gimped along, leaning on his staff at every other step, the tattered silvery cloak flapping around him. The ceramic coin burned at his chest.

"What must be will be. No. What *will* be . . ."

He felt like a puppet tugged here and there by invisible forces. Or a leaf, a poor dead husk of a leaf swept along on the river. Everything from now until his death bent toward fulfillment of what had already happened.

"What must be will be. What must be . . ."

He was on a path at the top of an embankment. Beyond the flooded fields, the peel-house stood atop the skull-shaped bluff which overlooked the Great River. Its towers pricked the blue-white curve of the Galaxy. He could go there and reconcile himself with the Aedile. He could go back in time and rescue Telmon. He could not save the world after all, but perhaps he could save all he loved. But first he must find the boy. That was the key.

He flung out his arms, raised his face to the black, empty sky, and screamed in defiance.

"I will not serve!"

Hurrying now. He was late, but surely not too late. Not too late to save himself from himself. If this was still the same story, the boy would be with Derev and Ananda. But he had not gone back in time to tell Beatrice and Osric his story, so they would not have set Derev's parents on the road to Aeolis, and so she would not be here . . .

He had forgotten about Lud and Lob.

The twins ambushed him by a wayside shrine, where the embankment sloped down to the old road. They rose from their hiding place in a thicket of chayote vine, crashing through curtains of scarlet, hand-shaped leaves with hoarse whoops. They were just as he remembered them, big and flabbily muscular, wearing only simple white kilts.

Lud grinned, showing his tusks. "Ho, and who are you, stranger?"

"Maybe he's with Dr. Dismas," Lob said.

"This culler? He's just a crazy."

"Let me pass," Yama said. He held the staff on guard, ready to brain them if they came too close.

Lud crossed his meaty arms over his bare chest. "You don't go anywhere without paying. This is our town."

Lob said uneasily, "Leave it. If he's just a crazy he won't have any gelt. We don't have time."

"This won't take long."

"Dismas will skin us alive if we fuck up again."

"I'm not frightened of him." Lud pointed at Yama. "What's that around your neck, eh? You give it as a toll and maybe we let you pass."

"It is not for you," Yama said, half-angry, half-amused by their foolish presumption. "Let me pass!"

"We'll need a toll," Lud said. He advanced, grinning horribly, but danced back when Yama screamed and jabbed the metal-shod tip of the staff at his face. Lob stooped and picked up a stone and said, "Ho, that's how it is, eh?"

Yama was able to dodge the first stones they threw. He screamed and capered angrily, swinging his staff with careless abandon. They could not kill him. History was on his side. Then a stone smashed into his forehead. There was a moment of stunning pain, a white flash like the beginning of the Universe, and he realized that he might die here. If history was changed, then anything could happen.

He wiped blood from his eyes with his forearm and whirled his staff, driving the twins backward, but it was only a temporary victory.

A stone struck his elbow and he nearly dropped the staff. Before he could recover, Lob and Lud roared, rushed at him from either side, and knocked him down. He surged up and struck Lob about the head, but Lud grabbed him from behind. He fell beneath Lud's weight, and Lob snatched up the staff and made to break it.

And then the boy stepped onto the road, brandishing a slim trident. The sizar of Aeolis's temple was behind him, his yellow robe glimmering in the half-light. Both looked very young and very scared.

"What is this, Lob?" the boy asked, and then Yama heard little more because Lud thrust his face into the dirt and cuffed him when he tried to struggle. Voices raised in anger, a howl that had to be Lob's, for the weight left his back as Lud jumped up. He rolled over. Lob was on his knees, gasping for breath, and Lud was advancing on the boy, holding a crooked knife up by his face. The boy had the staff and was watching Lud carefully, and was taken by surprise when Lob grabbed at his legs from behind. He staggered and hammered at Lob's back, but Lob dragged him down.

Yama tried to get to his feet. There were no machines near enough to help. No. This could not happen. He could not let them kill the boy.

And then the tree burst into flame and he thought his heart might explode with joy.

Derev was alive. She was here.

———

After Lud and Lob had been driven off, Yama had eyes only for Derev as she followed her shadow out of the brilliant light of the burning tree. She said something to the boy, her arms rising and falling gracefully. How beautiful she was!

The tree burned with fierce ardor, its trunk a shadow inside a roaring pillar of blue flame. Oceans of sparks swept high into the night, like stars playfully seized by the Preservers.

The yellow-robed sizar, Ananda, helped Yama sit up. He dabbed at his wounds, which were only superficial, and managed to stand. The boy held out the staff and Yama took it and bowed. It was a solemn, thrilling moment.

The boy did not recognize him, of course. He did not even see that Yama was of his bloodline. But Yama was suddenly frightened by the boy's searching stare and he could not, dared not, speak. Once again he felt that he was at the cusp of a delicate balance—the slightest movement in any direction could cause disaster. Everything had changed in the moment the tree had caught fire. The tumble of crazy ideas about altering the course of history had fallen away. He had nothing left now but the truth.

Fearing that his voice might betray him, Yama used the sign language which the old guard, Coronetes, had taught him when he had been imprisoned in the stacks of the Department of Indigenous Affairs. Ananda caught the gist of it, even if he mangled the meaning.

I went crazy when I was searching for you, but now I know, he signed.

Ananda said, "He wants you to know that he has been searching for you," and suggested that he might be a priest.

Yama shook his head, suppressing the urge to laugh, and signed again. *How happy I am that all is as I remembered.*

Ananda said uncertainly, "He says that he is glad that he remembered all this. I think he must mean that he will always remember this."

Yama pulled the leather thong over his head and dangled the coin from his left hand while he signed with his right. *Use this if you are to come here again,* which Ananda badly scrambled on the first attempt, but got right on the second.

The whistles of the militia sounded, far off in the night. Yama thrust the coin into the boy's hand, cast a last longing look at Derev, and turned and ran up the embankment, toward the mazed tombs of the City of the Dead.

He had not run very far when the ship overtook him. It had hidden itself in the deeps of the Great River, far from shore; now it dropped out of the night and hung just above the surface of a flooded paeonin field, tilted so that one wing tip touched the top of the embankment. Yama climbed aboard, and at once it rose high above the world.

"I saw her," he told the ship, "and I will see her again. I must. What must be will be, despite ourselves."

The ship's aspect, the solemn little girl, clasped her hands beneath her chin as Yama explained what he wanted. Behind her, the glassy plain with its freight of statues receded into the starless dark. She said, "You are still not well, master."

"No. Of course I am not well. I will never be well. I have seen too much. I have done too much. I think that I have been mad for a long time, but did not know it." Yama felt the craziness again, his thoughts dividing and dividing, impossible to stop.

"The loop will be very short, master. I cannot guarantee its accuracy."

Yama began to laugh and the laughter went on and on until he clamped his hands over his mouth because the laughter scared him. It bubbled through him. It might never stop. He choked it back and said, "Just do it."

"I will do my best, master." The ship was wounded. It had been built to take a pride in what it did.

"Take me there, ship. I know you will do it. What must be will be."

———

Night, summer, the Eye of the Preservers a smudged bloody thumbprint high in the black sky. Dr. Dismas's tower was a burnt-out ruin. Fragments of charred furniture were scattered outside its broken door. It was almost midnight, but the lights of the city of Aeolis burned brightly within its high wall.

Because of the summer heat, the citizens of Aeolis, the Amnan, slept in their cool seeps and wallows by day and began work at sunset. Sodium vapor lights blazed in the streets and lamps shone in every window. The doors of workshops, chandlers and taverns were flung open. Crowds swirled up and down the long road at the top of the old waterfront, where tribesmen from the dry hills downriver of the city had set up their blanket stalls and vendors of fried waterweed and nuts cried their wares. A mountebank stood halfway up a folding ladder, declaiming the wonders of a patent elixir; an auction of bacts was under way by the gate where Yama entered, clad in his tattered silvery cloak and leaning on his staff.

Hardly anyone marked his passing. He was almost certainly a mendicant; although Aeolis was a poor city, it was often visited by mendicants because it had once been one of the most holy cities on Confluence. Yama made his way through the crowds of large, ill-made, blubbery men with hardly a comment or a glance.

The steel door of the godown owned by Derev's father was open, guarded by a man with a carbine who gave Yama a hard look as he went past and walked around the corner to the family entrance.

The words which opened the door's lock had not been changed— even if they had, Yama could have forced it to open in an instant. Calling Derev's name, he went through the archway into a little courtyard where a fountain tiled with blue mosaic splashed. She would not be there. He knew that she would not be there, but there she was, floating down the spiral stair, her feathery white hair lifting around her pale face.

She stopped at a turn of the stair a little way above him. She wore a silk tabard the color of old ivory, and a long skirt of many layers of fine white gauzy stuff. She said, "Who let you in, dominie? I do not think my father has business with anyone this night."

"You do not recognize me?"

Her large dark eyes searched his face. Then she said, "You are the anchorite whose life Yama saved. Why have you come back? How did you get in? Do you know something about Yama? Is he—"

"He is here, Derev."

"Where? Is he hurt? Did something happen to him in Ys? Your face is so grave, dominie. O, do not tell me he is dead!"

Yama laughed. "My love, I am twice as alive as any other man in the world."

Derev's expression suddenly changed. She vaulted the rail of the stair and floated down into his arms. Her height, her heat, her fierce gaze searching his. The staff fell with a clatter, unnoticed, as they took each other into their arms.

"You," she said, leaning down into Yama's embrace. "I knew it was you, but I did not let myself believe it."

"You must believe it now, Derev. We have only a little time here."

She drew away from him, still holding his hands. "But you are hurt."

For a moment, Yama did not know what she meant; he had let the ship tend to the small cuts and bruises inflicted during the fight with Lud and Lob. Then he touched the ridges of scarred skin on the left side of his face and said, "These are old wounds."

"I did not mean those," she said. And then, "Yama. Yama!"

At first, she tried to hold him up. Then she eased him to the ground, and went to fetch her father.

It was almost dawn by the time Yama had recovered enough to be able to tell something of his story. He was bathed and perfumed, his hair and beard combed and trimmed. He was dressed in a clean shirt and trews, and had been fed with a salty beef broth and sweet fried shrimp. He sat with Derev and her mother and father, Calev and Carenon, in the roof garden of the godown. He told them of how he had escaped Prefect Corin at Ys and boarded a ship which had taken him downriver toward the war, of how he had been infected by Dr. Dismas and forced to fight on the side of the heretics, of how he had fallen beyond the edge of the world and traveled back in time through a shortcut.

He left much out. The friendship of Pandaras and brave, foolish Tamora, and all their adventures in Ys and the Palace of the Memory of the People; the miracle he had been allowed to perform; the destruction of Dr. Dismas's paramour in the Glass Desert; his adventures on the great ship with the last of his people. There was not enough time for that now.

"There is not enough time," he said, "because Aeolis will soon be attacked. I do not know exactly when, but certainly by tomorrow night."

Derev's father, Carenon, said, "We are still a long way from the heretics, I think. If an army or fleet is bent upon us, there would have been warnings, surely."

"It will not be attacked by heretics, but by a warship out of Ys, a warship commanded by someone who wishes to do me harm."

"Then we must prevent it. We will warn the Aedile, to begin with." Carenon stood, very tall and very thin in his black jacket and leggings. For a moment it seemed that he would raise his arms and leap into the sky. He said, "I will take you to the peel-house at once, Yamamanama."

"No," Yama said. "No, you will not."

Calev said, "How many will die, Yamamanama, when this warship comes?"

"The city will be destroyed. Many will escape and flee to the far side. I do not know how many will not."

Carenon said, "And you will allow no warning of this?"

Yama bowed his head. All his dead. The thousands he had killed while under the spell of Dr. Dismas. Dr. Dismas himself, and Prefect Corin. The crew of the *Weazel*. The soldiers who had captured him in the City of the Dead, and their mage. The regulator, and the last of his bloodline in the deep past. Tamora. And in only a few days his step-father would die of shame and exhaustion on the far side of the river, after he failed to prevent the sacking of Aeolis.

Derev took his hand in hers and said, "Don't you see that he would save them if he could?"

Yama said, "I thought so long on this that it drove me mad. If I could I would save them all, friends and enemies alike. But then who else might die? And all those I tried to save might still die . . ."

The silence that followed was punctuated by the distant ringing of signal bells; fishing boats were turning into the channel toward the end of the New Quay, where they would tie up and unload their catches. It was almost dawn. The city was shutting down, getting ready for the long, hot, lazy day.

At last, Carenon said, "I will warn my workers, at least. If I know, then they deserve to know too."

"No," Yama said. "They have families here. They will want to take them, and the news will spread until all the city will know. It does not end. Do one thing and it branches and branches until you are far from where you began. No. What will happen must happen."

Carenon gave him a sharp, troubled look. "Where did you hear that?"

"He knows about Beatrice and Osric," Derev said.

"I can take you away from here," Yama told Carenon. "You can come with me into the past, for that is where I must go."

Derev said, "Where we must go, I think."

His love for her returned in all its fierce wildness, and for a moment he thought that he might faint again.

Calev said with grave astonishment, "Then you are—"

"We did not know," her husband said. "I suppose it was for the best that we did not know, but it would have helped us. I hoped that you and Derev might make a match, Yamamanama, and perhaps things would not be as hard as has been foretold." He laughed and said, "What a fool I have been!"

"You always knew it would be a hard road when we came here," Calev said. "But you came here anyway."

Yama had never paid much attention to Derev's parents. They had always been formal and reserved, for all that they had encouraged Derev in her trysts with him. He had thought that it was because of his position. He had been the son of a high official of the Department of Indigenous Affairs, even if he had been an adopted son. Derev's father had been mocked in the city for being ambitious and grasping, for pushing his daughter into a relationship that would bring him greater profit and power. Yama saw now that Carenon and Calev were no more than ordinary people who had taken up an extraordinary burden; that they were willing to sacrifice their daughter to help save the world.

He said again, "I can save you. I know that you will flee the city before the attack. I can take you to the safest place of all, into the past."

Carenon ran his fingers over the leaves of one of the geraniums that grew along the edge of the roof garden, releasing a sweet dusky scent into the air. His fine white hair lifted in the breeze that had sprung up from the river. It was growing warmer. Light touched the rim of the sky.

Carenon said, "No, we will stay. I mean, we will flee the city, but we stay in this time. We built up one fortune, and we can take a little of that with us. Perhaps we can build another before the world ends. How long, before that happens?"

Yama lowered his head. He was ashamed and frightened. He had still to face that failure. He said, "I do not know."

Carenon said, "But surely the end of the world is already set in motion. The Great River fails steadily, although the Aedile has calculated that it will not run dry for many years. If the end comes before then, we might live to see the new worlds we were promised."

"Don't you see?" Derev said. "Everything must happen so that he can come here again."

Yama said quietly, "Besides, I have not yet done it."

Derev said, "But the river is failing. And Beatrice said—"

"The first part, diverting the end of the river into the future, was easy. But I failed at the second part. I thought instead that I could change things, and find a new way . . ."

Derev smiled. "And destroy the heretics? You always wanted to fight them, Yama, never more so than after Telmon died. Yet if you destroy the heretics, then you would only promote the cause of the Committee for Public Safety, and I know that you could not allow that."

Yama nodded. "They destroyed my father."

Carenon nodded. "A disgrace, the way they exiled so many loyal to the Department."

"I mean that they will. It is one of the Committee for Public Safety who will set fire to the city, and it will be the end of my father."

"They would be worse than the heretics," Derev said.

"It has happened before," Yama said. "A tyranny may conquer every one of its enemies, but will ultimately destroy itself from the inside. The wheel turns, and all is renewed."

Derev said, "And is that what you want? That the world can go on forever and ever without change?"

"No. That is not possible. I was allowed to perform a miracle, Derev. The indigenous peoples will become like us. They will gain self-awareness and at last achieve enlightenment. That is no small thing. If that was all I could do, then I could be content."

"But it is not."

"No. No, it is not. I was going to tell the boy, my younger self. Tell him everything and let him decide what to do. But that would do no more than pass the burden to another. And so I turned aside, and came here."

Derev said, "I cannot decide for you."

"I would not ask you to. Besides, I have already decided."

Carenon said, "I suppose that if we tried to stop you, or if I tried to tell my poor workers their fate, you would have the power to prevent it."

Behind him, far beyond the shadowy hills of the vast necropolis, the first rays of the sun touched the peaks of the Rim Mountains.

Yama said, "I will not force any of you, but I hope that you will help me."

26

Until the End of the World

EARLY ONE WINTER, one of the goats was taken by a leopard. It was the piebald nanny which in her short life had given birth to six fine healthy kids, and only one of them a billy. The winter looked to be a hard one. It had been raining for more than a decad, which was why Beatrice had not yet moved the goats from the thorn scrub pasture to their winter quarters, and perhaps the rain had driven the leopard from its usual range in the spruce forests in the mountains. Beatrice found its pugmarks by the swift stream at the edge of the pasture, but no trace of the goat, not so much as a drop of blood. She told Osric the news and said there was no helping it, and then added, "Why are you weeping, husband? It was only a goat."

"It is the sign."

Beatrice took off her wet oilskin and hung it on the hook by the kitchen door. The end of her long, feathery white hair had got wet. She wrapped it around her strong, capable hands and squeezed water from it onto the stone floor. She said, "It is a sign that means more winter fodder for the other goats, and less milk for us next spring."

"It will begin soon. He will come to us . . ."

Beatrice gave him a sharp look. "The boy."

"Next spring."

"We won't see Derev until then, that's certain. She won't want to make her way from Aeolis to the keelroad head in weather like this. And I will not risk sending out any doves in this weather, either. But never mind, there's plenty of time to tell her what she must do. Husband, what is it now?"

Osric was troubled, teary and weak. So often these days his mind seemed to catch on unimportant things. He would find himself in the middle of one of the little stone-walled gardens on top of the tower and not know whether he had come to harvest or water or weed. He said, "What will I tell him, wife?"

"I'm sure you'll remember when the time comes. That's how it is, isn't it? What must be will be."

Osric watched his wife putter about the kitchen. She built up the fire which he had forgotten to tend while she was out in the cold rain rounding up the surviving goats. Wind hunted at the slit windows. A loose shutter banged. The left side of his face ached, as it always did in cold wet weather. But they were snug here, with plenty of canned and pickled vegetables, and sacks of dry beans and wild rice for which they had traded goat's milk cheese with the local tribe of mountaineers. They would sleep in the niches on either side of the stone fireplace. And in spring . . .

Osric began to weep again, choking with frustration. He was too weak, too old, and too confused. He was older than Bryn, and Bryn had considered himself very old. He slept more than half the day, and could not work for more than an hour without having to rest for twice as long. He could not remember exactly what would happen, but he knew that it was so very important that he must try and recall every detail. He must tell the boy enough, but not too much.

Beatrice noticed her husband's distress and made him a beaker of camomile tea. "Well," she said, "as the fox said when he first saw the grapes, what are we going to do about it?"

"I suppose I must try and remember everything. I will tell the story again. I will tell it and you will write it down, wife."

"And I suppose that is more important than the half hundred things I must do before winter really comes."

"It is more important than anything in the world."

Beatrice warmed her hands at the fire, thinking about it. At last, she said, "We will do it a little at a time. An hour or two a day. We're old, husband, and we don't want to tire ourselves out."

Osric stroked her long white hair. She leaned into his attention, like a cat. He said, "I have to live until spring, at least."

"Longer than that, I hope. Well, where should we begin?"

Osric thought hard. He said, "I suppose the proper place might be when Dr. Dismas came back to Aeolis from Ys. That is how it really began. But any place is as good as any other. It is all a circle, like the river."

"As the river was, but is no more. Not for . . . ach, I always get confused over the ins and outs of it all."

"The point is that it does not matter where it begins, or where it ends."

"Of course it matters. Beginnings are as important as endings, and it's just the same the other way around. I think we had better write it all down, or we will begin at the end or somewhere in the middle, and never get ourselves straight."

"Perhaps that is the place to begin. The middle, I mean. Most people would start with the child and the dead woman in the white boat on the Great River. But I think it should begin with the goat, and how the boy will be brought here."

"I can see that I will have to find pen and paper straightaway," Beatrice said. "Think about what you want to say while I go and look."

It took most of the winter to tell the tale, until at last they reached the point where Yama had returned home for the last time, and where their own story, the story of the two of them, husband and wife, had really begun.

"Do you remember," Beatrice said fondly, "do you remember how shocked Father Quine was, when we burst in like that at dawn, waking him and Ananda and demanding that we be married at once?"

Osric smiled. "Ananda knew. He knew right away who I was."

Carenon told Father Quine that the marriage would take place at gunpoint if it had to, but Father Quine assured him that his threats were not necessary. All the while, the young sizar, Ananda, stared at Yama until he could contain his amazement no longer, and plunged into a breathless series of questions.

"Why have you returned? Did you go to Ys? What happened there? Did you run away from Prefect Corin? Did he do that to your face?"

And so on, until Yama burst into laughter. "I came back because something both wonderful and terrible happened," he said. "You will understand soon enough, Ananda. I wish I could tell you everything, but there is no time."

"But you did go to Ys."

"Yes. Yes, I did. And after many adventures I am back, but only for a little while, and in secret. The Aedile must not know. No one must know but the people in this room."

Ananda smiled. "Well, I am glad to see you again."

Father Quine cleared his throat, and Ananda bit back his next question. "I think you should fetch the oil," the priest told his sizar.

It did not take long; it was, after all, a metic marriage, the ceremony more in the nature of a blessing than a service. Afterward, Father Quine broke open a cruse of wine, and as they all sat around the kitchen table in the priest's house, Ananda dug out a little more of Yama's story. He was convinced that Yama had come straight back from Ys, and Yama did not disabuse him. There was not enough time.

"I will not see you again," Ananda said at last, ending an uncomfortable pause.

"I do not think so. You will stay in the temple . . ."

Yama meant that Father Quine and Ananda would be placed under house arrest when Prefect Corin came. The temple would be left standing when Aeolis was razed because it belonged to the Department. But he could not tell Ananda any of that.

"O yes," Ananda said quietly. "And become priest after Quine." He looked sideways at the priest, who was talking with Derev and her parents. He bent closer to Yama and added in a whisper, "Not that the dry old stick looks like withering away in my lifetime. I'll be a hundred years sweeping out the naos and polishing the shrine while you and Derev are off adventuring. At least, that's what you will be doing, I suppose."

"We will make a home together," Yama said, "with a little garden, and goats and doves. But not quite yet, I think. I am glad we met again, Ananda. I did not like the way we parted."

"I had not attended an execution before," Ananda said. "I was sick afterward. Quine was furious. Because I was sick, and because he knew then that I had broken the fast."

"Pistachios," Yama said, remembering that day.

Ananda grinned. "I have not eaten them since. Now, have some more wine."

"It is time we said a prayer, I think," Yama said. He drew Derev aside and told her to make her farewells to her parents.

They went together as man and wife before the shrine where so often as a child Yama had helped the Aedile perform the long and meaningless rituals which were part of the duties of his office, and where the aspect of Angel had first found him, so badly frightening the Aedile that he had damaged the shrine's mechanism.

But it still functioned as a shortcut mouth. Yama and Derev stepped through to a place far away, a bubble hung above a vast chamber deep in the keelways. The chamber was hundreds of leagues long. Machines as big as cities crouched on its floor. Lights came on around the rim of the bubble; lighted windows opened in the air. Some showed views of similar chambers, one for each section of the world.

A voice spoke out of the air and welcomed Yama, and asked him what he wished to do.

And so the end of the world was set in motion.

Afterward, Yama called down the ship and it took them out in a loop that compressed forty years into a few days, so that they could glimpse the end of the world before plunging down a shortcut into the deep past. They emerged around one of the stars mentioned by the Gatekeeper when Yama had first returned to Confluence, a star which had moved closer to the star of Confluence after the Preservers had quit the Galaxy.

One of the worlds which orbited the star had been reshaped into something like the world which had been the cradle of the race which had, over millions of years, changed the orbit of every star of the Galaxy and become at last the Preservers. There were many such worlds, the ship told them; it was possible that one of them might even be the true, ancient Earth which Angel's crewmates had left Confluence to search for. But Yama and Derev were content to explore the world they had, and afterward returned to Confluence, arriving fifty years before Yama cast his own self upon the waters of the Great River.

They found the tower at the far edge of the City of the Dead, in the foothills of the Rim Mountains. It was abandoned and open to the weather, and they spent some time restoring it before tracking Derev's grandparents to a small town several hundred leagues downriver of Aeolis. They took new names from an ancient poem Derev loved. Her grandparents refused to take up the burdens of the Department of the Curators of the City of the Dead; their parents had given up their family's traditional service because there was no longer any need for it, and they would not be persuaded to see a need for it now. But they had a son, ambitious and restless, and he remembered the story Beatrice and Osric told his parents. After they died, more than twenty years later, he sent a message to the new curators of the City of the Dead, saying that he would move to Aeolis if they could help him establish his business there.

"And a few years later he married, and a few years after that I was born," Beatrice said. "Unless you want to put in the business about the goat, I think you are done, for nothing has happened to us since."

"Perhaps I should say more about the end of the world," Osric said.

"It will happen soon enough, and there will be enough stories about it, too. At least one for every world the great ships will settle." Beatrice set aside the sheaf of paper and went to the window and opened the shutter a little and looked out. "It is still raining, but it looks like it might end soon. A long, cold, wet winter it has been, but at least we found something to fill it, eh, husband?"

"It is not very satisfactory as a tale. There are too many repetitions, and too many words wasted on adventures anyone could have had, or on diversions which led to nothing in particular."

"Well, that's how it always is with life. Cut short too soon, with too many loose ends."

"I wonder about the Ancients of Days. Will they ever find Old Earth? And what about poor Dreen, the Commissioner of Sensch, who went with them?"

"There are many Earths," Beatrice said. "No doubt they will find one to their liking, but people might already be living there. The Ancients of Days went the long way, remember. They are still traveling on it, and will not arrive anywhere for at least a hundred and fifty thousand years. Everyone else will fall through the shortcuts. Their descendants will be scattered across the Galaxy long before the Ancients of Days arrive."

"Yes," Osric said. "The Preservers abandoned the Galaxy and then the Universe, but the ten thousand bloodlines will inherit it. There will be room for everyone, even the heretics. There might be wars more terrible than the war I thought to end, but I do not think the heretics will survive for long. Their philosophy has been defeated before; it will be defeated again."

"And the indigenous peoples. Do not forget them, husband. You always said that they were the hope that things would be different."

"*They* are different. They are not marked by the Preservers. I wonder if that is what the Preservers wanted. We are the servants of the Preservers, but perhaps the indigenous peoples are their true heirs. Perhaps they will triumph over those from whom the Preservers fled. Or perhaps, by the working of some strange plan, they will become the Preservers' nemesis."

"We cannot know what the Preservers wanted," Beatrice said.

"But we can wonder about them. I wonder about the enlightened bloodlines too. About all those who became so holy that they vanished from the world. Perhaps they found a way through the event horizon of the Eye, and followed the Preservers to their new universe. We did not explore everything the shrines could do."

"Most likely they became so holy that they simply died out, like the people of Gond. But what is the use of speculating on things we cannot know? We cannot know about the fate of the Preservers because they fled the Universe so completely that nothing can return from them, not even light. You will waste your life, husband, thinking on questions which have no answers because they could have any answer."

"And there is the ghost ship," Osric said stubbornly. "I had thought that it would be me who would help save the boy when he escaped Enobarbus and Dr. Dismas. That I would invoke the vision of the ghost ship which stopped them from chasing the boy after he jumped over-board. But I forgot. I went directly to you. Perhaps the boy will not escape Dr. Dismas and Enobarbus, wife, and so will not come here. This may be a different time-line."

Beatrice was putting on her yellow oilskin. She said, "Every story must have a mystery, husband. No one likes a story in which everything is explained. How could you explain why people do the things they do, for instance? Now, I am going to see to the goats. Will you be all right while I am gone? Will you watch the fire?"

"Yes, of course," Osric said, as she went out.

But he was thinking of the ghost ship, and the way it had dissolved into a bank of fog which had hid him from the pinnace commanded by Enobarbus after he had escaped from it. The ghost ship had surely been an illusion conjured by a machine, for he had seen a machine rising out of the fog. But who had commanded the machine? Perhaps it had been his first miracle, and he had not known it. Or perhaps the machines he believed to be his to command had been working for some other power's subtle plan, of which he was but a part. But it did not do to think of these things. If anything was possible, then everything was possible. No. What will be must be. He had made that the core of his life when he had chosen to find Derev, and had closed his part of the tale by beginning the end of the world.

He remembered seeing how it would end. They had gone there after he had woken the great engines in the keelways. The ship had hung high above the long plane of the world and they had watched as it broke apart. At the beginning of his adventures, he had seen a picture slate which had shown one of his bloodline at the time of the construction of Confluence (he would have to find that slate, Osric thought). Behind the man had been a hundred shining splinters hung against a starry sky, but he had not realized then what they were: the elements of the world, the great ships which the Builders had joined together in the first act of the creation of the world.

He had reversed the process. He had saved the world and its people by destroying it. The Great River had failed; the engines in the keelways had been woken from their long slumber and had slowly resumed their functions. It took forty years. And then the shrines woke and warned the peoples of the world, telling them what would happen, and where they could find shelter. And less than a year later the world broke apart into its original sections, and those sections fell in different directions across the sky toward the expanding throats of the shortcuts: a field of blue rings flowering in the empty blackness of space and a cloud of splinters shining in the light of the lonely star.

How many had died, in the last days of Confluence? There had been terrible famines when the river had finally run dry, and earthquakes had thrown all of the cities into ruin. Certainly almost all of the heretics had died, for they had silenced most of the shrines in the cities they had captured, and so had no warning of the world's end. But many others had died, too, and many more would die when the great ships reached their destinations, and the reoccupation of the Galaxy began.

But many more would live, and prosper, and multiply.

He dozed a little, and woke, and remembered that after the boy came they would have to think of Pandaras. The boy would find Pandaras in Ys (or had it been the other way around?) and take him on his adventures, and Pandaras's own story would begin when the boy's ended. Although he had been charged with changing all the indigenous peoples of Confluence, Pandaras would not stop searching for his master. He would return at last to Ys, the place he loved most and knew best. They would track him down by the coin he carried, and explain how his master's story had ended. He must remember to tell Beatrice, Osric thought, and fell asleep again.

The door banged open and Beatrice came in, shaking water from her long hair. Osric stirred. "Look," she said. "See what I found."

It was a bunch of violets. She found a bowl and set them in it. Their sweet scent slowly filled the kitchen, promising the end of winter and the beginning of spring.

Soon the story would be over, and they could leave. They would find Pandaras, and call down the ship. They would embark for the last time. Where would they go? To the deep past, or to the deep future? All of history stood before him like a book. He could open it at any page.

He would have to think hard about it. Spring had only just begun, but soon Derev would find the boy in the ancient tomb in the Silent Quarter of the City of the Dead, and bring him here. And the story would begin again, and in its beginning would be its end.